True Blood Omnibus III

True Blood Omnibus III

All Together Dead
From Dead to Worse
Dead and Gone

Charlaine Harris

GOLLANCZ
London

This collection first published in Great Britain in 2011 by Gollancz
An imprint of the Orion Publishing Group
Orion House, 5 Upper St Martin's Lane, London WC2H 9EA
An Hachette UK Company

A CIP catalogue record for this book is available
from the British Library

ISBN 978 0 575 09939 5

1 3 5 7 9 10 8 6 4 2

Typeset by Input Data Services Ltd,
Bridgwater, Somerset

Printed in Great Britain by CPI Mackays, Chatham, Kent

The Orion Publishing Group's policy is to use papers that are natural,
renewable and recyclable products and made from wood grown
in sustainable forests. The logging and manufacturing processes are
expected to conform to the environmental regulations of the country of origin.

www.charlaineharris.com

www.orionbooks.co.uk

Contents

All Together Dead

This book is dedicated to a few of the women I'm proud to call 'friend': Jodi Dabson Bollendorf, Kate Buker, Toni Kelner, Dana Cameron, Joan Hess, Eve Sandstrom, Paula Woldan, and Betty Epley. All of you have meant something different to me, and I feel grateful to know you.

Chapter 1

The Shreveport Vampire Bar would be opening late tonight. I was running behind, and I'd automatically gone to the front door, the public door, only to be halted by a neatly lettered sign, red Gothic script on white cardboard: WE'LL BE READY TO GREET YOU WITH A BITE TONIGHT, AT EIGHT O'CLOCK. PLEASE EXCUSE OUR DELAYED OPENING. It was signed 'The Staff of Fangtasia.'

It was the third week in September, so the red neon FANGTASIA sign was already on. The sky was almost pitch-black. I stood with one foot inside my car for a minute, enjoying the mild evening and the faint, dry smell of vampire that lingered around the club. Then I drove around to the back and parked beside several other cars lined up at the employee entrance. I was only five minutes late, but it looked like everyone else had beaten me to the meeting. I rapped on the door. I waited.

I'd raised my hand to knock again when Pam, Eric's second-in-command, opened the door. Pam was based at the bar, but she had other duties in Eric's various business dealings. Though vampires had gone public almost four years ago and turned their best face to the world, they were still pretty secretive about their moneymaking methods, and sometimes I wondered how much of America the undead actually owned. Eric, the owner of Fangtasia, was a true vampire in the keeping-things-to-himself department. Of course, in his long, long existence he'd had to be.

'Come in, my telepathic friend,' Pam said, gesturing dramatically. She was wearing her work outfit: the filmy, trailing black gown that all the tourists who came into the bar seemed to expect from female vampires. (When Pam got to pick her own clothing, she was a pastels-and-twinset kind of woman.) Pam had the palest, straightest blond hair you ever saw; in fact, she was ethereally lovely, with a kind of deadly edge. The deadly edge was what a person shouldn't forget.

'How you doing?' I asked politely.

'I am doing exceptionally well,' she said. 'Eric is full of happiness.'

Eric Northman, the vampire sheriff of Area Five, had made Pam a vampire, and she was both obliged and compelled to do his bidding. That was part of the deal of becoming undead: you were always in sway to your maker. But Pam had told me more than once that Eric was a good boss to have, and that he would let her go her own way if and when she desired to do so. In fact, she'd been living in Minnesota until Eric had purchased Fangtasia and called her to help him run it.

Area Five was most of northwestern Louisiana, which until a month ago had been the economically weaker half of the state. Since Hurricane Katrina, the balance of power in Louisiana had shifted dramatically, especially in the vampire community.

'How is that delicious brother of yours, Sookie? And your shape-shifting boss?' Pam said.

'My delicious brother is making noises about getting married, like everyone else in Bon Temps,' I said.

'You sound a bit depressed.' Pam cocked her head to one side and regarded me like a sparrow eyeing a worm.

'Well, maybe a tad wee bit,' I said.

'You must keep busy,' Pam said. 'Then you won't have time to mope.'

Pam *loved* 'Dear Abby'. Lots of vampires scrutinized the column daily. Their solutions to some of the writers' problems would just make you scream. Literally. Pam had already advised me that I could only be imposed on if I permitted it, and that I needed to be more selective in picking my friends. I was getting emotional-health counseling from a vampire.

'I am,' I said. 'Keeping busy, that is. I'm working, I've still got my roommate from New Orleans, and I'm going to a wedding shower tomorrow. Not for Jason and Crystal. Another couple.'

Pam had paused, her hand on the doorknob of Eric's office. She considered my statement, her brows drawn together. 'I am not remembering what a wedding shower is, though I've heard of it,' she said. She brightened. 'They'll get married in a bathroom? No, I've heard the term before, surely. A woman wrote to Abby that she hadn't gotten a thank-you note for a large shower gift. They get . . . presents?'

'You got it,' I said. 'A shower is a party for someone who's about to get married. Sometimes the shower is for the couple, and they're both there. But usually only the bride is the honoree, and all the other people at the party are women. Everyone brings a gift. The theory is that this way the couple can start life with everything they need. We do the same thing when a couple's expecting a baby. Course, then it's a baby shower.'

'Baby shower,' Pam repeated. She smiled in a chilly way. It was enough to put frost on your pumpkin, seeing that up- curve of the lips. 'I like the term,' she said. She knocked on Eric's office door and then opened it. 'Eric,' she said, 'maybe someday one of the waitresses will get pregnant, and we can go to a *baby shower*!'

'That would be something to see,' said Eric, lifting his golden head from the papers on his desk. The sheriff registered my presence, gave me a hard look, and decided to ignore me. Eric and I had issues.

Despite the fact that the room was full of people waiting for his attention, Eric lay down his pen and stood to stretch his tall and magnificent body, perhaps for my benefit. As usual, Eric was in tight jeans and a Fangtasia T-shirt, black with the white stylized fangs that the bar used as its trademark. 'Fangtasia' was written in jazzy red script across the white points in the same style as the neon sign outside. If Eric turned around, the back would read 'The Bar with a Bite'. Pam had given me one when Fangtasia first got into marketing its own stuff.

Eric made the shirt look good, and I remembered all too well what was underneath it.

I tore my gaze away from Eric's stretch to look around the room. There were lots of other vampires crammed into the smallish space, but till you saw them you didn't know they were there, they were so still and silent. Clancy, the bar manager, had claimed one of the two visitor chairs before the desk. Clancy had just barely survived the previous year's Witch War, but he hadn't come out unscathed. The witches had drained Clancy near to the point of no return. By the time Eric discovered Clancy, tracing his smell to a Shreveport cemetery, Clancy was one Vacutainer short of dead. During his long recovery, the red-haired vamp had grown bitter and snappish. Now he grinned at me, showing some fang. 'You can sit in my lap, Sookie,' he said, patting his thighs.

I smiled back, but not like my heart was in it. 'No, thanks, Clancy,' I said politely. Clancy's flirting had always had an edge to it, and now that edge was razor sharp. He was one of those vamps I'd rather not be alone with. Though he ran the bar capably, and he had never laid a finger on me, he still set off warning bells. I can't read vampire minds, which was why I found it refreshing to hang with them, but when I felt that tingle of warning, I did find myself wishing I could just dip into Clancy's head and find out what was going on in there.

Felicia, the newest bartender, was sitting on the couch, along with Indira and Maxwell Lee. It was like the vampire Rainbow Coalition meeting. Felicia was a happy mixture of African and Caucasian, and she was almost six feet tall, so there was more loveliness to appreciate. Maxwell Lee was one of the darkest men I'd ever seen. Little Indira was the daughter of Indian immigrants.

There were four more people in the room (using the term 'people' loosely), and each one of them upset me, though in varying degrees.

One of them was someone I didn't acknowledge. I'd taken a page from the Were rule book and treated him like an outlawed member of my pack: I abjured him. I didn't speak his name, I didn't speak to him, I didn't recognize his existence. (Of course, this was my ex, Bill Compton – not that I recognized that he was in the room, brooding away in a corner.)

Leaning against the wall next to him was ancient Thalia, who was possibly even older than Eric. She was as small as Indira and very pale, with tightly waving black hair – and she was extremely rude.

To my amazement, some humans found that a complete turn-on.

Thalia actually had a devoted following who seemed thrilled when she used her stilted English to tell them to fuck off. I'd discovered she even had a website, established and maintained by fans. Go figure. Pam had told me that when Eric had agreed to let Thalia live in Shreveport, it was the equivalent of keeping a badly trained pit bull tethered in the yard. Pam had not approved.

These undead citizens all lived in Area Five. To live and work under Eric's protection, they'd all sworn fealty to him. So they were required to devote a certain amount of their time to doing his bidding, even if they didn't work at the bar. There were a few extra vampires in Shreveport these days, since Katrina; just like a lot of humans, they had to go somewhere. Eric hadn't decided what to do about the undead refugees, and they hadn't been invited to the meeting.

Tonight there were two visitors in Fangtasia, one of whom outranked Eric.

Andre was the personal bodyguard of Sophie-Anne Leclerq, the Queen of Louisiana. The queen, at present, was an evacuee in Baton Rouge. Andre looked very young, maybe sixteen; his face was baby smooth, his pale hair was close-cut. Andre had lived a long existence caring only for Sophie-Anne, his maker and savior. He was not wearing his saber tonight, because he wasn't acting as her bodyguard, but I was sure Andre was armed with something – knife or gun. Andre himself was a lethal weapon, with or without an aid.

Just as Andre was about to speak to me, from beyond his chair a deep voice said, 'Hey, Sookie.' Our second visitor, Jake Purifoy. I made myself hold still when every impulse I had was telling me to get out of the office. I was being an idiot. If I hadn't run screaming at the sight of Andre, Jake shouldn't make me think of bolting. I forced myself to nod to the nice-looking young man who still looked alive. But I knew my greeting didn't look natural. He filled me with a terrible blend of pity and fear.

Jake, born a Were, had been attacked by a vampire and bled to the point of death. In what had been perhaps a mistaken gesture of mercy, my cousin Hadley (another vampire) had discovered Jake's nearly lifeless body and brought Jake over. This might have been considered a good deed; but as it turned out, no one had really appreciated Hadley's kindness … not even Jake himself. No one had ever heard of a turned Were before: Weres disliked and distrusted vampires, and the feeling was heartily reciprocated. The going was very rough for Jake, who occupied a lonely no-man's-land. The queen had given him a place in her service, since no one else had stepped forward.

Jake, blind with bloodlust, had gone after me as his first vampire snack. I had a still-red scar on my arm as a result.

What a wonderful evening this was turning out to be.

'Miss Stackhouse,' said Andre, rising from Eric's second guest chair. He bowed. This was a true tribute, and it lifted my spirits a bit.

'Mr Andre,' I said, bowing back. Andre swept his hand to indicate his politely vacated seat, and since that solved my placement problem, I accepted.

Clancy looked chagrined. He should have given me his chair, since he was the lower-ranked vampire. Andre's action had pointed that out as clearly as a blinking neon arrow. I tried hard not to smile.

'How is Her Majesty?' I asked, trying to be just as courteous as Andre had been. It would be stretching it to say I liked Sophie-Anne, but I sure respected her.

'That's part of the reason I am here tonight,' he said. 'Eric, can we get started now?' A gentle chiding for Eric's time-wasting tactics, I thought. Pam folded to the floor beside my chair, crouched on the balls of her feet.

'Yes, we're all here. Go ahead, Andre. You have the floor,' Eric said with a little smile at his own modern terminology. He slumped back down into his chair, extending his long legs to rest his feet on the corner of his desk.

'Your queen is living in the Area Four sheriff's house in Baton Rouge,' Andre said to the little assemblage. 'Gervaise was very gracious in extending his hospitality.'

Pam cocked an eyebrow at me. Gervaise would have lost his head if he *hadn't* extended his hospitality.

'But staying at Gervaise's place can only be a temporary solution,' Andre continued. 'We've been down to New Orleans several times since the disaster. Here's a report of our property's condition.'

Though none of the vampires moved, I felt their attention had heightened.

'The queen's headquarters lost most of its roof, so there was extensive water damage on the second floor and in the attic area. Furthermore, a large piece of someone else's roof landed inside the building, causing a pileup of debris and some holes in walls – problems like that. While we're drying the inside, the roof is still covered with blue plastic. One reason I came up this way is to find a contractor who will start reroofing immediately. So far, I haven't had any luck, so if any of you have personal influence with some human who does this kind of work, I need your help. On the ground floor, there was a lot of cosmetic damage. Some water came in. We had some looters, too.'

'Maybe the queen should remain in Baton Rouge,' Clancy said maliciously. 'I'm sure Gervaise would be overwhelmed with delight at the prospect of hosting her permanently.'

So Clancy was a suicidal idiot.

'A delegation of New Orleans leaders came to visit our queen in Baton Rouge to ask that she return to the city,' Andre said, ignoring Clancy completely. 'The human leaders think that if the vampires will return to New Orleans, tourism will pick up again.' Andre fixed Eric with a cold gaze. 'In the meantime, the queen has talked to the four other sheriffs about the financial aspect of restoring the New Orleans buildings.'

Eric gave an almost imperceptible inclination of the head. Impossible to say what he felt about being taxed for the queen's repairs.

New Orleans had been the place to go for vampires and those who wanted to be around them ever since Anne Rice had been proven right about their existence. The city was like Disneyland for vamps. But since Katrina, all that had gone to hell, of course, along with so much else. Even Bon Temps was feeling the storm's effect, and had been ever since Katrina had hit land. Our little town was still crowded with people who had fled from the south.

'What about the queen's entertainment estate?' asked Eric. The queen had bought an old monastery at the edge of the Garden District for entertaining large numbers of people, both vamp and non-vamp. Though surrounded by a wall, the estate was not considered easily defensible (since it was a registered building, historic and unchange-able, the windows couldn't be blocked up), so the queen couldn't actually live there. I thought of it as her party barn.

'It didn't suffer much damage,' Andre said. 'There were looters there, too. Of course, they left a trace of their smell.' Vampires were second only to Weres in their tracking abilities. 'One of them shot the lion.'

I felt sorry for that. I'd liked the lion, sort of.

'Do you need help with the apprehension?' Eric asked. Andre arched an eyebrow.

'I only ask because your numbers are low,' Eric said.

'No, already taken care of,' Andre said, and smiled just a tad.

I tried not to think about that.

'Aside from the lion and the looting, how was the estate?' Eric said to get the discussion of the storm damage back on track.

'The queen can stay there while she views the other properties,' Andre continued, 'but at the most for a night or two only.'

There were tiny nods all around.

'Our loss of personnel,' Andre said, moving on in his agenda. All the vampires tensed a bit, even Jake, the newbie. 'Our initial assessment was modest, as you know. We assumed some would come forward after the impact of the storm was absorbed. But only ten have surfaced: five here, three in Baton Rouge, two in Monroe. It seems that we have lost thirty of our number just in Louisiana. Mississippi has lost at least ten.'

There were tiny sounds and movements all over the room as the Shreveport vampires reacted to the news. The concentration of vamps, both resident and visiting, had been high in New Orleans. If Katrina had visited Tampa with that much force, the number of dead and missing would have been much lower.

I raised my hand to speak. 'What about Bubba?' I asked when Andre nodded at me. I hadn't seen or heard of Bubba since Katrina. You'd know Bubba if you saw him. Anyone on earth would know him; at least, anyone over a certain age. He hadn't quite died on that bathroom floor in Memphis. Not quite. But his brain had been affected before he was brought over, and he wasn't a very good vampire.

'Bubba's alive,' said Andre. 'He hid in a crypt and survived on small mammals. He isn't doing too well mentally, so the queen has sent him up to Tennessee to stay with the Nashville community for a while.'

'Andre has brought me a list of those that are missing,' Eric said. 'I'll post it after the meeting.'

I'd known a few of the queen's guards, too, and I would be glad to find out how they'd fared.

I had another question, so I waved my hand.

'Yes, Sookie?' Andre asked. His empty gaze fixed me in place, and I was sorry I'd asked to speak.

'You know what I wonder, y'all? I wonder if one of the kings or queens attending this summit, or whatever you all call it, has a – like a weather predictor, or something like that on staff.'

Plenty of blank stares were aimed my way, though Andre was interested.

'Because, look, the summit, or conference, or whatever, was supposed to take place in late spring originally. But – delay, delay, delay, right? And then Katrina hit. If the summit had started when it was supposed to, the queen could have gone in a powerful position. She would have had a big war chest and a full quiver of vamps, and maybe they wouldn't have been so anxious to prosecute her for the king's death. The queen would have gotten anything she asked for, probably. Instead, she's going in as' – I started to say 'a beggar,' but I considered Andre just in time – 'much less powerful.' I'd been afraid they'd laugh or maybe ridicule me, but the silence that followed was intensely thoughtful.

'That's one of the things you'll need to look for at the summit,' Andre said. 'Now that you've given me the idea, it seems oddly possible. Eric?'

'Yes, I think there is something in that,' Eric said, staring at me. 'Sookie is good at thinking outside the box.'

Pam smiled up at me from beside my elbow.

'What about the suit filed by Jennifer Cater?' Clancy asked Andre. He'd been looking increasingly uncomfortable in the chair he'd thought he was so clever to snag.

You could have heard a pin drop. I didn't know what the hell the red-haired vampire was talking about, but I thought it would be better to find out from the conversation than to ask.

'It's still active,' Andre said.

Pam whispered, 'Jennifer Cater was in training to become Peter Threadgill's lieutenant. She was in Arkansas managing his affairs when the violence erupted.'

I nodded to let Pam know I appreciated her filling me in. The Arkansas vampires, though they hadn't gone through a hurricane, had undergone quite a reduction in their own ranks, thanks to Louisiana's group.

Andre said, 'The queen has responded to the suit by testifying that she had to kill Peter to save her own life. Of course, she offered reparation to the common fund.'

'Why not to Arkansas?' I whispered to Pam.

'Because the queen maintains that since Peter is dead, Arkansas goes to her, according to the marriage contract,' Pam murmured. 'She can't make reparation to herself. If Jennifer Cater wins her suit, not only will the queen lose Arkansas, she'll have to pay Arkansas a fine. A huge one. And make other restitution.'

Andre began to drift around the room soundlessly, the only indication that he was unhappy about the topic.

'Do we even have that much money after the disaster?' Clancy asked. It was an unwise question.

'The queen hopes the suit will be dismissed,' Andre said, again ignoring Clancy. Andre's permanently teenage face was quite blank. 'But apparently the court is prepared to hear a trial. Jennifer is charging that our queen lured Threadgill to New Orleans, away from his own territory, having planned all along to start the war and assassinate him.' This time Andre's voice came from behind me.

'But that wasn't what happened at all,' I said. And Sophie-Anne hadn't killed the king. I'd been present at his death. The vampire standing behind me right at this moment had killed Threadgill, and I'd thought at the time he was justified.

I felt Andre's cold fingers brush my neck as I sat there. How I knew the fingers were Andre's, I couldn't tell you; but the light touch, the second of contact, made me suddenly focus on an awful fact: I was the only witness to the death of the king, besides Andre and Sophie-Anne.

I'd never put it to myself in those terms, and for a moment, I swear, my heart stopped beating. At that skipped beat, I drew the gaze of at least half the vamps in the room. Eric's eyes widened as he looked at my face. And then my heart beat again, and the moment was over as if it never had been. But Eric's hand twitched on the desk, and I knew that he would not forget that second, and he would want to know what it meant.

'So you think the trial will be held?' Eric asked Andre.

'If the queen had been going to the summit as the ruler of New Orleans – New Orleans as it was – I believe the sitting court would have negotiated some kind of settlement between Jennifer and the queen. Maybe something involving Jennifer being raised to a position of power as the queen's deputy and getting a large bonus; something like that. But as things are now . . .' There was a long silence while we filled in the blanks. New Orleans wasn't as it had been, might never be so again. Sophie-Anne was a lame duck right now. 'Now, because of Jennifer's persistence, I think the court will pursue it,' Andre said, and then fell silent.

'We know there's no truth to the allegations,' a clear, cold voice said from the corner. I'd been doing a good job of ignoring the presence of my ex, Bill. But it didn't come naturally to me. 'Eric was there. I was there. Sookie was there,' the vampire (Nameless, I told myself) continued.

That was true. Jennifer Cater's allegation, that the queen had lured her king to her party barn in order to kill him, was completely bogus. The bloodbath had been precipitated by the decapitation of one of the queen's men by one of Peter Threadgill's.

Eric smiled reminiscently. He'd enjoyed the battle. 'I accounted for the one who started it,' he said. 'The king did his best to trap the queen in an indiscretion, but he didn't, thanks to our Sookie. When his plot didn't work, he resorted to a simple frontal attack.' Eric added, 'I haven't seen Jennifer in twenty years. She's risen fast. She must be ruthless.'

Andre had stepped to my right and within my line of vision, which was a relief. He nodded. Again, all the vampires in the room made a little group movement, not quite in unison but eerily close. I had seldom felt so alien: the only warmblood in a room full of animated dead creatures.

'Yes,' Andre said. 'Ordinarily the queen would want a full contingent there to support her. But since we're forced to practice economy, the numbers going have been cut.' Again, Andre came near enough to touch me, just a brush of my cheek.

The idea triggered a kind of mini-revelation: *This was how it felt to be a normal person.* I hadn't the slightest idea of the true intentions and plans of my companions. This was how real people lived every day of their lives. It was frightening but exciting; a lot like walking through a crowded room blindfolded. How did regular people stand the suspense of day-to-day living?

'The queen wants this woman close to her in meetings, since other humans will be there,' Andre continued. He was speaking strictly to Eric. The rest of us might as well not have been in the room. 'She wants to know their thoughts. Stan is bringing his telepath. Do you know the man?'

'I'm sitting right here,' I muttered, not that anyone paid any attention but Pam, who gave me a sunny smile. Then, with all those cold eyes fixed on me, I realized that they were waiting for me, that Andre had been addressing me directly. I'd become so used to the vamps talking over and around me that I'd been taken by surprise. I mentally replayed Andre's remarks until I understood he was asking me a question.

'I've only met one other telepath in my life, and he was living in Dallas, so I'm supposing it's the same guy – Barry the Bellboy. He was working at the vamp hotel in Dallas when I picked up on his, ah, gift.'

'What do you know about him?'

'He's younger than me, and he's weaker than me – or at least he was at the time. He'd never accepted what he was, the way that I had.' I shrugged. That was the sum total of my knowledge.

'Sookie will be there,' Eric told Andre. 'She is the best at what she does.'

That was flattering, though I faintly recalled Eric saying he'd encountered only one telepath previously. It was also infuriating, since he was implying to Andre that my excellence was to Eric's credit instead of my own.

Though I was looking forward to seeing something outside of my little town, I found myself wishing I could think of a way to back out of the trip to Rhodes. But months ago I'd agreed to attend this vampire summit as a paid employee of the queen's. And for the past month, I'd been working long hours at Merlotte's Bar to bank enough time so the other barmaids wouldn't mind covering for me for a week. My boss, Sam, had been helping me keep track of my overage with a little chart.

'Clancy will stay here to run the bar,' Eric said.

'This human gets to go while I have to remain?' the red- haired manager said. He was really, really unhappy with Eric's decision. 'I won't get to see any of the fun.'

'That's right,' Eric said pleasantly. If Clancy had thought of saying something else negative, he took one look at Eric's face and clamped down on it. 'Felicia will stay to help you. Bill, you will stay.'

'No,' said that calm, cool voice from the corner. 'The queen requires me. I worked hard on that database, and she's asked me to market it at the summit to help recoup her losses.'

Eric looked like a statue for a minute, and then he moved, a little lift of his eyebrows. 'Yes, I'd forgotten your computer skills,' he said. He might have been saying, 'Oh, I'd forgotten you can spell *cat*,' for all the interest or respect he showed. 'I suppose you need to be with us, then. Maxwell?'

'If it's your will, I will stay.' Maxwell Lee wanted to make it clear that he knew a thing or two about being a good underling. He glanced around at the assemblage to underscore his point.

Eric nodded. I guessed that Maxwell would get a nice toy for Christmas, and Bill – whoops, Nameless – would get ashes and switches. 'Then you'll remain here. And you, too, Thalia. But you must promise me that you will be good in the bar.' Thalia's required tour of duty in the bar, which simply consisted of sitting around being mysterious and vampiric a couple of evenings a week, did not always go by without incident.

Thalia, perpetually sullen and broody, gave a curt nod. 'I don't want to go, anyway,' she muttered. Her round black eyes showed nothing but contempt for the world. She had seen too much in her very long life, and she hadn't enjoyed herself in a few centuries, was the way I read it. I tried to avoid Thalia as much as possible. I was surprised she'd even hang with the other vamps; she seemed like a rogue to me.

'She has no desire to lead,' Pam breathed into my ear. 'She only wants to be left in peace. She was thrown out of Illinois because she was too aggressive after the Great Revelation.' The Great Revelation was the vampire term for the night that they'd gone on television all over the world to let us know that they actually existed and, furthermore, that they wanted to come out of the shadows and into the economic and social flow of human society.

'Eric lets Thalia do what she wants as long as she follows the rules and shows up on time for her hours at the bar,' Pam continued in her tiny whisper. Eric was ruler of this little world, and no one was forgetting it. 'She knows what the punishment will be if she steps out of line. Sometimes she seems to forget how little she would like that punishment. She should read Abby, get some ideas.'

If you weren't getting any joy out of your life, you needed to . . . oh, do something for others, or take up a new hobby, or something like that, right? Wasn't that the usual advice? I flashed on Thalia volunteering to take the night shift at a hospice, and I shuddered. The idea of Thalia knitting, with two long, sharp needles, gave me another frisson of horror. To heck with the therapy.

'So, the only ones attending the summit are Andre, our queen, Sookie, myself, Bill, and Pam,' Eric said. 'Cataliades the lawyer and his niece as his runner. Oh, yes, Gervaise from Four and his human woman, a concession since Gervaise has been hosting the queen so generously. Rasul, as driver. And Sigebert, of course. That's our party. I know some of you are disappointed, and I can only hope that next year will be a better year for Louisiana. And for Arkansas, which we now consider part of our territory.'

'I think that's all that we needed to talk about with all of you present,' Andre said. The rest of the stuff he and Eric had to discuss would be done in private. Andre didn't touch me again, which was a good thing. Andre scared me down to my polished pink toenails. Of course, I should feel that way about everyone in the room. If I'd had good sense, I would move to Wyoming, which had the lowest vamp population (two; there'd been an article about them in *American Vampire*). Some days I was sorely tempted.

I whipped a little notepad out of my purse as Eric went over the date of our departure, the date of our return, the time our chartered Anubis Airline plane was arriving from Baton Rouge to pick up the Shreveport contingent, and a rundown of the clothes we would need. With some dismay, I realized I would have to go borrowing from my friends again. But Eric added, 'Sookie, you wouldn't need these clothes if it wasn't for the trip. I've called your friend's store and you have credit there. Use it.'

I could feel my cheeks redden. I felt like the poor cousin until he added, 'The staff has an account at a couple of stores here in Shreveport, but that would be inconvenient for you.' My shoulders relaxed, and I hoped he was telling the truth. Not one flicker of an eyelid told me any different.

'We may have suffered a disaster, but we won't go in looking poor,' Eric said, being careful to give me only a fraction of his stare.

'Don't look poor,' I made a note.

'Is everyone clear? Our goals for this conference are to support the queen as she tries to clear herself of these ridiculous charges, and to let everyone know that Louisiana is still a prestigious state. None of the Arkansas vampires who came to Louisiana with their king survived to tell the tale.' Eric smiled, and it wasn't a pleasant smile.

I hadn't known that before this night.

Gosh, wasn't that convenient.

Chapter 2

'**H**alleigh, since you're marrying a policeman, maybe you'll be able to tell me ... just how big is a cop's nightstick?' Elmer Claire Vaudry asked.

I was sitting beside the bride-to-be, Halleigh Robinson, since I'd been given the all-important task of recording each gift and its giver as Halleigh opened all the white-and-silver wrapped boxes and flowered gift bags.

No one else seemed the least surprised that Mrs Vaudry, a fortyish grade school teacher, was asking a bawdy question at this firmly middle-class, church lady event.

'Why, I wouldn't know, Elmer Claire,' Halleigh said demurely, and there was a positive chorus of disbelieving sniggers.

'Well, now, what about the handcuffs?' Elmer Claire asked. 'You ever use those handcuffs?'

A fluttering of southern lady voices rose in the living room of Marcia Albanese, the hostess who'd agreed to let her house be the sacrificial lamb: the actual shower site. The other hostesses had had the lesser problems of bringing the food and the punch.

'You are just *something*, Elmer Claire,' Marcia said from her spot by the refreshments table. But she was smiling. Elmer Claire had her role as the Daring One, and the others were glad to let her enjoy it.

Elmer Claire would never have been so vulgar if old Caroline Belle-fleur had been present at the shower. Caroline was the social ruler of

Bon Temps. Miss Caroline was about a million years old and had a back stiffer than any soldier. Only something extreme would keep Miss Caroline home from a social event of this importance to her family, and something extreme had happened. Caroline Bellefleur had suffered a heart attack, to the amazement of everyone in Bon Temps. To her family, the event had not been a tremendous surprise.

The grand Bellefleur double wedding (Halleigh and Andy's, Portia and her accountant's) had been set for the previous spring. It had been organized in a rush because of Caroline Bellefleur's sudden deterioration in health. As it happened, even before the hurried-up wedding could be held, Miss Caroline had been felled by the attack. Then she'd broken her hip.

With the agreement of Andy's sister, Portia, and her groom, Andy and Halleigh had postponed the wedding until late October. But I'd heard Miss Caroline was not recovering as her grandchildren had hoped, and it seemed unlikely she ever would be back to her former self.

Halleigh, her cheeks flushed, was struggling with the ribbon around a heavy box. I handed her a pair of scissors. There was some tradition about not cutting the ribbon, a tradition that somehow tied into predicting the number of children the bridal couple would produce, but I was willing to bet that Halleigh was ready for a quick solution. She snipped the ribbon on the side closest to her so no one would notice her callous disregard for custom. She flashed me a grateful look. We were all in our party best, of course, and Halleigh looked very cute and young in her light blue pantsuit with pink roses splashed on the jacket. She was wearing a corsage, of course, as the honoree.

I felt like I was observing an interesting tribe in another country, a tribe that just happened to speak my language. I'm a barmaid, several rungs below Halleigh on the social ladder, and I'm a telepath, though people tended to forget about it since it is hard to believe, my outside being so normal. But I'd been on the guest list, so I'd made a big effort to fit in sartorially. I was pretty sure I'd succeeded. I was wearing a sleeveless tailored white blouse, yellow slacks, and orange-and-yellow sandals, and my hair was down and flowing smoothly past my shoulder blades. Yellow earrings and a little gold chain tied me all together. It might be late September, but it was hot as the six shades of hell. All the ladies were still dressed in their hot-weather finery, though a few brave souls had donned fall colors.

I knew everyone at the shower, of course. Bon Temps is not a big place, and my family has lived in it for almost two hundred years. Knowing who people are is not the same as being comfortable with them, and I'd been glad to be given the job of recording the gifts. Marcia Albanese was sharper than I'd given her credit for being.

I was certainly learning a lot. Though I was trying hard not to listen in, and my little task helped in that, I was getting a lot of mental overflow.

Halleigh was in hog heaven. She was getting presents, she was the center of attention, and she was getting married to a great guy. I didn't think she really knew her groom that well, but I was certainly willing to believe that there were wonderful sides to Andy Bellefleur that I'd never seen or heard. Andy had more imagination than the average middle-class man in Bon Temps; I knew that. And Andy had fears and desires he'd buried deeply; I knew that, too.

Halleigh's mother had come from Mandeville to attend the shower, of course, and she was doing her smiling best to support her daughter. I thought I was the only one who realized that Halleigh's mother hated crowds, even crowds this small. Every moment she sat in Marcia's living room was very uncomfortable for Linette Robinson. At this very moment, while she was laughing at another little sally by Elmer Claire, she was wishing passionately that she was home with a good book and a glass of iced tea.

I started to whisper to her that it would all be over in (I cast a glance at my watch) another hour, hour-fifteen at the outside – but I remembered in time that I'd just freak her out worse than she already was. I jotted down 'Selah Pumphrey – dish towels,' and sat poised to record the next gift. Selah Pumphrey had expected me to give her a Big Reaction when she'd sailed in the door, since for weeks Selah had been dating that vampire I'd abjured. Selah was always imagining I'd jump on her and whack her in the head. Selah had a low opinion of me, not that she knew me at all. She certainly didn't realize that the vampire in question was simply off my radar now. I was guessing she'd been invited because she'd been Andy and Halleigh's real estate agent when they'd bought their little house.

'Tara Thornton – lace teddy,' I wrote, and smiled at my friend Tara, who'd selected Halleigh's gift from the stock at her clothing store. Of course, Elmer Claire had a lot to say about the teddy, and a good time was had by all – at least on the face of it. Some of the assembled women weren't comfortable with Elmer Claire's broad humor, some of them were thinking that Elmer Claire's husband had a lot to put up with, and some of them just wished she would shut up. That group included me, and Linette Robinson, and Halleigh.

The principal at the school where Halleigh taught had given the couple some perfectly nice place mats, and the assistant principal had gotten napkins to match. I recorded those with a flourish and stuffed some of the torn wrapping paper into the garbage bag at my side.

'Thanks, Sookie,' Halleigh said quietly, as Elmer Claire was telling another story about something that had happened at her wedding involving a chicken and the best man. 'I really appreciate your help.'

'No big,' I said, surprised.

'Andy told me that he got you to hide the engagement ring when he proposed,' she said, smiling. 'And you've helped me out other times, too.' Then Andy had told Halleigh *all* about me.

'Not a problem,' I said, a little embarrassed.

She shot a sideways glance at Selah Pumphrey, seated two folding chairs away. 'Are you still dating that beautiful man I saw at your place?' she asked rather more loudly. 'The handsome one with the gorgeous black hair?'

Halleigh had seen Claude when he dropped me off at my temporary lodging in town; Claude, the brother of Claudine, my fairy godmother. Yes, really. Claude *was* gorgeous, and he could be absolutely charming (to women) for about sixty seconds. He'd made the effort when he'd met Halleigh, and I could only be thankful, since Selah's ears had pricked up just like a fox's.

'I saw him maybe three weeks ago,' I said truthfully. 'But we're not dating now.' We never had been, actually, because Claude's idea of a good date was someone with a little beard stubble and equipment I'd never possess. But not everyone had to know that, right? 'I'm seeing someone else,' I added modestly.

'Oh?' Halleigh was all innocent interest. I was getting fonder of the girl (all of five years younger than me) by the second.

'Yes,' I said. 'A consultant from Memphis.'

'You'll have to bring him to the wedding,' Halleigh said. 'Wouldn't that be great, Portia?'

This was another kettle of fish entirely. Portia Bellefleur, Andy's sister and the other bride-to-be in the double Bellefleur wedding, had asked me to be there to serve alcohol, along with my boss, Sam Merlotte. Now Portia was in a bind. She would never have invited me other than as a worker. (I sure hadn't been invited to any showers for *Portia*.) Now I beamed at Portia in an innocent, I'm-so-happy way.

'Of course,' Portia said smoothly. She had not trained in the law for nothing. 'We'd be delighted if you'd bring your boyfriend.'

I had a happy mental picture of Quinn transforming into a tiger at the reception. I smiled at Portia all the more brightly. 'I'll see if he can come with me,' I said.

'Now, y'all,' Elmer Claire said, 'a little bird told me to write down what Halleigh said when she unwrapped her gifts, cause you know, that's what you'll say on your wedding night!' She waved a legal pad.

Everyone fell silent with happy anticipation. Or dread.

'This is the first thing Halleigh said: "Oh, what pretty wrapping!"' A chorus of dutiful laughter. 'Then she said, let's see: "That's going to fit; I can hardly wait!"' Snickers. 'Then she said, "Oh, I needed one of those!"' Hilarity.

After that, it was time for cake and punch and peanuts and the cheese ball. We'd all resumed our seats, carefully balancing plates and cups, when my grandmother's friend Maxine opened a new topic of discussion.

'How's your new friend, Sookie?' Maxine Fortenberry asked. Maxine was clear across the room, but projecting was no problem for Maxine. In her late fifties, Maxine was stout and hearty, and she'd been a second mother to my brother, Jason, who was best friends with her son Hoyt. 'The gal from New Orleans?'

'Amelia's doing well.' I beamed nervously, all too aware I was the new center of attention.

'Is it true that she lost her house in the flooding?'

'It did sustain quite a bit of damage, her tenant said. So Amelia's waiting to hear from the insurance company, and then she'll decide what to do.'

'Lucky she was here with you when the hurricane hit,' Maxine said.

I guess poor Amelia had heard that a thousand times since August. I think Amelia was pretty tired of trying to feel lucky. 'Oh, yes,' I said agreeably. 'She sure was.'

Amelia Broadway's arrival in Bon Temps had been the subject of lots of gossip. That's only natural.

'So for right now, Amelia'll just stay on with you?' Halleigh asked helpfully.

'For a while,' I said, smiling.

'That's just real sweet of you,' Marcia Albanese said approvingly.

'Oh, Marcia, you know I got that whole upstairs that I never use. She's actually improved it for me; she got a window air conditioner put in up there, so it's much nicer. It doesn't put me out one bit.'

'Still, lots of people wouldn't want someone living in their home that long. I guess I should take in one of the poor souls staying at the Days Inn, but I just can't bring myself to let someone else in my house.'

'I like the company,' I said, which was mostly true.

'Has she been back to check on her house?'

'Ah, only once.' Amelia had to get in and out of New Orleans real quick, so none of her witch friends could track her down. Amelia was in a bit of hot water with the witch community of the Big Easy.

'She sure loves that cat of hers,' Elmer Claire said. 'She had that big old tom at the vet the other day when I took Powderpuff in.' Powderpuff, Elmer Claire's white Persian, was about a million years old. 'I asked her why she didn't get that cat neutered, and she just covered that cat's ears like he could hear me, and she asked me not to talk about it in front of Bob, just like he was a person.'

'She's real fond of Bob,' I said, not quite knowing whether I wanted to gag or laugh at the idea of the vet neutering Bob.

'You know that Amelia how?' Maxine asked.

'You remember my cousin Hadley?'

Everyone in the room nodded, except newcomer Halleigh and her mother.

'Well, when Hadley lived in New Orleans, she rented the upstairs of Amelia's house from her,' I said. 'And when Hadley passed away' – here there were solemn nods all around – 'I went down to New Orleans to clean out Hadley's things. And I met Amelia, and we became friends, and she just decided she'd visit Bon Temps for a while.'

All the ladies looked at me with the most expectant expressions, as if they couldn't wait to hear what would come next. Because there had to be more explanation, right?

There was indeed a lot more to the story, but I didn't think they were ready to hear that Amelia, after a night of great loving, had accidentally turned Bob into a cat during a sexual experiment. I'd never asked Amelia to describe the circumstances, because I was pretty sure I didn't want to get a visual on that scene. But they were all waiting for a little more explanation. Any explanation.

'Amelia had a bad breakup with her boyfriend,' I said, keeping my tone low and confidential.

All the other ladies' faces were both titillated and sympathetic.

'He was a Mormon missionary,' I told them. Well, Bob had *looked* like a Mormon missionary, in dark slacks and a white short-sleeved shirt, and he'd even arrived at Amelia's on a bicycle. He was actually a witch, like Amelia. 'But he knocked on Amelia's door and they just fell in love.' Actually, into bed. But you know – same thing, for the purposes of this story.

'Did his parents know?'

'Did his church find out?'

'Don't they get to have more than one wife?'

The questions crowded in too thick for me to deal with, and I waited until the attendees had subsided into their waiting mode again. I was not used to making up fabrications, and I was running out of truth to base the rest of the story on. 'I really don't know much about the Mormon church,' I told the last questioner, and that was the absolute truth. 'Though I think modern Mormons aren't supposed to have more than one wife. But what happened to them was his relatives

found out and got real mad because they didn't think Amelia was good
enough for the man, and they snatched him away and made him go
home. So she wanted to leave New Orleans to get a change of scene,
forget about the past, you know.'

They all nodded, absolutely fascinated by Amelia's big drama. I felt
a twinge of guilt. For a minute or two, everyone gave her opinion
about the sad story. Maxine Fortenberry summed it all up.

'Poor girl,' said Maxine. 'He should've stood up to them.'

I passed Halleigh another present to open. 'Halleigh, you know that
won't happen to you,' I said, diverting the conversation back to its
proper topic. 'Andy is just nuts about you; anyone can tell.'

Halleigh blushed, and her mother said, 'We all love Andy,' and the
shower was back on track. The rest of the conversation veered from
the wedding to the meals each church was taking in turn to cook for
the evacuees. The Catholics had tomorrow night, and Maxine sounded
a little relieved when she said the number to cook for had dropped to
twenty-five.

As I drove home afterward, I was feeling a little frazzled from the
unaccustomed sociability. I also faced the prospect of telling Amelia
about her new invented background. But when I saw the pickup
standing in my yard, all such thoughts flew out of my head.

Quinn was here – Quinn the weretiger, who made his living arranging and producing special events for the world of the weird – Quinn,
my honey. I pulled around back and practically leaped out of my car
after an anxious glance in my rearview mirror to make sure my
makeup was still good.

Quinn charged out of the back door as I hurried up to the steps, and
I gave a little jump. He caught me and whirled me around, and when
he put me down he was kissing me, his big hands framing my face.

'You look so beautiful,' he said, coming up for air. A moment later,
he gasped. 'You smell so good.' And then he was back into the kissing.

We finally broke it off.

'Oh, I haven't seen you in so long!' I said. 'I'm so glad you're here!'
I hadn't seen Quinn in weeks, and then I'd been with him only briefly
as he'd passed through Shreveport on his way to Florida with a load
of props for the coming-of-age ceremony for a packleader's daughter.

'I've missed you, babe,' he said, his big white teeth gleaming. His shaved head shone in the sunlight, which was coming at quite an angle this late in the afternoon. 'I had a little time to catch up with your roomie while you were at the shower. How'd it go?'

'Like showers usually do. Lots of presents and lots of gossip. This was the second shower I've been to for this gal, plus I gave them a plate in their everyday china for a wedding present, so I've done them proud.'

'You can go to more than one shower for the same person?'

'In a small town like this, yeah. And she went home to have a shower and a dinner party in Mandeville during the summer. So I guess Andy and Halleigh are set up pretty well.'

'I thought they were supposed to get married last April.'

I explained about Caroline Bellefleur's heart attack. 'By the time she was getting over that and they were talking wedding dates again, Miss Caroline fell and broke her hip.'

'Wow.'

'And the doctors didn't think she'd get over *that*, but she survived that, too. So I think Halleigh and Andy and Portia and Glen are actually going to have the most-anticipated wedding of the Bon Temps year sometime next month. And you're invited.'

'I am?'

We were heading inside by this time, since I wanted to take off my shoes and I also wanted to scout out what my housemate was up to. I was trying to think of some long errand I could send her off on, since I so seldom got to see Quinn, who was kind of my boyfriend, if at my age (twenty- seven), I could use that term.

That is, I thought he would be my boyfriend if he could ever slow down enough to latch on to me.

But Quinn's job, working for a subsidiary of Extreme(ly Elegant) Events, covered a lot of territory, literally and figuratively. Since we'd parted in New Orleans after our rescue from Were abductors, I'd seen Quinn three times. He'd been in Shreveport one weekend as he passed through on his way to somewhere else, and we'd gone out to dinner at Ralph and Kacoo's, a popular restaurant. It had been a good evening, but he'd taken me home at the end of it since he had to start driving at seven the next morning. The second time, he'd dropped into Merlotte's while I was at work, and since it was a slow night, I'd taken an hour off to sit and talk to him, and we'd held hands a little. The third time, I'd kept him company while he was loading up his trailer at a U-RENT-SPACE storage shed. It had been in the middle of summer, and we'd both been sweating up a storm. Streaming sweat, lots of dust, storage sheds, the occasional vehicle trolling through the lot . . . not a romantic ambience.

And even though Amelia was now obligingly coming down the stairs with her purse over her shoulder and clearly planning to head into town to give us some privacy, it hardly seemed promising that we'd have to grab an instant to consummate a relationship that had had so little face time.

Amelia said, 'Good-bye!' She had a big smile all over her face, and since Amelia has the whitest teeth in the world, she looked like the Cheshire cat. Amelia's short hair was sticking out all over (she says no one in Bon Temps can cut it right) and her tan face was bare of makeup. Amelia looks like a young suburban mom who has an infant seat strapped into the back of her minivan; the kind of mom who takes time off to run and swim and play tennis. In point of fact, Amelia did run three times a week and practiced tai chi out in my backyard, but she hated getting in the water and she thought tennis was for (and I quote) 'mouth-breathing idiots'. I'd always admired tennis players myself, but when Amelia had a point of view, she stuck to it.

'Going to the mall in Monroe,' she said. 'Shopping to do!' And with an I'm-being-a-good-roommate kind of wave, she hopped into her Mustang and vanished . . .

. . . leaving Quinn and me to stare at each other.

'That Amelia!' I said lamely.

'She's . . . one of a kind,' Quinn said, just as uneasy as I was.

'The thing is—' I began, just as Quinn said, 'Listen, I think we ought—' and we both floundered to a halt. He made a gesture that indicated I should go first.

'How long are you here for?' I asked.

'I have to leave tomorrow,' he said. 'I could stay in Monroe or Shreveport.'

We did some more staring. I can't read were minds, not like regular humans. I can get the intent, though, and the intent was . . . intent.

'So,' he said. He went down on one knee. 'Please,' he said.

I had to smile, but then I looked away. 'The only thing is,' I began again. This conversation would come much more easily to Amelia, who was frank to a very extreme point. 'You know that we have, uh, a lot of . . .' I gestured back and forth with my hand.

'Chemistry,' he said.

'Right,' I said. 'But if we never get to see any more of each other than we have the past six months, I'm not really sure I want to make that next step.' I hated to say it, but I had to. I didn't need to cause myself pain. 'I have big lust,' I said. 'Big, big lust. But I'm not a one-night-stand kind of woman.'

'When the summit is over; I'm taking a long time off,' Quinn said, and I could tell he was absolutely sincere. 'A month. I came here to ask you if I could spend it with you.'

'Really?' I couldn't help sounding incredulous. 'Really?'

He smiled up at me. Quinn has a smooth, shaved head, an olive complexion, a bold nose, and a smile that makes these little dimples in the corners of his mouth. His eyes are purple, like a spring pansy. He is as big as a pro wrestler, and just as scary. He held up a huge hand, as if he were swearing an oath. 'On a stack of Bibles,' he said.

'Yes,' I said after a moment's scan of my inner qualms to make sure they were minor. And also, I may not have a built-in truth detector, but I could have told if he'd been thinking, *I'm saying that to get in her pants.* Shifters are very hard to read, their brains are all snarly and semiopaque, but I would've picked up on that. 'Then . . . yes.'

'Oh, boy.' Quinn took a deep breath and his grin lit up the room. But in the next moment, his eyes got that focused look men get when they're thinking about sex very specifically. And then, lickety-split, Quinn was on his feet and his arms were around me as tightly as ropes tying us together.

His mouth found mine. We picked up where we'd left off with the kissing. His mouth was a very clever one and his tongue was very warm. His hands began examining my topography. Down the line of my back to the curve of my hips, back up to my shoulders to cup my face for a moment, down to brush my neck teasingly with the lightest of fingertips. Then those fingers found my breasts, and after a second he tugged my top out of my pants and began exploring territory he'd only visited briefly before. He liked what he found, if 'Mmmmm' was a statement of delight. It spoke volumes to me.

'I want to see you,' he said. 'I want to see all of you.'

I had never made love in the daytime before. It seemed very (excitingly) sinful to be struggling with buttons before the sun had even set, and I was so grateful I'd worn an extra-nice white lace bra and little bitty panties. When I dress up, I like to dress up all the way down to the skin.

'Oh,' he said when he saw the bra, which contrasted nicely with my deep summer tan. 'Oh, *boy*.' It wasn't the words; it was the expression of deep admiration. My shoes were already off. Luckily that morning. I'd dispensed with handy-but-totally-unsexy knee-high hose in favor of bare legs. Quinn spent some quality time nuzzling my neck and kissing his way down to the bra while I was struggling to undo his belt, though since he would bend while I was trying to deal with the stiff buckle, that wasn't working out fast enough.

'Take off your shirt,' I said, and my voice came out as hoarse as his. 'I don't have a shirt, you shouldn't have a shirt.'

'Fine,' he said, and presto, the shirt was off. You'd expect Quinn to be hairy, but he isn't. What he is, is muscular to the nth degree, and right at the moment his olive skin was summer-tan. His nipples were surprisingly dark and (not so surprisingly) very hard. Oh, boy – right at my eye level. He began dealing with his own damn belt while I began to explore one hard nub with my mouth, the other with my hand. Quinn's whole body jerked, and he stopped what he was doing. He ran his fingers into my hair to hold my head against him, and he sighed, though it came out more like a growl, vibrating through his body. My free hand yanked at his pants, and he resumed working on the belt but in an unfocused and distracted way.

'Let's move into the bedroom,' I said, but it didn't come out like a calm and collected suggestion, more a ragged demand.

He swooped me up, and I latched my arms around his neck and kissed him on his beautiful mouth again.

'No fair,' he muttered. 'My hands are full.'

'Bed,' I said, and he deposited me on the bed and then simply fell on top of me.

'Clothes,' I reminded him, but he had a mouthful of white lace and breast, and he didn't reply. 'Oh,' I said. I may have said 'Oh' a few more times; and 'Yes,' too. A sudden thought yanked me right out of the flow of the moment.

'Quinn, do you have, you know . . .' I had never needed to have such items before, since vamps can't get a girl pregnant or give her a disease.

'Why do you think I still have my pants on?' he said, pulling a little package out of his back pocket. His smile this time was far more feral.

'Good,' I said from my heart. I would have thrown myself from a window if we'd had to quit. 'And you might take the pants off now.'

I'd seen Quinn naked before but under decidedly stressful circumstances – in the middle of a swamp, in the rain, while we were being pursued by werewolves. Quinn stood by the bed and took off his shoes and socks and then his pants, moving slowly enough to let me watch. He stepped out of his pants, revealing boxer briefs that were suffering their own kind of stress. In one quick movement he eased them off, too. He had a tight, high butt, and the line from his hip to his thigh was just mouthwatering. He had fine, thin white scars striping him at random, but they seemed like such a natural part of him that they didn't detract from his powerful body. I was kneeling on the bed while I admired him, and he said, 'Now you.'

I unhooked my bra and slid it off my arms, and he said, 'Oh, God. I am the luckiest man alive.' After a pause, he said, 'The rest.'

I stood by the bed and eased the little white lacey things off.

'This is like standing in front of a buffet,' he said. 'I don't know where to begin.'

I touched my breasts. 'First course,' I suggested.

I discovered that Quinn's tongue was just a bit raspier than a regular man's. I was gasping and making incoherent noises when he moved from my right breast to my left as he tried to decide which one he liked best. He couldn't make up his mind immediately, which was fine with me. By the time he settled on the right breast, I was pushing against him and making sounds that couldn't be mistaken for anything but desperate.

'I think I'll skip the second course and go right to dessert,' he whispered, his voice dark and ragged. 'Are you ready, babe? You sound ready. You feel ready.'

'I am so ready,' I said, reaching down between us to wrap my hand around his length. He quivered all over when I touched him. He rolled on the condom.

'Now,' he growled. 'Now!' I guided him to my entrance, thrust my hips up to meet him. 'I dreamed of this,' he said, and shoved inside me up to the hilt. That was the last thing either of us was able to say.

Quinn's appetite was as outstanding as his equipment.

He enjoyed dessert so much, he came back for seconds.

Chapter 3

We were in the kitchen when Amelia returned. I'd fed Bob, her cat, since she'd been so tactful earlier and deserved some reward. Tact does not come naturally to Amelia.

Bob ignored his kibble in favor of watching Quinn fry bacon, and I was slicing tomatoes. I'd gotten out the cheese and the mayonnaise and the mustard and the pickles, anything I could imagine a man might want on a bacon sandwich. I'd pulled on some old shorts and a T-shirt, while Quinn had gotten his bag from his truck and put on his workout clothes – a tank top and worn shorts made from sweat material.

Amelia gave Quinn a top-to-bottom scan when he turned back to the stove, and then she looked at me, grinning broadly. 'You guys have a good reunion?' she said, tossing her shopping bags on the kitchen table.

'Up to your room, please,' I said, because otherwise Amelia would want us to admire every single thing she'd bought. With a pout, Amelia snagged the bags and carried them upstairs, returning in a minute to ask Quinn if there was enough bacon for her.

'Sure,' Quinn said obligingly, taking out some strips and putting a few more in the pan.

I liked a man who could cook. While I set out plates and silverware, I was pleasantly aware of the tenderness I felt south of my belly button and of my overwhelmingly relaxed mood. I got three glasses out of the cabinet but kind of forgot what I was doing on my way to the refrigerator, since Quinn stepped away from the stove to give me a quick kiss. His lips were so warm and firm, they reminded me of something else that had been warm and firm. I flashed on my astonished moment of revelation when Quinn had slid into me for the first time. Considering that my only previous sexual encounters had been with vampires, who are definitely on the cool side, you can imagine what a startling experience a breathing lover with a heartbeat and a warm penis would be. In fact, shape-shifters tended to run a bit warmer than regular humans. Even through the condom, I'd been able to feel the heat.

'What?' Quinn asked. 'Why the look?' He was smiling quizzically.

I smiled. 'I was just thinking of your temperature,' I said.

'Hey, you knew I was hot,' he said with a grin. 'What about the thought reading?' he said more seriously. 'How did that work out?'

I thought it was great that he'd even wondered. 'I can't call your thoughts any trouble,' I said, unable to suppress a huge grin. 'It might be a stretch to count 'yesyesyesyespleasepleaseplease' as a thought.'

'Not a problem then,' he said, totally unembarrassed.

'Not a problem. As long as you're wrapped in the moment and you're happy, I'm gonna be happy.'

'Well, hot damn.' Quinn turned back to the stove. 'That's just *great*.'

I thought it was, too.

Just great.

Amelia ate her sandwich with a good appetite and then picked Bob up to feed him little bits of bacon she'd saved. The big black-and-white cat purred up a storm.

'So,' said Quinn, after his first sandwich had disappeared with amazing quickness, 'this is the guy you changed by accident?'

'Yeah,' said Amelia, scratching Bob's ears. 'This is the guy.' Amelia was sitting cross-legged in the kitchen chair, which is something I simply couldn't do, and she was focused on the cat. 'The little fella,' she crooned. 'My fuzzy wuzzy honey, isn't he? Isn't he?' Quinn looked mildly disgusted, but I was just as guilty of talking baby talk to Bob when I was alone with him. Bob the witch had been a skinny, weird guy with a kind of geeky charm. Amelia had told me Bob had been a hairdresser; I'd decided if that were true, he'd fixed hair at a funeral parlor. Black pants, white shirt, bicycle? Have you ever known a hairdresser who presented himself that way?

'So,' Quinn said. 'What are you doing about it?'

'I'm studying,' Amelia said. 'I'm trying to figure out what I did wrong, so I can make it right. It would be easier if I could . . .' Her voice trailed off in a guilty kind of way.

'If you could talk to your mentor?' I said helpfully.

She scowled at me. 'Yeah,' she said. 'If I could talk to my mentor.'

'Why don't you?' Quinn asked.

'One, I wasn't supposed to use transformational magic. That's pretty much a no-no. Two, I've looked for her online since Katrina, on every message board witches use, and I can't find any news of her. She might have gone to a shelter somewhere, she might be staying with her kids or some friend, or she might have died in the flooding.'

'I believe you had your main income from your rental property. What are your plans now? What's the state of your property?' Quinn asked, carrying his plate and mine to the sink. He wasn't being bashful with the personal questions tonight. I waited with interest to hear Amelia's answers. I'd always wanted to know a lot of things about Amelia that were just plain rude to ask: like, What was she living on now? Though she had worked part-time for my friend Tara Thornton at Tara's Togs while Tara's help was sick, Amelia's outgo far exceeded her visible income. That meant she had good credit, some savings, or another source of income besides the tarot readings she'd done in a shop off Jackson Square and her rent money, which now wasn't coming in. Her mom had left her some money. It must have been a chunk.

'Well, I've been back into New Orleans once since the storm,' Amelia said. 'You've met Everett, my tenant?'

Quinn nodded.

'When he could get to a phone, he reported some damage to the bottom floor, where I live. There were trees and branches down, and of course there wasn't electricity or water for a couple of weeks. But the neighborhood didn't suffer as badly as some, thank God, and when the electricity was back on, I snuck down there.' Amelia took a deep breath. I could hear right from her brain that she was scared to venture into the territory she was about to reveal to us. 'I, um, went to talk to my dad about fixing the roof. Right then, we had a blue roof like half the people around us.' The blue plastic that covered damaged roofs was the new norm in New Orleans.

This was the first time Amelia had mentioned her family to me, in more than a very general way. I'd learned more from her thoughts than I'd learned from her conversation, and I had to be careful not to mix the two sources when we talked. I could see her dad's presence in her head, love and resentment mixing in her thoughts to form a confused mishmash.

'Your dad is going to repair your house?' Quinn asked casually. He was excavating in my Tupperware box in which I stored any cookies that happened to cross my threshold – not a frequent occurrence, since I have a tendency to put on weight when sweets are in the house. Amelia had no such problem, and she'd stocked the box with a couple of kinds of Keebler cookies and told Quinn he was welcome to help himself.

Amelia nodded, much more fascinated by Bob's fur than she had been a moment before. 'Yeah, he's got a crew on it,' she said.

This was news to me.

'So who is your dad?' Quinn was keeping up the directness. So far it had worked for him.

Amelia squirmed on the kitchen chair, making Bob raise his head in protest.

'Copley Carmichael,' she muttered.

We were both silent with shock. After a minute, she looked up at us. 'What?' she said. 'Okay, so he's famous. Okay, so he's rich. So?'

'Different last name?' I said.

'I use my mom's. I got tired of people being weird around me,' Amelia said pointedly.

Quinn and I exchanged glances. Copley Carmichael was a big name in the state of Louisiana. He had fingers in all kinds of financial pies, and all those fingers were pretty dirty. But he was an old-fashioned human wheeler-dealer: no whiff of the supernatural around Copley Carmichael.

'Does he know you're a witch?' I asked.

'He doesn't believe it for a minute,' Amelia said, sounding frustrated and forlorn. 'He thinks I'm a deluded little wannabe, that I'm hanging with weird little people and doing weird little jobs to stick my tongue out at him. He wouldn't believe in vampires if he hadn't seen them over and over.'

'What about your mom?' Quinn asked. I got myself a refill on my tea. I knew the answer to this one.

'Dead,' Amelia told him. 'Three years ago. That's when I moved out of my dad's house and into the bottom floor of the house on Chloe. He'd given it to me when I graduated from high school so I'd have my own income, but he made me manage it myself so I'd have the experience.'

That seemed like a pretty good deal to me. Hesitantly I said, 'Wasn't that the right thing to do? Get you to learn by doing?'

'Well, yeah,' she admitted. 'But when I moved out, he wanted to give me an allowance ... at my age! I knew I had to make it on my own. Between the rent, and the money I picked up doing fortunes, and magic jobs I got on my own, I've been making a living.' She threw up her head proudly.

Amelia didn't seem to realize the rent was income from a gift of her father's, not something she'd actually earned. Amelia was truly pleased as punch with her own self-sufficiency. My new friend, whom I'd acquired almost by accident, was a bundle of contradictions. Since she was a very clear broadcaster, I got her thoughts loud and clear. When I was alone with Amelia, I had to shield like crazy. I'd relaxed with Quinn around, but I shouldn't have. I was getting a whole mess from Amelia's head.

'So, could your dad help you find your mentor?' Quinn asked.

Amelia looked blank for a moment, as if she was considering that. 'I don't see how,' she said slowly. 'He's a powerful guy; you know that. But he's having as much trouble in New Orleans since Katrina as the rest of the people are.'

Except he had a lot more money and he could go somewhere else, returning when he pleased, which most of the inhabitants of the city could not. I closed my mouth to keep this observation to myself. Time to change the topic.

'Amelia,' I said. 'How well did you know Bob, anyway? Who's looking for him?'

She looked a little frightened, not Amelia's normal thing. 'I'm wondering, too,' she said. 'I just knew Bob to speak to, before that night. But I do know that Bob had – has – great friends in the magic community. I don't think any of them know we got together. That night, two nights before the queen's ball when the shit hit the fan between the Arkansas vamps and our vamps, Bob and I went back to my place after we'd left Terry and Patsy at the pizza place. Bob called in sick to work the next day, since we had celebrated so hard, and then he spent that day with me.'

'So it's possible Bob's family has been looking for him for months? Wondering if he's dead or alive?'

'Hey, chill. I'm not that awful. Bob was raised by his aunt, but they don't get along at all. He hasn't had much contact with her for years. I'm sure he does have friends that are worrying, and I'm really, really sorry about that. But even if they knew what had happened, that wouldn't help Bob, right? And since Katrina, everyone in New Orleans has a lot to worry about.'

At this interesting point in the discussion, the phone rang. I was closest, so I picked it up. My brother's voice was almost electric with excitement.

'Sookie, you need to come out to Hotshot in about an hour.'

'Why?'

'Me and Crystal are getting married. Surprise!'

While this was not a total shock (Jason had been 'dating' Crystal Norris for several months), the suddenness of the ceremony made me anxious.

'Is Crystal pregnant again?' I asked suspiciously. She'd miscarried a baby of Jason's not long ago.

'Yes!' Jason said, like that was the best news he could possibly impart. 'And this time, we'll be married when the baby comes.'

Jason was ignoring reality, as he was increasingly willing to do. The reality was that Crystal had been pregnant at least once before she was pregnant by Jason, and she had lost that child, too. The community at Hotshot was a victim of its own inbreeding.

'Okay, I'll be there,' I said. 'Can Amelia and Quinn come, too?'

'Sure,' Jason said. 'Crystal and me'll be proud to have them.'

'Is there anything I can bring?'

'No, Calvin and them are getting ready to cook. It's all going to be outside. We got lights strung up. I think they'll have a big pot of jambalaya, some dirty rice, and coleslaw, and me and my buddies are bringing the alcohol. Just come looking pretty! See you at Hotshot in an hour. Don't be late.'

I hung up and sat there for a minute, my hand still clutching the cordless phone. That was just like Jason: come in an hour to a ceremony planned at the last minute for the worst possible reason, and don't be late! At least he hadn't asked me to bring a cake.

'Sookie, you okay?' Quinn asked.

'My brother Jason's getting married tonight,' I said, trying to keep my voice even. 'We're invited to the wedding, and we need to be there in an hour.' I'd always figured Jason wouldn't marry a woman I truly adored; he'd always shown a partiality to tough sluts. And that was Crystal, sure enough.

Crystal was also a werepanther, a member of a community that guarded its own secrets jealously. In fact, my brother was now a werepanther himself because he'd been bitten over and over by a rival for Crystal's attentions.

Jason was older than I, and God knows, he'd had his share of women. I had to assume he knew when one suited him.

I emerged from my thoughts to find that Amelia was looking startled and excited. She loved to go out and party, and the chances for that around Bon Temps were limited. Quinn, who'd met Jason when he was visiting me, looked at me with a skeptical raised eyebrow.

'Yeah, I know,' I said. 'It's crazy and dumb. But Crystal's pregnant again, and there's no stopping him. Do you two want to come along with me? You don't have to. I'm afraid I've got to get ready right now.'

Amelia said, 'Oh, goody, I can wear my new outfit,' and sped upstairs to tear the tags off.

Quinn said, 'Babe, do you want me to come?'

'Yes, please,' I said. He came over to me and wrapped his heavy arms around me. I felt comforted, even though I knew Quinn was thinking what a fool Jason was.

I pretty much agreed with him.

Chapter 4

It was still warm at night, but not oppressively so, not this late in September. I wore a sleeveless white dress with red flowers on it, one I'd worn before when I had a date with Bill (whom I *wouldn't* think about). Out of sheer vanity, I put on my high-heeled red sandals, though they were hardly practical footwear for a wedding on a roughly paved road. I put on some makeup while Quinn was showering, and I wasn't displeased with my reflection. There's nothing like great sex to give you a glow. I came out of my room and glanced at the clock. We needed to leave pretty quickly.

Amelia was wearing a short-sleeved dress, beige with a tiny navy pattern. Amelia loved to buy clothes and considered herself a snappy dresser, but her taste was strictly suburban young matron. She wore little navy sandals with flowers on the straps, much more appropriate than my heels.

Just when I was beginning to worry, Quinn came out of my room wearing a brown silk dress shirt and khakis.

'What about a tie?' he asked. 'I've got some in my bag.'

I thought of the rural setting and vast lack of sophistication in the little community of Hotshot. 'I don't think a tie will be necessary,' I said, and Quinn looked relieved.

We piled into my car and drove west and then south. On the drive, I had a chance to explain to my out-of-town guests about the isolated band of werepanthers and their small cluster of houses grouped together in rural Renard Parish. I was driving, since that was just simplest. Once out of sight of the old railroad tracks, the country became increasingly unpopulated until for two or three miles we saw no lights of any kind. Then we saw cars and lights at a crossroads ahead. We were there.

Hotshot was out in the middle of nowhere, set in a long depression in the middle of gently rolling land, swells that were too ill-defined to be called hills. Formed around an ancient crossroads, the lonely community had a powerful vibration of magic. I could tell that Amelia was feeling that power. Her face became sharper and wiser as we got closer. Even Quinn inhaled deeply. As for me, I could detect the presence of magic, but it didn't affect non-supernatural me.

I pulled over to the side of the road behind Hoyt Fortenberry's truck. Hoyt was Jason's best friend and lifelong shadow. I spied him right ahead of us, trudging down the road to a well-lit area. I'd handed Amelia and Quinn a flashlight, and I kept one aimed at my feet.

'Hoyt,' I called. I hurried to catch up with him, at least as much as was practical in the red heels. 'Hey, are you okay?' I asked when I saw his downcast face. Hoyt was not a very good-looking guy, or very bright, but he was steady and tended to see past the moment to its consequences, something my brother had never mastered.

'Sook,' Hoyt said. 'I can't believe he's getting hitched. I guess I thought me and Jason would be bachelors forever.' He attempted to smile.

I gave him a pat on the shoulder. Life would've been neat 'n' tidy if I could have fallen in love with Hoyt, thus attaching him to my brother forever, but Hoyt and I had never had the slightest interest in each other.

Hoyt's mind was radiating a dull misery. He was certain that his life was changing forever this night. He expected Jason to mend his ways completely, to stay in with his wife like a husband should, and to forsake all others.

I sure hoped Hoyt's expectations were right on the money.

On the edges of the crowd, Hoyt met up with Catfish Hennessy, and they began making loud jokes about Jason's breaking down and marrying.

I hoped the male bonding would help Hoyt get through the ceremony. I didn't know if Crystal truly loved my brother – but Hoyt did.

Quinn took my hand, and with Amelia in our wake we forged
through the little crowd until we reached the center.

Jason was wearing a new suit, and the blue of it was only a bit darker
than the blue of his eyes. He looked great, and he was smiling to beat
the band. Crystal was wearing a leopard-print dress cut as low in the
front as you could get and still term the garment a dress. I didn't know
if the leopard motif was an ironic statement on her part or a simple
expression of her fashion sense. I suspected the latter.

The happy couple was standing in the middle of an empty space,
accompanied by Calvin Norris, leader of the Hotshot community. The
crowd kept respectfully back, forming an uneven circle.

Calvin, who happened to be Crystal's uncle, was holding Crystal's
arm. He smiled at me. Calvin had trimmed his beard and dug out a
suit for the occasion, but he and Jason were the only men wearing ties.
Quinn noticed that and thought relieved thoughts.

Jason spotted me right after Calvin did, and he beckoned to me.
I stepped forward, suddenly realizing that I was going to have a part
in the ceremony. I hugged my brother, smelling his musky cologne . . .
but no alcohol. I relaxed a fraction. I had suspected Jason had fortified
himself with a drink or two, but he was quite sober.

I let go of Jason and glanced behind me to see what had become
of my companions, so I knew the moment when the werepanthers
realized Quinn was there. There was a sudden hush among the
two-natured, and I heard his name ripple through them like a little
wind.

Calvin whispered, 'You brought *Quinn?*' as if I'd arrived with Santa
Claus or some other mythical creature.

'Is that okay?' I said, since I'd had no clue it would create such a stir.

'Oh, yes,' he said. 'He's your man now?' Calvin's face held such a
mixture of startled reevaluation and speculation that I immediately
began wondering what I didn't know about my new lover.

'Um, well, sorta,' I said with sudden caution.

'We're honored to have him here,' Calvin assured me.

'Quinn,' Crystal breathed. Her pupils were dilating, and I felt her brain focus on my date with a sort of groupie longing. I wanted to kick her. *Here to marry my brother, remember?*

Jason looked as puzzled as I was. Since he'd been a panther only a few months, there was a lot about the hidden world of the two-natured he hadn't picked up on yet.

Me, too.

Crystal made an effort to quell herself and get back into the moment. She was naturally enjoying being the center of attention, but she spared a moment to reassess her prospective sister-in-law. Her respect for me (pretty much nonexistent, heretofore) had just shot off the charts.

'What's the procedure?' I asked briskly, trying to get us all back on track.

Calvin reverted to his practical self. 'Since we have human guests, we've adapted the ceremony,' he explained in a very low voice. 'Here's how it goes . . . you vouch for Jason as his closest living relative, because he ain't got no one older than you to do it. I'm Crystal's oldest living relative, so I vouch for her. We offer to take the penalty if either of them does wrong.'

Ah-oh. I didn't like the sound of that. I darted a quick look at my brother, who (naturally) didn't seem to think twice about the commitment I was making. I shouldn't have expected anything else.

'Then the minister comes forward and the service proceeds just like any other wedding,' Calvin said. 'If there weren't outsiders here, it would be different.'

I was curious about that, but this wasn't the time to ask lots of questions. However, there were a few that had to be answered. 'What penalty am I promising to pay? What constitutes 'doing wrong'?'

Jason huffed a sigh, exasperated that I wanted to find out what I was promising. Calvin's calm golden-green eyes met mine, and they were full of understanding.

'Here's what you're vowing,' Calvin said in a voice that was quiet but intense. We huddled around him. 'Jason, you listen hard. We went over this, but I don't think you were giving me your full attention.' Jason was listening now, but I could feel his impatience.

'Being married here' – and Calvin waved a hand to indicate the little

Hotshot community – 'means being faithful to your mate, unless the mate has to breed to keep the group up. Since Crystal's pretty much out of the running on that, Jason, that means she has to be faithful to you, and you to her. You don't have mating obligations like the purebloods do.' Jason flushed at this reminder that his status was lesser since he was only a shifter because he'd been bitten by one, not because he'd been born with the gene. 'So if Crystal runs around on you and a member of the community can attest to it, and if she can't pay the price for some reason – pregnancy, or illness, or a kid to raise – I have to do it. We're not talking money here, you understand?'

Jason nodded. 'You're talking physical punishment,' he said.

'Yes,' Calvin said. 'Not only are you promising to be faithful, you're also swearing to keep our secret.'

Jason nodded again.

'And to help out other members of the community if they're in need.'

Jason scowled.

'Example?' I said.

'If Maryelizabeth's roof needs replacing, we might all chip in a bit to buy the material and we'd all make time to do the work. If a kid needs a place to stay, your home is open to that kid. We take care of each other.'

Jason nodded again. 'I understand,' he said. 'I'm willing.' He would have to give up some of his buddy time, and I felt sad for Hoyt; and I confess I felt a little sad for myself. I wasn't gaining a sister; I was losing my brother, at least to some degree.

'Mean this from the heart or call it off now,' I said, keeping my voice very low. 'You're committing my life to this, too. Can you keep the promises you're making to this woman and her community, or not?'

Jason looked at Crystal for a long moment, and I had no right to be in his head, so I pulled out and instead cast through the crowd for random thoughts. They were mostly what you'd expect: a bit of excitement at being at a wedding, a bit of pleasure at seeing the parish's most notorious bachelor shackled to a wild young woman, a bit of curiosity about the odd Hotshot ritual. *Hotshot* was a byword in the parish – 'as weird as a guy from Hotshot' had been a saying for years, and Hotshot kids who attended the Bon Temps school often had a hard time of it until after the first few playground fights.

'I'll keep my promises,' Jason said, his voice hoarse.

'I'll keep mine,' Crystal said.

The difference between the two was this: Jason was sincere, though I doubted his ability to stick to his word. Crystal had the ability, but she wasn't sincere.

'You don't mean it,' I said to her.

'The hell you say,' she retorted.

'I don't usually say one way or another,' I said, making the effort to keep my voice low. 'But this is too serious to keep silent. I can see inside your head, Crystal. Don't you ever forget I can.'

'I ain't forgetting nothing,' she said, making sure each word had weight. 'And I'm marrying Jason tonight.'

I looked at Calvin. He was troubled, but in the end, he shrugged. 'We can't stop this,' he said. For a second, I was tempted to struggle with his pronouncement. *Why not?* I thought. *If I hauled off and slapped her, maybe that would be enough disruption to stall the whole thing.* Then I reconsidered. They were both grown-ups, at least theoretically. They would get married if they chose, either here and now or somewhere else on some other night. I bowed my head and sucked up my misgivings.

'Of course,' I said, raising my face and smiling that bright smile I got when I was really anxious. 'Let's get on with the ceremony.' I caught a glimpse of Quinn's face in the crowd. He was looking at me, concerned by the low-voiced argument. Amelia, on the other hand, was happily chatting with Catfish, whom she'd met at the bar. Hoyt was by himself right under one of the portable lights rigged up for the occasion. He had his hands thrust in his pockets, and he looked more serious than I'd ever seen him. There was something strange about the sight, and after a second I figured out why.

It was one of the few times I'd ever seen Hoyt alone.

I took my brother's arm, and Calvin again gripped Crystal's. The priest stepped into the center of the circle, and the ceremony began. Though I tried hard to look happy for Jason, I had a difficult time holding back my tears while my brother became the bridegroom of a wild and willful girl who had been dangerous from birth.

There was dancing afterward, and a wedding cake, and lots of alcohol. There was food galore, and consequently there were huge trash cans that filled up with paper plates, cans, and crumpled paper napkins. Some of the men had brought cases of beer and wine, and some had hard liquor, too. No one could say that Hotshot couldn't throw a party.

While a zydeco band from Monroe played, the crowd danced in the street. The music echoed across the fields in an eerie way. I shivered and wondered what was watching from the dark.

'They're good, aren't they?' Jason asked. 'The band?'

'Yeah,' I said. He was flushed with happiness. His bride was dancing with one of her cousins.

'That's why we hurried this wedding up,' he said. 'She found out she was pregnant, and we decided to go on and do it – just do it. And her favorite band was free for tonight.'

I shook my head at my brother's impulsiveness. Then I reminded myself to keep visible signs of disapproval at a minimum. The bride's family might take issue.

Quinn was a good dancer, though I had to show him some of the Cajun steps. All the Hotshot belles wanted a dance with Quinn, too, so I had a turn with Calvin, and Hoyt, and Catfish. Quinn was having a good time, I could tell, and on one level I was, too. But around two thirty a.m., we gave each other a little nod. He had to leave the next day, and I wanted to be alone with him. Plus, I was tired of smiling.

As Quinn thanked Calvin for the wonderful evening, I watched Jason and Crystal dancing together, both apparently delighted with each other. I knew right from Jason's brain that he was infatuated with the shifter girl, with the subculture that had formed her, with the newness of being a supernatural. I knew from Crystal's brain that she was exultant. She'd been determined to marry someone that hadn't grown up in Hotshot, someone who was exciting in bed, someone able to stand up to not only her but her extended family . . . and now she had.

I made my way over to the happy couple and gave each of them a kiss on the cheek. Now Crystal was family, after all, and I would have to accept her as such and leave the two to work out their own life together. I gave Calvin a hug, too, and he held me for a second before releasing me and *giving* me a reassuring pat on the back. Catfish danced me around in a circle, and a drunken Hoyt took up where he'd left off. I had a hard time convincing the two that I really meant to leave, but finally Quinn and I began to make our way back to my car.

As we wended through the edges of the crowd, I spotted Amelia dancing with one of her Hotshot beaux. They were both in high spirits, both literally and libation-wise. I called to Amelia that we were leaving, and she yelled, 'I'll get a ride with someone later!'

Though I enjoyed seeing Amelia happy, it must have been Misgiving Night, because I worried about her a little. However, if anyone could take care of herself, it was Amelia.

We were moving slow when we let ourselves into the house. I didn't check out Quinn's head, but mine was muzzy from the noise, the clamor of all the brains around me, and the extra surges of emotion. It had been a long day. Some of it had been excellent, though. As I recalled the very best parts, I caught myself smiling down at Bob. The big cat rubbed himself against my ankles, meowing in an inquiring kind of way.

Oh, geez.

I felt like I had to explain Amelia's absence to the cat. I squatted down and scratched Bob's head, and (feeling incredibly foolish) I said, 'Hey, Bob. She's going to be real late tonight; she's still dancing at the party. But don't you worry, she'll be home!' The cat turned his back on me and stalked out of the room. I was never sure how much human was lurking in Bob's little feline brain, but I hoped he'd just fall asleep and forget all about our strange conversation.

Just at that moment, I heard Quinn call to me from my bedroom, and I put thoughts about Bob on hold. After all, it was our last night together for maybe weeks.

While I brushed my teeth and washed, my face, I had one last flare of worry about Jason. My brother had made his bed. I hoped he could lie comfortably in it for some time. *He's a grown-up*, I told myself over and over as I went into the bedroom in my nicest nightgown.

Quinn pulled me to him, said, 'Don't worry, babe, don't worry. . . .'

I banished my brother and Bob from my thoughts and this bedroom. I brought a hand up to trace the curve of Quinn's scalp, kept those fingers going down his spine, loved it when he shivered.

Chapter 5

I was walking in my sleep. It was a good thing I knew every inch of Merlotte's like I knew my own house, or I'd have bumped into every table and chair. I yawned widely as I took Selah Pumphrey's order. Ordinarily Selah irritated the hell out of me. She'd been dating Nameless Ex-Lover for several weeks – well, months now. No matter how invisible Ex had become, she'd never be my favorite person.

'Not getting enough rest, Sookie?' she asked, her voice sharp.

'Excuse me,' I apologized. 'I guess not. I was at my brother's wedding last night. What kind of dressing did you want on that salad?'

'Ranch.' Selah's big dark eyes were examining me like she was thinking of etching my portrait. She really wanted to know all about Jason's wedding, but asking me would be like surrendering ground to the enemy. Silly Selah.

Come to think of it, what was Selah doing here? She'd never come in without Bill. She lived in Clarice. Not that Clarice was far; you could get there in fifteen or twenty minutes. But why would a real estate saleswoman from Clarice be . . . oh. She must be showing a house here. Yes, the brain was moving slowly today.

'Okeydokey. Coming right up,' I said, and turned to go.

'Listen,' Selah said. 'Let me be frank.'

Oh, boy. In my experience, that meant, 'Let me be openly mean.'

I swung around, trying to look anything but massively irritated, which was what I actually was. This was not the day to screw with me. Among my many worries, Amelia hadn't come home the night before, and when I'd gone upstairs to look for Bob, I'd found that he'd thrown up in the middle of Amelia's bed . . . which would have been okay by me, but it had been covered with my great-grandmother's quilt. It had fallen to me to clean up the mess and get the quilt to soaking in the washing machine. Quinn had left early that morning, and I was simply sad about that. And then there was Jason's marriage, which had such potential to be a disaster.

I could think of a few more items to add to the list (down to the dripping tap in my kitchen), but you get that my day was not a happy one.

'I'm here working, Selah. I'm not here to have any personal chitchats with you.'

She ignored that.

'I know you're going on a trip with Bill,' she said. 'You're trying to steal him back from me. How long have you been scheming about this?'

I know my mouth was hanging open, because I just hadn't gotten enough warning that was coming. My telepathy was affected when I was tired – just as my reaction time and thought processes were – and I was heavily shielded when I worked, as a matter of course. So I hadn't picked up on Selah's thoughts. A flash of rage passed through me, lifting my palm and raising it to slap the shit out of her. But a warm, hard hand took mine, gripped it, brought it down to my side. Sam was there, and I hadn't even seen him coming. I was missing everything today.

'Miss Pumphrey, you'll have to get your lunch somewhere else,' Sam said quietly. Of course, everyone was watching. I could feel all the brains go on alert for fresh gossip as eyes drank in every nuance of the scene. I could feel my face redden.

'I have the right to eat here,' Selah said, her voice loud and arrogant. That was a huge mistake. In an instant, the sympathies of the spectators switched to me. I could feel the wave of it wash over me. I widened my eyes and looked sad like one of those abnormally big-eyed kids in the awful waif paintings. Looking pathetic was no big stretch. Sam put an arm around me as though I were a wounded child and looked at

Selah with nothing on his face but a grave disappointment in her behavior.

'I have the right to tell you to go,' he said. 'I can't have you insulting my staff.'

Selah was never likely to be rude to Arlene or Holly or Danielle. She hardly knew they existed, because she wasn't the kind of woman who really looked at a server. It had always stuck in her craw that Bill had dated me before he'd met her. ('Dated', in Selah's book, being a euphemism for 'had enthusiastic and frequent sex with'.)

Selah's body was jerky with anger as she threw her napkin on the floor. She got to her feet so abruptly that her chair would have fallen if Dawson, a boulder of a werewolf who ran a motorcycle repair business, hadn't caught it with one huge hand. Selah grabbed up her purse to stalk out of the door, narrowly avoiding a collision with my friend Tara, who was entering.

Dawson was highly amused by the whole scene. 'All that over a vamp,' he said. 'Them cold-blooded things must be something, to get fine-looking women so upset.'

'Who's upset?' I said, smiling and standing straighter to show Sam I was unfazed. I doubt he was fooled, since Sam knows me pretty well, but he got my emotional drift and went back behind the bar. The buzz of discussion of this juicy scene rose from the lunch crowd. I strode over to the table where Tara was sitting. She had JB du Rone in tow.

'Looking good, JB,' I said brightly, pulling the menus from between the napkin box and the salt and pepper shakers in the middle of the table and handing one to him and one to Tara. My hands were shaking, but I don't think they noticed.

JB smiled up at me. 'Thanks, Sookie,' he said in his pleasant baritone. JB was just beautiful, but really short on the brains. However, that gave him a charming simplicity. Tara and I had watched out for him in school, because once that simplicity was observed and targeted by other, less handsome boys, JB had been in for some rough patches . . . especially in junior high. Since Tara and I also both had huge flaws in our own popularity profiles, we'd tried to protect JB as much as we were able. In return, JB had squired me to a couple of dances I'd wanted to go to very badly, and his family had given Tara a place to stay a couple of times when I couldn't.

Tara had had sex with JB somewhere along this painful road. I hadn't. It didn't seem to make any difference to either relationship.

'JB has a new job,' Tara said, smiling in a self-satisfied way. So that was why she'd come in. Our relationship had been uneasy for the past few months, but she knew I'd want to share in her pride at having done a good thing for JB.

That was great news. And it helped me not think about Selah Pumphrey and her load of anger.

'Whereabouts?' I asked JB, who was looking at the menu as if he'd never seen it before.

'At the health club in Clarke,' he said. He looked up and smiled. 'Two days a week, I sit at the desk wearing this.' He waved a hand at his clean and tight-fitting golf shirt, striped burgundy and brown, and his pressed khakis. 'I get the members to sign in, I make healthy shakes, and I clean the equipment and hand out towels. Three days a week, I wear workout clothes and I spot for all the ladies.'

'That sounds great,' I said, awestruck at the perfection of the job for JB's limited qualifications. JB was lovely: impressive muscles, handsome face, straight white teeth. He was an ad for physical health. Also, he was naturally good-natured and neat.

Tara looked at me, expecting her due praise. 'Good work,' I told her. We gave each other a high five.

'Now, Sookie, the only thing that would make life perfect is you calling me some night,' JB said. No one could project a wholesome, simple lust like JB.

'Thanks so much, JB, but I'm seeing someone now,' I said, not troubling to keep my voice down. After Selah's little exhibition, I felt the need to brag a little.

'Oooh, that Quinn?' Tara asked. I may have mentioned him to her once or twice. I nodded, and we did another high five. 'Is he in town now?' she asked in a lower voice, and I said, 'Left this morning,' just as quietly.

'I want the Mexican cheeseburger,' JB said.

'Then I'll get you one,' I said, and after Tara had ordered, I marched to the kitchen. Not only was I delighted for JB, I was happy that Tara and I seemed to have mended our fences. I had needed a little upswing to my day, and I had gotten it.

When I reached home with a couple of bags of groceries, Amelia was back and my kitchen sparkled like an exhibit in a Southern Homes show. When she was feeling stressed or bored, Amelia cleaned, which was a fantastic habit to have in a housemate – especially when you're not used to having one at all. I like a neat house myself, and I get cleaning spurts from time to time, but next to Amelia I was a slob.

I looked at the clean windows. 'Feeling guilty, huh?' I said.

Amelia's shoulders slumped. She was sitting at the kitchen table with a mug of one of her weird teas, steam rising from the dark liquid.

'Yeah,' she said glumly. 'I saw the quilt was in the washing machine. I worked on the spot, and it's hanging out back on the line now.'

Since I'd noted that when I came in, I just nodded. 'Bob retaliated,' I said.

'Yeah.'

I started to ask her who she'd stayed with, then realized it was really none of my business. Besides, though I was very tired, Amelia was a broadcaster of the first order, and within seconds I knew she'd stayed with Calvin's cousin Derrick and the sex hadn't been good; also, Derrick's sheets had been very dirty and that had made her nuts. Plus, when Derrick had woken up this morning, he'd indicated that in his mind, a night together made them a couple. Amelia had had a hard time getting Derrick to give her a ride back to the house. He wanted her to stay with him, in Hotshot.

'Weirded out?' I asked, putting the hamburger meat in the refrigerator drawer. It was my week to cook, and we were going to have hamburger steak, baked potatoes, and green beans.

Amelia nodded, lifting her mug to take a sip. It was a homemade hangover restorative she'd concocted, and she shuddered as she experimented on herself. 'Yeah, I am. Those Hotshot guys are a little strange,' she said.

'Some of them.' Amelia had adjusted better to my telepathy than anyone I'd ever encountered. Since she was frank and open anyway –

sometimes way too much – I guess she never felt she had secrets to hide.

'What are you gonna do?' I asked. I sat down opposite her.

'See, it's not like I'd been dating Bob for a long time,' she said, jumping right into the middle of the conversation without bothering with preliminaries. She knew I understood. 'We'd only gotten together twice. Believe me, it was great. He really *got* me. That's why we began, ah, experimenting.'

I nodded, tried to look understanding. To me, experimenting was, well, licking a place you'd never licked before, or trying a position that gave you a cramp in your thigh. Like that. It did not involve turning your partner into an animal. I'd never worked up enough nerve to ask Amelia what their goal had been, and it was one thing her brain wasn't throwing out.

'I guess you like cats,' I said, following my train of thought to its logical conclusion. 'I mean, Bob is a cat, but a small one, and then you picked Derrick out of all the guys who would have been thrilled to spend the night with you.'

'Oh?' Amelia said, perking up. She tried to sound casual. 'More than one?'

Amelia did have the tendency to think way too well of herself as a witch, but not enough of herself as a woman.

'One or two,' I said, trying not to laugh. Bob came in and wreathed himself around my legs, purring loudly. It could hardly have been more pointed, since he walked around Amelia as if she were a pile of dog poop.

Amelia sighed heavily. 'Listen, Bob, you've gotta forgive me,' she said to the cat. 'I'm sorry. I just got carried away. A wedding, a few beers, dancing in the street, an exotic partner . . . I'm sorry. Really, really sorry. How about I promise to be celibate until I can figure out a way to turn you back into yourself?'

This was a huge sacrifice on Amelia's part, as anyone who'd read her thoughts for a couple of days (and more) would know. Amelia was a very healthy girl and she was a very direct woman. She was also fairly diverse in her tastes. 'Well,' she said, on second thought, 'what if I just promise not to do any guys?'

Bob's hind end sat while his front end stood, and his tail wrapped around his front paws. He looked adorable as he stared up at Amelia, his large yellow eyes unblinking. He appeared to be thinking it over. Finally, he said, 'Rohr.'

Amelia smiled.

'You taking that as a yes?' I said. 'If so, remember . . . I just do guys, so don't go looking my way.'

'Oh, I probably wouldn't try to hook up with you anyway,' Amelia said.

Did I mention Amelia is a little tactless? 'Why not?' I asked, insulted.

'I didn't pick Bob at random,' Amelia said, looking as embarrassed as it is possible for Amelia to look. 'I like 'em skinny and dark.'

'I'll just have to live with that,' I said, trying to look deeply disappointed. Amelia threw a tea ball at me, and I caught it in midair.

'Good reflexes,' she said, startled.

I shrugged. Though it had been ages since I'd had vampire blood, a trace seemed to linger on in my system. I'd always been healthy, but now I seldom even got a headache. And I moved a little quicker than most people. I wasn't the only person to enjoy the side effects of vamp blood ingestion. Now that the effects have become common knowledge, vampires have become prey themselves. Harvesting that blood to sell on the black market is a lucrative and highly perilous profession. I'd heard on the radio that morning that a drainer had disappeared from his Texarkana apartment after he'd gotten out on parole. If you make an enemy of a vamp, he can wait it out a lot longer than you can.

'Maybe it's the fairy blood,' Amelia said, staring at me thoughtfully.

I shrugged again, this time with a definite drop-this-subject air. I'd learned I had a trace of fairy in my lineage only recently, and I wasn't happy about it. I didn't even know which side of my family had bequeathed me this legacy, much less which individual. All I knew was that at some time in the past, someone in my family had gotten up close and personal with a fairy. I'd spent a couple of hours poring over the yellowing family trees and the family history my grandmother had worked so hard to compile, and I hadn't found a clue.

As if she'd been summoned by the thought, Claudine knocked at the back door. She hadn't flown on gossamer wings; she'd arrived in her car. Claudine is a full-blooded fairy, and she has other ways of getting places, but she uses those ways only in emergencies. Claudine is very tall, with a thick fall of dark hair and big, slanted dark eyes. She has to cover her ears with her hair, since unlike her twin, Claude, she hasn't had the pointy parts surgically altered.

Claudine hugged me enthusiastically but gave Amelia a distant wave. They are not nuts about each other. Amelia has acquired magic, but Claudine is magic to the bone. Neither quite trusts the other.

Claudine is normally the sunniest creature I ever met. She is very kind, and sweet, and helpful, like a supernatural Girl Scout, because it's her nature and because she's trying to work her way up the magical ladder to become an angel. Tonight, Claudine's face was unusually serious. My heart sank. I wanted to go to bed, and I wanted to miss Quinn in private, and I wanted to get over the jangling my nerves had taken at Merlotte's. I didn't want bad news.

Claudine settled at the kitchen table across from me and held my hands. She spared a look for Amelia. 'Take a hike, witch,' she said, and I was shocked.

'Pointy-eared bitch,' muttered Amelia, getting up with her mug of tea.

'Mate killer,' responded Claudine.

'He's not dead!' shrieked Amelia. 'He's just – different!'

Claudine snorted, and actually that was an adequate response.

I was too tired to scold Claudine for her unprecedented rudeness, and she was holding my hands too tight for me to be pleased about her comforting presence. 'What's up?' I asked. Amelia stomped out of the room, and I heard her shoes on the stairs up to the second floor.

'No vampires here?' Claudine said, her voice anxious. You know how a chocoholic feels about chunky fudge ice cream, double dipped in dark chocolate? That's how vamps feel about fairies.

'Yeah, the house is empty except for me, you, Amelia, and Bob,' I said. I was not going to deny Bob his person-hood, though sometimes it was pretty hard to recall, especially when his litter box needed cleaning.

'You're going to this summit?'

'Yes.'

'Why?'

That was a good question. 'The queen is paying me,' I said.

'Do you need the money so badly?'

I started to dismiss her concern, but then I gave it some serious thought. Claudine had done a lot for me, and the least I could do for her was think about what she said.

'I can live without it,' I said. After all, I still had some of the money Eric had paid me for hiding him from a group of witches. But a chunk of it had gone, as money seems to; the insurance hadn't covered everything that had been damaged or destroyed by the fire that had consumed my kitchen the winter before, and I'd upgraded my appliances, and I'd made a donation to the volunteer fire department. They'd come so quickly and tried so hard to save the kitchen and my car.

Then Jason had needed help to pay the doctor's bill for Crystal's miscarriage.

I found I missed that layer of padding between being solvent and being broke. I wanted to reinforce it, replenish it. My little boat sailed on precarious financial waters, and I wanted to have a towboat around to keep it afloat.

'I can live without it,' I said, more firmly, 'but I don't want to.'

Claudine sighed. Her face was full of woe. 'I can't go with you,' she said. 'You know how vampires are around us. I can't even put in an appearance.'

'I understand,' I said, a bit surprised. I'd never dreamed of Claudine's going.

'And I think there's going to be trouble,' she said.

'What kind?' The last time I'd gone to a vampire social gathering, there had been big trouble, major trouble, the bloodiest kind of trouble.

'I don't know,' Claudine said. 'But I feel it coming, and I think you should stay home. Claude does, too.'

Claude didn't give a rat's ass what happened to me, but Claudine was generous enough to include her brother in her kindness. As far as I could tell, Claude's benefit to the world was strictly as a decoration.

He was utterly selfish, had no social skills, and was absolutely beautiful.

'I'm sorry, Claudine, and I'll miss you while I'm in Rhodes,' I said. 'But I've obligated myself to go.'

'Going in the train of a vampire,' Claudine said dismally. 'It'll mark you as one of their world, for good. You'll never be an innocent bystander again. Too many creatures will know who you are and where you can be found.'

It wasn't so much what Claudine said as the way she said it that made cold prickles run up my spine and crawl along my scalp. She was right. I had no defense, though I rather thought that I was already into the vamp world too deeply to opt out.

Sitting there in my kitchen with the late afternoon sun slanting through the window, I had one of those illuminations that changes you forever. Amelia was silent upstairs. Bob had come back into the room to sit by his food bowl and stare at Claudine. Claudine herself was gleaming in a beam of sunlight that hit her square in the face. Most people would be showing every unattractive skin flaw. Claudine still looked perfect.

I wasn't sure I would ever understand Claudine and her thinking about the world, and I still knew frighteningly little about her life; but I felt quite sure that she had devoted herself to my well-being, for whatever reason, and that she was really afraid for me. And yet I knew I was going to Rhodes with the queen, and Eric, and the abjured one, and the rest of the Louisiana contingent.

Was I just curious about what the agenda might be at a vampire summit? Did I want the attention of more undead members of society? Did I want to be known as a fangbanger, one of those humans who simply adored the walking dead? Did some corner of me long for a chance to be near Bill without seeking him out, still trying to make some emotional sense of his betrayal? Or was this about Eric? Unbeknownst to myself, was I in love with the flamboyant Viking who was so handsome, so good at making love, and so political, all at the same time?

This sounded like a promising set of problems for a soap opera season.

'Tune in tomorrow,' I muttered. When Claudine looked at me

askance, I said, 'Claudine, I feel embarrassed to tell you I'm doing something that really doesn't make much sense in a lot of ways, but I want the money and I'm going to do it. I'll be back here to see you again. Don't worry, please.'

Amelia clomped back into the room, began making herself some more tea. She was going to float away.

Claudine ignored her. 'I'm going to worry,' she said simply. 'There is trouble coming, my dear friend, and it will fall right on your head.'

'But you don't know how or when?'

She shook her head. 'No, I just know it's coming.'

'Look into my eyes,' muttered Amelia. 'I see a tall, dark man . . .'

'Shut up,' I told her.

She turned her back to us, made a big fuss out of pinching the dead leaves off some of her plants.

Claudine left soon after. For the remainder of her visit, she didn't recover her normal happy demeanor. She never said another word about my departure.

Chapter 6

On the second morning after Jason's wedding. I was feeling much more myself. Having a mission helped. I needed to be at Tara's Togs right after it opened at ten. I had to pick out the clothes Eric said I needed for the summit. I wasn't due at Merlotte's until five thirty or so that night, so I had that pleasant feeling of the whole day stretching ahead of me.

'Hey, girl!' Tara said, coming from the back of the shop to greet me. Her part-time assistant, McKenna, glanced at me and resumed moving clothes around. I assumed she was putting misplaced items back into their correct positions; clothing store employees seem to spend a lot of time doing that. McKenna didn't speak, and unless I was much mistaken, she was trying to avoid talking to me at all. That hurt, since I'd gone to see her in the hospital when she'd had her appendix out two weeks ago, and I'd taken her a little present, too.

'Mr Northman's business associate Bobby Burnham called down here to say you needed some clothes for a trip?' Tara said. I nodded, trying to look matter of fact. 'Would casual clothes be what you needed? Or suits, something of a business nature?' She gave me an utterly false bright smile, and I knew she was angry with me because she was scared for me. 'McKenna, you can take that mail to the post office,' Tara told McKenna with an edge to her voice. McKenna scuttled out the back door, the mail stuffed under her arm like a riding crop.

'Tara,' I said, 'it's not what you think.'

'Sookie, it's none of my business,' she said, trying hard to sound neutral.

'I think it is,' I said. 'You're my friend, and I don't want you thinking I'm just going traveling with a bunch of vampires for fun.'

'Then why are you going?' Tara's face dropped all the false cheer. She was deadly serious.

'I'm getting paid to go with a few of the Louisiana vamps to a big meeting. I'll act as their, like, human Geiger counter. I'll tell them if a human's trying to bullshit them, and I'll know what the other vamps' humans are thinking. It's just for this one time.' I couldn't explain more fully. Tara had been into the world of the vampires more heavily than she needed to be, and she'd almost gotten killed. She wanted nothing more to do with it, and I couldn't blame her. But she still couldn't tell me what to do. I'd gone through my own soul searching over this issue, even before Claudine's lecture, and I wasn't going to permit anyone else to second-guess me once I'd made up my mind. Getting the clothes was okay. Working for the vamps was okay ... as long as I didn't turn humans over to get killed.

'We've been friends for a coon's age,' Tara said quietly. 'Through thick and thin. I love you, Sookie, I always will; but this is a real thin time.' Tara had had so much disappointment and worry in her life that she simply wasn't willing to undertake any more. So she was cutting me loose, and she thought she would call JB that night and renew their carnal acquaintance, and she would do that almost in memory of me.

It was a strange way to write my premature epitaph.

'I need an evening dress, a cocktail-type dress, and some nice day clothes,' I said, checking my list quite unnecessarily. I wasn't going to fool with Tara anymore. I was going to have fun, no matter how sour she looked. She'd come around, I told myself.

I was going to enjoy buying clothes. I started off with an evening dress and a cocktail dress. And I got two suits, like business suits (but not really, since I can't see myself in black pinstripes). And two pants outfits. And hose and knee-highs and a nightgown or two. And a bit of lingerie.

I was swinging between guilt and delight. I spent more of Eric's money than I absolutely had to, and I wondered what would happen if Eric asked to see the things he'd bought. I'd feel pretty bad then. But it was like I'd been caught up in a buying frenzy, partly out of the sheer delight of it, and partly out of anger at Tara, and partly to deny the fear I was feeling at the prospect of accompanying a group of vampires anywhere.

With another sigh, this one a very quiet and private one, I returned the lingerie and the nightgowns to their tables. Nonessentials. I felt sad to part with them, but I felt better overall. Buying clothes to suit a specific need, well, that was okay. That was a meal. But buying underthings, that was something else entirely. That was like a MoonPie. Or Ding Dongs. Sweet, but bad for you.

The local priest, who had started attending Fellowship of the Sun meetings, had suggested to me that befriending vamps, or even working for them, was a way of expressing a death wish. He'd told me this over his burger basket the week before. I thought about that now, standing at the cash register while Tara rang up all my purchases, which would be paid for with vampire money. Did I believe I wanted to die? I shook my head. No, I didn't. And I thought the Fellowship of the Sun, which was the ultra right-wing anti-vampire movement that was gaining an alarming stronghold in America, was a crock. Their condemnation of all humans who had any dealings with vampires, even down to visiting a business owned by a vamp, was ridiculous. But why was I even drawn to vamps to begin with?

Here was the truth of it: I'd had so little chance of having the kind of life my classmates had achieved – the kind of life I'd grown up thinking was the ideal – that any other life I could shape for myself seemed interesting. If I couldn't have a husband and children, worry about what I was going to take to the church potluck and if our house needed another coat of paint, then I'd worry about what three-inch heels would do to my sense of balance when I was wearing several extra pounds in sequins.

When I was ready to go, McKenna, who'd come back from the post office, carried my bags out to my car while Tara cleared the amount with Eric's day man, Bobby Burnham. She hung up the phone, looking pleased.

'Did I use it all up?' I asked, curious to find out how much Eric had invested in me.

'Not nearly,' she said. 'Want to buy more?'

But the fun was over. 'No,' I said. 'I've gotten enough.' I had a definite impulse to ask Tara to take every stitch back. Then I thought what a shabby thing that would be to do to her. 'Thanks for helping me, Tara.'

'My pleasure,' she assured me. Her smile was a little warmer and more genuine. Tara always liked making money, and she'd never been able to stay mad at me long. 'You need to go to World of Shoes in Clarice to get something to go with the evening gown. They're having a sale.'

I braced myself. This was the day to get things done. Next stop, World of Shoes.

I would be leaving in a week, and work that night went by in a blur as I grew more excited about the trip. I'd never been as far from home as Rhodes, which was way up there by Chicago; actually, I'd never been north of the Mason-Dixon Line. I'd flown only once, and that had been a short flight from Shreveport to Dallas. I would have to get a suitcase, one that rolled. I'd have to get ... I thought of a long list of smaller items. I knew that some hotels had hair dryers. Would the Pyramid of Gizeh? The Pyramid was one of the most famous vampire-oriented hotels that had sprung up in major American cities.

Since I'd already arranged my time off with Sam, that night I told him when I was scheduled to leave. Sam was sitting behind his desk in the office when I knocked on the door – well, the door frame, because Sam almost never shut the door. He looked up from his bill paying. He was glad to be interrupted. When he worked on the books, he ran his hands through his reddish blond hair, and now he looked a little electrified as a result. Sam would rather be tending bar than doing this task, but he'd actually hired a substitute for tonight just for the purpose of getting his books straight.

'Come in, Sook,' he said. 'How's it going out there?'

'Pretty busy; I haven't got but a second. I just wanted to tell you I'll be leaving next Thursday.'

Sam tried to smile, but he ended up simply looking unhappy. 'You have to do this?' he asked.

'Hey, we've talked about this,' I said, sounding a clear warning.

'Well, I'll miss you,' he explained. 'And I'll worry a little. You and lots of vamps.'

'There'll be humans there, like me.'

'*Not* like you. They'll be humans with a sick infatuation with the vampire culture, or deaddiggers, looking to make a buck off the undead. None of these are healthy people with long life expectancies.'

'Sam, two years ago I didn't have any idea of what the world around me was really like. I didn't know what you really were; I didn't know that vampires were as different from each other as we are. I didn't know that there were real fairies. I couldn't have imagined any of that.' I shook my head. 'What a world this is, Sam. It's wonderful and it's scary. Each day is different. I never thought I would have any kind of life for myself, and now I do.'

'I'd be the last person in the world to block your place in the sun, Sookie,' Sam said, and he smiled at me. But it didn't escape my attention that his statement was a wee bit ambiguous.

Pam came to Bon Temps that night, looking bored and cool in a pale green jumpsuit with navy piping. She was wearing navy penny loafers ... no kidding. I hadn't even realized those were still for sale. The dark leather was polished to a high shine, and the pennies were new. She got plenty of admiring looks in the bar. She perched at a table in my section and sat patiently, her hands clasped on the table in front of her. She went into the vampire state of suspension that was so unnerving to anyone who hadn't seen it yet – her eyes open but not seeing, her body totally unmoving, her expression blank. Since she was having some downtime, I waited on a few people before I went to her table. I was sure I knew why she was there, and I wasn't looking forward to the conversation.

'Pam, can I get you a drink?'

'What's with the tiger, then?' she asked, going straight for the conversational jugular.

'Quinn is who I'm seeing now,' I said. 'We don't get to stay together much because of his job, but we'll see each other at the summit.' Quinn had been hired to produce some of the summit's expected ceremonies and rituals. He'd be busy, but I'd catch glimpses of him, and I was already excited about the prospect. 'We're spending a month together after the summit,' I told Pam.

Ah-oh, maybe I'd over-shared on that one. Pam's face lost its smile.

'Sookie, I don't know what strange game you and Eric have going, but it's not good for us.'

'I have nothing going! Nothing!'

'You may not, but he does. He has not been the same since the time you two spent together.'

'I don't know what I can do about that,' I said weakly.

Pam said, 'I don't either, but I hope he can resolve his feelings for you. He doesn't enjoy having conflicts. He doesn't enjoy feeling attached. He is not the carefree vampire he used to be.'

I shrugged. 'Pam, I've been as straight with him as I can be. I think maybe he's worried about something else. You're exaggerating my importance in Eric's scheme of things. If he has any kind of undying love for me, then he's sure not telling me about it. And I never see him. And he knows about Quinn.'

'He made Bill confess to you, didn't he?'

'Well, Eric was there,' I said uncertainly.

'Do you think Bill would ever have told you if Eric hadn't commanded him to?'

I'd done my best to forget that night altogether. In the back of my mind, I'd known the strange timing of Bill's revelation was significant, but I just hadn't wanted to think about it.

'Why do you think Eric would give a flying fuck what Bill had been ordered to do, much less reveal it to a human woman, if he didn't have inappropriate feelings for you?'

I'd never put it to myself quite like that. I'd been so ripped up by Bill's confession – the queen had planted him to seduce me (if necessary) to gain my trust – that I hadn't thought of why Eric had forced Bill into the position of telling me about the plot.

'Pam, I don't know. Listen, I'm working here, and you need to order something to drink. I gotta take care of my other tables.'

'O-negative, then. TrueBlood.'

I hurried to get the drink out of the cooler, and I warmed it up in the microwave, shaking it gently to make sure the temperature was even. It coated the sides of the bottle in an unpleasant way, but it certainly looked and tasted like real blood. I'd poured a few drops into a glass one time at Bill's so I could have the experience. As far as I could tell, drinking synthetic blood was exactly like drinking real blood. Bill had always enjoyed it, though he'd remarked more than once that flavor wasn't the thing; it was the sensation of biting into flesh, feeling the heartbeat of the human, that made being a vampire fun. Glugging out of a bottle just didn't do the trick. I took the bottle and a wineglass to Pam's table and deposited both before her, along with a napkin, of course.

'Sookie?' I looked up to see that Amelia had come in.

My roomie had come into the bar often enough, but I was surprised to see her tonight. 'What's up?' I asked.

'Um ... hi,' Amelia said to Pam. I took in Amelia's pressed khakis, her neat white golf shirt, her equally white tennis shoes. I glanced at Pam, whose pale eyes were wider than I'd ever seen them.

'This is my roommate, Amelia Broadway,' I told Pam. 'Amelia, this is Pam the vampire.'

'I am pleased to meet you,' Pam said.

'Hey, neat outfit,' Amelia said.

Pam looked pleased. 'You look very nice, too,' she said.

'You a local vamp?' Amelia asked. Amelia was nothing if not blunt. And chatty.

Pam said, 'I'm Eric's second-in-command. You do know who Eric Northman is?'

'Sure,' Amelia said. 'He's the blond hunk of burning love who lives in Shreveport, right?'

Pam smiled. Her fangs popped out a little. I looked from Amelia to the vampire. Geez Louise.

'Perhaps you would like to see the bar some night?' Pam said.

'Oh, sure,' Amelia said, but not as if she were particularly excited. Playing hard to get. For about ten minutes, if I knew Amelia.

I left to answer a customer beckoning from another table. Out of the corner of my eye, Amelia sat down with Pam, and they talked for a few minutes before Amelia got up and stood by the bar, waiting for me to return.

'And what brings you here tonight?' I asked maybe a little too abruptly.

Amelia raised her eyebrows, but I didn't apologize.

'I just wanted to tell you, you got a phone call at the house.'

'Who from?'

'From Quinn.'

I felt a smile spread across my face, a real one. 'What did he say?'

'He said he'd see you in Rhodes. He misses you already.'

'Thanks, Amelia. But you could've just called here to tell me, or told me when I got home.'

'Oh, I got a little bored.'

I'd known she would be, sooner or later. Amelia needed a job, a full-time job. She missed her city and her friends, of course. Even though she'd left New Orleans before Katrina, she'd suffered a little every day since the storm's aftermath had devastated the city. Amelia missed the witchcraft, too. I'd hoped she'd pal around with Holly, another barmaid and a dedicated Wiccan. But after I'd introduced the two and they'd had some conversations, Amelia had told me glumly that she and Holly were very different sorts of witches. Amelia herself was (she considered) a true witch, while Holly was a Wiccan. Amelia had a thinly veiled contempt for the Wiccan faith. Once or twice, Amelia had met with Holly's coven, partly to keep her hand in . . . and partly because Amelia yearned for the company of other practitioners.

At the same time, my houseguest was very anxious she might be discovered by the witches of New Orleans and made to pay a high price for her mistake in changing Bob. To add yet another emotional layer, since Katrina, Amelia feared for the safety of these same former companions. She couldn't find out if they were okay without them discovering her in return.

Despite all this, I'd known the day (or night) would come when Amelia would be restless enough to look outside my house and yard and Bob.

I tried not to frown as Amelia went over to Pam's table to visit some more. I reminded my inner worrier that Amelia could take care of herself. Probably. I'd been more certain the night before in Hotshot. As I went about my work, I switched my thoughts to Quinn's call. I wished I'd had my new cell phone (thanks to Amelia's paying me a little rent, I could afford one) with me, but I didn't think it was right to carry it at work, and Quinn knew I wouldn't have it with me and turned on unless I was at liberty to answer it. I wished Quinn would be waiting at home when I left the bar in an hour. The strength of that fantasy intoxicated me.

Though it would have been pleasant to roll in that feeling, indulging myself in the flush of my new relationship, I concluded it was time to back down and face a little reality. I concentrated on serving my tables, smiling and chatting as needed, and refreshing Pam's TrueBlood once or twice. Otherwise, I left Amelia and Pam to their tête-à-tête.

Finally, the last working hour was over, and the bar cleared out. Along with the other servers, I did my closing-up chores. When I was sure the napkin holders and salt shakers were full and ready for the next day, I went down the little hall into the storeroom to deposit my apron in the large laundry basket. After listening to us hint and complain for years, Sam had finally hung a mirror back there for our benefit. I found myself standing absolutely still, staring into it. I shook myself and began to untie my apron. Arlene was fluffing her own bright red hair. Arlene and I were not such good friends these days. She'd gotten involved in the Fellowship of the Sun. Though the Fellowship represented itself as an informational organization, dedicated to spreading the 'truth' about vampires, its ranks were riddled with those who believed all vampires were intrinsically evil and should be eliminated, by violent means. The worst among the Fellowship took out their anger and fear on the humans who consorted with vampires.

Humans like me.

Arlene tried to meet my eyes in the mirror. She failed.

'That vamp in the bar your buddy?' she asked, putting a very unpleasant emphasis on the last word.

'Yes,' I said. Even if I hadn't liked Pam, I would have said she was my buddy. Everything about the Fellowship made the hair rise up on my neck.

'You need to hang around with humans more,' Arlene said. Her mouth was set in a solid line, and her heavily made-up eyes were narrow with intensity. Arlene had never been what you'd call a deep thinker, but I was astonished and dismayed by how fast she'd been sucked into the Fellowship way of thinking.

'I'm with humans ninety-five percent of the time, Arlene.'

'You should make it a hundred.'

'Arlene, how is this any of your business?' My patience was stretched to its breaking point.

'You been putting in all these hours because you're going with a bunch of vamps to some meeting, right?'

'Again, what business of yours?'

'You and me were friends for a long time, Sookie, until that Bill Compton walked into the bar. Now you see vamps all the time, and you have strange people staying at your house.'

'I don't have to defend my life to you,' I said, and my temper utterly snapped. I could see inside her head, see all the smug and satisfied righteous judgment. It hurt. It rankled. I had babysat her children, consoled her when she was left high and dry by a series of unworthy men, cleaned her trailer, tried to encourage her to date men who wouldn't walk all over her. Now she was staring at me, actually surprised at my anger.

'Obviously you have some big holes in your own life if you have to fill them with this Fellowship crap,' I said. 'Look at what sterling guys you pick to date and marry.' With that unchristian dig, I spun on my heel and walked out of the bar, thankful I'd already gotten my purse from Sam's office. Nothing's worse than having to stop in the middle of a righteous walkout.

Somehow Pam was beside me, having joined me so quickly that I hadn't seen her move. I looked over my shoulder. Arlene was standing with her back flat against the wall, her face distorted with pain and anger. My parting shot had been a true one. One of Arlene's boyfriends had stolen the family silverware, and her husbands ... hard to know where to start.

Pam and I were outside before I could react to her presence.

I was rigid with the shock of Arlene's verbal attack and my own fury. 'I shouldn't have said anything about him,' I said. 'Just because one of Arlene's husbands was a murderer is no reason for me to be ugly.' I was absolutely channeling my grandmother, and I gave a shaky hoot of laughter.

Pam was a little shorter than I, and she looked up into my face curiously as I struggled to control myself.

'She's a whore, that one,' Pam said.

I pulled a Kleenex out of my purse to blot my tears. I often cried when I got angry; I hated that. Crying just made you look weak, no matter what triggered it.

Pam held my hand and wiped my tears off with her thumb. The tender effect was a little weakened when she stuck the thumb in her mouth, but I figured she meant well.

'I wouldn't call her a whore, but she's truly not as careful as she might be about who she goes with,' I admitted.

'Why do you defend her?'

'Habit,' I said. 'We were friends for years and years.'

'What did she do for you, with her friendship? What benefit was there?'

'She . . .' I had to stop and think. 'I guess I was just able to say I had a friend. I cared about her kids, and I helped her out with them. When she couldn't work, I'd take her hours, and if she worked for me, I'd clean her trailer in return. She'd come see me if I was sick and bring me food. Most of all, she was tolerant of my differences.'

'She used you and yet you felt grateful,' Pam said. Her expressionless white face gave me no clue to her feelings.

'Listen, Pam, it wasn't like that.'

'How was it, Sookie?'

'She really did like me. We really did have some good times.'

'She's lazy. That extends to her friendships. If it's easy to be friendly, she will be. If the wind blows the other way, her friendship will be gone. And I'm thinking the wind is blowing the other way. She has found some other way to be an important person in her own right, by hating others.'

'Pam!'

'Is this not true? I've watched people for years. I know people.'

'There's true stuff you should say, and true stuff that's better left unsaid.'

'There's true stuff you would *rather* I left unsaid,' she corrected me.

'Yes. As a matter of fact, that's ... true.'

'Then I'll leave you and go back to Shreveport.' Pam turned to walk around the building to where her car was parked in front.

'Whoa!'

She turned back. 'Yes?'

'Why were you here in the first place?'

Pam smiled unexpectedly. 'Aside from asking you questions about your relationship with my maker? And the bonus of meeting your delectable roommate?'

'Oh. Yeah. Aside from all that.'

'I want to talk to you about Bill,' she said to my utter surprise. 'Bill, and Eric.'

Chapter 7

'I don't have anything to say.' I unlocked my car and tossed my purse inside. Then I turned to face Pam, though I was tempted to get in the car and go home.

'We didn't know,' the vampire said. She walked slowly, so I could see her coming. Sam had left two lawn chairs out in front of his trailer, set at right angles to the rear of the bar, and I got them out of his yard and set them by the car. Pam took the hint and perched in one while I took the other.

I drew a deep, silent breath. I had wondered ever since I returned from New Orleans if all the vamps in Shreveport had known Bill's secret purpose in courting me. 'I wouldn't have told you,' Pam said, 'even if I had known Bill had been charged with a mission, because . . . vampires first.' She shrugged. 'But I promise you that I didn't know.'

I bobbed my head in acknowledgment, and a little pocket of tension in me finally relaxed. But I had no idea how to respond.

'I must say, Sookie, that you have caused a tremendous amount of trouble in our area.' Pam didn't seem perturbed by that; she was just stating a fact. I hardly felt I could apologize. 'These days Bill is full of anger, but he doesn't know who to hate. He feels guilty, and no one likes that. Eric is frustrated that he can't remember the time he was in hiding at your house, and he doesn't know what he owes you. He's angry that the queen has annexed you for her own purposes, through Bill, and thus poached on Eric's territory, as he sees it. Felicia thinks you are the bogeyman, since so many of the Fangtasia bartenders have died while you were around. Longshadow, Chow.' She smiled. 'Oh, and your friend, Charles Twining.'

'None of that was my fault.' I'd listened to Pam with growing agitation. It's so not good to have vampires angry with you. Even the current Fangtasia bartender, Felicia, was much stronger than I would ever be, and she was definitely the low vamp on the totem pole.

'I don't see that that makes any difference,' Pam said, her voice curiously gentle. 'Now that we know you have fairy blood, thanks to Andre, it would be easy to write all this off. But I don't think that's it, do you? I've known many humans descended from the fae, and none of them have been telepathic. I think that's just you, Sookie. Of course, knowing you have this streak of fairy makes one wonder how you would taste. I certainly enjoyed the sip I got when the maenad maimed you, though that was tainted with her poison. We love fairies, as you know.'

'Love them to death,' I said under my breath, but of course Pam heard.

'Sometimes,' she agreed with a little smile. That Pam.

'So what's the bottom line here?' I was ready to go home and just be human, all by myself.

'When I say "we" didn't know about Bill's agreement with the queen, that includes Eric,' Pam said simply.

I looked down at my feet, struggling to keep my face under control.

'Eric feels especially angry about this,' Pam said. She was picking her words now. 'He is angry at Bill because Bill made an agreement with the queen that bypassed Eric. He is angry that he didn't discern Bill's plan. He is angry at you because you got under his skin. He is angry at the queen because she is more devious than he is. Of course, that's why she's the queen. Eric will never be a king, unless he can control himself better.'

'You're really worried about him?' I'd never known Pam to be seriously concerned about much of anything. When she nodded, I found myself saying, 'When did you meet Eric?' I'd always been curious, and tonight Pam seemed to be in a sharing mood.

'I met him in London the last night of my life.' Her voice was level, coming out of the shadowy darkness. I could see half her face in the overhead security light, and she looked quite calm. 'I risked everything for *love*. You'll laugh to hear this.'

I wasn't remotely close to laughing.

'I was a very wild girl for my times. Young ladies weren't supposed to be alone with gentlemen, or any males, for that matter. A far cry from now.' Pam's lips curved upward in a brief smile. 'But I was a romantic, and bold. I slipped out of my house late at night to meet the cousin of my dearest friend, the girl who lived right next door. The cousin was visiting from Bristol, and we were very attracted to each other. My parents didn't consider him to be my equal in social class, so I knew they wouldn't let him court me. And if I were caught alone with him at night, it would be the end of me. No marriage, unless my parents could force him to wed me. So, no future at all.' Pam shook her head. 'Crazy to think of now. Those were the times women didn't have choices. The ironic part is, our meeting was quite innocent. A few kisses, a lot of sentimental claptrap, undying love. Yada yada yada.'

I grinned at Pam, but she didn't look up to catch the smile.

'On my way back to my house, trying to move so silently through the garden, I met Eric. There was no way to slip silently enough to avoid *him*.' For a long moment, she was quiet. 'And it really was the end of me.'

'Why'd he turn you?' I settled lower in my chair and crossed my legs. This was an unexpected and fascinating conversation.

'I think he was lonely,' she said, a faint note of surprise in her voice. 'His last companion had struck out on her own, since children can't stay with their maker for long. After a few years, the child must strike out on its own, though it may come back to the maker, and must if the maker calls.'

'Weren't you angry with him?'

She seemed to be trying to remember. 'At first, I was shocked,' Pam said. 'After he'd drained me, he put me in bed in my own room, and of course my family thought I'd died of some mysterious ailment, and they buried me. Eric dug me up, so I wouldn't wake up in my coffin and have to dig my own way out. That was a great help. He held me and explained it all to me. Up until the night I died, I'd always been a very conventional woman underneath my daring tendencies. I was used to wearing layers and layers of clothes. You would be amazed at the dress I died in: the sleeves, the trim. The fabric in the skirt alone could make you three dresses!' Pam looked fondly reminiscent, nothing more. 'After I'd awakened, I discovered being a vampire freed some wild thing in me.'

'After what he did, you didn't want to kill him?'

'No,' she said instantly. 'I wanted to have sex with him, and I did. We had sex many, many times.' She grinned. 'The tie between maker and child doesn't have to be sexual, but with us it was. That changed quite soon, actually, as my tastes broadened. I wanted to try everything I'd been denied in my human life.'

'So you actually liked it, being a vampire? You were glad?'

Pam shrugged. 'Yes, I've always loved being what I am. It took me a few days to understand my new nature. I'd never even heard of a vampire before I became one.'

I couldn't imagine the shock of Pam's awakening. Her self-proclaimed quick adjustment to her new state amazed me.

'Did you ever go back to see your family?' I asked. Okay, that was tacky, and I regretted it as soon as the words passed my lips.

'I saw them from a distance, maybe ten years later. You understand, the first thing a new vampire needed to do was leave her home area. Otherwise she ran the risk of being recognized and hunted down. Now you can parade around as much as you like. But we were so secret, so careful. Eric and I headed out of London as quickly as we could go, and after spending a little time in the north of England while I became accustomed to my state, we left England for the continent.'

This was gruesome but fascinating. 'Did you love him?'

Pam looked a little puzzled. There was a tiny wrinkle in her smooth forehead. 'Love him? No. We were good companions, and I enjoyed the sex and the hunting. But love? No.' In the glare of the overhead security lights, which cast curious dark shadows in the corners of the lot, I watched Pam's face relax into its normal smooth lines. 'I owe him my loyalty,' Pam said. 'I have to obey him, but I do it willingly. Eric is intelligent, ambitious, and very entertaining. I would be crumbled to nothing in my grave by now if he hadn't been watching me slip back to my house from meeting that silly young man. I went my own way for many, many years, but I was glad to hear from him when he opened the bar and called me to serve him.'

Was it possible for anyone in the world to be as detached as Pam over the whole 'I was murdered' issue? There was no doubt Pam relished being a vampire, seemed to genuinely harbor a mild contempt for humans; in fact, she seemed to find them amusing. She had thought it was hilarious when Eric had first exhibited feelings for me. Could Pam truly be so changed from her former self?

'How old were you, Pam?'

'When I died? I was nineteen.' Not a flicker of feeling crossed her face.

'Did you wear your hair up every day?'

Pam's face seemed to warm a little. 'Yes, I did. I wore it in a very elaborate style; my maid had to help me. I put artificial pads underneath my hair to give it height. And the underwear! You would laugh yourself sick to see me get into it.'

As interesting as this conversation had been, I realized I was tired and ready to go home. 'So the bottom line is, you're really loyal to Eric, and you want me to know that neither of you knew that Bill had a hidden agenda when he came to Bon Temps.' Pam nodded. 'So, you came here tonight to . . .?'

'To ask you to have mercy on Eric.'

The idea of Eric needing my mercy had never crossed my mind. 'That's as funny as your human underwear,' I said. 'Pam, I know you believe you owe Eric, even though he killed you – honey, he *killed* you – but I don't owe Eric a thing.'

'You care for him,' she said, and for the first time she sounded a little angry. 'I know you do. He's never been so entangled in his emotions. He's never been at such a disadvantage.' She seemed to gather herself, and I figured our conversation was over. We got up, and I returned Sam's chairs.

I had no idea what to say.

Fortunately, I didn't have to think of anything. Eric himself walked out of the shadows at the edge of the lot.

'Pam,' he said, and that one word was loaded. 'You were so late, I followed your trail to make sure all was well.'

'Master,' she said, which was something I'd never heard from Pam. She went down on one knee on the gravel, which must have been painful.

'Leave,' Eric said, and just like that, Pam was gone.

I kept silent. Eric was giving me that vampiric fixed stare, and I couldn't read him at all. I was pretty sure he was mad – but about what, at whom, and with what intensity? That was the fun part of being with vampires, and the scary part of being with vampires, all at the same time.

Eric decided action would speak louder than words. Suddenly, he was right in front of me. He put a finger under my chin and lifted my face to his. His eyes, which looked simply dark in the irregular light, latched on to mine with an intensity that was both exciting and painful. Vampires; mixed feelings. One and the same.

Not exactly to my astonishment, he kissed me. When someone has had approximately a thousand years to practice kissing, he can become very good at it, and I would be lying if I said I was immune to such osculatory talent. My temperature zoomed up about ten degrees. It was everything I could do to keep from stepping into him, wrapping my arms around him, and stropping myself against him. For a dead guy, he had the liveliest chemistry – and apparently all my hormones were wide awake after my night with Quinn. Thinking of Quinn was like a dash of cold water.

With an almost painful reluctance, I pulled away from Eric. His face had a focused air, as if he was sampling something and deciding if it was good enough to keep.

'Eric,' I said, and my voice was shaking. 'I don't know why you're here, and I don't know why we're having all this drama.'

'Are you Quinn's now?' His eyes narrowed.

'I'm my own,' I said. 'I choose.'

'And have you chosen?'

'Eric, this is beyond gall. You haven't been dating me. You haven't given me any sign that was on your mind. You haven't treated me as though I had any significance in your life. I'm not saying I would have been open to those things, but I'm saying in their *absence* I've been free to find another, ah, companion. And so far, I like Quinn just fine.'

'You don't know him any more than you really knew Bill.'

That sliced down where it hurt.

'At least I'm pretty damn sure he wasn't ordered to get me in bed so I'd be a political asset!'

'It's better that you knew about Bill,' Eric said.

'Yes, it's better,' I agreed. 'That doesn't mean I enjoyed the process.'

'I knew that would be hard. But I had to make him tell you.

'Why?'

Eric seemed stumped. I don't know any other way to put it. He looked away, off into the darkness of the woods. 'It wasn't right,' he said at last.

'True. But maybe you just wanted to be sure I wouldn't ever love him again?'

'Maybe both things,' he said.

There was a sharp moment of silence, as if something big was drawing in breath.

'Okay,' I said slowly. This was like a therapy session. 'You've been moody around me for months, Eric. Ever since you were . . . you know, not yourself. What's up with you?'

'Ever since that night I was cursed, I've wondered why I ended up running down the road to your house.'

I took a step or two back and tried to pull some evidence, some indication of what he was thinking, from his white face. But it was no use.

It had never occurred to me to wonder why Eric had been there. I'd been so astounded over so many things that the circumstances of finding Eric alone, half naked, and clueless, early in the morning on the first day of the New Year, had been buried in the aftermath of the Witch War.

'Did you ever figure out the answer?' I asked, realizing after the words had left my mouth how stupid the question was.

'No,' he said in a voice that was just short of a hiss. 'No. And the witch who cursed me is dead, though the curse was broken. Now she can't tell me what her curse entailed. Was I supposed to look for the person I hated? Loved? Could it have been random that I found myself running out in the middle of nowhere . . . except that nowhere was on the way to your house?'

A moment of uneasy silence on my part. I had no idea what to say, and Eric was clearly waiting for a response.

'Probably the fairy blood,' I said weakly, though I had spent hours telling myself that my fraction of fairy blood was not significant enough to cause more than a mild attraction on the part of the vampires I met.

'No,' he said. And then he was gone.

'Well,' I said out loud, unhappy with the quiver in my voice. 'As exits go, that was a good one.' It was pretty hard to have the last word with a vampire.

Chapter 8

'**M**y bags are packed . . .' I sang.

'Well, I'm not so lonesome I could cry,' Amelia said. She'd kindly agreed to drive me to the airport, but I should have made her promise to be pleasant that morning, too. She'd been a little broody the whole time I was putting on my makeup.

'I wish I was going, too,' she said, admitting what had been sticking in her craw. Of course, I'd known Amelia's problem before she'd said it out loud. But there wasn't a thing I could do.

'It's not up to me to invite or not invite,' I said. 'I'm the hired help.'

'I know,' she said grumpily. 'I'll get the mail, and I'll water the plants, and I'll brush Bob. Hey, I heard that the Bayou State insurance salesman needs a receptionist, since the mom of the woman who worked for him got evacuated from New Orleans and has to have full-time care.'

'Oh, do go in to apply for that job,' I said. 'You'll just love it.' My insurance guy was a wizard who backed up his policies with spells. 'You'll really like Greg Aubert, and he'll interest you.' I wanted Amelia's interview at the insurance agency to be a happy surprise.

Amelia looked at me sideways with a little smile. 'Oh, is he cute and single?'

'Nope. But he has other interesting attributes. And remember, you promised Bob you wouldn't do guys.'

'Oh, yeah.' Amelia looked gloomy. 'Hey, let's look up your hotel.'

Amelia was teaching me how to use my cousin Hadley's computer.

I'd brought it back with me from New Orleans, thinking I'd sell it, but Amelia had coaxed me to set it up here at the house. It looked funny on a desk in the corner of the oldest part of the house, the room now used as a living room. Amelia paid for an extra phone line for the Internet, since she needed it for her laptop upstairs. I was still a nervous novice.

Amelia clicked on Google and typed in 'Pyramid of Gizeh hotel'. We stared at the picture that popped up on the screen. Most of the vampire hotels were in large urban centers, like Rhodes, and they were also tourist attractions. Often called simply 'the Pyramid', the hotel was shaped like one, of course, and it was faced with bronze-colored reflective glass. There was one band of lighter glass around one of the floors close to the base.

'Not exactly . . . hmmm.' Amelia looked at the building, her head tilted sideways.

'It needs to slant more,' I said, and she nodded.

'You're right. It's like they wanted to have a pyramid, but they didn't really need enough floors to make it look right. The angle's not steep enough to make it look really grand.'

'And it's sitting on a big rectangle.'

'That, too. I expect those are the convention rooms.'

'No parking,' I said, peering at the screen.

'Oh, that'll be below the building. They can build 'em that way up there.'

'It's on the lakefront,' I said. 'Hey, I get to see Lake Michigan. See, there's just a little park between the hotel and the lake.'

'And about six lanes of traffic,' Amelia pointed out.

'Okay, that, too.'

'But it's close to major shopping,' Amelia said.

'It's got an all-human floor,' I read. 'I'll bet that's this floor, the one that's lighter. I thought that was just the design, but it's so humans can go somewhere to have light during the day. People need that for their well-being.'

'Translation: it's a law,' Amelia said. 'What else is there? Meeting rooms, blah blah blah. Opaque glass throughout except for the human floor. Exquisitely decorated suites on the highest levels, blab blah blah.

Staff thoroughly trained in vampires' needs. Does that mean they're all willing to be blood donors or fuck buddies?'

Amelia was so cynical. But now that I knew who her father was, that kind of made sense.

'I'd like to see the very top room, the tip of the pyramid,' I said.

'Can't. It says here that that's not a real guest floor. It's actually where all the air conditioner stuff is.'

'Well, hell. Time to go,' I said, glancing at my watch.

'Oh, yeah.' Amelia stared gloomily at the screen.

'I'll only be gone a week,' I said. Amelia was definitely a person who didn't like to be by herself. We went downstairs and carried my bags to the car.

'I got the hotel number to call in case of emergency. I got your cell phone number, too. You pack your charger?' She maneuvered down the long gravel driveway and out onto Hummingbird Road. We'd go right around Bon Temps to get to the interstate.

'Yeah.' And my toothbrush and toothpaste, my razor, my deodorant, my hair dryer (just in case), my makeup, all my new clothes and some extras, lots of shoes, a sleeping outfit, Amelia's traveling alarm clock, underwear, a little jewelry, an extra purse, and two paperbacks. 'Thanks for loaning me the suitcase.' Amelia had contributed her bright red roller bag and a matching garment bag, plus a carry-on I'd crammed with a book, a crossword puzzle compendium, a portable CD player, and a headset, plus a small CD case.

We didn't talk much on the drive. I was thinking how strange it was going to be, leaving Amelia alone in my family home. There had been Stackhouses in residence on the site for over a hundred and seventy years.

Our sporadic conversation died by the time we neared the airport. There didn't seem to be anything else to be said. We were right by the main Shreveport terminal, but we were going to a small private hangar. If Eric hadn't booked an Anubis charter plane weeks ago, he would've been up a creek, because the summit was definitely taxing Anubis's capabilities. All the states involved were sending delegations, and a big hunk of Middle America, from the Gulf to the Canadian border, was included in the American Central division.

A few months ago, Louisiana would have needed two planes. Now one would suffice, especially since a few of the party had gone ahead. I'd read the list of missing vampires after the meeting at Fangtasia, and to my regret, Melanie and Chester had been on it. I'd met them at the queen's New Orleans headquarters, and though we hadn't had time to become bosom buddies or anything, they'd seemed like good vamps.

There was a guard at the gate in the fence enclosing the hangar, and he checked my driver's license and Amelia's before he let us in. He was a regular human off-duty cop, but he seemed competent and alert. 'Turn to the right, and there's parking by the door in the east wall,' he said.

Amelia leaned forward a little as she drove, but the door was easy enough to see, and there were other cars parked there. It was about ten in the morning, and there was a touch of cool in the air, just below the surface warmth. It was an early breath of fall. After the hot, hot summer, it was just blissful. It would be cooler in Rhodes, Pam had said. She'd checked the temperatures for the coming week, on the Internet and called me to tell me to pack a sweater. She'd sounded almost excited, which was a big deal for Pam. I'd been getting the impression that Pam was a wee bit restless, a bit tired of Shreveport and the bar. Maybe it was just me.

Amelia helped me unload the suitcases. Amelia had had to take a number of spells off the red Samsonite before she could hand it over to me. I hadn't asked what would have happened if she'd forgotten. I pulled up the handle on the rolling bag and slung the carry-on bag across my shoulder. Amelia took the hanging bag and opened the door.

I'd never been in an airplane hangar before, but it was just like the ones in the movies: cavernous. There were a few small planes parked inside, but we proceeded as Pam had instructed to the large opening in the west wall. The Anubis Air jet was parked outside, and the coffins were being loaded onto the luggage belt by the uniformed Anubis employees. They all wore black relieved only by a stylized jackal's head on the chest of the uniform, an affectation that I found irritating. They glanced at us casually, but no one challenged us or asked to see identification until we got to the steps leading up to the plane.

Bobby Burnham was standing at the foot of the steps with a clip-board. Of course, since it was daylight, it was obvious Bobby wasn't a vamp, but he was nearly pale and stern enough to be one. I'd never met him before, but I knew who he was, and he certainly recognized me. I plucked that right from his brain. But his certainty didn't stop him from checking my ID against his damn list, and he was giving Amelia the big glare, like she couldn't turn him into a toad. (That was what Amelia was thinking.)

'He'd have to croak,' I murmured, and she smiled.

Bobby introduced himself, and when we nodded, he said, 'Your name is on the list, Miss Stackhouse, but Miss Broadway's isn't. I'm afraid you'll have to get your luggage up by yourself.' Bobby was loving the power.

Amelia was whispering something under her breath, and in a rush Bobby blurted, 'I'll carry the heavy bag up the stairs, Miss Stackhouse. Can you handle the other bag? If that's not something you want to do, I'll be back down in a minute and take them up for you.' The astonishment on his face was priceless, but I tried not to enjoy it too much. Amelia was playing a slightly mean trick.

'Thanks, I can manage,' I reassured him, and took the hanging bag from Amelia while he bumped up the stairs with the heavier piece of luggage.

'Amelia, you rascal,' I said, but not too angrily.

'Who's the asshole?' she asked.

'Bobby Burnham. He's Eric's daytime guy.' All vamps of a certain rank had one. Bobby was a recent acquisition of Eric's.

'What does he do? Dust the coffins?'

'No, he makes business arrangements, he goes to the bank, he picks up the dry cleaning, he deals with the state offices that are open only in the day, and so forth.'

'So he's a gofer.'

'Well, yeah. But he's an important gofer. He's Eric's gofer.'

Bobby was coming back down the steps now, still looking surprised that he'd been polite and helpful. 'Don't do anything else to him,' I said, knowing that she was considering it.

Amelia's eyes flashed before she got the sense of what I was saying.

'Yeah, petty of me,' she admitted. 'I just hate power-mad jerks.'

'Who doesn't? Listen, I'll see you in a week. Thanks for bringing me to the plane.'

'Yeah, yeah.' She gave me a forlorn smile. 'You have a good time, and don't get killed or bitten or anything.'

Impulsively, I hugged her, and after a second's surprise, she hugged me back.

'Take good care of Bob,' I said, and up the stairs I went.

I couldn't help feeling a little anxious, since I was cutting my ties with my familiar life, at least temporarily. The Anubis Air employee in the cabin said, 'Choose your seat, Miss Stackhouse.' She took the hanging bag from me and put it away. The interior of the aircraft was not like that of any human plane, or at least that was what the Anubis website had alleged. The Anubis fleet had been designed and outfitted for the transportation of sleeping vamps, with human passengers coming in second. There were coffin bays around the wall, like giant luggage bins, and at the front end of the aircraft there were three rows of seats, on the right three seats, and on the left two, for people like me ... or, at least, people who were going to be helpful to the vamps at this conference in some capacity. At present, there were only three other people sitting in the seats. Well, one other human and two part-humans.

'Hi, Mr Cataliades,' I said, and the round man rose from his seat, beaming.

'Dear Miss Stackhouse,' he said warmly, because that was the way Mr Cataliades talked, 'I am so very glad to see you again.'

'Pleased to see you, too, Mr Cataliades.'

His name was pronounced Ka-TAL-ee-ah-deez, and if he had a first name, I didn't know it. Sitting next to him was a very young woman with bright red spiked hair: his niece, Diantha. Diantha wore the strangest ensembles, and tonight she'd topped herself. Maybe five feet tall, bony thin, Diantha had chosen orange calf-length leggings, blue Crocs, a white ruffled skirt, and a tie-dyed tank top. She was dazzling to the eye.

Diantha didn't believe in breathing while she talked. Now she said, 'Goodtoseeya.'

'Right back at ya,' I said, and since she didn't make any other move, I gave her a nod. Some supes shake hands, others don't, so you have to be careful. I turned to the other passenger. With another human, I thought I was on firmer ground, so I held out my right hand. As if he'd been offered a dead fish, the man extended his own hand after a perceptible pause. He pressed my palm in a limp way and withdrew his fingers as if he could just barely refrain from wiping them on his suit pants.

'Miss Stackhouse, this is Johan Glassport, a specialist in vampire law.'

'Mr Glassport,' I said politely, struggling not to take offense.

'Johan, this is Sookie Stackhouse, the queen's telepath,' Mr Cataliades said in his courtly way. Mr Cataliades's sense of humor was as abundant as his belly. There was a twinkle in his eye even now. But you had to remember that the part of him that wasn't human – the majority of Mr Cataliades – was a demon. Diantha was half-demon; her uncle even more.

Johan gave me a brief up-and-down scan, almost audibly sniffed, and returned to the book he had in his lap.

Just then, the Anubis stewardess began giving us the usual spiel, and I buckled myself into my seat. Soon after that, we were airborne. I didn't have a twinge of anxiety, because I was so disgusted by Johan Glassport's behavior.

I didn't think I'd ever encountered such in-your-face rudeness. The people of northern Louisiana may not have much money, and there may be a high teen pregnancy rate and all kinds of other problems, but by God, we're polite.

Diantha said, 'Johan'sanasshole.'

Johan paid absolutely no attention to this accurate assessment but turned the page of his book.

'Thanks, dear,' Mr Cataliades said. 'Miss Stackhouse, bring me up to date on your life.'

I moved to sit opposite the trio. 'Not much to tell, Mr Cataliades. I got the check, as I wrote you. Thanks for tying up all the loose ends on Hadley's estate, and if you'd reconsider and send me a bill, I'd be glad to pay it.' Not exactly glad, but relieved of an obligation.

'No, child. It was the least I could do. The queen was happy to express her thanks in that way, even though the evening hardly turned out like she'd planned.'

'Of course, none of us imagined it would end that way.' I thought of Wybert's head flying through the air surrounded by a mist of blood, and I shuddered.

'You are the witness,' Johan said unexpectedly. He slipped a bookmark into his book and closed it. His pale eyes, magnified behind his glasses, were fixed on me. From being dog poop on his shoe, I had been transformed into something quite interesting and remarkable.

'Yeah. I'm the witness.'

'Then we must talk, now.'

'I'm a little surprised, if you're representing the queen at this very important trial, that you haven't gotten around to talking to me before,' I said in as mild a voice as I could manage.

'The queen had trouble contacting me, and I had to finish with my previous client,' Johan said. His unlined face didn't exactly change expression, but it did look a bit tenser.

'Johan was in jail,' Diantha said very clearly and distinctly.

'Oh, my goodness,' I said, truly startled.

Johan said, 'Of course, the charges were completely unfounded.'

'Of course, Johan,' Mr Cataliades said with absolutely no inflection in his voice.

'Ooo,' I said. 'What were those charges that were so false?'

Johan looked at me again, this time with less arrogance. 'I was accused of striking a prostitute in Mexico.'

I didn't know much about law enforcement in Mexico, but it did seem absolutely incredible to me that an American could get arrested in Mexico for hitting a prostitute, if that was, the only charge. Unless he had a lot of enemies.

'Did you happen to have something in your hand when you struck her?' I asked with a bright smile.

'I believe Johan had a knife in his hand,' Mr Cataliades said gravely.

I know my smile vanished right about then. 'You were in jail in Mexico for knifing a woman,' I said. Who was dog poop now?

'A prostitute,' he corrected. 'That was the charge, but of course, I was completely innocent.'

'Of course,' I said.

'Mine is not the case on the table right now, Miss Stackhouse. My job is to defend the queen against the very serious charges brought against her, and you are an important witness.'

'I'm the only witness.'

'Of course – to the actual death.'

'There were several actual deaths.'

'The only death that matters at this summit is the death of Peter Threadgill.'

I sighed at the image of Wybert's head, and then I said, 'Yeah, I was there.'

Johan may have been lower than pond scum, but he knew his stuff. We went through a long question and answer session that left the lawyer knowing more about what had happened than I did, and I'd been there. Mr Cataliades listened with great interest, and now and then threw in a clarification or explained the layout of the queen's monastery to the lawyer.

Diantha listened for a while, sat on the floor and played jacks for half an hour, then reclined her seat and went to sleep.

The Anubis Airline attendant came through and offered drinks and snacks from time to time on the three-hour flight north, and after I'd finished my session with the trial lawyer, I got up to use the bathroom. That was an experience; I'd never been in an airplane bathroom before. Instead of resuming my seat, I walked down the plane, taking a look at each coffin. There was a luggage tag on each one, attached to the handles. With us in the plane today were Eric, Bill, the queen, Andre, and Sigebert. I also found the coffin of Gervaise, who'd been hosting the queen, and Cleo Babbitt, who was the sheriff of Area Three. The Area Two sheriff, Arla Yvonne, had been left in charge of the state while the queen was gone.

The queen's coffin was inlaid with mother-of-pearl designs, but the others were quite plain. They were all of polished wood: no modern metal for these vamps. I ran my hand over Eric's, having creepy mental pictures of him lying inside, quite lifeless.

'Gervaise's woman drove ahead by night with Rasul to make sure all the queen's preparations were in place,' Mr Cataliades's voice said from my right shoulder. I jumped and shrieked, which tickled the queen's civil lawyer pink. He chuckled and chuckled.

'Smooth move,' I said, and my voice was sour as a squeezed lemon.

'You were wondering where the fifth sheriff was.'

'Yes, but you were maybe a thought or two behind.'

'I'm not telepathic like you, my dear. I was just following your facial expressions and body language. You counted the coffins and began reading the luggage tags.'

'So the queen is not only the queen, but the sheriff of her own area.'

'Yes; it eliminates confusion. Not all the rulers follow that pattern, but the queen found it irksome to constantly consult another vampire when she wanted to do something.'

'Sounds like the queen.' I glanced forward at our companions. Diantha and Johan were occupied: Diantha with sleep, Johan with his book. I wondered if it was a dissection book, with diagrams – or perhaps an account of the crimes of Jack the Ripper, with the crime scene photographs. That seemed about Johan's speed. 'How come the queen has a lawyer like him?' I asked in as low a voice as I could manage. 'He seems really . . . shoddy.'

'Johan Glassport is a great lawyer, and one who will take cases other lawyers won't,' said Mr Cataliades. 'And he is also a murderer. But then, we all are, are we not?' His beady dark eyes looked directly into mine.

I returned the look for a long moment. 'In defense of my own life or the life of someone I loved, I would kill an attacker,' I said, thinking before every word left my mouth.

'What a diplomatic way to put it, Miss Stackhouse. I can't say the same for myself. Some things I have killed, I tore apart for the sheer joy of it.'

Oh, *ick*. More than I wanted to know.

'Diantha loves to hunt deer, and she has killed people in my defense. And she and her sister even brought down a rogue vampire or two.'

I reminded myself to treat Diantha with more respect. Killing a vampire was a very difficult undertaking. And she could play jacks like a fiend.

'And Johan?' I asked.

'Perhaps I'd better leave Johan's little predilections unspoken for the moment. He won't step out of line while he's with us, after all. Are you pleased with the job Johan is doing, briefing you?'

'Is that what he's doing? Well, yes, I guess so. He's been very thorough, which is what you want.'

'Indeed.'

'Can you tell me what to expect at the summit? What the queen will want?'

Mr Cataliades said, 'Let's sit and I'll try to explain it to you.'

For the next hour, he talked, and I listened and asked questions.

By the time Diantha sat up and yawned, I felt a bit more prepared for all the new things I faced in the city of Rhodes. Johan Glassport closed his book and looked at us, as if he were now ready to talk.

'Mr Glassport, have you been to Rhodes before?' Mr Cataliades asked.

'Yes,' the lawyer answered. 'I used to practice in Rhodes. Actually, I used to commute between Rhodes and Chicago; I lived midway between.'

'When did you go to Mexico?' I asked.

'Oh, a year or two ago,' he answered. 'I had some disagreements with business associates here, and it seemed a good time to . . .'

'Get the heck out of the city?' I supplied helpfully.

'Run like hell?' Diantha suggested.

'Take the money and vanish?' Mr Cataliades said.

'All of the above,' said Johan Glassport with the faintest trace of a smile.

Chapter 9

It was midafternoon when we arrived in Rhodes. There was an Anubis truck waiting to onload the coffins and transport them to the Pyramid of Gizeh. I looked out the limo windows every second of the ride into the city, and despite the overwhelming presence of the chain stores we also saw in Shreveport, I had no doubt I was in a different place. Heavy red brick, city traffic, row houses, glimpses of the lake . . . I was trying to look in all directions at once. Then we came into view of the hotel; it was amazing. The day wasn't sunny enough for the bronze glass to glint, but the Pyramid of Gizeh looked impressive anyway. Sure enough, there was the park across the six-lane street, which was seething with traffic, and beyond it the vast lake.

While the Anubis truck pulled around to the back of the Pyramid to discharge its load of vampires and luggage, the limo swept up to the front of the hotel. As we daytime creatures scooted out of the car, I didn't know what to look at first: the broad waters or the decorations of the structure itself.

The main doors of the Pyramid were manned by a lot of maroon-and-beige uniformed men, but there were silent guardians, too. There were two elaborate reproductions of sarcophagi placed in an upright position, one on each side of the main lobby doors. They were fascinating, and I would have enjoyed the chance to examine both of them, but we were swept into the building by the staff. One man opened the car door, one examined our identification to make sure we were registered guests – not human reporters, curiosity seekers, or assorted fanatics – and another pushed open the door of the hotel to indicate we should enter.

I'd stayed in a vampire hotel before, so I expected the armed guards and the lack of ground floor windows. The Pyramid of Gizeh was making more of an effort to look a bit like a human hotel than Dallas's Silent Shore had; though the walls held murals imitating Egyptian tomb art, the lobby was bright with artificial light and horribly perky with piped-in music – 'The Girl from Ipanema' in a vampire hotel.

The lobby was busier than the Silent Shore's, too.

There were lots of humans and other creatures striding around purposefully, lots of action at the check-in desk, and some milling around the hospitality booth put up by the host city's vampire nest. I'd gone with Sam to a bar supply convention in Shreveport once when he was shopping for a new pump system, and I recognized the general setup. Somewhere, I was sure, there would be a convention hall with booths, and a schedule of panels or demonstrations.

I hoped there would be a map of the hotel, with all events and locations noted, in our registration packet. Or were the vampires too snooty for such mundane aids? No, there was a hotel diagram framed and lit for the perusal of guests and scheduled tours. This hotel was numbered in reverse order. The top floor, the penthouse, was numbered 1. The bottom, largest floor – the human floor – was numbered 15. There was a mezzanine between the human floor and lobby, and there were large convention rooms in the annex to the northern side of the hotel, the rectangular windowless projection that had looked so odd in the Internet picture.

I eyed people scurrying through the lobby – maids, bodyguards, valets, bellmen. . . . Here we were, all us little human beavers, scurrying around to get things ready for the undead conventioneers. (Could you call them that, when this was billed as a summit? What was the difference?) I felt a little sour when I wondered why this was the order of things, when a few years ago, the vampires were the ones doing the scurrying, and that was back into a dark corner where they could hide. Maybe that had been the more natural way. I slapped myself mentally. I might as well go join the Fellowship, if that was how I really felt. I'd noticed the protesters in the little park across the street from the Pyramid of Gizeh, which some of the signs referred to as 'The Pyramid of Geezers'.

'Where are the coffins?' I asked Mr Cataliades.

'They're coming in through a basement entrance,' he said.

There had been a metal detector at the hotel door. I'd tried hard not to look when Johan Glassport had emptied his pockets. The detector had gone off like a siren when he'd passed through. 'Do the coffins have to go through a metal detector, too?' I asked.

'No. Our vampires have wooden coffins, but the hardware on them is metal, and you can't empty the vampires out to search their pockets for other metal objects, so that wouldn't make any sense,' Mr Cataliades answered, for the first time sounding impatient. 'Plus, some vampires have chosen the modern metal caskets.'

'The demonstrators across the street,' I said. 'They have me spooked. They'd love to sneak in here.'

Mr Cataliades smiled, a terrifying sight. 'No one will get in here, Miss Sookie. There are other guards that you can't see.'

While Mr Cataliades checked us in, I stood to his side and turned to look around at the other people. They were all dressed very nicely, and they were all talking. About us. I felt instantly anxious at the looks we were getting from the others, and the buzzing thoughts from the few live guests and staff reinforced my anxiety. We were the human entourage of the queen who had been one of the most powerful vampire rulers in America. Now she was not only weakened economically, but she was going on trial for murdering her husband. I could see why the other flunkies were interested – I would've found us interesting – but I was uncomfortable. All I could think about was how shiny my nose must be, and how much I wanted to have a few moments alone.

The clerk went over our reservations very slowly and deliberately, as if to keep us on exhibit in the lobby for as long as possible. Mr Cataliades dealt with him with his usual elaborate courtesy, though even that was getting strained after ten minutes.

I'd been standing at a discreet distance during the process, but when I could tell the clerk – fortyish, recreational drug user, father of three –

was just fucking us over to entertain himself, I took a step closer. I laid a hand on Mr C's sleeve to indicate that I wanted to join in the conversation. He interrupted himself to turn an interested face toward me.

'You give us our keys and tell us where our vamps are, or I'll tell your boss that you're the one selling Pyramid of Gizeh items on eBay. And if you bribe a maid to even *touch* the queen's panties, much less steal 'em, I'll sic Diantha on you.' Diantha had just returned from tracking down a bottle of water. She obligingly revealed her sharp, pointed teeth in a lethal smile.

The clerk turned white and then red in an interesting display of blood flow patterns. 'Yes, ma'am,' he stammered, and I wondered if he would wet himself. After my little rummage through his head, I didn't much care.

In very short order, we all had keys, we had a list of 'our' vampires' resting places, and the bellman was bringing our luggage in one of those neat carts. That reminded me of something.

Barry, I said in my head. *You here?*

Yeah, said a voice that was far from the faltering one it had been the first time I'd heard it. *Sookie Stackhouse?*

It's me. We're checking in. I'm in 1538. You?

I'm in 1576. How are you doing?

Good, personally. But Louisiana ... we've had the hurricane, and we've got the trial. I guess you know all about that?

Yeah. You saw some action.

You could say that, I told him, wondering if my smile was coming across in my head.

Got that loud and clear.

Now I had an inkling of how people must feel when they were faced with me.

I'll see you later, I told Barry. *Hey, what's your real last name?*

You started something when you brought my gift out into the open, he told me. *My real name is Barry Horowitz. Now I just call myself Barry Bellboy. That's how I'm registered, if you forget my room number.*

Okay. Looking forward to visiting with you.

Same here.

And then Barry and I both turned our attention to other things, and that strange tickling feeling of mind-to-mind communication was gone.

Barry's the only other telepath I've ever encountered.

Mr Cataliades had discovered that the humans – well, the non-vampires – in the party had each been put in a room with another person. Some of the vampires had roommates, too. He hadn't been pleased that he himself was sharing a room with Diantha, but the hotel was extremely crowded, the clerk had said. He may have been lying about a lot of other things, but that much was clearly true.

I was sharing a room with Gervaise's squeeze, and as I slid the card into the slot on the door, I wondered if she'd be in. She was. I'd been expecting a woman like the fangbangers who hang around at Fangtasia, but Carla Danvers was another kind of creature entirely.

'Hey, girl!' she said, as I entered. 'I figured you'd be along soon when they brought your bags up. I'm Carla, Gerry's girlfriend.'

'Nice to meet you,' I said, shaking hands. Carla was a prom queen. Maybe she hadn't been, literally; maybe she hadn't made homecoming queen, either, but she'd surely been on the court. Carla had dark brown chin-length hair, and big brown eyes, and teeth that were so straight and white that they were an advertisement for her orthodontist. Her breasts had been enhanced, and her ears were pierced, and her belly button, too. She had a tattoo on her lower back, some black vines in a vee pattern with a couple of roses with green leaves in the middle. I could see all this because Carla was naked, and she didn't seem to have the slightest idea that her nudity was a little on the 'too much information' side to suit me.

'Have you and Gervaise been going together long?' I asked to camouflage how uncomfortable I was.

'I met Gerry, let's see, seven months ago. He said it would be better for me to have a separate room because he might have to have business meetings in his, you know? Plus, I'm going shopping while I'm here – retail therapy! Big city stores! And I wanted someplace to store my shopping bags so he won't ask me how much it all costs.' She gave me a wink I can only say was roguish.

'Okay,' I said. 'Sounds good.' It really didn't, but Carla's program was hardly my business. My suitcase was waiting for me on a stand, so I opened it and started to unpack, noting that my hanging bag with my good dresses was already in the closet. Carla had left me exactly half the closet space and drawer space, which was decent. She had brought about twenty times more clothes than I had, which made her fairness all the more remarkable.

'Whose girlfriend are you?' Carla asked. She was giving herself a pedicure. When she drew up one leg, the overhead light winked on something metallic between her legs. Completely embarrassed, I turned away to straighten my evening dress on the hanger.

'I'm dating Quinn,' I said.

I glanced over my shoulder, keeping my gaze high.

Carla looked blank.

'The weretiger,' I said. 'He's arranging the ceremonies here.'

She looked marginally more responsive.

'Big guy, shaved head,' I said.

Her face brightened. 'Oh, yeah, I saw him this morning! He was eating breakfast in the restaurant when I was checking in.'

'There's a restaurant?'

'Yeah, sure. Though of course it's tiny. And there's room service.'

'You know, in vampire hotels there often isn't a restaurant,' I said, just to make conversation. I'd read an article about it in *American Vampire*.

'Oh. Well, that makes no sense at all.' Carla finished one set of toes and began another.

'Not from a vampire point of view.'

Carla frowned. 'I know they don't eat. But people do. And this is a people world, right? That's like not learning English when you emigrate to America.'

I turned around to check out Carla's face, make sure she was serious. Yeah, she was.

'Carla,' I said, and then stopped. I didn't have any idea what to say, how to get across to Carla that a four-hundred-year-old vamp really didn't care very much about the eating arrangements of a twenty-year-old human. But the girl was waiting for me to finish. 'Well, it's good that there's a restaurant here,' I said weakly.

She nodded. 'Yeah, 'cause I need my coffee in the morning,' she said. 'I just can't get going without it. Course, when you date a vamp, your morning is liable to begin at three or four in the afternoon.' She laughed.

'True,' I said. I'd finished unpacking, so I went over to our window and looked out. The glass was so heavily tinted that it was hard to make out the landscape, but it was seeable. I wasn't on the Lake Michigan side of the hotel, which was a pity, but I looked at the buildings around the west side of the hotel with curiosity. I didn't see cities that often, and I'd never seen a northern city. The sky was darkening rapidly, so between that and the tinted windows I really couldn't see too much after ten minutes. The vampires would be awake soon, and my workday would begin.

Though she kept up a sporadic stream of chatter, Carla didn't ask what my role was at this summit. She assumed I was there as arm candy. For the moment, that was all right with me. Sooner or later, she'd find out what my particular talent was, and then she'd be nervous around me. On the other hand, now she was a little *too* relaxed.

Carla was getting dressed (thank God) in what I thought of as 'classy whore'. She was wearing a glittery green cocktail dress that almost didn't have a top to it, and fuck-me shoes, and what amounted to a see-through thong. Well, she had her working clothes, and I had mine. I wasn't too pleased with myself for being so judgmental, and maybe I was a little envious that my working clothes were so conservative.

For tonight, I had chosen a chocolate brown lace handkerchief dress. I put in my big gold earrings and slid into brown pumps, put on some lipstick, and brushed my hair really well. Sticking my keycard into my little evening purse, I headed to the front desk to find out which suite was the queen's, since Mr Cataliades had told me to present myself there.

I had hoped to run into Quinn along the way, but I didn't see hide nor hair of him. What with me having a roommate, and Quinn being so busy all the time, this summit might not promise as much fun on the side as I'd hoped.

The desk clerk blanched when he saw me coming, and he looked around to see if Diantha was with me. While he was scrawling the queen's room number on a piece of notepaper with a shaking hand, I looked around me with more attention.

There were security cameras in a few obvious locations, pointed at the front doors and at the registration desk. And I thought I could see one at the elevators. There were the usual armed guards – usual for a vampire hotel, that is. The big selling point for any vampire hotel was the security and privacy of its guests. Otherwise, vampires could stay more cheaply and centrally in the special vampire rooms of mainstream hotels. (Even Motel 6 had one vampire room at almost every location.) When I thought about the protesters outside, I really hoped the security crew here at the Pyramid was on the ball.

I nodded at another human woman as I crossed the lobby to the central bank of elevators. The rooms got ritzier the higher up you went, I gathered, since there were fewer on the floor. The queen had one of the fourth floor suites, since she'd booked for this event a long time ago, before Katrina – and probably while her husband was still alive. There were only eight doors on her floor, and I didn't have to see the number to know which room was Sophie-Anne's. Sigebert was standing in front of it. Sigebert was a boulder of a man. He had guarded the queen for hundreds of years, as had Andre. The ancient vampire looked lonely without his brother, Wybert. Otherwise, he was the same old Anglo-Saxon warrior he'd been the first time I'd met him – shaggy beard, physique of a wild boar, missing a tooth or two in crucial places.

Sigebert grinned at me, a terrifying sight. 'Miss Sookie,' he said by way of greeting.

'Sigebert,' I said, carefully pronouncing it 'See-ya-bairt.' 'Are you doing okay?' I wanted to convey sympathy without dipping into too-sentimental waters.

'My brother, he died a hero,' Sigebert said proudly. 'In battle.'

I thought of saying, 'You must miss him so much after a thousand years.' Then I decided that was exactly like reporters asking the parents of missing children, 'How do you feel?'

'He was a great fighter,' I said instead, and that was exactly what Sigebert wanted to hear. He clapped me on the shoulder, almost knocking me to the ground. Then his look got a little absent, as if he were listening to an announcement.

I'd suspected that the queen could talk to her 'children' telepathically, and when Sigebert opened the door for me without another word, I knew that was true. I was glad she couldn't talk to me. Being able to communicate with Barry was kind of fun, but if we hung out together all the time I was sure it would get old in a hurry. Plus, Sophie-Anne was a heck of a lot scarier.

The queen's suite was lavish. I'd never seen anything like it. The carpet was as thick as a sheep's pelt, and it was off-white. The furniture was upholstered in shades of gold and dark blue. The slanting slab of glass that enclosed the outside wall was opaque. I have to say, the large wall of darkness made me feel twitchy.

In the midst of this splendor, Sophie-Anne sat curled on a couch. Small and extremely pale, with her shining brown hair swept up in a chignon, the queen was wearing a raspberry-colored silk suit with black piping and black alligator heels. Her jewelry was heavy, gold, and simple.

Sophie-Anne would have looked more age-appropriate wearing a Gwen Stefani L.A.M.B. outfit. She'd died as a human when she'd been maybe fifteen or sixteen. In her time, that would have made her a fully-grown woman and mother. In our time, that made her a mall rat. To modern eyes, her clothes were too old for her, but it would take an insane person to tell her so. Sophie-Anne was the world's most dangerous teenager, and the second most dangerous had her back. Andre was standing right behind Sophie-Anne, as always. When he'd given me a thorough look, and the door had closed behind me, he actually sat beside Sophie-Anne, which was some kind of signal that I was a member of the club, I guess. Andre and his queen had both been drinking TrueBlood, and they looked rosy as a result – almost human, in fact.

'How are your accommodations?' Sophie-Anne asked politely.

'Fine. I'm rooming with a . . . girlfriend of Gervaise's,' I said.

'With *Carla*? Why?' Her brows rose up like dark birds in a clear sky.

'The hotel's crowded. It's no big thing. I figure she'll be with Gervaise most of the time, anyway,' I said.

Sophie-Anne said, 'What did you think of Johan?'

I could feel my face harden. 'I think he belongs in jail.'

'But he will keep me out of it.'

I tried to imagine what a vampire jail would be like, gave up. I couldn't give her any positive feedback on Johan, so I just nodded.

'You are still not telling me what you picked up from him.'

'He's very tense and conflicted.'

'Explain.'

'He's anxious. He's scared. He's fighting different loyalties. He only wants to come out alive. He doesn't care for anyone but himself.'

'So how does that make him different from any other human?' Andre commented.

Sophie-Anne responded with a twitch of one side of her mouth. That Andre, what a comedian.

'Most humans don't stab women,' I said as quietly and calmly as I could. 'Most humans don't enjoy that.'

Sophie-Anne was not completely indifferent to the violent death Johan Glassport had meted out, but naturally she was a little more concerned with her own legal defense. At least, that was how I read her, but with vampires, I had to go on subtle body language rather than the sure knowledge right out of their brains. 'He'll defend me, I'll pay him, and then he's on his own,' she said. 'Anything might happen to him then.' She gave me a clear-eyed look.

Okay, Sophie-Anne, I got the picture.

'Did he question you thoroughly? Did you feel he knew what he was doing?' she asked, returning to the important stuff.

'Yes, ma'am,' I said promptly. 'He did seem to be really competent.'

'Then he'll be worth the trouble.'

I didn't even let my eyes flicker.

'Did Cataliades tell you what to expect?'

'Yes, ma'am, he did.'

'Good. As well as your testimony at the trial, I need you to attend every meeting with me that includes humans.'

This was why she was paying me the big bucks.

'Ah, do you have any schedule of meetings?' I asked. 'It's just, I'd be ready and waiting if I had any idea when you needed me.'

Before she could answer, there was a knock at the door. Andre rose and moved to answer it so smoothly and fluidly that you would have sworn he was part cat. His sword was in his hand, though I hadn't seen it before. The door opened a bit just as Andre reached it, and I heard Sigebert's bass rumble.

After they'd exchanged a few sentences, the door opened wider, and Andre said, 'The King of Texas, my lady.' There was only a hint of pleased surprise in his voice, but it was the equivalent of Andre doing cartwheels across the carpet. This visit was a show of support for Sophie-Anne, and all the other vampires would notice.

Stan Davis came in, trailing a group of vamps and humans.

Stan was a nerd's nerd. He was the kind of guy who you checked out for a pocket protector. You could see the comb marks in his sandy hair, and his glasses were heavy and thick. They were also quite unnecessary. I'd never met a vamp who didn't have excellent vision and very precise hearing. Stan was wearing a wash 'n' wear white shirt with a Sears brand logo and some navy Dockers. And brown leather moccasins. Hoo, boy. He'd been a sheriff when I'd met him, and now that he was king, he was maintaining the same low-key approach.

Behind Stan came his sergeant at arms, Joseph Velasquez. A short, burly Hispanic with spiky hair, Joseph never seemed to crack a smile. By his side was a red-haired female vamp named Rachel; I remembered her, too, from my trip to Dallas. Rachel was a savage one, and she didn't like cooperating with humans in the least. Trailing the two was Barry the Bellboy, looking good in designer jeans and a taupe silk T-shirt, a discreet gold chain around his neck. Barry had matured in an almost scary way since I'd last seen him. He'd been a handsome, gawky boy of maybe nineteen when I'd first spotted him working as a bellboy at the Silent Shore Hotel in Dallas. Now Barry had had a manicure, a very good haircut, and the wary eyes of someone who'd been swimming in the shark pool.

We smiled at each other, and Barry said, *Good to see you. Looking pretty, Sookie.*

Thanks, and likewise, Barry.

Andre was doing the proper vampire greeting thing, which did not include handshaking. 'Stan, we are pleased to see you. Who have you brought to meet us?'

Stan gallantly bent to kiss Sophie-Anne's hand. 'Most beautiful queen,' he said. 'This vampire is my second, Joseph Velasquez. And this vampire is my nest sister Rachel. This human is the telepath Barry Bellboy. Indirectly, I have you to thank for him.'

Sophie-Anne actually smiled. She said, 'Of course, I am always delighted to do you any sort of favor in my power, Stan.' She gestured to him to sit opposite her. Rachel and Joseph took up flanking positions. 'It's so good to see you here in my suite. I had been concerned that I wouldn't have any visitors at all.'

('Since I'm under indictment for killing my husband, and since I've also sustained a staggering economic blow,' was the subtext.)

'I extend my sympathies to you,' Stan said with a completely inflectionless voice. 'The losses in your country have been extreme. If we can help . . . I know the humans from my state have helped yours, and it's only right that the vampires do likewise.'

'Thank you for your kindness,' she said. Sophie-Anne's pride was hurting in a major way. She had to struggle to paste that smile back on her face. 'I believe you know Andre,' she continued. 'Andre, you now know Joseph. And I believe all of you know our Sookie.'

The phone rang, and since I was closest to it, I answered it.

'Am I speaking to a member of the Queen of Louisiana's party?' the gruff voice asked.

'Yes, you are.'

'One of you needs to come down to the loading bay to get a suitcase that belongs to your party. We can't read the label.'

'Oh . . . okay.'

'Sooner the better.'

'All right.'

He hung up. Okay, that was a little abrupt.

Since the queen was waiting for me to tell her who had called, I relayed the request, and she looked equally puzzled for all of a millisecond. 'Later,' she said dismissively.

In the meantime, the light eyes of the King of Texas were focused on me like laser beams. I inclined my head to him, which I hoped was

the correct response. It seemed to be adequate. I would have liked to
have had time to go over the protocol with Andre before the queen
began receiving guests, but truthfully, I hadn't expected there to be
any, much less a powerful guy like Stan Davis. This had to mean
something good for the queen, or maybe it was a subtle vampire insult.
I was sure I'd find out.

I felt the tickle of Barry in my mind. *She good to work for?* Barry
asked.

I just help her out from time to time, I said. *I still have a day job.*

Barry looked at me with surprise. *You kidding? You could be raking it
in, if you go to a good state like Ohio or Illinois where there's real money.*

I shrugged. *I like where I live*, I said.

Then we both became aware that our vampire employers were
watching our silent exchange. Our faces were changing expression,
I guess, like faces do during a conversation . . . except our conversation
had been silent.

'Excuse me,' I said. 'I didn't mean to be rude. I just don't see people
like me very often, and it's kind of a treat to talk to another telepath.
I beg your pardon, ma'am, sir.'

'I could almost hear it,' Sophie-Anne marveled. 'Stan, he has been
very useful?' Sophie-Anne could talk to her own children mentally,
but it must be as rare an ability among vampires as it was among
people.

'Very useful,' Stan confirmed. 'The day that your Sookie brought
him to my attention was a very good day for me. He knows when
the humans are lying; he knows what their ulterior motives are. It's
wonderful insight.'

I looked at Barry, wondering if he ever thought of himself as a traitor
to humankind or just as a vendor supplying a needed good. He met
my eyes, his own face hard. Sure, he was conflicted about serving a
vampire, revealing human secrets to his employer. I struggled with
that idea myself from time to time.

'Hmmm. Sookie only works for me on occasion.' Sophie-Anne was
staring at me, and if I could characterize her smooth face, I would say
she was thoughtful. Andre had something going on behind his pink-
tinged teenage facade, and it was something I had better watch out

for. He wasn't just thoughtful, he was interested; engaged, for want of a better description.

'Bill brought her to Dallas,' Stan observed, not quite asking a question.

'He was her protector at the time,' Sophie-Anne said.

A brief silence. Barry leered at me hopefully, and I gave him an in-your-dreams look. Actually, I felt like hugging him, since that little exchange broke up the silence into something I could handle.

'Do you really need Barry and me here, since we're the only humans, and it might not be so productive if we just sat around and read each other's minds?'

Joseph Velasquez actually smiled before he could stop himself.

After a silent moment, Sophie-Anne nodded, and then Stan. Queen Sophie and King Stan, I reminded myself. Barry bowed in a practiced way, and I felt like sticking out my tongue at him. I did a sort of bob and then scuttled out of the suite. Sigebert eyed us with a questioning face. 'The queen, she not need you?' he asked.

'Not right now,' I said. I tapped a pager that Andre had handed me at the last minute. 'The pager will vibrate if she needs me,' I said.

Sigebert eyed the device mistrustfully. 'I think it would be better if you just stayed here,' he said.

'The queen, she says I can go,' I told him.

And off I went, Barry trailing along behind me. We took the elevator down to the lobby, where we found a secluded corner where no one could sneak up on us to eavesdrop.

I'd never conversed with someone entirely in my head, and neither had Barry, so we played around with that for a while. Barry would tell me the story of his life while I tried to block out all the other brains around me; then I'd try to listen to everyone else *and* to Barry.

This was actually a lot of fun.

Barry turned out to be better than I was at picking out who was thinking what in a crowd. I was a bit better at hearing nuance and detail, not always easy to pick up in thoughts. But we had some common ground.

We agreed on who the best broadcasters in the room were; that is, our 'hearing' was the same. He would point at someone (in this case it was my roommate, Carla) and we would both listen to her thoughts, then rate them on a scale of one to five, five being the loudest, clearest broadcast. Carla was a three. After that agreement, we rated other people, and we found ourselves reacting almost as one over that.

Okay, this was interesting.

Let's try touching, I suggested.

Barry didn't even leer. He was into this, too. Without further ado, he took my hand, and we faced in nearly opposite directions.

The voices came in so clearly, it was like having a full-voice conversation with everyone in the room, all at once. Like pumping up the volume on a DVD, with the treble and bass perfectly balanced. It was elating and terrifying, all at once. Though I was facing away from the reception desk, I clearly heard a woman inquiring about the arrival of the Louisiana vamps. I caught my own image in the brain of the clerk, who was feeling delighted at doing me a bad turn.

Here comes trouble, Barry warned me.

I swung around to see a vampire advancing on me with not a very pleasant expression on her face. She had hot hazel eyes and straight light brown hair, and she was lean and mean.

'Finally, one of the Louisiana party. Are the rest of you in hiding? Tell your bitch whore of a mistress that I'll nail her hide to the wall! She won't get away with murdering my king! I'll see her staked and exposed to the sun on the roof of this hotel!'

I said the first thing that came into my head, unfortunately. 'Save the drama for your mama,' I told her, just like an eleven-year-old. 'And by the way, who the heck are you?'

Of course, this had to be Jennifer Cater. I started to tell her that her king's character had been really substandard, but I liked my head right where it sat on my shoulders, and it wouldn't take much to tip this gal over the edge.

She gave good glare, I'd say that for her.

'I'll drain you dry,' she said, harshly. We were attracting a certain amount of attention by then.

'Ooooo,' I said, exasperated beyond wisdom. 'I'm so scared. Wouldn't the court love to hear you say that? Correct me if I'm wrong, but aren't vampires prevented by – oh, yes – the *law* from threatening humans with death, or did I just read that wrong?'

'As if I give a snap of my fingers for human law,' Jennifer Cater said, but the fire was dying down in her eyes as she realized that the whole lobby was listening to our exchange, including many humans and possibly some vampires who'd love to see her out of the way.

'Sophie-Anne Leclerq will be tried by the laws of our people,' Jennifer said as a parting shot. 'And she will be found guilty. I'll hold Arkansas, and I'll make it great.'

'That'll be a first,' I said with some justification. Arkansas, Louisiana, and Mississippi were three poor states huddled together, much to our mutual mortification. We were all grateful for each other, because we got to take turns being at the bottom of almost every list in the United States: poverty level, teen pregnancy, cancer death, illiteracy. . . . We pretty much rotated the honors.

Jennifer marched off, not wanting to try a comeback. She was determined, and she was vicious, but I thought Sophie-Anne could outmaneuver Jennifer any day. If I were a betting woman, I'd put money on the French nag.

Barry and I gave each other a shrug. Incident over. We joined hands again.

More trouble, Barry said, sounding resigned.

I focused my brain where his was going. I heard a weretiger heading our way in a big, big hurry.

I dropped Barry's hand and turned, my arms out already and my whole face smiling. 'Quinn!' I said, and after a moment where he looked very uncertain, Quinn swung me up in his arms.

I hugged him as hard as I could, and he returned the hug so emphatically that my ribs creaked. Then he kissed me, and it took all my strength of character to keep the kiss within social boundaries.

When we parted to breathe, I realized Barry was standing awkwardly a few feet away, not sure what to do.

'Quinn, this is Barry Bellboy,' I said, trying not to feel embarrassed. 'He's the only other telepath I know. He works for Stan Davis, the King of Texas.'

Quinn extended a hand to Barry, who I now realized was standing awkwardly for a reason. We'd transmitted a bit too graphically. I felt a tide of red sweep over my cheeks. The best thing to do was pretend I hadn't noticed, of course, and that's what I did. But I could feel a little smile twitching the corners of my mouth, and Barry looked more amused than angry.

'Good to meet you, Barry,' Quinn rumbled.

'You're in charge of the ceremony arrangements?' Barry asked.

'Yep, that's me.'

'I've heard of you,' Barry said. 'The great fighter. You've got quite a rep among the vamps, man.'

I cocked my head. Something I wasn't getting here. 'Great fighter?' I said.

'I'll tell you about it later,' Quinn said, and his mouth set in a hard line.

Barry looked from me to Quinn. His own face did some hardening, and I was surprised to see that much toughness in Barry. 'He hasn't told you?' he asked, and then read the answer right from my head. 'Hey, man, that's not right,' he said to Quinn. 'She should know.'

Quinn almost snarled. 'I'll tell her about it soon.'

'Soon?' Quinn's thoughts were full of turmoil and violence. 'Like now?'

But at that moment, a woman strode across the lobby toward us. She was one of the most frightening women I'd ever seen, and I've seen some scary women. She was probably five foot eight, with inky black curls that hugged her head, and she was holding a helmet under her arm. It matched her armor. The armor itself, black and lusterless, was very much like a rather tailored baseball catcher's outfit: a chest guard, thigh protectors, and shin guards, with the addition of thick leather braces that strapped around the forearms. She had some heavy boots on, too, and she carried a sword, a gun, and a small crossbow draped about her in appropriate holsters.

I could only gape.

'You are the one they call Quinn?' she asked, coming to a halt a yard away. She had a heavy accent, one I couldn't trace.

'I am,' Quinn said. I noticed Quinn didn't seem to be as amazed as I was at the appearance of this lethal being.

'I'm Batanya. You are in charge of special events. Does that include security? I wish to discuss my client's special needs.'

'I thought security, was your job,' Quinn said.

Batanya smiled, and it would really make your blood run cold. 'Oh, yes, that's my job. But guarding him would be easier if—'

'I'm not in charge of security,' he said. 'I'm only in charge of the rituals and procedures.'

'All right,' she said, her accent making the casual phrase into something serious. 'Then whom do I talk to?'

'A guy named Todd Donati. His office is in the staff area behind the registration desk. One of the clerks can show you.'

'Excuse me,' I said.

'Yes?' She looked down an arrow-straight nose at me. But she didn't look hostile or snooty, just worried.

'I'm Sookie Stackhouse,' I said. 'Who do you work for, Miss Batanya?'

'The King of Kentucky,' she said. 'He has brought us here at great expense. So it's a pity there's nothing I can do to keep him from being killed, as things stand now.'

'What do you mean?' I was considerably startled and alarmed.

The bodyguard looked like she was willing to give me an earful, but we were interrupted.

'Batanya!' A young vampire was hurrying across the lobby, his crew cut and all-black Goth ensemble looking all the more frivolous when he stood by the formidable woman. 'The master says he needs you by his side.'

'I am coming,' Batanya said. 'I know my place. But I had to protest the way the hotel is making my job much harder than it needs to be.'

'Complain on your own dime,' the youngster said curtly.

Batanya gave him a look I wouldn't have wanted to have earned. Then she bowed to us, each in turn. 'Miss Stackhouse,' she said, extending her hand for me to shake. I hadn't realized hands could be characterized as muscular. 'Mr Quinn.' Quinn got the shake, too, while Barry got a nod, since he hadn't introduced himself. 'I will call this Todd Donati. Sorry I filled your ears, when this is not your responsibility.'

'Wow,' I said, watching Batanya stride away. She was wearing pants like liquid leather, and you could see each buttock flex and relax with her movement. It was like an anatomy lesson. She had muscles in her butt.

'What galaxy did she come from?' Barry asked, sounding dazed.

Quinn said, 'Not galaxy. Dimension. She's a Britlingen.'

We waited for more enlightenment.

'She's a bodyguard, a super-bodyguard,' he explained. 'Britlingens are the best. You have to be really rich to hire a witch who can bring one over, and the witch has to negotiate the terms with their guild. When the job's over, the witch has to send them back. You can't leave them here. Their laws are different. Way different.'

'You're telling me the King of Kentucky paid gobs of money to bring that woman to this . . . this dimension?' I'd heard plenty of unbelievable things in the past two years, but this topped them all.

'It's a very extreme action. I wonder what he's so afraid of. Kentucky isn't exactly rolling in money.'

'Maybe he bet on the right horse,' I said, since I had my own royalty to worry about. 'And I need to talk to you.'

'Babe, I gotta get back to work,' Quinn said apologetically. He shot an unfriendly look at Barry. 'I know we need to talk. But I've got to line up the jurors for the trial, and I've got to set up a wedding ceremony. Negotiations between the King of Indiana and the King of Mississippi have been concluded, and they want to tie the knot while everyone's here.'

'Russell's getting married?' I smiled. I wondered if he'd be the bride or the groom, or a little bit of both.

'Yeah, but don't tell anyone yet. They're announcing it tonight.'

'So when are we gonna talk?'

'I'll come to your room when the vamps are in bed for the day. Where are you?'

'I have a roommate.' I gave him the room number anyway.

'If she's there, we'll find somewhere else to go,' he said, glancing at his watch. 'Listen, don't worry; everything's okay.'

I wondered what I should be worrying about. I wondered where another dimension was, and how hard it would be to bring over bodyguards from it. I wondered why anyone would go to the expense. Not that Batanya hadn't seemed pretty damn effective; but the extreme effort Kentucky had gone to, that sure seemed to argue extreme fear. Who was after him?

My waist buzzed at me, and I realized I was being summoned back up to the queen's suite. Barry's pager went off, too. We looked at each other.

Back to work, he said, as we went toward the elevator. *I'm sorry if I caused trouble between you and Quinn.*

You don't mean that.

He glanced at me. He had the grace to look ashamed. *I guess I don't. I had a picture built up of how you and me would be, and Quinn kind of intruded on my fantasy life.*

Ah . . . ah.

Don't worry – you don't have to think of something to say. It was one of those fantasies. Now that I'm really with you, I have to adjust.

Ah.

But I shouldn't have let my disappointment make me a jerk.

Ah. Okay. I'm sure Quinn and I can work it out.

So, I kept the fantasy screened from you, huh?

I nodded vigorously.

Well, at least that's something.

I smiled at him. *Everyone's got to have a fantasy,* I told him. *My fantasy is finding out where Kentucky got that money, and who he hired to bring that woman here. Was she not the scariest thing you've ever seen?*

No, Barry answered, to my surprise. *The scariest thing I've ever seen . . . well, it wasn't Batanya.* And then he locked the communicating door between our brains and threw away the key. Sigebert was opening the door into the queen's suite, and we were back at work.

After Barry and his party left, I kind of waved my hand in the air to let the queen know I had something to say if she wanted to listen. She and Andre had been discussing Stan's motivation in paying the significant visit, and they paused in identical attitudes. It was just weird. Their heads were cocked at the same angle, and with their extreme pallor and stillness, it was like being regarded by works of art carved in marble: Nymph and Satyr at Rest, or something like that.

'You know what Britlingens are?' I asked, stumbling over the unfamiliar word.

The queen nodded. Andre just waited.

'I saw one,' I said, and the queen's head jerked.

'Who has gone to the expense to hire a Britlingen?' Andre asked.

I told them the whole story.

The queen looked – well, it was hard to say how she looked. Maybe a little worried, maybe intrigued, since I'd garnered so much news in the lobby.

'I never knew how useful I'd find it, having a human servant,' she said to Andre. 'Other humans will say anything around her, and even the Britlingen spoke freely.'

Andre was perhaps a tad jealous if the look on his face was any indication.

'On the other hand, I can't do a damn thing about any of this,' I said. 'I can just tell you what I heard, and it's hardly classified information.'

'Where did Kentucky get the money?' Andre said.

The queen shook her head, as if to say she hadn't a clue and really didn't care that much. 'Did you see Jennifer Cater?' she asked me.

'Yes, ma'am.'

'What did she say?' asked Andre.

'She said she'd drink my blood, and she'd see you staked and exposed on the hotel roof.'

There was a moment of utter silence.

Then Sophie-Anne said, 'Stupid Jennifer. What's that phrase Chester used to use? She's getting too big for her britches. What to do ...? I wonder if she would accept a messenger from me?'

She and Andre looked at each other steadily, and I decided they were doing a little telepathic communication of their own.

'I suppose she's taken the suite Arkansas had reserved,' the queen said to Andre, and he picked up the in-house phone and called the front desk. It wasn't the first time I'd heard the king or queen of a state referred to as the state itself, but it seemed a really impersonal way to refer to your former husband, no matter how violently the marriage had ended.

'Yes,' he said after he'd hung up.

'Maybe we should pay her a visit,' the queen said. She and Andre indulged in some of that silent to and fro that was their way of conversing. Probably like watching Barry and me, I figured. 'She'll admit us, I'm sure. There'll be something she wants to say to me in person.' The queen picked up the phone, but not as if that was something she did every day. She dialed the room number with her own fingers, too.

'Jennifer,' she said charmingly. She listened to a torrent of words that I could hear only a bit. Jennifer didn't sound any happier than she'd been in the lobby.

'Jennifer, we need to talk.' The queen sounded much more charming and a lot tougher. There was silence on the other end of the line. 'The doors are not closed to discussion or negotiation, Jennifer,' Sophie-Anne said. 'At least, my doors aren't. What about yours?' I think Jennifer spoke again. 'All right, that's wonderful, Jennifer. We'll be down in a minute or two.' The queen hung up and stood silent for a long moment.

It seemed to me like going to visit Jennifer Cater, when she was bringing a lawsuit against Sophie-Anne for murdering Peter Thread-gill, was a real bad idea. But Andre nodded approvingly at Sophie-Anne.

After Sophie-Anne's conversation with her archenemy, I thought we'd head to the Arkansas group's room any second. But maybe the queen wasn't as confident as she'd sounded. Instead of starting out briskly for the showdown with Jennifer Cater, Sophie-Anne dawdled. She gave herself a little extra grooming, changed her shoes, searched around for her room key, and so on. Then she got a phone call about what room service charges the humans in her group could put on the room bill. So it was more than fifteen minutes before we managed to leave the room. Sigebert was coming out of the staircase door, and he fell into place with Andre at the waiting elevator.

Jennifer Cater and her party were on floor seven. There was no one standing at Jennifer Cater's door: I guessed she didn't rate her own bodyguard. Andre did the knocking honors, and Sophie-Anne straight-ened expectantly. Sigebert hung back, giving me an unexpected smile. I tried not to flinch.

The door swung open. The interior of the suite was dark.
The smell that wafted from the door was unmistakable.
'Well,' said the Queen of Louisiana briskly. 'Jennifer's dead.'

Chapter 10

'**G**o see,' the queen told me.

'What? But all y'all are stronger than I am! And less scared!'

'And we're the ones she's suing,' Andre pointed out. 'Our smell cannot be in there. Sigebert, you must go see.'

Sigebert glided into the darkness.

A door across the landing opened, and Batanya stepped out.

'I smell death,' she said. 'What's happened?'

'We came calling,' I said. 'But the door was unlocked already. Something's wrong in there.'

'You don't know what?'

'No, Sigebert is exploring,' I explained. 'We're waiting.'

'Let me call my second. I can't leave Kentucky's door unguarded.' She turned to call back into the suite, 'Clovache!' At least, I guess that was how it was spelled, it was pronounced 'Kloh-VOSH.'

A kind of Batanya Junior emerged – same armor, but smaller scale; younger, brown-haired, less terrifying ... but still plenty formidable.

'Scout the place,' Batanya ordered, and without a single question Clovache drew her sword and eased into the apartment like a dangerous dream.

We all waited, holding our breaths – well, I was, anyway. The vamps didn't have breath to hold, and Batanya didn't seem at all agitated. She had moved to a spot where she could watch the open door of Jennifer

Cater's place and the closed door of the King of Kentucky. Her sword was drawn.

The queen's face looked almost tense, perhaps even excited; that is, slightly less blank than usual. Sigebert came out and shook his head without a word.

Clovache appeared in the doorway. 'All dead,' she reported to Batanya.

Batanya waited.

'By decapitation,' Clovache elaborated. 'The woman was, ah' – Clovache appeared to be counting mentally – 'in six pieces.'

'This is bad,' the queen said at the same moment Andre said, 'This is good.' They exchanged exasperated glances.

'Any humans?' I asked, trying to keep my voice small because I didn't want their attention, but I did want to know, very badly.

'No, all vampires,' Clovache said after she got a go-ahead nod from Batanya. 'I saw three. They're flaking off pretty fast.'

'Clovache, go in and call that Todd Donati.' Clovache went silently into the Kentucky suite and placed a call, which had an electrifying effect. Within five minutes, the area in front of the elevator was crammed with people of all sorts and descriptions and degrees of living.

A man wearing a maroon jacket with *Security* on the pocket seemed to be in charge, so he must be Todd Donati. He was a policeman who'd retired from the force early because of the big money to be made guarding and aiding the undead. But that didn't mean he liked them. Now he was furious that something had happened so early in the summit, something that would cause him more work than he was able to handle. He had cancer, I heard clearly, though I wasn't able to discern what kind. Donati wanted to work as long as he could to provide for his family after he was gone, and he was resentful of the stress and strain this investigation would cause, the energy it would drain. But he was doggedly determined to do his job.

When Donati's vampire boss, the hotel manager, showed up, I recognized him. Christian Baruch had been on the cover of *Fang* (the vamp version of *People*) a few months ago. Baruch was Swiss born. As a human, he'd designed and managed a bunch of fancy hotels in

Western Europe. When he'd told a vampire in the same line of business that if he was 'brought over' (not only to the vampire life but to America), he could run outstanding and profitable hotels for a syndicate of vampires, he'd been obliged in both ways.

Now Christian Baruch had eternal life (if he avoided pointy wooden objects), and the vampire hotel syndicate was raking in the money. But he wasn't a security guy or a law enforcement expert, and he wasn't the police. Sure, he could decorate the hell out of the hotel and tell the architect how many suites needed a wet bar, but what good would he be in this situation? His human hireling looked at Baruch sourly. Baruch was wearing a suit that looked remarkably wonderful, even to inexperienced eyes like mine. I was sure it had been made for him, and I was sure it had cost a bundle.

I had been pushed back by the crowd until I was pressed against the wall by one of the suite doors – Kentucky's, I realized. It hadn't opened yet. The two Britlingens would have to guard their charge extra carefully with this mob milling around. The hubbub was extraordinary. I was next to a woman in a security uniform; it was just like the ex-cop's, but she didn't have to wear a tie.

'Do you think letting all these people into this space is a good idea?' I asked. I didn't want to be telling the woman her business, but dang. Didn't she ever watch *CSI*?

Security Woman gave me a dark look. 'What are *you* doing here?' she asked, as if that made some big point.

'I'm here because I was with the group that found the bodies.'

'Well, you just need to keep quiet and let us do our work.'

She said this in the snottiest tone possible. 'What work would that be? You don't seem to be doing anything at all,' I said.

Okay, maybe I shouldn't have said that, but she *wasn't* doing anything. It seemed to me that she should be —

And then she grabbed me and slammed me into the wall and handcuffed me.

I gave a kind of yelp of surprise. 'That really wasn't what I meant you to do,' I said with some difficulty, since my face was mashed against the door of the suite.

There was a large silence from the crowd behind us. 'Chief, I got a woman here causing trouble,' said Security Woman.

Maroon looked awful on her, by the way.

'Landry, what are you doing?' said an overly reasonable male voice. It was the kind of voice you use with an irrational child.

'She was telling me what to do,' replied Security Woman, but I could tell her voice was deflating even as she spoke.

'What was she telling you to do, Landry?'

'She wondered what all the people were doing here, sir.'

'Isn't that a valid question, Landry?'

'Sir?'

'Don't you think we should be clearing out some of these people?'

'Yes, sir, but she said she was here because she was in the party that found the bodies.'

'So she shouldn't leave.'

'Right. Sir.'

'Was she trying to leave?'

'No, sir.'

'But you handcuffed her.'

'Ah.'

'Take the fucking handcuffs off her, Landry.'

'Yes, sir.' Landry was a flat pancake by now, no air left in her at all.

The handcuffs came off, to my relief, and I was able to turn around. I was so angry I could have decked Landry. But since I would've been right back in the handcuffs, I held off. Sophie-Anne and Andre pushed through the crowd; actually, it just kind of melted in front of them. Vampires and humans alike were glad to get out of the way of the Queen of Louisiana and her bodyguard.

Sophie-Anne glanced at my wrists, saw that they really weren't hurt at all, and correctly diagnosed the fact that my worst injury was to my pride.

'This is my employee,' Sophie-Anne said quietly, apparently address-ing Landry but making sure everyone there heard her. 'An insult or injury to this woman is an insult or injury to me.'

Landry didn't know who the hell Sophie-Anne was, but she could tell power when she saw it, and Andre was just as scary. They were the two most frightening teenagers in the world, I do believe.

'Yes, ma'am, Landry will apologize in writing. Now can you tell me what happened here just now?' Todd Donati asked in a very reasonable voice.

The crowd was silent and waiting. I looked for Batanya and Clovache and saw they were missing. Suddenly Andre said, 'You are the chief of security?' in a rather loud voice, and as he did, Sophie-Anne leaned very close to me to say, 'Don't mention the Britlingens.'

'Yes, sir.' The policeman ran a hand over his mustache. 'I'm Todd Donati, and this is my boss, Mr Christian Baruch.'

'I am Andre Paul, and this is my queen, Sophie-Anne Leclerq. This young woman is our employee Sookie Stackhouse.' Andre waited for the next step.

Christian Baruch ignored me. But he gave Sophie-Anne the look I'd give a roast I was thinking of buying for Sunday dinner. 'Your presence is a great honor to my hotel,' he murmured in heavily accented English, and I glimpsed the tips of his fangs. He was quite tall, with a large jaw and dark hair. But his small eyes were arctic gray.

Sophie-Anne took the compliment in stride, though her brows drew together for a second. Showing fang wasn't an exactly subtle way of saying, 'You shake my world.' No one spoke. Well, not for a long, awkward second. Then I said, 'Are you all going to call the police, or what?'

'I think we must consider what we have to tell them,' Baruch said, his voice smooth, sophisticated, and making fun of rural-southern-human me. 'Mr Donati, will you go see what's in the suite?'

Todd Donati pushed his way through the crowd with no subtlety at all. Sigebert, who'd been guarding the open doorway (for lack of anything better to do), stood aside to let the human enter. The huge bodyguard worked his way over to the queen, looking happier when he was in proximity to his ruler.

While Donati examined whatever was left in the Arkansas suite, Christian Baruch turned to address the crowd. 'How many of you came down here after you heard something had happened?'

Maybe fifteen people raised their hands or simply nodded.

'You will please make your way to the Draft of Blood bar on the ground level, where our bartenders will have something special for all of you.' The fifteen moved out pretty quickly after that. Baruch knew his thirsty people. Vamps. Whatever.

'How many of you were not here when the bodies were discovered?' Baruch said after the first group had left. Everyone raised a hand except the four of us: me, the queen, Andre, Sigebert.

'Everyone else may feel free to leave,' Baruch said as civilly as if he was extending a pleasant invitation. And they did. Landry hesitated and got a look that sent her hurtling down the stairs.

The area around the central elevator seemed spacious now, since it was so much emptier.

Donati came back out. He didn't look deeply disturbed or sick, but he did look less composed.

'There's only bits of them left now. There's stuff all over the floor, though; residue, I guess you'd call it. I think there were three of them. But one of them is in so many pieces, that it might be two of them.'

'Who's on the registration?'

Donati referred to a palm-held electronic device. 'Jennifer Cater, of Arkansas. This room was rented to the delegation of Arkansas vampires. The remaining Arkansas vampires.'

The word *remaining* possibly got a little extra emphasis. Donati definitely knew the queen's history.

Christian Baruch raised a thick, dark brow. 'I do know my own people, Donati.'

'Yes, sir.'

Sophie-Anne's nose might have wrinkled delicately with distaste. *His own people, my ass*, that nose said. Baruch was at most four years old, as a vampire.

'Who's been in to see the bodies?' Baruch asked.

'Neither of us,' Andre said promptly. 'We haven't set foot in the suite.'

'Who did?'

'The door was unlocked, and we smelled death. In view of the situation between my queen and the vampires of Arkansas, we thought it was unwise to go inside,' Andre said. 'We sent Sigebert, the queen's guard.'

Andre simply omitted Clovache's exploration of the suite. So Andre and I did have something in common: we could skirt the truth with something that wasn't quite a lie. He'd done a masterful job.

As the questions continued – mostly unanswered or unanswerable – I found myself wondering if the queen would still have to go to trial now that her main accuser was dead. I wondered whom the state of Arkansas belonged to; it was reasonable to assume that the wedding contract had given the queen some rights regarding Peter Threadgill's property, and I knew Sophie-Anne needed every bit of income she could claim, since Katrina. Would she still have those rights to Arkansas, since Andre had killed Peter? I hadn't thought through how much was hanging over the queen's head at this summit.

But after I'd finished asking myself all these questions, I realized that the most immediate issue had yet to be addressed. Who'd killed Jennifer Cater and her companions? (How many Arkansas vamps could be left, after the battle in New Orleans and today's slaughter? Arkansas wasn't that big a state, and it had very few population centers.)

I was recalled to the here and now when Christian Baruch caught my eyes. 'You're the human who can read minds,' he said so suddenly that I jerked.

'Yes,' I said, because I was tired of sirring and ma'aming everyone.

'Did you kill Jennifer Cater?'

I didn't have to fake astonishment. 'That's giving me a lot of credit,' I said. 'Thinking I could have gotten the drop on three vampires. No, I didn't kill her. She came up to me in the lobby this evening, talking trash, but that's the only time I ever even saw her.'

He looked a little taken aback, as if he'd expected another answer or maybe a humbler attitude.

The queen took a step to stand beside me, and Andre mirrored her, so that I was bracketed by ancient vampires. What a warm and cozy feeling. But I knew they were reminding the hotelier that I was their special human and not to be harassed.

At that very opportune moment, a vampire flung open the door from the stairs and hurtled toward the death suite. But Baruch was just as swift, and he barred the way so that the new vampire bounced off him and onto the floor. The small vamp was up in a movement so quick my eyes couldn't break it down and was making a desperate effort to get Baruch out of the doorway.

But the newcomer couldn't, and finally he took a step away from the hotelier. If the smaller vampire had been human, he'd have been panting, and as it was his body shook with tremors of delayed action. He had brown hair and a short beard, and he was wearing a suit, a regular old JCPenney one. He looked like an ordinary guy until you saw his wide eyes and realized that he was some kind of lunatic.

'Is it true?' he asked, his voice low and intent.

'Jennifer Cater and her companions are dead,' Christian Baruch said, not without compassion.

The small man howled, literally howled, and the hair on my arms stood up. He sank to his knees, his body swaying back and forth in a transport of grief.

'I take it you are one of her party?' the queen said.

'Yes, yes!'

'Then now I am your queen. I offer you a place at my side.'

The howling stopped as if it had been lopped off by a pair of scissors.

'But you had our king killed,' the vampire said.

'I was the spouse of your king, and as such, I'm entitled to inherit his state in the event of his death,' Sophie-Anne said, her dark eyes looking almost benevolent, almost luminous. 'And he is undoubtedly dead.'

'That's what the fine print said,' Mr Cataliades murmured in my ear, and I barely suppressed a yelp of astonishment. I'd always thought that what people said about big men moving lightly was total bullshit. Big people move bigly. But Mr Cataliades walked as lightly as a butterfly, and I had no idea he was nearby until he spoke to me.

'In the queen's wedding contract?' I managed to say.

'Yes,' he said. 'And Peter's attorney went over it very thoroughly indeed. The same applied in the event of Sophie-Anne's death, too.'

'I guess there were a lot of clauses hanging on that?'

'Oh, just a few. The death had to be witnessed.'

'Oh, gosh. That's me.'

'Yes, indeed it is. The queen wants you in her sight and under her thumb for a very good reason.'

'And other conditions?'

'There could be no second-in-command alive to take the state over. In other words, a great catastrophe had to occur.'

'And now it has.'

'Yes, it seems that it has.' Mr Cataliades appeared quite pleased about that.

My mind was tumbling around like one of those wire bins they draw bingo numbers from at the fair.

'My name is Henrik Feith,' the small vamp said. 'And there are only five vampires left in Arkansas. I am the only one here in Rhodes, and I am only alive because I went down to complain about the towels in the bathroom.'

I had to slap a hand over my own mouth to keep from laughing, which would have been, shall we say, inappropriate. Andre's gaze remained fixed on the man kneeling before us, but somehow his hand wandered over and gave me a pinch. After that it was easy to not laugh. In fact, it was hard not to shriek.

'What was wrong with the towels?' Baruch said, completely sidetracked by this slur on his hotel.

'Jennifer alone used up three,' Henrik began explaining, but this fascinating byway was cut short when Sophie-Anne said, 'Enough. Henrik, you come with us to my suite. Mr Baruch, we look forward to receiving updates from you on this situation. Mr Donati, are you intending to call the Rhodes police?'

It was polite of her to address Donati as though he actually had a say in what was done. Donati said, 'No, ma'am, this seems like a vampire matter to me. There's no body to examine now, there's no film since there's no security camera in the suite, and if you'll look up . . .' We all did, of course, to the corner of the hallway. 'You'll notice that someone has very accurately thrown a piece of gum over the lens of the security camera. Or perhaps, if it was a vampire, he jumped up and planted the gum on the lens. Of course I'm going to review the tapes, but as fast as vampires can jump, it may well be impossible to determine who the individual is. At the moment, there aren't any vampires on the homicide squad in the Rhodes police force, so I'm not sure there's anyone we can call. Most human cops won't investigate vampire crime, unless they have a vampire partner to get their backs.'

'I can't think of anything more we can do here,' Sophie-Anne said, exactly as if she could not care less. 'If you don't need us any longer, we'll go to the opening ceremony.' She had looked at her watch a few times during this conversation. 'Master Henrik, if you are up to it, come with us. If you're not up to it, which of course we would understand, Sigebert will take you up to my suite and you may remain there.'

'I would like to go somewhere quiet,' Henrik Feith said. He looked like a beaten puppy.

Sophie-Anne nodded to Sigebert, who didn't look happy about getting his marching orders. But he had to obey her, of course, so off he went with the little vampire who was one-fifth of all that was left of the Arkansas undead.

I had so much to think about that my brain went into a stall. Just when I believed nothing more could happen, the elevator dinged and the doors swept open to allow Bill to leap out. He didn't arrive as dramatically as Henrik, but he made a definite entrance. He stopped dead and assessed the situation. Seeing we were all standing there calmly, he gathered his composure around him and said, 'I hear there has been trouble?' He addressed this to the air in between us, so anyone could answer him.

I was tired of trying to think of him as Nameless. Hell, it was Bill. I might hate every molecule in his body, but he was undeniably there. I wondered if the Weres really managed to keep the abjured off their radar, and how they dealt with it. I wasn't managing very well.

'There is trouble,' the queen said. 'Though I don't understand what your presence will achieve.'

I'd never seen Bill looking abashed, but he did now. 'I apologize, my queen,' he said. 'If you need me for something, I'll have returned to my booth in the convention hall.'

In icy silence, the elevator doors slid shut, blocking out my first lover's face and form. It was possible that Bill was trying to show he cared about me by showing up with such haste when he was supposed to be doing business for the queen elsewhere. If this demonstration was supposed to soften my heart, it failed.

'Is there anything I can be doing to help you in your investigation?' Andre asked Donati, though his words were really aimed at Christian Baruch. 'Since the queen is the legal heir of Arkansas, we stand ready to assist.'

'I would expect nothing less of such a beautiful queen, one also well-known for her business acumen and tenacity.' Baruch bowed to the queen.

Even Andre blinked at the convoluted compliment, and the queen gave Baruch a narrow-eyed look. I kept my gaze fixed on the potted plant, and I kept my face absolutely blank. I was in danger of snickering. This was brownnosing on a scale I'd never encountered.

There really didn't seem to be any more to say, and in subdued silence I got on the elevator with the vampires and Mr Cataliades, who had remained most remarkably quiet.

Once the doors shut, he said, 'My queen, you must marry again immediately.'

Let me tell you, Sophie-Anne and Andre had quite a reaction to this bombshell; their eyes widened for all of a second.

'Marry anyone: Kentucky, Florida, I would add even Mississippi, if he were not negotiating with Indiana. But you need an alliance, someone lethal to back you up. Otherwise jackals like this Baruch will circle around, yipping for your attention.'

'Mississippi's out of the running, thankfully. I don't think I could stand all the men. Once in a while, of course, but not day in, day out, scores of them,' Sophie-Anne said.

It was the most natural and unguarded thing I'd ever heard her say. She almost sounded human. Andre reached out and punched the button to stop the elevator between floors. 'I wouldn't advise Kentucky,' he said. 'Anyone who needs Britlingens is in enough trouble of his own.'

'Alabama is lovely,' Sophie-Anne said. 'But she enjoys some things in bed that I object to.'

I was tired of being in the elevator and also of being regarded as part of the scenery. 'May I ask a question?' I said.

After a moment's silence, Sophie-Anne nodded.

'How come you get to keep your children with you, and you've gone to bed with them, and most vampires aren't able to do that? Isn't it supposed to be a short-term relationship, sire and child?'

'Most vampire children don't stay with their makers after a certain time,' Sophie-Anne agreed. 'And there are very few cases of children staying with their maker as long as Andre and Sigebert have been with me. That closeness is my gift, my talent. Every vampire has a gift: some can fly, some have special skills with the sword. I can keep my children with me. We can talk to each other, as you and Barry can. We can love each other physically.'

'If all that's so, why don't you just name Andre the King of Arkansas and marry him?'

There was a long, total silence. Sophie-Anne's lips parted a couple of times as if she was about to explain to me why that was impossible, but both times she pressed them shut again. Andre stared at me with such intensity that I expected to see two spots on my face begin smoking. Mr Cataliades just looked shocked, as if a monkey had begun to speak to him in iambic pentameter.

'Yes,' said Sophie-Anne finally. 'Why don't I do that? Have as king and spouse my dearest friend and lover.' In the blink of an eye, she looked positively radiant. 'Andre, the only drawback is that you will have to spend some time apart from me when you return to Arkansas to take care of the state's affairs. My oldest child, are you willing?'

Andre's face was transformed with love. 'For you, anything,' he said.

We had us a Kodak moment going. I actually felt a little choked up.

Andre pressed the button again and down we went.

Though I am not immune to romance – far from it – in my opinion, the queen needed to focus on finding out who'd killed Jennifer Cater and the remaining Arkansas vampires. She needed to be grilling Towel Guy, the surviving vampire – Henrik Whatever. She didn't need to be trailing around meeting and greeting. But Sophie-Anne didn't ask me what I thought, and I'd volunteered enough of my ideas for the day.

The lobby was thronged. Plunged into such a crowd, my brain would normally be going into overload unless I was very careful indeed. But when the majority of the beings with brains were vampires, I got a lobby full of nothing, just a few flutters from the human flunky brains. Watching all the movement and not hearing much was strange, like watching birds' wings beating and yet not hearing the movement. I was definitely working now, so I sharpened up and scanned the individuals who had circulating blood and beating hearts.

One male witch, one female. One lover/blood donor – in other words, a fangbanger, but a high-class one. When I tracked him down visually, I saw a very handsome young man wearing everything designer down to his tighty whities, and proud of it. Standing beside the King of Texas was Barry the Bellboy: he was doing his job as I was doing mine. I tracked a few hotel employees going about their business. People aren't always thinking about interesting stuff like, 'Tonight I'm in on a plot to assassinate the hotel manager,' or something like that, even if they *are*. They're thinking stuff like, 'The room on eleven needs soap, the room on eight has a heater that won't work, the room service cart on four needs to be moved . . .'

Then I happened upon a whore. Now, *she* was interesting. Most of the whores I knew were of the amateur variety, but this woman was a thorough professional. I was curious enough to make eye contact. She was fairly attractive in the face department, but would never have been a candidate for Miss America or even homecoming queen – definitely not the girl next door, unless you lived in a red-light district. Her platinum hair was in a tousled, bedtime hairdo, and she had rather narrow brown eyes, an allover tan, enhanced breasts, big earrings, stiletto heels, bright lipstick, a dress that was mostly red spangles – you couldn't say she didn't advertise. She was accompanying a man who'd been made vamp when he was in his forties. She held on to his arm as if she couldn't walk without help, and I wondered if the stiletto heels were responsible for that, or if she held on because he liked it.

I was so interested in her – she was projecting her sexuality so strongly, she was so very much a prostitute – that I slipped through the crowd to track her more closely. Absorbed in my goal, I didn't think about her noticing me, but she seemed to feel my eyes on her and she looked over her shoulder to watch me approach. The man she was with was talking to another vampire, and she didn't have to kowtow to him just for the moment, so she had time to eye me with sharp suspicion. I stood a few feet away to listen to her, out of sheer ill-bred curiosity.

Freaky girl, not one of us, does she want him? She can have him; I can't stand that thing he does with his tongue, and after he does me he'll want me to do him and that other guy – geez, do I have some spare batteries? Maybe she could go away and stop staring?

'Sure, sorry,' I said, ashamed of myself, and plunged back into the crowd. Next I went over the servers hired by the hotel, who were busy circulating through the crowd with trays of glasses filled with blood and a few actual drinks for the humans scattered around. The servers were all preoccupied with dodging the milling crowd, not spilling, sore backs and tender feet, things like that. Barry and I exchanged nods, and I caught a trailing thought that had Quinn's name embedded, so I followed that trail until I found it led to an employee of E(E)E. I knew this because she was wearing the company T-shirt. This gal was a young woman with a very short haircut and very long legs. She was talking to one of the servers, and it was definitely a one-sided conversation. In a crowd that was noticeably dressed up, this woman's jeans and sneakers stood out.

'—and a case of iced soft drinks,' she was saying. 'A tray of sandwiches, and some chips. Okay? In the ballroom, within an hour.' She swung around abruptly and came face-to-face with me. She scanned me up and down and was little impressed.

'You dating one of the vamps, blondie?' she asked. Her voice was harsh to my ears, a northeastern clipped accent.

'No, I'm dating Quinn,' I said. 'Blondie, yourself.' Though at least I was naturally blond. Well, *assisted* natural. This gal's hair looked like straw . . . if straw had dark roots.

She didn't like that at all, though I wasn't sure which part of it displeased her most. 'He didn't say he had a new woman,' she said, and of course she said it in the most insulting way possible.

I felt free to dip into her skull, and I found there a deep affection for Quinn. She didn't think any other women were worthy of him. She thought I was a slow southern girl who hid behind men.

Since this was based on our conversation of less than sixty seconds, I could excuse her for being wrong. I could excuse her for loving

Quinn. I couldn't forgive her overwhelming contempt.

'Quinn doesn't have to tell you his personal information,' I said. What I really wanted was to ask her where Quinn was now, but that would definitely hand the advantage to her, so I was going to keep that question to myself. 'If you'll excuse me, I have to get back to work, and I assume you do, too.'

Her dark eyes flashed at me, and she strode off. She was at least four inches taller than me, and very slim. She hadn't bothered with a bra, and she had little plum-like boobs that jiggled in an eye-catching way. This was a gal who'd always want to be on top. I wasn't the only one who watched her cross the room. Barry had jettisoned his fantasy about me for a brand-new one.

I returned to the queen's side because she and Andre were moving into the convention hall from the lobby. The wide double doors were propped open by a really beautiful pair of urns that held huge arrangements of dried grasses.

Barry said, 'Have you ever been to a real convention, a normal one?'

'No,' I said, trying to keep my scan of the surrounding crowd up. I wondered how Secret Service agents coped. 'Well, I went to one with Sam, a bartending supplies convention, but just for a couple of hours.'

'Everyone wore a badge, right?'

'If you can call a thing on a lanyard around your neck a badge, yeah.'

'That's so workers at the door can be sure you've paid your admittance, and so that unauthorized people won't come in.'

'Yeah, so?'

Barry went silent. *So, you see anyone with a badge? You see anyone checking?*

No one but us. And what do we know? The whore might be an undercover spy for the northeastern vampires. Or something worse, I added more soberly.

They're used to being the strongest and scariest, Barry said. *They might fear each other, but they don't seriously fear humans, not when they're together.*

I took his point. The Britlingen had already aroused my concern, and now I was even more worried.

Then I looked back at the doors to the hotel. They were guarded, now that it was dark, by armed vampires instead of armed humans.

The front desk, too, was staffed with vampires wearing the hotel uniform, and those vampires were scanning each and every person who walked in the doors. This building was not as laxly protected as it might seem. I relaxed and decided to check out the booths in the convention hall.

There was one for prosthetic fangs that you could have implanted; they came in natural ivory, silver, or gold, and the really expensive ones retracted by means of a tiny motor when your tongue pressed a tiny button in your mouth. 'Undetectable from the real thing,' an elderly man was assuring a vampire with a long beard and braided hair. 'And sharp, oh goodness, yes!' I couldn't figure out who would want a pair. A vamp with a broken tooth? A vamp wannabe who wanted to pretend? A human looking for a little role-playing?

The next booth sold CDs of music from various historical eras, like *Russian Folk Songs of the Eighteenth Century* or *Italian Chamber Music, the Early Years*. It was doing a brisk business. People always like the music of their prime, even if that prime was centuries past.

The next booth was Bill's, and it had a large sign arching over the temporary 'walls' of the enclosure. VAMPIRE IDENTIFICATION, it said simply. TRACK DOWN ANY VAMPIRE, ANYWHERE, ANYTIME. ALL YOU NEED IS A COMPUTER-SMART MINION, said a smaller sign. Bill was talking to a female vamp who was extending her credit card to him, and Pam was popping a CD case into a little bag. Pam caught my eye and winked. She was wearing a campy harem outfit, which I would have supposed she'd refuse to do. But Pam was actually smiling. Maybe she was enjoying the break in her routine.

HAPPY BIRTHDAY PRESS PRESENTS: SANGUINARY SOUP FOR THE SOUL was the sign over the next booth, at which sat a bored and lonely vampire with a stack of books in front of her.

The next exhibit took up several spaces and needed no explanation. 'You should definitely upgrade,' an earnest salesman was telling a black vampire whose hair was braided and tied with a thousand colored strings. She listened intently, eyeing one of the sample miniature coffins open in front of her. 'Certainly, wood's biodegradable and it's traditional, but who needs that? Your coffin is your home; that's what my daddy always said.'

There were others, including one for Extreme(ly Elegant) Events. That one was a large table with several price brochures and photo albums lying open to tempt the passersby. I was ready to check it out when I noticed that the booth was being 'manned' by Miss Snooty Long-Legs. I didn't want to talk to her again, so I sauntered on, though I never lost sight of the queen. One of the human waiters was admiring Sophie-Anne's ass, but I figured that wasn't punishable by death, so I let it go.

By that time the queen and Andre had met with the sheriffs Gervaise and Cleo Babbitt. The broad-faced Gervaise was a small man, perhaps five foot six. He appeared to be about thirty-five, though you could easily add a hundred years to that and be closer to his true age. Gervaise had borne the burden of Sophie-Anne's maintenance and amusement for the past few weeks, and the wear and tear was showing. I'd heard he'd been renowned for his sophisticated clothing and debonair style. The only time I'd seen him before, his light hair had been combed as smooth as glass on his sleek round head. Now it was definitely disheveled. His beautiful suit needed to go to the cleaner, and his wing tips needed polishing. Cleo was a husky woman with broad shoulders and coal black hair, a wide face with a full-lipped mouth. Cleo was modern enough to want to use her last name; she'd been a vampire for only fifty years.

'Where is Eric?' Andre asked the other sheriffs.

Cleo laughed, the kind of deep-throated laugh that made men look. 'He got conscripted,' she said. 'The priest didn't show up, and Eric's taken a course, so he's going to officiate.'

Andre smiled. 'That'll be something to watch. What's the occasion?'

'It'll be announced in a second,' Gervaise said.

I wondered what church would have Eric as a priest. The Church of High Profits? I drifted over to Bill's booth and attracted Pam's attention.

'Eric's a priest?' I murmured

'Church of the Loving Spirit,' she told me, bagging three copies of the CD and handing them to a fangbanger sent by his master to pick them up. 'He got his certificate from the online course, with Bobby Burnham's help. He can perform marriage services.'

A waiter somehow outmaneuvered all the guests around the queen and approached her with a tray full of wineglasses brimming with blood. In the blink of an eye Andre was between the waiter and the queen, and in the blink of another eye, the waiter swiveled and walked in another direction.

I tried to look in the waiter's mind but found it perfectly blank. Andre had grabbed control of the guy's will and sent him on his way. I hoped the waiter was okay. I followed his progress to a humble door set in a corner until I was sure that he was going back to the kitchen. Okay, incident averted.

There was a ripple in the currents of the display hall, and I turned to see what was happening. The King of Mississippi and the King of Indiana had come in together hand in hand, which seemed to be a public signal that they'd concluded their marriage negotiations. Russell Edgington was a slight, attractive vampire who liked other men – exclusively and extensively. He could be good company, and he was a good fighter, too. I liked him. I was a little anxious about seeing Russell, since a few months before I'd left a body in his pool. I tried to look on the bright side. The body was a vampire's, so it should have disintegrated before the pool covering had been removed in the spring.

Russell and Indiana stopped in front of Bill's booth. Indiana, incidentally, was a big bull-like guy with brown curly hair and a face I thought of as no-nonsense.

I drifted closer, because this could be trouble.

'Bill, you look good,' Russell said. 'My staff tells me you had a hard time at my place. You seem to have recovered nicely. I'm not sure how you got free, but I'm glad.' If Russell was pausing for a reaction, he didn't get one. Bill's face was just as impassive as if Russell had been commenting on the weather, not Bill's torture. 'Lorena was your sire, so I couldn't interfere,' Russell said, his voice just as calm as Bill's face. 'And here you are, selling your own little computer thing that Lorena was trying so hard to get from you. As the Bard said, "All's well that ends well."'

Russell had been too verbose, which was the only indication that the king was anxious about Bill's reaction. And sure enough, Bill's voice was like cold silk running over glass. But all he said was, 'Think nothing of it, Russell. Congratulations are in order, I understand.'

Russell smiled up at his groom.

'Yes, Mississippi and I are tying the knot,' the King of Indiana said. He had a deep voice. He would look at home beating up some welsher in an alley or sitting in a bar with sawdust on the floor. But Russell did everything but blush.

Maybe this was a love match.

Then Russell spotted me. 'Bart, you have to meet this young woman,' he said immediately. I about had a panic attack, but there was no way out of the situation without simply turning tail and running. Russell pulled his intended over to me by their linked hands. 'This young woman was staked while she was in Jackson. Some of those Fellowship thugs were in a bar, and one of them stabbed her.'

Bart looked almost startled. 'You survived, obviously,' he said. 'But how?'

'Mr Edgington here got me some help,' I said. 'In fact, he saved my life.'

Russell tried to look modest, and he almost succeeded. The vampire was trying to look good in front of his intended, such a human reaction that I could scarcely believe it.

'However, I believe you took something with you when you left,' Russell said severely, shaking a finger at me.

I tried to glean something from his face that would tell me which way to jump with my answer. I'd taken a blanket, sure enough, and some loose clothes the young men in Russell's harem had left lying around. And I'd taken Bill, who'd been a prisoner in one of the out-buildings. Probably Russell was referring to Bill, huh?

'Yessir, but I left something behind in return,' I said, since I couldn't stand this verbal cat and mouse. All right, already! I'd rescued Bill and killed the vampire Lorena, though that had been more or less by accident. And I'd dumped her evil ass in the pool.

'I did think there was some sludge at the bottom when we got the pool ready for the summer,' Russell said, and his bitter chocolate eyes examined me thoughtfully. 'What an enterprising young woman you are, Miss . . .'

'Stackhouse. Sookie Stackhouse.'

'Yes, I remember now. Weren't you at Club Dead with Alcide Herveaux? He's a Were, honey,' Russell said to Bart.

'Yessir,' I said, wishing he hadn't remembered that little detail.

'Didn't I hear Herveaux's father was campaigning for packleader in Shreveport?'

'That's right. But he . . . ah, he didn't get it.'

'So that was the day Papa Herveaux died?'

'It was,' I said. Bart was listening intently, his hand running up and down Russell's coat sleeve all the while. It was a lusty little gesture.

Quinn appeared at my side just then and put his arm around me, and Russell's eyes widened. 'Gentlemen,' Quinn said to Indiana and Mississippi, 'I believe we have your wedding ready and waiting.'

The two kings smiled at each other. 'No cold feet?' Bart asked Russell.

'Not if you keep them warm,' Russell said with a smile that would have melted an iceberg. 'Besides, our lawyers would kill us if we reneged on those contracts.'

They both nodded at Quinn, who loped to the dais at one end of the exhibit hall. He stood at the highest level and stretched out his arms. There was a microphone up there, and his deep voice boomed out over the crowd. 'Your attention, ladies and gentlemen, kings and commoners, vampires and humans! You are all requested and invited to attend the union of Russell Edgington, King of Mississippi, and Bartlett Crowe, King of Indiana, in the Ritual Room. The ceremony will begin in ten minutes. The Ritual Room is through the double doors in the east wall of the hall.' Quinn pointed regally at the double doors.

I'd had time to appreciate his outfit while he spoke. He was wearing full trousers that gathered at the waist and the ankle. They were deep scarlet. He had cinched the trousers with a wide gold belt like a prizefighter's, and he was wearing black leather boots with the trouser legs tucked in. He wasn't wearing a shirt. He looked like a genie who'd just popped out of a really big bottle.

'This is your new man?' Russell said. 'Quinn?'

I nodded, and he looked impressed.

'I know you got things on your mind right now,' I said impulsively.

'I know you're about to get married. But I just want to say I hope that we're even-steven, right? You're not mad at me, or holding a grudge at me, or anything?'

Bart was accepting the congratulations of assorted vampires, and Russell glanced his way. Then he did me the courtesy of concentrating on me, though I knew he had to turn away and enjoy his evening in a very short time, which was only right.

'I hold no grudge against you,' he said. 'Fortunately, I have a sense of humor, and fortunately, I didn't like Lorena worth a damn. I lent her the room in the stable because I'd known her for a century or two, but she always was a bitch.'

'Then let me ask you, since you're not mad at me,' I said. 'Why does everyone seem so in awe of Quinn?'

'You really don't know, and you've got the tiger by his tail?' Russell looked happily intrigued. 'I don't have time to tell you the whole story, because I want to be with my husband-to-be, but I'll tell you what, Miss Sookie, your man has made a lot of people a lot of money.'

'Thanks,' I said, a bit bewildered, 'and best wishes to you and, ah, Mr Crowe. I hope you'll be very happy together.' Since shaking hands was not a vampire custom, I bowed and tried to sort of back away quickly while we were still on such good terms with each other.

Rasul popped up at my elbow. He smiled when I jumped. Those vamps. Gotta love their sense of humor.

I'd only seen Rasul in SWAT gear, and he'd looked good in that. Tonight he was wearing another uniform, but it was also pretty military looking, in a kind of Cossack way. He wore a long-sleeved tunic and tailored pants in a deep plum with black trim and bright brass buttons. Rasul was deeply brown, quite naturally, and had the large, dark liquid eyes and black hair of someone from the Middle East.

'I knew you were supposed to be here, so it's nice to run into you,' I said.

'She sent Carla and me ahead of time,' he said lightly in his exotic accent. 'You are looking lovelier than ever, Sookie. How are you enjoying the summit?'

I ignored his pleasantries. 'What's with the uniform?'

'If you mean, whose uniform is it, it's the new house uniform of our queen,' he said. 'We wear this instead of the armor when we're not out on the streets. Nice, huh?'

'Oh, you're stylin',' I said, and he laughed.

'Are you going to the ceremony?' he said.

'Yeah, sure. I've never seen a vampire wedding. Listen, Rasul, I'm sorry about Chester and Melanie.' They'd been on guard duty with Rasul in New Orleans.

For a second, all the humor left the vampire's face. 'Yes,' he said after a moment of stiff silence. 'Instead of my comrades, now I have the Formerly Furred.' Jake Purifoy was approaching us, and he was wearing the same uniform as Rasul. He looked lonely. He hadn't been a vampire long enough to maintain the calm face that seemed to be second nature to the undead.

'Hi, Jake,' I said.

'Hi, Sookie,' he said, sounding forlorn and hopeful.

Rasul bowed to both of us and set off in another direction. I was stuck with Jake. This was too much like grade school for my taste. Jake was the kid who'd come to school wearing the wrong clothes and packing a weird lunch. Being a combo vamp-Were had ruined his chances with either crowd. It was like trying to be a Goth jock.

'Have you had a chance to talk to Quinn yet?' I asked for lack of anything better to say. Jake had been Quinn's employee before his change had effectively put him out of a job.

'I said hello in passing,' Jake said. 'It's just not fair.'

'What?'

'That he should be accepted no matter what he's done, and I should be ostracized.'

I knew what *ostracized* meant, because it had been on my Word of the Day calendar. But my brain was just snagging on that word because the bigger meaning of Jake's comment was affecting my equilibrium. 'No matter what he's done?' I asked. 'What would that mean?'

'Well, of course, you know about Quinn,' Jake said, and I thought I might jump on his back and beat him around the head with something heavy.

'The wedding begins!' came Quinn's magnified voice, and the crowd began streaming into the double doors he'd indicated earlier. Jake and

I streamed right along with them. Quinn's bouncy-boobed assistant was standing just inside the doors, passing out little net bags of pot-pourri. Some were tied with blue and gold ribbon, some with blue and red.

'Why the different colors?' the whore asked Quinn's assistant. I appreciated her asking, because it meant I didn't have to.

'Red and blue from the Mississippi flag, blue and gold from the Indiana,' the woman said with an automatic smile. She still had it pasted on her face when she handed me a red-and-blue tied bag, though it faded in an almost comical way when she realized who I was.

Jake and I worked our way to a good spot a bit to the right of center. The stage was bare except for a few props, and there were no chairs. They weren't expecting this to take very long, apparently. 'Answer me,' I hissed. 'About Quinn.'

'After the wedding,' he said, trying not to smile. It had been a few months since Jake had had the upper hand on anyone, and he couldn't hide the fact that he was enjoying it. He glanced behind us, and his eyes widened. I looked in that direction to see that the opposite end of the room was set up as a buffet, though the main feature of the buffet was not food but blood. To my disgust, there were about twenty men and women standing in a line beside the synthetic blood fountain, and they all had name tags that read simply, 'Willing Donor.' I about gagged. Could that be legal? But they were all free and unrestrained and could walk out if they chose, and most of them looked pretty eager to begin their donation. I did a quick scan of their brains. Yep, willing.

I turned to the platform, only eighteen inches high, which Mississippi and Indiana had just mounted. They'd put on elaborate costumes, which I remembered seeing before in a photo album at the shop of a photographer who specialized in recording supernatural rituals. At least these were easy to put on. Russell was wearing a sort of heavy brocade, open-fronted robe that fit over his regular clothes. It was a splendid garment of gleaming gold cloth worked in a pattern of blue and scarlet. Bart, King of Indiana, was wearing a similar robe in a copper brown color, embroidered with a design in green and gold.

'Their formal robes,' Rasul murmured. Once again, he'd drifted to my side without me noticing. I jumped and saw a little smile twitch the corners of his generous mouth. To my left, Jake sidled a little closer to me, as if he were trying to hide from Rasul by concealing himself behind my body.

But I was more interested in this ceremony than I was in vampire one-upmanship. A giant ankh was the prop at the center of the group onstage. Off to one side, there was a table bearing two thick sheaves of paper with two plumed pens arranged between them. A female vampire was standing behind the table, and she was wearing a business suit with a knee-length skirt. Mr Cataliades stood behind her, looking benevolent, his hands clasping each other across his belly.

Standing on the opposite side of the stage from the table, Quinn, my honey (whose background I was determined to learn pretty shortly), was still in his Aladdin's genie outfit. He waited until the crowd's murmur died to nothing and then he made a great gesture to stage right. A figure came up the steps and onto the platform. He was wearing a cloak of black velvet, and it was hooded. The hood was drawn well forward. The ankh symbol was embroidered in gold on the shoulders of the cloak. The figure took its position between Mississippi and Indiana, its back to the ankh, and raised its arms.

'The ceremony begins,' Quinn said. 'Let all be silent and witness this joining.'

When someone tells a vampire to be quiet, you can be sure the silence is absolute. Vampires don't have to fidget, sigh, sneeze, cough, or blow their nose like people do. I felt noisy just breathing.

The cloaked figure's hood fell back. I sighed. Eric. His wheat-colored hair looked beautiful against the black of the cloak, and his face was solemn and commanding, which was what you want in an officiant.

'We are here to witness the joining of two kings,' he said, and every word carried to the corners of the room. 'Russell and Bart have agreed, both verbally and by written covenant, to ally their states for a hundred years. For a hundred years, they may not marry any other. They may not form an alliance with any other, unless that alliance is mutually agreed and witnessed. Each must pay the other a conjugal visit at least once a year. The welfare of Russell's kingdom shall come second only to his own in Bart's sight, and the welfare of Bart's kingdom shall come second only to his own in Russell's sight. Russell Edgington, King of Mississippi, do you agree to this covenant?'

'Yes, I do,' Russell said clearly. He held out his hand to Bart.

'Bartlett Crowe, King of Indiana, do you agree to this covenant?'

'I do,' Bart said, and took Russell's hand. Awwww.

Then Quinn stepped forward and knelt, holding a goblet under the joined hands, and Eric whipped out a knife and cut the two wrists with two movements too quick to separate.

Oh, *ick*. As the two kings bled into the chalice, I chided myself. I might have known that a vampire ceremony would include a blood exchange.

Sure enough, when the wounds closed, Russell took a sip from the chalice, and then handed it to Bart, who drained it dry. Then they kissed, Bart holding the smaller man tenderly. And then they kissed some more. Evidently the mingled blood was a real turn-on.

I caught Jake's eye. *Get a room*, he mouthed, and I looked down to hide my smile.

Finally, the two kings moved on to the next step, a ceremonious signing of the contract they'd agreed upon. The business-suit woman turned out to be a vampire lawyer from Illinois, since a lawyer from another state had to draw up the contract. Mr Cataliades had been a neutral lawyer, too, and he signed the documents after the kings and the vampire lawyer.

Eric stood in his black-and-gold glory while all this was done, and once the pens were back on their elaborate stands, he said, 'The marriage is sacred for one hundred years!' and a cheer went up. Vampires aren't big on cheering, either, so it was mostly the humans and the other supes in the crowd who did the hurrahing, but the vampires all made an appreciative murmur – not as good, but the best they could do, I guess.

I sure wanted to find out more about how Eric had qualified as a priest, or whatever they called the officiant, but first I was going to make Jake tell me about Quinn. He was trying to wriggle away in the crowd, but I caught up with him pretty quick. He wasn't a good enough vampire yet to get away from me.

'Spill,' I said, and he tried to act like he didn't know what I was talking about, but he saw from my face I wasn't buying it.

So, while the crowd eddied around us, trying not to speed toward the open bar, I waited for Quinn's story.

'I can't believe he hasn't told you this himself,' Jake said, and I was tempted to slap him upside the head.

I glared at him to let him know I was *waiting*.

'Okay, okay,' he said. 'I heard all this when I was still a Were. Quinn is like a rock star in the shifter world, you know. He's one of the last weretigers, and he's one of the most ferocious.'

I nodded. So far, that paralleled my knowledge of Quinn.

'Quinn's mom was captured one full moon when she changed. A bunch of hunters were out camping, set up a trap because they wanted a bear for their illegal dogfights. Something new to bet on, you know? A pack of dogs versus a bear. This was somewhere in Colorado, and snow was on the ground. His mom was out on her own, and somehow she fell into the trap, didn't sense it.'

'Where was his dad?'

'He had died when Quinn was little. Quinn was about fifteen when this happened.'

I had a feeling worse was coming, and I was right.

'He changed, of course, the same night, soon as he found she was missing. He tracked them to the camp. His mom had turned back into a woman under the stress of the capture, and one of them was raping her.' Jake took a deep breath. 'Quinn killed them all.'

I looked down at the floor. I couldn't think of anything to say.

'The campsite had to be cleaned up. There wasn't a pack around to step in – course, tigers don't hang in packs – and his mother was hurt bad and in shock, so Quinn went to the local vampire nest. They agreed to do the job, if he'd be indebted to them for three years.' Jake shrugged. 'He agreed.'

'What exactly did he agree to do?' I asked.

'To fight in the pits for them. For three years or until he died, whichever came first.'

I began to feel cold fingers moving up my spine, and this time it wasn't creepy Andre ... it was just fear. 'The pits?' I said, but if he hadn't had vampire hearing, he wouldn't have been able to make my words out.

'There's a lot of bets placed on pit fighting,' Jake said. 'It's like the dogfights the hunters wanted the bear for. Humans aren't the only ones who like to watch animals kill each other. Some vamps love it. So do some other supes.'

My lips curled in disgust. I felt almost nauseated.

Jake was looking at me, troubled by my reaction, but also giving me time to understand the sad story was not at an end. 'Obviously Quinn survived his three years,' Jake said. 'He's one of the few who've lived that long.' He looked at me sideways. 'He kept winning and winning. He was one of the most savage fighters anyone's ever seen. He fought bears, lions, you name it.'

'Aren't they all really rare?' I asked.

'Yeah, they are, but I guess even rare Were creatures need money,' Jake said with, a toss of his head. 'And you can make big bucks pit fighting, when you've earned enough to bet on yourself.'

'Why did he stop?' I asked. I regretted more than I could say that I had been curious about Quinn. I should have waited until he volunteered all this. He would have, I hoped. Jake caught a human servant walking by and snagged a glass of synthetic blood off the tray. He drained it in one gulp.

'His three years ended, and he had to take care of his sister.'

'Sister?'

'Yeah, his mom got pregnant that night, and the result was the dyed blonde who gave us the potpourri bags at the door. Frannie gets into trouble from time to time, and Quinn's mother can't handle her, so she sends her to stay with Quinn for a while. Frannie turned up here last night.'

I'd had as much as I could stomach. I turned in one quick movement and walked away from Jake. And to his credit, he didn't try to stop me.

Chapter 11

I was so anxious to get out of the crowd in the wedding hall that I collided with a vampire, who whirled and grabbed my shoulders in a blur of darkness. He had a long Fu Manchu mustache and a mane of hair that would have done a couple of horses credit. He was wearing a solid black suit. At another time, I might have enjoyed the total package. Now I just wanted him to move.

'Why in such a hurry, my sweet maid?' he asked.

'Sir,' I said politely, since he must be older than I, 'I really am in a hurry. Excuse me for bumping into you, but I need to leave.'

'You're not a donor, by any chance?'

'Nope, sorry.'

Abruptly he let go of my shoulders and turned back to the conversation I'd interrupted. With a great wave of relief, I continued to pick my way through the assemblage, though with more care now that I'd already had one tense moment.

'There you are!' Andre said, and he almost sounded cross. 'The queen needs you.'

I had to remind myself that I was there to work, and it really didn't matter how much inner drama I was experiencing. I followed Andre over to the queen, who was in conversation with a knot of vamps and humans.

'Of course I am on your side, Sophie,' said a female vampire. She was wearing an evening gown of pink chiffon joined at one shoulder with a big broach sparkling with diamonds. They might be Swarovski crystals, but they looked real to me. What do I know? The pale pink looked real pretty against her chocolate skin. 'Arkansas was an asshole, anyway. I was only astonished that you married him in the first place.'

'So if I come to trial, you will be kind, Alabama?' Sophie-Anne asked, and you would have sworn she wasn't a day over sixteen. Her upturned face was smooth and firm, her big eyes gleamed, her makeup was subtle. Her brown hair was loose, which was unusual for Sophie-Anne.

The vamp seemed to soften visibly. 'Of course,' she said.

Her human companion, the designer-clad fangbanger I'd noticed earlier, thought, *That'll last ten minutes, until she turns her back on Sophie-Anne. Then they'll be plotting again. Sure, they all say they like crackling fires and long walks on the beach by moonlight, but whenever you go to a party, it's maneuver, maneuver, maneuver, and lie, lie, lie.*

Sophie-Anne's gaze just brushed mine, and I gave a tiny shake of my head. Alabama excused herself to go congratulate the newlyweds, and her human tagged along. Mindful of all the ears around us, most of which could hear far better than I could, I said, 'Later,' and got a nod from Andre.

Next to court Sophie-Anne was the King of Kentucky, the man who was guarded by Britlingens. Kentucky turned out to look a lot like Davy Crockett. All he needed was a ba'ar and a coonskin cap. He was actually wearing leather pants and a suede shirt and jacket, fringed suede boots, and a big silk kerchief tied around his neck. Maybe he needed the bodyguards to protect him from the fashion police.

I didn't see Batanya and Clovache anywhere, so I assumed he'd left them in his room. I didn't see what good it was to hire expensive and otherworldly bodyguards if they weren't around your body to guard it. Then, since I didn't have another human to distract me, I noticed something odd: there was a space behind Kentucky that stayed constantly empty, no matter what the flow of the crowd might be. No matter how natural it would be for someone passing behind Kentucky to step in that area, somehow no one ever did. I figured the Britlingens were on duty, after all.

'Sophie-Anne, you're a sight for sore eyes,' said Kentucky. He had a drawl that was thick as honey, and he made a point of letting Sophie-Anne see his fangs were partially out. Ugh.

'Isaiah, it's always good to see you,' Sophie-Anne said, her voice and face smooth and calm as always. I couldn't tell whether or not Sophie-Anne knew the bodyguards were right behind him. As I drew a little closer, I found that though I couldn't see Clovache and Batanya, I could pick up their mental signatures. The same magic that cloaked their physical presence also muffled their brain waves, but I could get a dull echo off both of them. I smiled at them, which was really dumb of me, because Isaiah, King of Kentucky, picked up on it right away. I should have known he was smarter than he looked.

'Sophie-Anne, I want to have a chat with you, but you gotta get that little blond gal out of here for the duration,' Kentucky said with a broad grin. 'She pure-dee gives me the willies.' He nodded toward me, as if Sophie-Anne had lots of blond human women trailing her.

'Of course, Isaiah,' Sophie-Anne said, giving me a very level look. 'Sookie, please go down to the lower level and fetch the suitcase the staff called about earlier.'

'Sure,' I said. I didn't mind a humble errand. I'd almost forgotten the gruff voice on the phone earlier in the evening. I thought it was stupid that procedure required us to come down to the bowels of the hotel, rather than allowing a bellman to bring us the suitcase, but red tape is the same everywhere you go, right?

As I turned to go, Andre's face was quite blank, as usual, but when I was almost out of earshot, he said, 'Excuse me, your majesty, we didn't tell the girl about your schedule for the night.' In one of those disconcerting flashes of movement, he was right beside me, hand on my arm. I wondered if he'd gotten one of those telepathic communications from Sophie-Anne. Without a word, Sigebert had moved into Andre's place beside Sophie-Anne, a half step back.

'Let's talk,' said Andre, and quick as a wink he guided me to an EXIT sign. We found ourselves in a blank beige service corridor that extended for maybe ten yards, then made a right-angle turn. Two laden waiters came around the corner and passed us, giving us curious glances, but when they met Andre's eyes they hurried away on their task.

'The Britlingens are there,' I said, assuming that was why Andre had wanted to talk to me in private. 'They're trailing right behind Kentucky. Can all Britlingens become invisible?'

Andre did another movement that was so fast it was a blur, and then his wrist was in front of me, dripping blood. 'Drink,' he said, and I felt him pushing at my mind.

'No,' I said, outraged and shocked at the sudden movement, the demand, the blood. 'Why?' I tried to back away, but there was no place to go and no help in sight.

'You have to have a stronger connection to Sophie-Anne or me. We need you bound to us by more than a paycheck. Already you've proved more valuable than we'd imagined. This summit is critical to our survival, and we need every advantage we can get.'

Talk about brutal honesty.

'I don't want you to have control over me,' I told him, and it was awful to hear my voice going wavery with fear. 'I don't want you to know how I'm feeling. I got hired for this job, and after it, I'm going back to my real life.'

'You don't have a real life anymore,' Andre said. He didn't look unkind; that was the weird, and most frightening, thing. He looked absolutely matter-of-fact.

'I do! You guys are the blip on the radar, not me!' I wasn't totally sure what I meant by that, but Andre got my drift.

'I don't care what your plans are for the rest of your human existence,' he said, and shrugged. *Phooey for your life.* 'Our position will be strengthened if you drink, so you must. I've explained this to you, which I wouldn't bother to do if I didn't respect your ability.'

I pushed at him, but it was like shoving an elephant. It would work only if the elephant felt like moving. Andre didn't. His wrist came closer to my mouth, and I clamped my lips together, though I was sure Andre would break my teeth if he had to. And if I opened my mouth to scream, he'd have that blood in my mouth before you could say Jack Robinson.

Suddenly there was a third presence in the stark beige corridor. Eric, still wearing the black velvet cape, hood thrown back, was standing right by us, his face uncharacteristically uncertain.

'Andre,' he said, his voice sounding deeper than usual. 'Why are you doing this?'

'Are you questioning the will of your queen?'

Eric was in a bad place, because he was definitely interfering with the execution of the queen's orders – at least, I assumed the queen knew about this – but I could only pray he stayed to help me. I begged him with my eyes.

I could name several vamps I'd rather have a connection to than Andre. And, stupidly, I couldn't help but feel hurt. I'd given Andre and Sophie-Anne such a good idea about him being King of Arkansas, and this was the way I got repaid. That would teach me to keep my mouth shut. That would teach me to treat vampires like they were people.

'Andre, let me offer a suggestion,' Eric said in a much cooler, calmer voice. Good. He was keeping his head together. One of us needed to. 'She must be kept happy, or she won't cooperate anymore.'

Oh, crap. Somehow I knew his suggestion wasn't going to be, 'Let her go or I'll break your neck,' because Eric was way too canny for that. Where was John Wayne when you needed him? Or Bruce Willis? Or even Matt Damon? I would be glad to see Jason Bourne right now.

'We've exchanged blood several times, Sookie and I,' Eric said. 'In fact, we've been lovers.' He took a step closer. 'I think she wouldn't be so balky if I were the blood giver. Would that suit your purposes? I'm under oath to you.' He bowed his head respectfully. He was being careful, so careful. That made me more frightened of Andre.

Andre let me go while he pondered. His wrist had almost healed up, anyway. I took a few long, shaky breaths. My heart was racing.

Andre looked at Eric, and I thought I could detect a certain amount of distrust in his gaze. Then he looked at me.

'You look like a rabbit hiding under a bush while the fox tracks her,' he said. There was a long pause. 'You did do my queen and me a large service,' he said. 'More than once. If the end result will be the same, why not?'

I started to say, 'And I'm the only witness to Peter Threadgill's death,' but my guardian angel shut my mouth to seal in the words. Well, maybe it wasn't my *actual* guardian angel, but my subconscious, which told me not to speak. Whatever. I was grateful.

'All right, Eric,' Andre said. 'As long as she's bonded to someone in our kingdom. I've only had a drop of her blood, to find out if she was part fae. If you've exchanged blood with her more than once, the bond is already strong. Has she answered well to your call?'

What? What call? When? Eric had never called me. In fact, I'd out and out defied him before.

'Yes, she heels nicely,' Eric said without a blink of an eye. I about choked, but that would have ruined the effect of Eric's words, so I looked down at my chest as if I was embarrassed by my thralldom.

'Well, then,' Andre said with an impatient gesture of his hand. 'Go on.'

'Right here? I'd prefer somewhere more private,' Eric said.

'Here and now.' Andre was not going to compromise any further.

Eric said, 'Sookie.' He looked at me intently.

I looked right back at him. I understood what that one word was saying. There was no way out of this. No struggling or screaming or refusal would prevent this procedure. Eric might have spared me from submitting to Andre, but that was as far as he could go.

Eric raised one eyebrow.

With that arched eyebrow, Eric was telling me that this was my best bet, that he would try not to hurt me, that being tied to him was infinitely preferable to being tied to Andre.

I knew all this not only because I wasn't stupid, but because we *were* bound together. Both Eric and Bill had had my blood, and I theirs. For the first time, I understood there was a real connection. Didn't I see the two of them as more human than vampire? Didn't they have the power to wound me more than any others? It wasn't only my past relationships with the two that kept me tied to them. It was the blood exchange. Maybe because of my unusual heritage, they couldn't order me around. They didn't have mind control over me, and they couldn't read my thoughts; and I couldn't do any of those things to them. But we did share a tie. How often had I heard their lives humming away in the background, without realizing what I was listening to?

It takes way longer to tell this than it did to think it.

'Eric,' I said, and tilted my head to one side. He read as much from the gesture and word as I had from his. He stepped over to me and extended his arms to hold the black cloak out as he leaned over me, so the cloak and the hood could give us some illusion of privacy. The gesture was hokey, but the idea was nice. 'Eric, no sex,' I said in a voice as hard as I could make it. I could tolerate this if it wasn't like a lovers' blood exchange. *I wouldn't* have sex in front of another person. Eric's mouth was in the bend of my neck and shoulder, and his body pressed against mine. My arms slid around him, because that was simply the easiest way to stand. Then he bit, and I couldn't choke back a gasp of pain.

He didn't stop, thank God, because I wanted to get this over with. One of his hands stroked my back as if he was trying to soothe me.

After a long few seconds, Eric licked my neck to be sure his coagulant-laden saliva had coated the little wounds. 'Now, Sookie,' he said right into my ear. I couldn't reach his neck unless we were lying down, not without him bending over awkwardly. He started to hold his wrist up to my mouth, but we'd have to rearrange ourselves for that to work. I unbuttoned his shirt and, pushed it open. I hesitated. I always hated this part, because human teeth are not nearly as sharp as vampire teeth, and I knew it would be messy when I bit. Eric did something that surprised me, then; he produced the same small ceremonial knife he'd used in marrying Mississippi and Indian. With the same quick motion he'd used on their wrists, Eric sliced a cut in his chest right below his nipple. The blood oozed out sluggishly, and I took advantage of the flow to latch on. This was embarrassingly intimate, but at least I didn't have to look at Andre, and he couldn't see me.

Eric moved restlessly, and I realized he was getting aroused. There was nothing I could do about it, and I held our bodies apart that crucial couple of inches. I sucked hard, and Eric made a small noise, but I was strictly trying to get this over with. Vampire blood is thick and almost sweet, but when you think about what you're actually doing and you're not sexually aroused, it's not pleasant at all. When I thought I'd done it long enough, I let go and rebuttoned Eric's shirt with unsteady hands, thinking this little incident was over and I could hide somewhere until my heart stopped pounding.

And then Quinn flung open the door and stepped into the corridor.

'What the hell are you doing?' he roared, and I wasn't sure if he meant me, or Eric, or Andre.

'They are obeying orders,' Andre said sharply.

'My woman doesn't have to take orders from you,' Quinn said.

I opened my mouth to protest, but under these circumstances, it was hard to hand Quinn the line that I could take care of myself.

There was no social guideline to cover a calamity like this, and even my grandmother's all-purpose rule of etiquette ('Do what will make everyone most comfortable') could not remotely stretch to encompass my situation. I wondered what Dear Abby would say.

'Andre,' I said, trying to sound firm instead of cowed and scared, 'I'll finish the job I undertook to do for the queen here, because I shook on it. But I'll never work for you two again. Eric, thank you for making that as pleasant for me as you could.' (Though *pleasant* hardly seemed the right word.)

Eric had staggered a step over to lean against the wall. He'd allowed the cloak to fall open, and the stain on his pants was clearly visible. 'Oh, no problem,' Eric said dreamily.

That didn't help. I suspected he was doing it on purpose. I felt heat rise in my cheeks. 'Quinn, I'll talk to you later, as we agreed,' I snapped. Then I hesitated. 'That is, if you're still willing to talk to me.' I thought, but couldn't say because it would have been too grossly unfair, that it would have been more help to me if he'd come ten minutes earlier . . . or not at all.

Looking neither to the right nor the left, I made myself march down that hall, took the right-angle turn, and walked through a swinging doorway directly into the kitchen.

This clearly wasn't where I wanted to be, but at least it was away from the three men in the hall. 'Where's the baggage area?' I asked the first uniformed staff person I saw. She was a server loading glasses of synthetic blood onto a huge round tray, and she didn't pause in her task but nodded her head toward a door in the south wall marked EXIT. I was taking a lot of those this evening.

This door was heavier and led to a flight of stairs descending to a lower level, which I figured was actually under the ground. We don't have basements where I come from (the water table's too high), so it gave me a little frisson to be below street level.

I'd been walking as if something was chasing me, which in a non-literal way was absolutely true, and I'd been thinking about the damn suitcase so I wouldn't have to think about anything else. But when I reached the landing, I came to a complete stop.

Now that I was out of sight and truly alone, I took a moment to stand still, one hand resting against the wall. I let myself react to what had just happened. I began shaking, and when I touched my neck, I realized my collar felt funny. I pulled the material out and away and did a sort of sideways downward squinch to have a look at it. The collar was stained with my blood. Tears began flooding my eyes, and I sank to my haunches on the landing of that bleak staircase in a city far from home.

Chapter 12

I simply couldn't process what had just happened; it didn't jibe with my inner picture of myself or how I behaved. I could only think, *You had to be there.* And even then that didn't sound convincing.

Okay, Sookie, I said to myself. *What else could you have done?* It wasn't the time to do a lot of detailed thinking, but a quick scan of my options came up zero. I couldn't have fought off Andre or persuaded him to leave me alone. Eric could have fought Andre, but he chose not to because he wanted to keep his place in the Louisiana hierarchy, and also because he might have lost. Even if he'd chanced to win, the penalty would have been incredibly heavy. Vampires didn't fight over humans.

Likewise, I could have chosen to die rather than submit to the blood exchange, but I wasn't quite sure how I would have achieved that, and I was quite sure I didn't want to.

There was simply nothing I could have done, at least nothing that popped to my mind as I squatted there in the beigeness of the back stairway.

I shook myself, blotted my face with a tissue from my pocket, and smoothed my hair. I stood up straighter. I was on the right track to regaining my self-image. I would have to save the rest for later.

I pushed open the metal door and stepped into a cavernous area floored with concrete. As I'd progressed farther into the working area of the hotel (beginning with the first plain beige corridor), the decor had scaled back to minimal. This area was absolutely functional.

No one paid the least attention to me, so I had a good look around. It's not like I was anxious to hurry back to the queen, right? Across the floor, there was a huge industrial elevator. This hotel had been designed with as few openings onto the outside world as possible, to minimize the chance of intrusion, both of humans and the enemy sun. But the hotel had to have at least one large dock to load and unload coffins and supplies. This was the elevator that served that dock. The coffins entered here before they were taken to their designated rooms. Two uniformed men armed with shotguns stood facing the elevator, but I have to say that they looked remarkably bored, not at all like the alert watchdogs in the lobby.

In an area by the far wall, to the left of the huge elevator, some suitcases were slumped together in a forlorn sort of suitcase corral, an area delineated by those posts that contain retractable strips that are used to direct crowds in airports. No one appeared to be in charge of them, so I walked over – and it was a long walk – and began reading labels. There was already another lackey like me searching through the luggage, a young man with glasses and wearing a business suit.

'What are you looking for?' I asked. 'If I see it while I'm looking, I can pull it out for you.'

'Good idea. The desk called to say we had a suitcase down here that hadn't made it to the room, so here I am. The tag should say 'Phoebe Golden, Queen of Iowa' or something like that. You?'

'Sophie-Anne Leclerq, Louisiana.'

'Wow, you work for her? Did she do it?'

'Nope, and I know because I was there,' I said, and his curious face got even more curious. But he could tell I wasn't going to say any more about it, and he resumed looking.

I was surprised at the number of suitcases in the corral.

'How come,' I asked the young man, 'they can't just bring these up and leave them in the rooms? Like the rest of the luggage?'

He shrugged. 'I was told it's some kind of liability issue. We have to identify our suitcases personally, so they can say we were the ones who picked them out. Hey, this is the one I want,' he said after a moment. 'I can't read the name of the owner, but it does say Iowa, so it must belong to someone in our group. Well, bye, nice to talk to you.' He set off briskly with a black rolling bag.

Immediately after that, I hit luggage pay dirt. A blue leather suitcase was tagged with 'Sheriff, Area' – well, that was too scribbled to make out. The vampires used all kinds of scripts, depending on the education they'd had in the age they were born. 'Louisiana': the label did say that. I picked up the old suitcase and lifted it over the barrier. The writing wasn't any clearer closer to my eyes. Like my opposite number in Iowa, I decided the best course would be to take it upstairs and show it around until someone claimed it.

One of the armed guards had turned halfway from his post to figure out what I was doing. 'Where you going with that, beautiful?' he called.

'I work for the Queen of Louisiana. She sent me down to get it,' I said.

'Your name?'

'Sookie Stackhouse.'

'Hey, Joe!' he called to a fellow employee, a heavy guy who was sitting behind a really ugly desk on which sat a battered computer. 'Check out the name Stackhouse, will ya?'

'Sure thing,' Joe said, wrenching his gaze from the young Iowan, who was just barely visible over on the other side of the cavernous space. Joe regarded me with the same curiosity. When he saw that I'd noticed, he looked guilty and tapped away at the keyboard. He eyed the computer screen like it could tell him everything he needed to know, and for the purposes of his job, maybe he was right.

'Okay,' Joe called to the guard. 'She's on the list.' His was the gruff voice that I remembered from the phone conversation. He resumed staring at me, and though all the other people in the cavernous space were having blank, neutral thoughts, Joe's were not blank. They were shielded. I'd never encountered anything like it. Someone had put a metaphysical helmet on his head. I tried to get through it, around, under it, but it stayed in place. While I fumbled around, trying to get inside his thoughts, Joe was looking at me with a cross expression. I don't think he knew what I was doing. I think he was a grouch.

'Excuse me,' I asked, calling so my question could reach Joe's ears. 'Is my picture by my name on your list?'

'No,' he said, snorting as if I'd asked a strange question. 'We got a list of all the guests and who they brought with them.'

'So, how do you know I'm me?'

'Huh?'

'How do you know I'm Sookie Stackhouse?'

'Aren't you?'

'Yeah.'

'Then what you bitching about? Get outta here with the damn suitcase.' Joe looked down at his computer, and the guard swung around to face the elevator. *This must be the legendary Yankee rudeness,* I thought.

The bag didn't have a roller mechanism; no telling how long the owner had had it. I picked it up and marched back over to the door to the stairs. There was another elevator close to the door, I noticed, but it wasn't half as large as the huge one that had access to the outside. It could take up coffins, true, but perhaps only one at a time.

I'd already opened the stair door when I realized that if I went up that way I'd have to pass through the service corridor again. What if Eric, Andre, and Quinn were still there? What if they'd ripped each other's throats out? Though just at the moment such a scenario wouldn't have devastated me, I decided to forgo the chance of an encounter. I took the elevator instead. Okay, cowardly, but a woman can handle only so much in one night.

This elevator was definitely for the peons. It had pads on the walls to prevent cargo from being damaged. It serviced only the first four floors: basement levels, lobby, mezzanine, human floor. After that, the shape of the pyramid dictated that to rise, you had to go to the center to catch one of elevators that went all the way up. This would make taking the coffins around a slow process, I thought. The staff of the Pyramid worked hard for their money.

I decided to take the suitcase straight to the queen's suite. I didn't know what else to do with it.

When I stepped off at Sophie-Anne's floor, the lobby area around the elevator was silent and empty. Probably all the vampires and their attendants were downstairs at the soiree. Someone had left a discarded soda can lying in a large, boldly patterned urn holding some kind of small tree. The urn was positioned against the wall between the two elevators. I think the tree was supposed to be some kind of short palm tree, to maintain the Egyptian theme. The stupid soda can bothered me. Of course, there were maintenance people in the hotel whose job it was to keep everything clean, but the habit of picking up was ingrained in me. I'm no neat freak, but still. This was a nice place, and some idiot was strewing garbage around. I bent over to pick the darn thing up with my free right hand, intending to toss it into the first available garbage can.

But it was a lot heavier than it should have been.

I set down the suitcase to look at the can closely, cradling it in both my hands. The colors and the design made the cylinder look like a Dr Pepper can in almost every respect, but it just wasn't. The elevator doors whooshed open again, and Batanya stepped off, a strange-looking gun in one hand, a sword in the other. Looking over the bodyguard's shoulder into the elevator car, I saw the King of Kentucky, who looked back at me curiously.

Batanya seemed a bit surprised to see me standing there, smack-dab in front of the door. She scanned the area, then pointed her gunlike weapon carefully at the floor. The sword remained ready in her left hand. 'Could you step to my left?' she asked very courteously. 'The king wants to visit in that room.' Her head nodded toward one of the rooms to the right.

I didn't move, couldn't think of what to say.

She took in the way I was standing and the expression on my face. She said in a sympathetic way, 'I don't know why you people drink those carbonated things. They give me gas, too.'

'It's not that.'

'Is something wrong?'

'This isn't an empty can,' I said.

Batanya's face froze. 'What do you think it is?' she asked very, very calmly. That was the voice of Big Trouble.

'It might be a spy camera,' I said hopefully. 'Or, see, I'm thinking it might be a bomb. Because it's not a real can. It's full of something heavy, and that heaviness is not fluid.' Not only was the tab top not on the can, but the innards didn't slosh.

'I understand,' Batanya said. Again with the calm. She pressed a little panel on the armor over her chest, a dark blue area about the size of a credit card. 'Clovache,' she said. 'Unknown device on four. I'm bringing the king back down.'

Clovache's voice said, 'How large is the device?' Her accent was sort of like Russian, at least to my untravelled ears. ('Hau larch . . .?')

'The size of one of those cans of sweetened syrup,' Batanya answered.

'Ah, the burping drinks,' Clovache said. *Good memory, Clovache*, I thought.

'Yes. The Stackhouse girl noticed it, not me,' Batanya said grimly. 'And now she is standing with it in her hand.'

'Tell her to put it down,' advised the invisible Clovache with the simplicity of one who was stating an obvious fact.

Behind Batanya, the King of Kentucky was beginning to look very nervous. Batanya glanced over her shoulder at him. 'Get a bomb team up here from the local policing unit,' Batanya said to Clovache. 'I'm bringing the king back down.'

'The tiger is here, too,' Clovache said., 'She is his woman.'

Before I could say, 'For God's sake, don't send him up,' Batanya pressed the rectangle again, and it went dark.

'I have to protect the king,' Batanya said with an apology in her voice. She stepped back into the elevator, punched a button, and gave me a nod.

Nothing had scared me as much as that nod. It was a good-bye look. And the door swooshed shut.

There I stood, alone on the silent hotel floor, holding an instrument of death. Maybe.

Neither of the elevators gave any signs of life. No one came out of the doors on the fourth floor, and no one went into them. The stair door didn't budge. There was a long, dead time in which I did nothing but stand and hold a fake Dr Pepper can. I did a little breathing, too, but nothing too violent.

With an explosion of sound that startled me so much I nearly dropped the can, Quinn burst onto the floor. He'd taken the stairs in a huge hurry if his breathing was any indication. I couldn't spare the brainpower to find out what was going on in his head, but his face was showing nothing but the same kind of calm mask that Batanya wore. Todd Donati, the security guy, was right on Quinn's heels. They stopped dead about four feet away from me.

'The bomb squad is coming,' Donati said, leading off with the good news.

'Put it down where it was, babe,' Quinn said.

'Oh, yeah, I *want* to put it back where it was,' I said. 'I'm just scared to.' I hadn't moved a muscle in what felt like a million years, and I was becoming tired already. But still I stood looking down at the can I was holding in both hands. I promised myself I would never drink another Dr Pepper as long as I lived, and I'd been real fond of them before tonight.

'Okay,' Quinn said, holding out his hand. 'Give it to me.'

I'd never wanted to do anything more in my life.

'Not till we know what it is,' I said. 'Maybe it's a camera. Maybe some tabloid is trying to get insider shots of the big vampire summit.' I tried to smile. 'Maybe it's a little computer, counting vampires and humans as they go by. Maybe it's a bomb Jennifer Cater planted before she got offed. Maybe she wanted to blow up the queen.' I'd had a couple of minutes to think about this.

'And maybe it'll take your hand off,' he said. 'Let me take it, babe.'

'You sure you want to do that, after tonight?' I asked dismally.

'We can talk about that later. Don't worry about it. Just give me the damn can.'

I noticed Todd Donati wasn't offering, and he already had a fatal disease. Didn't he want to go out as a hero? What was wrong with him? Then I was ashamed of myself for even thinking that. He had a family, and he'd want every minute with them.

Donati was sweating visibly, and he was white as a vampire. He was talking into the little headset he wore, relaying what he was seeing to . . . someone.

'No, Quinn. Someone with one of those special suits on needs to take it,' I said. 'I'm not moving. The can's not moving. We're okay. Till one of those special guys gets here. Or special gal,' I added in the interest of fairness. I was feeling a little light-headed. The multiple shocks of the night were taking their toll on me, and I was beginning to tremble. Plus, I thought I was nuts for doing this; and yet here I was, doing it. 'Anyone got X-ray vision?' I asked, trying to smile. 'Where's Superman when you need him?'

'Are you trying to be a martyr for these damn things?' Quinn asked, and I figured the 'damn things' were the vampires.

'Ha,' I said. 'Oh, ha-ha. Yeah, 'cause they *love* me. You see how many vampires are up here? Zero, right?'

'One,' said Eric, stepping out of the stairwell. 'We're bound a bit too tightly to suit me, Sookie.' He was visibly tense; I couldn't remember ever seeing Eric so notably anxious. 'I'm here to die right along with you, it seems.'

'Good. To make my day absolutely effing complete, here's Eric again,' I said, and if I sounded a little sarcastic, well, I was due. 'Are you all completely nuts? Get the hell out of here!'

In a brisk voice, Todd Donati said; 'Well, *I* will. You won't let anyone take the can, you won't put it down, and you haven't blown up yet. So I think I'll go downstairs to wait for the bomb squad.'

I couldn't fault his logic. 'Thanks for calling in the troops,' I said, and Donati took the stairs, because the elevator was too close to me. I could read his head easily, and he felt deep shame that he hadn't actually offered to help me in any more concrete way. He planned to go down a floor to where no one could see him and then take the elevator to save his strength. The stairwell door shut behind him, and then we three stood by ourselves in a triangular tableau: Quinn, Eric, and me. Was this symbolic, or what?

My head was feeling light.

Eric began to move very slowly and carefully – I think so I wouldn't be startled. In a moment, he was at my elbow. Quinn's brain was throbbing and pulsating like a disco ball farther to my right. He didn't know how to help me, and of course, he was a bit afraid of what might happen.

Who knew, with Eric? Aside from being able to locate him and determine how he was oriented to me, I couldn't see more.

'You'll give it to me and leave,' Eric said. He was pushing his vampire influence at my head with all his might. 'Won't work, never did,' I muttered.

'You are a stubborn woman,' he said.

'I'm *not*,' I said, on the verge of tears at being first accused of nobility, then stubbornness. 'I just don't want to move it! That's safest!'

'Some might think you suicidal.'

'Well, "some" can stick it up their ass.'

'Babe, put it down on the urn. Just lay it down re-a-a-llll easy,' Quinn said, his voice very gentle. 'Then I'll get you a big drink with lots of alcohol. You're a real strong gal, you know that? I'm proud of you, Sookie. But if you don't put that down now and get out of here, I'm gonna be real mad, hear me? I don't want anything to happen to you. That would be nuts, right?'

I was saved from further debate by the arrival of another entity on the scene. The police sent up a robot in the elevator.

When the door swooshed open we all jumped, because we'd been too wrapped up in the drama to notice the noise of the elevator. I actually giggled when the stubby robot rolled off the elevator. I started to hold the bomb out to it, but I figured the robot wasn't supposed to take it. It seemed to be operating on remote control, and it turned slightly right to face me. It remained motionless for a couple of minutes to have a good look at me and what was in my hand. After a minute or two of examination, the robot retreated onto the elevator, and its arm jerkily reached up to punch the correct button. The doors swished shut, and it left.

'I hate modern technology,' Eric said quietly.

'Not true,' I said. 'You love what computers can do for you. I know that for a fact. Remember how happy you got when you saw the Fangtasia employee roster, with all the work hours filled in?'

'I don't like the impersonality of it. I like the knowledge it can hold.'

This was just too weird a conversation for me to continue under the circumstances.

'Someone's coming up the stairs,' Quinn said, and opened the stair door.

Into our little group strode the bomb disposal guy. The homicide squad might not have boasted any vampire cops, but the bomb squad did. The vampire wore one of those space suit – looking outfits. (Even if you can survive it, I guess getting blown up is not a good experience.) Someone had written 'BOOM' on his chest where a name tag would normally be. Oh, that was *so funny*.

'You two civilians need to leave the floor to the lady and me,' Boom said, moving slowly across the floor to me. 'Take a hike, guys,' he said when neither man moved.

'No,' said Eric.

'Hell, no,' said Quinn.

It isn't easy to shrug in one of those suits, but Boom managed. He was holding a square container. Frankly, I was in no mood to have a look at it, and all I cared about was that he opened the lid and held it out, carefully placing it under my hands.

Very, very carefully I lowered the can into the padded interior of the container. I let it go and brought my hands out of the container with a relief that I can't even describe, and Boom closed the container, still grinning merrily through his clear face guard. I shuddered all over, my hands trembling violently from the release of the position.

Boom turned, slowed, by the suit, and gestured to Quinn to open the stairwell door again. Quinn did, and down the stairs the vampire went: slowly, carefully, evenly. Maybe he smiled all the way. But he didn't blow up, because I didn't hear a noise, and I've got to say we all stood frozen in our places for a good long while.

'Oh,' I said, 'Oh.' This was not brilliant, but I was in about a thousand emotional pieces. My knees gave way.

Quinn pounced on me and wrapped his arms around me. 'You idiot,' he said. 'You idiot.' It was like he was saying, 'Thank you, God.' I was smothered in weretiger, and I rubbed my face against his E(E)E shirt to wipe up the tears that had leaked from my eyes.

When I peered under his arm, there was no one else in the area. Eric had vanished. So I had a moment to enjoy being held, to know that Quinn still liked me, that the thing with Andre and Eric hadn't killed all feeling he had begun to have for me. I had a moment to feel the absolute relief of escaping death.

Then the elevator and the stair door opened simultaneously, and all manner of people wanted to talk to me.

Chapter 13

'It was a bomb,' Todd Donati said. 'A quick crude bomb. The police will be telling me more, I hope, after they've finished their examination.' The security chief was sitting in the queen's suite. I had finally gotten to stow the blue suitcase by one of her couches, and, boy, was I glad to be rid of it. Sophie-Anne hadn't bothered to thank me for its return, but I hadn't really expected her to, I guess. When you had underlings, you sent them on errands and you didn't have to thank them. That's why they were underlings. For that matter, I wasn't sure the stupid thing was even hers.

'I expect I'll get fired over it, especially after the murders,' the security chief said. His voice was calm, but his thoughts were bitter. He needed the health insurance.

Andre gave the security chief one of his long, blue gazes. 'And how did the can come to be on the queen's floor, in that area?' Andre couldn't have cared less about Todd Donati's job situation. Donati glared back, but it was a weary kind of glare.

'Why on earth would you be fired, just because someone was able to bring a bomb in and plant it? Maybe because you are in charge of the safety of everyone in the hotel?' Gervaise asked, definitely on the cruel side. I didn't know Gervaise very well, and I was beginning to feel that was just fine with me. Cleo slapped him on the arm hard enough to make Gervaise wince.

Donati said, 'That's it in a nutshell. Obviously someone brought that bomb up and put it on the potted plant by the elevator door. It might have been meant for the queen, since it was closest to her door. Almost equally, it might have been meant for anyone else on the floor, or it might have been planted at random. So I think the bomb and the murder of the Arkansas vampires are two different cases. In our questioning, we're finding Jennifer Cater didn't have a lot of friends. Your queen isn't the only one with a grudge against her, though your queen's is the most serious. Possibly Jennifer planted the bomb, or arranged to have someone else do it, before she was murdered.' I saw Henrik Feith sitting in a corner of the suite, his beard quivering with the shaking of his head. I tried to picture the one remaining member of the Arkansas contingent creeping around with a bomb, and I just couldn't feature it. The small vampire seemed convinced that he was in a nest of vipers. I was sure he was regretting his acceptance of the queen's protection, because right now that was looking like it wasn't a very reliable prospect.

'There is much to do here and now,' Andre said. He sounded just a shade concerned, and he was riding his own conversational train. 'It was rash of Christian Baruch to threaten to fire you now, when he needs your loyalty the most.'

'The guy's got a temper on him,' Todd Donati said, and I knew without a doubt that he wasn't a native of Rhodes. The more stressed he got, the more he sounded like home; not Louisiana, maybe, but northern Tennessee. 'The ax hasn't fallen yet. And if we can get to the bottom of what's happening, maybe I'll get reinstated. Not too many people would cotton to this job. Lots of security people don't like—'

Working with the damn vampires, Donati completed his sentence silently to everyone but me and him. He reminded himself harshly to stick to the immediate present. 'Don't like the hours it takes to run security in a big place like this,' he finished out loud, for the vampires' benefit. 'But I enjoy the work.' *My kids will need the benefits when I die. Just two more months and coverage will stay with them after I pass.*

He'd come to the queen's suite to talk to me about the Dr Pepper incident (as had the police, and the ever-present Christian Baruch), but he was staying to chat. Though the vampires didn't seem to notice, Donati was so chatty because he had taken some heavy pain medication. I felt sorry for him, and at the same time I realized that someone with so many distractions wasn't likely to be doing a good job. What had gotten by Donati in the past couple of months, since his illness had begun affecting his daily life?

Maybe he'd hired the wrong people. Maybe he'd omitted some vital step in protecting the guests of the hotel. Maybe – I was distracted by a wave of warmth.

Eric was coming.

I'd never had such a clear sense of his presence, and my heart sank as I knew the blood exchange had been an important one. If my memory was clear, it was the third time I'd taken Eric's blood, and three is always a significant number. I felt a constant awareness of his presence when he was anywhere near me, and I had to believe it was the same for him. There might be even more to the tie now, more that I just hadn't experienced yet. I closed my eyes and leaned over to rest my forehead on my knees.

There was a knock at the door, and Sigebert answered it after a careful look through the peephole. He admitted Eric. I could scarcely bring myself to look at him or to give him a casual greeting. I should be grateful to Eric, and I knew it; and on one level I was. Sucking blood from Andre would have been intolerable. Scratch that: I would've had to tolerate it. It would have been disgusting. But exchanging blood at all had not been a choice I got to make, and I wasn't *going* to forget it.

Eric sat on the couch beside me. I jumped up as if I'd been poked by a cattle prod and went across the room to the bar to pour myself a glass of water. No matter where I went, I could feel Eric's presence; to make that even more unsettling, I found his nearness was somehow comforting, as if it made me more secure.

Oh, just *great*.

There wasn't anywhere else for me to sit. I settled miserably by the Viking, who now owned a piece of me. Before this night, when I'd seen Eric, I'd felt simply a casual pleasure – though I had thought of him perhaps more often than a woman ought to think about a man who would outlive her for centuries.

I reminded myself that this was not Eric's fault. Eric might be political, and he might be focused on looking out for number one (which was spelled E-R-I-C), but I didn't see how he could have sur-mised Andre's purpose and caught up with us to reason with Andre, with any degree of premeditation. So I owed Eric a big thank-you, no matter how you looked at it, but that wasn't going to be a conversation we had anywhere in the vicinity of the queen and the aforesaid Andre.

'Bill is still selling his little computer disk downstairs,' Eric remarked to me.

'So?'

'I thought perhaps you were wondering why I showed up when you were in dire straits, and he didn't.'

'It never crossed my mind,' I said, wondering why Eric was bringing this up.

'I made him stay downstairs,' Eric said. 'After all, I'm his area sheriff.'

I shrugged.

'He wanted to hit me,' Eric said with only the hint of a smile on his lips. 'He wanted to take the bomb from you and be your hero. Quinn would have done that, too.'

'I remember that Quinn offered,' I said.

'I did, too,' Eric said. He seemed a bit shocked at the fact.

'I don't want to talk about it,' I said, and I hoped my tone made it clear I was serious. It was getting close to dawn, and I'd had a stressful night (which was the mildest way I could put it). I managed to catch Andre's eye and give him the tiny nod toward Todd Donati. I was trying to clue him in that Donati was not entirely okay. In fact, he was as gray as a snow sky.

'If you'll excuse us, Mr Donati. . . . We've enjoyed your company, but we have much to discuss about our plans for tomorrow night,' Andre said smoothly, and Donati tensed, since he knew quite well he'd been dismissed.

'Of course, Mr Andre,' the security chief said. 'I hope all of you sleep well this day, and I'll see you tomorrow night.' He rose to his feet with a lot more effort than it should have taken, and he suppressed a flinch at the pain. 'Miss Stackhouse, I hope you get over your bad experience real soon.'

'Thank you,' I said, and Sigebert opened the door for Donati to leave.

'If you'll excuse me,' I said the minute he was gone, 'I'll just go to my room now.'

The queen gave me a sharp look. 'Are you unhappy about something, Sookie?' she said, though she sounded like she didn't really want to hear my answer.

'Oh, why would I be unhappy? I *love* having things done to me without my will,' I said. The pressure had built up and up, and the words came out like lava erupting from a volcano, even though my more intelligent self kept telling me to put a plug in it. 'And then,' I said very loudly, not listening to myself one little bit, 'I like hanging around the ones responsible. That's *even better!*' I was losing coherence and gaining momentum.

There was no telling what I would have said next if Sophie-Anne hadn't held up one little white hand. She seemed a weensy bit perturbed, as my grandmother would have put it.

'You are assuming I know what you are talking about, and that I want to hear a human yelling at me,' Sophie-Anne said.

Eric's eyes were glowing as if a candle burned behind them, and he was so lovely I could have drowned in him. God help me. I made myself look at Andre, who was examining me as if he was deciding where the best cut of meat was. Gervaise and Cleo just looked interested.

'Excuse me,' I said, returning to the world of reality with a thud. It was so late, and I was so tired, and the night had been filled with so many incidents that I thought for a split second that I might actually faint. But the Stackhouses don't produce fainters, and neither do the fairies, I guess. It was time I gave a nod to that little percentage of my heritage. 'I'm very tired.' I had no fight left in me all of a sudden. I really wanted to go to bed. Not a word was spoken as I trudged to the door, which was almost a miracle. Though, as I closed it behind me, I heard the queen say, 'Explain, Andre.'

Quinn was waiting by the door to my room. I didn't know if I even had the energy to be glad or sad to see him. I got out the plastic rectangle and opened the door, and after I'd scanned the interior and seen that my roommate was gone (though I wondered where, since Gervaise had been by himself), I jerked my head to tell Quinn he could come in.

'I have an idea,' he said quietly.

I raised my eyebrows, too exhausted to speak.

'Let's just climb in the bed and sleep.'

I finally managed to smile at him. 'That's the best offer I've had all day,' I said. At that second, I saw how I could come to love Quinn. While he visited the bathroom, I pulled off my clothes, folded them, and slipped into my pajamas, short and pink and silky to the touch.

Quinn came out of the bathroom in his briefs, but I was just too worn out to appreciate the view. He got into the bed while I brushed my teeth and washed my face. I slid in beside him. He turned on his side and his arms opened, and I just kept on sliding right into them. We hadn't showered, but he smelled good to me: he smelled alive and vital.

'Good ceremony tonight,' I remembered to say after I'd switched off the bedside lamp.

'Thanks.'

'Got any more coming up?'

'Yeah, if your queen goes on trial. Now that Cater was killed, who knows if that's still on. And tomorrow night is the ball, after the trial.'

'Oh, I get to wear my pretty dress.' A little pleasure stirred in me at the prospect. 'You got to work?'

'No, the ball's being run by the hotel,' he said. 'You gonna dance with me or the blond vampire?'

'Oh, hell,' I said, wishing Quinn hadn't reminded me.

And right on cue, he said, 'Forget it now, babe. We're here, now, in bed together like we ought to be.'

Like we ought to be. That sounded good.

'You heard about me tonight, right?' he asked.

The night had contained so many incidents it took me a moment to remember that I'd learned about the things he'd had to do to survive.

And that he had a half sister. A troublesome, nutty, dependent half sister who hated me on sight.

He was a little tense, waiting for my reaction. I could feel it in his head, in his body. I tried to think of a sweet, wonderful way to put how I felt. I was too tired.

'Quinn, I've got no problem with you,' I said. I kissed his cheek, kissed his mouth. 'No problem at all. And I'll try to like Frannie.'

'Oh,' he said, sounding simply relieved. 'Well, then.' He kissed my forehead, and we fell asleep.

I slept like a vampire. I didn't wake to make a trip to the bathroom, even, or to turn over. I swam almost up to consciousness once to hear Quinn was snoring, just a faint ruffle of sound, and I snuggled closer to him. He stopped, murmured, and fell silent.

I looked at the bedside clock when I finally, really, woke up. It was four in the afternoon; I'd slept for twelve hours. Quinn was gone, but he'd drawn a big pair of lips (with my lipstick) on a piece of hotel stationery and laid it on his pillow. I smiled. My roommate hadn't come in. Maybe she was spending the day in Gervaise's coffin. I shuddered. 'He leaves *me* cold,' I said out loud, wishing Amelia was there to respond. Speaking of Amelia . . . I fished my cell phone out of my purse and called her.

'Hey,' she said. 'What's up?'

'What are you doing?' I asked, trying not to feel homesick.

'Brushing Bob,' she said. 'He had a hair ball.'

'Aside from that?'

'Oh, I worked at the bar a little,' Amelia said, trying to sound casual.

I was dumbfounded. 'Doing what?'

'Well, serving drinks. What else is there to do?'

'How come Sam needed you?'

'The Fellowship is having a big rally in Dallas, and Arlene wanted time off to go with that asshole she's dating. Then Danielle's kid got pneumonia. So Sam was really worried, and since I happened to be in the bar, he asked me if I knew how to do the job. I said, "Hey, how hard could it be?"'

'Thanks, Amelia.'

'Oh, okay, I guess that sounded pretty disrespectful.' Amelia laughed. 'So, it is a little tricky. Everyone wants to talk to you, but you have to hurry, and you can't spill their drinks on 'em, and you have to remember what everyone was drinking, and who's paying for the round, and who's on a tab. And you have to stand up for hours and hours.'

'Welcome to my world.'

'So, how's Mr Stripes?'

I realized she was talking about Quinn. 'We're okay,' I said, pretty sure that was true. 'He did one big ceremony last night; it was so cool. A vampire wedding. You would've loved it.'

'What's on for tonight?'

'Well, maybe a trial.' I didn't feel like explaining, especially over a cell phone. 'And a ball.'

'Wow, like Cinderella.'

'Remains to be seen.'

'How's the business part of it going?'

'I'll have to tell you about that when I get back,' I said, suddenly not so cheerful. 'I'm glad you're busy and I'm glad everything's going okay.'

'Oh, Terry Bellefleur called to ask if you wanted a puppy. You remember when Annie got out?'

Annie was Terry's very expensive and much-loved Catahoula. He'd come out to my place looking for Annie when she'd roamed away, and by the time he'd found her, she had had some close encounters.

'What do the puppies look like?'

'He said you had to see them to believe them. I told him you'd come by next week, maybe. I didn't commit you to anything.'

'Okay, good.'

We chatted a minute more but since I'd been gone from Bon Temps less than forty-eight hours, there really wasn't that much to say.

'So,' she said in closing, 'I miss you, Stackhouse.'

'Yeah? I miss you, too, Broadway.'

'Bye. Don't get any strange fangs on you.'

Too late for that. 'Bye. Don't spill any beer on the sheriff.'

'If I do, it'll be on purpose.'

I laughed, because I'd felt like dousing Bud Dearborn, too. I hung up feeling pretty good. I ordered room service, very tentatively. That was not something I got to do every day; even every year. Or ever.

I was a little nervous about letting the waiter into my room, but Carla wandered in at just the same moment. She was decorated with hickeys and wearing last night's dress.

'That smells good,' she said, and I handed her a croissant. She drank my orange juice while I had the coffee. It worked out okay. Carla did the talking for both of us, telling me all about the things I'd experienced. She didn't seem to realize I'd been with the queen when the slaughter of Jennifer Cater's group was discovered, and though she'd heard I'd found the Dr Pepper bomb, she told me all about it anyway, as though I hadn't been there. Maybe Gervaise made her keep silent, and the words just built up.

'What are you wearing to the ball tonight?' I asked, feeling impossibly hokey to even be asking such a question. She showed me her dress, which was black, spangled, and almost nonexistent above the waist, like all her other evening wear. Carla definitely believed in emphasizing her assets.

She asked to see my dress, and we both made insincere noises about what good taste the other had.

We had to take turns in the bathroom, of course, which I wasn't used to doing. I was pretty exasperated by the time Carla emerged. I hoped the entire city hadn't run out of hot water. Of course, there was plenty left, and despite the scattering of her cosmetics on the bathroom counter, I managed to get clean and get made-up on time. In honor of my beautiful dress, I tried to put my hair up, but I'm no good with anything more complex than a ponytail. The hair would be down. I went a little heavier on the makeup than I do in the daytime, and I had some big earrings that Tara had told me were just right. I turned my head experimentally and watched them swing and glitter. They were silvery and white, just like the beading on the bodice of my evening dress. *Which it is now time to put on*, I told myself with a little jolt of anticipation.

Oh, boy. My dress was ice blue, and had silver and white beads, and was cut just the right depth in the front and back. It had a built-in bra so I didn't have to wear one, and I pulled on some blue panties that would never leave a line on me. Then thigh-high hose. Then my shoes, which were high heeled and silvery.

I'd done my nails while Water Woman was in the shower, and I put on my lipstick and had a final look in the mirror.

Carla said, 'You look real pretty, Sookie.'

'Thanks.' I knew I was smiling a big smile. There's nothing like dressing up once in a while. I felt like my prom date was picking me up with a corsage to pin to my dress. JB had taken me to my senior prom, though other girls had asked him because he would look so good in the photographs. My aunt Linda had made my dress.

No more homemade dresses for me.

A knock at the door had me looking anxiously in the mirror. But it was Gervaise, checking to see if Carla was ready. She smiled and turned around to garner the admiration due her, and Gervaise gave her a kiss on the cheek. I wasn't too impressed with Gervaise's character, and he wasn't my cup of tea physically, either, with his broad, bland face and his light mustache, but I had to hand it to him for generosity: he fastened a diamond tennis bracelet around Carla's wrist then and there, with no further ado than if he were giving her a bauble. Carla tried to restrain her excitement, but then she cast that to the winds and threw her arms around Gervaise's neck. I was embarrassed to be in the room, because some of the pet names she used while thanking him were sort of anatomically correct.

After they left, well pleased with each other, I stood in the middle of the bedroom. I didn't want to sit down in my dress until I had to, because I knew it would wrinkle and lose that perfect feeling. That left me with very little to do, other than trying not to get miffed about the chaos Carla had left on her side and feeling a bit at a loss. Surely Quinn had said he'd come by the room to get me? We hadn't been supposed to meet downstairs, right?

My purse made a noise, and I realized I'd stuck the queen's pager in there. Oh, surely not!

'Get down here,' read the message. 'Trial is now.'

At the same moment, the room phone rang. I picked it up, trying to catch my breath.

'Babe,' said Quinn. 'I'm sorry. In case you hadn't heard, the council has decided that the queen will have to go on trial, right now, and you gotta hustle down here. I'm sorry,' he said again, 'I'm in charge of setting up. I gotta work. Maybe this won't take long.'

'Okay,' I said weakly, and he hung up.

So much for my glamorous evening with my new guy.

But, dammit, I wasn't going to change into anything less festive. Everyone else would have party clothes on, and even if my role in the evening had altered, I deserved to look pretty, too. I rode down on the elevator with one of the hotel employees, who couldn't tell if I was a vampire or not. I made him very nervous. It always tickles me when people can't tell. To me, vampires sort of glow, just a bit.

Andre was waiting for me when I got off the elevator. He was as flustered as I'd ever seen him; I could tell because his fingers were clenching and unclenching, and his lip was bloody where he'd bitten it, though it healed as I watched. Before last night, Andre had just made me nervous. Now I loathed him. But it was evident I had to put personal issues aside until another time.

'How could this happen?' he asked. 'Sookie, you need to learn everything you can about this. We have more enemies than we knew.'

'I thought there wouldn't be a trial after Jennifer got killed. Since she was the queen's chief accuser—'

'That's what we all thought. Or, if there was a trial, it would be an empty form, staged simply so the charges could be dismissed. But we got down here tonight and they were waiting for us. They've put off the start of the ball to do this. Take my arm,' he said, and I was so taken by surprise that I slid my arm through his.

'Smile,' he said. 'Look confident.'

And we walked into the convention hall with bold faces – me and my good buddy Andre.

It was lucky I'd had plenty of practice in insincere smiling, because this was like the marathon of Saving Face. All the vampires and their human entourages parted way for us. Some of them were smiling, too, though not pleasantly, and some looked concerned, and some just looked mildly anticipatory, as if they were about to watch a movie that had gotten good buzz.

And the rush of thoughts engulfed me. I smiled and walked on automatic while I listened in. *Pretty . . . Sophie-Anne'll get what's coming to her . . . maybe I can call her lawyer, see if she's open to an approach from our king . . . nice boobs . . . my man needs a telepath . . . hear she's fucking Quinn . . . hear she's fucking the queen and Baby Boy Andre . . . found her at a bar . . . Sophie-Anne's washed up, serves her right . . . hear she's fucking Cataliades . . . stupid trial, where's the band? . . . hope they have some food at the dance, people food . . .*

And on and on. Some of it pertaining to me, the queen, and/or Andre, some of it the simple thoughts of people who are tired of waiting and want to get the party started.

We strolled the gauntlet until it terminated in the room where the wedding had been held. The crowd in this room was almost 100 percent vampire. A notable absence: human servers, and any other human hotel staff. The only ones circulating with drinks trays were vampires. Things were going to happen in this room that weren't for human consumption. If it was possible for me to feel more anxious, I did.

I could see Quinn had been busy. The low platform had been rearranged. The giant ankh had been put away, and two lecterns had been added. On the spot where Mississippi and his loved one had taken their vows, about midway between the two lecterns, there sat a thronelike chair. In it was an ancient woman with wild white hair. I had never seen a vampire who had been turned when she was so old, and though I'd sworn I wasn't going to speak to him, I said as much to Andre.

'That is the Ancient Pythoness,' he said absently. He was scanning the crowd, trying to find Sophie-Anne, I supposed. I spotted Johan Glassport, who was going to get his moment in the limelight after all, and the rest of the Louisiana contingent was with the murderous lawyer – all except the queen and Eric and Pam, whom I'd glimpsed standing near the stage.

Andre and I took our seats at the right front. On the left front was a clump of vampires who were no fans of ours. Chief among them was Henrik Feith. Henrik had transformed himself from a panicky scaredy-cat to a ball of wrath. He glowered at us. He did everything but throw spitballs.

'What crawled up his ass and died?' muttered Cleo Babbitt, dropping into the seat to my right. 'The queen offers to take him under her wing when he's alone and defenseless, and this is the thanks she gets?' Cleo was wearing a traditional tuxedo, and she looked pretty, darn good in it. The severity of it suited her. Her boy toy looked much more feminine than she did. I wondered at his inclusion in the crowd, which was all supe and overwhelmingly vampire. Diantha leaned forward from the row behind us to tap me on the shoulder. She was wearing a red bustier with black ruffles and a black taffeta skirt, also ruffled. Her bustier didn't have much bust to fill it. She was clutching a handheld computer game. 'Goodtoseeya,' she said, and I made the effort of smiling at her. She returned her attention to the computer game.

'What will happen to us if Sophie-Anne is found guilty?' Cleo asked, and we all fell silent.

What *would* happen to us if Sophie-Anne were convicted? With Louisiana in a weakened position, with the scandal surrounding Peter's death, we were all at risk.

I don't know why I hadn't thought this through, but I hadn't.

In a moment, I understood that I hadn't even thought about worrying because I'd grown up a free United States human citizen; I wasn't used to worrying about my fate being in question. Bill had joined the little group surrounding the queen, and as I peered across the room at them, he knelt, along with Eric and Pam. Andre leaped up from his seat to my left, and in one of his lightning moves he crossed the room to kneel with them. The queen stood before them like a Roman goddess accepting tribute. Cleo followed my gaze, and her shoulder twitched. Cleo wasn't going to go do any kneeling.

'Who's on the council?' I asked the dark-haired vamp, and she nodded to the group of five vampires seated right before the low stage, facing the Ancient Pythoness.

'The King of Kentucky, the Queen of Iowa, the King of Wisconsin, the King of Missouri, the Queen of Alabama,' she said, pointing to them in order. The only one I'd met was Kentucky, though I recognized the sultry Alabama from her conversation with Sophie-Anne.

The lawyer for the other side joined Johan Glassport on the stage. Something about the Arkansans' lawyer reminded me of Mr Cataliades, and when he nodded in our direction, I saw Mr Cataliades nod back.

'They related?' I asked Cleo.

'Brothers-in-law,' Cleo said, leaving me to imagine what a female demon would look like. Surely they didn't all look like Diantha.

Quinn leaped up on the stage. He was wearing a gray suit, white shirt, and tie, and he carried a long staff covered with carvings. He beckoned to Isaiah, King of Kentucky, who floated onto the stage. With a flourish, Quinn handed the staff to Kentucky, who was dressed much more stylishly than he had been earlier. The vampire thudded the staff against the floor, and all conversation ceased. Quinn retreated to the back of the stage.

'I am the elected master-at-arms of this judicial session,' Kentucky announced in a voice that carried easily to the corners of the room. He held the staff up so it could not be ignored. 'Following the traditions of the vampire race, I call you all to witness the trial of Sophie-Anne Leclerq, Queen of Louisiana, on the charge that she murdered her signed and sealed spouse, Peter Threadgill, King of Arkansas.'

It sounded very solemn, in Kentucky's deep, drawling voice.

'I call the lawyers for the two parties to be ready to present their cases.'

'I am ready,' said the part-demon lawyer. 'I am Simon Maimonides, and I represent the bereaved state of Arkansas.'

'I am ready,' said our murderous lawyer, reading from a pamphlet. 'I am Johan Glassport, and I represent the bereaved widow, Sophie-Anne Leclerq, *falsely* charged with the murder of her signed and sealed spouse.'

'Ancient Pythoness, are you ready to hear the case?' Kentucky asked, and the crone turned her head toward him.

'Is she blind?' I whispered.

Cleo nodded. 'From birth,' she said.

'How come she's the judge?' I asked. But the glares of the vampires around us reminded me that their hearing hardly made whispering worthwhile, and it was only polite to shut up.

'Yes,' said the Ancient Pythoness. 'I am ready to hear the case.' She had a very heavy accent that I couldn't begin to identify. There was a stirring of anticipation in the crowd.

Okay. Let the games begin.

Bill, Eric, and Pam went to stand against the wall, while Andre sat by me.

King Isaiah did a little staff-pounding again. 'Let the accused be brought forth,' he said with no small amount of drama.

Sophie-Anne, looking very delicate, walked up to the stage, escorted by two guards. Like the rest of us, she'd gotten ready for the ball, and she was wearing purple. I wondered if the royal color had been a coincidence. Probably not. I had a feeling Sophie-Anne arranged her own coincidences.

The dress was high-collared and long-sleeved, and it actually had a train.

'She is beautiful,' said Andre, his voice full of reverence.

Yeah, yeah, yeah. I had more on my mind than admiring the queen. The guards were the two Britlingens, probably pressed into service by Isaiah, and they had packed some dress armor in their interdimensional trunks. It was black, too, but it gleamed dully, like slowly moving dark water. It was just as figure-hugging as the first set of armor. Clovache and Batanya lifted Sophie-Anne onto the low platform and then retreated a bit. This way, they were close to both the prisoner and their employer, so it worked out great, I suppose, from their point of view.

'Henrik Feith, state your case,' Isaiah said with no further ado.

Henrik's case was long and ardent and full of accusations. Boiled down, he testified that Sophie-Anne had married his king, signed all the usual contracts, and then immediately began maneuvering Peter into his fatal fight, despite the king's angelic temperament and his adoration of his new queen. It sounded like Henrik was talking about Kevin and Britney, rather than two ancient and crafty vampires.

Blah blah blah. Henrik's lawyer let him go on and on, and Johan did not object to any of Henrik's highly colored statements. Johan thought (I checked) that Henrik would lose sympathy by being so fervent and immoderate – and boring – and he was quite right, if the slight movements and shifts in body language in the crowd were anything to go by.

'And now,' Henrik concluded, faint pink tears running down his face, 'there are only a handful of us left in the whole state. She, who killed my king and his lieutenant Jennifer, she has offered me a place with her. And I was almost weak enough to accept, for fear of being rogue. But she is a liar and she will kill me, too.'

'Someone told him that,' I murmured.

'What?' Andre's mouth was right by my ear. Keeping a conversation private in a group of vampires is not an easy thing.

I held up a hand to request his silence. No, I wasn't listening to Henrik's brain but to Henrik's lawyer's, who didn't have as much demon blood as Cataliades. Without realizing I was doing it, I was leaning forward in my seat and craning toward the stage to hear better. Hear with my head, that is.

Someone had told Henrik Feith that the queen planned to kill him. He had been willing to let the lawsuit slide, since Jennifer Cater's murder had taken out the chief complainant. He had never rated high enough in the ranks to take up the mantle of leadership; he didn't have the wit or the desire. He would rather go into the service of the queen. But if she really meant to kill him . . . he would try to kill her first by the only means he might survive, and that was through the law.

'She doesn't want to kill you,' I called, hardly knowing what I was doing.

I wasn't even aware I'd gotten to my feet until I felt the eyes of everyone in the audience on me. Henrik Feith was staring at me, his face stunned, his mouth still open. 'Tell us who told you that, and we'll know who killed Jennifer Cater, because—'

'Woman,' said a stentorian voice, and I was drowned out and shut up very effectively. 'Be silent. Who are you and what right do you have to intrude on these solemn proceedings?' The Pythoness was surprisingly forceful for someone as frail as she appeared. She was leaning forward on her throne, glaring in my direction with her blind eyes.

Okay, standing in a roomful of vampires and interrupting their ritual was a pretty good way to get bloodstains all over my beautiful new dress.

'I don't have any right in the world, Your Majesty,' I said, and from a few yards to my left, I heard Pam snicker. 'But I know the truth.'

'Oh, then I have no role in these proceedings, do I?' croaked the Ancient Pythoness in her heavily accented English. 'Why should I have come forth from my cave to give judgment?'

Why, indeed.

'I may hear the truth, but I don't have the juice to get justice done,' I said honestly.

Pam snickered again. I just knew it was her.

Eric had been standing to the side of the room with Pam and Bill, but now he moved forward. I could feel his presence, cold and steady, very near to me. He gave me some courage. I don't know how. I felt it, though, felt a rising strength where there had been only my shaking knees. A shocking suspicion hit me with the force of a Mack truck. Eric had given me enough blood now that I qualified, hemoglobin-wise, as being close to a vampire; and my strange gift had slopped over into fatal territory. I wasn't reading Henrik's lawyer's mind. I was reading *Henrik's*.

'Then come tell me what I must do,' said the Ancient Pythoness with a sarcasm so sharp it could have sliced a meat loaf.

I needed a week or two to get over the shock of my terrible suspicion, and I had a renewed conviction that I really ought to kill Andre, and maybe Eric, too, even if a corner of my heart would weep for the loss.

I had all of twenty seconds to process this.

Cleo gave me a sharp pinch. 'Cow,' she said furiously. 'You will ruin everything.' I edged left out of the row, stepping over Gervaise as I did so. I ignored his glare and Cleo's pinch. The two were fleas compared to the other powers that might want a piece of me first. And Eric stepped up behind me. My back was covered.

As I moved closer to the platform, it was hard to tell what Sophie-Anne was thinking of this new turn in her unexpected trial. I concentrated on Henrik and his lawyer.

'Henrik thinks that the queen decided to have him killed. He was told that, so he would testify against her in self-defense,' I said.

Now I was behind the judges' chairs on the floor, with Eric by my side.

'The queen didn't decide to have me killed?' Henrik said, looking hopeful, confused, and betrayed all at the same time. That was a tall order for a vampire, since facial expressions are not their foremost means of communication.

'No, she didn't. She was sincere in offering you a place.' I kept my eyes fixed on his, trying to drill my sincerity into his frightened brain. I'd moved almost squarely in front of him now.

'You're probably lying, too. You're in her pay, after all.'

'Perhaps I might have a word?' the Ancient Pythoness said, with acid sarcasm.

Oops. There was a silence that was just chilling.

'Are you a seer?' she asked, speaking very slowly so that I could understand her.

'No, ma'am, I'm a telepath.' This close, the Ancient Pythoness looked even older, which I wouldn't have thought possible.

'You can read minds? Vampire minds?'

'No, ma'am, those are the only ones I can't read,' I said very firmly. 'I pieced all this together from the lawyer's thoughts.'

Mr Maimonides was not happy about that.

'All this was known to you?' the Ancient P. asked the lawyer.

'Yes,' he said. 'I did know that Mr Feith felt he was threatened with death.'

'And you knew the queen had offered to accept him into her service?'

'Yes, he told me she said so.' That was said in so doubtful a tone that you didn't have to be an A.P. to read between the lines.

'And you did not believe the word of a vampire queen?'

Okay, that was a stumper for Maimonides. 'I felt it my duty to protect my client, Ancient Pythoness.' He struck just the right note of humble dignity.

'Hmmm,' said the A.P., sounding as skeptical as I felt. 'Sophie-Anne Leclerq, it is your turn to present your side of the story. Will you proceed?'

Sophie-Anne said, 'What Sookie has said is true. I offered Henrik a place with me and protection. When we get to call witnesses, Ancient One, you will hear that Sookie is my witness and was there during the final fight between Peter's people and mine. Though I knew that Peter married me with a secret agenda, I didn't lift a hand against him until his people attacked on the night of our celebratory feast. Due to many circumstances, he didn't get to pick his best moment to go after me, and as a result, his people died and most of mine lived. He actually began the attack when there were others there not of our blood.' Sophie-Anne managed to look shocked and saddened. 'It has taken me all these months to be sure the accounts were hushed.'

I thought I'd gotten most of the humans and Weres out before the slaughter started, but apparently there'd been some around.

Probably they weren't 'around' anymore.

'In the time since that night, you have suffered many other losses,' the Ancient Pythoness observed. This sounded quite sympathetic.

I began to sense that the deck had been stacked in Sophie-Anne's favor. Was it significant that Kentucky, who'd been courting Sophie-Anne, was the council member in charge of the proceedings?

'As you say, I've had many losses – both in terms of my people and in terms of my income,' Sophie-Anne agreed. 'This is why I need my inheritance from my husband, to which I'm entitled as part of our marriage covenant. He thought he would inherit the rich kingdom of Louisiana. Now I will be glad if I can get the poor one of Arkansas.'

There was a long silence.

'Shall I call our witness?' Johan Glassport said. He sounded very hesitant and uncertain, for a lawyer. But in this courtroom, it wasn't hard to understand why. 'She's already right here, and she was witness to Peter's death.' He held out his hand to me, and I had to mount the platform. Sophie-Anne looked relaxed, but Henrik Feith, a few inches to my left, was gripping the arms of his chair.

Another silence. The wild white hair of the ancient vampire hung forward to hide her face as she stared at her own lap. Then she looked up, and her sightless eyes went unerringly to Sophie-Anne. 'Arkansas is yours by law, and now yours by right. I declare you innocent of conspiring to murder your husband,' the Ancient Pythoness said, almost casually.

Well . . . *yippee.* I was close enough to see that Sophie-Anne's eyes widened with relief and surprise, and Johan Glassport gave a private little grin to his lectern. Simon Maimonides looked down at the five judges to see how they'd take the A.P.'s pronouncement, and when none of them voiced a word of protest, the lawyer shrugged.

'Now, Henrik,' croaked the Ancient Pythoness, 'your safety is assured. Who has told you lies?'

Henrik hardly looked assured. He looked scared witless. He rose to his feet to stand by me.

Henrik was smarter than we were. There was a flash through the air.

The next time an expression crossed his face, it was utter horror. He looked down, and we all followed his eyes. There was a thin wooden shaft protruding from his chest, and as soon as his eyes identified it, Henrik's hand rose to touch it, and he swayed. A human crowd would have erupted in chaos, but the vampires threw themselves on the floor in near silence. The only person who shrieked was the blind Ancient Pythoness, who demanded to know what had happened and why everyone was so tense. The two Britlingens leaped across the stage to Kentucky and stood in front of him, their weapons in their hands and ready. Andre literally flew out of his seat in the audience to land in front of Sophie-Anne. And Quinn leaped across the stage to knock me down, and he took the second arrow, the insurance arrow, that was meant for Henrik. It was quite unnecessary. Henrik was dead when he hit the floor.

Chapter 14

Batanya killed the assassin with a throwing star. She was facing the crowd, so she saw the vampire left standing after all the others had prudently hit the floor. This vampire wasn't firing the arrows from a bow; he was *throwing* them, which was why he'd managed to remain inconspicuous. Even in that group, someone carrying in a bow would have attracted a certain amount of attention.

Only a vampire could throw an arrow and kill someone. Perhaps only a Britlingen could throw a razor-sharp star in such a way as to decapitate a vampire.

I've seen vampires decapitated before, and it's not as messy as you'd think; not like cutting off the head of a human. But it's not pleasant, either, and as I watched the head topple off the shoulders, I had a moment of knee-knocking nausea from my position on the floor. I scrambled to my knees to check on Quinn.

'I'm not bad,' he said instantly. 'Not bad. It's in my shoulder, not my heart.' He rolled over to lie on his back. The Louisiana vamps had all leaped up to the platform to circle the queen, just a second behind Andre. Once they were sure the threat was over, they clustered around us.

Cleo threw off her tuxedo jacket and ripped off the pleated white shirt. She folded it into a pad in movements so fast I could hardly follow them. 'Hold this,' she said, pressing it into my hand and placing my hand close to the wound. 'Prepare to press hard.' She didn't wait for me to nod. 'Hold on,' she said to Quinn. And she put her strong hands on his shoulders to hold him still while Gervaise pulled the arrow out.

Quinn bellowed, not too surprisingly. The next few minutes were pretty bad. I pressed the pad against the wound, and while Cleo pulled on the tuxedo jacket over her black lace bra, she directed Herve, her human squeeze, to donate his shirt, too. I've got to say, he whipped it right off. There was something really shocking about seeing a bare hairy chest in the middle of all this evening finery. And it was beyond weird that I would note that, after I'd just seen a guy's head separated from his body.

I knew Eric was beside me before he spoke, because I felt less terrified. He knelt down to my level. Quinn was concentrating on not yelling, so his eyes were shut as though he was unconscious and there was still lots of action going on all around me. But Eric was next to me, and I felt . . . not exactly calm, but not as upset. Because he was there.

I just hated that.

'He's going to heal,' Eric said. He didn't sound especially happy about it, but not sad, either.

'Yes,' I said.

'I know. I didn't see it coming.'

'Oh, would you have flung yourself in front of me?'

'No,' Eric said simply. 'Because it might have hit me in the heart, and I would die. But I would have dived in and tackled you to take you out of the arrow's path if there had been time.'

I couldn't think of a thing to say.

'I know you may come to hate me because I spared you the bite of Andre,' he said quietly. 'But I really am the lesser of two evils.'

I glanced sideways at him. 'I know that,' I said, Quinn's blood staining my hands as it soaked through the makeshift pad. 'I wouldn't have rather died than get bit by Andre, but it was a close thing.'

He laughed, and Quinn's eyes flickered. 'The weretiger is regaining consciousness,' Eric said. 'Do you love him?'

'Don't know yet.'

'Did you love me?'

A team of stretcher bearers came over. Of course, these weren't regular paramedics. Regular paramedics wouldn't have been welcome in the Pyramid of Gizeh. These were Weres and shifters who worked for the vamps, and their leader, a young woman who looked like a honey bear, said, 'We'll make sure he gets healed in record time, lady.'

'I'll check on him later.'

'We'll take care of him,' she said. 'Among us, he'll do better. It's a privilege to take care of Quinn.'

Quinn nodded. 'I'm ready to be moved,' he said, but he was clenching the words between his teeth.

'See you later,' I said, taking his hand in mine. 'You're the bravest of the brave, Quinn.'

'Babe,' he said, biting his lower lip from the pain. 'Be careful.'

'Don't you be worrying about her,' said a black guy with a short, clipped Afro. 'She's got guardians.' He gave Eric a cool look. Eric held out his hand and I took it to stand up. My knees were aching a little after their acquaintance with the hard floor.

As they got him onto the stretcher and lifted him, Quinn seemed to lose consciousness. I started forward, but the black guy held out his arm. It looked like carved ebony, the muscles were so defined. 'Sister, you just stay here,' he said. 'We're on the job now.'

I watched them carry him off. Once he was out of sight, I looked down at my dress. Amazingly, it was all right. Not dirty, not bloody, and the wrinkles were at a minimum.

Eric waited.

'Did I love you?' I knew Eric wasn't going to give up, and I might as well figure out an answer. 'Maybe. Sort of. But I knew all along that whoever was with me, it wasn't the real you. And I knew sooner or later you'd remember who you were and what you were.'

'You don't seem to have yes or no answers about men,' he said.

'You don't exactly seem to know how you feel about me, either,' I said.

'You're a mystery,' he said. 'Who was your mother, and who was your father? Oh, I know, you'll say they raised you from a child and died when you were a little girl. I remember you telling me the story. But I don't know if it's exactly true. If it is, when did the fairy blood enter your family tree? Did it come in with one of your grandparents? That's what I'm supposing.'

'And what business is it of yours?'

'You know it is my business. Now we are tied.'

'Is this going to fade? It will, right? We won't always be like this?'

'I like being like this. You'll like it, too,' he said, and he seemed mighty damn sure.

'Who was the vampire who tried to kill us?' I asked, to change the subject. I was hoping he wasn't right, and anyway, we'd said everything there was to say on the subject, as far as I was concerned.

'Let's go find out,' he said, and took my hand. I trailed along with him, simply because I wanted to know.

Batanya was standing by the vampire's body, which had begun the rapid disintegration of its kind. She'd retrieved her throwing star, and she was polishing it on her pants leg.

'Good throw,' Eric said. 'Who was he?'

She shrugged. 'I dunno. The guy with the arrows, was all I know. All I care.'

'He was the only one?'

'Yes.'

'Can you tell me what he looked like?'

'I was sitting next to him,' said a very small male vampire. He was perhaps five feet tall, and slim besides. His hair trailed down his back. If he went to jail, he'd have guys knocking on his cell door within thirty minutes. They'd be sorry, of course, but to the unobservant eye, he did look like the world's easiest target. 'He was a rough one, and not dressed for the evening. Khakis and a striped dress shirt ... well, you can see.'

Though the body was blackening and flaking away as vamp corpses did, naturally the clothes were intact.

'Maybe he had a driver's license?' I suggested. That was almost a given with humans, but not with vampires. However, it was worth a shot.

Eric squatted and inserted his fingers into the man's front pocket.

Nothing came out, or from the other front pocket, so without further ado Eric rolled him over. I took a couple of steps back to avoid the flurry of flakes of ash. There was something in the rear pocket: a regular wallet. And inside it, sure enough, was a driver's license.

It had been issued by Illinois. Under blood type was the designation 'NA.' Yep, a vamp, for sure. Reading over Eric's shoulder, I could see that the vamp's name had been Kyle Perkins. Perkins had put '3V' as his age, so he had been a vamp for only three years.

'He must have been an archer before he died,' I said. 'Because that's not a skill you'd pick up right away, especially that young.'

'I agree,' Eric said. 'And in the daytime, I want you to check all the local places you can practice archery. Throwing arrows is not a skill you can improvise. He trained. The arrow was specially made. We need to find out what happened to Kyle Perkins, and why this rogue accepted the job to attend this meeting and kill whomever necessary.'

'So he was a . . . vampire hit man?'

'Yes, I think so,' Eric said. 'Someone is maneuvering us very carefully. Of course, this Perkins was simply backup in case the trial went wrong. And if it hadn't been for you, the trial might well have gone wrong. Someone went to a lot of trouble to play on Henrik Feith's fears, and stupid Henrik was about to give that someone up. This Kyle, he was planted to prevent just that.'

Then the cleanup crew arrived: a group of vampires with a body bag and cleaning supplies. The human maids would not be asked to mop up Kyle. Luckily, they were all occupied in refreshing the vampire rooms, which were off-limits to them during the day.

In very short order, the residue of Kyle Perkins was bagged up and taken away, with one vampire remaining behind to wield a little handheld vacuum. Let Rhodes CSI try to get ahold of *that*.

I sensed a lot of movement and looked up to see that the service doors were open and staff was pouring into the large room to pack away the chairs. In less than fifteen minutes, Quinn's judicial paraphernalia was being stored away, his sister directing the work. Then a band set up on the platform, and the room was cleared for dancing. I'd never seen anything like it. First a trial, then a few murders, then dancing. Life goes on. Or, in this case, death continues.

Eric said, 'You had better check in with the queen.'

'Oh. Yeah, she might have a few words to say to me.' I glanced around and spotted Sophie-Anne pretty quickly. She was surrounded by a crowd of people congratulating her on the favorable verdict. Of course, they would have been just as glad to see her executed, or whatever would have happened if the Ancient Pythoness had turned thumbs down. Speaking of the A.P. . . .

'Eric, where'd the old gal go?' I asked.

'The Ancient Pythoness is the original oracle that Alexander consulted,' he said, his voice quite neutral. 'She was considered so revered that even in her old age, she was converted by the very primitive vampires of her time. And now she has outlasted all of them.'

I didn't want to think about how she'd fed before the advent of the synthetic blood that had changed the vampire world. How'd she hobble after her human prey? Maybe they'd brought people to her, like snake owners bring live mice to their pets?

'To answer your question, I would guess her handmaidens have removed her to her suite. She is brought out for special occasions.'

'Like the good silver,' I said seriously, and then burst into giggles. To my surprise, Eric smiled, too, that big smile that made multiple little arcs appear in the corners of his mouth.

We took our places behind the queen. I wasn't sure she'd even registered my presence, she was so busy being the belle of the ball. But in a momentary lull in the chitchat, she reached behind her and took my hand, squeezing it very lightly. 'We'll talk later,' she said, and then greeted a stout female vampire in a sequined pantsuit. 'Maude,' Sophie-Anne said, 'how good to see you. And how are things going in Minnesota?'

Just then a tap on the music stand drew everyone's attention to the band. It was all vampire, I noticed with a start. The slick-haired guy at the podium said, 'If all you hot vamps and vampesses are ready to rumble, we're ready to play! I'm Rick Clark, and this is . . . the Dead Man Dance Band!'

There was a polite smattering of applause.

'Here to open the evening are two of Rhodes's finest dancers, courtesy of Blue Moon Productions. Please welcome . . . Sean and Layla!'

The pair who stepped out into the middle of the dance floor were striking, whether you were human or vamp. They were both of the cold-blooded variety themselves, though he was very old and she was freshly turned, I thought. She was one of the most beautiful women I'd ever seen, and she was wearing a beige lace dress that drifted around her world-class legs like snow falling around trees. Her partner was maybe the only vampire I'd ever seen with freckles, and his dusty red hair was as long as hers.

They only had eyes for each other, and they danced together as if they were gliding through a dream.

I had never seen anything like it, and from the rapt attention of the audience, no one else had, either. As the music drew to a conclusion – and to this day, I can't remember what they danced to – Sean flung Layla back over his arm, bent over her, and bit. I was shocked, but the others seemed to expect it, and it turned them on no little amount. Sophie-Anne smoldered up at Andre (though she didn't have far to smolder, since he wasn't much taller than she), and Eric looked down at me with that hot light in his eyes that made me wary.

I turned my attention to the dance floor with determination and clapped like a maniac when the two took their bow and more couples began to join them as the music started up again. From habit I looked around for Bill, who was nowhere to be seen.

Then Eric said, 'Let's dance,' and I found I couldn't say no.

We took the floor along with the queen and her potential king, and I saw Russell Edgington and his husband, Bart, step out to dance, too. They looked almost as enthralled with each other as the two exhibition dancers.

I can't sing, but by golly, I can dance. And Eric had had a few ballroom lessons along the way, some century or other. My hand rested on his back, his on mine, our free hands clasped, and off we went. I wasn't sure exactly what the dance was, but he was a strong leader, so it was easy to follow along. More like the waltz than anything else, I decided.

'Pretty dress,' said the dancer Layla as we swung by them.

'Thank you,' I said, and beamed at her. From someone as lovely as she was, that was a great compliment. Then her partner leaned over to give her a kiss, and they swirled away into the crowd.

'That *is* a pretty dress,' Eric said. 'And you are a beautiful woman.'

I was oddly embarrassed. I'd gotten compliments before – you can't be a barmaid and not get compliments – but most of them had consisted of (various degrees of drunk) guys telling me I was really cute – or, in one man's case, how impressive my 'rack' was. (Somehow, JB du Rone and Hoyt Fortenberry had managed to stomp on that guy's toes and spill a drink all over him at the same time, just accidentally.)

'Eric,' I said, but I couldn't finish the sentence because I couldn't think of what to say next. I had to concentrate on the speed with which my feet were moving. We were dancing so fast I felt like I was flying. Suddenly Eric dropped my hand to grip my waist, and as we turned, he swung me up, and then I was really flying, with a little help from a Viking. I laughed like a loon, my hair billowing out around my head, and then he let me go and caught me, just inches away from the floor, and then he did it again and again, until at last I was standing on the floor and the music was over.

'Thank you,' I said, knowing I must look like I'd been standing in a high gale. 'Excuse me while I go to the ladies' room.'

I scooted off through the crowd, trying not to grin like an idiot. I should be with – oh, yeah – *my boyfriend*. Instead of dancing with another guy until I felt tingly with happiness. And it didn't do any good, excusing myself on account of our blood tie.

Sophie-Anne and Andre had stopped dancing, and they were standing with a group of other vampires. She couldn't need me, then, since there were no humans for me to 'listen' to. I spotted Carla dancing with Gervaise, and they seemed happy enough. Carla was getting lots of admiring looks from other vampires, and that would make Gervaise swell with pride. Having his fellow vampires craving what he was already getting was sweet.

I knew how Gervaise felt.

I stopped in my tracks.

Had I . . . I wasn't really reading his mind, was I? No, I couldn't. The only times I'd caught a fragment of vampire thought prior to tonight, that fragment had felt cold and snaky.

But I knew how Gervaise felt, for sure, just as I'd read Henrik's thoughts. Was it just my knowledge of men and their reactions or my knowledge of vampires, or could I really follow vampire emotions better since I'd had Eric's blood for a third time? Or had my skill, or my talent, or my curse – whatever I called it – broadened to include vampires since I was closer to being one myself?

No. No, no, no. I felt like myself. I felt human. I felt warm. I was breathing. I had to use the bathroom. I was hungry, too. I thought about old Mrs Bellefleur's famous chocolate cake. My mouth watered. Yep, human.

Okay, then, this new affinity for vamps would fade, like my extra strength would fade, in time. I'd had two drinks from Bill, I thought; maybe more. And three from Eric. And every time I'd had their blood, two or three months had seen the waning of the strength and acuity I'd gained from the intake. So that would happen this time, too, right? I shook myself briskly. Sure, it would.

Jake Purifoy was leaning against the wall, watching the couples dance. I'd glimpsed him earlier steering a young vampire woman around the floor, and she'd been laughing. So it wasn't all melancholy for Jake, and I was glad.

'Hey,' I said.

'Sookie, that was quite some action at the trial.'

'Yeah, it was scary.'

'Where'd that guy come from?'

'Rogue, I guess. Eric's got me looking at archery ranges tomorrow to track him down, try to find out who hired him.'

'Good. That was a close call for you. I'm sorry,' he said awkwardly. 'I know you must have been frightened.'

I'd really been too worried about Quinn to think about the arrow being aimed at me. 'I guess I was. You have a good time, now.'

'Something's got to make up for not being able to change anymore,' Jake said.

'I didn't know you'd tried.' I couldn't think of anything else to say.

'Over and over,' he said. We looked at each other for a long, long moment. 'Well, I'm off to find another partner,' he told me, and headed purposefully in the direction of a vampire who'd come with Stan Davis's group from Texas. She looked glad to see him coming.

By that time I was ducking into the ladies' room, which was small, of course; most of the females at the Pyramid of Gizeh wouldn't need to use such a facility, except to comb their hair. There was an attendant, a nicety I'd never seen before though I'd read about it in books. I was supposed to tip her. I still had my little evening purse with my room key in it, and I was relieved to recall I'd slipped a few dollars in there, along with some tissues and breath mints and a tiny brush. I nodded to the attendant, a squatty, dark-skinned woman with an unhappy face.

I took care of business in the nice clean stall and then emerged to wash my hands and to try to smooth out my hair. The attendant, wearing a name tag that read 'Lena', turned on the water for me, which kind of weirded me out. I mean, I can turn a faucet. But I washed my hands and used the towel she extended to me, figuring this was the routine and I shouldn't act ignorant. I dropped two dollars in the tip bowl, and she tried to smile at me, but she looked too unhappy to manage it. She must be having a bad night.

'Thanks,' I said, and turned to leave. I don't know why, but I glanced into the mirror on the inside of the door before I pulled on the handle. There Lena was, staring a hole into my back. She'd looked so unhappy because she'd been having to suppress how much she loathed me.

That's always a bad feeling, when you know someone hates you; especially when it's for no good reason. But her problems were not mine, and if she didn't want to turn on the faucet for women who dated vampires, she could find another job. I didn't want her damn faucet-turning-on, anyway, by God.

So I forged my way through the crowd, checking with the queen to see if she had any humans around who needed scanning (no), checking to see if I could find a Were or shifter to give me an update on Quinn (no).

By a stroke of luck, I did find the weather witch, the male witch I'd spotted earlier. I confess it made me a little proud to find my conjecture had actually been right. His being here tonight was his reward for good service, though I couldn't detect who his patron was. The weather witch had a drink in his hand and a middle-aged woman on his arm. Mrs Witch, I discovered with another quick dip into his mental pool. He was hoping she hadn't observed that he was very interested in the beautiful vampire dancer and the pretty blond human coming toward him, the one who'd looked at him earlier like she knew him. Oh . . . that would be me.

I couldn't pick up his name, which would have greased the skids, and I didn't know what to say to him. But this was a person who should be brought to Sophie-Anne's attention. Someone had used him against her.

'Hello,' I said, giving them my biggest smile. The wife smiled back, a little cautiously, because the sedate couple weren't normally approached by young single women (she'd glanced at my left hand) during glamorous parties. The weather witch's smile was more on the frightened side. 'Are you all enjoying the party?' I asked.

'Yes, quite an evening,' the wife said.

'My name is Sookie Stackhouse,' I said, oozing charm.

'Olive Trout,' she replied, and we shook hands. 'This is my husband, Julian.' She had no idea what her husband was.

'Are you all from around here?' I was scanning the crowd as unobtrusively as possible. I had no idea what to do with them now that I'd found them.

'You haven't watched our local stations,' Olive said proudly. 'Julian is the Channel 7 weatherman.'

'How interesting,' I said, with absolute sincerity. 'If you two would just come with me, I know someone who'd just love to meet you.' As I dragged the two through the crowd, I began to have second thoughts. What if Sophie-Anne intended retribution? But that wouldn't make sense. The important fact was not that there *was* a weather witch; the important fact was that someone had hired Julian Trout to predict the weather outlook for Louisiana and had somehow postponed the summit until Katrina had wreaked its havoc.

Julian was bright enough to figure out something was wrong with my enthusiasm, and I was afraid they'd both balk. I was mighty relieved to spot Gervaise's blond head. I called his name in a hearty voice as if I hadn't talked to him in a coon's age. By the time I reached him I was almost out of breath from herding the Trouts with such speed and anxiety.

'Gervaise, Carla,' I said, depositing the Trouts in front of the sheriff as if I'd drug them out of the water. 'This is Olive Trout and her husband, Julian. The queen's been anxious to meet someone like Julian. He's *really into the weather.*' Okay, not subtle. But Julian's face turned white. Yeah, a little knowledge of wrongdoing definitely present in Julian's conscience.

'Honey, are you sick?' Olive asked.

'We need to go home,' he said.

'No, no, no,' Carla said, leaping into the conversation. 'Gervaise, honey, you remember Andre said if we heard of anyone who was really a weather authority, he and the queen especially wanted to have a word with 'em?' She tucked her arms around the Trouts and beamed at them. Olive looked uncertain.

'Of course,' said Gervaise, the lightbulb finally switching on above his head. 'Thank you, Sookie. Please, come with us.' And they guided the Trouts away.

I felt a little giddy with the pleasure of having been proved right.

Looking around, I spotted Barry sticking a little plate on an empty tray.

'You wanna dance?' I asked, because the Dead Man Dance Band was playing a great cover of an old Jennifer Lopez song. Barry looked reluctant, but I pulled him by his hand, and pretty soon we were shaking our bonbons all over the place and having a great time. Nothing's like dancing for relaxing tension and losing yourself, just for a little while. I wasn't as good as Shakira at muscle control, but maybe if I practiced once in a while . . .

'What are you doing?' Eric asked, and he wasn't being facetious. He was glacial with disapproval.

'Dancing, why?' I gave a wave to signal Eric to scoot. But Barry had stopped, already, and given me a little goodbye wave.

'I was having a good time,' I protested.

'You were twitching your assets in front of every male in the room,' he said. 'Like a . . .'

'You hold up, buddy! You stop right there!' I held up a finger, warning him.

'Take your finger out of my face,' he said.

I inhaled to say something unforgivable, welcoming the tide of anger with actual delight – I was *not* tied to him at the waist – when a strong, wiry arm clamped around me, and an unfamiliar Irish-accented voice said, 'Dance, darling?' As the red-haired dancer who'd opened the night's shindig swung me off in a more sedate but complicated set of steps, I spotted his partner seizing Eric's wrist to do the same.

'Just follow while you calm down, girl. I'm Sean.'

'Sookie.'

'Pleased to meet you, young woman. You're a fine dancer.'

'Thank you. That's a high compliment, coming from you. I really enjoyed your routine earlier.' I could feel the rush of anger draining away.

'It's my partner,' he said, smiling. It didn't look easy for him, that smile, but it transformed him from a thin-faced freckled man with a blade of a nose to a man with sexiness to spare. 'My Layla is a dream to dance with.'

'She's very beautiful.'

'Oh, yes, inside and out.'

'How long have you been partners?'

'In dancing, two years. In life, over a year.'

'From your accent, I guess you came here in a roundabout way.' I glimpsed Eric and the beautiful Layla. Layla had an easy smile on her lips, and she was talking to Eric, who was still looking sort of grim. But not angry.

'You could say so,' he agreed. 'Of course, I'm from Ireland, but I've been over here for . . .' His brow furrowed in thought, and it was like watching marble ripple. 'Been here for a hundred years, anyway. From time to time, we think about moving back to Tennessee, where Layla's from, but we haven't made up our minds.'

This was a lot of conversation from a quiet-looking guy. 'You're just getting tired of living in the city?'

'Too much anti-vampire stuff going around lately. The Fellowship of the Sun, the Take the Night from the Dead movement: we seem to breed 'em here.'

'The Fellowship is everywhere,' I said. The very name made me feel gloomy. 'And what'll happen when they get to hear about Weres?'

'Aye. And I think that'll be soon. I keep hearing from Weres that it's just around the corner.'

You'd think, that out of all the supes I knew, one of them would let me know what was up. Sooner or later the Weres and the shifters would have to let the world in on their big secret, or they'd get outed by the vampires, either intentionally or unintentionally.

'There might even be a civil war,' Sean said, and I forced my mind back to the topic at hand.

'Between the Fellowship and the supers?'

He nodded. 'I'm thinking that could happen.'

'What would you do in that case?'

'I've been through a few wars, and I don't want to go through another one,' he said promptly. 'Layla hasn't seen the Old World, and she would enjoy it, so we'd go to England. We could dance there, or we could just find a place to hide out.'

As interesting as this was, it wasn't getting me any closer to solving the numerous problems facing me right at the moment, which I could count off on my fingers. Who had paid Julian Trout? Who had planted the Dr Pepper bomb? Who had killed the rest of the Arkansas vampires? Was it the same person who'd had Henrik killed, the employer of the rogue vamp?

'What was the result?' I said out loud, to the red-haired vamp's confusion.

'I beg your pardon?'

'Just talking to myself. It's been a pleasure to dance with you. Excuse me; I have to go find a friend.'

Sean danced me to the edge of the crowd, and we parted ways. He was already looking for his mate. Vampire couples didn't stay together for long, as a rule. Even the hundred-year marriages of kings and queens required only a once-a-year nuptial visit. I hoped Sean and Layla would prove to be the exception.

I decided I should check on Quinn. That might be a lengthy process, since I had no idea where the Weres had taken him. I was so confused by the effect Eric was having on me, all mixed up with the beginnings of affection for Quinn. But I knew whom I was beholden to. Quinn had saved my life tonight. I started my search by calling his room but got no answer.

If I was a Were, where would I take a wounded tiger? Well, nowhere public, because Weres were secretive. They wouldn't want the hotel staff to catch a word or a phrase that would tip them off to the existence of the other supes. So they'd take Quinn to a private room, right? So, who had a private room and was sympathetic to the Weres?

Jake Purifoy, of course – former Were, current vamp. Quinn could be there – or he could be down in the hotel garage somewhere, or in the security chief's room, or in the infirmary, if there was such a thing. I had to start somewhere. I inquired at the front desk, where the clerk didn't seem to have any problem releasing the room number to me, though it's true Jake and I were flagged as being members of the same party. The clerk was not the one who'd been so rude when we'd checked in. She thought my dress was very pretty, and she wanted one just like it.

Jake's room was a floor up from mine, and as I raised my hand to knock on the door, I casually scanned inside to count the brains. There was the hole in the air that marked a vampire brain (that's the best way I can describe it), and a couple of human signatures. But I picked up on a thought that froze my fist before it had a chance to touch the door.

. . . *they should all die*, came the faint fragment of thought. Nothing followed it, though – no other thought that clarified or elaborated on that malign idea. So I knocked, and the pattern in the room changed instantly. Jake answered the door. He didn't look welcoming.

'Hi, Jake,' I said, making my smile as bright and innocent as I could. 'How you doing? I came by to check if Quinn was with you.'

'With me?' Jake sounded startled. 'Since I turned, I've hardly talked to Quinn, Sookie. We just don't have anything to talk about.' I must have looked disbelieving, because he said in a rush, 'Oh, it's not Quinn; it's me. I just can't bridge the chasm between who I was and who I am now. I'm not even sure who I am.' His shoulders slumped.

That sounded honest enough. And I felt a lot of sympathy for him. 'Anyway,' Jake said, 'I helped carry him to the infirmary, and I bet he's still there. There's a shifter called Bettina and a Were called Hondo with him.'

Jake was holding the door shut. He didn't want me to see his companions. Jake didn't know that I could tell that he had people in his room.

It wasn't any of my business, of course. But it was disquieting. Even as I thanked him and turned to leave, I was thinking the situation over. The last thing in the world I wanted to do was to cause the troubled Jake any more problems, but if he was somehow involved in the plot that seemed to be snaking through the halls of the Pyramid of Gizeh, I had to find out.

First things first. I went down to my room and called the desk to get directions to the infirmary, and I carefully wrote them on the phone pad. Then I sneaked back up the stairs to stand outside Jake's door again, but in the time I'd been gone, the party had begun to disperse. I saw two humans from the rear. Strange; I couldn't be certain, but one of them looked like the surly Joe, the computer-consulting employee from the luggage area. Jake had been meeting with some of the hotel staff in his room. Maybe he still felt more at home with humans than he did with vampires. But surely Weres would have been his choice. . . .

As I stood there in the corridor, feeling sorry for him, Jake's door opened and he stepped out. I hadn't checked for blank spots, only live signatures. My bad. Jake looked a bit suspicious when he saw me, and I couldn't blame him.

'Do you want to go with me?' I asked.

'What?' He looked startled. He hadn't been a vampire long enough to get the inscrutable face down pat.

'To see Quinn?' I said. 'I got directions to the infirmary, and you said you hadn't talked to him in a while, so I thought you might want to go with me if I'd kind of smooth the way?'

'That's a nice idea, Sookie,' he said. 'I think I'll pass. The fact is, most shifters don't want me around anymore. Quinn is better than most, I'm sure, but I make him uneasy. He knows my mom, my dad, my ex-girlfriend; all the people in my former life, the ones who don't want to hang with me now.'

I said impulsively, 'Jake, I'm so sorry. I'm sorry Hadley turned you if you would rather have passed on. She was fond of you, and she didn't want you to die.'

'But I did die, Sookie,' Jake said. 'I'm not the same guy anymore. As you know.' He picked up my arm and looked at the scar on it, the one he'd left with his teeth. 'You won't ever be the same, either,' he said, and he walked away. I'm not sure he knew where he was going, but he just wanted to get away from me.

I watched him until he was out of sight. He didn't turn to look back at me.

My mood had been fragile anyway, and that encounter pretty much started it on the downslope. I trudged to the elevators, determined to find the damn infirmary. The queen hadn't buzzed me, so presumably she was hobnobbing with other vampires, trying to find out who had hired the weather witch, and generally reveling in her relief. No more trial, a clear inheritance, the chance to put her beloved Andre in power. Things were coming up roses for the Queen of Louisiana, and I tried not to be bitter. Or did I have a right to be? Hmmm, let's see. I'd helped stop the trial, though I hadn't counted on it stopping as finally and completely as it had for, say, the hapless Henrik. Since she'd been found innocent, she'd get the inheritance as promised in her marriage contract. And who'd had the idea about Andre? And I'd been proved right about the witch. Okay, maybe I could be a little bitter at my own unbenevolent fortune. Plus, sooner or later I'd have to choose between Quinn and Eric, through no fault of my own. I'd stood holding a bomb for a very long time. The Ancient Pythoness was not a member of my fan club, and she was an object of reverence to most of the vampires. I'd almost been killed with an arrow.

Well, I'd had worse nights.

I found the infirmary, which was easier to locate than I'd thought, because the door was open and I could hear a familiar laugh coming from the room. I stepped in to find that Quinn was talking to the honey bear – looking woman, who must be Bettina, and the black guy, who must be Hondo. Also, to my astonishment, Clovache was there.

Her armor was not off, but she managed to give the impression of a guy who'd loosened his tie.

'Sookie,' said Quinn. He smiled at me, but the two shape-changers didn't. I was definitely an unwelcome visitor.

But I hadn't come to see them. I'd come to see the man who'd saved my life. I walked over to him, letting him watch me, giving him a little smile. I sat on the plastic chair by the bed and took his hand.

'Tell me how you're feeling,' I said.

'Like I had a real close shave,' he said. 'But I'm gonna be fine.'

'Could you all excuse us a moment, please?' I was at my most polite as I met the eyes of the three others in the room.

Clovache said, 'Back to guarding Kentucky,' and took off. She might have winked at me before she vanished. Bettina looked a bit disgruntled, as if she'd been student teaching on her own and now the teacher had returned and snatched back her authority.

Hondo gave me a dark look that held more than a hint of threat. 'You treat my man right,' he said. 'Don't give him no hard time.'

'Never,' I said. He couldn't think of a way to stay, since Quinn apparently wanted to talk to me, so he left.

'My fan base just gets bigger and bigger,' I said, watching them go. I got up and shut the door behind them. Unless a vampire, or Barry, stood outside the door, we were reasonably private.

'Is this where you dump me for the vampire?' Quinn asked. All trace of good humor had vanished from his face, and he was holding very still.

'No. This is where I tell you what happened, and you listen, and then we talk.' I said this as if I was sure he'd go along with it, but that was far from the case, and my heart was thudding in my throat as I waited for his reply. Finally he nodded, and I closed my eyes in relief, clutching his left hand in both of mine. 'Okay,' I said, bracing myself, and then I was off and running with my narrative, hoping that he would see that Eric really was the lesser of two evils.

Quinn didn't pull his hand away, but he didn't hold mine, either. 'You're bound to Eric,' he said.

'Yes.'

'You've exchanged blood with him at least three times.'

'Yes.'

'You know he can turn you whenever he feels like it?'

'Any of us could be turned whenever the vampires feel like it, Quinn. Even you. It might take two of them to hold you down and one to take all your blood and give you his, but it still could happen.'

'It wouldn't take that long if he made up his mind, now that you two have swapped so often. And this is Andre's fault.'

'There's nothing I can do about that now. I wish there were. I wish I could cut Eric out of my life. But I can't.'

'Unless he gets staked,' Quinn said.

I felt a pang in my heart that almost had me clapping a hand to my chest.

'You don't want that to happen.' Quinn's mouth was compressed in a hard line.

'No, of course not!'

'You care about him.'

Oh, *crap*. 'Quinn, you know Eric and I were together for a while, but he had amnesia and he doesn't remember it. I mean, he knows it's a fact, but he doesn't remember it at all.'

'If anyone besides you told me that story, you know what I'd think.'

'Quinn. I'm not anybody else.'

'Babe, I don't know what to say. I care about you, and I love spending time with you. I love going to bed with you. I like eating at the table with you. I like cooking together. I like almost everything about you, including your gift. But I'm not good at sharing.'

'I don't go with two guys at the same time.'

'What are you saying?'

'I'm saying, I'm going with you, unless you tell me different.'

'What will you do when Mr Big and Blond tells you to hop in bed with him?'

'I'll tell him I'm spoken for . . . if you're going to speak.'

Quinn shifted restlessly on the narrow bed. 'I'm healing, but I'm hurting,' he admitted. He looked very tired.

'I wouldn't trouble you with all this if it didn't seem pretty important to me,' I said. 'I'm trying to be honest with you. Absolutely honest. You took the arrow for me, and it's the least I can do in return.'

'I know that. Sookie, I'm a man who almost always knows his own mind, but I have to tell you . . . I don't know what to say. I thought we were just about ideal for each other until this.' Quinn's eyes blazed in his face suddenly. 'If he died, we'd have no problems.'

'If you killed him, I'd have a problem,' I said. I couldn't get any plainer than that.

Quinn closed his eyes. 'We have to think about this again when I'm all healed and you've had sleep and time to relax,' he said. 'You gotta meet Frannie, too. I'm so . . .' To my horror, I thought Quinn was going to choke up. If he cried, I would, too, and the last thing I needed was tears. I leaned over so far I thought I was going to fall on top of him, and I kissed him, just a quick pressure of my mouth on his. But then he held my shoulder and pulled me back to him, and there was much more to explore, his warmth and intensity . . . but then his gasp drew us out of the moment. He was trying not to grimace with pain.

'Oh! I'm sorry.'

'Don't ever apologize for a kiss like that,' he said. And he didn't look teary anymore. 'We definitely have something going on, Sookie. I don't want Andre's vampire crap to ruin it.'

'Me, either,' I said. I didn't want to give Quinn up, not the least because of our sizzling chemistry. Andre terrified me, and who knew what his intentions were? I certainly didn't. I suspected Eric didn't know, either, but he was never averse to power.

I said good-bye to Quinn, a reluctant good-bye, and began finding my way back to the dance. I felt obliged to check in with the queen to make sure she didn't need me, but I was exhausted, and I needed to get out of my dress and collapse on my bed.

Clovache was leaning against a wall in the corridor ahead, and I had the impression she was waiting for me. The younger Britlingen was less statuesque than Batanya, and while Batanya looked like a striking hawk with dark curls, Clovache was lighter altogether, with feathery ash-brown hair that needed a good stylist and big green eyes with high, arched brows.

'He seems like a good man,' she said in her harsh accent, and I got the strong feeling that Clovache was not a subtle woman.

'He seems that way to me, too.'

'While a vampire, by definition, is twisty and deceptive.'

'By definition? You mean, without exception?'

'I do.'

I kept silent as we walked. I was too tired to figure out the warrior's purpose in telling me this. I decided to ask. 'What's up, Clovache? What's the point?'

'Did you wonder why we were here, guarding the King of Kentucky? Why he had decided to pay our truly astronomical fees?'

'Yes, I did, but I figured it wasn't my business.'

'It's very much your business.'

'Then tell me. I'm not up to guessing.'

'Isaiah caught a Fellowship spy in his entourage a month ago.'

I stopped dead, and Clovache did, too. I processed her words. 'That's really bad,' I said, knowing the words were inadequate.

'Bad for the spy, of course. But she gave up some information before she went to the vale of shadows.'

'Wow, that's a pretty way to put it.'

'It's a load of crap. She died, and it *wasn't* pretty. Isaiah is an old-fashioned guy. Modern on the surface, a traditional vampire underneath. He had a wonderful time with the poor bitch before she gave it up.'

'You think you can trust what she said?'

'Good point. I'd confess to anything if I thought it would spare me some of the things his cronies did to her.'

I wasn't sure that was true. Clovache was made of pretty stern stuff.

'But I think she told him the truth. Her story was, a splinter group in the Fellowship got wind of this summit and decided it would be a golden opportunity to come out in the open with their fight against the vampires. Not simply protests and sermons against the vamps, but out-and-out warfare. This isn't the main body of the Fellowship . . . the leaders are always careful to say, "Oh, gosh, no, we don't condone violence against anyone. We're only cautioning people to be aware that if they consort with vampires, they're consorting with the devil."'

'You know a lot about things in this world,' I said.

'Yes,' she agreed. 'I do a lot of research before we take a job.'

I wanted to ask her what her world was like, how she got from one to the other, how much she charged, if all the warriors on (in?) her world were women or could the guys kick butt, too; and if so, what they looked like in the wonderful pants. But this wasn't the time or the place.

'So, what's the bottom line on this?' I asked.

'I think maybe the Fellowship is trying to mount some major offensive here.'

'The bomb in the soda can?'

'Actually, that baffles me. But it was outside Louisiana's room, and the Fellowship has to know by now that their operative didn't succeed, if it was their work.'

'And there are also the three murdered vampires in the Arkansas suite,' I pointed out.

'Like I say, baffled,' Clovache said.

'Would they have killed Jennifer Cater and the others?'

'Certainly, if they had a chance. But to tip their hand in such a small way when according to the spy they have planned something really big – that seems very unlikely. Also, how could a human get into the suite and kill three vampires?'

'So, what was the result of the Dr Pepper bomb?' I asked, trying hard to figure out the thinking behind it. We'd resumed walking, and now we were right outside the ceremonies room. I could hear the orchestra.

'Well, it gave you a few new white hairs,' Clovache said, smiling.

'I can't think that was the goal,' I said. 'I'm not that egocentric.'

Clovache had made up her mind. 'You're right,' she said, 'because the Fellowship wouldn't have planted it. They wouldn't want to draw attention to their larger plan with the little bomb.'

'So it was there for some other purpose.'

'And what was that purpose?'

'The end result of the bomb, if it had gone off, would have been that the queen got a big scare,' I said slowly.

Clovache looked startled. 'Not killed?'

'She wasn't even in the room.'

'It should have gone off earlier than it did,' Clovache said.

'How do you know that?'

'Security guy. Donati. That's what the police told him. Donati sees us as fellow professionals.' Clovache grinned. 'He likes women in armor.'

'Hey, who doesn't?' I grinned back.

'And it was a weak bomb, if any bomb can be called weak. I'm not saying there wouldn't have been damage. There would have. Maybe even someone killed, like you could have been. But the episode seems to be ineffective and ill-planned.'

'Unless it was designed only to scare. Designed to be spotted. Designed to be disarmed.'

Clovache shrugged.

'I don't understand,' I said. 'If not the Fellowship, who? What does the Fellowship plan to do? Charge the lobby armed with sharpened baseball bats?'

'The security here is not so good,' Clovache said.

'Yeah, I know. When I was down in the basement, getting a suitcase for the queen, the guards were pretty lazy, and I don't think the employees are searched as they come in, either. And they got a lot of suitcases mixed up.'

'And the vampires hired these people. Unbelievable. On one level vampires realize they're not immortal. They can be killed. On another, they've survived for so long, it makes them feel omnipotent.' Clovache shrugged. 'Well, back to duty.' We'd reached the ballroom. The Dead Man Dance Band was still playing.

The queen was standing very close to Andre, who no longer stood behind her but to her side. I knew this was significant, but it wasn't plain enough to cause Kentucky to give up hope. Christian Baruch was also in close attendance. If he'd had a tail, it would have been wagging, he was so anxious to please Sophie-Anne. I glanced around the room at the other kings and queens, recognizable by their entourages. I hadn't seen them in a room all together before, and I counted. There were only four queens. The other twelve rulers were males. Of the four queens, Minnesota appeared to be mated with the King of Wisconsin. Ohio had his arm around Iowa, so they were a couple. Besides Alabama, the only unmated queen was Sophie-Anne.

Though many vampires tend to be elastic about the gender of their sexual partner, or at least tolerant of those who prefer something different, some of them definitely aren't. No wonder Sophie-Anne was shining so brightly, even from under the lifted cloud of Peter Threadgill's death. Vampires didn't seem to be afraid of merry widows.

Alabama's boy toy scuttled his fingers up her bare back, and she shrieked in pretended fear. 'You know I hate spiders,' she said playfully, looking almost human, clutching him close to her. Though he'd played at frightening her, she clung closer.

Wait, I thought. *Wait just a minute*. But the idea wouldn't form.

Sophie-Anne noticed me lurking, and she beckoned. 'I think most of the humans are gone for the night,' she said.

A glance around the room told me that was true. 'What did you think of Julian Trout?' I asked, to allay my fear that she'd do something awful to him.

'I think he doesn't understand what he did,' Sophie-Anne said. 'At least to some extent. But he and I will come to an understanding.' She smiled. 'He and his wife are quite all right. I don't need you anymore tonight. Go amuse yourself,' she said, and it didn't sound condescending. Sophie-Anne really wanted me to have a good time, though, granted, she wasn't too particular about how I did it.

'Thanks,' I said, and then recalled that I'd better dress that up a bit. 'Thank you, ma'am, and you have a good night. See you tomorrow evening.'

I was glad to get out of there. With the room chock full o' vampires, the glances I was getting were a little on the pointy-toothed side. Individual bloodsuckers had an easier time of it sticking to the artificial blood than a group did. Something about the memory of the good ole days just made them want something warm from the source, rather than a liquid created in a lab and heated up in a microwave. Right on schedule, the crowd of Willing Donors returned through a back door and lined up, more or less, against the back wall. In very short order, they were all occupied, and (I suppose) happy.

After Bill had taken my blood during lovemaking, he'd told me blood from the neck of a human – after a diet of TrueBlood, say – was like going to Ruth's Chris Steak House after many meals at McDonald's. I saw Gervaise nuzzling Carla off in a corner, and I wondered if she needed help; but when I saw her face, I decided not.

Carla didn't come in that night, either, and without the distraction of Quinn, I was kind of sorry. I had too much to think about. It seemed that trouble was looking for me in the corridors of the Pyramid of Gizeh, and no matter which turn I took, it was going to find me.

Chapter 15

I'd finally gone to bed at four in the morning, and I woke at noon. That eight hours wasn't a good eight hours. I kept starting half awake, and I couldn't regulate my temperature, which might have had something to do with the blood exchange . . . or not. I had bad dreams, too, and twice I thought I heard Carla entering the room, only to open my eyes enough to see she wasn't there. The weird light that entered through the heavily colored glass of the human-only floor was not like real daylight, not at all. It was throwing me off.

I felt a tad bit better after a long shower, and I lifted the phone to call room service to get something to eat. Then I decided to go down to the little restaurant. I wanted to see other humans.

There were a few there; not my roommate, but a human playmate or two, and Barry. He gestured to the empty chair at his table, and I dropped into it, looking around for the waiter to signal for coffee. It came right away, and I shuddered with pleasure at the first sip. After I'd finished the first cup, I said – in my way – *How are you today? Were you up all night?*

No, Stan went to bed early with his new girlfriend, so I wasn't needed. They're still in the honeymoon stage. I went to the dance for a while, then I hung out with the makeup girl the Queen of Iowa brought with her. He waggled his eyebrows to tell me that the makeup girl was hot.

So, what's your program for today?

Did you get one of these slid under your door? Barry pushed a stapled sheaf of papers across the table to me just as the waiter brought my English muffin and eggs.

Yeah, I stuffed it in my purse. Wow, I could talk to Barry while I ate, the neatest answer to talking with your mouth full I could ever devise.

Take a look.

While Barry cut open a biscuit to slather it with butter, I scanned the pages. An agenda for the night, which was very helpful. Sophie-Anne's trial had been the most serious case that had to be adjudicated, the only one involving royalty. But there were a couple of others. The first session was set for 8:00, and it was a dispute over a personal injury. A Wisconsin vampire named Jodi (which seemed unlikely in and of itself) was being sued by an Illinois vampire named Michael. Michael alleged that Jodi had waited until he had dozed off for the day and then broken off one of his canines. With pliers.

Wow. That sounds . . . interesting. I raised my eyebrows. *How come the sheriffs aren't handling this?* Vampires really didn't like airing their dirty laundry.

'Interstate,' Barry said succinctly. The waiter had just brought a whole pot of coffee, so Barry topped off my cup and filled his own.

I flipped over a page. The next case involved a Kansas City, Missouri, vampire named Cindy Lou Suskin, who'd turned a child. Cindy Lou claimed that the child was dying of a blood disorder anyway, and she'd always wanted a child; so now she had a perpetual vampire preteen. Furthermore, the boy had been turned with his parents' consent, gotten in writing. Kate Book, the Kansas City, Kansas, lawyer appointed by the state to supervise the child's welfare, was complaining that now the child refused to see his human parents or to have any interaction with them, which was contrary to the agreement between the parents and Cindy Lou.

Sounded like something on daytime television. *Judge Judy, anyone?*

So, tonight is court cases, I summarized after scanning the remaining sheets. 'I guess we're needed?'

'Yes, I guess so. There'll be human witnesses for the second case. Stan wants me to be there, and I'm betting your queen will want you there, too. Her subject Bill is one of the appointed judges. Only kings and queens can judge other kings and queens, but for cases involving lesser vampires, the judges are picked from a pool. Bill's name came out of the hat.'

'Oh, goody.'

You got a history with him?

Yeah. But I think he'd probably be a good judge. I wasn't sure why I believed this; after all, Bill had shown he was capable of great deception. But I thought he would try to be fair and dispassionate.

I had noticed that the 'court' cases would take up the hours between eight and eleven. After that, midnight to four a.m. was blocked out as 'Commerce'. Barry and I looked at each other and shrugged.

'Swap meet?' I suggested. 'Flea market?'

Barry had no idea.

The fourth night of the conference was the last, and the first half of it was marked 'Free Time for Everyone in Rhodes'. Some of the suggested activities: seeing the Blue Moon dancers again, or their more explicit division, Black Moon. The difference wasn't spelled out, but I got the definite idea that the Black Moon employees did much more sexually oriented performances. Different dance teams from the studio were listed as appearing at different venues. The visiting vampires were also advised to visit the zoo, which would be open at night by special arrangement, or the city museum, ditto. Or they could visit a club 'for the particular enjoyment of those who enjoy their pleasures on the darker side'. It was called Kiss of Pain. *Remind me to walk down the other side of the street from that one*, I told Barry.

You never enjoy a little bite? Barry touched his tongue to his own blunt canines so I couldn't miss the implication.

There's lots of pleasure in that, I said, because I could hardly deny it. *But I think this place probably goes a little beyond a nip in the neck. Are you busy right now? Because I have to do some legwork for Eric, and I could use some help.*

'Sure,' Barry said. 'What's up?'

'We need to find archery places,' I said.

'This was left for you at the desk, miss,' said our waiter, who dropped a manila envelope on the table and retreated as if he suspected we had rabies. Evidently our silent exchanges had freaked someone out.

I opened the envelope to find a picture of Kyle Perkins inside. There was a note paper-clipped to it in Bill's familiar cramped handwriting. 'Sookie: Eric says you need this to do some detective work, and that this picture is necessary. Please be cautious. William Compton.' And just when I was thinking about asking the waiter for a phone book, I saw there was a second sheet. Bill had searched the Internet and made a list of all the archery practice places in the city. There were only four. I tried not to be impressed by Bill's thoughtfulness and assistance. I'd done with being impressed by Bill.

I called the hotel garage to get one of the cars brought by the Arkansas contingent. The queen had assumed ownership of them, and Eric had offered me one of them.

Barry had run up to his room to get a jacket, and I was standing by the front door, waiting for the car to be brought around and wondering how much I should tip the valet when I spotted Todd Donati. He came over to me, walking slowly and somehow heavily, though he was a thin man. He looked bad today, the scalp exposed by his receding hairline gray and damp looking, even his mustache sagging.

He stood facing me for a moment, not speaking. I thought he was gathering his courage, or his hopelessness. If ever I saw death riding on a man's shoulder, it was on Todd Donati's.

'My boss is trying to interest your boss in hooking up,' he said abruptly. If I'd imagined how he'd open our conversation, it had never included that line.

'Yeah, now that she's a widow, she's attracting quite a lot of interest,' I said.

'He's an old-fashioned guy in a lot of ways,' Todd Donati said. 'Comes from an old family, doesn't like modern thinking.'

'Um-hum,' I said, trying to sound neutral but encouraging.

'He don't believe in women making up their own minds, being able to fend for themselves,' the security chief said.

I couldn't look like I understood what Donati was talking about, because I sure didn't.

'Even vampire women,' he said, and looked at me squarely and directly.

'Okay,' I said.

'Think about it,' Donati said. 'Get your queen to ask him where the security tape is that shows that area in front of her room.'

'I will,' I said, having no idea why I was agreeing. Then the ailing man spun on his heel and walked away with an air of having discharged his duty.

Then the car came around, Barry hurried out of the elevator and came over to join me, and any thinking I might have done about the encounter faded in my fear of driving in the city. I don't think Eric ever considered how hard it would be for me to drive in Rhodes, because he just didn't think about stuff like that. If I hadn't had Barry with me, it would have been nearly impossible. I could cope with the driving, or I could look at the map the parking attendant loaned us, but not both.

I didn't do too bad, though the traffic was heavy and the weather was cold and raining. I hadn't been out of the hotel since we'd arrived, and it was kind of refreshing to see the outside world. Also, this was probably the only glimpse of the rest of the city I would get. I did as much looking as I could. Who knew if I'd ever come back? And this was so far north.

Barry plotted our course, and we began our archery tour of Rhodes.

We started with the farthest business, called Straight Arrow. It was a long, narrow place on a very busy avenue. It was gleaming, well-lit – and had qualified instructors behind the counter who were heavily armed. I knew this, because a big sign said so. The men there were not impressed by Barry's southern accent. They thought it made him sound stupid. Though when I talked, they thought I was cute. Okay, how insulting is that? The subtext, which I read very clearly from their minds, was: women sound stupid anyway, so a southern accent just enhances that adorable dimness. Men are supposed to sound crisp and direct, so southern men sound stupid and weak.

Anyway, aside from their built-in prejudices, these men were not helpful. They'd never seen Kyle Perkins at any of their night classes, and they didn't think he'd ever rented time to practice at their place.

Barry was fuming at the disrespect he'd endured, and he didn't even want to go in the second place. I trotted in by myself with the picture, and the one guy at work at the second archery supply store, which had no range, said, 'No,' immediately. He didn't discuss the picture, ask me why I wanted to know about Kyle Perkins, or wish me a nice day. He didn't have a sign to tell me how formidable he was. I figured he just ruded people to death.

The third place, housed in a building that I thought might at one time have been a bowling alley, had a few cars in the parking lot and a heavy opaque door. STOP AND BE IDENTIFIED a sign said. Barry and I could read it from the car. It seemed a little ominous.

'I'm tired of being in the car anyway,' he said gallantly, and got out with me. We stood where we could be seen, and I alerted Barry when I spotted the camera above our heads. Barry and I both looked as pleasant as we could. (In Barry's case, that was pretty pleasant. He just had a way about him.) After a few seconds, we heard a loud click, and the door unlocked. I glanced at Barry, and he pulled open the heavy door while I stepped inside the room and to one side so he could enter, too.

We were faced with a long counter extending the length of the opposite wall. There was a woman about my age behind the counter, with coppery hair and skin, the product of an interesting racial blend. She'd dyed her eyebrows black, which added a touch of the bizarre to the whole uni-color effect.

She looked us over just as carefully in person as she had over the camera, and I could read the thought that she was much happier to see Barry than she was to see me. I told Barry, *You better take this one.*

Yeah, I'm getting the idea, he answered, and while I laid Kyle's picture on the counter, he said, 'Could you tell us if this guy ever came in here to buy arrows or to practice?'

She didn't even ask why we wanted to know. She bent over to look at the picture, maybe a little farther than necessary to give Barry the benefit of her neckline. She scanned Kyle's picture and immediately made a face. 'Yeah, he came in here right after dark yesterday,' she said. 'We'd never had a vampire customer, and I didn't really want to serve him, but what are you gonna do? He had the money, and the law says we can't discriminate.' She was a woman who was ready and willing to discriminate, no doubt about it.

'Was anyone with him?' Barry asked.

'Oh, let me think.' She posed, her head thrown back, for Barry's benefit. *She* didn't think his southern accent sounded stupid. She thought it was adorable and sexy. 'I just can't remember. Listen, I'll tell ya what I'll do. I'll get the security tape for last night; we've still got it. And I'll let you have a look at it, okay?'

'Can we do that right now?' I asked, smiling sweetly.

'Well, I can't leave the counter right now. There's no one else here to watch the store if I have to go to the back. But if you'll come to look tonight after my replacement gets here' – she cast a very pointed glance at Barry, to make sure I realized I need not come – 'I'll let you have a peek.'

'What time?' Barry said, rather reluctantly.

'Shall we say seven? I get off right after that.'

Barry didn't touch the hint, but he agreed to be back at seven.

'Thanks, Barry,' I said as we buckled up again. 'You're really helping me out.' I called the hotel and left a message for the queen and Andre, explaining where I was and what I was doing, so they wouldn't get mad when I wasn't at their disposal the moment they woke, which should be very soon. After all, I was following Eric's orders.

'You gotta come in with me,' Barry said. 'I'm not seeing that woman by myself. She'll eat me alive. That was the War of Northern Aggression, for sure.'

'Okay. I'll stay out in the car, and you can yell to me from your head if she climbs on top of you.'

'It's a deal.'

To fill the time, we had a cup of coffee and some cake at a bakery. It was great. My grandmother had always believed that northern women couldn't cook. It was delightful to find out exactly how untrue that conviction had been. My appetite was also delightful. It was a continuing relief to find that I was just as hungry as I normally was. Nothing vampy about me, no sir!

After we filled up the tank and checked our route back to the Pyramid, it was finally time to return to the archery range to talk to Copper. The sky was full dark, and the city glowed with light. I felt sort of urban and glamorous, driving around such a large and famous city. And I'd been given a task and performed it successfully. No country mouse, me.

My feeling of happiness and superiority didn't last long.

Our first clue that all was not well at the Monteagle Archery Company was the heavy metal door hanging askew.

'Shit,' said Barry, which summed up my feelings in a nutshell.

We got out – very reluctantly – and, with many glances from side to side, we went up to the door to examine it.

'Blown or ripped?' I said.

Barry knelt on the gravel to have a closer look.

'I'm no 007,' he said, 'but I think this was ripped off.'

I looked at the door doubtfully. But when I bent over to look more closely, I saw the twisted metal of the hinges. Chalk one up for Barry.

'Okay,' I said. *Here's the part where we actually have to go in.*

Barry's jaw tightened. *Yeah,* he said, but he didn't sound too sure. Barry was definitely not into violence or confrontations. Barry was into money, and he had the best-paying employer. Right now, he was wondering if any amount of money would be enough to compensate for this, and he was thinking if he weren't with a woman, he'd just get in the car and drive away.

Sometimes male pride can be a good thing. I sure didn't want to do this by myself.

I shoved the door, which responded in a spectacular way by falling off its hinges and crashing to the gravel.

'Hi, we're here,' Barry said weakly. 'Anyone who didn't know before . . .'

After the noise had stopped and nothing had leaped out of the building to eat us, Barry and I straightened up from our instinctive crouching positions. I took a deep breath. This was my task, since this had been my errand. I stepped into the stream of light coming from the empty doorway. I took one big step forward over the threshold of the building. A quick scan hadn't given me a brain signal, so I pretty much figured what I was going to find.

Oh, yeah, Copper was dead. She was on top of the counter, laid out in a sprawl of limbs, her head canting off to one side. There was a knife protruding from her chest. Someone had been sick about a yard to the left of my foot – not blood – so there'd been at least one human on-site. I heard Barry step into the building and pause, just as I had.

I'd noted two doors from the room on our earlier visit. There was a door to the right, outside the counter, that would admit customers to the range. There was a door behind the counter that would allow employees to duck back for breaks and to attend customers in the range area. I was sure the tape we'd come to watch had been back there, because that would be the natural place for the security equipment. Whether it was still back there, that was the big question.

I wanted to turn around and leave without a backward glance, and I was scared out of my mind, but she'd died because of that tape, I figured, and it seemed like I'd be discarding her unwilling sacrifice if I discarded the tape. That didn't really make much sense, but that was how I felt.

I'm not finding anyone else in the area, Barry told me.

Me, either, I said, after I'd performed my second, more thorough, scan.

Barry, of course, knew exactly what I planned to do, and he said, *Do you want me to come with you?*

No, I want you to wait outside. I'll call you if I need you. In truth, it would have been nice to have him closer, but it smelled too bad in the room for anyone to stand around for more than a minute, and our minute was up.

Without protesting, Barry went back outside, and I crept down the counter to a clear area. It felt indescribably creepy to scramble over, avoiding Copper's body. I was glad her sightless eyes were not aimed in my direction as I used a tissue to wipe the area my hands had gripped.

On the employee side of the counter, there was evidence of a considerable struggle. She'd fought hard. There were smears of blood here and there, and paperwork had gotten knocked to the floor. There was a panic button clearly visible, below the top of the counter, but I guess she hadn't had time to punch it.

The lights were on in the office behind the counter, too, as I could see through the partially open door. I pushed it with my foot, and it swung away from me with a little creak. Again, nothing leaped out at me. I took a deep breath and stepped through.

The room was a combination security room/office/breakroom.

There were counters built around the walls with rolling chairs pulled up to them, and there were computers and a microwave and a little refrigerator: the usual stuff. And there were the security tapes, heaped in a pile on the floor and smoldering. All the other smells in the outer room had been so bad we simply hadn't gotten around to this one. There was another door leading out; I didn't go check to see where it led to, because there was a body blocking it. It was a man's body, and it was lying facedown, which was a blessing. I didn't need to go over to check to see if he was dead. He was surely dead. Copper's replacement, I assumed.

'Well, crap,' I said out loud. And then I thought, *Thank God I can get the hell out of here.* One thing about the security tapes having been burned: any record of our earlier visit was gone, too.

On my way, I pressed the panic button with my elbow. I hoped it was ringing somewhere at a police station, and that they'd get here soon.

Barry was waiting for me outside, as I'd been 99 percent sure he would be. Though I confess I wouldn't have been completely surprised if he'd left. 'Let's book! I set off the alarm,' I said, and we jumped into the car and got the hell out of there.

I was driving, because Barry was looking green. We had to pull over once (and in Rhodes traffic that wasn't easy) for him to be sick. I didn't blame him one little bit. What we'd seen was awful. But I've been blessed with a strong stomach, and I'd seen worse.

We got back to the hotel in time for the judicial session. Barry looked at me with gaping astonishment when I commented that I'd better get ready for it. He hadn't had an inkling what I'd been thinking, so I knew he was really feeling bad.

'How can you think of going?' he said. 'We have to tell someone what happened.'

'I called the police, or at least a security company who'll report it,' I said. 'What else can we do?' We were in the elevator rising from the parking garage to the lobby.

'We have to talk to them.'

'Why?' The doors opened and we stepped out into the hotel lobby. 'To tell them.'

'What?'

'That someone tried to kill you last night here by . . . okay, throwing an arrow at you.' He fell silent.

'Right. See?' I was getting his thoughts now, and he'd come to the correct conclusion. 'Would it help solve her murder? Probably not, because the guy is dead and the tapes are destroyed. And they'd come here asking questions of the master vampires of a third of the United States. Who would thank me for that? No one, that's who.'

'We can't stand by and do nothing.'

'This isn't perfect. I know that. But it's realistic. And practical.'

'Oh, so now you're *practical*?' Barry was getting shrieky.

'And you're yelling at my – at Sookie,' said Eric, earning another shriek (this one wordless) from Barry. By that time, Barry didn't care if he ever saw me again in his life. Though I didn't feel quite that drastic, I didn't think we were going to become pen pals, either.

If Eric didn't know how to pick a term for what I was to him, I was equally stumped. 'Do you need something?' I asked him in a voice that warned him I wasn't in the mood for any double entendres.

'What did you find out today?' he asked, all business, and the starch ran out of me in a stream.

'You go on,' I told Barry, who didn't need telling twice.

Eric looked around for a safe place to talk, didn't see one. The lobby was busy with vampires who were going to the judicial proceedings, or chatting, or flirting. 'Come,' he said, not as rudely as it sounds, and we went to the elevators and up to his room. Eric was on the ninth floor, which covered a much larger area than the queen's. There were twenty rooms on nine, at least. There was a lot more traffic, too; we passed quite a few vamps on the way to Eric's room, which he told me he was sharing with Pam.

I was a little curious about seeing a regular vampire room, since I'd seen only the living room of the queen's suite. I was disappointed to find that aside from the traveling coffins, it looked quite ordinary. Of course, that was kind of a big 'aside'. Pam's and Eric's coffins were resting on fancy trestles covered with fake hieroglyphics in gilt on black-painted wood, which gave them a neat atmospheric touch. There were two double beds, too, and a very compact bathroom. Both towels were hung up, which I could see because the door was open. Eric had never hung up his towels when he lived with me, so I was willing to bet that Pam had folded them and hung them on the rack. It seemed oddly domestic. Pam had probably picked up for Eric for over a century. Good God. I hadn't even managed two weeks.

What with the coffins and the beds, the room was a bit crowded, and I wondered what the lower echelon vamps had to put up with, say, on floor twelve. Could you arrange coffins in a bunk configuration? But I was just waffling, trying not to think about being alone with Eric. We sat down, Eric on one bed and I on another, and he leaned forward. 'Tell me,' he said.

'Well, it's not good,' I said, just to put him on the right track.

His face darkened, the blond brows drawing in to meet, his mouth turning down.

'We did find an archery range that Kyle Perkins visited. You were right about that. Barry went with me to be nice, and I really appreciated it,' I said, getting my opening credits in. 'To condense the whole afternoon, we found the right range at our third stop, and the gal behind the counter said we could look at the security tape from the night Kyle visited. I thought we might see someone we knew coming in with him. But she wanted us to come back at the end of her shift, seven o'clock.' I paused to take a deep breath. Eric's face didn't change at all. 'We came back at the appointed time, and she was dead, murdered, in the store. I went past her to look in the office, and the tapes had been burned.'

'Killed how?'

'She'd been stabbed, and the knife was left in her chest, and the killer or someone with him had thrown up food. Also, a guy who worked at the store was killed, but I didn't check him out to see how.'

'Ah.' Eric considered this. 'Anything else?'

'No,' I said, and got to my feet to leave.

'Barry was angry with you,' he observed.

'Yeah, he was, but he'll get over it.'

'What's his problem?'

'He doesn't think I handled the ... He doesn't think we should've left. Or ... I don't know. He thinks I was unfeeling.'

'I think you did exceptionally well.'

'Well, *great!*' Then I clamped down on myself. 'Sorry,' I said. 'I know you meant to compliment me. I'm not feeling all that good about her dying. Or leaving her. Even if it was the practical thing to do.'

'You're second-guessing yourself.'

'Yes.'

A knock at the door. Since Eric didn't shift himself, I got up to answer it. I didn't think it was a sexist thing; it was a status thing. I was definitely the lower dog in the room.

Completely and totally not to my surprise, the knocker was Bill. That just made my day complete. I stood aside to let him enter. Darn if I was going to ask Eric if I should let him in.

Bill looked me up and down, I guess to check that my clothes were in order, then strode by me without a word. I rolled my eyes at his back. Then I had a brilliant idea: instead of turning back into the room for further discussion, I stepped out of the open door and shut it behind me. I marched off quite briskly and grabbed the elevator with hardly any wait. In two minutes, I was unlocking my door.

End of problem.

I felt quite proud of myself.

Carla was in our room, naked again.

'Hi,' I said. 'Please put on a robe.'

'Well, hey, if it bothers you,' she said in a fairly relaxed manner, and pulled on a robe. Wow. End of another problem. Direct action, straightforward statements; obviously, those were the keys to improving my life.

'Thanks,' I said. 'Not going to the judicial stuff?'

'Human dates aren't invited,' she said. 'It's Free Time for us. Gervaise and I are going out nightclubbing later. Some really extreme place called Kiss of Pain.'

'You be careful,' I said. 'Bad things can happen if there are lots of vamps together and a bleeding human or two.'

'I can handle Gervaise,' Carla said.

'No, you can't.'

'He's nuts about me.'

'Until he stops being nuts. Or until a vamp older than Gervaise takes a shine to you, and Gervaise gets all conflicted.'

She looked uncertain for a second, an expression I felt sure Carla didn't wear too often.

'What about you? I hear you're tied to Eric now.'

'Only for a while,' I said, and I meant it. 'It'll wear off.'

I will never go anywhere with vampires again, I promised myself. *I let the lure of the money and the excitement of the travel pull me in. But I won't do that again. As God is my witness* . . . Then I had to laugh out loud. Scarlett O'Hara, I wasn't. 'I'll never be hungry again,' I told Carla.

'Why, did you eat a big supper?' she asked, focused on the mirror because she was plucking her eyebrows.

I laughed. And I couldn't stop.

'What's up with you?' Carla swung around to eye me with some concern. 'You're not acting like yourself, Sookie.'

'Just had a bad shock,' I said, gasping for breath. 'I'll be okay in a minute.' It was more like ten before I gathered my control back around me. I was due at the judicial meeting, and frankly, I wanted to have something to occupy my mind. I scrubbed my face and put on some makeup, changed into a bronze silk blouse and tobacco-colored pants with a matching cardigan, and put on some brown leather pumps. With my room key in my pocket and a relieved good-bye from Carla, I was off to find the judicial sessions.

Chapter 16

The vampire Jodi was pretty formidable. She put me in mind of Jael, in the Bible. Jael, a determined woman of Israel, put a tent peg through the head of Sisera, an enemy captain, if I was remembering correctly. Sisera had been asleep when Jael did the deed, just as Michael had been when Jodi broke off his fang. Even though Jodi's name made me snicker, I saw in her a steely strength and resolve, and I was immediately on her side. I hoped the panel of judges could see past the vampire Michael's whining about his damn tooth.

This wasn't set up like the previous evening, though the session took place in the same room. The panel of judges, I guess you'd call them, were on the stage and seated at a long table facing the audience. There were three of them, all from different states: two men and a woman. One of the males was Bill, who was looking (as always) calm and collected. I didn't know the other guy, a blond. The female was a tiny, pretty vamp with the straightest back and longest rippling black hair I ever saw. I heard Bill address her as 'Dahlia.' Her round little face whipped back and forth as she listened to the testimony of first Jodi, then Michael, just as if she was watching a tennis match. Centered on the white tablecloth before the judges was a stake, which I guess was the vampire symbol of justice.

The two complaining vampires were not represented by lawyers. They said their piece, and then the judges got to ask questions before they decided the verdict by a majority vote. It was simple in form, if not in fact.

'You were torturing a human woman?' Dahlia asked Michael.

'Yes,' he said without blinking an eye. I glanced around. I was the only human in the audience. No wonder there was a certain simplicity to the proceedings. The vampires weren't trying to dress it up for a warm-blooded audience. They were behaving as they would if they were by themselves. I was sitting by those of my party who'd attended – Rasul, Gervaise, Cleo – and maybe their closeness masked my scent, or maybe one tame human didn't count.

'She'd offended me, and I enjoy sex that way, so I abducted her and had a little fun,' Michael said. 'Then Jodi goes all ballistic on me and breaks my fang. See?' He opened wide enough to show the judges the fang's stump. (I wondered if he'd gone by the booth that was still set up out in the vendors' area, the one that had such amazing artificial fangs.)

Michael had the face of an angel, and he didn't get that what he'd done was wrong. He had wanted to do it, so he did it. Not all people who've been brought over to be vampires are mentally stable to start with, and some of them are utterly conscienceless after decades, or even centuries, of disposing of humans as they damn well please. And yet, they enjoy the openness of the new order, getting to stride around being themselves, with the right not to be staked. They don't want to pay for that privilege by adhering to the rules of common decency.

I thought breaking off one fang was a very light punishment. I couldn't believe he'd had the gall to bring a case against anyone. Apparently, neither did Jodi, who was on her feet and going for him again. Maybe she meant to snap off his other fang. This was way better than *The Peoples' Court* or *Judge Judy*.

The blond judge tackled her. He was much larger than Jodi, and she seemed to accept that she wasn't going to heave him off. I noticed Bill had moved his chair back so he could leap up if further developments required quick action.

The tiny Dahlia said, 'Why did you take such exception to Michael's actions, Jodi?'

'The woman was the sister of one of my employees,' Jodi said, her voice shaking with anger. 'She was under my protection. And stupid Michael will cause all of us to be hunted again if he continues his ways. He can't be corrected. Nothing stops him, not even losing the fang. I warned him three times to stay away, but the young woman spoke back to him when he propositioned her yet again on the street, and his pride was more important than his intelligence or discretion.'

'Is this true?' the little vamp asked Michael.

'She insulted me, Dahlia,' he said smoothly. 'A human publicly insulted me.'

'This one's easy,' said Dahlia. 'Do you both agree?' The blond male restraining Jodi nodded, and so did Bill, who was still perched on the edge of his chair to Dahlia's right.

'Michael, you will bring retribution on us by your unwise actions and your inability to control your impulses,' Dahlia said. 'You have ignored warnings, and you ignored the fact that the young woman was under the protection of another vampire.'

'You can't mean this! Where is your pride?' Michael was yelling and on his feet.

Two men stepped forward out of the shadows at the back of the stage. They were both vampires, of course, and they were both good-sized men. They held Michael, who put up quite a fight. I was a little shocked by the noise and the violence, but in a minute they'd take Michael off to some vampire prison, and the calm proceedings would continue.

To my absolute astonishment, Dahlia nodded to the vamp sitting on Jodi, who got up and assisted her to rise. Jodi, smiling broadly, was across the stage in one leap, like a panther. She grabbed up the stake lying on the judges' table, and with one powerful swing of her lean arm, she buried the stake in Michael's chest.

I was the only one who was shocked, and I clapped both hands over my mouth to keep from squeaking.

Michael looked at her with utter rage, and he even kept struggling, I suppose to free his arms so he could pull the stake out, but in a few seconds it was all over. The two vamps holding the new corpse hauled it off, and Jodi stepped off the stage, still beaming.

'Next case,' called Dahlia.

The next was the one about the vampire kid, and there were humans involved in this one. I felt less conspicuous when they came in: the hangdog parents with their vampire representative (was it possible that humans couldn't testify before this court?) and the 'mother' with her 'child'.

This was a longer, sadder case, because the parents' suffering over the loss of their son – who was still walking and talking, but not to them – was nearly palpable. I wasn't the only one who cried, 'For shame!' when Cindy Lou revealed the parents were giving her monthly payments for the boy's upkeep. The vampire Kate argued for the parents ferociously, and it was clear she thought Cindy Lou was a trailer-trash vampire and a bad mother, but the three judges – different ones this time, and I didn't know any of them – abided by the written contract the parents had signed and refused to give the boy a new guardian. However, they ruled, the contract had to be equally enforced on the parents' behalf, and the boy was required to spend time with his biological parents as long as they chose to enforce the right.

The head judge, a hawk-faced guy with dark, liquid eyes, called the boy up to stand before them. 'You owe these people respect and obedience, and you signed this contract, too,' he said. 'You may be a minor in human law, but to us, you are as responsible as . . . *Cindy Lou.*' Boy, it just killed him, having to admit there was a vampire named Cindy Lou. 'If you try to terrorize your human parents, or coerce them, or drink their blood, we will amputate your hand. And when it grows back, we'll amputate it again.'

The boy could hardly be whiter than he was, and his human mother fainted. But he'd been so cocky, so sure of himself, and so dismissive of his poor parents, I thought the strong warning was necessary. I caught myself nodding.

Oh, yeah, this was fair, to threaten a kid with having his hand amputated.

But if you'd seen this kid, you might have agreed. And Cindy Lou was no prize; whoever had turned her must have been mentally and morally deficient.

I hadn't been needed after all. I was wondering about the rest of the evening when the queen came through the double doors at the end of the room, Sigebert and Andre in close attendance. She was wearing a sapphire blue silk pantsuit with a beautiful diamond necklace and small diamond earrings. She looked classy, absolutely smooth, sleek, and perfect. Andre made a beeline to me.

'I know,' he said, 'that is, Sophie-Anne tells me that I have done wrong to you. I'm not sorry, because I will do anything for her. Others don't mean anything to me. But I do regret that I have not been able to refrain from causing something that distresses you.'

If that was an apology, it was the most half-assed one I'd ever received in my life. It left almost everything to be desired. All I could do was say, 'I hear you.' It was the most I'd ever get.

By then, Sophie-Anne was standing in front of me. I did my head-bob thing. 'I will need you with me during the next few hours,' she said, and I said, 'Sure.' She glanced up and down my clothes, as if wishing I had dressed up a little more, but no one had warned me that a part of the night marked off for Commerce meant fancy clothes were appropriate.

Mr Cataliades steamed up to me, wearing a beautiful suit and a dark red-and-gold silk tie, and he said, 'Good to see you, my dear. Let me brief you on the next item on the schedule.'

I spread my hands to show I was ready. 'Where's Diantha?' I asked.

'She is working something out with the hotel,' Cataliades said. He frowned. 'It's most peculiar. There was an extra coffin downstairs, apparently.'

'How could that be?' Coffins belonged to somebody. It's not like a vampire was going to be traveling with a spare, like you had to have a dress coffin and an everyday coffin. 'Why did they call you?'

'It had one of our tags on it,' he said.

'But all of our vamps are accounted for, right?' I felt a tingle of anxiety in my chest. Just then, I saw the usual waiters moving among the crowd, and I saw one spot me and turn away. Then he saw Barry, who'd come in with the King of Texas. The waiter turned away yet again.

I actually started to call to a nearby vampire to hold the guy so I could have a look into his head, and then I realized I was acting as high-handed as the vampires themselves. The waiter vanished, and

I hadn't had a close look at him, so I wasn't sure I could even identify him in a crowd of other servers in the same outfit. Mr Cataliades was talking, but I held up a hand. 'Hold it for a sec,' I murmured. The waiter's quick turn had reminded me of something, something else that had seemed odd.

'Please pay attention, Miss Stackhouse,' the lawyer said, and I had to stow the thread of thought away. 'Here's what you need to do. The queen will be negotiating for a few favors she needs to help rebuild her state. Just do what you do best to discover if everyone dealing with her is honorable.'

This was not a very specific guideline. 'Do my best,' I said. 'But I think you should go find Diantha, Mr C. I think there's something really strange and wrong about this extra coffin they're talking about. There was that extra suitcase, too,' I said. 'I carried it up to the queen's suite.'

Mr Cataliades looked at me blankly. I could see that he considered the small problem of extra items turning up in a hotel to be a small one and below his concern. 'Did Eric tell you about the murdered woman?' I asked, and his attention sharpened.

'I haven't seen Master Eric this evening,' he said. 'I'll be sure to track him down.'

'Something's up; I just don't know what,' I muttered more or less to myself, and then I turned away to catch up with Sophie-Anne.

Commerce was conducted in a sort of bazaar style. Sophie-Anne positioned herself by the table where Bill was sitting, back at work selling the computer program. Pam was helping him, but she was in her regular clothes, and I was glad the harem costume was getting a rest. I wondered what the procedure was, but I adopted a wait-and-see attitude, and I found out soon enough. The first to approach Sophie-Anne was the big blond vampire who'd served as a judge earlier. 'Dear madam,' he said, kissing her hand. 'I am charmed to see you, as always, and devastated by the destruction of your beautiful city.'

'A small portion of my beautiful city,' Sophie-Anne said with the sweetest of smiles.

'I am in despair at the thought of the straits you must be in,' he continued after a brief pause to register her correction. 'You, the ruler of such a profitable and prestigious kingdom . . . now brought so low. I hope to be able to assist you in my humble fashion.'

'And what form would that assistance take?' Sophie-Anne inquired.

After much palaver, it turned out that Mr Flowery was willing to bring a gazillion board feet of lumber to New Orleans if Sophie-Anne would give him 2 percent of her next five years' revenue. His accountant was with him. I looked into his eyes with great curiosity. I stepped back, and Andre slithered to my side. I turned so that no one could read my lips.

'Quality of the lumber,' I said as quietly as a hummingbird's wings.

That took forever to hammer out, and it was boring, boring, boring. Some of the wannabe providers didn't have humans with them, and I was no help with those; but most of them did. Sometimes the human had paid the vampire a substantial sum to 'sponsor' him, so he could just be in the hall and pitch his woo in a one-on-one setting. By the time vendor number eight simpered to a stop in front of the queen, I was unable to suppress my yawns. I'd noticed Bill was doing a landmark business selling copies of his vampire database. For a reserved kind of guy, he did a good job of explaining and promoting his product, considering some of the vampires were very mistrustful of computers. If I heard about the 'Yearly Update Package' one more time, I was gonna puke. There were lots of humans clustering around Bill, because they were more computer savvy than the vamps as a whole. While they were absorbed, I tried to get a scan in here and there, but they were just thinking megahertz and RAM and hard drives – stuff like that.

I didn't see Quinn. Since he was a wereanimal, I figured he'd be completely over his wound of the night before. I could only take his absence as a signal. I was heart-heavy and weary.

The queen invited Dahlia, the little, pretty vampire who'd been so direct in her judgment, up to her suite for a drink. Dahlia accepted regally, and our whole party moved up to the suite. Christian Baruch tagged along; he'd been hovering around Sophie-Anne all evening.

His courtship of Sophie-Anne was heavy-handed, to say the least. I thought again of the boy toy I'd watched the previous evening, tickling the back of his ladylove in imitation of a spider, because he knew she was frightened of them, and how he'd gotten her to snuggle closer to him. I felt a lightbulb come on over my head and wondered if it was visible to anyone else.

My opinion of the hotelier plummeted. If he thought such a strategy would work on Sophie-Anne, he had a lot of thinking to do.

I didn't see Jake Purifoy anywhere around, and I wondered what Andre had him doing. Something innocuous probably, like checking to make sure all the cars were gassed up. He wasn't really trusted to handle anything more taxing, at least not yet. Jake's youth and his Were heritage counted against him, and he'd have to bust his tail to earn points. But Jake didn't have that fire in him. He was looking to the past, to his life as a Were. He had a backlog of bitterness.

Sophie's suite had been cleaned; all the vampire suites had to be cleaned at night, of course, while the vamps were out of them. Christian Baruch started telling us about the extra help he'd had to take on to cope with the summit crowd and how nervous some of them were about cleaning rooms occupied by vampires. I could tell Sophie-Anne was not impressed by Baruch's assumption of superiority. He was so much younger than her, he must seem like a swaggering teenager to the centuries-old queen.

Jake came in just then, and after paying his respects to the queen and meeting Dahlia, he came to sit by me. I was slumping in an uncomfortable straight chair, and he pulled a matching one over.

'What's up, Jake?'

'Not much. I've been getting the queen and Andre tickets to a show for tomorrow night. It's an all-vampire production of *Hello, Dolly!*'

I tried to imagine that, found I couldn't. 'What are you going to be doing? It's marked as free time on the schedule.'

'I don't know,' he said, a curiously remote tone in his voice. 'My life has changed so much I just can't predict what will happen. Are you going out tomorrow in the day, Sookie? Shopping, maybe? There are some wonderful stores on Widewater Drive. That's down by the lake.'

Even I had heard of Widewater Drive, and I said, 'I guess it's possible. I'm not much of a shopper.'

'You really should go. There're some great shoe stores, and a big Macy's – you'd love Macy's. Make a day of it. Get away from this place while you can.'

'I'll sure think about it,' I said, a little puzzled. 'Um, have you seen Quinn today?'

'Glimpsed him. And I talked to Frannie for a minute. They've been busy getting props ready for the closing ceremonies.'

'Oh,' I said. Right. Sure. That took loads of time.

'Call him, ask him to take you out tomorrow,' Jake said.

I tried to picture me asking Quinn to take me shopping. Well, it wasn't totally out of the question, but it wasn't likely, either. I shrugged. 'Maybe I'll get out some.'

He looked pleased.

'Sookie, you can go,' Andre said. I was so tired I hadn't even noticed him glide up.

'Okay. Good night, you two,' I said, and stood to stretch. I noticed the blue suitcase was still where I'd dropped it two nights ago. 'Oh, Jake, you need to take that suitcase back down to the basement. They called me and told me to bring it up here, but no one's claimed it.'

'I'll ask around,' he said vaguely, and took off for his own room. Andre's attention had already returned to the queen, who was laughing at the description of some wedding Dahlia had attended.

'Andre,' I said in a very low voice, 'I gotta tell you, I think Mr Baruch had something to do with that bomb outside the queen's door.'

Andre looked as if someone had stuck a nail up his fundament. 'What?'

'I'm thinking that he wanted Sophie-Anne scared,' I said. 'I'm thinking that he thought she'd be vulnerable and need a strong male protector if she felt threatened.'

Andre was not Mr Expressive, but I saw incredulity, disgust, and belief cross his face in quick order.

'And I'm also thinking maybe he told Henrik Feith that Sophie-Anne was going to kill him. Because he's the hotel owner, right? And he'd have a key to get into the queen's room, where we thought Henrik was safe, right? So Henrik would continue the queen's trial, because he'd been persuaded she would do him in. Again, Christian Baruch would be there, to be her big savior. Maybe he had Henrik killed, after he'd set him up, so he could do a tah-*dah* reveal and dazzle Sophie-Anne with his wonderful care of her.'

Andre had the strangest expression on his face, as if he was having trouble following me. 'Is there proof?' he asked.

'Not a smidge. But when I talked to Mr Donati in the lobby this morning, he hinted that there was a security tape I might want to watch.'

'Go see,' Andre said.

'If I go ask for it, he'll get fired. You need to get the queen to ask Mr Baruch point-blank if she can see the security tape for the lobby outside during the time the bomb was planted. Gum on the camera or not, that tape will show something.'

'Leave first, so he won't connect you to this.' In fact, the hotelier had been absorbed in the queen and her conversation, or his vampire hearing would have tipped him off that we were talking about him.

Though I was exhausted, I had the gratifying feeling that I was earning the money they were paying me for this trip. And it was a load off my mind to feel that the Dr Pepper thing was solved. Christian Baruch would not be doing any more bomb planting now that the queen was on to him. The threat the splinter group of the Fellowship posed … well, I'd only heard of that from hearsay, and I didn't have any evidence of what form it would take. Despite the death of the woman at the archery place, I felt more relaxed than I had since I'd walked into the Pyramid of Gizeh, because I was inclined to attribute the killer archer to Baruch, too. Maybe when he saw that Henrik would actually take Arkansas from the queen, he'd gotten greedy and had the assassin take out Henrik, so the queen would get everything. There was something confusing and wrong about that scenario, but I was too tired to think it through, and I was content to let the whole tangled web lie until I was rested.

I crossed the little lobby to the elevator and pressed the button. When the doors dinged open, Bill stepped out, his hands full of order forms.

'You did well this evening,' I said, too tired to hate him. I nodded at the forms.

'Yes, we'll all make a lot of money from this,' he said, but he didn't sound particularly excited.

I waited for him to step out of my way, but he didn't do that, either.

'I would give it all away if I could erase what happened between us,' he said. 'Not the times we spent loving each other, but . . .'

'The times you spent lying to me? The times you pretended you could hardly wait to date me when it turns out you were under order to? Those times?'

'Yes,' he said, and his deep brown eyes didn't waver. 'Those times.'

'You hurt me too much. That's not ever gonna happen.'

'Do you love any man? Quinn? Eric? That moron JB?'

'You don't have the right to ask me that,' I said. 'You don't have any rights at all where I'm concerned.'

JB? Where'd that come from? I'd always been fond of the guy, and he was lovely, but his conversation was about as stimulating as a stump's. I was shaking my head as I rode down in the elevator to the human floor.

Carla was out, as usual, and since it was five in the morning the chances seemed good that she'd stay out. I put on my pink pajamas and put my slippers beside the bed so I wouldn't have to grope around for them in the darkened room in case Carla came in before I awoke.

Chapter 17

My eyes snapped open like shades that were wound too tight.

Wake up, wake up, wake up! Sookie, something's wrong.

Barry, where are you?

Standing at the elevators on the human floor.

I'm coming. I pulled on last night's outfit, but without the heels. Instead, I slid my feet into my rubber-soled slippers. I grabbed the slim wallet that held my room key, driver's license, and credit card, and stuffed it in one pocket, jammed my cell phone into the other, and hurried out of the room. The door slammed behind me with an ominous thud. The hotel felt empty and silent, but my clock had read 9:50.

I had to run down a long corridor and turn right to get to the elevators. I didn't meet a soul. A moment's thought told me that was not so strange. Most humans on the floor would still be asleep, because they kept vampire hours. But there weren't even any hotel employees cleaning the halls.

All the little tracks of disquiet that had crawled through my brain, like slug tracks on your back doorstep, had coalesced into a huge throbbing mass of uneasiness.

I felt like I was on the *Titanic*, and I'd just heard the hull scrape against the iceberg.

I finally spotted someone, lying on the floor. I'd been woken so suddenly and sharply that everything I did had a dreamlike quality to it, so finding a body in the hall was not such a jolt.

I let out a cry, and Barry came bounding around the corner. He crouched down with me. I rolled over the body. It was Jake Purifoy, and he couldn't be roused.

Why isn't he in his room? What was he doing out so late? Even Barry's mental voice sounded panicked.

Look, Barry, he's lying sort of pointing toward my room. Do you think he was coming to see me?

Yes, and he didn't make it.

What could have been so important that Jake wasn't prepared for his day's sleep? I stood up, thinking furiously. I'd never, ever heard of a vampire who didn't know instinctively that the dawn was coming. I thought of the conversations I'd had with Jake, and the two men I'd seen leaving his room.

'You *bastard*,' I hissed through my teeth, and I kicked him as hard as I could.

'Jesus, Sookie!' Barry grabbed my arm, horrified. But then he got the picture from my brain.

'We need to find Mr Cataliades and Diantha,' I said. 'They can get up; they're not vamps.'

'I'll get Cecile. She's human, my roommate,' Barry said, and we both went off in different directions, leaving Jake to lie where he was. It was all we could do.

We were back together in five minutes. It had been surprisingly easy to raise Mr Cataliades, and Diantha had been sharing his room. Cecile proved to be a young woman with a no-nonsense haircut and a competent way about her, and I wasn't surprised when Barry introduced her as the king's new executive assistant.

I'd been a fool to discount, even for a minute, the warning that Clovache had passed along. I was so angry at myself I could hardly stand to be inside my own skin. But I had to shove that aside and we had to act now.

'Listen to what I think,' I said. I'd been putting things together in my head. 'Some of the waiters have been avoiding Barry and me over the past couple of days, as soon as they found out what we were.'

Barry nodded. He'd noticed, too. He looked oddly guilty, but that had to wait.

'They know what we are. They didn't want us to know what they're about to do, I'm assuming. So I'm also assuming it must be something really, really bad. And Jake Purifoy was in on it.'

Mr Cataliades had been looking faintly bored, but now he began to look seriously alarmed. Diantha's big eyes went from face to face.

'What shall we do?' Cecile asked, which earned her high marks in my book.

'It's the extra coffins,' I said. 'And the blue suitcase in the queen's suite. Barry, you were asked to bring up a suitcase, too, right? And it didn't belong to anyone?'

Barry said, 'Right. It's still sitting in the foyer of the king's suite, since everyone passes through there. We thought someone would claim it. I was going to take it back to the luggage department today.'

I said, 'The one I went down for is sitting in the living room of the queen's suite. I think the guy who was in on it was Joe, the manager down in the luggage and, delivery area. He's the one who called me down to get the suitcase. No one else seemed to know anything about it.'

'The suitcases will blow up?' Diantha said in her shrill voice. 'The unclaimed coffins in the basement, too? If the basement goes, the building will collapse!' I'd never heard Diantha sound so human.

'We have to wake them up,' I said. 'We have to get them out.'

'The building's going to blow,' said Barry, trying to process the idea.

'The vamps won't wake up.' Cecile the practical. 'They can't.'

'Quinn!' I said. I was thinking of so many things at once that I was standing rooted in place. Fishing my phone from my pocket, I punched his number on speed dial and heard his mumble at the other end. 'Get out,' I said. 'Quinn, get your sister and get out. There's going to be an explosion.' I only waited to hear him sound more alert before I shut the phone.

'We have to save ourselves, too,' Barry was saying.

Brilliantly, Cecile ran down the hall to a red fixture and flipped the fire alarm. The clamor almost split our eardrums, but the effect was wonderful on the sleeping humans on this floor. Within seconds, they began to come out of the rooms.

'Take the stairs,' Cecile directed them in a bellow, and obediently, they did. I was glad to see Carla's dark head among them. But I didn't see Quinn, and he was always easy to spot.

'The queen is high up,' said Mr Cataliades.

'Can those glass panels be busted from the inside?' I asked.

'They did it on *Fear Factor*,' Barry said.

'We could try sliding the coffins down.'

'They'd break on impact,' Cecile said.

'But the vamps would survive the explosion,' I pointed out.

'To be burned up by the sun,' Mr Cataliades said. 'Diantha and I will go up and try to get out the queen's party, wrapped up in blankets. We'll take them . . .' He looked at me desperately.

'Ambulances! Call 911 now! They can figure out where to take them!'

Diantha called 911 and was incoherent and desperate enough to get ambulances started to an explosion that had not happened yet. 'The building's on fire,' she said, which was like a future truth.

'Go,' I told Mr Cataliades, actually shoving the demon, and off he sped to the queen's suite.

'Go try to get your party out,' I said to Barry, and he and Cecile ran for the elevator, though at any minute it might be unworkable.

I'd done everything about getting humans out that I could. Cataliades and Diantha could take care of the queen and Andre. Eric and Pam! I knew where Eric's room was, thank God. I took the stairs. As I ran up, I met a party coming down: the two Britlingens, both with large packs on their backs, carrying a wrapped bundle. Clovache had the feet, Batanya the head. I had no doubt that the bundle was the King of Kentucky, and that they were doing their duty. They both nodded as I hugged the wall to let them by. If they weren't as calm as if they were out for a stroll, they were close to it.

'You set off the fire alarm?' Batanya said. 'Whatever the Fellowship is doing, it's today?'

'Yes,' I said.

'Thanks. We're getting out now, and you should, too,' Clovache said.

'We'll go back to our place after we deposit him,' Batanya said. 'Good-bye.'

'Good luck,' I told them stupidly, and then I was running upstairs as if I'd trained for this. As a result, I was huffing like a bellows when I flung open the door to the ninth floor. I saw a lone maid pushing a cart down a long corridor. I ran up to her, frightening her even more than the fire alarm already had.

'Give me your master key,' I said.

'No!' She was middle-aged and Hispanic, and she wasn't about to give in to such a crazy demand. 'I'll get fired.'

'Then open this door' – I pointed to Eric's – 'and get out of here.' I'm sure I looked like a desperate woman, and I was. 'This building is going to blow up any minute.'

She flung the key at me and made tracks down the hallway to the elevators. Dammit.

And then the explosions began. There was a deep, resounding quiver and a boom from way below my feet, as if some gargantuan sea creature were making its way to the surface. I staggered over to Eric's room, thrusting the plastic key into the slot and shoving open the door in a moment of utter silence. The room was in complete darkness.

'Eric, Pam!' I yelled. I fumbled for a light switch in the pitch-black room, felt the building sway. At least one of the upper charges had gone off. Oh, shit! Oh, shit! But the light came on, and I saw that Eric and Pam had gotten in the beds, not the coffins.

'Wake up!' I said, shaking Pam since she was closest. She didn't stir at all. It was exactly like shaking a doll stuffed with sawdust. 'Eric!' I screamed right in his ear.

This got a bit of a reaction; he was much older than Pam. His eyes opened a slit and tried to focus. 'What?' he said.

'You have to get up! You have to! You have to go out!'

'Daytime,' he whispered. He began to flop over on his side.

I slapped him harder than I've ever hit anyone in my life. I screamed, 'Get up!' until my voice would hardly work. Finally Eric stirred and managed to sit up. He was wearing black silk pajama bottoms, thank God, and I spied the ceremonial black cloak tossed over his coffin. He hadn't returned it to Quinn, which was huge luck. I arranged it over him and fastened it at the neck. I pulled the hood over his face. 'Cover your head!' I yelled, and I heard a burst of noise above my head: shattering glass, followed by shrieks.

Eric would drop back to sleep if I didn't keep him awake. At least he was trying. I remembered that Bill had managed to stagger, under dire circumstances, at least for a few minutes. But Pam, though roughly the same age as Bill, simply could not be roused. I even pulled her long pale hair.

'You have to help me get Pam out,' I said finally, despairing. 'Eric, you just have to.' There was another roar and a lurch in the floor. I screamed, and Eric's eyes went wide. He staggered to his feet. As if we'd shared thoughts like Barry and I could, we both shoved his coffin off its trestle and onto the carpet. Then we slid it over to the opaque slanting glass panel forming the side of the building.

Everything around us trembled and shook. Eric's eyes were a little wider now, and he was concentrating so heavily on keeping himself moving that his strength was pulling on mine.

'Pam,' I said, trying to push him into more action. I opened the coffin, after some desperate fumbling. Eric went over to his sleeping child, walking like his feet were sticking to the floor with each step. He took Pam's shoulders and I took her feet, and we picked her up, blanket and all. The floor shook again, more violently this time, and we lurched over to the coffin and tossed Pam into it. I shut the lid and latched it, though a corner of Pam's nightgown was sticking out.

I thought about Bill, and Rasul flashed across my mind, but there was nothing I could do, and there wasn't any time left. 'We have to break the glass!' I shrieked at Eric. He nodded very slowly. We knelt to brace ourselves against the end of the coffin and we pushed as hard as we could till it slammed into the glass, which cracked into about a thousand pieces. They hung together, amazingly – the miracle of safety glass. I could have screamed from frustration. We needed a *hole*, not a curtain of glass. Crouching lower, digging our toes into the carpet, trying to ignore the rumbling noises in the building below us, Eric and I shoved with all our strength.

Finally! We punched the coffin all the way through. The window let go of its frame and cascaded down the side of the building.

And Eric saw sunlight for the first time in a thousand years. He screamed, a terrible, gut-wrenching noise. But in the next instant, he pulled the cloak tight around him. He grabbed me and hopped astride the coffin, and we pushed off with our feet. For just a fraction of a minute, we hung in the balance, and then we tilted forward. In the most awful moment of my life, we went out the window and began tobogganing down the building on the coffin. We would crash unless —

Suddenly we were off the coffin and kind of staggering through the air, Eric holding me to him with dogged persistence.

I exhaled with profound relief. Of course, Eric could fly.

In his light-stunned stupor, he couldn't fly very well. This was not the smooth progress I'd experienced before; we had more of a zigzag, bobbing descent.

But it was better than a free fall.

Eric could delay our descent enough to keep me from being dashed to my death on the street outside the hotel. However, the coffin with Pam inside had a bad landing, and Pam came catapulting out of the remains of the wood and into the sunlight where she lay motionless. Without making a sound, she began to burn. Eric landed on top of her and used the blanket to cover both of them. One of Pam's feet was exposed, and the flesh was smoking. I covered it up.

I also heard the sound of sirens. I flagged down the first ambulance I saw, and the medics leaped out.

I pointed to the blanketed heap. 'Two vampires – get them out of the sun!' I said.

The pair of EMTs, both young women, exchanged an incredulous glance. 'What do we do with them?' asked the dark one.

'You take them to a nice basement somewhere, one without any windows, and you tell the owners to keep that basement open, because there are gonna be more.'

High up, a smaller explosion blew out one of the suites. A suitcase bomb, I thought, wondering how many Joe had talked us into carrying up into the rooms. A fine shower of glass sparkled in the sun as we looked up, but darker things were following the glass out of the window, and the EMTs began to move like the trained team they were. They didn't panic, but they definitely moved with haste, and they were already debating which building close at hand had a large basement.

'We'll tell everyone,' said the dark woman. Pam was now in the ambulance and Eric halfway there. His face was bright red and steam was rising from his lips. Oh, my God. 'What you going to do?'

'I have to go back in there,' I said.

'Fool,' she said, and then threw herself in the ambulance, which took off.

There was more glass raining down, and part of the bottom floor appeared to be collapsing. That would be due to some of the larger explosive-packed coffin bombs in the shipping and receiving area. Another explosion came from about the sixth floor, but on the other side of the pyramid. My senses were so dulled by the sound and the sight that I wasn't surprised when I saw a blue suitcase flying through the air. Mr Cataliades had succeeded in breaking the queen's window. Suddenly I realized the suitcase was intact, had not exploded, and was hurtling straight at me.

I began to run, flashing back to my softball days when I had sprinted from third to home and had to slide in. I aimed for the park across the street, where traffic had come to a stop because of the emergency vehicles: cop cars, ambulances, fire engines. There was a cop just ahead of me who was facing away, pointing something out to another cop. 'Down!' I yelled. 'Bomb!' and she swung around to face me and I tackled her, taking her down to the ground with me. Something hit me in the middle of the back, whoosh, and the air was shoved out of my lungs. We lay there for a long minute, until I pushed myself off of her and climbed unsteadily to my feet. It was wonderful to inhale, though the air was acrid with flames and dust. She might have said something to me, but I couldn't hear her.

I turned around to face the Pyramid of Gizeh.

Parts of the structure were crumbling, folding in and down, all the glass and concrete and steel and wood separating from the whole into discrete parts, while most of the walls that had created the spaces – of rooms and bathrooms and halls – collapsed. That collapse trapped many of the bodies that had occupied these arbitrarily divided areas. They were all one now: the structure, its parts, its inhabitants.

Here and there were still bits that had held together. The human floor, the mezzanine, and the lobby level were partially intact, though the area around the registration desk was destroyed.

I saw a shape I recognized, a coffin. The lid had popped clean off with the impact of its fall. As the sun hit the creature inside, it let out a wail, and I rushed over. There was a hunk of drywall by it, and I hauled that over the coffin. There was silence as soon as the sun was blocked from touching the vampire inside.

'Help!' I yelled. 'Help!'

A few policemen moved toward me.

'There are people and vamps still alive,' I said. 'The vamps have to be covered.'

'People first,' said one beefy veteran.

'Sure,' I agreed automatically, though even as I said it, I thought, *Vampires didn't set these bombs.* 'But if you can cover the vamps, they can last until ambulances can take them to a safe place.'

There was a chunk of hotel still standing, a bit of the south part. Looking up, I saw Mr Cataliades standing at an empty frame where the glass had fallen away. Somehow, he had worked his way down to the human floor. He was holding a bundle wrapped in a bedspread, clutching it to his chest.

'Look!' I called, to get a fireman's attention. 'Look!'

They leaped into action at seeing a live person to rescue. They were far more enthusiastic about that than about rescuing vamps who were possibly smoldering to death in the sunlight and could easily be saved by being covered. I tried to blame them, but I couldn't.

For the first time I noticed that there was a crowd of regular people who had stopped their cars and gotten out to help – or gawk. There were also people who were screaming, 'Let them burn!'

I watched the firemen go up in a bucket to fetch the demon and his burden, and then I turned back to working my way through the rubble.

After a time, I was flagging. The screams of the human survivors, the smoke, the sunlight muted by the huge cloud of dust, the noise of the groaning structure settling, the hectic noise of the rescue workers and the machinery that was arriving and being employed ... I was overwhelmed.

By that time, since I'd stolen one of the yellow jackets and one of the hard hats all the rescuers were wearing, I'd gotten close enough to find two vampires, one of whom I knew, in the ruins of the check-in area, heavily overlaid by debris from the floors above. A big piece of wood survived to identify the reception desk. One of the vampires was very burned, and I had no idea if he'd survive it or not. The other vamp had hidden beneath the largest piece of wood, and only his feet and hands had been singed and blackened. Once I yelled for help, the vamps were covered with blankets. 'We got a building two blocks away; we're using it for the vampire repository,' said the dark-skinned ambulance driver who took the more seriously injured one, and I realized it was the same woman who'd taken Eric and Pam.

In addition to the vampires, I uncovered a barely alive Todd Donati. I spent a few moments with him until a stretcher got there. And I found, near to him, a dead maid. She'd been crushed.

I had a smell in my nose that just wouldn't go away, and I hated it. It was coating my lungs inside, I thought, and I'd spend the rest of my life breathing it in and breathing it out. The odor was composed of burning building materials, scorched bodies, and disintegrating vampires. It was the smell of hatred.

I saw some things so awful I couldn't even think about them then.

Suddenly, I didn't feel I could search anymore. I had to sit down. I was drawn to a pile created by the chance arrangement of a large pipe and some drywall. I perched on it and wept. Then the whole pile shifted sideways, and I landed on the ground, still weeping.

I looked into the opening revealed by the shifted debris.

Bill was crouched inside, half his face burned away. He was wearing the clothes I'd last seen him in the night before. I arched myself over him to keep the sun off, and he said, 'Thanks,' through cracked and bloody lips. He kept slipping in and out of his comatose daytime sleep.

'Jesus God,' I said. 'Come help!' I called, and saw two men start toward me with a blanket.

'I knew you'd find me,' Bill said, or did I imagine that?

I stayed hunched in the awkward position. There just wasn't anything near enough to grab that would cover as much of him as I did. The smell was making me gag, but I stayed. He'd lasted this long only because he'd been covered by accident.

Though one fireman threw up, they covered him and took him away.

Then I saw another yellow-jacketed figure tear off across the debris field toward the ambulances as fast as anyone could move without breaking a leg. I got the impression of a live brain, and I recognized it at once. I scrambled over piles of rubble, following the signature of the brain of the man I wanted most to find. Quinn and Frannie lay half- buried under a pile of loose rubble. Frannie was unconscious, and she'd been bleeding from the head, but it had dried. Quinn was dazed but coming to full awareness. I could see that fresh water had cut a path in the dust on his face, and I realized the man who'd just dashed away had given Quinn some water to drink and was returning with stretchers for the two.

He tried to smile at me. I fell to my knees beside him. 'We might have to change our plans, babe,' he said. 'I may have to take care of Frannie for a week or two. Our mom's not exactly Florence Nightingale.'

I tried not to cry, but it was like, once turned to 'on', I couldn't tell my tear ducts to switch off. I wasn't sobbing anymore, but I was trickling steadily. Stupid. 'You do what you have to do,' I said. 'You call me when you can. Okay?' I hated people who said 'Okay?' all the time, like they were getting permission, but I couldn't help that, either. 'You're alive; that's all that matters.'

'Thanks to you,' he said. 'If you hadn't called, we'd be dead. Even the fire alarm might not have gotten us out of the room in time.'

I heard a groan from a few feet away, a breath on the air. Quinn heard it, too. I crawled away from him, pushing aside a large chunk of toilet and sink. There, covered with dust and debris, under several large bits of drywall, lay Andre, completely out of it. A quick glance told me he had several serious injuries. But none of them was bleeding. He would heal them all. Dammit.

'It's Andre,' I told Quinn. 'Hurt, but alive.' If my voice was grim, I felt grim. There was a nice, long wood splinter right by his leg, and I was so tempted. Andre was a threat to my freedom of will, to everything I enjoyed about my life. But I'd seen so much death that day already.

I crouched there beside him, hating him, but after all ... I knew him. That should have made it easier, but it didn't.

I duckwalked out of the little alcove where he lay, scuttled back to Quinn.

'Those guys are coming back to get us,' he told me, sounding stronger every minute. 'You can leave now.'

'You want me to leave?'

His eyes were telling me something. I wasn't reading it.

'Okay,' I said hesitantly. 'I'll go.'

'I've got help coming,' he said gently. 'You could be finding someone else.'

'All right,' I said, not knowing how to take this, and pushed to my feet. I'd gone maybe two yards when I heard him begin to move. But after a moment of stillness, I kept walking.

I returned to a big van that had been brought in and parked close to the rescue command center. This yellow jacket had been a magic pass, but it might run out any minute. Someone would notice I was wearing bedroom slippers, and they were ripping up, since they'd hardly been intended for ruin-scrambling. A woman handed me a bottle of water from the van, and I opened it with unsteady hands. I drank and drank, and poured the rest of the water over my face and hands. Despite the chill in the air, it felt wonderful.

By then, two (or four, or six) hours must have passed since the first explosion. There were now scores of rescuers there who had equipment, machinery, blankets. I was casting around for someone who looked authoritative, intending to find out where the other human survivors had been taken, when a voice spoke in my head.

Sookie?

Barry!

What kind of shape are you in?

Pretty rocky, but not much hurt. You?

Same. Cecile died.

I'm so sorry. I couldn't think of anything else to say.

I've thought of something we can do.

What? I probably didn't sound very interested.

We can find living people. We'll be better, together.

That's what I've been doing, I told him. *But you're right, together we'll be stronger.* At the same time, I was so tired that something inside of me cringed at the thought of making further effort. *Of course we can,* I said.

If this pile of debris had been as horrifyingly huge as the Twin Towers, we couldn't have done it. But this site was smaller and more contained, and if we could get anyone to believe us, we had a chance.

I found Barry close to the command center, and I took his grimy hand. He was younger than me, but now he didn't look it, and I didn't think he'd ever act it again. When I scanned the line of bodies on the grass of the little park, I saw Cecile, and I saw what might have been the maid I'd accosted in the hallway. There were a few flaking, vaguely manlike shapes that were disintegrating vampires. I could have known any of them, but it was impossible to tell.

Any humiliation would be a small thing to pay if we could save someone. So Barry and I prepared to be humiliated and mocked.

At first, it was hard to get anyone to listen. The professionals kept referring us to the casualty center or to one of the ambulances parked nearby ready to take survivors to one of Rhodes's hospitals.

Finally, I was face-to-face with a thin, gray-haired man who listened to me without any expression on his face at all.

'I never thought I'd be rescuing vampires, either,' he said, as though that explained his decision, and maybe it did. 'So, take these two men with you, and show 'em what you can do. You have fifteen minutes of these men's valuable time. If you waste it, you might be killing someone.'

Barry had had the idea, but now he seemed to want me to speak for us. His face was blackened with smears of soot. We had a silent conference about the best way to go about our task, and at the end of it, I turned to the firemen and said, 'Put us up in one of those bucket things.'

For a wonder, they did, without further argument. We were lifted out over the debris, and yes, we knew it was dangerous, and yes, we were prepared to take the consequences. Still holding hands, Barry and I shut our eyes and *searched*, flinging our minds open and outward.

'Move us left,' I said, and the fireman in the bucket with us gestured to the man in the cab of the machine. 'Watch me,' I said, and he looked back. 'Stop,' I said, and the bucket stopped. We searched again. 'Directly below,' I said. 'Right below here. It's a woman named something Santiago.'

After a few minutes, a roar went up. They'd found her alive.

We were popular after that, and there were no more questions about how we did it, as long as we kept it up. Rescue people are all about rescuing. They were bringing dogs, and they were inserting microphones, but Barry and I were quicker and more articulate than the dogs, and more precise than the microphones. We found four more live people, and we found a man who died before they could get to him, a waiter named Art who loved his wife and suffered terribly right up until the end. Art was especially heartbreaking, because they were trying like hell to dig the guy out, and I had to tell them it was no good. Of course, they didn't take my word for it; they kept excavating, but he had passed. By that time, the searchers were really excited about our ability and wanted us to work through the night, but Barry was failing and I wasn't much better. Worse, dark was closing in.

'The vampires'll be rising,' I reminded the fire chief. He nodded and looked at me for further explanation. 'They'll be hurt bad,' I said. He still didn't get it. 'They'll need blood instantly, and they won't have any control. I wouldn't send any rescue workers out on the debris alone,' I said, and his face went blank with thought.

'You don't think they're all dead? Can't you find them?'

'Well, actually, no. We can't find vamps. Humans, yes. But not undead. Their brains don't give off any, ah, waves. We've got to go now. Where are the survivors?'

'They're all in the Thorne Building, right down there,' he said, pointing. 'In the basement.' We turned to walk away. By this time, Barry had slung his arm around my shoulders, and not because he was feeling affectionate. He needed the support.

'Let me get your names and addresses, so the mayor can thank you,' the gray-haired man said, holding a pen and clipboard at the ready.

No! Barry said, and my mouth snapped shut.

I shook my head. 'We're going to pass on that,' I said. I'd had a quick look in his head, and he was greedy for more of our help. Suddenly

I understood why Barry had stopped me so abruptly, though my fellow telepath was so tired he couldn't tell me himself. My refusal didn't go over big.

'You'll work for vamps, but you don't want to stand and be counted as someone who helped on this terrible day?'

'Yes,' I answered. 'That's just about right.'

He wasn't happy with me, and I thought for a minute he was going to force the issue: grab my wallet out of my pants, send me to jail, or something. But he reluctantly nodded his head and jerked it in the direction of the Thorne Building.

Someone will try to find out, Barry said. *Someone will want to use us.*

I sighed, and I hardly had the energy to take in more air. I nodded. *Yeah, someone will. If we go to the shelter, someone will be watching for us there, and they'll ask for our names from someone who recognizes us, and after that, it's only a matter of time.*

I couldn't think of a way to dodge going in there. We had to have help, we had to find our parties and discover how and when we could leave the city, and we had to find out who had lived and who hadn't.

I patted my back pocket, and to my amazement, my cell phone was still in it and still had bars. I called Mr Cataliades. If anyone besides me had come out of the Pyramid of Gizeh with a cell phone, the lawyer would be the one.

'Yes,' he said cautiously. 'Miss St—'

'Shhh,' I said. 'Don't say my name out loud.' It was sheer paranoia talking.

'Very well.'

'We helped them out down here, and now they really want to get to know us better,' I said, feeling very clever for talking so guardedly. I was very tired. 'Barry and I are outside the building where you are. We need to stay somewhere else. Too many people making lists in there, right?'

'That is a popular activity,' he said.

'You and Diantha okay?'

'She has not been found. We were separated.'

I didn't speak for a few seconds. 'I'm so sorry. Who were you holding when I saw them rescue you?'

'The queen. She is here, though badly injured. We can't find Andre.'

He paused, and because I couldn't help it, I said, 'Who else?'

'Gervaise is dead. Eric, Pam, Bill . . . burned, but here. Cleo Babbitt is here. I haven't seen Rasul.'

'Is Jake Purifoy there?'

'I haven't seen him, either.'

'Because you might want to know he's at least partially responsible if you do see him. He was in on the Fellowship plot.'

'Ah.' Mr Cataliades registered that. 'Oh, yes, I certainly did want to know that. Johan Glassport will be especially interested, since he has several broken ribs and a broken collarbone. He's very, very angry.' It said something about Johan Glassport's viciousness, that Mr Cataliades thought him capable of exacting as much vengeance as a vampire would. 'How did you come to know there was a plot at all, Miss Sookie?'

I told the lawyer the story Clovache had told me; I figured now that she and Batanya had gone back to wherever they came from, that would be okay.

'Hiring them proved to be worth the money for King Isaiah.' Cataliades sounded thoughtful rather than envious. 'Isaiah is here and completely uninjured.'

'We need to go find somewhere to sleep. Can you tell Barry's king that he's with me?' I asked, knowing I needed to get off the phone and make a plan.

'He is too injured to care. He is not aware.'

'All right. Just someone from the Texas party.'

'I see Joseph Velasquez. Rachel is dead.' Mr Cataliades couldn't help himself; he had to tell me all the bad news.

'Cecile, Stan's assistant, is dead,' I told him.

'Where are you going to go?' Cataliades asked.

'I don't know what to do,' I said. I felt exhausted and hopeless, and I'd had too much bad news and gotten too battered to rally one more time.

'I will send a cab for you,' Mr Cataliades offered. 'I can get a number from one of the nice volunteers. Tell the driver you are rescue workers and you need a ride to the nearest inexpensive hotel. Do you have a credit card?'

'Yeah, and my debit card,' I said, blessing the impulse that had led me to stuff the little wallet in my pocket.

'No, wait, they'll track you very easily if you use it. Cash?'

I checked. Thanks largely to Barry, we had a hundred ninety dollars between us. I told Mr Cataliades we could swing it.

'Then spend the night in a hotel, and tomorrow call me again,' he said, sounding unutterably weary.

'Thanks for the plan.'

'Thanks for your warning,' the courtly demon said. 'We would all be dead if you and the Bellboy hadn't wakened us.'

I ditched the yellow jacket and the hard hat. Barry and I tottered along, more or less holding each other up. We found a concrete barricade to lean against, our arms around each other. I tried to tell Barry why we were doing this, but he didn't care. I was worried that at any minute some firefighter or cop from the scene would spot us and stop to find out what we were doing, where we were going, who we were. I was so relieved that I felt sick when I spied a cab cruising slowly, the driver peering out the window. Had to be for us. I waved my free arm frantically. I had never hailed a cab before in my life. It was just like the movies.

The cab driver, a wire-thin guy from Guyana, wasn't too excited about letting filthy creatures like us get into his cab, but he couldn't turn down people as pitiful as we were. The nearest 'inexpensive' hotel was a mile back into the city, away from the water. If we'd had the energy, we could have walked it. At least the cab ride wasn't too pricey.

Even at the mid-range hotel, the desk clerks were less than thrilled with our appearance; but after all, it was a day for charity to people who were involved in the blast. We got a room at a price that would have made me gasp if I hadn't seen the room rates at the Pyramid. The room itself wasn't much, but we didn't need much. A maid knocked on the door right after we got in and said she'd like to wash our clothes for us, since we didn't have any more. She looked down when she said that, so she wouldn't embarrass me. Trying not to choke up at her kindness, I looked down at my shirt and slacks and agreed.

I turned to Barry to find he was absolutely out cold. I maneuvered him into the bed. It was unpleasantly like handling one of the vampires, and I held my lips pressed together in a tight line the whole time I undressed his limp body. Then I shucked my own clothes, found a plastic bag in the closet to hold them, and handed the soiled clothes out to her. I got a washcloth and wiped off Barry's face and hands and feet, and then I covered him up.

I had to shower, and I thanked God for the complimentary shampoo and soap and cream rinse and skin lotion. I also thanked God for hot and cold running water, particularly hot. The kind maid had even handed me two toothbrushes and a little packet of toothpaste, and I scrubbed my mouth clean of the flavor of ashes. I washed my panties and bra in the sink and rolled them up in a towel before I hung them up to dry. I'd given the lady every stitch of Barry's clothes.

Finally, there was nothing else to do, and I crawled into the bed beside Barry. Now that I smelled so good, I noticed that he didn't, but that was just tough for me, right? I wouldn't have woken him for anything. I turned on my side away from him, thought about how frightening that long, empty corridor had been – isn't it funny that that was what I picked out as scary, after such a horrific day?

The hotel room was so very quiet after the tumult of the scene of the explosions, and the bed was so very comfortable, and I smelled so much better and hardly hurt at all.

I slept and didn't dream.

Chapter 18

I know there are many worse things than waking up naked in a bed with someone you don't know very well. But when my eyes fluttered open the next day, I couldn't think of any, for five long minutes. I knew Barry was awake. You can tell when a brain pops into awareness. To my relief, he slipped out of the bed and into the bathroom without speaking, and I heard the drumming of the water in the shower stall soon after.

Our clean clothes were in a bag hanging on our inside doorknob, and there was a USA Today, too. After hastily donning my clothes, I spread the newspaper out on the small table while I brewed a pot of the free coffee. I also extended the bag with Barry's clothes in it into the bathroom and dropped it on the floor, waving it a little first to attract his attention.

I'd looked at the room service menu, and we didn't have enough cash to get anything on it. We had to reserve some of our funds for a cab, because I didn't know what our next move would be. Barry came out, looking as refreshed as I'd been last night. To my surprise, he kissed me on the cheek, and then sat opposite me with his own insulated cup that contained something that bore a faint relationship to brewed coffee.

'I don't remember much about last night,' he said. 'Fill me in on why we're here.'

I did.

'That was good thinking on my part,' he said. 'I'm in awe of myself.'

I laughed. He might be feeling a little male chagrin that he had wilted before I did, but at least he could make fun of himself.

'So, I guess we need to call your demon lawyer?'

I nodded. It was eleven by then, so I called.

He answered right away. 'There are many ears here,' he said without preamble. 'And I understand these phones aren't too secure. Cell phones.'

'All right.'

'So I will come to you in a while, bringing some things you'll need. You are where?'

With a twinge of misgiving, since the demon was a guy people would notice, I told him the name of the hotel and our room number, and he told me to be patient. I'd been feeling fine until Mr Cataliades said that, and all of a sudden I began to twitch inwardly. I felt like we were on the run now, when we in no way deserved to be. I'd read the newspaper, and the story about the Pyramid said the catastrophe was due to 'a series of explosions' that Dan Brewer, head of the state terrorist task force, attributed to several bombs. The fire chief was less committal: 'An investigation is underway.' I should damn well hope so.

Barry said, 'We could have sex while we wait.'

'I liked you better unconscious,' I said. I knew Barry was only trying not to think about stuff, but still.

'You undress me last night?' he said with a leer.

'Yeah, that was me, lucky me,' I said. I smiled at him, surprising myself.

A knock at the door had us both staring at it like startled deer.

'Your demon guy,' said Barry after a second of mental checking.

'Yep,' I said, and got up to answer it.

Mr Cataliades hadn't had the kindness of a maid, so he was still in the soiled clothes of the day before. But he managed to look dignified, anyway, and his hands and face were clean.

'Please, how is everyone?' I asked.

'Sophie-Anne has lost her legs, and I don't know if they'll come back,' he said.

'Oh, geez,' I said, wincing.

'Sigebert fought free of the debris after dark,' he continued. 'He'd hidden in a safe pocket in the parking garage, where he landed after the explosions. I suspect he found someone to feed off, because he was healthier than he ought to have been. But if that's the case, he shoved the body into one of the fires, because we would have heard if a drained body had been found.'

I hoped the donor had been one of the Fellowship guys.

'Your king,' Mr Cataliades said to Barry, 'is so injured it may take him a decade to recover. Until the situation is clear, Joseph leads, though he'll be challenged soon. The king's child Rachel is dead; perhaps Sookie told you?'

'Sorry,' I said. 'I just had too much bad news to finish getting through it all.'

'And Sookie has told me the human Cecile perished.'

'What about Diantha?' I asked, hesitating to do so. It had to be significant that Mr Cataliades hadn't' mentioned his niece.

'Missing,' he said briefly 'And yet that piece of filth, Glassport, survived.'

'I'm sorry for both things,' I said.

Barry seemed numb. All traces of his flippant mood had vanished. He looked smaller, sitting on the edge of the bed. The cocky sharp dresser I'd met in the lobby of the Pyramid had gone underground, at least for a while.

'I told you about Gervaise,' Mr Cataliades said. 'I identified his woman's body this morning. What was her name?'

'Carla. I can't remember her last name. It'll come to me.'

'The first name will probably be enough for them to identify her. One of the corpses in hotel uniform had a computer list in his pocket.'

'They weren't all in on it,' I said with some certainty.

'No, of course not,' Barry said. 'Only a few.'

We looked at him.

'How do you know?' I asked.

'I overheard them.'

'When?'

'The night before.'

I bit the inside of my mouth, hard.

'What did you hear?' Mr Cataliades asked in a level voice.

'I was with Stan in the, you know, the buy-and-sell thing. I had noticed the waiters and so on were dodging me, and then I watched to see if they were avoiding Sookie as well. So I thought, 'They know what you are, Barry, and there's something they don't want you to know. You better check it out.' I found a good place to sort of skulk behind some of those fake palm trees, close by the service door, and I could get a reading on what they were thinking inside. They didn't spell it out or anything, okay?' He had gotten an accurate reading on our thoughts, too. 'It was just, like, "Okay, we're gonna get those vamps, damn them, and if we take some of their human slaves, well, that's just too bad, we'll live with it. Damned, by association."'

I could only sit there and look at him.

'No, I didn't know when or what they were going to do! I went to bed finally kind of worrying about them, what the plan was, and when I couldn't settle into a good sleep, I finally quit trying and called you. And we tried to get everyone out,' he said, and began crying.

I sat beside him and put my arm around him. I didn't know what to say. Of course, he could tell what I was thinking.

'Yes, I wish I'd said something before I did,' he said in a choked voice. 'Yes, I did the wrong thing. But I thought if I spoke up before I knew something for sure, the vamps would fall on them and drain them. Or they'd want me to point out who knew and who didn't. And I couldn't do that.'

There was a long silence.

'Mr Cataliades, have you seen Quinn?' I asked to break the silence.

'He's at the human hospital. He couldn't stop them from taking him.'

'I have to go see him.'

'How serious is your fear that the authorities will try to coerce you into doing their bidding?'

Barry raised his head and looked at me. 'Pretty serious,' we said simultaneously.

'It's the first time I've ever shown anyone, aside from local people, what I can do,' I said.

'Me, too.' Barry wiped his eyes with the back of his hand. 'You should have seen that guy's face when he finally believed that we could find people. He thought we were psychics or something, and he couldn't understand that what we were doing was registering a live brain signature. Nothing mystical about it.'

'He was all over the idea once he believed us,' I said. 'You could hear in his head that he was thinking of the hundred different ways we could be of use to rescue operations, to the government at conferences, police interrogations.'

Mr Cataliades looked at us. I couldn't pick out all his snarly demon thoughts, but he was having a lot of them.

'We'd lose control over our lives,' Barry said. 'I like my life.'

'I guess I could be saving a lot of people,' I said. I'd just never thought about it before. I'd never been faced with a situation like the one we'd faced the previous day. I hoped I never was again. How likely was it I would ever be on-site again at a disaster? Was I obligated to give up a job I liked, among people I cared about, to work for strangers in far away places? I shivered when I thought of it. I felt something harden within me when I realized that the advantage Andre had taken of me would only be the beginning, in situations like that. Like Andre, everyone would want to own me.

'No,' I said. 'I won't do it. Maybe I'm just being selfish and I'm damning myself, but I won't do it. I don't think we're exaggerating how bad that would be for us, not a bit.'

'Then going to the hospital is not a good idea,' Cataliades said.

'I know, but I have to, anyway.'

'Then you can stop by on your way to the airport.'

We sat up straighter.

'There's an Anubis plane flying out in three hours. It'll go to Dallas first, then Shreveport. The queen and Stan are paying for it jointly. It'll have all the survivors of both parties on it. The citizens of Rhodes have donated used coffins for the trip.' Mr Cataliades made a face, and honestly, I couldn't blame him. 'Here's all the cash we can spare,' he continued, handing me a short stack of bills, 'Make it to the Anubis terminal in time, and you'll both go home with us. If you don't make it, I'll assume something happened to stop you and you'll have to call to make some other arrangement. We know we owe you a great debt, but we have wounded to get home ourselves, and the queen's credit cards and so on were lost in the fire. I'll have to call her credit company for emergency service, but that won't take much time.'

This seemed a little cold, but after all, he wasn't our best friend, and as the daytime guy for the queen, he had a lot to do and many more problems to solve.

'Okay,' I said. 'Hey, listen, is Christian Baruch at the shelter?'

His face sharpened. 'Yes. Though somewhat burned, he's hanging around the queen in Andre's absence as if he would take Andre's place.'

'He wants to, you know. He wants to be the next Mr Queen of Louisiana.'

'Baruch?' Cataliades could not have been more scornful if a goblin had applied for the job.

'No, he's gone to extreme lengths.' I already told Andre about this. Now I had to explain again. 'That's why he planted that Dr Pepper bomb,' I said about five minutes later.

'How do you know this?' Mr Cataliades asked.

'I figured it out, from this and that,' I said modestly. I sighed. Here came the yucky part. 'I found him yesterday, hiding underneath the registration desk. There was another vampire with him, badly burned. I don't even know who that one was. And in the same area was Todd Donati, the security guy, alive but hurt, and a dead maid.' I felt the exhaustion all over again, smelled the awful smell, tried to breathe the thick air. 'Baruch was out of it, of course.'

I was not exactly proud of this, and I looked down at my hands. 'Anyway, I was trying to read Todd Donati's mind, to find out how hurt he was, and he was just hating Baruch and blaming him, too. He was willing to be frank, this time. No more job to worry about. Todd told me he'd watched all the security tapes over and over again, and he'd finally figured out what he was seeing. His boss was leaping up to block the camera with gum so he could plant the bomb. Once he'd figured that out, Donati knew that Baruch had wanted to alarm the queen, make her insecure, so she'd take a new husband. And that would be Christian Baruch. But guess why he wants to marry her?'

'I can't imagine,' said Mr Cataliades, thoroughly shocked.

'Because he wants to open a new vampire hotel in New Orleans.

Blood in the Quarter got flooded and closed, and Baruch thought he could rebuild and reopen.'

'But Baruch didn't have anything to do with the other bombs?'

'I sure don't think so, Mr Cataliades. I think that was the Fellowship, just like I said yesterday.'

'Then who killed the vampires from Arkansas?' Barry asked. 'I guess the Fellowship did that, too? No, wait . . . why would they? Not that they'd quibble at killing some vampires, but they'd know the vampires would probably get killed in the big explosion.'

'We have an overload of villains,' I said. 'Mr Cataliades, you got any ideas about who might have taken out the Arkansas vampires?' I gave Mr Cataliades a straight-in-the-eyes stare.

'No,' Mr Cataliades said. 'If I did, I would *never* say those ideas out loud. I think you should be concentrating on your man's injuries and getting back to your little town, not worrying about three deaths among so many.'

I wasn't exactly worried about the deaths of the three Arkansas vampires, and it seemed like a really good idea to take Mr Cataliades's advice to heart. I'd had the odd moment to think about the murders, and I'd decided that the simplest answer was often the best.

Who'd thought she had a good chance of skipping a trial altogether, if Jennifer Cater was silenced?

Who'd prepared the way to be admitted to Jennifer's room, by the simple means of a phone call?

Who'd had a good long moment of telepathic communication with her underlings before she began the artificial flurry of primping for the impromptu visit?

Whose bodyguard had been coming out of the stairway door just as we were exiting the suite?

I knew, just as Mr Cataliades knew, that Sophie-Anne had ensured Sigebert would be admitted to Jennifer Cater's room by calling down ahead and telling Jennifer she herself was on her way. Jennifer would look out the peephole, recognize Sigebert, and assume the queen was right behind him. Once inside, Sigebert would unsheath his sword and kill everyone in the place.

Then he would hurry back up the stairs to appear in time to escort the queen right back down to the seventh floor. He'd enter the room again so there'd be a reason for his scent to be on the air.

And at the time I'd suspected absolutely nothing.

What a shock it must have been to Sophie-Anne when Henrik Feith had popped up alive; but then the problem had been solved when he accepted her protection.

The problem reasserted itself when someone talked him into accusing her anyway.

And then, amazingly, problem solved again: the nervous little vampire had been assassinated in front of the court.

'I do wonder how Kyle Perkins was hired,' I said. 'He must have known he was on a suicide mission.'

'Perhaps,' Mr Cataliades said carefully, 'he had decided to meet the sun anyway. Perhaps he was looking for a spectacular and interesting way to go, earning a monetary legacy for his human descendants.'

'It seems strange that I was sent looking for information about him by a member of our very own party,' I said, my voice neutral.

'Ah, not everyone needs to know everything,' Mr Cataliades said, his voice just as neutral.

Barry could hear my thoughts, of course, but he wasn't getting what Mr Cataliades was saying, which was just as well. It was stupid that it made me feel better, Eric and Bill not knowing the queen's deep game. Not that they weren't capable of playing deep games themselves, but I didn't think Eric would have sent me on the wild goose chase for the archery range where Kyle Perkins had trained if Eric had known the queen herself had hired Perkins.

The poor woman behind the counter had died because the queen hadn't told her left hand what her right hand was doing. And I wondered what had happened to the human, the one who'd thrown up on the murder scene, the one who'd been hired to drive Sigebert or Andre to the range ... after I'd so thoughtfully left a message to tell them when Barry and I were going back to collect the evidence. I'd sealed the woman's fate myself by leaving that phone message.

Mr Cataliades took his departure, shaking our hands with his beaming smile, almost normal. He urged us once again to get to the airport.

'Sookie?' said Barry.

'Yeah.'

'I really want to be on that plane.'

'I know.'

'What about you?'

'I don't think I can do it. Sit on the same plane with them.'

'They all got hurt,' Barry said.

'Yeah, but that isn't payback.'

'You took care of that, didn't you?'

I didn't ask him what he meant. I knew what he could pick up out of my head.

'As much as I could,' I said.

'Maybe I don't want to be on the same plane with *you*,' Barry said.

Of course it hurt, but I guess I deserved it.

I shrugged. 'You gotta decide that on your own. All of us have different things we can live with.'

Barry considered that. 'Yeah,' he said. 'I know. But for right now, it's better that we go our separate ways, here. I'm leaving for the airport to hang around until I can leave. Are you going to the hospital?'

I was too wary now to tell him. 'I don't know,' I said. 'But I'm finding a car or a bus to take me home.'

He hugged me, no matter how upset he was about the choices I'd made. I could feel the affection and regret in his heart. I hugged him back. He'd made his own choices.

I left the maid ten dollars when I departed on foot about five minutes after Barry got in a cab. I waited until I got two blocks from the hotel, and then I asked a passerby how to get to St. Cosmas. It was a long ten-block hike, but the day was beautiful, cool and crisp with a bright sun. It felt good to be by myself. I might be wearing rubber-soled slippers, but I was dressed nicely enough, and I was clean. I ate a hot dog on my way to the hospital, a hot dog I'd bought from a street vendor, and that was something else I'd never done before. I bought a shapeless hat from a street vender, too, and stuffed all my hair up under it. The same guy had some dark glasses for sale. With the sky being so bright and the wind blowing in off the lake, the combination didn't look too odd.

St. Cosmas was an old edifice, with lots of ornate architectural embellishment on the outside. It was huge, too. I asked about Quinn's condition, and one of the women stationed at the busy visitors' desk said she couldn't give out that information. But to see if he was registered at the hospital, she'd had to look up his records, and I plucked his room number from her thoughts. I waited until all three of the women were occupied with other queries, and I slipped into the elevator and rode up.

Quinn was on the tenth floor. I'd never seen a hospital so large, and I'd never seen one so bustling. It was easy to stride around like I had a purpose and knew where I was going.

There was no one on guard outside his room.

I knocked lightly, and there wasn't a sound from inside. I pushed open the door very gently and stepped inside. Quinn was asleep in the bed, and he was attached to machines and tubes. And he was a fast-healing shifter, so his injuries must have been grievous. His sister was by his side. Her bandaged head, which had been propped on her hand, jerked up as she became aware of my presence. I pulled off the sunglasses and the hat.

'You,' she said.

'Yeah, me, Sookie. What's Frannie short for, anyway?'

'It's really Francine, but everyone calls me Frannie.' She looked younger as she said it.

Though I was pleased at the decreased hostility, I decided I'd better stay on my side of the room. 'How is he?' I asked, jerking my chin at the sleeping man.

'He fades in and out.' There was a moment of silence while she took a drink from a white plastic cup on the bedside table. 'When you woke him up, he got me up,' she said abruptly. 'We started down the stairs. But a big piece of ceiling fell on him, and the floor went out from beneath us, and the next thing I knew, some firemen are telling me some crazy woman found me while I was still alive, and they're giving me all kinds of tests, and Quinn's telling me he was going to take care of me until I was well. Then they told me he had two broken legs.'

There was an extra chair, and I collapsed onto it. My legs just wouldn't hold me. 'What does the doctor say?'

'Which one?' Frannie said bleakly.

'Any. All.' I took one of Quinn's hands. Frannie almost reached out as if she thought I'd hurt him, but then she subsided. I had the hand that was free of tubes, and I held it for a while.

'They can't believe how much better he is already,' Frannie said just when I'd decided she wasn't going to answer. 'In fact, they think it's something of a miracle. Now we're gonna have to pay someone to get his records out of the system.' Her dark-rooted hair was in clumps, and she was still filthy from the blast site.

'Go buy some clothes and come back and have a shower,' I said. 'I'll sit with him.'

'Are you really his girlfriend?'

'Yes, I am.'

'He said you had some conflicts.'

'I do, but not with him.'

'So, okay. I will. You got any money?'

'Not a lot, but here's what I can spare.'

I handed her seventy-five dollars of Mr Cataliades's money.

'Okay, I can stretch it,' she said. 'Thanks.' She said it without enthusiasm, but she said it.

I sat in the quiet room and held Quinn's hand for almost an hour. In that time, his eyes had flickered open once, registered my presence, and closed again. A very faint smile curved his lips for a moment. I knew that while he was sleeping, his body was healing, and when he woke, he might be able to walk again. I would have found it very comforting to climb on that bed and snuggle with Quinn for a while, but it might be bad for him if I did that; I might jostle him or something.

After a while, I began talking to him. I told him why I thought the crude bomb had been left outside the queen's door, and I told him my theory about the deaths of the three Arkansas vampires. 'You gotta agree, it makes sense,' I said, and then I told him what I thought about the death of Henrik Feith and the execution of his murderer. I told him about the dead woman in the shop. I told him about my suspicions about the explosion.

'I'm sorry it was Jake that was in with them,' I told him. 'I know you used to like him. But he just couldn't stand being a vamp. I don't know if he approached the Fellowship or the Fellowship approached him. They had the guy at the computer, the one who was so rude to me. I think he called a delegate from each party to have them come pick up a suitcase. Some of them were too smart or too lazy to pick them up, and some of them returned the suitcases when no one claimed them. But not me, oh no, I put it in the queen's effing living room.' I shook my head. 'I guess not too many of the staff were in on it, because otherwise Barry or I would've picked up on something way before Barry did.'

Then I slept for a few minutes, I think, because Frannie was there when I looked around, and she was eating from a McDonald's bag. She was clean, and her hair was wet.

'You love him?' she asked, sucking up some Coke through a straw.

'Too soon to tell.'

'I'm going to have to take him home to Memphis,' she said.

'Yeah, I know. I may not get to see him for a while. I've got to get home, too, somehow.'

'The Greyhound station is two blocks away.'

I shuddered. A long, long bus ride was not a prospect that I could look forward to.

'Or you could take my car,' Frannie said.

'What?'

'Well, we got here separately. He drove here with all the props and a trailer, and I left out of my mama's in a hurry in my little sports car. So there are two cars here, and we only need one. I'm going to have to go home with him and stay for a while. You have to get back to work, right?'

'Right.'

'So, drive my car home, and we'll pick it up when we're able.'

'That's very nice of you,' I said. I was surprised by her generosity, because I'd definitely had the impression she wasn't keen on Quinn having a girlfriend, and she wasn't keen on me, specifically.

'You seem okay. You tried to get us out of there in time. And he really cares about you.'

'And you know this how?'

'He told me so.'

She'd gotten part of the family directness, I could tell.

'Okay,' I said. 'Where are you parked?'

Chapter 19

I'd been terrified the whole two-day drive: that I'd be stopped and they wouldn't believe I'd gotten permission to use the car, that Frannie would change her mind and tell the police I'd stolen it, that I'd have an accident and have to repay Quinn's sister for the vehicle. Frannie had an old red Mustang, and it was fun to drive. No one stopped me. The weather was good all the way back to Louisiana. I thought I'd see a slice of America, but along the interstate, everything looks the same. I imagined that in any small town I passed through, there was another Merlotte's, and maybe another Sookie.

I didn't sleep well on the trip, either, because I dreamed of the floor shaking under my feet and the dreadful moment we went out the hole in the glass. Or I saw Pam burning. Or other things, things I'd done and seen during the hours we patrolled the debris, looking for bodies.

When I turned into my driveway, having been gone a week, my heart began to pound as if the house was waiting for me. Amelia was sitting on the front porch with a bright blue ribbon in her hand, and Bob was sitting in front of her, batting at the dangling ribbon with a black paw. She looked up to see who it was, and when she recognized me behind the wheel, she leaped to her feet. I didn't pull around back; I stopped right there and jumped out of the driver's seat. Amelia's arms wrapped around me like vines, and she shrieked, 'You're back! Oh, blessed Virgin, you're back!'

We danced around and hopped up and down like teenagers, whooping with sheer happiness.

'The paper listed you as a survivor,' she said. 'But no one could find you the day after. Until you called, I wasn't sure you were alive.'

'It's a long story,' I said. 'A long, long story.'

'Is it the right time to tell it to me?'

'Maybe after a few days,' I said.

'Do you have anything to carry in?'

'Not a thing. All my stuff went up in smoke when the building went down.'

'Oh, my God! Your new clothes!'

'Well, at least I have my driver's license and my credit card and my cell phone, though the battery's flat and I don't have the charger.'

'And a new car?' She glanced back at the Mustang.

'A borrowed car.'

'I don't think I have a single friend who would loan me a whole car.'

'Half a car?' I asked, and she laughed.

'Guess what?' Amelia said. 'Your friends got married.'

I stopped dead. 'Which friends?' Surely she couldn't mean the Bellefleur double wedding; surely they hadn't changed the date yet again.

'Oh, I shouldn't have said anything,' Amelia said, looking guilty. 'Well, speak of the devil!' There was another car coming to a stop right by the red Mustang.

Tara scrambled out. 'I saw you driving by the shop,' she called. 'I almost didn't recognize you in the new car.'

'Borrowed it from a friend,' I said, looking at her askance.

'You did *not* tell her, Amelia Broadway!' Tara was righteously indignant.

'I didn't,' Amelia said. 'I started to, but I stopped in time!'

'Tell me what?'

'Sookie, I know this is going to sound crazy,' Tara said, and I felt my brows draw together. 'While you were gone, everything just clicked in a strange way, like something I'd known should happen, you know?'

I shook my head. I didn't know.

'JB and I got married!' Tara said, and the expression on her face was full of so many things: anxiety, hopefulness, guilt, wonder.

I ran that incredible sentence through my head several times before I was sure I understood the meaning of it. 'You and JB? Husband and wife?' I said.

'I know, I know, it seems maybe a little strange . . .'

'It seems perfect,' I said with all the sincerity I could scrape together. I wasn't really sure how I felt, but I owed my friend the happy face and cheerful voice I offered her. At the moment, this was the true stuff, and vampire fangs and blood under the bright searchlights seemed like the dream, or a scene from a movie I hadn't much enjoyed. 'I'm so happy for you. What do you need for a wedding present?'

'Just your blessing, we put the announcement in the paper yesterday,' she said, burbling away like a happy brook. 'And the phone just hasn't stopped ringing off the wall since then. People are so nice!'

She truly believed she'd swept all her bad memories into a corner. She was in the mood to credit the world with benevolence.

I would try that, too. I would do my best to smother the memory of that moment when I'd glanced back to see Quinn pulling himself along by his elbows. He'd reached Andre, who lay mute and stricken. Quinn had propped himself on one elbow, reached out with his other hand, grabbed the piece of wood lying by Andre's leg and jammed it into Andre's chest. And, just like that, Andre's long life was over.

He'd done it for me.

How could I be the same person? I wondered. How could I be happy that Tara had gotten married and yet remember such a thing – not with horror, but with a savage sense of pleasure? I had wanted Andre to die, as much as I had wanted Tara to find someone to live with who would never tease her for her awful past, someone who would care for her and be sweet to her. And JB would do that. He might not be much on intellectual conversation, but Tara seemed to have made her peace with that.

Theoretically, then, I was delighted and hopeful for my two friends. But I couldn't feel it. I'd seen awful things, and I'd felt awful things. Now I felt like two different people trying to exist inside the same space.

If I just stay away from the vampires for a while, I told myself, smiling and nodding the whole time as Tara talked on and Amelia patted my shoulder or my arm. *If I pray every night, and hang around with humans, and leave the Weres alone, I'll be okay.*

I hugged Tara, squeezing her until she squeaked.

'What do JB's parents say?' I asked. 'Where'd you get the license? Up in Arkansas?'

As Tara began to tell me all about it, I winked at Amelia, who winked back and bent down to scoop up Bob in her arms. Bob blinked when he looked into my face, and he rubbed his head against my offered fingers and purred. We went inside with the sun bright on our backs and our shadows preceding us into the old house.

From Dead to Worse

*Though she can't walk or see quite as well as she used to,
my mother, Jean Harris, remains the most complete person
I have ever met. She's been the bulwark of my existence,
the foundation I was built on, and the best mother
a woman could have.*

If this was *The Lord of the Rings* and I had a smart British voice like Cate Blanchett, I could tell you the background of the events of that fall in a really suspenseful way. And you'd be straining to hear the rest.

But what happened in my little corner of northwest Louisiana wasn't an epic story. The vampire war was more of the nature of a small-country takeover, and the Were war was like a border skirmish. Even in the annals of supernatural America – I guess they exist somewhere – they were minor chapters . . . unless you were actively involved in the takeovers and skirmishes.

Then they became pretty damn major.

And everything was due to Katrina, the disaster that just kept on spreading grief, woe, and permanent change in its wake.

Before Hurricane Katrina, Louisiana had a flourishing vampire community. In fact, the vampire population of New Orleans had burgeoned, making it the place to go if you wanted to see vampires; and lots of Americans did. The undead jazz clubs, featuring musicians no one had seen playing in public in decades, were special draws. Vamp strip clubs, vamp psychics, vamp sex acts; secret and not-so-secret places where you could get bitten and have an orgasm on the spot: all this was available in southern Louisiana.

In the northern part of the state . . . not so much. I live in the northern part in a small town called Bon Temps. But even in my area, where vamps are relatively thin on the ground, the undead were making economic and social strides.

All in all, vampire business in the Pelican State was booming. But then came the death of the King of Arkansas while his wife, the Queen of Louisiana, was entertaining him soon after their wedding. Since the corpse vanished and all the witnesses – except me – were supernaturals, human law took no notice. But the other vampires did, and the queen, Sophie-Anne Leclerq, landed in a very dicey legal position. Then came Katrina, which wiped out the financial base of Sophie-Anne's empire. Still, the queen was floundering back from those disasters, when another one followed hard on their heels. Sophie-Anne and some of her strongest adherents – and me, Sookie Stackhouse, telepath and human – were caught in a terrible explosion in Rhodes, the destruction of the vampire hotel called the Pyramid of Gizeh. A splinter group of the Fellowship of the Sun claimed responsibility, and while the leaders of that anti-vampire 'church' decried the hate crime, everyone knew that the Fellowship was hardly agonizing over those who were terribly wounded in the blast, much less over the (finally, absolutely) dead vampires or the humans who served them.

Sophie-Anne lost her legs, several members of her entourage, and her dearest companion. Her life was saved by her half-demon lawyer, Mr Cataliades. But her recuperation time was going to be lengthy, and she was in a position of terrible vulnerability.

What part did I play in all this?

I'd helped save lives after the pyramid went down, and I was terrified I was now on the radar of people who might want me to spend my time in their service, using my telepathy for their purposes. Some of those purposes were good, and I wouldn't mind lending a hand in rescue services from time to time, but I wanted to keep my life to myself. I was alive; my boyfriend, Quinn, was alive; and the vampires most important to me had survived, too. As far as the troubles Sophie-Anne faced, the political consequences of the attack and the fact that supernatural groups were circling the weakened state of Louisiana like hyenas around a dying gazelle . . . I didn't think about it at all.

I had other stuff on my mind, personal stuff. I'm not used to thinking much further than the end of my fingertips; that's my only excuse.

Not only was I not thinking about the vampire situation, there was another supernatural situation I didn't ponder that turned out to be just as crucial to my future.

Close to Bon Temps, in Shreveport, there's a Were pack whose ranks are swollen by the men and women from Barksdale Air Force Base. During the past year, this Were pack had become sharply divided between two factions. I'd learned in American History what Abraham Lincoln, quoting the Bible, had to say about houses divided.

To assume that these two situations would work themselves out, to fail to foresee that their resolution would involve me, well . . . that was where I was almost fatally blind. I'm telepathic, not psychic. Vampire minds are big relaxing blanks to me. Weres are difficult to read, though not impossible. That's my only excuse for being unaware of the trouble brewing all around me.

What was I so busy thinking about? Weddings – and my missing boyfriend.

Chapter 1

I was making a neat arrangement of liquor bottles on the folding table behind the portable bar when Halleigh Robinson rushed up, her normally sweet face flushed and tear-streaked. Since she was supposed to be getting married within an hour and was still wearing blue jeans and a T-shirt, she got my immediate attention.

'Sookie!' she said, rounding the bar to grab my arm. 'You have to help me.'

I'd already helped her by putting on my bartending clothes instead of the pretty dress I'd planned on wearing. 'Sure,' I said, imagining Halleigh wanted me to make her a special drink – though if I'd listened in to her thoughts, I'd have known differently already. However, I was trying to be on my best behavior, and I was shielding like crazy. Being telepathic is no picnic, especially at a high-tension event like a double wedding. I'd expected to be a guest instead of a bartender. But the caterer's bartender had been in a car wreck on her way over from Shreveport, and Sam, who'd been unhired when E(E)E had insisted on using their own bartender, was abruptly hired again.

I was a little disappointed to be on the working side of the bar, but you had to oblige the bride on her special day. 'What can I do for you?' I asked.

'I need you to be my bridesmaid,' she said.

'Ah . . . what?'

'Tiffany fainted after Mr Cumberland took the first round of pictures. She's on her way to the hospital.'

It was an hour before the wedding, and the photographer had been trying to get a number of group shots out of the way. The bridesmaids and the groomsmen were already togged out. Halleigh should have been getting into her wedding finery, but instead here she was in jeans and curlers, no makeup, and a tear-streaked face.

Who could resist that?

'You're the right size,' she said. 'And Tiffany is probably just about to have her appendix out. So, can you try on the dress?'

I glanced at Sam, my boss.

Sam smiled at me and nodded. 'Go on, Sook. We don't officially open for business until after the wedding.'

So I followed Halleigh into Belle Rive, the Bellefleur mansion, recently restored to something like its antebellum glory. The wooden floors gleamed, the harp by the stairs shone with gilt, the silverware displayed on the big sideboard in the dining room glowed with polishing. There were servers in white coats buzzing around everywhere, the E(E)E logo on their tunics done in an elaborate black script. Extreme(ly Elegant) Events had become the premier upscale caterer in the United States. I felt a stab in my heart when I noticed the logo, because my missing guy worked for the supernatural branch of E(E)E. I didn't have long to feel the ache, though, because Halleigh was dragging me up the stairs at a relentless pace.

The first bedroom at the top was full of youngish women in gold-colored dresses, all fussing around Halleigh's soon-to-be sister-in-law, Portia Bellefleur. Halleigh zoomed past that door to enter the second room on the left. It was equally full of younger women, but these were in midnight blue chiffon. The room was in chaos, with the bridesmaids' civilian clothes piled here and there. There was a makeup and hair station over by the west wall, staffed by a stoic woman in a pink smock, curling-rod in her hand.

Halleigh tossed introductions through the air like paper pellets. 'Gals, this is Sookie Stackhouse. Sookie, this is my sister Fay, my cousin Kelly, my best friend Sarah, my other best friend Dana. And here's the dress. It's an eight.'

I was amazed that Halleigh had had the presence of mind to divest
Tiffany of the bridesmaid dress before her departure for the hospital.
Brides are ruthless. In a matter of minutes, I was stripped down to the
essentials. I was glad I'd worn nice underwear, since there wasn't any
time for modesty. How embarrassing it would have been to be in
granny panties with holes! The dress was lined, so I didn't need a slip,
another stroke of luck. There was a spare pair of thigh-highs, which
I pulled on, and then the dress went over my head. Sometimes I wear
a ten – in fact, most of the time – so I was holding my breath while
Fay zipped it up.

If I didn't breathe a lot, it would be okay.

'Super!' one of the other women (Dana?) said with great happiness.
'Now the shoes.'

'Oh, God,' I said when I saw them. They were very high heels
dyed to match the midnight blue dress, and I slid my feet into them,
anticipating pain. Kelly (maybe) buckled the straps, and I stood up. All
of us held our breath as I took a step, then another. They were about
half a size too small. It was an important half.

'I can get through the wedding,' I said, and they all clapped.

'Over here then,' said Pink Smock, and I sat in her chair and had
more makeup reapplied over my own and my hair redone while the
real bridesmaids and Halleigh's mother assisted Halleigh into her dress.
Pink Smock had a lot of hair to work with. I've only had light trims in
the past three years, I guess, and it's way down past my shoulder blades
now. My roommate, Amelia, had put some highlights in, and that had
turned out real good. I was blonder than ever.

I examined myself in the full-length mirror, and it seemed impossible I could have been so transformed in twenty minutes. From
working barmaid in a white ruffled tux shirt and black trousers to
bridesmaid in a midnight blue dress – and three inches taller, to boot.

Hey, I looked *great*. The dress was a super color for me, the skirt
was gently A-line, the short sleeves weren't too tight, and it wasn't low
cut enough to look slutty. With my boobs, the slut factor kicks in if
I'm not careful.

I was yanked out of self-admiration by the practical Dana, who said,
'Listen, here's the drill.' From that moment on, I listened and nodded.

I examined a little diagram. I nodded some more. Dana was one organized gal. If I ever invaded a small country, this was the woman I wanted on my side.

By the time we made our way carefully down the stairs (long skirts and high heels, not a good combination), I was fully briefed and ready for my first trip down the aisle as a bridesmaid.

Most girls have done this a couple of times before they reach twenty-six, but Tara Thornton, the only friend I had close enough to ask me, had up and eloped while I was out of town.

The other wedding party was assembled downstairs when we descended. Portia's group would precede Halleigh's. The two grooms and their groomsmen were already outside if all was going smoothly, because now it was five minutes until liftoff.

Portia Bellefleur and her bridesmaids averaged seven years older than Halleigh's posse. Portia was the big sister of Andy Bellefleur, Bon Temps police detective and Halleigh's groom. Portia's dress was a little over-the-top – it was covered with pearls and so much lace and sequins I thought it could stand by itself – but then, it was Portia's big day and she could wear whatever she damn well pleased. All Portia's bridesmaids were wearing gold.

The bridesmaids' bouquets all matched – white and dark blue and yellow. Coordinated with the dark blue of Halleigh's bridesmaid selection, the result was very pretty.

The wedding planner, a thin nervous woman with a big cloud of dark curly hair, counted heads almost audibly. When she was satisfied everyone she needed was present and accounted for, she flung open the double doors to the huge brick patio. We could see the crowd, backs to us, seated on the lawn in two sections of white folding chairs, with a strip of red carpet running between the two sides. They were facing the platform where the priest stood at an altar decked in cloth and gleaming candlesticks. To the right of the priest, Portia's groom, Glen Vick, was waiting, facing the house. And, therefore, us. He looked very, very nervous, but he was smiling. His groomsmen were already in position flanking him.

Portia's golden bridesmaids stepped out onto the patio, and one by one they began their march down the aisle through the manicured garden. The scent of wedding flowers made the night sweet. And the Belle Rive roses were blooming, even in October.

Finally, to a huge swell of music, Portia crossed the patio to the end of the carpet, the wedding coordinator (with some effort) lifting the train of Portia's dress so it wouldn't drag on the bricks.

At the priest's nod, everyone stood and faced the rear so they could see Portia's triumphal march. She'd waited years for this.

After Portia's safe arrival at the altar, it was our party's turn. Halleigh gave each one of us an air kiss on the cheek as we stepped past her out onto the patio. She even included me, which was sweet of her. The wedding coordinator sent us off one by one, to stand reflecting our designated groomsman up front. Mine was a Bellefleur cousin from Monroe who was quite startled to see me coming instead of Tiffany. I walked at the slow pace Dana had emphasized and held my bouquet in my clasped hands at the desired angle. I'd been watching the other maids like a hawk. I wanted to get this right.

All the faces were turned to me, and I was so nervous I forgot to block. The thoughts of the crowd rushed at me in a gush of unwanted communication. *Looks so pretty . . . What happened to Tiffany . . .? Wow, what a rack. . . . Hurry it up, I need a drink. . . . What the hell am I doing here? She drags me to every dog fight in the parish . . . I love wedding cake.*

A photographer stepped in front of me and took a picture. It was someone I knew, a pretty werewolf named Maria-Star Cooper. She was the assistant of Al Cumberland, a well-known photographer based in Shreveport. I smiled at Maria-Star and she took another shot. I continued down the carpet, held on to my smile, and pushed away all the racket in my head.

After a moment I noticed there were blank spots in the crowd, which signaled the presence of vampires. Glen had requested a night wedding specifically so he could invite some of his more important vampire clients. I'd been sure Portia truly loved him when she agreed to that, because Portia didn't like bloodsuckers at all. In fact, they gave her the creeps.

I kind of liked vampires in general, because their brains were closed to me. Being in their company was oddly restful. Okay, a strain in other ways, but at least my brain could relax.

Finally, I arrived at my designated spot. I'd watched Portia and Glen's attendants arrange themselves in an inverted V, with a space at the front for the nuptial couple. Our group was doing the same thing. I'd nailed it, and I exhaled in relief. Since I wasn't taking the place of the maid of honor, my work was over. All I had to do was stand still and look attentive, and I thought I could do that.

The music swelled to a second crescendo, and the priest gave his signal again. The crowd rose and turned to look at the second bride. Halleigh began moving slowly toward us. She looked absolutely radiant. Halleigh had selected a much simpler dress than Portia's, and she looked very young and very sweet. She was at least five years younger than Andy, maybe more. Halleigh's dad, as tanned and fit as his wife, stepped out to take Halleigh's arm when she drew abreast; since Portia had come down the aisle alone (her father was long dead), it had been decided Halleigh would, too.

After I'd had my fill of Halleigh's smile, I looked over the crowd who'd rotated to follow the bride's progress.

There were so many familiar faces: teachers from the elementary school where Halleigh taught, members of the police department where Andy worked, the friends of old Mrs Caroline Bellefleur who were still alive and tottering, Portia's fellow lawyers and other people who worked in the justice system, and Glen Vick's clients and other accountants. Almost every chair was occupied.

There were a few black faces to be seen, and a few brown faces, but most of the wedding guests were middle-class Caucasians. The palest faces in the crowd were the vampires', of course. One of them I knew well. Bill Compton, my neighbor and former lover, was sitting about halfway back, wearing a tuxedo and looking very handsome. Bill managed to seem at home in whatever he chose to wear. Beside him sat his human girlfriend, Selah Pumphrey, a real estate agent from Clarice. She was wearing a burgundy gown that set off her dark hair. There were perhaps five vamps I didn't recognize. I assumed they were clients of Glen's. Though Glen didn't know it, there were several other attendees who were more (and less) than human.

My boss, Sam, was a rare true shapeshifter who could become any animal. The photographer was a werewolf like his assistant. To all the regular wedding guests, he looked like a well-rounded, rather short African-American male wearing a nice suit and carrying a big camera. But Al turned into a wolf at the full moon just like Maria-Star. There were a few other Weres in the crowd, though only one I knew – Amanda, a red-haired woman in her late thirties who owned a bar in Shreveport called the Hair of the Dog. Maybe Glen's firm handled the bar's books.

And there was one werepanther, Calvin Norris. Calvin had brought a date, I was glad to see, though I was less than thrilled after I identified her as Tanya Grissom. Blech. What was she doing back in town? And why had Calvin been on the guest list? I liked him, but I couldn't figure out the connection.

While I'd been scanning the crowd for familiar faces, Halleigh had assumed her position by Andy, and now all the bridesmaids and groomsmen had to face forward to listen to the service.

Since I didn't have a big emotional investment in this proceeding, I found myself mentally wandering while Father Kempton Littrell, the Episcopal priest who ordinarily came to the little Bon Temps church once every two weeks, conducted the service. The lights that had been set up to illuminate the garden glinted off Father Littrell's glasses and bleached some of the color out of his face. He looked almost like a vampire.

Things proceeded pretty much on the standard plan. Boy, it was lucky I was used to standing up at the bar, because this was a lot of standing, and in high heels, too. I seldom wore heels, much less three-inch ones. It felt strange being five foot nine. I tried not to shift around, possessed my soul with patience.

Now Glen was putting the ring on Portia's finger, and Portia looked almost pretty as she looked down at their clasped hands. She'd never be one of my favorite people – nor I hers – but I wished her well. Glen was bony and had darkish receding hair and major glasses. If you called central casting and ordered an 'accountant type', they'd send you Glen. But I could tell directly from his brain that he loved Portia, and she loved him.

I let myself shift a bit, put my weight a little more on my right leg.

Then Father Littrell started all over again on Halleigh and Andy.

I kept my smile pasted to my face (no problem there; I did it all the time at the bar) and watched Halleigh become Mrs Andrew Bellefleur. I was lucky. Episcopalian weddings can be long, but the two couples had opted for having the shorter form of the service.

At last the music swelled to triumphant strains, and the newlyweds exited to the house. The wedding party trailed after them in reverse order. On my way down the aisle, I felt genuinely happy and a weensy bit proud. I'd helped Halleigh in her time of need ... and very soon I was going to get to take these shoes off.

From his chair, Bill caught my eye and silently put his hand over his heart. It was a romantic and totally unexpected gesture, and for a moment I softened toward him. I very nearly smiled, though Selah was right there by his side. Just in time, I reminded myself that Bill was a no-good rat bastard, and I swept on my painful way. Sam was standing a couple of yards past the last row of chairs, wearing a white tux shirt like the one I'd had on and black dress pants. Relaxed and at ease, that was Sam. Even his tangled halo of strawberry blond hair somehow fit in.

I flashed him a genuine smile, and he grinned back. He gave me a thumbs-up, and though shifter brains are hard to read, I could tell he approved of the way I looked and the way I'd conducted myself. His bright blue eyes never left me. He's been my boss for four years, and we've gotten along great for the most part. He'd been pretty upset when I'd started dating a vampire, but he'd gotten over it.

I needed to get to work, and pronto. I caught up with Dana. 'When can we change?' I asked.

'Oh, we have pictures to do yet,' Dana said cheerfully. Her husband had come up to put his arm around her. He was holding their baby, a tiny thing swaddled in sex-neutral yellow.

'Surely I won't be needed for those,' I said. 'You-all took a lot of pictures earlier, right? Before what's-her-name got sick.'

'Tiffany. Yes, but there'll be more.'

I seriously doubted the family would want me in them, though my absence would unbalance the symmetry in the group pictures. I found Al Cumberland.

'Yes,' he said, snapping away at the brides and grooms as they beamed at each other. 'I do need some shots. You got to stay in costume.'

'Crap,' I said, because my feet hurt.

'Listen, Sookie, the best I can do is to shoot your group first. Andy, Halleigh! That is . . . Mrs Bellefleur! If you-all will come this way, let's get your pictures done.'

Portia Bellefleur Vick looked a little astonished that her group wasn't going first, but she had way too many people to greet to really get riled. While Maria-Star snapped away at the touching scene, a distant relative wheeled old Miss Caroline up to Portia, and Portia bent to kiss her grandmother. Portia and Andy had lived with Miss Caroline for years, after their own parents had passed away. Miss Caroline's poor health had delayed the weddings at least twice. The original plan had been for last spring, and it had been a rush job because Miss Caroline was failing. She'd had a heart attack and then recovered. After that, she'd broken her hip. I had to say, for someone who'd survived two major health disasters, Miss Caroline looked . . . Well, to tell the truth, she looked just like a very old lady who'd had a heart attack and a broken hip. She was all dressed up in a beige silk suit. She even had on some makeup, and her snow-white hair was arranged à la Lauren Bacall. She'd been a beauty in her day, an autocrat her entire life, and a famous cook until the recent past.

Caroline Bellefleur was in her seventh heaven this night. She'd married off both her grandchildren, she was getting plenty of tribute, and Belle Rive was looking spectacular, thanks to the vampire who was staring at her with an absolutely unreadable face.

Bill Compton had discovered he was the Bellefleurs' ancestor, and he had anonymously given Miss Caroline a whacking big bunch of money. She'd enjoyed spending it so much, and she had had no idea it had come from a vampire. She'd thought it a legacy from a distant relative. I thought it was kind of ironic that the Bellefleurs would just as soon have spit on Bill as thanked him. But he was part of the family, and I was glad he'd found a way to attend.

I took a deep breath, banished Bill's dark gaze from my consciousness, and smiled at the camera. I occupied my designated space in the pictures to balance out the wedding party, dodged the googly-eyed cousin, and finally hotfooted it up the stairs to change into my bartender's rig.

There was no one up here, and it was a relief to be in the room by myself.

I shimmied out of the dress, hung it up, and sat on a stool to unbuckle the straps of the painful shoes.

There was a little sound at the door, and I looked up, startled. Bill was standing just inside the room, his hands in his pockets, his skin glowing gently. His fangs were out.

'Trying to change here,' I said tartly. No point in making a big show of modesty. He'd seen every inch of me.

'You didn't tell them,' he said.

'Huh?' Then my brain caught up. Bill meant that I hadn't told the Bellefleurs that he was their ancestor. 'No, of course not,' I said. 'You asked me not to.'

'I thought, in your anger, you might give them the information.'

I gave him an incredulous look. 'No, some of us actually have honor,' I said. He looked away for a minute. 'By the way, your face healed real well.'

During the Fellowship of the Sun bombing in Rhodes, Bill's face had been exposed to the sun with really stomach-churning results.

'I slept for six days,' he said. 'When I finally got up, it was mostly healed. And as for your dig about my failing in honor, I haven't any defense . . . except that when Sophie-Anne told me to pursue you . . . I was reluctant, Sookie. At first, I didn't want to even pretend to have a permanent relationship with a human woman. I thought it degraded me. I only came into the bar to identify you when I couldn't put it off any longer. And that evening didn't turn out like I'd planned. I went outside with the drainers, and things happened. When you were the one who came to my aid, I decided it was fate. I did what I had been told to do by my queen. In so doing, I fell into a trap I couldn't escape. I still can't.'

The trap of LUUUUVVVV, I thought sarcastically. But he was too serious, too calm, to mock. I was simply defending my own heart with the weapon of bitchiness.

'You got you a girlfriend,' I said. 'You go on back to Selah.' I looked down to make sure I'd gotten the little strap on the second sandal unlatched. I worked the shoe off. When I glanced back up, Bill's dark eyes were fixed on me.

'I would give anything to lie with you again,' he said.

I froze, my hands in the act of rolling the thigh-high hose off my left leg.

Okay, that pretty much stunned me on several different levels. First, the biblical 'lie with'. Second, my astonishment that he considered me such a memorable bed partner.

Maybe he only remembered the virgins.

'I don't want to fool with you tonight, and Sam's waiting on me down there to help him tend bar,' I said roughly. 'You go on.' I stood and turned my back to him while I pulled on my pants and my shirt, tucking the shirt in. Then it was time for the black running shoes. After a quick check in the mirror to make sure I still had on some lipstick, I faced the doorway.

He was gone.

I went down the wide stairs and out the patio doors into the garden, relieved to be resuming my more accustomed place behind a bar. My feet still hurt. So did the sore spot in my heart labeled Bill Compton.

Sam gave me a smiling glance as I scurried into place. Miss Caroline had vetoed our request to leave a tip jar out, but bar patrons had already stuffed a few bills into an empty highball glass, and I intended to let that stay in position.

'You looked real pretty in the dress,' Sam said as he mixed a rum and Coke. I handed a beer across the bar and smiled at the older man who'd come to fetch it. He gave me a huge tip, and I glanced down to see that in my hurry to get downstairs I'd skipped a button. I was showing a little extra cleavage. I was momentarily embarrassed, but it wasn't a slutty button, just a 'Hey, I've got boobs' button. So I let it be.

'Thanks,' I said, hoping Sam hadn't noticed this quick evaluation. 'I hope I did everything right.'

'Of course you did,' Sam said, as if the possibility of me blowing my new role had never crossed his mind. This is why he's the greatest boss I've ever had.

'Well, good evening,' said a slightly nasal voice, and I looked up from the wine I was pouring to see that Tanya Grissom was taking up space and breathing air that could be better used by almost anyone else. Her escort, Calvin, was nowhere in sight.

'Hey, Tanya,' Sam said. 'How you doing? It's been a while.'

'Well, I had to tie up some loose ends in Mississippi,' Tanya said. 'But I'm back here visiting, and I wondered if you needed any part-time help, Sam.'

I pressed my mouth shut and kept my hands busy. Tanya stepped to the side nearest Sam when an elderly lady asked me for some tonic water with a wedge of lime. I handed it to her so quickly she looked astonished, and then I took care of Sam's next customer. I could hear from Sam's brain that he was pleased to see Tanya. Men can be idiots, right? To be fair, I did know some things about her that Sam didn't.

Selah Pumphrey was next in line, and I could only be amazed at my luck. However, Bill's girlfriend just asked for a rum and Coke.

'Sure,' I said, trying not to sound relieved, and began putting the drink together.

'I heard him,' Selah said very quietly.

'Heard who?' I asked, distracted by my effort to listen to what Tanya and Sam were saying – either with my ears or with my brain.

'I heard Bill when he was talking to you earlier.' When I didn't speak, she continued, 'I snuck up the stairs after him.'

'Then he knows you were there,' I said absently, and handed her the drink. Her eyes flared wide at me for a second – alarmed, angry? She stalked off. If wishes could kill, I would be lifeless on the ground.

Tanya began to turn away from Sam as if her body was thinking of leaving, but her head was still talking to my boss. Finally, her whole self went back to her date. I looked after her, thinking dark thoughts.

'Well, that's good news,' Sam said with a smile. 'Tanya's available for a while.'

I bit back my urge to tell him that Tanya had made it quite clear she was available. 'Oh, yeah, great,' I said. There were so many people I liked. Why were two of the women I really didn't care for at this wedding tonight? Well, at least my feet were practically whimpering with pleasure at getting out of the too-small heels.

I smiled and made drinks and cleared away empty bottles and went to Sam's truck to unload more stock. I opened beers and poured wine and mopped up spills until I felt like a perpetual-motion machine.

The vampire clients arrived at the bar in a cluster. I uncorked one bottle of Royalty Blended, a premium blend of synthetic blood and the real blood of actual European royalty. It had to be refrigerated, of course, and it was a very special treat for Glen's clients, a treat he'd personally arranged. (The only vampire drink that exceeded Royalty Blended in price was the nearly pure Royalty, which contained only a trace of preservatives.) Sam lined up the wineglasses. Then he told me to pour it out. I was extraspecial careful not to spill a drop. Sam handed each glass to its recipient. The vampires, including Bill, all tipped very heavily, big smiles on their faces as they lifted their glasses in a toast to the newlyweds.

After a sip of the dark fluid in the wineglasses, their fangs ran out to prove their enjoyment. Some of the human guests looked a smidge uneasy at this expression of appreciation, but Glen was right there smiling and nodding. He knew enough about vampires not to offer to shake hands. I noticed the new Mrs Vick was not hobnobbing with the undead guests, though she made one pass through the cluster with a strained smile fixed on her face.

When one of the vampires came back for a glass of ordinary True-Blood, I handed him the warm drink. 'Thank you,' he said, tipping me yet again. While he had his billfold open, I saw a Nevada driver's license. I'm familiar with a wide variety of licenses from carding kids at the bar; he'd come far for this wedding. I really looked at him for the first time. When he knew he'd caught my attention, he put his hands together and bowed slightly. Since I'd been reading a mystery set in Thailand, I knew this was a *wai*, a courteous greeting practiced by Buddhists – or maybe just Thai people in general? Anyway, he meant to be polite. After a brief hesitation, I put down the rag in my hand and copied his movement. The vampire looked pleased.

'I call myself Jonathan,' he said. 'Americans can't pronounce my real name.'

There might have been a touch of arrogance and contempt there, but I couldn't blame him.

'I'm Sookie Stackhouse,' I said.

Jonathan was a smallish man, maybe five foot eight, with the light copper coloring and dusky black hair of his country. He was really handsome. His nose was small and broad, his lips plump. His brown eyes were topped with absolutely straight black brows. His skin was so fine I couldn't detect any pores. He had that little shine vampires have.

'This is your husband?' he asked, picking up his glass of blood and tilting his head in Sam's direction. Sam was busy mixing a piña colada for one of the bridesmaids.

'No, sir, he's my boss.'

Just then, Terry Bellefleur, second cousin to Portia and Andy, lurched up to ask for another beer. I was real fond of Terry, but he was a bad drunk, and I thought he was well on his way to achieving that condition. Though the Vietnam vet wanted to stand and talk about the president's policy on the current war, I walked him over to another family member, a distant cousin from Baton Rouge, and made sure the man was going to keep an eye on Terry and prevent him from driving off in his pickup.

The vampire Jonathan was keeping an eye on *me* while I did this, and I wasn't sure why. But I didn't observe anything aggressive or lustful in his stance or demeanor, and his fangs were in. It seemed safe to disregard him and take care of business. If there was some reason Jonathan wanted to talk to me, I'd find out about it sooner or later. Later was fine.

As I fetched a case of Cokes from Sam's truck, my attention was caught by a man standing alone in the shadows cast by the big live oak on the west side of the lawn. He was tall, slim, and impeccably dressed in a suit that was obviously very expensive. The man stepped forward a little and I could see his face, could realize he was returning my gaze. My first impression was that he was a lovely creature and not a man at all. Whatever he was, human wasn't part of it. Though he had some age on him, he was extremely handsome, and his hair, still pale gold, was as long as mine. He wore it pulled back neatly. He was slightly withered, like a delicious apple that had been in the crisper too long, but his back was absolutely straight and he wore no glasses. He did carry a cane, a very simple black one with a gold head.

When he stepped out of the shadows, the vampires turned as a group to look. After a moment they slightly inclined their heads. He returned the acknowledgment. They kept their distance, as if he was dangerous or awesome.

This episode was very strange, but I didn't have time to think about it. Everyone wanted one last free drink. The reception was winding down, and people were filtering to the front of the house for the leave-taking of the happy couples. Halleigh and Portia had disappeared upstairs to change into their going-away outfits. The E(E)E staff had been vigilant about clearing up empty cups and the little plates that had held cake and finger food, so the garden looked relatively neat.

Now that we weren't busy, Sam let me know he had something on his mind. 'Sookie, am I getting the wrong idea, or do you dislike Tanya?'

'I do have something against Tanya,' I said. 'I'm just not sure I should tell you about it. You clearly like her.' You'd think I'd been sampling the bourbon. Or truth serum.

'If you don't like to work with her, I want to hear the reason,' he said. 'You're my friend. I respect your opinion.'

This was very pleasant to hear.

'Tanya is pretty,' I said. 'She's bright and able.' Those were the good things.

'And?'

'And she came here as a spy,' I said. 'The Pelts sent her, trying to find out if I had anything to do with the disappearance of their daughter Debbie. You remember when they came to the bar?'

'Yes,' said Sam. In the illumination that had been strung up all around the garden, he looked both brightly lit and darkly shadowed. 'You did have something to do with it?'

'Everything,' I said sadly. 'But it was self-defense.'

'I know it must have been.' He'd taken my hand. My own jerked in surprise. 'I know you,' he said, and didn't let go.

Sam's faith made me feel a little warm glow inside. I'd worked for Sam a long time now, and his good opinion meant a lot to me. I felt almost choked up, and I had to clear my throat. 'So, I wasn't happy to see Tanya,' I continued. 'I didn't trust her from the start, and when

I found out why she'd come to Bon Temps, I got really down on her. I don't know if she still gets paid by the Pelts. Plus, tonight she's here with Calvin, and she's got no business hitting on you.' My tone was a lot angrier than I'd intended.

'Oh.' Sam looked disconcerted.

'But if you want to go out with her, go ahead,' I said, trying to lighten up. 'I mean – she can't be all bad. And I guess she thought she was doing the right thing, coming to help find information on a missing shifter.' That sounded pretty good and might even be the truth. 'I don't have to like who you date,' I added, just to make it clear I understood I had no claim on him.

'Yeah, but I feel better if you do,' he said.

'Same here,' I agreed, to my own surprise.

Chapter 2

We began packing up in a quiet and unobtrusive way, since there were still lingering guests.

'As along as we're talking about dates, what happened to Quinn?' he asked as we worked. 'You've been moping ever since you got back from Rhodes.'

'Well, I told you he got hurt pretty bad in the bombing.' Quinn's branch of E(E)E staged special events for the supe community: vampire hierarchal weddings, Were coming of age parties, packleader contests, and the like. That was why Quinn had been in the Pyramid of Gizeh when the Fellowship did its dirty deed.

The FotS people were anti-vampire, but they had no idea that vampires were just the visible, public tip of the iceberg in the supernatural world. No one knew this; or at least only a few people like me, though more and more were in on the big secret. I was sure the Fellowship fanatics would hate werewolves or shapeshifters like Sam just as much as they hated vampires . . . if they knew they existed. That time might come soon.

'Yeah, but I would have thought . . .'

'I know, I would have thought Quinn and I were all set, too,' I said, and if my voice was dreary, well, thinking about my missing weretiger made me feel that way. 'I kept thinking I'd hear from him. But not a word.'

'You still got his sister's car?' Frannie Quinn had loaned me her car so I could get home after the Rhodes disaster.

'No, it vanished one night when Amelia and I were both at work. I called and left a voice mail on his cell to say it had been taken, but I never heard back.'

'Sookie, I'm sorry,' Sam said. He knew that was inadequate, but what could he say?

'Yeah, me, too,' I said, trying not to sound too depressed. It was an effort to keep from retreading tired mental ground. I knew Quinn didn't blame me in any way for his injuries. I'd seen him in the hospital in Rhodes before I'd left, and he'd been in the care of his sister, Frannie, who didn't seem to hate me at that point. No blame, no hate – why no communication?

It was like the ground had opened to swallow him up. I threw up my hands and tried to think of something else. Keeping busy was the best remedy when I was worried. We began to shift some of our things to Sam's truck, parked about a block away. He carried most of the heavier stuff. Sam is not a big guy, but he's really strong, as all shifters are.

By ten thirty we were almost finished. From the cheers at the front of the house, I knew that the brides had descended the staircase in their honeymoon clothes, thrown their bouquets, and departed. Portia and Glen were going to San Francisco, and Halleigh and Andy were going to Jamaica to some resort. I couldn't help but know.

Sam told me I could leave. 'I'll get Dawson to help me unload at the bar,' he said. Since Dawson, who'd been standing in for Sam at Merlotte's Bar tonight, was built like a boulder, I agreed that was a good plan.

When we divided the tips, I got about three hundred dollars. It had been a lucrative evening. I tucked the money in my pants pocket. It made a big roll, since it was mostly ones. I was glad we were in Bon Temps instead of a big city, or I'd worry that someone would hit me on the head before I got to my car.

'Well, night, Sam,' I said, and checked my pocket for my car keys. I hadn't bothered with bringing a purse. As I went down the slope of the backyard to the sidewalk, I patted my hair self-consciously. I'd been able to stop the pink smock lady from putting it on top of my head, so she'd done it puffy and curly and sort of Farrah Fawcett. I felt silly.

There were cars going by, most of them wedding guests taking their departure. There was some regular Saturday night traffic. The line of vehicles parked against the curb stretched for a very long way down the street, so all traffic was moving slowly. I'd illegally parked with the driver's side against the curb, not usually a big deal in our little town.

I bent to unlock my car door, and I heard a noise behind me. In a single movement, I palmed my keys and clenched my fist, wheeled, and hit as hard as I could. The keys gave my fist quite a core, and the man behind me staggered across the sidewalk to land on his butt on the slope of the lawn.

'I mean you no harm,' said Jonathan.

It isn't easy to look dignified and nonthreatening when you have blood running from one corner of your mouth and you're sitting on your ass, but the Asian vampire managed it.

'You surprised me,' I said, which was a gross understatement.

'I can see that,' he said, and got easily to his feet. He brought out a handkerchief and patted his mouth.

I wasn't going to apologize. People who sneak up on me when I'm alone at night, well, they deserve what they get. But I reconsidered. Vampires move quietly. 'I'm sorry I assumed the worst,' I said, which was sort of a compromise. 'I should have identified you.'

'No, it would have been too late by then,' Jonathan said. 'A woman alone must defend herself.'

'I appreciate your understanding,' I said carefully. I glanced behind him, tried not to register anything on my face. Since I hear so many startling things from people's brains, I'm used to doing that. I looked directly at Jonathan. 'Did you . . . Why were you here?'

'I'm passing through Louisiana, and I came to the wedding as a guest of Hamilton Tharp,' he said. 'I'm staying in Area Five, with the permission of Eric Northman.'

I had no idea who Hamilton Tharp was – presumably some buddy of the Bellefleurs'. But I knew Eric Northman quite well. (In fact, at one time I'd known him from his head to his toes, and all points in between.) Eric was the sheriff of Area Five, a large chunk of northern Louisiana. We were tied together in a complex way, which most days I resented like hell.

'Actually, what I was asking you was – why did you approach me just now?' I waited, keys still clutched in my hand. I'd go for his eyes, I decided. Even vampires are vulnerable there.

'I was curious,' Jonathan said finally. His hands were folded in front of him. I was developing a strong dislike for the vamp.

'Why?'

'I heard a little at Fangtasia about the blond woman Eric values so highly. Eric has such a hard nose that it didn't seem likely any human woman could interest him.'

'So how'd you know I was going to be here, at this wedding, tonight?'

His eyes flickered. He hadn't expected me to persist in questioning. He had expected to be able to calm me, maybe at this moment was trying to coerce me with his glamour. But that just didn't work on me.

'The young woman who works for Eric, his child Pam, mentioned it,' he said.

Liar, liar, pants on fire, I thought. I hadn't talked to Pam in a couple of weeks, and our last conversation hadn't been girlish chatter about my social and work schedule. She'd been recovering from the wounds she'd sustained in Rhodes. Her recovery, and Eric's, and the queen's, had been the sole topic of our conversation.

'Of course,' I said. 'Well, good evening. I need to be leaving.' I unlocked the door and carefully slid inside, trying to keep my eyes fixed on Jonathan so I'd be ready for a sudden move. He stood as still as a statue, inclining his head to me after I started the car and pulled off. At the next stop sign, I buckled my seat belt. I hadn't wanted to pin myself down while he was so close. I locked the car doors, and I looked all around me. No vampires in sight. I thought, *That was really, really weird*. In fact, I should probably call Eric and relate the incident to him.

You know what the weirdest part was? The withered man with the long blond hair had been standing in the shadows behind the vampire the whole time. Our eyes had even met once. His beautiful face had been quite unreadable. But I'd known he didn't want me to acknowledge his presence. I hadn't read his mind – I couldn't – but I'd known this nonetheless.

And weirdest of all, Jonathan hadn't known he was there. Given the acute sense of smell that all vampires possessed, Jonathan's ignorance was simply extraordinary.

I was still mulling over the strange little episode when I turned off Hummingbird Road and onto the long driveway through the woods that led back to my old house. The core of the house had been built more than a hundred and sixty years before, but of course very little of the original structure remained. It had been added to, remodeled, and reroofed a score of times over the course of the decades. A two-room farmhouse to begin with, it was now much larger, but it remained a very ordinary home.

Tonight the house looked peaceful in the glow of the outside security light that Amelia Broadway, my housemate, had left on for me. Amelia's car was parked in back, and I pulled alongside it. I kept my keys out in case she'd gone upstairs for the night. She'd left the screen door unlatched, and I latched it behind me. I unlocked the back door and relocked it. We were hell on security, Amelia and I, especially at night.

A little to my surprise, Amelia was sitting at the kitchen table, waiting for me. We'd developed a routine after weeks of living together, and generally Amelia would have retired upstairs by this time. She had her own TV, her cell phone, and her laptop up there, and she'd gotten a library card, so she had plenty to read. Plus, she had her spell work, which I didn't ask questions about. Ever. Amelia is a witch.

'How'd it go?' she asked, stirring her tea as if she had to create a tiny whirlpool.

'Well, they got married. No one pulled a Jane Eyre. Glen's vampire customers behaved themselves, and Miss Caroline was gracious all over the place. But I had to stand in for one of the bridesmaids.'

'Oh, wow! Tell me.'

So I did, and we shared a few laughs. I thought of telling Amelia about the beautiful man, but I didn't. What could I say? 'He looked at me'? I did tell her about Jonathan from Nevada.

'What do you think he really wanted?' Amelia said.

'I can't imagine.' I shrugged.

'You need to find out. Especially since you'd never heard of the guy whose guest he said he was.'

'I'm going to call Eric – if not tonight, then tomorrow night.'

'Too bad you didn't buy a copy of that database Bill is peddling. I saw an ad for it on the Internet yesterday, on a vampire site.' This might seem like a sudden change of subject, but Bill's database contained pictures and/or biographies of all the vampires he'd been able to locate all over the world, and a few he'd just heard about. Bill's little CD was making more money for his boss, the queen, than I could ever have imagined. But you had to be a vampire to purchase a copy, and they had ways of checking.

'Well, since Bill is charging five hundred dollars a pop, and impersonating a vampire is a dangerous risk . . .' I said.

Amelia waved her hand. 'It'd be worth it,' she said.

Amelia is a lot more sophisticated than I am . . . at least in some ways. She grew up in New Orleans, and she'd lived there most of her life. Now she was living with me because she'd made a giant mistake. She'd needed to leave New Orleans after her inexperience had caused a magical catastrophe. It was lucky she'd departed when she had, because Katrina followed soon after. Since the hurricane, her tenant was living in the top-floor apartment of Amelia's house. Amelia's own apartment on the bottom floor had sustained some damage. She wasn't charging the tenant rent because he was overseeing the repair of the house.

And here came the reason Amelia wasn't moving back to New Orleans any time soon. Bob padded into the kitchen to say hello, rubbing himself affectionately against my legs.

'Hey, my little honey bunny,' I said, picking up the longhaired black-and-white cat. 'How's my precious? I wuv him!'

'I'm gonna barf,' Amelia said. But I knew that she talked just as disgustingly to Bob when I wasn't around.

'Any progress?' I said, raising my head from Bob's fur. He'd had a bath this afternoon – I could tell from his fluffy factor.

'No,' she said, her voice flat with discouragement. 'I worked on him for an hour today, and I only gave him a lizard tail. Took everything I had to get it changed back.'

Bob was really a guy, that is, a man. A sort of nerdy-looking man with dark hair and glasses, though Amelia had confided he had some outstanding attributes that weren't apparent when he was dressed for the street. Amelia wasn't supposed to be practicing transformational magic when she turned Bob into a cat; they were having what must have been very adventurous sex. I'd never had the nerve to ask her what she'd been trying to do. It was clear that it was something pretty exotic.

'The deal is,' Amelia said suddenly, and I went on the alert. The real reason she'd stayed up to see me was about to be revealed. Amelia was a very clear broadcaster, so I picked it right up from her brain. But I let her go on and speak, because people *really* don't like it if you tell them they don't have to actually speak to you, especially when the topic is something they've had to build up to. 'My dad is going to be in Shreveport tomorrow, and he wants to come by Bon Temps to see me,' she said in a rush. 'It'll be him and his chauffeur, Marley. He wants to come for supper.'

The next day would be Sunday. Merlotte's would be open only in the afternoon, but I wasn't scheduled to work anyway, I saw with a glance at my calendar. 'So I'll just go out,' I said. 'I could go visit JB and Tara. No big.'

'Please be here,' she said, and her face was naked with pleading. She didn't spell out why. But I could read the reason easy enough. Amelia had a very conflicted relationship with her dad; in fact, she'd taken her mother's last name, Broadway, though in part that was because her father was so well-known. Copley Carmichael had lots of political clout and he was rich, though I didn't know how Katrina had affected his income. Carmichael owned huge lumberyards and was a builder, and Katrina might have wiped out his businesses. On the other hand, the whole area needed lumber and rebuilding.

'What time's he coming?' I asked.

'Five.'

'Does the chauffeur eat at the same table as him?' I'd never dealt with employees. We just had the one table here in the kitchen. I sure wasn't going to make the man sit on the back steps.

'Oh, God,' she said. This had clearly never occurred to her. 'What will we do about Marley?'

'That's what I'm asking you.' I may have sounded a little too patient.

'Listen,' Amelia said. 'You don't know my dad. You don't know how he is.'

I knew from Amelia's brain that her feelings about her father were really mixed. It was very difficult to pick through the love, fear, and anxiety to get to Amelia's true basic attitude. I knew few rich people, and even fewer rich people who employed full-time chauffeurs.

This visit was going to be interesting.

I said good night to Amelia and went to bed, and though there was a lot to think about, my body was tired and I was soon asleep.

Sunday was another beautiful day. I thought of the newlyweds, safely launched on their new lives, and I thought of old Miss Caroline, who was enjoying the company of a couple of her cousins (youngsters in their sixties) by way of watchdogs and companions. When Portia and Glen returned, the cousins would go back to their more humble home, probably with some relief. Halleigh and Andy would move into their own small house.

I wondered about Jonathan and the beautiful withered man.

I reminded myself to call Eric the next night when he was up.

I thought about Bill's unexpected words.

For the millionth time, I speculated about Quinn's silence.

But before I could get too broody, I was caught up in Hurricane Amelia.

There are lots of things I've come to enjoy, even love, about Amelia. She's straightforward, enthusiastic, and talented. She knows all about the supernatural world, and my place in it. She thinks my weird 'talent' is really cool. I can talk to her about anything. She's never going to react with disgust or horror. On the other hand, Amelia is impulsive and headstrong, but you have to take people like they are. I've really enjoyed having Amelia living with me.

On the practical side, she's a decent cook, she's careful about keeping our property separate, and God knows she's tidy. What Amelia really does well is *clean*. She cleans when she's bored, she cleans when she's nervous, and she cleans when she feels guilty. I am no slouch in the housekeeping department, but Amelia is world-class. The day she had a near-miss auto accident, she cleaned my living room furniture, upholstery and all. When her tenant called her to tell her the roof had to be replaced, she went down to EZ Rent and brought home a machine to polish and buff the wooden floors.

When I got up at nine, Amelia was already deep in a cleaning frenzy because of her father's impending visit. By the time I left for church at about ten forty-five, Amelia was on her hands and knees in the downstairs hall bathroom, which admittedly is very old-fashioned looking with its tiny octagonal black-and-white tiles and a huge old claw-footed bathtub; but (thanks to my brother, Jason) it has a more modern toilet. This was the bathroom Amelia used, since there wasn't one upstairs. I had a small, private one off my bedroom, added in the fifties. In my house, you could see several major decorating trends over the past few decades all in one building.

'You really think it was that dirty?' I said, standing in the doorway. I was talking to Amelia's rump.

She raised her head and passed a rubber-gloved hand over her forehead to push her short hair out of the way.

'No, it wasn't bad, but I want it to be great.'

'My house is just an old house, Amelia. I don't think it can look great.' There was no point in my apologizing for the age and wear of the house and its furnishings. This was the best I could do, and I loved it.

'This is a wonderful old home, Sookie,' Amelia said fiercely. 'But I have to be busy.'

'Okay,' I said. 'Well, I'm going to church. I'll be home by twelve thirty.'

'Can you go to the store after church? The list is on the counter.'

I agreed, glad to have something to do that would keep me out of the house longer.

The morning felt more like March (March in the south, that is) than

October. When I got out of my car at the Methodist church, I raised my face to the slight breeze. There was a touch of winter in the air, a little taste of it. The windows in the modest church were open. When we sang, our combined voices floated out over the grass and trees. But I saw some leaves blow past as the pastor preached.

Frankly, I don't always listen to the sermon. Sometimes the hour in church is just a time to think, a time to consider where my life is going. But at least those thoughts are in a context. And when you watch leaves falling off trees, your context gets pretty narrow.

Today I listened. Reverend Collins talked about giving God the things that were due him while giving Caesar the things due *him*. That seemed like an April fifteenth type sermon to me, and I caught myself wondering if Reverend Collins paid his taxes quarterly. But after a while, I figured he was talking about the laws we break all the time without feeling guilty – like the speed limit, or sticking a letter in with some presents in a box you're mailing at the post office, without paying the extra postage.

I smiled at Reverend Collins on my way out of the church. He always looks a little troubled when he sees me.

I said hello to Maxine Fortenberry and her husband, Ed, as I reached the parking lot. Maxine was large and formidable, and Ed was so shy and quiet he was almost invisible. Their son, Hoyt, was my brother Jason's best friend. Hoyt was standing behind his mother. He was wearing a nice suit, and his hair had been trimmed. Interesting signs.

'Sugar, you give me a hug!' Maxine said, and of course I did. Maxine had been a good friend to my grandmother, though she was more the age my dad would have been. I smiled at Ed and gave Hoyt a little wave.

'You're looking nice,' I told him, and he smiled. I didn't think I'd ever seen Hoyt smile like that, and I glanced at Maxine. She was grinning.

'Hoyt, he's dating that Holly you work with,' Maxine said. 'She's got a little one, and that's a thing to think about, but he's always liked kids.'

'I didn't know,' I said. I really had been out of it lately. 'That's just great, Hoyt. Holly's a real nice girl.'

I wasn't sure I would have put it quite that way if I'd had time to think, so maybe it was lucky I didn't. There were some big positives about Holly (devoted to her son, Cody; loyal to her friends; a competent worker). She'd been divorced for several years, so Hoyt wasn't a rebound. I wondered if Holly had told Hoyt she was a Wiccan. Nope, she hadn't, or Maxine wouldn't be smiling so broadly.

'We're meeting her for lunch at the Sizzler,' she said, referring to the steakhouse up by the interstate. 'Holly's not much of a churchgoer, but we're working on getting her to come with us and bring Cody. We better get moving if we're gonna be on time.'

'Way to go, Hoyt,' I said, patting his arm as he went by me. He gave me a pleased look.

Everyone was getting married or falling in love. I was happy for them. Happy, happy, happy. I pasted a smile on my face and went to Piggly Wiggly. I fished Amelia's list out of my purse. It was pretty long, but I was sure there'd be additions by now. I called her on my cell phone, and she had already thought of three more items to add, so I was some little while in the store.

My arms were weighed down with plastic bags as I struggled up the steps to the back porch. Amelia shot out to the car to grab the other bags. 'Where have you been?' she asked, as if she'd been standing by the door tapping her toe.

I looked at my watch. 'I got out of church and went to the store,' I said defensively. 'It's only one.'

Amelia passed me again, heavily laden. She shook her head in exasperation as she went by, making a noise that could only be described as 'Urrrrrrgh.'

The rest of the afternoon was like that, as though Amelia were getting ready for the date of her life.

I'm not a bad cook, but Amelia would let me do only the most menial chores in fixing the dinner. I got to chop onions and tomatoes. Oh, yeah, she let me wash the preparation dishes. I'd always wondered if she could do the dishes like the fairy godmothers in *Sleeping Beauty*, but she just snorted when I brought it up.

The house was spanky clean, and though I tried not to mind, I noticed that Amelia had even given the floor of my bedroom a once-over. As a rule, we didn't go into each other's space.

'Sorry I went in your room,' Amelia said suddenly, and I jumped – me, the telepath. Amelia had beaten me at my own game. 'It was one of those crazy impulses I get. I was vacuuming, and I just thought I'd get your floor, too. And before I thought about it, I was done. I put your slippers up under your bed.'

'Okay,' I said, trying to sound neutral.

'Hey, I *am* sorry.'

I nodded and went back to drying the dishes and putting them away. The menu, as decided by Amelia, was tossed green salad with tomatoes and slivered carrots, lasagna, hot garlic bread, and steamed fresh mixed vegetables. I don't know diddly-squat about steamed vegetables, but I had prepared all the raw materials – the zucchini, bell peppers, mushrooms, cauliflower. Late in the afternoon, I was deemed capable of tossing the salad, and I got to put the cloth and the little bouquet of flowers on the table and arrange the place settings. Four place settings.

I'd offered to take Mr Marley into the living room with me, where we could eat on TV trays, but you would have thought I'd offered to wash his feet, Amelia was so horrified.

'No, you're sticking with me,' she said.

'You gotta talk to your dad,' I said. 'At some point, I'm leaving the room.'

She took a deep breath and let it out. 'Okay, I'm a grownup,' she muttered.

'Scaredy-cat,' I said.

'You haven't met him yet.'

Amelia hurried upstairs at four fifteen to get ready. I was sitting in the living room reading a library book when I heard a car on the gravel driveway. I glanced at the clock on the mantel. It was four forty-eight. I yelled up the staircase and stood to look out the window. The afternoon was drawing to a close, but since we hadn't reverted to standard time yet, it was easy to see the Lincoln Town Car parked in front. A man with clipped dark hair, wearing a business suit, got out of the driver's seat. This must be Marley. He wasn't wearing a chauffeur's hat, somewhat to my disappointment. He opened a rear door. Out stepped Copley Carmichael.

Amelia's dad wasn't very tall, and he had short thick gray hair that looked like a really good carpet, dense and smooth and expertly cut. He was very tan, and his eyebrows were still dark. No glasses. No lips. Well, he did have lips, but they were really thin, so his mouth looked like a trap.

Mr Carmichael looked around him as if he were doing a tax assessment.

I heard Amelia clattering down the stairs behind me as I watched the man in my front yard complete his survey. Marley the chauffeur was looking right at the house. He'd spotted my face at the window.

'Marley's sort of new,' Amelia said. 'He's been with my dad for just two years.'

'Your dad's always had a driver?'

'Yeah. Marley's a bodyguard, too,' Amelia said casually, as if everyone's dad had a bodyguard.

They were walking up the gravel sidewalk now, not even looking at its neat border of ilex. Up the wooden steps. Across the front porch. Knocking.

I thought of all the scary creatures that had been in my house: Weres, shifters, vampires, even a demon or two. Why should I be worried about this man? I straightened my spine, chilled my anxious brain, and went to the front door, though Amelia almost beat me to it. After all, this was my house.

I put my hand on the knob, and I got my smile ready before I opened the door.

'Please come in,' I said, and Marley opened the screen door for Mr Carmichael, who came in and hugged his daughter but not before he'd cast another comprehensive look around the living room.

He was as clear a broadcaster as his daughter.

He was thinking this looked mighty shabby for a daughter of his. . . . Pretty girl Amelia was living with . . . Wondered if Amelia was having sex with her . . . The girl was probably no better than she should be. . . . No police record, though she had dated a vampire and had a wild brother . . .

Of course a rich and powerful man like Copley Carmichael would have his daughter's new housemate investigated. Such a procedure had simply never occurred to me, like so many things the rich did.

I took a deep breath. 'I'm Sookie Stackhouse,' I said politely. 'You must be Mr Carmichael. And this is?' After shaking Mr Carmichael's hand, I extended mine to Marley.

For a second, I thought I'd caught Amelia's dad off-footed. But he recovered in record time.

'This is Tyrese Marley,' Mr Carmichael said smoothly.

The chauffeur shook my hand gently, as if he didn't want to break my bones, and then he nodded to Amelia. 'Miss Amelia,' he said, and Amelia looked angry, as if she was going to tell him to cut the 'Miss,' but then she reconsidered. All these thoughts, pinging back and forth . . . It was enough to keep me distracted.

Tyrese Marley was a very, very light-skinned African-American. He was far from black; his skin was more the color of old ivory. His eyes were bright hazel. Though his hair was black, it wasn't curly, and it had a red cast. Marley was a man you'd always look at twice.

'I'll take the car back to town and get some gas,' he said to his boss. 'While you spend time with Miss Amelia. When you want me back?'

Mr Carmichael looked down at his watch. 'A couple of hours.'

'You're welcome to stay for supper,' I said, managing a very neutral tone. I wanted what made everyone feel comfortable.

'I have a few errands I need to run,' Tyrese Marley said with no inflection. 'Thanks for the invitation. I'll see you later.' He left.

Okay, end of my attempt at democracy.

Tyrese couldn't have known how much I would have preferred going into town rather than staying in the house. I braced myself and began the social necessities. 'Can I get you a glass of wine, Mr Carmichael, or something else to drink? What about you, Amelia?'

'Call me Cope,' he said, smiling. It was way too much like a shark's grin to warm my heart. 'Sure, a glass of whatever's open. You, baby?'

'Some of the white,' she said, and I heard her telling her dad to be seated as I went to the kitchen.

I served the wine and added it to the tray with our hors d'oeuvres: crackers, a warm Brie spread, and apricot jam mixed with hot peppers.

We had some cute little knives that looked good with the tray, and Amelia had gotten cocktail napkins for the drinks.

Cope had a good appetite, and he enjoyed the Brie. He sipped the wine, which was an Arkansas label, and nodded politely. Well, at least he didn't spit it out. I seldom drink, and I'm no kind of wine connoisseur. In fact, I'm not a connoisseur of anything at all. But I enjoyed the wine, sip by sip.

'Amelia, tell me what you're doing with your time while you're waiting for your home to be repaired,' Cope said, which I thought was a reasonable opening.

I started to tell him that for starters, she wasn't screwing around with me, but I thought that might be a little too direct. I tried very hard not to read his thoughts, but I swear, with him and his daughter in the same room, it was like listening to a television broadcast.

'I've done some filing for one of the local insurance agents. And I'm working part-time at Merlotte's Bar,' Amelia said. 'I serve drinks and the occasional chicken basket.'

'Is the bar work interesting?' Cope didn't sound sarcastic, I'll give him that. But, of course, I was sure he'd had Sam researched, too.

'It's not bad,' she said with a slight smile. That was a lot of restraint for Amelia, so I checked into her brain to see that she was squeezing herself into a conversational girdle. 'I get good tips.'

Her father nodded. 'You, Miss Stackhouse?' Cope asked politely.

He knew everything about me but the shade of fingernail polish I was wearing, and I was sure he'd add that to my file if he could. 'I work at Merlotte's full-time,' I said, just as if he didn't know that. 'I've been there for years.'

'You have family in the area?'

'Oh, yes, we've been here forever,' I said. 'Or as close to forever as Americans get. But our family's dwindled down. It's just me and my brother now.'

'Older brother? Younger?'

'Older,' I said. 'Married, real recently.'

'So maybe there'll be other little Stackhouses,' he said, trying to sound like he thought that would be a good thing.

I nodded as if the possibility pleased me, too. I didn't like my brother's wife much, and I thought it was entirely possible that any kids they had would be pretty rotten. In fact, one was on the way right now, if Crystal didn't miscarry again. My brother was a werepanther (bitten, not born), and his wife was a born . . . a pure . . . werepanther, that is. Being raised in the little werepanther community of Hotshot was not an easy thing, and would be even harder for kids who weren't pure.

'Dad, can I get you some more wine?' Amelia was out of her chair like a shot, and she sped on her way to the kitchen with the half-empty wineglass. Good, quality alone time with Amelia's dad.

'Sookie,' Cope said, 'you've been very kind to let my daughter live with you all this time.'

'Amelia pays rent,' I said. 'She buys half the groceries. She pays her way.'

'Nonetheless, I wish you'd let me give you something for your trouble.'

'What Amelia gives me on rent is enough. After all, she's paid for some improvements to the property, too.'

His face sharpened then, as if he was on the scent of something big. Did he think I'd talked Amelia into putting a pool in the backyard?

'She got a window air conditioner put in her bedroom upstairs,' I said. 'And she got an extra phone line for the computer. And I think she got a throw rug and some curtains for her room, too.'

'She lives upstairs?'

'Yes,' I said, surprised he didn't somehow know already. Perhaps there were a few things his intelligence net hadn't scooped up. 'I live down here, she lives up there, and we share the kitchen and living room, though I think Amelia's got a TV upstairs, too. Hey, Amelia!' I called.

'Yeah?' Her voice floated down the hall from the kitchen.

'You still got that little TV up there?'

'Yeah, I hooked it up to the cable.'

'Just wondered.'

I smiled at Cope, indicating the conversational ball was in his court. He was thinking of several things to ask me, and he was thinking of the best way to approach me to get the most information. A name popped to the surface in the whirlpool of his thoughts, and it took everything I had to keep a polite expression.

'The first tenant Amelia had in the house on Chloe – she was your cousin, right?' Cope said.

'Hadley. Yes.' I kept my face calm as I nodded. 'Did you know her?'

'I know her husband,' he said, and smiled.

Chapter 3

I knew Amelia had returned and was standing by the wingback chair where her father sat, and I knew she was frozen in place. I knew I didn't breathe for a second.

'I never met him,' I said. I felt as if I'd been walking in a jungle and fallen into a concealed pit. I was sure glad I was the only telepath in the house. I hadn't told anyone, anyone at all, about what I'd found in Hadley's lockbox when I'd cleaned it out that day at a bank in New Orleans. 'They'd been divorced for a while before Hadley died.'

'You should take the time to meet him someday. He's an interesting man,' Cope said, as if he wasn't aware he was dropping a bombshell on me. Of course he was waiting for my reaction. He'd hoped I hadn't known about the marriage at all, that I'd be taken completely by surprise. 'He's a skilled carpenter. I'd love to track him down and hire him again.'

The chair he was sitting on had been upholstered in a cream-colored material with lots of tiny blue flowers on green arching stems embroidered on it. It was still pretty, if faded. I concentrated on the pattern of the chair so I wouldn't show Copley Carmichael how very angry I was.

'He doesn't mean anything to me, no matter how interesting he is,' I said in a voice so level you could've played pool on it. 'Their marriage was over and done. As I'm sure you know, Hadley had another partner at the time she died.' Was murdered. But the government hadn't

gotten around to taking much notice of vampire deaths unless those
deaths were caused by humans. Vampires did most of their own self-
policing.

'I'd think you'd want to see the baby, though,' Copley said.

Thank God I picked this out of Copley's head a second or two before
he actually spoke the words. Even knowing what he was going to say,
I felt his oh-so-casual remark hit me like a blow to the stomach. But
I didn't want to give him the satisfaction of letting him see that. 'My
cousin Hadley was wild. She used drugs and people. She wasn't the
most stable person in the world. She was really pretty, and she had a
way about her, so she always had admirers.' There, I'd said everything
pro and con about my cousin Hadley. And I hadn't said the word
'baby'. *What baby?*

'How'd your family feel when she became a vampire?' Cope said.

Hadley's change was a matter of public record. 'Turned' vampires
were supposed to register when they entered their altered state of
being. They had to name their maker. It was a kind of governmental
vampire birth control. You can bet the Bureau of Vampire Affairs
would come down like a ton of bricks on a vampire who made too
many other little vampires. Hadley had been turned by Sophie-Anne
Leclerq herself.

Amelia had put her father's wineglass down within his reach and
resumed her seat on the sofa beside me. 'Dad, Hadley lived upstairs
from me for two years,' she said. 'Of course we knew she was a
vampire. For goodness sake, I thought you'd want to tell me all the
hometown news.'

God bless Amelia. I was having a hard time holding myself together,
and only years of doing that very thing when I telepathically overheard
something awful was keeping me glued.

'I need to check on the food. Excuse me,' I murmured, and rose and
left the room. I hoped I didn't scurry. I tried to walk normally. But
once in the kitchen, I kept on going out the back door and across the
back porch, out the screen door and into the yard.

If I thought I'd hear Hadley's ghostly voice telling me what to do,
I was disappointed. Vampires don't leave ghosts, at least as far as I know.
Some vampires believe they don't possess souls. I don't know. That's

up to God. And here I was babbling to myself, because I didn't want to think about Hadley's baby, about the fact that I hadn't known about the child.

Maybe it was just Copley's way. Maybe he always wanted to demonstrate the extent of his knowledge, as a way of showing his power to the people he dealt with.

I had to go back in there for Amelia's sake. I braced myself, put my smile back on – though I knew it was a creepy, nervous smile – and back I went. I perched by Amelia and beamed at both of them. They looked at me expectantly, and I realized a conversational lull had fallen.

'Oh,' said Cope suddenly. 'Amelia, I forgot to tell you. Someone called the house for you last week, someone I didn't know.'

'Her name?'

'Oh, let me think. Mrs Beech wrote it down. Ophelia? Octavia? Octavia Fant. That was it. Unusual.'

I thought Amelia was going to faint. She turned a funny color and she braced her hand against the arm of the couch. 'You're sure?' she asked.

'Yes, I'm sure. I gave her your cell phone number, and I told her you were living in Bon Temps.'

'Thanks, Dad,' Amelia croaked. 'Ah, I'll bet supper's done; let me go check.'

'Didn't Sookie just look at the food?' He wore the broad tolerant smile a man wears when he thinks women are being silly.

'Oh, sure, but it's in the end stage,' I said while Amelia shot out of the room as swiftly as I'd just done. 'It would be awful if it burned. Amelia worked so hard.'

'Do you know this Ms Fant?' Cope asked.

'No, I can't say as I do.'

'Amelia looked almost scared. No one's trying to hurt my girl, right?'

He was a different man when he said that, and one I could almost like. No matter what else he was, Cope didn't want anyone hurting his daughter. Anyone except him, that is.

'I don't think so.' I knew who Octavia Fant was because Amelia's brain had just told me, but she herself hadn't spoken it out loud, so it wasn't a thing I could share. Sometimes the things I hear out loud and the things I hear in my head become really tangled and confused – one of the reasons why I have a reputation for being borderline crazy. 'You're a contractor, Mr Carmichael?'

'Cope, please. Yes, among other things.'

'I guess your business must be booming right now,' I said.

'If my company was twice as big, we couldn't keep up with the jobs there are to do,' he said. 'But I hated to see New Orleans all torn up.'

Oddly enough, I believed him.

Supper went smoothly enough. If Amelia's father was disconcerted at eating in the kitchen, he didn't give a sign of it. Since he was a builder, he noticed that the kitchen portion of the house was new and I had to tell him about the fire, but that could have happened to anyone, right? I left out the part about the arsonist.

Cope seemed to enjoy his food and complimented Amelia, who was mighty pleased. He had another glass of wine with his meal, but no more than that, and he ate moderately, too. He and Amelia talked about friends of the family and some relatives, and I was left alone to think. Believe me, I had a lot of thinking to do.

Hadley's marriage license and divorce decree had been in her lockbox at her bank when I'd opened it after her death. The box had contained some family things – a few pictures, her mother's obituary, several pieces of jewelry. There'd also been a lock of fine hair, dark and wispy, with a bit of Scotch tape to keep it together. It had been placed in a little envelope. I'd wondered when I'd noticed how fine the hair was. But there hadn't been a birth certificate or any other scrap of evidence that Hadley had had a baby.

Up until now, I'd had no clearly defined reason to contact Hadley's former husband. I hadn't even known he existed until I'd opened her lockbox. He wasn't mentioned in her will. I'd never met him. He hadn't shown up while I was in New Orleans.

Why hadn't she mentioned the child in her will? Surely any parent would do that. And though she'd named Mr Cataliades and me as the joint executors, she hadn't told either of us – well, she hadn't told me – that she had relinquished her rights to her child, either.

'Sookie, would you pass the butter?' Amelia asked, and I could tell from her tone it wasn't the first time she'd spoken to me.

'Of course,' I said. 'Can I get either of you any more water or another glass of wine?'

They both declined.

After supper, I volunteered to do the dishes. Amelia accepted my offer after a brief pause. She and her father had to have some time alone, even if Amelia didn't relish the prospect.

I washed and dried and put away the dishes in relative peace. I wiped down the counters and whipped the tablecloth off the table and popped it into the washer on the enclosed back porch. I went into my room and read for a while, though I didn't take in much of what was happening on the page. Finally, I laid the book aside and got a box out of my underwear drawer. This box contained everything I'd retrieved from Hadley's lockbox. I checked the name on the marriage certificate. On impulse, I called information.

'I need a listing for a Remy Savoy,' I said.

'What city?'

'New Orleans.'

'That number's been disconnected.'

'Try Metairie.'

'No, ma'am.'

'Okay, thanks.'

Of course, a lot of people had moved since Katrina, and a lot of those moves were permanent. People who had fled the hurricane had no reason to come back, in many cases. There was nowhere to live and no job to go to, in all too many cases.

I wondered how to search for Hadley's ex-husband.

A very unwelcome solution crept into my head. Bill Compton was a computer whiz. Maybe he could track down this Remy Savoy, find out where he was now, discover if the child was with him.

I rolled the idea around in my head like a mouthful of doubtful wine. Given our exchange of the night before at the wedding, I could not imagine myself approaching Bill to ask for a favor, though he'd be the right man for the job.

A wave of longing for Quinn almost took me to my knees. Quinn was a smart and well-traveled man, and he would surely have a good piece of advice for me. If I ever saw him again.

I shook myself. I could just hear a car pulling into the parking area by the sidewalk at the front of the house. Tyrese Marley was returning for Cope. I straightened my back and left my room, my smile fixed firmly on my face.

The front door was open, and Tyrese was standing in it, pretty much filling it up from side to side. He was a big man. Cope was leaning over to give his daughter a peck on the cheek, which she accepted without a hint of a smile. Bob the cat came through the door and sat down beside her. The cat was looking up at Amelia's father with his wide-eyed stare.

'You have a cat, Amelia? I thought you hated cats.'

Bob switched his gaze to Amelia. Nothing can stare like a cat.

'Dad! That was years ago! This is Bob. He's great.' Amelia picked up the black-and-white cat and held him to her chest. Bob looked smug and began purring.

'Hmmm. Well, I'll be calling you. Please take care. I hate to think about you being up here at the other end of the state.'

'It's just a few hours' ride away,' Amelia said, sounding all of seventeen.

'True,' he said, trying for rueful but charming. He missed by a foot or two. 'Sookie, thanks for the evening,' he called over his daughter's shoulder.

Marley had gone to Merlotte's to see if he could scope out any information on me, I heard clearly from his brain. He'd picked up quite a few odds and ends. He'd talked to Arlene, which was bad, and to our current cook and our busboy, which was good. Plus assorted bar patrons. He'd have a mixed report to convey.

The moment the car pulled away, Amelia collapsed onto the sofa with relief 'Thank God he's gone,' she said. 'Now do you see what I mean?'

'Yeah,' I said. I sat beside her. 'He's a mover and a shaker, isn't he?'

'Always has been,' she said. 'He's trying to maintain a relationship, but our ideas don't match.'

'Your dad loves you.'

'He does. But he loves power and control, too.'

That was putting it conservatively.

'And he doesn't know you have your own form of power.'

'No, he doesn't believe in it at all,' Amelia said. 'He'll tell you he's a devout Catholic, but that's not the truth.'

'In a way, that's good,' I said. 'If he believed in your witch power, he'd try to make you do all kinds of things for him. You wouldn't want to do some of them, I bet.' I could have bitten my tongue, but Amelia didn't take offense.

'You're right,' she said. 'I wouldn't want to help him advance his agenda. He's capable of doing that without my assistance. If he'd just leave me alone, I'd be content. He's always trying to improve my life, on his terms. I'm really doing okay.'

'Who was that who had called you in New Orleans?' Though I knew, I had to pretend. 'Fant, her name was?'

Amelia shuddered. 'Octavia Fant is my mentor,' she said. 'She's the reason I left New Orleans. I figured my coven would do something awful to me when they found out about Bob. She's the head of my coven. Or what's left of it. If anything's left of it.'

'Ooops.'

'Yeah, no shit. I'm going to have to pay the price now.'

'You think she'll come up here?'

'I'm only surprised she's not here already.'

Despite her expressed fear, Amelia had been worried sick about the welfare of her mentor after Katrina. She had made a huge effort to track the woman, though she didn't want Octavia to find *her*.

Amelia feared being discovered, especially with Bob still in his cat form. She'd told me that her dabbling in transformational magic would be considered all the more reprehensible because she was still an intern, or something along those lines . . . a step above novice, anyway. Amelia didn't discuss the witch infrastructure.

'You didn't think of telling your father not to reveal your location?'

'Asking him to do that would have made him so curious he'd have torn up my entire life to find out why I'd asked. I never thought Octavia would call him, since she knows how I feel about him.'

Which was, to say the least, conflicted.

'I have something to tell you that I forgot,' Amelia said abruptly. 'Speaking of phone calls, Eric called you.'

'When?'

'Ah, last night. Before you got home. You were so full of news when you got here, I just forgot to tell you. Plus, you'd said you were going to call him anyway. And I was really upset about my dad coming. I'm sorry, Sookie. I promise I'll write a note next time.'

This was not the first time Amelia had neglected to tell me about a caller. I wasn't pleased, but it was water under the bridge, and our day had been stressful enough. I hoped Eric had found out about the money the queen owed me for my services in Rhodes. I hadn't gotten a cheque yet, and I hated to bug her since she'd been hurt so badly. I went to the phone in my room to call Fangtasia, which should be in full blast. The club was open every night except Monday.

'Fangtasia, the bar with a bite,' Clancy said.

Oh, great. My least favorite vampire. I phrased my request carefully. 'Clancy, it's Sookie. Eric asked me to return his call.'

There was a moment of silence. I was willing to bet that Clancy was trying to figure out if he could block my access to Eric. He decided he couldn't. 'One moment,' he said. A brief pause while I listened to 'Strangers in the Night'. Then Eric picked up the phone.

'Hello?' he said.

'I'm sorry I didn't call you back before now. I just got your message. Did you call about my money?'

A moment of silence. 'No, about something else entirely. Will you go out with me tomorrow night?'

I stared at the telephone. I couldn't manage a coherent thought. Finally I said, 'Eric, I'm dating Quinn.'

'And how long has it been since you've seen him?'

'Since Rhodes.'

'How long has it been since you heard from him?'

'Since Rhodes.' My voice was wooden. I was unwilling to talk to Eric about this, but we had shared blood often enough to have a much stronger tie than I liked. In fact, I loathed our bond, one we'd been compelled to forge. But when I heard his voice, I felt content. When I was with him, I felt beautiful and happy. And there was nothing I could do about it.

'I think you can give me one evening,' Eric said. 'It doesn't sound as though Quinn has you booked.'

'That was mean.'

'It's Quinn who's cruel, promising you he'd be here and then not keeping his word.' There was a dark element in Eric's voice, an undertone of anger.

'Do you know what's happened to him?' I asked. 'Do you know where he is?'

There was a significant silence. 'No,' Eric said very gently. 'I don't know. But there is someone in town who wants to meet you. I promised I would arrange it. I'd like to take you to Shreveport myself.'

So this wasn't a *date* date.

'You mean that guy Jonathan? He came to the wedding and introduced himself. I've got to say, I didn't much care for the guy. No offense, if he's a friend of yours.'

'Jonathan? What Jonathan?'

'I'm talking about the Asian guy; he's maybe Thai? He was at the Bellefleur wedding last night. He said he wanted to see me because he was staying in Shreveport and he'd heard a lot about me. He said he'd checked in with you, like a good little visiting vampire.'

'I don't know him,' Eric said. His voice was much sharper. 'I'll ask here at Fangtasia to see if anyone has seen him. And I'll prompt the queen about your money, though she is . . . not herself. Now, will you please do what I'm asking you to do?'

I made a face at the telephone. 'I guess,' I said. 'Who'm I meeting? And where?'

'I'll have to let the "who" remain a mystery,' Eric said. 'As to where, we'll go to dinner at a nice restaurant. The kind you'd call casual dressy.'

'You don't eat. What will you do?'

'I'll introduce you and stay as long as you need me to.'

A crowded restaurant should be all right. 'Okay,' I said, not very graciously. 'I'll get off work about six or six thirty.'

'I'll be there to pick you up at seven.'

'Give me till seven thirty. I need to change.' I knew I sounded grumpy, and that was exactly how I felt. I hated the big mystery around this meeting.

'You'll feel better when you see me,' he said. Dammit, he was absolutely right.

Chapter 4

I checked my Word of the Day calendar while I was waiting for my hair-straightening iron to heat up. 'Epicene'. Huh.

Since I didn't know what restaurant we were going to, and I didn't know who we'd meet there, I picked my most comfortable option and wore a sky blue silk T-shirt that Amelia had said was too big for her, and some black dress slacks with black heels. I don't wear a lot of jewelry, so a gold chain and some little gold earrings did the decorating for me. I'd had a tough day at work, but I was too curious about the evening ahead to feel tired.

Eric was on time, and I felt (surprise) a rush of pleasure when I saw him. I don't think that was entirely due to the blood bond between us. I think any heterosexual woman would feel a rush of pleasure at the sight of Eric. He was a tall man and must have been seen as a giant in his time. He was built to swing a heavy sword to hew down his enemies. Eric's golden blond hair sprang back like a lion's mane from a bold forehead. There was nothing *epicene* about Eric, nothing ethereally beautiful, either. He was all male.

Eric bent to kiss me on the cheek. I felt warm and safe. This was the effect Eric had on me now that we'd swapped blood more than three times. The blood sharing hadn't been for pleasure but a necessity – at least I'd thought so – every time, but the price I paid was steep. We were bonded now, and when he was near, I was absurdly happy.

I tried to enjoy the sensation, but knowing it wasn't completely natural made that hard to do.

Since Eric had come in his Corvette, I was extra glad I'd worn pants. Getting into and out of a Corvette modestly was a very difficult procedure if you were wearing a dress. I made small talk on the way to Shreveport, but Eric was uncharacteristically silent. I tried to question him about Jonathan, the mysterious vampire at the wedding, but Eric said, 'We'll talk about that later. You haven't seen him again, have you?'

'No,' I said. 'Should I expect to?'

Eric shook his head. There was an uncomfortable pause. From the way he was gripping the wheel, I could tell that Eric was building up to saying something he didn't want to say.

'I'm glad for your sake that it appears Andre didn't survive the bombing,' he said.

The queen's dearest child, Andre, had died in the bombing in Rhodes. But it hadn't been the bomb that had killed him. Quinn and I knew what had done the deed: a big splinter of wood that Quinn had driven into Andre's heart while the vampire lay disabled. Quinn had killed Andre for my sake, because he knew Andre had plans for me that made me sick with fear.

'I'm sure the queen will miss him,' I said carefully.

Eric shot me a sharp glance. 'The queen is distraught,' he said. 'And her healing will take months more. What I was beginning to say . . .' His voice trailed off.

This wasn't like Eric. 'What?' I demanded.

'You saved my life,' he said. I'd turned to look at him, but he was looking straight ahead at the road. 'You saved my life, and Pam's, too.'

I shifted uncomfortably. 'Yeah, well.' Miss Articulate. The silence lengthened until I felt I had to say something else. 'We do have the blood tie thing going.'

Eric didn't respond for a stretch of time. 'That's not why you came to wake me, first of all, the day the hotel blew up,' he said. 'But we won't talk further about this now. You have a big evening ahead.'

Yes, boss, I said snippily, but only to myself.

★

We were in a part of Shreveport I didn't know too well. It was definitely out of the main shopping area, with which I was fairly familiar. We were in a neighborhood where the houses were large and the lawns were groomed. The businesses were small and pricey . . . what retailers called 'boutiques'. We pulled into a group of such shops. It was arranged in an L, and the restaurant was at the rear of the L. It was called Les Deux Poissons. There were maybe eight cars parked there, and each one of them represented my yearly income. I looked down at my clothes, feeling suddenly uneasy.

'Don't worry, you're beautiful,' Eric said quietly. He leaned over to unbuckle my seat belt (to my astonishment), and as he straightened he kissed me again, this time on the mouth. His bright blue eyes blazed out of his white face. He looked as if a whole story was on the tip of his tongue. But then he swallowed it back and unfolded himself from the car to walk around to my side to open the door for me. Maybe I wasn't the only one this blood bond worked on, huh?

From his tension I realized that some major event was coming at me fast, and I began to be afraid. Eric took my hand as we walked across to the restaurant, and he ran his thumb absently across my palm. I was surprised to find out there was a direct line from my palm to my, my, hootchie.

We stepped into the foyer, where there was a little fountain and a screen that blocked the view of the diners. The woman standing at the podium was beautiful and black, her hair shaved very close to her skull. She wore a draped dress of orange and brown and the highest heels I had ever seen. She might as well have been wearing toe shoes. I looked at her closely, and I sampled the signature of her brain, and I found she was human. She smiled brilliantly at Eric and had the sense to give me a share of that smile.

'A party of two?' she said.

'We're meeting someone,' Eric said.

'Oh, the gentleman . . .'

'Yes.'

'Right this way, please.' Her smile replaced by a look almost of envy, she turned and walked gracefully into the depths of the restaurant. Eric gestured for me to follow her. The interior was fairly dark, and candles flickered on the tables, which were covered with snowy white cloths and elaborately folded napkins.

My eyes were on the hostess's back, so when she came to a halt, I didn't immediately recognize that she'd stopped at the table where we were to sit. She stepped aside. Seated facing me was the lovely man who'd been at the wedding two nights before.

The hostess spun on her high heel, touched the back of the chair to the man's right to indicate I should sit there, and told us our server would be with us. The man rose to pull out my chair and hold it for me. I glanced back at Eric. He gave me a reassuring nod. I slipped in front of the chair and the man pushed it forward with perfect timing.

Eric didn't sit. I wanted him to explain what was happening, but he didn't speak. He looked almost sad.

The beautiful man was looking at me intently. 'Child,' he said to get my attention. Then he pushed back his long, fine golden hair. None of the other diners were positioned to see what he was showing me.

His ear was pointed. He was a fairy.

I knew two other fairies. But they avoided vampires at all costs, because the smell of a fairy was as intoxicating to a vampire as honey is to a bear. According to a vampire who was particularly gifted in the scent sense, I had a trace of fairy blood.

'Okay,' I said, to let him know the ears had registered.

'Sookie, this is Niall Brigant,' Eric said. He pronounced it 'Nye-all.' 'He's going to talk to you over supper. I'll be outside if you need me.' He inclined his head stiffly to the fairy and then he was gone.

I watched Eric walk away, and I was bowled over with a rush of anxiety. Then I felt a hand on top of my own. I turned to meet the eyes of the fairy.

'As he said, my name is Niall.' His voice was light, sexless, resonant. His eyes were green, the deepest green you can imagine. In the flickering candlelight, the color hardly mattered – it was the depth you noticed. His hand on mine was light as a feather but very warm.

'Who are you?' I asked, and I wasn't asking him to repeat his name.

'I'm your great-grandfather,' Niall Brigant said.

'Oh, *shit*,' I said, and covered my mouth with my hand. 'Sorry, I just

. . .' I shook my head. 'Great-grandpa?' I said, trying out the concept. Niall Brigant winced delicately. On a real man, the gesture would have looked effeminate, but on Niall it didn't.

Lots of kids in our neck of the woods call their grandfathers 'Papaw'. I'd *love* to see his reaction to that. The idea helped me recover my scattered sense of self.

'Please explain,' I said very politely. The waiter came to inquire after our drink orders and recite the specials of the day. Niall ordered a bottle of wine and told him we would have the salmon. He did not consult me. High-handed.

The young man nodded vigorously. 'Great choice,' he said. He was a Were, and though I would have expected him to be curious about Niall (who after all was a supernatural being not often encountered), I seemed to be of more interest. I attributed that to the waiter's youth and my boobs.

See, here's the weird thing about meeting my self-proclaimed relative: I never doubted his truthfulness. This was my true great-grandfather, and the knowledge just clicked into place as if it fit into a puzzle.

'I'll tell you all about it,' Niall said. Very slowly, telegraphing his intention, he leaned over to kiss my cheek. His mouth and eyes crinkled as his facial muscles moved to frame the kiss. The fine cobweb of wrinkles did not in any way detract from his beauty; he was like very old silk or a crackled painting by an ancient master.

This was a big night for getting kissed.

'When I was still young, perhaps five or six hundred years ago, I used to wander among the humans,' Niall said. And every now and then, as a male will, I'd see a human woman I found appealing.'

I glanced around so I wouldn't be staring at him every second, and I noticed a strange thing: no one was looking at us but our waiter. I mean, not even a casual glance strayed our way. And no human brains in the room were even registering our presence. My great-grandfather paused while I did this, and resumed speaking when I'd finished evaluating the situation.

'I saw such a woman in the woods one day, and her name was Einin. She thought I was an angel.' He was silent for a moment. 'She was delicious,' he said. 'She was lively, and happy, and simple.' Niall's eyes were fixed on my face. I wondered if he thought I was like Einin: simple. 'I was young enough to be infatuated, young enough to be able to ignore the inevitable end of our connection as she aged and I did not. But Einin got pregnant, which was a shock. Fairies and humans don't crossbreed often. Einin gave birth to twins, which is quite common among the fae. Einin and both boys lived through the birthing, which in those times was far from certain. She called our older son Fintan. The second was Dermot.'

The waiter brought our wine, and I was jerked out of the spell Niall's voice had laid on me. It was like we'd been sitting around a campfire in the woods listening to an ancient legend, and then snap! We were in a modern restaurant in Shreveport, Louisiana, and there were other people around who had no idea what was going on. I automatically lifted my glass and took a sip of wine. I felt I was entitled.

'Fintan the Half Fairy was your paternal grandfather, Sookie,' Niall said.

'No. I know who my grandfather was.' My voice was shaking a little, I noticed, but it was still very quiet. 'My grandfather was Mitchell Stackhouse and he married Adele Hale. My father was Corbett Hale Stackhouse, and he and my mom died in a flash flood when I was a little girl. Then I was raised by my grandmother Adele.' Though I remembered the vampire in Mississippi who'd told me he detected a trace of fairy blood in my veins, and I believed this was my great-grandfather, I just couldn't adjust my inner picture of my family.

'What was your grandmother like?' Niall asked.

'She raised me when she didn't have to,' I said. 'She took me and Jason into her home, and she worked hard to raise us right. We learned everything from her. She loved us. She had two children herself and buried them both, and that must have about killed her, but still she was strong for us.'

'She was beautiful when she was young,' Niall said. His green eyes lingered on my face as if he were trying to find some trace of her beauty in her granddaughter.

'I guess,' I said uncertainly. You don't think about your grandmother in terms of beauty, at least in the normal way of things.

'I saw her after Fintan made her pregnant,' Niall said. 'She was lovely. Her husband had told her he could not give her children. He'd had mumps at the wrong time. That's a disease, isn't it?' I nodded. 'She met Fintan one day when she was beating a rug out on the clothesline, in back of the house where you now live. He asked her for a drink of water. He was smitten on the spot. She wanted children so badly, and he promised her he could give them to her.'

'You said fairies and people weren't usually fertile when they cross-breed.'

'But Fintan was only half fairy. And he already knew that he was able to give a woman a child.' Niall's mouth quirked. 'The first woman he loved died in childbirth, but your grandmother and her son were more fortunate, and then two years later she was able to carry Fintan's daughter to completion.'

'He raped her,' I said, almost hoping it was so. My grandmother had been the most true-blue woman I'd ever met. I couldn't picture her cheating anyone out of anything, particularly since she'd promised in front of God to be faithful to my grandfather.

'No, he did not. She wanted children, though she didn't want to be unfaithful to her husband. Fintan didn't care about the feelings of others, and he wanted her desperately,' Niall said. 'But he was never violent. He would not have raped her. However, my son could talk a woman into anything, even into something against her moral judgment. . . . And if she was very beautiful, so was he.'

I tried to see the woman she must have been, in the grandmother I'd known. And I just couldn't.

'What was your father like, my grandson?' Niall asked.

'He was a handsome guy,' I said. 'He was a hard worker. He was a good dad.'

Niall smiled slightly. 'How did your mother feel about him?'

That question cut sharply into my warm memories of my father. 'She, ah, she was really devoted to him.' Maybe at the expense of her children.

'She was obsessed?' Niall's voice was not judgmental but certain, as if he knew my answer.

'Real possessive,' I admitted. 'Though I was only seven when they died, even I could see that. I guess I thought it was normal. She really wanted to give him all her attention. Sometimes Jason and I were in the way. And she was really jealous, I remember.' I tried to look amused, as if my mother being so jealous of my father was a charming quirk.

'It was the fairy in him that made her hold on so strongly,' Niall said. 'It takes some humans that way. She saw the supernatural in him, and it enthralled her. Tell me, was she a good mother?'

'She tried hard,' I whispered.

She had tried. My mother had known how to be a good mother theoretically. She knew how a good mother acted toward her children. She'd made herself go through all the motions. But all her true love had been saved for my father, who'd been bemused by the intensity of her passion. I could see that now, as an adult. As a child, I'd been confused and hurt.

The red-haired Were brought our salad and set it down in front of us. He wanted to ask us if we needed anything else, but he was too scared. He'd picked up on the atmosphere at the table.

'Why did you decide now to come meet me?' I asked. 'How long have you known about me?' I put my napkin in my lap and sat there holding the fork. I should take a bite. Wasting was not part of the way I'd been raised. By my grandmother. Who'd had sex with a half fairy (who'd wandered into the yard like a stray dog). Enough sex over enough time to produce two children.

'I've known about your family for the past sixty years, give or take. But my son Fintan forbade me seeing any of you.' He carefully put a bit of tomato into his mouth, held it there, thought about it, chewed it. He ate the way I would if I was visiting an Indian or Nicaraguan restaurant.

'What changed?' I said, but I figured it out. 'So your son is dead now.'

'Yes,' he said, and put down the fork. 'Fintan is dead. After all, he was half human. And he'd lived for seven hundred years.'

Was I supposed to have an opinion about this? I felt so numb, as though Niall had shot Novocain into my emotional center. I probably should ask how my – my *grandfather* had come to die, but I couldn't bring myself to do it.

'So you decided to come tell me about this – why?' I was proud of how calm I sounded.

'I'm old, even for my kind. I would like to know you. I can't atone for the way your life has been shaped by the heritage Fintan gave you. But I will try to make your life a little easier, if you'll permit me.'

'Can you take the telepathy away?' I asked. A wild hope, not unmixed with fear, flared in me like a sunspot.

'You are asking if I can remove something from the fiber of your being,' Niall said. 'No, I can't do that.'

I slumped in my chair. 'Thought I'd ask,' I said, fighting away tears. 'Do I get three wishes, or is that with genies?'

Niall regarded me with no humor at all. 'You wouldn't want to meet a genie,' he said. 'And I'm not a figure of fun. I am a prince.'

'Sorry,' I said. 'I'm having a little trouble coping with all this . . . Great-grandfather.' I didn't remember my human great-grandfathers. My grandfathers – okay, I guess one of them hadn't truly been my grandfather – hadn't looked or acted a thing like this beautiful creature. My grandfather Stackhouse died sixteen years ago, and my mother's parents had died before I was into my teens. So I'd known my grandmother Adele much better than any of the others, actually much better than I'd known my true parents.

'Hey,' I said. 'How come Eric fetched me for you? You're fairy, after all. Vampires go nuts when they smell fairies.'

In fact, most vampires lost their self-control when they were around fairies. Only a very disciplined vampire could behave when a fairy got within smelling distance. My fairy godmother, Claudine, was terrified of being anywhere around a bloodsucker.

'I can suppress my essence,' Niall said. 'They can see me but not smell me. It's a convenient magic. I can keep humans from even noticing me, as you have observed.'

The way he said this let me know that he was not only very old and very powerful, but he was also very proud. 'Did you send Claudine to me?' I said.

'Yes. I hope she's been of use. Only people of part-fae blood can have such a relationship with a fairy. I knew you needed her.'

'Oh, yes, she's saved my life,' I said. 'She's been wonderful.' She'd even taken me shopping. 'Are all fairies as nice as Claudine, or as beautiful as her brother?'

Claude, male stripper and now entrepreneur, was as handsome as a man could get, and he had the personality of a self-absorbed turnip.

'Dear one,' Niall said, 'we are all beautiful to humans; but some fairies are very nasty indeed.'

Okay, here came the downside. I had a strong feeling that finding out I had a great-grandfather who was a full-blooded fairy was supposed to be good news, from Niall's point of view – but that it wasn't a completely iced cupcake. Now I would get the bad news.

'You went many years without being found,' Niall said, 'in part because that was what Fintan wanted.'

'But he watched me?' I almost felt warmth in my heart at hearing that.

'My son was remorseful that he'd condemned two children to the half-in, half-out existence he'd experienced as a fairy who wasn't truly a fairy. I'm afraid the others of our race weren't kind to him.' My great-grandfather's gaze was steady. 'I did my best to defend him, but it wasn't enough. Fintan also found he wasn't human enough to pass as human, at least not for more than a short time.'

'You don't look like this normally?' I asked, very curious.

'No.' And just for a split second, I saw an almost blinding light, with Niall in the middle of it, beautiful and perfect. No wonder Einin had thought he was an angel.

'Claudine said she was working her way up,' I said. 'What does that mean?' I was floundering through this conversation. I felt like I'd been knocked down to my knees by all this information, and I was struggling to get to my emotional feet. I wasn't having a very successful time doing it.

'She shouldn't have told you that,' Niall said. He debated with himself for a second or two before continuing. 'Shifters are humans with a genetic twist, vampires are dead humans transformed into something different, but the fae have only a basic shape in common with humans. There are many kinds of fae – from the grotesque, like goblins, to the beautiful, like us.' He said this quite unself-consciously.

'Are there angels?'

'Angels are yet another form, and one which has undergone an almost complete transformation, physical and moral. It can take hundreds of years to become an angel.'

Poor Claudine.

'But enough about this,' Niall said. 'I want to know about you. My son kept me from your father and your aunt, and then from their children. His death came too late for me to know your cousin Hadley. But now I can see you and touch you.' Which, incidentally, Niall was doing in a way that wasn't exactly human: if his hand wasn't holding mine, it was placed flat against my shoulder, or my back. This wasn't exactly the way humans related, but it wasn't hurting me. I wasn't as freaked out as I might have been, since I'd noticed Claudine was very touchy-feely, too. Since I couldn't get telepathic vibes from fairies, this much contact was tolerable. With a regular human being, I'd be bombarded with thoughts, since touch increased my sensitivity to telepathic contact.

'Did Fintan have any other children or grandchildren?' I asked. It would be nice to have more family.

'We'll talk of that later,' Niall said, which sent up an immediate red flag. 'Now that you know me a little,' he said, 'please tell me what I can do for you.'

'Why should you do anything for me?' I said. We'd had the genie conversation. I wasn't going to revisit that.

'I can tell that your life has been hard. Now that I am allowed to see you, let me help you in some way.'

'You sent me Claudine. She's been a big help,' I repeated. Without the crutch of my sixth sense, I was having trouble understanding my great-grandfather's emotional and mental set. Was he grieving for his son? What had their relationship really been? Had Fintan thought he was doing us all a good deed in keeping his dad away from the Stackhouses all these years? Was Niall evil, or did he have bad intentions toward me? He could have done something awful to me from afar without going to the trouble of meeting me and paying for an expensive dinner.

'You wouldn't want to explain any more, huh?'

Niall shook his head, his hair brushing his shoulders like strands of gold and silver spun out to incredible fineness.

I had an idea. 'Can you find my boyfriend?' I asked hopefully.

'You have a man? Besides the vampire?'

'Eric is not my man, but since I've had his blood a few times, and he's had mine . . .'

'That's why I approached you through him. You have a tie to him.'

'Yes.'

'I have known Eric Northman for a long time. I thought you would come if he asked you to. Did I do wrong?'

I was startled at this appeal. 'No, sir,' I said. 'I don't think I'd have come if he hadn't told me it was okay. He wouldn't have brought me if he hadn't trusted you. . . . At least, I don't think so.'

'Do you want me to kill him? End the tie?'

'No!' I said, getting kind of excited in a bad way. 'No!'

A few people actually glanced at us for the first time, hearing my agitation despite my great-grandfather's *don't-look* influence.

'The other boyfriend,' Niall said, and took another bite of his salmon. 'Who is he and when did he vanish?'

'Quinn the weretiger,' I said. 'He's been gone since the explosion in Rhodes. He was hurt, but I saw him afterward.'

'I heard about the Pyramid,' Niall said. 'You were there?'

I told him about it, and my newly discovered great-grandfather listened with a refreshing lack of judgment. He was neither horrified nor appalled, and he didn't feel sorry for me. I really liked that.

While I talked, I had a chance to regroup my emotions. 'You know what?' I said when there was a natural pause. 'Don't look for Quinn. He knows where I am, and he's got my number.' *In more ways than one,* I thought sourly. 'He'll show up when he feels like he can, I guess. Or not.'

'But that leaves me with nothing to do as a gift for you,' my great-grandfather said.

'Just give me a raincheck,' I said, smiling, and then had to explain the term to him. 'Something'll come up. Am I . . . Can I talk about you? To my friends?' I asked. 'No, I guess not.' I couldn't imagine telling my friend Tara that I had a new great-grandfather who was a fairy. Amelia might be more understanding.

'I want to keep our relationship a secret,' he said. 'I am so glad to know you finally, and I want to know you better.' He laid his hand against my cheek. 'But I have powerful enemies, and I wouldn't want them to think of harming you to get at me.'

I nodded. I understood. But it was kind of deflating to have a brand-new relative and be forbidden to talk about him. Niall's hand left my cheek to drift down to my own hand.

'What about Jason?' I asked. 'Are you gonna talk to him, too?'

Jason,' he said, his face showing distaste. 'Somehow the essential spark passed Jason by. I know he is made of the same material as you, but in him the blood has only shown itself in his ability to attract lovers, which after all is not much recommendation. He wouldn't understand or appreciate our connection.'

Great-grandfather sounded pretty snotty when he said that. I started to say something in Jason's defense, but then I closed my mouth. I had to admit to my most secret self that Niall was almost certainly right. Jason would be full of demands, and he would talk.

'How often are you going to be around?' I said instead, striving hard to sound nonchalant. I knew I was expressing myself clumsily, but I didn't know how else to establish some framework for this new and awkward relationship.

'I'll try to visit you like any other relative would,' he said.

I tried hard to picture that. Niall and I eating at the Hamburger Palace? Sharing a pew at church on a Sunday? I didn't think so.

'I feel like there's a lot you're not telling me,' I said bluntly.

'Then we'll have something to talk about next time,' he said, and one sea green eye winked at me. Okay, that was unexpected. He handed me a business card, another thing I didn't anticipate. It said simply, 'Niall Brigant', with a telephone number centered beneath. 'You can reach me at that number any time. Someone will answer.'

'Thanks,' I said. 'I guess you know my phone number?' He nodded. I'd thought he was ready to leave, but he lingered. He seemed as reluctant to part as I was. 'So,' I began, clearing my throat. 'What do you do all day?' I can't tell you how strange and neat it felt to be with a family member. I only had Jason, and he wasn't exactly a close brother, the kind you told everything to. I could count on him in a pinch, but hanging out together? Not going to happen.

My great-grandfather answered my question, but when I tried to recall it afterward, I couldn't come up with anything specific. I guess he did secret fairy-prince stuff He did tell me he had part ownership in a bank or two, a company that made lawn furniture, and – and this seemed odd to me – a company that created and tested experimental medicine.

I looked at him doubtfully. 'Medicine for humans,' I said, to be sure I understood.

'Yes. For the most part,' he responded. 'But a few of the chemists make special things for us.'

'For the fae.'

He nodded, fine corn-silk hair falling around his face as his head moved. 'There is so much iron now,' he said. 'I don't know if you realize that we are very sensitive to iron? And yet if we wear gloves every moment, we're too conspicuous in today's world.' I looked at his right hand as it lay over mine on the white tablecloth. I extracted my fingers, stroked his skin. It felt oddly smooth.

'It's like an invisible glove,' I said.

'Exactly.' He nodded. 'One of their formulas. But enough about me.'

Just when it was getting interesting, I thought. But I could see that my great-grandfather had no real reason to trust me with all his secrets yet.

Niall asked me about my job, and my boss, and my routine, like a real great-grandfather would. Though he clearly didn't like the idea of his great-granddaughter working, the bar part of it didn't seem to disturb him. As I've said, Niall wasn't easy to read. His thoughts were his own as far as I was concerned; but I did notice that every now and then he stopped himself from speaking.

Eventually, dinner got eaten, and I glanced at my watch, astounded at how many hours had passed. I needed to go. It was getting late. I excused myself, thanking my great- grandfather (it still made me shiver, thinking of him that way) for the meal and very hesitantly leaning forward to kiss his cheek as he'd kissed mine. He seemed to hold his breath while I did so, and his skin felt soft and lustrous as a silky plum under my lips. Even though he could look like a human, he didn't feel like one.

He stood when I left, but he remained at the table – to take care of the bill, I assumed. I went outside without registering anything my eyes saw along the way. Eric was waiting for me in the parking lot. He'd had some TrueBlood while he was waiting, and he'd been reading in the car, which was parked under a light.

I was exhausted.

I didn't realize how nerve-wracking my dinner with Niall had been until I was out of his presence. Though I'd been sitting in a comfortable chair the whole meal, I was as tired as if we'd been talking while we were running.

Niall had been able to mask the fairy odor from Eric in the restaurant, but I saw from the flare of Eric's nostrils that the intoxicating scent clung to me. Eric's eyes closed in ecstasy, and he actually licked his lips. I felt like a T-bone just out of reach of a hungry dog.

'Snap out of it,' I said. I wasn't in the mood.

With a huge effort, Eric reined himself in. 'When you smell like that,' he said, 'I just want to fuck you and bite you and rub myself all over you.'

That was pretty comprehensive, and I won't say I didn't have a second (split evenly between lust and fear) of picturing such activity. But I had larger issues to think about.

'Hold your horses,' I said. 'What do you know about fairies? Aside from how they taste?'

Eric looked at me with clearer eyes. 'They're lovely, male and female both. Incredibly tough and ferocious. They aren't immortal, but they live a very long time unless something happens to them. You can kill them with iron, for example. There are other ways to kill them, but it's hard work. They like to keep to themselves for the most part. They like moderate climates. I don't know what they eat or drink when they're by themselves. They sample the food of other cultures; I've even seen a fairy try blood. They have a higher opinion of themselves than they have any right to. When they give their word, they keep it.'

He thought for a moment. 'They have different magics. They can't all do the same things. And they are very magical. It's their essence. They have no gods but their own race, for they've often been mistaken for gods. In fact, some of them have taken on the attributes of a deity.'

I gaped at him. 'What do you mean?'

'Well, I don't mean they're *holy*,' Eric said. 'I mean that the fairies who inhabit the woods identify with the woods so strongly that to hurt one is to hurt the other. So they've suffered a great drop in numbers. Obviously, we vampires are not going to be up on fairy politics and survival issues, since we are so dangerous to them … simply because we find them intoxicating.'

I'd never thought to ask Claudine about any of this. For one thing, she didn't seem to enjoy talking about being a fairy, and when she popped up, it was usually when I was in trouble and therefore sadly self-absorbed. For another thing, I'd imagined there were maybe a small handful of fairies left in the world, but Eric was telling me there once were as many fairies as there were vampires, though the fairy race was on the wane.

In sharp contrast, vampires – at least in America – were definitely on the increase. There were three bills wending their way through Congress dealing with vampire immigration. America had the distinction (along with Canada, Japan, Norway, Sweden, England, and Mexico) of being a country that had responded to the Great Revelation with relative calm.

The night of the carefully orchestrated Great Revelation, vampires all over the world had appeared on television, radio, in person, whatever the best means of communication in the area might be, to tell the human population, 'Hey! We actually exist. But we're not life threatening! The new Japanese synthetic blood satisfies our nutritional requirements.'

The four years since then had been one big learning curve.

Tonight I'd added a huge amount to my store of supernatural lore.

'So the vampires have the upper hand,' I said.

'We're not at war,' Eric said. 'We haven't been at war for centuries.'

'So in the past the vampires and the fairies have fought each other? I mean, like, pitched battles?'

'Yes,' Eric said. 'And if it came to that again, the first one I'd take out is Niall.'

'Why?'

'He's very powerful in the fairy world. He is very magical. If he's sincere in his desire to take you under his wing, you're both very lucky and very unlucky.' Eric started the car and we pulled out of the parking lot. I hadn't seen Niall come out of the restaurant. Maybe he'd just poofed out of the dining room. I hoped he'd paid our bill first.

'I guess I have to ask you to explain that,' I said. But I had a feeling I didn't really want to know the answer.

'There were thousands of fairies in the United States once,' Eric said. 'Now there are only hundreds. But the ones that are left are very determined survivors. And not all of those are friends of the prince's.'

'Oh, good. I needed another supernatural group who dislikes me,' I muttered.

We drove through the night in silence, wending our way back to the interstate that would carry us east to Bon Temps. Eric seemed heavily thoughtful. I also had plenty of food for thought; more than I'd eaten at supper, that was for sure.

I found that on the whole, I felt cautiously happy. It was good to have a kind of belated great-grandfather. Niall seemed genuinely anxious to establish a relationship with me. I still had a heap of questions to ask, but they could wait until we knew each other better.

Eric's Corvette could go pretty damn fast, and Eric wasn't exactly sticking to the speed limit on the interstate. I wasn't awfully surprised when I saw the blinking lights coming up behind us. I was only astonished the cop car could catch up with Eric.

'A-hum,' I said, and Eric cursed in a language that probably hadn't been spoken out loud in centuries. But even the sheriff of Area Five has to obey human laws these days, or at least he has to pretend to. Eric pulled over to the shoulder.

'With a vanity plate like BLDSKR, what do you expect?' I asked, not so secretly enjoying the moment. I saw the dark shape of the trooper emerging from the car behind us, walking up with something in his hand – clipboard, flashlight?

I looked harder. I reached out. A snarled mass of aggression and fear met my inner ear.

'Were! There's something wrong,' I said, and Eric's big hand shoved me down into the floorboard, which would have provided a little more concealment if the car had been anything other than a Corvette.

Then the patrolman came up to the window and tried to shoot me.

Chapter 5

Eric had turned to fill the window and block the rest of the car from the shooter's aim, and he got it in the neck. For an awful moment, Eric slumped back in the seat, his face blank and dark blood flowing sluggishly down his white skin. I screamed as if noise would protect me, and the gun pointed at me as the gunman leaned into the car to aim past Eric.

But he'd been a fool to do that. Eric's hand clamped on the man's wrist, and Eric began squeezing. The 'patrolman' started doing a little shrieking of his own, flailing uselessly at Eric with his empty hand. The gun fell on top of me. I'm just lucky it didn't discharge when it fell. I don't know much about handguns, but this one was big and lethal-looking, and I scrambled to an upright position and aimed it at the shooter.

He froze in place, half in and half out of the window. Eric had already broken his arm and had kept a tight grip. The fool should have been more afraid of the vampire who had a hold on him than the waitress who hardly knew how to fire the gun, but the gun commanded his attention.

I was sure I would have heard if the highway patrol had decided to start shooting speeders instead of ticketing them.

'Who are you?' I said, and no one could blame me if my voice wasn't too steady. 'Who sent you?'

'They told me to,' the Were gasped. Now that I had time to notice details, I could see he wasn't wearing a proper highway patrol uniform. It was the right color, and the hat was right, but the pants weren't uniform pants.

'They, who?' I asked.

Eric's fangs clamped into the Were's shoulder. Despite his wound, Eric was pulling the faux patrolman, into the car inch by inch. It seemed only fair that Eric got some blood since he'd lost so much of his own. The assassin began crying.

'Don't let him turn me into one of them,' he appealed to me.

'You should be so lucky,' I said, not because I actually thought it was so darn great to be a vampire but because I was sure Eric had something much worse in mind.

I got out of the car because there was no point in trying to get Eric to release the Were. He wouldn't listen to me with the bloodlust on him so strong. My bond to Eric was the crucial factor in this decision. I was happy that he was enjoying himself, getting the blood he needed. I was furious that someone had tried to hurt him. Since both of these feelings would not normally be colors in my emotional palette, I knew what was to blame.

Plus, the inside of the Corvette had gotten unpleasantly crowded, what with me, Eric, and most of the Were.

Miraculously, no cars passed while I trotted along the shoulder to our attacker's vehicle, which (not so much to my surprise) turned out to be a plain white car with an illegal flashing attachment. I turned out the car's lights and, by punching or disconnecting every wire and button I could find, managed to kill the flashers, too. Now we were not nearly so conspicuous. Eric had shut down the Corvette's lights moments into the encounter.

I looked over the inside of the white car quickly but didn't see an envelope marked 'Revelation of who hired me, in case I get caught'. I needed a clue. There should at least have been a phone number on a scrap of paper, a phone number I could look up in a reverse directory. If I knew how to do such a thing. Rats. I trudged back to Eric's car, noticing in the lights of a passing semi that there weren't any legs sticking out of the driver's window anymore, which rendered the Corvette a lot less conspicuous. But we needed to get out of there.

I peered into the Corvette and found it empty. The only reminder of what had just happened was a smear of blood on Eric's seat, and I pulled a tissue out of my purse, spat on it, and rubbed the drying blood off; not a very elegant solution, but practical.

Suddenly, Eric was beside me, and I had to stifle a shriek. He was still excited by the unexpected attack, and he pinned me against the side of the car, holding my head at the correct angle for a kiss. I felt a lurch of desire and came very close to saying, 'What the hell, take me now, you big Viking.' It was not only the blood bond inclining me to accept his tacit offer, but my memory of how wonderful Eric was in bed. But I thought of Quinn and detached myself from Eric's mouth with a great effort.

For a second, I didn't think he was going to let go, but he did. 'Let me see,' I said in an unsteady voice, and pulled his shirt collar aside to look at the bullet wound. Eric had almost finished healing, but of course his shirt was still wet with blood.

'What was that about?' he asked. 'Was that an enemy of yours?'

'I have no idea.'

'He shot at you,' Eric said, as if I was just a wee bit slow. 'He wanted you first.'

'But what if he did that to hurt you? What if he would have blamed my death on you?' I was so tired of being the object of plots that I suspected I was trying to *will* Eric into being the target. Another idea struck me, and I veered into it. 'And how'd they find us?'

'Someone who knew we'd be driving back to Bon Temps tonight,' Eric said. 'Someone who knew what car I was in.'

'It couldn't have been Niall,' I said, and then rethought my flash of loyalty to my brand-new, self-proclaimed great- grandfather. After all, he might have been lying the whole time we were at the table. How would I know? I couldn't get in his head. The ignorance of my position felt strange to me.

But I didn't believe Niall had been lying.

'I don't think it was the fairy, either,' Eric said. 'But we'd better talk about it on the road. This isn't a good place for us to linger.'

He was right about that. I didn't know where he'd put the body, and I realized that I didn't really care. A year ago it would have torn me up, leaving a body behind as we sped away along the interstate. Now I was just glad it was him and not me who was lying in the woods.

I was a terrible Christian and a decent survivalist.

As we drove through the dark, I pondered the chasm yawning right in front of me, waiting for me to take that extra step. I felt stranded on that brink. I found it harder and harder to stick to what was right, when what was expedient made better sense. Really, my brain told me ruthlessly, didn't I understand that Quinn had dumped me? Wouldn't he have gotten in touch if he still considered us a couple? Hadn't I always had a soft spot for Eric, who made love like a train thundering into a tunnel? Didn't I have beaucoup evidence that Eric could defend me better than anyone I knew?

I could hardly summon the energy to be shocked at myself.

If you find yourself considering who to take for a lover because of his ability to defend you, you're getting pretty close to selecting a mate because you think he has desirable traits to pass along to future generations. And if there'd been a chance I could have had Eric's child (a thought that made me shiver), he would have been at the top of the list, a list I hadn't even known I'd been compiling. I pictured myself as a female peacock looking for the male peacock with the prettiest display of tail, or a wolf waiting for the leader (strongest, smartest, bravest) of the pack to mount her.

Okay, I'd yucked myself out. I was a human woman. I tried to be a good woman. I had to find Quinn because I had committed myself to him ... sort of.

No, no quibbling!

'What are you thinking about, Sookie?' Eric asked out of the darkness. 'Your face has had thoughts rippling across it too fast to follow.'

The fact that he could see me – not only in the dark, but while he was supposed to be watching the road – was exasperating and scary. And proof of his superiority, my inner cavewoman said.

'Eric, just get me home. I'm in emotional overload.'

He didn't speak again. Maybe he was being wise, or maybe the healing was painful.

'We need to talk about this again,' he said when he pulled into my driveway. He parked in front of the house, turned to me as much as he could in the little car. 'Sookie, I'm hurting. . . . Can I . . .' He leaned over, brushed his fingers over my neck.

At the very idea, my body betrayed me. A throbbing started down low, and that was just wrong. A person shouldn't get excited at the idea of being bitten. That's bad, right? I clenched my fists so tightly my fingernails made my palms hurt.

Now that I could see him better, now that the interior of the car was illuminated with the harsh glare of the security light, I realized that Eric was even paler than usual. As I watched, the bullet began exiting the wound, and he leaned back against his seat, his eyes shut. Millimeter by millimeter, the bullet was extruded until it dropped into my waiting hand. I remembered Eric getting me to suck out a bullet in his arm. Ha! What a fraud he'd been. The bullet would've come out on its own. My indignation made me feel more like myself.

'I think you can make it home,' I said, though I felt an almost irresistible urge to lean over to him and offer my neck or my wrist. I gritted my teeth and got out of the car. 'You can stop at Merlotte's and get bottled blood if you really need some.'

'You're hard-hearted,' Eric said, but he didn't sound truly angry or affronted.

'I am,' I said, and I smiled at him. 'You be careful, you hear?'

'Of course,' he said. 'And I'm not stopping for any policemen.'

I made myself march into the house without looking back. When I was inside the front door and had shut it firmly behind me, I felt an immediate relief. Thank goodness. I'd wondered if I was going to turn around at every step I took away from him. This blood tie thing was really irritating. If I wasn't careful and vigilant, I was going to do something I'd regret.

'I am woman, hear me roar,' I said.

'Gosh, what prompted that?' Amelia asked, and I jumped. She was coming down the hall from the kitchen in her nightgown and matching robe, peach with cream-colored lace trim. Everything of Amelia's was nice. She'd never sneer at anyone else's shopping habits, but she'd never wear anything from WalMart, either.

'I've had a trying evening,' I said. I looked down at myself. Only a little blood on the blue silk T-shirt. I'd have to soak it. 'How have things gone here?'

'Octavia called me,' Amelia said, and though she was trying to keep her voice steady, I could feel the anxiety coming off her in waves.

'Your mentor.' I wasn't at my brightest.

'Yep, the one and only.' She bent down to pick up Bob, who always seemed to be around if Amelia was upset. She held him to her chest and buried her face in his fur. 'She had heard, of course. Even after Katrina and all the changes it made in her life, she has to bring up *the mistake*.' (That was what Amelia called it – the mistake.)

'I wonder what Bob calls it,' I said.

Amelia looked over Bob's head at me, and I knew instantly I'd said a tactless thing. 'Sorry,' I said. 'I wasn't thinking. But maybe it's not too realistic to think you can get out of this without being called to account, huh?'

'You're right,' she said. She didn't seem too happy about my right-ness, but at least she said it. 'I did wrong. I attempted something I shouldn't have, and Bob paid the price.'

Wow, when Amelia decided to confess, she went whole hog.

'I'm going to have to take my licks,' she said. 'Maybe they'll take away my magic practice for a year. Maybe longer.'

'Oh. That seems harsh,' I said. In my fantasy, her mentor just scolded Amelia in front of a room full of magicians and sorcerers and witches or what-have-you, and then they transformed Bob back. He promptly forgave Amelia and told her he loved her. Since he forgave her, the rest of the assemblage did, too, and Amelia and Bob came back to my house and lived here together ... for a good long while. (I wasn't too specific about that part.)

'That's the mildest punishment possible,' Amelia said.

'Oh.'

'You don't want to know the other possible sentences.' She was right. I didn't. 'Well, what mysterious errand did Eric take you on?' Amelia asked.

Amelia couldn't have tipped off anyone to our destination or route; she hadn't known where we were going. 'Oh, ah, he just wanted to take me to a new restaurant in Shreveport. It had a French name. It was pretty nice.'

'So, this was like a date?' I could tell she was wondering what place Quinn played in my relationship with Eric.

'Oh, no, not a date,' I said, sounding unconvincing even to myself. 'No guy-girl action going on. Just, you know, hanging out.' Kissing. Getting shot.

'He sure is handsome,' Amelia said.

'Yeah, no doubt about it. I've met some toothsome guys. Remember Claude?' I'd shown Amelia the poster that had arrived in the mail two weeks before, a blowup of the romance novel cover for which Claude had posed. She'd been impressed – what woman wouldn't be?

'Ah, I went to watch Claude strip last week.' Amelia couldn't meet my eyes.

'And you didn't take me!' Claude was a very disagreeable person, especially when contrasted with his sister, Claudine, but he was beyond gorgeous. He was in the Brad Pitt stratosphere of male beauty. Of course, he was gay. Wouldn't you know it? 'You went while I was at work?'

'I thought you wouldn't approve of my going,' she said, ducking her head. 'I mean, since you're friends with his sister. I went with Tara. JB was working. Are you mad?'

'Nah. I don't care.' My friend Tara owned a dress shop, and her new husband, JB, worked at a women's exercise center. 'I would like to see Claude trying to act like he was enjoying himself.'

'I think he was having a good time,' she said. 'There's no one Claude loves better than Claude, right? So all these women looking at him and admiring him ... He's not into women, but he's sure into being admired.'

'True. Let's go see him together sometime.'

'Okay,' she said, and I could tell she was quite cheerful again. 'Now, tell me what you ordered at this new fancy restaurant.' So I told her. But all the while I was wishing I didn't have to keep silent about my great-grandfather. I wanted so badly to tell Amelia about Niall: how he looked, what he'd said, that I had a whole history I hadn't known. And it would take me a while to process what my grandmother had endured, to alter my picture of her in light of the facts I'd learned. And I had to rethink my unpleasant memories of my mother, too. She'd fallen for my dad like a ton of bricks, and she'd had his kids because she loved him . . . only to find that she didn't want to share him with them, especially with me, another female. At least, this was my new insight.

'There was more stuff,' I said, a yawn splitting my jaw in two. It was very late. 'But I've got to get to bed. I get any phone calls or anything?'

'That Were from Shreveport called. He wanted to talk to you, and I told him you were out for the evening and he should call you on your cell. He asked if he could meet up with you, but I said I didn't know where you were.'

'Alcide,' I said. 'I wonder what he wanted.' I figured I'd call him tomorrow.

'And some girl called. Said she'd been a waitress at Merlotte's before, and she'd seen you at the wedding last night.'

'Tanya?'

'Yeah, that was her name.'

'What did she want?'

'Don't know. She said she'd call back tomorrow or see you at the bar.'

'Crap. I hope Sam didn't hire her to fill in or something.'

'I thought I was the fill-in bargirl.'

'Yeah, unless someone's quit. I warn you, Sam likes her.'

'You don't?'

'She's a treacherous bitch.'

'Gosh, tell me what you really think.'

'No kidding, Amelia, she took a job at Merlotte's so she could spy on me for the Pelts.'

'Oh, *that's* the one. Well, she won't spy on you again. I'll take steps.'

That was a scarier thought than working with Tanya. Amelia was a strong and skillful witch, don't get me wrong, but she was also prone to attempt things beyond her experience level. Hence Bob.

'Check with me first, please,' I said, and Amelia looked surprised.

'Well, sure,' she said. 'Now, I'm off to bed.'

She made her way up the steps with Bob in her arms, and I went to my small bathroom to remove my makeup and put on my own nightgown. Amelia hadn't noticed the speckles of blood on the shirt, and I put it in the sink to soak.

What a day it had been. I'd spent time with Eric, who always rattled my chain, and I'd found a living relative, though not a human one. I'd learned a lot of stuff about my family, most of it unpleasant. I'd eaten in a fancy restaurant, though I could hardly recall the food. And finally, I'd been shot at.

When I crawled into bed, I said my prayers, trying to put Quinn at the top of the list. I thought the excitement of discovering a great-grandfather would keep me awake that night, but sleep claimed me right when I was in the middle of asking God to help me find my way through the moral morass of being party to a killing.

Chapter 6

There was a knock on the front door the next morning about an hour before I wanted to wake up. I heard it only because Bob had come into my room and jumped on my bed, where he wasn't supposed to be, settling into the space behind my knees while I lay on my side. He purred loudly, and I reached down to scratch behind his ears. I loved cats. That didn't stop me from liking dogs, too, and only the fact that I was gone so much kept me from getting a puppy. Terry Bellefleur had offered me one, but I'd wavered until his pups were gone. I wondered if Bob would mind a kitten companion. Would Amelia get jealous if I bought a female cat? I had to smile even as I snuggled deeper into the bed.

But I wasn't truly asleep, and I did hear the knock.

I muttered a few words about the person at the door, and I slid on my slippers and threw on my thin blue cotton bathrobe. The morning had a hint of chill, reminding me that despite the mild and sunny days, this was October. There were Halloweens when even a sweater was too warm, and there were Halloweens when you had to wear a light coat when you did your trick-or-treating.

I looked through the peephole and saw an elderly black woman with a halo of white hair. She was light-skinned and her features were narrow and sharp: nose, lips, eyes. She was wearing magenta lipstick and a yellow pantsuit. But she didn't seem armed or dangerous. This just goes to show how misleading first appearances can be. I opened the door.

'Young lady, I'm here to see Amelia Broadway,' the woman informed me in very precisely pronounced English.

'Please come in,' I said, because this was an older woman and I'd been brought up to revere old people. 'Have a seat.' I indicated the couch. 'I'll go up and get Amelia.'

I noticed she didn't apologize for getting me out of bed or for showing up unannounced. I climbed the stairs with a grim feeling that Amelia wasn't going to enjoy this message.

I so seldom went up to the second floor that it surprised me to see how nice Amelia had made it look. Since the upper bedrooms had only had basic furniture in them, she'd turned the one to the right, the larger one, into her bedroom. The one to the left was her sitting room. It held her television, an easy chair and ottoman, a small computer desk and her computer, and a plant or two. The bedroom, which I believed had been built for a generation of Stackhouses that had sired three boys in quick succession, had only a small closet, but Amelia had bought rolling clothes racks from somewhere on the Internet and assembled them handily. Then she'd bought a tri-fold screen at an auction and repainted it and arranged it in front of the racks to cam-ouflage them. Her bright bedspread and the old table she'd repainted to serve as her makeup table added to the color that jumped out from the white-painted walls. Amid all this cheer was one dismal witch.

Amelia was sitting up in bed, her short hair mashed into strange shapes. 'Who is that I hear downstairs?' she asked in a very hushed voice.

'Older black lady, light-skinned? Sharp way about her?'

'Omigod,' Amelia breathed, and slumped back against her dozen or so pillows. 'It's Octavia.'

'Well, you come down and have a word with her. I can't entertain her.'

Amelia snarled at me, but she accepted the inevitable. She got out of bed and pulled off her nightgown. She pulled on a bra and panties and some jeans, and she extracted a sweater from a drawer.

I went down to tell Octavia Fant that Amelia was coming. Amelia would have to walk right past her to get to the bathroom, since there was only the one staircase, but at least I could smooth the way.

'Can I get you some coffee?' I asked. The older woman was busy looking around the room with her bright brown eyes.

'If you have some tea, I'd like a cup,' Octavia Fant said.

'Yes, ma'am, we have some,' I said, relieved that Amelia had insisted on buying it. I had no idea what kind it was, and I hoped it was in a bag, because I'd never made hot tea in my life.

'Good,' she said, and that was that.

'Amelia's on her way down,' I said, trying to think of some graceful way to add, 'And she's going to have to hurry through the room to pee and brush her teeth, so pretend you don't see her.' I abandoned that lost cause and fled to the kitchen.

I retrieved Amelia's tea from one of her designated shelves, and while the water was getting hot, I got down two cups and saucers and put them on a tray. I added the sugar bowl and a tiny pitcher with milk and two spoons. *Napkins!* I thought, and wished I had some cloth ones instead of regular paper. (This was how Octavia Fant made me feel, without her using a bit of magic on me.) I heard the water running in the hall bathroom just as I put a handful of cookies on a plate and added that to the assemblage. I didn't have any flowers or a little vase, which was the only other thing I thought of that I could've added. I picked up the tray and made my way slowly down the hall to the living room.

I set the tray down on the coffee table in front of Ms Fant. She looked up at me with her piercing eyes and gave me a curt nod of thanks. I realized that I could not read her mind. I'd been holding off, waiting for a moment when I could really give her her proper due, but she knew how to block me out. I'd never met a human who could do that. For a second I felt almost irritated. Then I remembered who and what she was, and I scooted off to my room to make my bed and visit my own little bathroom. I passed Amelia in the hall, and she gave me a scared look.

Sorry, Amelia, I thought, as I closed my bedroom door firmly. *You're on your own.*

I didn't have to be at work until the evening, so I put on some old jeans and a Fangtasia T-shirt ('The Bar with a Bite'). Pam had given it to me when the bar first started selling them. I slid my feet into some

Crocs and went into the kitchen to fix my own beverage, coffee. I made some toast and got the local paper I'd grabbed when I'd answered the door. Rolling the rubber band off, I glanced at the front page. The school board had met, the local Wal-Mart had donated generously to the Boys and Girls Club's after-school program, and the state legislature had voted to recognize vampire-human marriages. Well, well. No one had thought that bill would ever pass.

I flipped open the paper to read the obituaries. First the local deaths – no one I knew, good. Then the area deaths – oh, *no*.

MARIA-STAR COOPER, read the heading. The item said only, 'Maria-Star Cooper, 25, a resident of Shreveport, died unexpectedly at her home yesterday. Cooper, a photographer, is survived by her mother and father, Matthew and Stella Cooper of Minden, and three brothers. Arrangements are pending.'

I felt suddenly out of breath and sank into the straight-back chair with a feeling of total disbelief. Maria-Star and I hadn't exactly been friends, but I'd liked her well enough, and she and Alcide Herveaux, a major figure in the Shreveport Were pack, had been going together for months. Poor Alcide! His first girlfriend had died violently, and now this.

The phone rang and I jumped. I grabbed it up with a terrible feeling of disaster. 'Hello?' I said cautiously, as if the phone could spit at me.

'Sookie,' said Alcide. He had a deep voice, and now it was husky with tears.

'I'm so sorry,' I said. 'I just read the paper.' There was nothing else to say. Now I knew why he'd called the night before.

'She was murdered,' Alcide said.

'Oh, my God.'

'Sookie, it was only the beginning. On the off chance that Furnan is after you, too, I want you to stay alert.'

'Too late,' I said after a moment given to absorbing this awful news. 'Someone tried to kill me last night.'

Alcide held the phone away from him and howled. Hearing this, in the middle of the day, over the telephone ... Even then, it was frightening.

Trouble within the Shreveport pack had been brewing for a while.

Even I, separated from Were politics, had known that. Patrick Furnan, the leader of the Long Tooth pack, had gotten his office by killing Alcide's father in combat. The victory had been legal – well, Were legal – but there had been a few not-so-legal plays along the way. Alcide – strong, young, prosperous, and packing a grudge – had always been a threat to Furnan, at least in Furnan's mind.

This was a tense topic, since Weres were secret from the human population, not out in the open like vampires. The day was coming, and coming soon, when the shifter population would step forward. I'd heard them speak of it over and over. But that hadn't happened yet, and it wouldn't be good if the first knowledge the humans had of the Weres was of bodies turning up all over the place.

'Someone will be over there right away,' Alcide said.

'Absolutely not. I have to go to work tonight, and I'm so utterly on the edge of this thing that I'm sure they won't try again. But I do need to know how the guy knew where and when to find me.'

'Tell Amanda the circumstances,' Alcide said, his voice thick with anger, and then Amanda came on. Hard to believe that when I'd seen her at the wedding we'd both been so cheerful.

'Tell me,' she said crisply, and I knew this was no time to argue. I told her the story as tersely as possible (leaving out Niall, and Eric's name, and most other details), and she was silent for a few seconds after I'd finished speaking.

'Since he was taken out, that's one less we have to worry about,' she said, sounding simply relieved. 'I wish you'd known who he was.'

'Sorry,' I said a bit acidly. 'I was thinking about the gun, not his ID. How come you-all can have a war with as few people as you have?' The Shreveport pack couldn't number over thirty.

'Reinforcements from other territories.'

'Why would anyone do that?' Why join in a war that wasn't yours? What was the point of losing your own people when it was the other pack's dispute?

'There are perks to backing the winning side,' Amanda said. 'Listen, you still got that witch living with you?'

'I do.'

'Then there's something you can do to help.'

'Okay,' I said, though I didn't recall offering. 'What would that be?'

'You need to ask your witch friend if she'll go to Maria-Star's apartment and get some kind of reading on what happened there. Is that possible? We want to know the Weres involved.'

'It's possible, but I don't know if she'll do it.'

'Ask her now, please.'

'Ah . . . let me call you back. She's got a visitor.'

Before I went out to the living room, I made a call. I didn't want to leave this message on the answering machine at Fangtasia, which wouldn't be open yet, so I called Pam's cell, something I'd never done before. As it rang, I found myself wondering if it was in the coffin with her. That was an eerie thing to picture. I didn't know if Pam actually slept in a coffin or not, but if she did . . . I shuddered. Of course, the phone went to voice mail, and I said, 'Pam, I've found out why Eric and I were pulled over last night, or at least I think so. There's a Were war brewing, and I think I was the target. Someone sold us out to Patrick Furnan. And I didn't tell anyone where I was going.' That was a problem Eric and I had been too shaken to discuss the night before. How had anyone, anyone at all, known where we'd be last night? That we'd be driving back from Shreveport.

Amelia and Octavia were in the middle of a discussion, but neither of them looked as angry or upset as I'd feared.

'I hate to intrude,' I said as both pairs of eyes turned to me. Octavia's eyes were brown, Amelia's bright blue, but at the moment they were eerily alike in expression.

'Yes?' Octavia was clearly queen of the situation.

Any witch worth her salt would know about Weres. I condensed the issues of the Were war down to a few sentences, told them about the attack the night before on the interstate, and explained Amanda's request.

'Is this something you should get involved with, Amelia?' Octavia asked, her voice making it quite clear there was only one answer she should give.

'Oh, I think so,' Amelia said. She smiled. 'Can't have someone shooting at my roomie. I'll help Amanda.'

Octavia couldn't have been more shocked if Amelia had spat a watermelon seed on her pants. 'Amelia! You're trying things beyond your ability! This will lead to terrible trouble! Look what you've already done to poor Bob Jessup.'

Oh, boy, I hadn't known Amelia that long, but I already knew that was a poor way to get her to comply with your wishes. If Amelia was proud of anything, it was her witchy ability. Challenging her expertise was a sure way to rattle her. On the other hand, Bob was a major fuckup.

'Can you change him back?' I asked the older witch.

Octavia looked at me sharply. 'Of course,' she said.

'Then why don't you do it, and we can go from there?' I said.

Octavia looked very startled, and I knew I shouldn't have gotten up in her face like that. On the other hand, if she wanted to show Amelia that her magic was more powerful, here was her chance. Bob the cat was sitting in Amelia's lap, looking unconcerned. Octavia reached in her pocket and pulled out a pill container filled with what looked like marijuana; but I guess any dried herb pretty much looks the same, and I haven't ever actually handled marijuana, so I'm no judge. Anyway, Octavia took a pinch of this dried green stuff and reached out to let the bits drop on the cat's fur. Bob didn't seem to mind.

Amelia's face was a picture as she watched Octavia casting a spell, which seemed to consist of some Latin, a few motions, and the afore-mentioned herb. Finally, Octavia uttered what must have been the esoteric equivalent of 'Allakazam!' and pointed at the cat.

Nothing happened.

Octavia repeated the phrase even more forcefully. Again with the finger pointing.

And again with the no results.

'You know what I think?' I said. No one seemed to want to know, but it was my house. 'I wonder if Bob was always a cat, and for some reason he was temporarily human. That's why you can't change him back. Maybe he's in his true form right now.'

'That's ridiculous,' the older witch snapped. She was some kind of put out at her failure. Amelia was trying hard to suppress a grin.

'If you're so sure after this that Amelia's incompetent, which I happen to know she isn't, you might want to consider coming to see

Maria-Star's apartment with us,' I said. 'Make sure Amelia doesn't get into any trouble.'

Amelia looked indignant for a second, but she seemed to see my plan, and she added her entreaty to mine.

'Very well. I'll come along,' Octavia said grandly.

I couldn't see into the old witch's mind, but I'd worked at a bar long enough to know a lonely person when I saw one.

I got the address from Amanda, who told me Dawson was guarding the place until we arrived. I knew him and liked him, since he'd helped me out before. He owned a local motorcycle repair shop a couple of miles out of Bon Temps, and he sometimes ran Merlotte's for Sam. Dawson didn't run with a pack, and the news that he was pitching in with Alcide's rebel faction was significant.

I can't say the drive to the outskirts of Shreveport was a bonding experience for the three of us, but I did fill Octavia in on the background of the pack troubles. And I explained my own involvement. 'When the contest for packmaster was taking place,' I said, 'Alcide wanted me there as a human lie detector. I actually did catch the other guy cheating, which was good. But after that, it became a fight to the death, and Patrick Furnan was stronger. He killed Jackson Herveaux.'

'I guess they covered up the death?' The old witch seemed neither shocked nor surprised.

'Yes, they put the body out at an isolated farm he owned, knowing no one would look there for a while. The wounds on the body weren't recognizable by the time he was found.'

'Has Patrick Furnan been a good leader?'

'I really don't know,' I admitted. 'Alcide has always seemed to have a discontented group around him, and they're the ones I know best in the pack, so I guess I'm on Alcide's side.'

'Did you ever consider that you could just step aside? Let the best Were win?'

'No,' I said honestly. 'I would have been just as glad if Alcide hadn't called me and told me about the pack troubles. But now that I know, I'll help him if I can. Not that I'm an angel or anything. But Patrick Furnan hates me, and it's only smart to help his enemy, point number one. And I liked Maria- Star, point number two. And someone tried to kill me last night, someone who may have been hired by Furnan, point number three.'

Octavia nodded. She was sure no wussy old lady.

Maria-Star had lived in a rather dated apartment building on Highway 3 between Benton and Shreveport. It was a small complex, just two buildings side by side facing a parking lot, right there on the highway. The buildings backed onto a field, and the adjacent businesses were day businesses: an insurance agency and a dentist's office.

Each of the two red brick buildings was divided into four apartments. I noticed a familiar battered pickup truck in front of the building on the right, and I parked by it. These apartments were enclosed; you went in the common entrance into a hall, and there was a door on either side of the stairway to the second floor. Maria-Star had lived on the ground-floor left apartment. This was easy to spot, because Dawson was propped against the wall beside her door.

I introduced him to the two witches as 'Dawson' because I didn't know his first name. Dawson was a supersized man. I'd bet you could crack pecans on his biceps. He had dark brown hair beginning to show just a little gray, and a neatly trimmed mustache. I'd known who he was all my life, but I'd never known him well. Dawson was probably seven or eight years older than me, and he'd married early. And divorced early, too. His son, who lived with the mother, was quite a football player for Clarice High School. Dawson looked tougher than any guy I'd ever met. I don't know if it was the very dark eyes, or the grim face, or simply the size of him.

There was crime scene tape across the apartment doorway. My eyes welled up when I saw it. Maria-Star had died violently in this space only hours before. Dawson produced a set of keys (Alcide's?) and unlocked the door, and we ducked under the tape to enter.

And we all stood frozen in silence, appalled at the state of the little living room. My way was blocked by an overturned occasional table with a big gash marring the wood. My eyes flickered over the irregular dark stains on the walls until my brain told me the stains were blood.

The smell was faint but unpleasant. I began to breathe shallowly so I wouldn't get sick.

'Now, what do you want us to do?' Octavia asked.

'I thought you'd do an ectoplasmic reconstruction, like Amelia did before,' I said.

'Amelia did an ectoplasmic reconstruction?' Octavia had dropped the haughty tone and sounded genuinely surprised and admiring. 'I've never seen one.'

Amelia nodded modestly. 'With Terry and Bob and Patsy,' she said. 'It worked great. We had a big area to cover.'

'Then I'm sure we can do one here,' Octavia said. She looked interested and excited. It was like her face had woken up. I realized that what I'd seen before had been her depressed face. And I was getting enough from her head (now that she wasn't concentrating on keeping me out) to let me know that Octavia had spent a month after Katrina wondering where her next meal would come from, where she'd lay her head from night to night. Now she lived with family, though I didn't get a clean picture.

'I brought the stuff with me,' Amelia said. Her brain was radiating pride and relief. She might yet get out from under the Bob contretemps without paying a huge price.

Dawson stood leaning against the wall, listening with apparent interest. Since he was a Were, it was hard to read his thoughts, but he was definitely relaxed.

I envied him. It wasn't possible for me to be at ease in this terrible little apartment, which almost echoed with the violence done in its walls. I was scared to sit on the love seat or the armchair, both upholstered in blue and white checks. The carpet was a darker blue, and the paint was white. Everything matched. The apartment was a little dull for my taste. But it had been neat and clean and carefully arranged, and less than twenty-four hours ago it had been a home.

I could see through to the bedroom, where the covers were thrown back. This was the only sign of disorder in the bedroom or the kitchen. The living room had been the center of the violence.

For lack of a better place to park myself, I went to lean against the bare wall beside Dawson.

I didn't think the motorcycle repairman and I had ever had a long conversation, though he'd gotten shot in my defense a few months before. I'd heard that *the law* (in this case, Andy Bellefleur and his fellow detective Alcee Beck) suspected more took place at Dawson's shop than motorcycle repairs, but they'd never caught Dawson doing anything illegal. Dawson also hired out as a bodyguard from time to time, or maybe he volunteered his services. He was certainly suited to the job.

'Were you friends?' Dawson rumbled, nodding his head at the bloodiest spot on the floor, the spot where Maria-Star had died.

'We were more like friendly acquaintances,' I said, not wanting to claim more grief than my due. 'I saw her at a wedding a couple of nights ago.' I started to say she'd been fine then, but that would have been stupid. You don't sicken before you're murdered.

'When was the last time anyone talked to Maria-Star?' Amelia asked Dawson. 'I need to establish some time limits.'

'Eleven last night,' he said. 'Phone call from Alcide. He was out of town, with witnesses. Neighbor heard a big to-do from in here about thirty minutes after that, called the police.' That was a long speech for Dawson. Amelia went back to her preparations, and Octavia read a thin book that Amelia had extracted from her little backpack.

'Have you ever watched one of these before?' Dawson said to me.

'Yeah, in New Orleans. I gather this is kind of rare and hard to do. Amelia's really good.'

'She's livin' with you?'

I nodded.

'That's what I heard,' he said. We were quiet for a moment. Dawson was proving to be a restful companion as well as a handy hunk of muscle.

There was some gesturing, and there was some chanting, with Octavia following her onetime student. Octavia might never have done an ectoplasmic reconstruction, but the longer the ritual went on the more power reverberated in the small room, until my fingernails seemed to hum with it. Dawson didn't exactly look frightened, but he was definitely on the alert as the pressure of the magic built. He uncrossed his arms and stood up straight, and I did, too.

Though I knew what to expect, it was still startling to me when Maria-Star appeared in the room with us. Beside me, I felt Dawson jerk with surprise. Maria-Star was painting her toenails. Her long dark hair was gathered into a ponytail on top of her head. She was sitting on the carpet in front of the television, a sheet of newspaper spread carefully under her foot. The magically re-created image had the same watery look I'd seen in a previous reconstruction, when I'd observed my cousin Hadley during her last few hours on earth. Maria-Star wasn't exactly in color. She was like an image filled with glistening gel. Because the apartment was no longer in the same order it had been when she'd sat in that spot, the effect was odd. She was sitting right in the middle of the overturned coffee table.

We didn't have long to wait. Maria-Star finished her toenails and sat watching the television set (now dark and dead) while she waited for them to dry. She did a few leg exercises while she waited. Then she gathered up the polish and the little spacers she'd had between her toes and folded the paper. She rose and went into the bathroom. Since the actual bathroom door was now half-closed, the watery Maria-Star had to walk through it. From our angle, Dawson and I couldn't see inside, but Amelia, whose hands were extended in a kind of sustaining gesture, gave a little shrug as if to say Maria-Star was not doing anything important. Ectoplasmic peeing, maybe.

In a few minutes, the young woman appeared again, this time in her nightgown. She went into the bedroom and turned back the bed. Suddenly, her head turned toward the door.

It was like watching a pantomime. Clearly Maria-Star had heard a sound at her door, and the sound was unexpected. I didn't know if she was hearing the doorbell, a knocking, or someone trying to pick the lock.

Her alert posture turned to alarm, even panic. She went back into the living room and picked up her cell phone – we saw it appear when she touched it – and punched a couple of numbers. Calling someone on speed dial. But before the phone could even have rung on the other end, the door exploded inward and a man was on her, a half wolf, half man. He showed up because he was a living thing, but he was clearer when he was close to Maria-Star, the focus of the spell. He pinned Maria-Star to the floor and bit her deeply on her shoulder. Her mouth opened wide, and you could tell she was screaming and she was fighting like a Were, but he'd caught her totally by surprise and her arms were pinned down. Gleaming lines indicated blood running down from the bite.

Dawson gripped my shoulder, a growl rising from his throat. I didn't know if he was furious at the attack on Maria- Star, excited by the action and the impression of flowing blood, or all of the above.

A second Were was right behind the first. He was in his human form. He had a knife in his right hand. He plunged it into Maria-Star's torso, withdrew it, reared back, and plunged it in again. As the knife rose and fell, it cast blood drops on the walls. We could see the blood drops, so there must be ectoplasm (or whatever it really is) in blood, too.

I hadn't known the first man. This guy, I recognized. He was Cal Myers, a henchman of Furnan's and a police detective on the Shreveport force.

The blitz attack had taken only seconds. The moment Maria-Star was clearly mortally wounded, they were out the door, closing it behind them. I was shocked by the sudden and dreadful cruelty of the murder, and I felt my breath coming faster. Maria-Star, glistening and almost clear, lay there before us for a moment in the middle of the wreckage, gleaming blood splotches on her shirt and on the floor around her, and then she just winked out of existence, because she had died in that moment.

We all stood in appalled silence. The witches were silent, their arms dropping down by their sides as if they were puppets whose strings had been cut. Octavia was crying, tears running down her creased cheeks. Amelia looked as though she were thinking of throwing up. I was shivering in reaction, and even Dawson looked nauseated.

'I didn't know the first guy since he'd only half changed,' Dawson said. 'The second one looked familiar. He's a cop, right? In Shreveport?'

'Cal Myers. Better call Alcide,' I said when I thought my voice would work. 'And Alcide needs to send these ladies something for their trouble, when he gets his own sorted out.' I figured Alcide might not think of that since he was mourning for Maria-Star, but the witches had done this work with no mention of recompense. They deserved to be rewarded for their effort. It had cost them dearly: both of them had folded onto the love seat.

'If you ladies can manage,' Dawson said, 'we better get our asses out of here. No telling when the police'll be back. The crime lab finished just five minutes before you got here.'

While the witches gathered their energy and all their paraphernalia, I talked to Dawson. 'You said Alcide's got a good alibi?'

Dawson nodded. 'He got a phone call from Maria-Star's neighbor. She called Alcide right after she called the police, when she heard all the ruckus. Granted, the call was to his cell phone, but he answered right away and she could hear the sounds of the hotel bar behind the conversation. Plus, he was in the bar with people he'd just met who swore he was there when he found out she'd been killed. They aren't likely to forget.'

'I guess the police are trying to find a motive.' That was what they did on the TV shows.

'She didn't have enemies,' Dawson said.

'Now what?' Amelia said. She and Octavia were on their feet, but they were clearly drained. Dawson shepherded us out of the apartment and relocked it.

'Thanks for coming, ladies,' Dawson told Amelia and Octavia. He turned to me. 'Sookie, could you come with me, explain to Alcide what we just saw? Can Amelia drive Miss Fant back?'

'Ah. Sure. If she's not too tired.'

Amelia said she thought she could manage. We'd come in my car, so I tossed her the keys. 'You okay driving?' I asked, just to reassure myself.

She nodded. 'I'll take it slow.'

I was scrambling into Dawson's truck when I realized that this step dragged me even further into the Were war. Then I figured, *Patrick Furnan already tried to kill me. Can't get any worse.*

Chapter 7

Dawson's pickup, a Dodge Ram, although battered on the outside, was orderly within. It wasn't a new vehicle by any means – probably ten years old – but it was very well-maintained both under the hood and in the cab.

'You're not a member of the pack, Dawson, right?'

'It's Tray. Tray Dawson.'

'Oh, I'm sorry.'

Dawson shrugged, as if to say *No big deal.* 'I never was a good pack animal,' he said. 'I couldn't keep in line. I couldn't follow the chain of command.'

'So why are you joining in this fight?' I said.

'Patrick Furnan tried to put me out of business,' Dawson said.

'Why'd he do that?'

'Aren't that many other motorcycle repair shops in the area, especially since Furnan bought the Harley-Davidson dealership in Shreveport,' Tray explained. 'That so-and-so's greedy. He wants it all for himself. He doesn't care who goes broke. When he realized I was sticking with my shop, he sent a couple of his guys down to see me. They beat me up, busted up the shop.'

'They must have been really good,' I said. It was hard to believe anyone could best Tray Dawson. 'Did you call the police?'

'No. The cops in Bon Temps aren't that crazy about me anyway. But I threw in with Alcide.'

Detective Cal Myers, obviously, was not above doing Furnan's dirty work. It was Myers who'd collaborated with Furnan in cheating in the packmaster contest. But I was truly shocked that he would go as far as murdering Maria-Star, whose only sin was being loved by Alcide. We'd seen it with our own eyes, though.

'What's the deal with you and the police in Bon Temps?' I asked, as long as we were talking about law enforcement.

He laughed. 'I used to be a cop; did you know that?'

'No,' I said, genuinely surprised. 'No kidding?'

'For real,' he said. 'I was on the force in New Orleans. But I didn't like the politics, and my captain was a real bastard, pardon me.'

I nodded gravely. It had been a long time since someone had apologized for using bad language within my hearing. 'So, something happened?'

'Yeah, eventually things came to a head. The captain accused me of taking some money this scuzzbag had left lying on a table when we arrested him in his home.' Tray shook his head in disgust. 'I had to quit then. I liked the job.'

'What did you like about it?'

'No two days were alike. Yeah, sure, we got in the cars and patrolled. That was the same. But every time we got out something different would happen.'

I nodded. I could understand that. Every day at the bar was a little different, too, though probably not as different as Tray's days had been in the patrol car.

We drove in silence for a while. I could tell Tray was thinking about the odds of Alcide overcoming Furnan in the struggle for dominance. He was thinking Alcide was a lucky guy to have dated Maria-Star and me, and all the luckier since that bitch Debbie Pelt had vanished. Good riddance, Tray thought.

'Now I get to ask you a question,' Tray said.

'Only fair.'

'You have something to do with Debbie disappearing?'

I took a deep breath. 'Yeah. Self-defense.'

'Good for you. Someone needed to do it.'

We were quiet again for at least ten minutes. Not to drag the past into the present too much, but Alcide had broken up with Debbie Pelt before I met him. Then he dated me a little. Debbie decided I was an enemy, and she tried to kill me. I got her first. I'd come to terms with it . . . as much as you ever do. However, it had been impossible for Alcide to ever look at me again in the same way, and who could blame him? He'd found Maria-Star, and that was a good thing.

Had been a good thing.

I felt tears well up in my eyes and looked out the window. We'd passed the racetrack and the turnoff to Pierre Bossier Mall, and we went a couple more exits before Tray turned the truck onto the off ramp.

We meandered through a modest neighborhood for a while, Tray checking his rearview mirror so often that even I realized he was watching for anyone following us. Tray suddenly turned into a driveway and pulled around to the back of one of the slightly larger homes, which was demurely clad in white siding. We parked under a porte cochere in the back, along with another pickup. There was a small Nissan parked off to the side. There were a couple of motorcycles, too, and Tray gave them a glance of professional interest.

'Whose place?' I was a little hesitant about asking yet another question, but after all, I did want to know where I was.

'Amanda's,' he said. He waited for me to precede him, and I went up the three steps leading up to the back door and rang the bell.

'Who's there?' asked a muffled voice.

'Sookie and Dawson,' I said.

The door opened cautiously, the entrance blocked by Amanda so we couldn't see past her. I don't know much about handguns, but she had a big revolver in her hand pointed steadily at my chest. This was the second time in two days I'd had a gun pointed at me. Suddenly, I felt very cold and a little dizzy.

'Okay,' Amanda said after looking us over sharply.

Alcide was standing behind the door, a shotgun at the ready. He'd stepped out into view as we came in, and when his own senses had checked us out, he stood down. He put the shotgun on the kitchen counter and sat at the kitchen table.

'I'm sorry about Maria-Star, Alcide,' I said, forcing the words through stiff lips. Having guns aimed at you is just plain terrifying, especially at close range.

'I haven't gotten it yet,' he said, his voice flat and even. I decided he was saying that the impact of her death hadn't hit him. 'We were thinking about moving in together. It would have saved her life.'

There wasn't any point in wallowing in what-might-have-been. That was only another way to torture yourself. What had actually happened was bad enough.

'We know who did it,' Dawson said, and a shiver ran through the room. There were more Weres in the house – I could sense them now – and they had all become alert at Tray Dawson's words.

'What? How?' Without my seeing the movement, Alcide was on his feet.

'She got her witch friends to do a reconstruction,' Tray said, nodding in my direction. 'I watched. It was two guys. One I'd never seen, so Furnan's brought in some wolves from outside. The second was Cal Myers.'

Alcide's big hands were clenched in fists. He didn't seem to know where to start speaking, he had so many reactions. 'Furnan's hired help,' Alcide said, finally picking a jumping-in point. 'So we're within our rights to kill on sight. We'll snatch one of the bastards and make him talk. We can't bring a hostage here; someone would notice. Tray, where?'

'Hair of the Dog,' he answered.

Amanda wasn't too crazy about that idea. She owned that bar, and using it as an execution or torture site didn't appeal to her. She opened her mouth to protest. Alcide faced her and snarled, his face twisting into something that wasn't quite Alcide. She cowered and nodded her assent.

Alcide raised his voice even more for his next pronouncement. 'Cal Myers is Kill on Sight.'

'But he's a pack member, and members get trials,' Amanda said, and then cowered, correctly anticipating Alcide's wordless roar of rage.

'You haven't asked me about the man who tried to kill me,' I said. I wanted to defuse the situation, if that was possible.

As furious as he was, Alcide was still too decent to remind me that

I'd lived and Maria-Star hadn't, or that he'd loved Maria-Star much more than he'd ever cared about me. Both thoughts crossed his mind, though.

'He was a Were,' I said. 'About five foot ten, in his twenties. He was clean-shaven. He had brown hair and blue eyes and a big birthmark on his neck.'

'Oh,' said Amanda. 'That sounds like what's-his-name, the brand-new mechanic at Furnan's shop. Hired last week. Lucky Owens. Ha! Who were you with?'

'I was with Eric Northman,' I said.

There was a long, not entirely friendly silence. Weres and vampires are natural rivals, if not out-and-out enemies.

'So, the guy's dead?' Tray asked practically, and I nodded.

'How'd he approach you?' Alcide asked in a voice that was more rational.

'That's an interesting question,' I said. 'I was on the interstate driving home from Shreveport with Eric. We'd been to a restaurant here.'

'So who would know where you were and who you were with?' Amanda said while Alcide frowned down at the floor, deep in thought.

'Or that you'd have to return home along the interstate last night.' Tray was really rising in my opinion; he was right in there with the practical and pertinent ideas.

'I only told my roommate I was going out to dinner, not where,' I said. 'We met someone there, but we can leave him out. Eric knew, because he was acting as chauffeur. But I know Eric and the other man didn't tip anyone off.'

'How can you be so sure?' Tray asked.

'Eric got shot protecting me,' I said. 'And the person he took me to meet was a relative.'

Amanda and Tray didn't realize how small my family was, so they didn't get how momentous that statement was. But Alcide, who knew more about me, glared. 'You're making this up,' he said.

'No, I'm not.' I stared back. I knew this was a terrible day for Alcide, but I didn't have to explain my life to him. But I had a sudden thought. 'You know, the waiter – he was a Were.' That would explain a lot.

'What's the name of the restaurant?'

'Les Deux Poissons.' My accent wasn't good, but the Weres nodded.

'Kendall works there,' Alcide said. 'Kendall Kent. Long reddish hair?' I nodded, and he looked sad. 'I thought Kendall would come around to our side. We had a beer together a couple of times.'

'That's Jack Kent's oldest. All he would have had to do was place a phone call,' Amanda said. 'Maybe he didn't know . . .'

'Not an excuse,' Tray said. His deep voice reverberated in the little kitchen. 'Kendall has to know who Sookie is, from the packmaster contest. She's a friend of the pack. Instead of telling Alcide she was in our territory and should be protected, he called Furnan and told him where Sookie was, maybe let him know when she started home. Made it easy for Lucky to lie in wait.'

I wanted to protest that there was no certainty that it had happened like that, but when I thought about it, it had to have been exactly that way or in some manner very close to it. Just to be sure I was remembering correctly, I called Amelia and asked her if she'd told any callers where I was the night before.

'No,' she said. 'I heard from Octavia, who didn't know you. I got a call from that werepanther boy I met at your brother's wedding. Believe me, you didn't come up in that conversation. Alcide called, real upset. Tanya. I told her nothing.'

'Thanks, roomie,' I said. 'You recovering?'

'Yeah, I'm feeling better, and Octavia left to go back to the family she's been staying with in Monroe.'

'Okay, see you when I get back.'

'You going to make it back in time for work?'

'Yeah, I *have* to make it to work.' Since I'd spent that week in Rhodes, I have to be careful to stick to the schedule for a while, otherwise the other waitresses would get up in my face about Sam giving me all the breaks. I hung up. 'She told no one,' I said.

'So you – and Eric – had a leisurely dinner at an expensive restaurant, with another man.'

I looked at him incredulously. This was so far off the point. I concentrated. I'd never poked a mental probe into such turmoil. Alcide was feeling grief for Maria-Star, guilt because he hadn't protected her, anger that I'd been drawn into the conflict, and above all, eagerness to

knock some skulls. As the cherry on top of all that, Alcide – irration-
ally – hated that I'd been out with Eric.

I tried to keep my mouth shut out of respect for his loss; I was no
stranger to mixed emotions myself. But I found I'd become abruptly
and completely tired of him. 'Okay,' I said. 'Fight your own battles.
I came when you asked me to. I helped you when you asked me to,
both at the battle for packleader and today, at expense and emotional
grief to myself. Screw you, Alcide. Maybe Furnan is the better Were.'
I spun on my heel and caught the look Tray Dawson was giving Alcide
while I marched out of the kitchen, down the steps, and into the
carport. If there'd been a can, I would've kicked it.

'I'll take you home,' Tray said, appearing at my side, and I marched
over to the side of the truck, grateful that he was giving me the
wherewithal to leave. When I'd stormed out, I hadn't been thinking
about what would happen next. It's the ruin of a good exit when you
have to go back and look in the phone book for a cab company.

I'd believed Alcide truly loathed me after the Debbie debacle. Apparently the loathing was not total.

'Kind of ironic, isn't it?' I said after a silent spell. 'I almost got shot
last night because Patrick Furnan thought that would upset Alcide.
Until ten minutes ago, I would have sworn that wasn't true.'

Tray looked like he would rather be cutting up onions than dealing
with this conversation. After another pause, he said, 'Alcide's acting
like a butthead, but he's got a lot on his plate.'

'I understand that,' I said, and shut my mouth before I said one
more word.

As it turned out, I *was* on time to go to work that night. I was so
upset while I was changing clothes that I almost split my black pants,
I yanked them on so hard. I brushed my hair with such unnecessary
vigor that it crackled.

'Men are incomprehensible assholes,' I said to Amelia.

'No shit,' she said. 'When I was searching for Bob today, I found a
female cat in the woods with kittens. And guess what? They were all
black-and-white.'

I really had no idea what to say.

'So to hell with the promise I made him, right? I'm going to have fun. He can go have sex; I can have sex. And if he vomits on my bedspread again, I'll get after him with the broom.'

I was trying not to look directly at Amelia. 'I don't blame you,' I said, trying to keep my voice steady. It was nice to be on the verge of laughter instead of wanting to smack someone. I grabbed up my purse, checked my ponytail in the mirror in the hall bathroom, and exited out the back door to drive to Merlotte's.

I felt tired before I even walked through the employees' door, not a good way to start my shift.

I didn't see Sam when I stowed my purse in the deep desk drawer we all used. When I came out of the hall that accessed the two public bathrooms, Sam's office, the storeroom, and the kitchen (though the kitchen door was kept locked from the inside, most of the time), I found Sam behind the bar. I gave him a wave as I tied on the white apron I'd pulled from the stack of dozens. I slid my order pad and a pencil into a pocket, looked around to find Arlene, whom I'd be replacing, and scanned the tables in our section.

My heart sank. No peaceful evening for me. Some asses in Fellowship of the Sun T-shirts were sitting at one of the tables. The Fellowship was a radical organization that believed (a) vampires were sinful by nature, almost demons, and (b) they should be executed. The Fellowship 'preachers' wouldn't say so publicly, but the Fellowship advocated the total eradication of the undead. I'd heard there was even a little primer to advise members of how that could be carried out. After the Rhodes bombing they'd become bolder in their hatred.

The FotS group was growing as Americans struggled to come to terms with something they couldn't understand – and as hundreds of vampires streamed into the country that had given them the most favorable reception of all the nations on earth. Since a few heavily Catholic and Muslim countries had adopted a policy of killing vampires on sight, the U.S. had begun accepting vampires as refugees from religious or political persecution, and the backlash against this policy was violent. I'd recently seen a bumper sticker that read, 'I'll say vamps are alive when you pry my cold dead fingers from my ripped-out throat.'

I regarded the FotS as intolerant and ignorant, and I despised those who belonged to its ranks. But I was used to keeping my mouth shut on the topic at the bar, the same way I was used to avoiding discussions on abortion or gun control or gays in the military.

Of course, the FotS guys were probably Arlene's buddies. My weak-minded ex-friend had fallen hook, line, and sinker for the pseudo religion that the FotS propagated.

Arlene curtly briefed me on the tables as she headed out the back door, her face set hard against me. As I watched her go, I wondered how her kids were. I used to babysit them a lot. They probably hated me now, if they listened to their mother.

I shook off my melancholy, because Sam didn't pay me to be moody. I made the rounds of the customers, refreshed drinks, made sure everyone had enough food, brought a clean fork for a woman who'd dropped hers, supplied extra napkins to the table where Catfish Hennessy was eating chicken strips, and exchanged cheerful words with the guys seated at the bar. I treated the FotS table just like I treated everyone else, and they didn't seem to be paying me any special attention, which was just fine with me. I had every expectation that they'd leave with no trouble . . . until Pam walked in.

Pam is white as a sheet of paper and looks just like Alice in Wonderland would look if she'd grown up to become a vampire. In fact, this evening Pam even had a blue band restraining her straight fair hair, and she was wearing a dress instead of her usual pants set. She was lovely – even if she looked like a vampire cast in an episode of *Leave It to Beaver*. Her dress had little puff sleeves with white trim, and her collar had white trim, too. The tiny buttons down the front of her bodice were white, to match the polka dots on the skirt. No hose, I noticed, but any hose she bought would look bizarre since the rest of her skin was so pale.

'Hey, Pam,' I said as she made a beeline for me.

'Sookie,' she said warmly, and gave me a kiss as light as a snowflake. Her lips felt cool on my cheek.

'What's up?' I asked. Pam usually worked at Fangtasia in the evening.

'I have a date,' she said. 'Do you think I look good?' She spun around.

'Oh, sure,' I said. 'You always look good, Pam.' That was only the truth. Though Pam's clothing choices were often ultraconservative and strangely dated, that didn't mean they didn't become her. She had a kind of sweet-but-lethal charm. 'Who's the lucky guy?'

She looked as arch as a vampire over two hundred years old can look. 'Who says it's a guy?' she said.

'Oh, right.' I glanced around. 'Who's the lucky person?'

Just then my roomie walked in. Amelia was wearing a beautiful pair of black linen pants and heels with an off-white sweater and a pair of amber and tortoiseshell earrings. She looked conservative, too, but in a more modern way. Amelia strode over to us, smiled at Pam, and said, 'Had a drink yet?'

Pam smiled in a way I'd never seen her smile before. It was . . . coy. 'No, waiting for you.'

They sat at the bar and Sam served them. Soon they were chatting away, and when their drinks were gone, they got up to leave.

When they passed me on their way out, Amelia said, 'I'll see you when I see you' – her way of telling me she might not be home tonight.

'Okay, you two have fun,' I said. Their departure was followed by more than one pair of male eyes. If corneas steamed up like glasses do, all the guys in the bar would be seeing blurry.

I made the round of my tables again, fetching new beers for one, leaving the bill at another, until I reached the table with the two guys wearing the FotS shirts. They were still watching the door as though they expected Pam to jump back inside and scream, 'BOO!'

'Did I just see what I thought I saw?' one of the men asked me. He was in his thirties, clean-shaven, brown-haired, just another guy. The other man was someone I would have eyed with caution if we'd been in an elevator alone. He was thin, had a beard fringe along his jaw, was decorated with a few tattoos that looked like home jobs to me – jail tats – and he was carrying a knife strapped to his ankle, a thing that hadn't been too hard for me to spot once I'd heard in his mind that he was armed.

'What do you think you just saw?' I asked sweetly. Brown Hair thought I was a bit simple. But that was a good camouflage, and it meant that Arlene hadn't sunk to telling all and sundry about my little peculiarities. No one in Bon Temps (if you asked them outside of church on Sunday) would have said telepathy was possible. If you'd asked them outside of Merlotte's on a Saturday night, they might have said there was something to it.

'I think I saw a vamp come in here, just like she had a right. And I think I saw a woman acting happy to walk out with her. I swear to God, I cannot believe it.' He looked at me as if I was sure to share his outrage. Jail Tat nodded vigorously.

'I'm sorry – you see two women walking out of a bar together, and that bothers you? I don't understand your problem with that.' Of course I did, but you have to play it out sometimes.

'Sookie!' Sam was calling me.

'Can I get you gentlemen anything else?' I asked, since Sam was undoubtedly trying to call me back to my senses.

They were both looking at me oddly now, having correctly deduced that I was not exactly down with their program.

'I guess we're ready to leave,' said Jail Tat, clearly hoping I'd be made to suffer for driving paying customers away. 'You got our check ready?' I'd *had* their check ready, and I laid it down on the table in between them. They each glanced at it, slapped a ten on top, and shoved their chairs back.

'I'll be back with your change in just a second,' I said, and turned.

'No change,' said Brown Hair, though his tone was surly and he didn't seem genuinely thrilled with my service.

'Jerks,' I muttered as I went to the cash register at the bar.

Sam said, 'Sookie, you have to suck it up.'

I was so surprised that I stared at Sam. We were both behind the bar, and Sam was mixing a vodka collins. Sam continued quietly, keeping his eyes on his hands, 'You have to serve them like they were anybody else.'

It wasn't too often that Sam treated me like an employee rather than a trusted associate. It hurt; the more so when I realized he was right. Though I'd been polite on the surface, I would have (and should have) swallowed their last remarks with no comment – if it hadn't been for the FotS T-shirts. Merlotte's wasn't my business. It was Sam's. If customers didn't come back, he'd suffer the consequences. Eventually, if he had to let barmaids go, I would, too.

'I'm sorry,' I said, though it wasn't easy to manage saying it. I smiled brightly at Sam and went off to do an unnecessary round of my tables, one that probably crossed the line from attentive and into irritating. But if I went into the employees' bathroom or the public ladies' room, I'd end up crying, because it hurt to be admonished and it hurt to be wrong; but most of all, it hurt to be put in my place.

When we closed that night, I left as quickly and quietly as possible. I knew I was going to have to get over being hurt, but I preferred to do my healing in my own home. I didn't want to have any 'little talks' with Sam – or anyone else, for that matter. Holly was looking at me with way too much curiosity.

So I scooted out to the parking lot with my purse, my apron still on. Tray was leaning against my car. I jumped before I could stop myself.

'You running scared?' he asked.

'No, I'm running upset,' I said. 'What are you doing here?'

'I'm going to follow you home,' he said. 'Amelia there?'

'No, she's out on a date.'

'Then I'm definitely checking out the house,' the big man said, and climbed into his truck to follow me out to Hummingbird Road.

There wasn't any reason to object that I could see. In fact, it made me feel good to have someone with me, someone I pretty much trusted.

My house was just as I'd left it, or rather, as Amelia had left it. The outside security lights had come on automatically, and she'd left the light over the sink on in the kitchen as well as the back porch light. Keys in hand, I crossed to the kitchen door.

Tray's big hand gripped my arm when I started to twist the door-knob.

'There's no one there,' I said, having checked in my own way. 'And it's warded by Amelia.'

'You stay here while I look around,' he said gently. I nodded and let him in. After a few seconds' silence, he opened the door to tell me I could come into the kitchen. I was ready to follow him through the house for the rest of his search, but he said, 'I'd sure like a glass of Coke, if you got any.'

He'd deflected me perfectly from following him by appealing to my hospitality. My grandmother would have hit me with a fly swatter if I hadn't gotten Tray a Coke right then.

By the time he arrived back in the kitchen and pronounced the house clear of intruders, the icy Coke was sitting in a glass on the table, and there was a meatloaf sandwich sitting by it. With a folded napkin.

Without a word, Tray sat down and put the napkin in his lap and ate the sandwich and drank the Coke. I sat opposite him with my own drink.

'I hear your man has vanished,' Tray said when he'd patted his lips with the napkin.

I nodded.

'What do you think happened to him?'

I explained the circumstances. 'So I haven't heard a word from him,' I concluded. This story was sounding almost automatic, like I ought to tape it.

'That's bad' was all he said. Somehow it made me feel better, this quiet, undramatic discussion of a very touchy subject. After a minute of thoughtful silence, Tray said, 'I hope you find him soon.'

'Thanks. I'm real anxious to know how he's doing.' That was a huge understatement.

'Well, I'd better be getting on,' he said. 'If you get nervous in the night, you call me. I can be here in ten minutes. It's no good, you being alone out here with the war starting.'

I had a mental image of tanks coming down my driveway.

'How bad do you think it could get?' I asked.

'My dad told me in the last war, which was when his daddy was little, the pack in Shreveport got into it with the pack in Monroe. The Shreveport pack was about forty then, counting the halfies.' Halfies was the common term for Weres who'd become wolves by being bitten. They could only turn into a kind of wolf-man, never achieving the perfect wolf form that born Weres thought was vastly superior. 'But the Monroe pack had a bunch of college kids in it, so it come up to forty, forty- five, too. At the end of the fighting, both packs were halved.'

I thought of the Weres I knew. 'I hope it stops now,' I said.

'It ain't gonna,' Tray said practically. 'They've tasted blood, and killing Alcide's girl instead of trying for Alcide was a cowardly way to open the fight. Them trying to get you, too; that only made it worse. You don't have a drop of Were blood. You're a friend of the pack. That should make you untouchable, not a target. And this afternoon, Alcide found Christine Larrabee dead.'

I was shocked all over again. Christine Larrabee was – had been – the widow of one of the previous packleaders. She had a high standing in the Were community, and she'd rather reluctantly endorsed Jackson Herveaux for packleader. Now she had gotten a delayed payback.

'He's not going after any men?' I finally managed to speak.

Tray's face was dark with contempt. 'Naw,' the Were said. 'The only way I can read it is, Furnan wants to set Alcide's temper off. He wants everyone to be on a hair trigger, while Furnan himself stays cool and collected. He's about got what he wants, too. Between grief and the personal insult, Alcide is aimed to go off like a shotgun. He needs to be more like a sniper rifle.'

'Isn't Furnan's strategy real . . . unusual?'

'Yes,' Tray said heavily. 'I don't know what's gotten into him. Apparently, he don't want to face Alcide in personal combat. He don't want to just beat Alcide. He's aiming to kill Alcide and all Alcide's people, as far as I can tell. A few of the Weres, the ones with little kids, they already repledged themselves to him. They're too scared of what he'd do to their kids, after the attacks against women.' The Were stood. 'Thanks for the food. I've got to go feed my dogs. You lock up good after me, you hear? And where's your cell phone?'

I handed it to him, and with surprisingly neat movements for such large hands, Tray programmed his cell phone number into my directory. Then he left with a casual wave of his hand. He had a small neat house by his repair shop, and I was really relieved to find he'd timed the journey from there to here at only ten minutes. I locked the door behind him, and I checked the kitchen windows. Sure enough, Amelia had left one open at some point during the mild afternoon. After that discovery, I felt compelled to check every window in the house, even the ones upstairs.

After that was done and I felt as secure as I was going to feel, I turned on the television and sat in front of it, not really seeing what was happening on the screen. I had a lot to think about.

Months ago, I'd gone to the packmaster contest at Alcide's request to watch for trickery. It was my bad luck that my presence had been noticed and my discovery of Furnan's treachery had been public. It griped me that I'd been drawn into this fight, which was none of my own. In fact, bottom line: knowing Alcide had brought me nothing but grief.

I was almost relieved to feel a head of anger building at this injustice, but my better self urged me to squash it in the bud. It wasn't Alcide's fault that Debbie Pelt had been such a murderous bitch, and it wasn't Alcide's fault that Patrick Furnan had decided to cheat in the contest. Likewise, Alcide wasn't responsible for Furnan's bloodthirsty and uncharacteristic approach to consolidating his pack. I wondered if this behavior was even remotely wolflike.

I figured it was just Patrick Furnan – like.

The telephone rang, and I jumped about a mile. 'Hello?' I said, unhappy at how frightened I sounded.

'The Were Herveaux called me,' Eric said. 'He confirms that he's at war with his packmaster.'

'Yeah,' I said. 'You needed confirmation from Alcide? My message wasn't enough?'

'I'd thought of an alternative to the theory that you were attacked in a strike against Alcide. I'm sure Niall must have mentioned that he has enemies.'

'Uh-huh.'

'I wondered if one of those enemies had acted very swiftly. If the Weres have spies, so may the fairies.'

I pondered that. 'So, in wanting to meet me, he almost caused my death.'

'But he had the wisdom to ask me to escort you to and from Shreveport.'

'So he saved my life, even though he risked it.'

Silence.

'Actually,' I said, leaping to firmer emotional ground, 'you saved my life, and I'm grateful.' I half expected Eric to ask me just how grateful I was, to refer to the kissing . . . but still he didn't speak.

Just as I was about to blurt out something stupid to break the silence, the vampire said, 'I'll only interfere in the Were war to defend our interests. Or to defend you.'

My turn for a silent spell. 'All right,' I said weakly.

'If you see trouble coming, if they try to draw you in further, call me immediately,' Eric told me. 'I believe the assassin truly was sent by the packmaster. Certainly he was a Were.'

'Some of Alcide's people recognized the description. The guy, Lucky somebody, had just been taken on by Furnan as a mechanic.'

'Strange that he'd entrust such an errand to someone he hardly knew.'

'Since the guy turned out to be so unlucky.'

Eric actually snorted. Then he said, 'I won't talk to Niall of this any further. Of course, I told him what occurred.'

I had a moment's ridiculous pang because Niall hadn't rushed to my side or called to ask if I was okay. I'd only met him once, and now I was sad he wasn't acting like my nursemaid.

'All right, Eric, thanks,' I said, and hung up as he was saying good-bye. I should have asked him about my money again, but I was too dispirited; besides, it wasn't Eric's problem.

I was jumpy the whole time I was getting ready for bed, but nothing happened to make me more anxious. I reminded myself about fifty times that Amelia had warded the house. The wards would work whether she was in the house or not.

I had some good locks on the doors.

I was tired.

Finally, I slept, but I woke up more than once, listening for an assassin.

Chapter 8

I got up with heavy eyes the next day. I felt groggy and my head hurt. I had what amounted to an emotional hangover. Something had to change. I couldn't spend another night like this. I wondered if I should call Alcide and see if he'd, ah, gone to the mattresses with his soldiers. Maybe they'd let me have a corner? But the very idea of having to do that to feel safe made me angry.

I couldn't stop the thought from going through my head – *If Quinn were here, I could stay in my own home without fear.* And for a moment, I wasn't just worried about my missing wounded boyfriend, I was mad at him.

I was ready to be mad at *someone*. There was too much loose emotion hanging around.

Well, this was the beginning of a very special day, huh?

No Amelia. I had to assume she'd spent the night with Pam. I didn't have any problem with their having a relationship. I simply wanted Amelia to be around because I was lonely and scared. Her absence left a little blank spot in my landscape.

At least the air was cooler this morning. You could feel clearly that fall was on the way, was already in the ground waiting to leap up and claim the leaves and grass and flowers. I put on a sweater over my nightgown and went out on the front porch to drink my first cup of coffee. I listened to the birds for a while; they weren't as noisy as they were in the spring, but their songs and discussions let me know that nothing unusual was in the woods this morning. I finished my coffee and tried to plan out my day, but I kept running up against a mental roadblock. It was hard to make plans when you suspected someone might try to kill you. If I could tear myself away from the issue of my possibly impending death, I needed to vacuum the downstairs, do a load of my laundry, and go to the library. If I survived those chores, I had to go to work.

I wondered where Quinn was.

I wondered when I'd hear from my new great-grandfather again.

I wondered if any more Weres had died during the night.

I wondered when my phone would ring.

Since nothing happened on my front porch, I dragged myself inside and did my usual morning get-ready routine. When I looked at the mirror, I was sorry I'd troubled. I didn't look rested and refreshed. I looked like a worried person who hadn't gotten any sleep. I dabbed some concealer beneath my eyes and put on a little extra eye shadow and blush to give my face some color. Then I decided I looked like a clown and rubbed most of it off. After feeding Bob and scolding him for the litter of kittens, I checked all my locks again and hopped in the car to go to the library.

The Renard Parish library, Bon Temps branch, is not a large building. Our librarian graduated from Louisiana Tech in Ruston, and she is a super lady in her late thirties named Barbara Beck. Her husband, Alcee, is a detective on the Bon Temps force, and I really hope Barbara doesn't know what he's up to. Alcee Beck is a tough man who does good things . . . sometimes. He also does quite a few bad things. Alcee was lucky when he got Barbara to marry him, and he knows it.

Barbara's the only full-time employee of the branch library, and I wasn't surprised to find her by herself when I pushed open the heavy door. She was shelving books. Barbara dressed in what I thought of as comfortable chic, meaning she picked out knits in bright colors and wore matching shoes. She favored chunky, bold jewelry, too.

'Good morning, Sookie,' she said, smiling her big smile.

'Barbara,' I said, trying to smile back. She noticed I wasn't my usual self, but she kept her thoughts to herself. Not really, of course, since I have my little disability, but she didn't say anything out loud. I put

the books I was returning on the appropriate desk, and I began looking
at the shelves of new arrivals. Most of them were some permutation
on self-help. Going by how popular these books were and how often
they were checked out, everyone in Bon Temps should have become
perfect by now.

I grabbed up two new romances and a couple of mysteries, and
even a science fiction, which I rarely read. (I guess I thought my reality
was crazier than anything a science fiction writer could dream up.)
While I was looking at the jacket of a book by an author I'd never read,
I heard a thunk in the background and knew someone had come in
the back door of the library. I didn't pay attention; some people
habitually used the back door.

Barbara made a little noise, and I looked up. The man behind her
was huge, at least six foot six, and whip thin. He had a big knife, and
he was holding it to Barbara's throat. For a second I thought he was a
robber, and I wondered who would ever think of robbing a library. For
the overdue-book money?

'Don't scream,' he hissed through long sharp teeth. I froze. Barbara
was in some space beyond fear. She was way into terror. But I could
hear another active brain in the building.

Someone else was coming in the back door very quietly.

'Detective Beck will kill you for hurting his wife,' I said very loudly.
And I said it with absolute certainty. 'Kiss your ass good-bye.'

'I don't know who that is and I don't care,' the tall man said.

'You better care, muthafucker,' said Alcee Beck, who'd stepped up
behind him silently. He put his gun to the man's head. 'Now, you let
go of my wife and you drop that knife.'

But Sharp Teeth wasn't about to do that. He spun, pushed Barbara
at Alcee, and ran right toward me, knife raised.

I threw a Nora Roberts hardback at him, whacking him upside his
head. I extended my foot. Blinded by the impact of the book, Sharp
Teeth tripped over the foot, just as I'd hoped. He fell on his own knife,
which I *hadn't* planned.

The library fell abruptly silent except for Barbara's gasping breath.
Alcee Beck and I stared down at the creeping pool of blood coming
out from under the man.

'Ah-oh,' I said.

'Welllllll . . . shit,' said Alcee Beck. 'Where'd you learn to throw like that, Sookie Stackhouse?'

'Softball,' I said, which was the literal truth.

As you can imagine, I was late to work that afternoon. I was even more tired than I had been to start with, but I was thinking that I might live through the day. So far, two times in a row, fate had intervened to prevent my assassination. I had to assume that Sharp Teeth had been sent to kill me and had botched it, just as the fake highway patrolman had done. Maybe my luck wouldn't hold a third time; but there was a chance it would. What were the odds that another vampire would take a bullet for me, or that, by sheer accident, Alcee Beck would drop off his wife's lunch that she'd left at home on the kitchen counter? Slim, right? But I'd beaten those odds twice.

No matter what the police were officially assuming (since I didn't know the guy and no one could say I did – and he'd seized Barbara, not me), Alcee Beck now had me in his sights. He was really good at reading situations, and he had seen that Sharp Teeth was focused on me. Barbara had been a means to get my attention. Alcee would never forgive me for that, even if it hadn't been my fault. Plus, I'd thrown that book with suspicious force and accuracy.

In his place, I would probably feel the same way.

So now I was at Merlotte's, going through the motions in a weary way, wondering where to go and what to do and why Patrick Furnan had gone nuts. And where had all these strangers come from? I hadn't known the Were who'd broken down Maria-Star's door. Eric had been shot by a guy who'd worked at Patrick Furnan's dealership only a few days. I'd never seen Sharp Teeth before, and he was an unforgettable kind of guy.

The whole situation made no sense at all.

Suddenly I had an idea. I asked Sam if I could make a phone call since my tables were quiet, and he nodded. He'd been giving me those narrow looks all evening, looks that meant he was going to pin me down and talk to me soon, but for now I had a breather. So I went into

Sam's office, looked in his Shreveport phone book to get the listing for
Patrick Furnan's home, and I called him.

'Hello?'

I recognized the voice.

'Patrick Furnan?' I said, just to be sure.

'Speaking.'

'Why are you trying to kill me?'

'What? Who is this?'

'Oh, come on. It's Sookie Stackhouse. Why are you doing this?'

There was a long pause.

'Are you trying to trap me?' he asked.

'How? You think I got the phone tapped? I want to know why.
I never did anything to you. I'm not even dating Alcide. But you're
trying to off me like I am powerful. You killed poor Maria-Star. You
killed Christine Larrabee. What's with this? I'm not important.'

Patrick Furnan said slowly, 'You really believe it's me doing this?
Killing female pack members? Trying to kill you?'

'Sure I do.'

'It's not me. I read about Maria-Star. Christine Larrabee is dead?'
He sounded almost frightened.

'Yes,' I said, and my voice was as uncertain as his. 'And someone's
tried to kill me twice. I'm afraid some totally innocent person is
going to get caught in the cross fire. And of course, I don't want to
die.'

Furnan said, 'My wife disappeared yesterday.' His voice was ragged
with grief and fear. And anger. 'Alcide's got her, and that fucker is going
to pay.'

'Alcide wouldn't do that,' I said. (Well, I was pretty sure Alcide
wouldn't do that.) 'You're saying you *didn't* order the hits on Maria-
Star and Christine? And me?'

'No, why would I go for the women? We never want to kill pure-
blooded female Weres. Except maybe Amanda,' Furnan added tact-
lessly. 'If we're going to kill someone, it'd be the men.'

'I think you and Alcide need to have a sit-down. He doesn't have
your wife. He thinks you've gone crazy, attacking women.'

There was a long silence. Furnan said, 'I think you're right about that sit-down, unless you made up this whole thing to get me into a position where Alcide can kill me.'

'I just want to live to see the next week myself.'

'I'll agree to meet with Alcide if you'll be there and if you'll swear to tell each of us what the other is thinking. You're a friend of the pack, *all* the pack. You can help us now.'

Patrick Furnan was so anxious to find his wife he was even willing to believe in me.

I thought of the deaths that had already taken place. I thought of the deaths that were to come, perhaps including my own. I wondered what the hell was going on. 'I'll do it if you and Alcide will sit down unarmed,' I said. 'If what I suspect is true, you have a common enemy who's trying to get you two to kill each other off.'

'If that black-haired bastard will agree to it, I'll give it a shot,' said Furnan. 'If Alcide has my wife, not a hair on her body better be disturbed, and he better bring her with him. Or I swear to God I'll dismember him.'

'I understand. I'll make sure he understands, too. We'll be getting back with you,' I promised, and I hoped with all my heart that I was telling the truth.

Chapter 9

It was the middle of the same night and I was about to walk into danger. It was my own damn fault. Through a swift series of phone calls, Alcide and Furnan had worked out where to meet. I'd envisioned them sitting down across a table, their lieutenants right behind them, and working this whole situation out. Mrs Furnan would appear and the couple would reunite. Everyone would be content, or at least less hostile. I would be nowhere around.

Yet here I was at an abandoned office center in Shreveport, the same one where the contest for packmaster had taken place. At least Sam was with me. It was dark and cool and the wind was lifting my hair from my shoulders. I shifted from foot to foot, anxious to get this over with. Though he was not as fidgety as I was, I could tell Sam felt the same way.

It was my fault he was here. When he'd become so curious about what was brewing with the Weres, I'd had to tell him. After all, if someone came through the door of Merlotte's trying to shoot me down, Sam at least deserved to know why his bar was full of holes. I'd argued bitterly with him when he'd told me he was coming with me, but here we both were.

Maybe I'm lying to myself. Maybe I simply wanted a friend with me, someone definitely on my side. Maybe I was just scared. Actually, no 'maybe' about that at all.

The night was brisk, and we were both wearing waterproof jackets with hoods. Not that we needed the hoods, but if it got any colder, we might be grateful for them. The abandoned office park stretched around us in gloomy silence. We stood in the loading bay of a firm that had accepted big shipments of something. The large metal pull-down doors where the trucks had been unloaded looked like big shiny eyes in the gleam of the remaining security lights.

Actually, there were lots of big shiny eyes around tonight. The Sharks and the Jets were negotiating. Oh, excuse me, the Furnan Weres and the Herveaux Weres. The two sides of the pack might come to an understanding, and they might not. And right smack dab in the middle stood Sam the Shapeshifter and Sookie the Telepath.

As I felt the hard red throbbing of Were brains approaching from both north and south, I turned to Sam and said from the bottom of my heart, 'I should never have let you come with me. I should never have opened my mouth.'

'You've gotten into the habit of not telling me things, Sookie. I want you to tell me what's going on with you. Especially if there's danger.' Sam's red gold hair blew around his head in the sharp little breeze wafting between the buildings. I felt his difference more strongly than I ever had. Sam is a rare true shapeshifter. He can change into anything. He prefers the form of a dog, because dogs are familiar and friendly and people don't shoot at them too often. I looked into his blue eyes and saw the wildness in them. 'They're here,' he said, raising his nose to the breeze.

Then the two groups were standing about ten feet away on either side of us, and it was time to concentrate.

I recognized the faces of a few of the Furnan wolves, who were more numerous. Cal Myers, the police detective, was among them. It took some kind of nerve for Furnan to bring Cal along when he was proclaiming his innocence. I also recognized the teenage girl Furnan had taken as part of his victory celebration after Jackson Herveaux's defeat. She looked a million years older tonight.

Alcide's group included auburn-haired Amanda, who nodded at me, her face serious, and some werewolves I'd seen at the Hair of the Dog the night Quinn and I had visited the bar. The scrawny girl who'd worn the red leather bustier that night was standing right behind

Alcide, and she was both intensely excited and deeply scared. To my surprise, Dawson was there. He wasn't as much of a lone wolf as he'd painted himself to be.

Alcide and Furnan stepped away from their packs.

This was the agreed-on format for the parley, or sit-down, or whatever you wanted to call it: I would stand between Furnan and Alcide. Each Were leader would grip one of my hands. I would be the human lie detector while they talked. I had sworn to tell each one if the other lied, at least to the best of my ability. I could read minds, but minds can be deceptive and tricky or just dense. I'd never done anything exactly like this, and I prayed my ability would be extra precise tonight and that I would use it wisely, so I could help to end this life taking.

Alcide approached me stiffly, his face harsh in the hard glare of the security lighting. For the first time, I noticed that he looked thinner and older. There was a little gray in the black hair that hadn't been there when his father had been alive. Patrick Furnan, too, didn't look well. He'd always had a tendency to porkiness, and now he looked as though he'd gained a good fifteen or twenty pounds. Being packmaster hadn't been good to him. And the shock of the abduction of his wife had laid its mark on his face.

I did something that I never imagined I would do. I held out my right hand to him. He took it, and the flood of his ideas washed through me instantly. Even his twisty Were brain was easy to read because he was so focused. I held out my left hand to Alcide, and he grasped it too tightly. For a long minute, I felt inundated. Then, with a huge effort, I channeled them into a stream so I wouldn't be overwhelmed. It would be easy for them to lie out loud, but it's not so easy to lie inside your own head. Not consistently. I closed my eyes. A flip of the coin had given Alcide the first question.

'Patrick, why did you kill my woman?' The words sounded like they were cutting up Alcide's throat. 'She was pure Were, and she was as gentle as a Were can be.'

'I never ordered any of my people to kill any of yours,' Patrick Furnan said. He sounded so tired he could hardly stand up, and his thoughts were proceeding in much the same way: slowly, wearily, on a track he'd worn in his own brain. He was easier to read than Alcide. He meant what he said.

Alcide was listening with great attention, and he said next, 'Did you tell anyone not in your pack to kill Maria-Star and Sookie and Mrs Larrabee?'

'I never gave orders to kill any of you, ever,' Furnan said.

'He believes that,' I said.

Unfortunately, Furnan wouldn't shut up. 'I hate you,' he said, sounding just as tired as he had before. 'I would be glad if a truck hit you. But I didn't kill anyone.'

'He believes that, too,' I said, maybe a little dryly.

Alcide demanded, 'How can you claim to be innocent with Cal Myers standing with your pack? He stabbed Maria-Star to death.'

Furnan looked confused. 'Cal wasn't there,' he said.

'He believes what he says,' I told Alcide. I turned my face to Furnan. 'Cal was there, and he murdered Maria-Star.' Though I dared not lose focus, I heard the whispering start all around Cal Myers, saw the rest of the Furnan Weres step away from him.

It was Furnan's turn to ask a question.

'My wife,' he said, and his voice cracked. 'Why her?'

'I didn't take Libby,' Alcide said. 'I would never abduct a woman, especially a Were woman with young. I would never order anyone else to do it.'

He believed that. 'Alcide didn't do it himself, and he didn't order it done.' But Alcide hated Patrick Furnan with a great ferocity. Furnan hadn't needed to kill Jackson Herveaux at the climax of the contest, but he had. Better to start his leadership with the elimination of his rival. Jackson would never have submitted to his rule, and would have been a thorn in his side for years. I was getting thoughts from both sides, wafts of ideas so strong it burned in my head, and I said, 'Calm down, both of you.' I could feel Sam behind me, his warmth, the touch of his mind, and I said, 'Sam, don't touch me, okay?'

He understood, and he moved away.

'Neither of you killed any of the people who have died. And neither of you ordered it done. As far as I can tell.'

Alcide said, 'Give us Cal Myers to question.'

'Then where is my wife?' Furnan growled.

'Dead and gone,' said a clear voice. 'And I'm ready to take her place. Cal is mine.'

We all looked up, because the voice had come from the flat roof of the building. There were four Weres up there, and the brunette female who'd spoken was closest to the edge. She had a sense of the dramatic, I'll give her that. Female Weres have power and status but they're not packleader ... ever. This woman was clearly large and in charge, though she was maybe five foot two. She had prepared to change; that is to say, she was naked. Or maybe she just wanted Alcide and Furnan to see what they could be getting. Which was a lot, both in quantity and in quality.

'Priscilla,' said Furnan.

It seemed like such an unlikely name for the Were that I felt myself actually smile, which was a bad idea under the circumstances.

'You know her,' Alcide said to Furnan. 'Is this part of your plan?'

'No,' I answered for him. My mind careened through the thoughts I could read and latched on to one thread in particular. 'Furnan, Cal is her creature,' I said. 'He's betrayed you.'

'I thought if I picked off a few key bitches, you two would kill each other off,' Priscilla said. 'Too bad it didn't work.'

'Who is this?' Alcide asked Furnan again.

'She's the mate of Arthur Hebert, a packleader from St. Catherine Parish.' St. Catherine was way south, just east of New Orleans. It had been hit hard by Katrina.

'Arthur is dead. We don't have a home anymore,' Priscilla Hebert said. 'We want yours.'

Well, that was clear enough.

'Cal, why have you done this?' Furnan asked his lieutenant. Cal should have gotten up on the roof while he was able. The Furnan wolves and the Herveaux wolves had formed a circle around him.

'Cal's my brother,' Priscilla called. 'You better not touch a hair on his body.' There was an edge of desperation to her voice that hadn't been there before. Cal looked up at his sister unhappily. He realized what a fix he was in, and I was pretty sure he wanted her to shut up. That would be his last thought.

Furnan's arm was suddenly out of its sleeve and covered with hair. With huge force, he swung at his former cohort, eviscerating the Were. Alcide's clawed hand took off the back of Cal's head as the traitor fell to the ground. Cal's blood sprayed over me in an arc. At my back, Sam was humming with the energy of his oncoming change, triggered by the tension, the smell of blood, and my involuntary yelp.

Priscilla Hebert roared in rage and anguish. With inhuman grace, she leaped from the top of the building to the parking lot, followed by her henchmen (henchwolves?).

The war had begun.

Sam and I had worked ourselves into the middle of the Shreveport wolves. As Priscilla's pack began closing in from each side, Sam said, 'I'm going to change, Sookie.'

I couldn't see what use a collie would be in this situation, but I said, 'Okay, boss.' He grinned at me in a lopsided way, stripped off his clothes, and bent over. All around us the Weres were doing the same. The chill night air was full of the gloppy sound, the sound of hard things moving through thick, sticky liquid, that characterizes the transformation from man to animal. Huge wolves straightened and shook themselves all around me; I recognized the wolf forms of Alcide and Furnan. I tried counting the wolves in our suddenly reunited pack, but they were milling around, positioning themselves for the coming battle, and there was no way to keep track of them.

I turned to Sam to give him a pat and found myself standing beside a lion.

'Sam,' I said in a whisper, and he roared.

Everyone froze in place for a long moment. The Shreveport wolves were just as scared as the St. Catherine's wolves at first, but then they seemed to realize that Sam was on their side, and yips of excitement echoed between the empty buildings.

Then the fighting started.

Sam tried to surround me, which was impossible, but it was a gallant attempt. As an unarmed human, I was basically helpless in this struggle. It was a very unpleasant feeling – in fact, a terrifying feeling.

I was the frailest thing on site.

Sam was magnificent. His huge paws flashed, and when he hit a wolf square on, that wolf went *down*. I danced around like a demented elf, trying to stay out the way. I couldn't watch everything that was going on. Clusters of St. Catherine wolves made for Furnan, Alcide, and Sam, while individual battles went on around us. I realized that these clusters had been charged with taking down the leaders, and I knew that a lot of planning had gone into this. Priscilla Hebert hadn't allowed for getting her brother out quickly enough, but that wasn't slowing her down any.

No one seemed to be too concerned with me, since I posed no threat. But there was every chance I'd get knocked down by the snarling combatants and be hurt as severely as I would if I had been the target. Priscilla, now a gray wolf, targeted Sam. I guess she wanted to prove she had more balls than anyone by going for the biggest and most dangerous target. But Amanda was biting at Priscilla's hind legs as Priscilla worked her way through the melee. Priscilla responded by turning her head to bare her teeth at the smaller wolf. Amanda danced away, and then when Priscilla turned to resume her progress, Amanda darted back to bite the leg again. Since Amanda's bite was powerful enough to break bone, this was more than an annoyance, and Priscilla rounded on her in full display. Before I could even think *Oh no*, Priscilla seized Amanda in her iron jaws and broke her neck.

While I stood staring in horror, Priscilla dropped Amanda's body on the ground and wheeled to leap onto Sam's back. He shook and shook but she had sunk her fangs into his neck and she would not be dislodged.

Something in me snapped as surely as the bones in Amanda's neck. I lost any sense I might have had, and I launched myself in the air as if I were a wolf, too. To keep from sliding off the heaving mass of animals, I wound my arms in the fur around Priscilla's neck, and I wound my legs around Priscilla's middle, and I tightened my arms until I was just about hugging myself. Priscilla didn't want to let go of Sam, so she flung herself from side to side to knock me loose. But I was clinging to her like a homicidal monkey.

Finally, she had to let go of his neck to deal with me. I squeezed and squeezed harder, and she tried to bite me, but she couldn't reach around properly since I was on her back. She was able to curve enough to graze my leg with her fangs, but she couldn't hold on. The pain hardly registered. I tightened my grip even more though my arms were aching like hell. If I let go one little bit, I would join Amanda.

Though all of this took place so quickly it was hard to believe, I felt as if I'd been trying to kill this woman/wolf for eternity. I wasn't really thinking, 'Die, die,' in my head; I just wanted her to *stop what she was doing*, and she wouldn't, dammit. Then there was another ear-shattering roar, and huge teeth flashed an inch away from my arms. I understood I should let go, and the second my arms loosened, I tumbled off the wolf, rolling over the pavement to land in a heap a few feet away.

There was a sort of *pop!* and Claudine was standing over me. She was in a tank top and pajama bottoms and she had a case of bedhead. From between her striped legs I saw the lion bite the wolf's head nearly off, then spit her out in a fastidious way. Then he turned to survey the parking lot, evaluating the next threat.

One of the wolves leaped at Claudine. She proved she was completely awake. While the animal was in midair her hands clamped on its ears. She swung him, using his own momentum. Claudine flung the huge wolf with the ease of a frat boy tossing a beer can, and the wolf smacked against the loading dock with a sound that seemed quite final. The speed of this attack and its conclusion was absolutely incredible.

Claudine didn't move from her straddling stance, and I was smart enough to stay put. Actually, I was exhausted, frightened, and a little bloody, though only the red spatter on my leg seemed to be my own. Fighting takes such a short time, yet it uses up the body's reserves with amazing speed. At least, that's the way it works with humans. Claudine looked pretty sparky.

'Bring it on, fur-ass!' she shrieked, beckoning with both hands to a Were who was slinking up on her from behind. She'd twisted around without moving her legs, a maneuver that would be impossible for a mundane human body. The Were launched and got exactly the same treatment as its packmate. As far as I could tell, Claudine wasn't even breathing heavy. Her eyes were wider and more intent than usual, and she held her body in a loose crouch, clearly ready for action.

There was more roaring, and barking, and growling, and shrieks of pain, and rending noises that didn't bear thinking about. But after maybe five more minutes of battle, the noise died down.

Claudine had not even glanced down at me during this time because she was guarding my body. When she did, she winced. So I looked pretty bad.

'I was late,' she said, shifting her feet so she was standing on one side of me. She reached down and I seized her hand. In a flash, I was on my feet. I hugged her. Not only did I want to, I needed to. Claudine always smelled so wonderful, and her body was curiously firmer to the touch than human flesh. She seemed happy to hug me back, and we clung together for a long moment while I regained my equilibrium.

Then I raised my head to look around, dreading what I would see. The fallen lay in heaps of fur around us. The dark stains on the pavement were not from oil drips. Here and there a bedraggled wolf nosed through the corpses, looking for someone in particular. The lion was crouched a couple of yards away, panting. Blood streaked his fur. There was an open wound on his shoulder, the one caused by Priscilla. There was another bite on his back.

I didn't know what to do first. 'Thanks, Claudine,' I said, and kissed her cheek.

'I can't always make it,' Claudine cautioned me. 'Don't count on an automatic rescue.'

'Am I wearing some kind of fairy Life Alert button? How'd you know to come?' I could tell she wasn't going to answer. 'Anyway, I sure appreciate this rescue. Hey, I guess you know I met my great-grandfather.' I was babbling. I was so glad to be alive.

She bowed her head. 'The prince is my grandfather,' she said.

'Oh,' I said. 'So, we're like cousins?'

She looked down at me, her eyes clear and dark and calm. She didn't look like a woman who'd just killed two wolves as quick as you could snap your fingers. 'Yes,' she said. 'I guess we are.'

'So what do you call him? Granddaddy? Popsy?'

'I call him "my lord".'

'Oh.'

She stepped away to check out the wolves she'd disposed of (I was pretty sure they were still dead), so I went over to the lion. I crouched beside him and put my arm around his neck. He rumbled. Automatically, I scratched the top of his head and behind his ears, just like I did with Bob. The rumble intensified.

'Sam,' I said. 'Thanks so much. I owe you my life. How bad are your wounds? What can I do about them?'

Sam sighed. He laid his head on the ground.

'You're tired?'

Then the air around him got hyper, and I pulled away from him. I knew what was coming. After a few moments, the body that lay beside me was human, not animal. I ran my eyes over Sam anxiously and I saw that he still had the wounds, but they were much smaller than they'd been on his lion form. All shape-shifters are great at healing. It says a lot about the way my life had changed that it didn't seem significant to me that Sam was buck naked. I had kind of gone beyond that now – which was good, since there were bare bodies all around me. The corpses were changing back, as well as the injured wolves.

It had been easier to look at the bodies in wolf form.

Cal Myers and his sister, Priscilla, were dead, of course, as were the two Weres Claudine had dispatched. Amanda was dead. The skinny girl I'd met in the Hair of the Dog was alive, though severely wounded in the upper thigh. I recognized Amanda's bartender, too; he seemed unscathed. Tray Dawson was cradling an arm that looked broken.

Patrick Furnan lay in the middle of a ring of the dead and wounded, all of them Priscilla's wolves. With some difficulty, I picked my way through broken, bloody bodies. I could feel all the eyes, wolf and human, focus on me as I squatted by him. I put my fingers on his neck and got nothing. I checked his wrist. I even put my hand against his chest. No movement.

'Gone,' I said, and those remaining in wolf form began to howl. Far more disturbing were the howls coming from the throats of the Weres in human form.

Alcide staggered over to me. He appeared to be more or less intact, though streaks of blood matted his chest hair. He passed the slain Priscilla, kicking her corpse as he went by. He knelt for a moment by Patrick Furnan, dipping his head as though he was bowing to the corpse. Then he rose to his feet. He looked dark, savage, and resolute.

'I am the leader of this pack!' he said in a voice of absolute certainty. The scene became eerily quiet as the surviving wolves absorbed that.

'You need to leave now,' Claudine said very quietly right behind me. I jumped like a rabbit. I'd been mesmerized by the beauty of Alcide, by the primitive wildness rolling off him.

'What? Why?'

'They're going to celebrate their victory and the ascension of a new packmaster,' she said.

The skinny girl clenched her hands together and brought them down on the skull of a fallen – but still twitching – enemy. The bones broke with a nasty crunch. All around me the defeated Weres were being executed, at least those who were severely wounded. A small cluster of three scrambled to kneel in front of Alcide, their heads tilted back. Two of them were women. One was an adolescent male. They were offering Alcide their throats in surrender. Alcide was very excited. All over. I remembered the way Patrick Furnan had celebrated when he got the packmaster job. I didn't know if Alcide was going to fuck the hostages or kill them. I took in my breath to exclaim. I don't know what I would've said, but Sam's grimy hand clapped over my mouth. I rolled my eyes to glare at him, both angry and agitated, and he shook his head vehemently. He held my gaze for a long moment to make sure I would stay silent, and then he removed his hand. He put his arm around my waist and turned me abruptly away from the scene. Claudine took the rear guard as Sam marched me rapidly away. I kept my eyes forward.

I tried not to listen to the noises.

Chapter 10

Sam had some extra clothes in his truck, and he pulled them on matter-of-factly. Claudine said, 'I have to get back to bed,' as if she'd been awoken to let the cat out or go to the bathroom, and then *pop!* she was gone.

'I'll drive,' I offered, because Sam was wounded.

He handed me his keys.

We started out in silence. It was an effort to remember the route to get back to the interstate to return to Bon Temps because I was still shocked on several different levels.

'That's a normal reaction to battle,' Sam said. 'The surge of lust.'

I carefully didn't look at Sam's lap to see if he was having his own surge. 'Yeah, I know that. I've been in a few fights now. A few too many.'

'Plus, Alcide did ascend to the packmaster position.' Another reason to feel 'happy'.

'But he did this whole battle thing because Maria-Star died.' So he should have been too depressed to think about celebrating the death of his enemy, was my point.

'He did this *whole battle thing* because he was threatened,' Sam said. 'It's really stupid of Alcide and Furnan that they didn't sit down and talk before it came to this point. They could have figured out what was happening much earlier. If you hadn't persuaded them, they'd still be getting picked off and they'd have started an all-out war. They'd have done most of Priscilla Hebert's work for her.'

I was sick of the Weres, their aggression and stubbornness. 'Sam, you went through all of this because of me. I feel terrible about that. I would have died if it wasn't for you. I owe you big-time. And I'm so sorry.'

'Keeping you alive,' Sam said, 'is important to me.' He closed his eyes and slept the rest of the way back to his trailer. He limped up the steps unaided, and his door shut firmly. Feeling a little forlorn and not a little depressed, I got in my own car and drove home, wondering how to fit what had happened that night into the rest of my life.

Amelia and Pam were sitting in the kitchen. Amelia had made some tea, and Pam was working on a piece of embroidery. Her hands flew as the needle pierced the fabric, and I didn't know what was most astonishing: her skill or her choice of pastimes.

'What have you and Sam been up to?' Amelia asked with a big smile. 'You look like you've been rode hard and put away wet.'

Then she looked more closely and said, 'What happened, Sookie?'

Even Pam put down her embroidery and gave me her most serious face. 'You smell,' she said. 'You smell of blood and war.'

I looked down at myself and registered what a mess I was. My clothes were bloody, torn, and dirty, and my leg ached. It was first aid time, and I couldn't have had better care from Nurse Amelia and Nurse Pam. Pam was a little excited by the wound, but she restrained herself like a good vampire. I knew she'd tell Eric everything, but I just couldn't find it in me to care. Amelia said a healing spell over my leg. Healing wasn't her strongest suit, she told me modestly, but the spell helped a bit. My leg did stop throbbing.

'Aren't you worried?' Amelia asked. 'This is from a Were. What if you caught it?'

'It's harder to catch than almost any communicable disease,' I said, since I'd asked almost every werecreature I'd met about the chances of their condition being transmitted by bite. After all, they have doctors, too. And researchers. 'Most people have to be bitten several times, all over their body, to get it, and even then it's not for sure.' It's not like the flu or the common cold. Plus, if you cleaned the wound soon afterward, your chances dropped considerably even from that.

I'd poured a bottle of water over my leg before I'd gotten in the car. 'So I'm not worried, but I *am* sore, and I think I might have a scar.'

'Eric won't be happy,' Pam said with an anticipatory smile. 'You endangered yourself because of the Weres. You know he holds them in low esteem.'

'Yeah, yeah, yeah,' I said not caring one little bit. 'He can go fly a kite.'

Pam brightened. 'I'll tell him that,' she said.

'Why do you like to tease him so much?' I asked, realizing I was almost sluggish with weariness.

'I've never had this much ammunition to tease him with,' she answered, and then she and Amelia were out of my room, and I was blessedly alone and in my own bed and alive, and then I was asleep.

The shower I took the next morning was a sublime experience. In the list of Great Showers I've Had, this one ranked at least number 4. (The best shower was the one I'd shared with Eric, and I couldn't even think of that one without shivering all over.) I scoured myself clean. My leg looked good, and though I was even more sore from pulling muscles I didn't use too much, I felt a disaster had been averted and that evil had been vanquished, at least in a gray sort of way.

As I stood under the pounding hot water, rinsing my hair, I thought about Priscilla Hebert. In my brief glimpse into her world, she'd been at least trying to find a place for her disenfranchised pack, and she'd done the research to find a weak area where she could establish a foothold. Maybe if she'd come to Patrick Furnan as a supplicant, he would have been glad to give a home to her pack. But he would never have surrendered leadership. He'd killed Jackson Herveaux to attain it, so he sure wouldn't have agreed to any kind of co-op arrangement with Priscilla – even if wolf society would permit that, which was doubtful, especially given her status as a rare female packleader.

Well, she wasn't one anymore.

Theoretically, I admired her attempt to reestablish her wolves in a new home. Since I'd met Priscilla in the flesh, I could only be glad she hadn't succeeded.

Clean and refreshed, I dried my hair and put on my makeup. I was working the day shift, so I had to be at Merlotte's at eleven. I pulled on the usual uniform of black pants and white shirt, decided to leave my hair loose for once, and tied my black Reeboks.

I decided I felt pretty good, all things considered.

A lot of people were dead, and a lot of grief was hanging around the events of last night, but at least the encroaching pack had been defeated and now the Shreveport area should be peaceful for a while. The war was over in a very short time. And the Weres hadn't been exposed to the rest of the world, though that was a step they'd have to take soon. The longer the vampires were public, the more likely it became that someone would out the Weres.

I added that fact to the giant box full of things that were not my problem.

The scrape on my leg, whether due to its nature or because of Amelia's ministrations, was already scabbed over. There were bruises on my arms and legs, but my uniform covered them. It was feasible to wear long sleeves today, because it was actually cool. In fact, a jacket would have been nice, and I regretted not having thrown one on as I drove to work. Amelia hadn't been stirring when I left, and I had no idea if Pam was in my secret vampire hidey-hole in the spare bedroom. Hey, not my concern!

As I drove, I was adding to the list of things I shouldn't have to worry about or consider. But I came to a dead halt when I got to work. When I saw my boss, a lot of thoughts came crowding in that I hadn't anticipated. Not that Sam looked beaten up or anything. He looked pretty much as usual when I stopped in his office to drop my purse in its usual drawer. In fact, the brawl seemed to have invigorated him. Maybe it had felt good to change into something more aggressive than a collie. Maybe he'd enjoyed kicking some werewolf butt. Ripping open some werewolf stomachs . . . breaking some werewolf spines.

Okay, well – whose life had been saved by the aforesaid ripping and breaking? My thoughts cleared up in a hurry. Impulsively, I bent to give him a kiss on the cheek. I smelled the smell that was Sam: aftershave, the woods, something wild yet familiar.

'How are you feeling?' he asked, as if I always kissed him hello.

'Better than I thought I would,' I said. 'You?'

'A little achy, but I'll do.'

Holly stuck her head in. 'Hey, Sookie, Sam.' She came in to deposit her own purse.

'Holly, I hear you and Hoyt are an item,' I said, and I hoped I looked smiling and pleased.

'Yeah, we're hitting it off okay,' she said, trying for nonchalance. 'He's really good with Cody, and his family's real nice.' Despite her aggressively dyed spiky black hair and her heavy makeup, there was something wistful and vulnerable about Holly's face.

It was easy for me to say, 'I hope it works out.' Holly looked very pleased. She knew as well as I did that if she married Hoyt she'd be for all intents and purposes my sister-in-law, since the bond between Jason and Hoyt was so strong.

Then Sam began telling us about a problem he was having with one of his beer distributors, and Holly and I tied on our aprons, and our working day began. I stuck my head through the hatch to wave at the kitchen staff. The current cook at Merlotte's was an ex-army guy named Carson. Short-order cooks come and go. Carson was one of the better ones. He'd mastered burgers Lafayette right away (hamburgers steeped in a former cook's special sauce), and he got the chicken strips and fries done exactly right, and he didn't have tantrums or try to stab the busboy. He showed up on time and left the kitchen clean at the end of his shift, and that was such a huge thing Sam would have forgiven Carson a lot of weirdness.

We were light on customers, so Holly and I were getting the drinks and Sam was on the phone in his office when Tanya Grissom came in the front door. The short, curvy woman looked as pretty and healthy as a milkmaid. Tanya went light on the makeup and heavy on the self-assurance.

'Where's Sam?' she asked. Her little mouth curved up in a smile. I smiled back just as insincerely. Bitch.

'Office,' I said, as if I always knew exactly where Sam was.

'That woman there,' Holly said, pausing on her way to the serving hatch. 'That gal is a deep well.'

'Why do you say that?'

'She's living out at Hotshot, rooming with some of the women out there,' Holly said. Of all the regular citizens of Bon Temps, Holly was one of the few who knew that there were such creatures as Weres and shifters. I didn't know if she'd discovered that the residents of Hotshot were werepanthers, but she knew they were inbred and strange, because that was a byword in Renard Parish. And she considered Tanya (a werefox) guilty by association, or at least *suspicious* by association.

I had a stab of genuine anxiety. I thought, *Tanya and Sam could change together. Sam would enjoy that. He could even change into a fox himself, if he wanted to.*

It was a huge effort to smile at my customers after I'd had that idea. I was ashamed when I realized I should be happy to see someone interested in Sam, someone who could appreciate his true nature. It didn't say much for me that I wasn't happy at all. But she wasn't good enough for him, and I'd warned him about her.

Tanya returned from the hallway leading to Sam's office and went out the front door, not looking as confident as she'd gone in. I smiled at her back. Ha! Sam came out to pull beers. He didn't seem nearly as cheerful.

That wiped the smile off my face. While I served Sheriff Bud Dearborn and Alcee Beck their lunch (Alcee glowering at me all the while), I worried about that. I decided to take a peek in Sam's head, because I was getting better at aiming my talent in certain ways. It was also easier to block it off and keep it out of my everyday activities now that I'd bonded with Eric, though I hated to admit that. It's not nice to flit around in someone else's thoughts, but I've always been able to do it, and it was just second nature.

I know that's a lame excuse. But I was used to knowing, not to wondering. Shifters are harder to read than regular people, and Sam was hard even for a shifter, but I got that he was frustrated, uncertain, and thoughtful.

Then I was horrified at my own audacity and lack of manners. Sam had risked his life for me the night before. He had *saved my life*. And here I was, rummaging around in his head like a kid in a box full of toys. Shame made my cheeks flush, and I lost the thread of what the gal at my table was saying until she asked me gently if I felt all right. I snapped out of it and focused and took her order for chili and crackers and a glass of sweet tea. Her friend, a woman in her fifties, asked for a hamburger Lafayette and a side salad. I got her choice of dressing and beer, and shot off to the hatch to turn in the order. I nodded at the tap when I stood by Sam, and he handed me the beer a second later. I was too rattled to talk to him. He shot me a curious glance.

I was glad to leave the bar when my shift was up. Holly and I turned over to Arlene and Danielle, and grabbed our purses. We emerged into near-darkness. The security lights were already on. It was going to rain later, and clouds obscured the stars. We could hear Carrie Underwood singing on the jukebox, faintly. She wanted Jesus to take the wheel. That seemed like a real good idea.

We stood by our cars for a moment in the parking lot. The wind was blowing, and it was downright chilly.

'I know Jason is Hoyt's best friend,' Holly said. Her voice sounded uncertain, and though her face was hard to decipher, I knew she wasn't sure I'd want to hear what she was going to say. 'I've always liked Hoyt. He was a good guy in high school. I guess – I hope you don't really get mad at me – I guess what stopped me from dating him earlier was his being so tight with Jason.'

I didn't know how to respond. 'You don't like Jason,' I said finally.

'Oh, sure, I like Jason. Who doesn't? But is he good for Hoyt? Can Hoyt be happy if that cord between them is weaker? 'Cause I can't think about getting closer to Hoyt unless I believe he can stick with me the way he's always stuck with Jason. You can see what I mean.'

'Yes,' I said. 'I love my brother. But I know Jason isn't really in the habit of thinking about the welfare of other people.' And that was putting it mildly.

Holly said, 'I like you. I don't want to hurt your feelings. But I figured you'd know, anyway.'

'Yeah, I kinda did,' I said. 'I like you, too, Holly. You're a good mother. You've worked hard to take care of your kid. You're on good terms with your ex. But what about Danielle? I would've said you were as tight with her as Hoyt is with Jason.' Danielle was another divorced mother, and she and Holly had been thick as thieves since they were in first grade. Danielle had more of a support system than Holly. Danielle's mother and father were still hale and were very glad to help out with her two kids. Danielle had been going with a guy for some time now, too.

'I would never have said anything could come between Danielle and me, Sookie.' Holly pulled on her Windbreaker and fished for her keys in the depths of her purse. 'But her and me, we've parted ways a little bit. We still see each other for lunch sometimes, and our kids still play together.' Holly sighed heavily. 'I don't know. When I got interested in something other than the world here in Bon Temps, the world we grew up in, Danielle started thinking there was something a little wrong with that, with my curiosity. When I decided to become a Wiccan, she hated that, still does hate it. If she knew about the Weres, if she knew what had happened to me . . .' A shapeshifting witch had tried to force Eric to give her a piece of his financial enterprises. She'd forced all the local witches she could round up into helping her, including an unwilling Holly. 'That whole thing changed me,' Holly said now.

'It does, doesn't it? Dealing with the supes.'

'Yeah. But they're part of our world. Someday everyone will know that. Someday . . . the whole world will be different.'

I blinked. This was unexpected. 'What do you mean?'

'When they all come out,' Holly said, surprised at my lack of insight. 'When they all come out and admit their existence. Everyone, everyone in the world, will have to adjust. But some people won't want to. Maybe there'll be a backlash. Wars maybe. Maybe the Weres will fight all the other shifters, or maybe the humans will attack the Weres and the vampires. Or the vampires – you know they don't like the wolves worth a durn – they'll wait until some fine night, and then they'll kill them all and get the humans to say thank you.'

She had a touch of the poet in her, did Holly. And she was quite a visionary, in a doom-ridden way. I'd had no idea Holly was that deep, and I was again ashamed of myself. Mind readers shouldn't be taken by surprise like that. I'd tried so hard to stay out of people's minds that I was missing important cues.

'All of that, or none of that,' I said. 'Maybe people will just accept it. Not in every country. I mean, when you think of what happened to the vampires in eastern Europe and some of South America . . .'

'The pope never sorted that one out,' Holly commented.

I nodded. 'Kind of hard to know what to say, I guess.' Most churches had had (excuse me) a hell of a time deciding on a scriptural and theological policy toward the undead. The Were announcement would sure add another wrinkle to that. They were definitely alive, no doubt about it. . . . But they had almost too much life, as opposed to already having died once.

I shifted my feet. I hadn't intended on standing out here and solving the world's problems and speculating on the future. I was still tired from the night before. 'I'll see you, Holly. Maybe you and me and Amelia can go to the movies in Clarice some night?'

'Sure,' she said, a little surprised. 'That Amelia, she doesn't think much of my craft, but at least we can talk the talk a little.'

Too late, I had a conviction the threesome wouldn't work out, but what the hell. We could give it a try.

I drove home wondering if anyone would be there waiting for me. The answer came when I parked beside Pam's car at the back door. Pam drove a conservative car, of course, a Toyota with a Fangtasia bumper sticker. I was only surprised it wasn't a minivan.

Pam and Amelia were watching a DVD in the living room. They were sitting on the couch but not exactly twined around each other. Bob was curled up in my recliner. There was a bowl of popcorn on Amelia's lap and a bottle of TrueBlood in Pam's hand. I stepped around so I could see what they were watching. *Underworld*. Hmmm.

'Kate Beckinsale is hot,' Amelia said. 'Hey, how was work?'

'Okay,' I said. 'Pam, how come you have two evenings off in a row?'

'I deserve it,' Pam said. 'I haven't had time off in two years. Eric agreed I was due. How do you think I would look in that black outfit?'

'Oh, as good as Beckinsale,' Amelia said, and turned her head to smile at Pam. They were at the ooey-gooey stage. Considering my own complete lack of ooey, I didn't want to be around.

'Did Eric find out any more about that Jonathan guy?' I asked.

'I don't know. Why don't you call him yourself?' Pam said with a complete lack of concern.

'Right, you're off duty,' I muttered, and stomped back to my room, grumpy and a little ashamed of myself. I punched in the number for

Fangtasia without even having to look it up. So not good. And it was on speed dial on my cell phone. Geez. Not something I wanted to ponder just at the moment.

The phone rang, and I put my dreary musing aside. You had to be on your game when you talked to Eric.

'Fangtasia, the bar with a bite. This is Lizbet.' One of the fang-bangers. I scrounged around my mental closet, trying to put a face with the name. Okay – tall, very round and proud of it, moon face, gorgeous brown hair.

'Lizbet, this is Sookie Stackhouse,' I said.

'Oh, hi,' she said, sounding startled and impressed.

'Um . . . hi. Listen, could I speak to Eric, please?'

'I'll see if the master is available,' Lizbet breathed, trying to sound reverent and all mysterious.

'Master,' my ass.

The fangbangers were men and women who loved vampires so much they wanted to be around them every minute the vampires were awake. Jobs at places like Fangtasia were bread and butter to these people, and the opportunity to get bitten was regarded as close to sacred. The fangbanger code required them to be *honored* if some bloodsucker wanted to sample them; and if they died of it, well, that was just about an honor, too. Behind all the pathos and tangled sexuality of the typical fangbanger was the underlying hope that some vampire would think the fangbanger was 'worthy' of being turned into a vampire. Like you had to pass a character test.

'Thanks, Lizbet,' I said.

Lizbet set the phone down with a thud and went off looking for Eric. I couldn't have made her happier.

'Yes,' said Eric after about five minutes.

'Busy, were you?'

'Ah having supper.'

I wrinkled my nose. 'Well, hope you had enough,' I said with a total lack of sincerity. 'Listen, did you find out anything about that Jonathan?'

'Have you seen him again?' Eric asked sharply.

'Ah, no. I was just wondering.'

'If you see him, I need to know immediately.'

'Okay, got that. What have you learned?'

'He's been seen other places,' Eric said. 'He even came here one night when I was away. Pam's at your house, right?'

I had a sinking feeling in my gut. Maybe Pam wasn't sleeping with Amelia out of sheer attraction. Maybe she'd combined business with a great cover story, and she was staying with Amelia to keep an eye on me. *Damn vampires*, I thought angrily, because that scenario was entirely too close to an incident in my recent past that had hurt me incredibly.

I wasn't going to ask. Knowing would be worse than suspecting.

'Yes,' I said between stiff lips. 'She's here.'

'Good,' Eric said with some satisfaction. 'If he appears again, I know she can take care of it. Not that that's why she's there,' he added unconvincingly. The obvious afterthought was Eric's attempt at pacifying what he could tell were my upset feelings; it sure didn't arise from any feeling of guilt.

I scowled at my closet door. 'Are you gonna give me any real information on why you're so jumpy about this guy?'

'You haven't seen the queen since Rhodes,' Eric said.

This was not going to be a good conversation. 'No,' I said. 'What's the deal with her legs?'

'They're growing back,' Eric said after a brief hesitation.

I wondered if the feet were growing right out of her stumps, or if the legs would grow out and then the feet would appear at the end of the process. 'That's good, right?' I said. Having legs had to be a good thing.

'It hurts very much,' Eric said, 'when you lose parts and they grow back. It'll take a while. She's very . . . She's incapacitated.' He said the last word very slowly, as if it was a word he knew but had never said aloud.

I thought about what he was telling me, both on the surface and beneath. Conversations with Eric were seldom single-layered.

'She's not well enough to be in charge,' I said in conclusion. 'Then who is?'

'The sheriffs have been running things,' Eric said. 'Gervaise perished in the bombing, of course; that leaves me, Cleo, and Arla Yvonne. It would have been clearer if Andre had survived.' I felt a twinge of panic and guilt. I could have saved Andre. I'd feared and loathed him, and I hadn't. I'd let him be killed.

Eric was silent for a minute, and I wondered if he was picking up on the fear and guilt. It would be very bad if he ever learned that Quinn had killed Andre for my sake. Eric continued, 'Andre could have held the center because he was so established as the queen's right hand. If one of her minions had to die, I wish I could have picked Sigebert, who's all muscles and no brains. At least Sigebert's there to guard her body, though Andre could have done that and guarded her territory as well.'

I'd never heard Eric so chatty about vampire affairs. I was beginning to have an awful creeping feeling that I knew where he was headed.

'You expect some kind of takeover,' I said, and felt my heart plummet. Not again. 'You think Jonathan was a scout.'

'Watch out, or I'll begin to think you can read my mind.' Though Eric's tone was light as a marshmallow, his meaning was a sharp blade hidden inside.

'That's impossible,' I said, and if he thought I was lying, he didn't challenge me. Eric seemed to be regretting telling me so much. The rest of our talk was very brief. He told me again to call him at the first sight of Jonathan, and I assured him I'd be glad to.

After I'd hung up, I didn't feel quite as sleepy. In honor of the chilly night I pulled on my fleecy pajama bottoms, white with pink sheep, and a white T-shirt. I unearthed my map of Louisiana and found a pencil. I sketched in the areas I knew. I was piecing my knowledge together from bits of conversations that had taken place in my presence. Eric had Area Five. The queen had had Area One, which was New Orleans and vicinity. That made sense. But in between, there was a jumble. The finally deceased Gervaise had had the area including Baton Rouge, and that was where the queen had been living since Katrina damaged her New Orleans properties so heavily. So that should have been Area Two, due to its prominence. But it was called Area Four. Very lightly, I traced a line that I could erase, and would, after I'd looked at it for a bit.

I mined my head for other bits of information. Five, at the top of the state, stretched nearly all the way across. Eric was richer and more powerful than I'd thought. Below him, and fairly even in territory, were Cleo Babbitt's Area Three and Arla Yvonne's Area Two. A swoop down to the Gulf from the southwesternmost corner of Mississippi marked off the large areas formerly held by Gervaise and the queen, Four and One respectively. I could only imagine what vampiric political contortions had led to the numbering and arrangement.

I looked at the map for a few long minutes before I erased all the light lines I'd drawn. I glanced at the clock. Nearly an hour had passed since my conversation with Eric. In a melancholy mood, I brushed my teeth and washed my face. After I climbed into bed and said my prayers, I lay there awake for quite a while. I was pondering the undeniable truth that the most powerful vampire in the state of Louisiana, at this very point in time, was Eric Northman, my blood-bonded, once-upon-a-time lover. Eric had said in my hearing that he didn't want to be king, didn't want to take over new territory; and since I'd figured out the extent of his territory right now, the size of it made that assertion a little more likely.

I believed I knew Eric a little, maybe as much as a human can know a vampire, which doesn't mean my knowledge was profound. I didn't believe he wanted to take over the state, or he would have done so. I did think his power meant there was a giant target pinned to his back. I needed to try to sleep. I glanced at the clock again. An hour and a half since I'd talked to Eric.

Bill glided into my room quite silently.

'What's up?' I asked, trying to keep my voice very quiet, very calm, though every nerve in my body had started shrieking.

'I'm uneasy,' he said in his cool voice, and I almost laughed. 'Pam had to leave for Fangtasia. She called me to take her place here.'

'Why?'

He sat in the chair in the corner. It was pretty dark in my room, but the curtains weren't drawn completely shut and I got some illumination from the yard's security light. There was a night-light in the bathroom, too, and I could make out the contours of his body and the blur of his face. Bill had a little glow, like all vampires do in my eyes.

'Pam couldn't get Cleo on the phone,' he said. 'Eric left the club to run an errand, and Pam couldn't raise him, either. But I got his voice mail; I'm sure he'll call back. It's Cleo not answering that's the rub.'

'Pam and Cleo are friends?'

'No, not at all,' he said, matter-of-factly. 'But Pam should be able to talk to her at her all-night grocery. Cleo always answers.'

'Why was Pam trying to reach her?' I asked.

'They call each other every night,' Bill said. 'Then Cleo calls Arla Yvonne. They have a chain. It should not be broken, not in these days.' Bill stood up with a speed that I couldn't follow. 'Listen!' he whispered, his voice as light on my ear as a moth wing. 'Do you hear?'

I didn't hear jack shit. I held still under the covers, wishing passionately that this whole thing would just go away. Weres, vampires, trouble, strife . . . But no such luck. 'What do you hear?' I asked, trying to be as quiet as Bill was being, an effort doomed in the attempt.

'Someone's coming,' he said.

And then I heard a knock on the front door. It was a very quiet knock.

I threw back the covers and got up. I couldn't find my slippers because I was so rattled. I started for the bedroom door on my bare feet. The night was chilly, and I hadn't turned on the heat yet; my soles pressed coldly against the polished wood of the floor.

'I'll answer the door,' Bill said, and he was ahead of me without my having seen him move.

'Jesus Christ, Shepherd of Judea,' I muttered, and followed him. I wondered where Amelia was: asleep upstairs or on the living room couch? I hoped she was only asleep. I was so spooked by that time that I imagined she might be dead.

Bill glided silently through the dark house, down the hall, to the living room (which still smelled like popcorn), to the front door, and then he looked through the peephole, which for some reason I found funny. I had to slap a hand over my mouth to keep from giggling.

No one shot Bill through the peephole. No one tried to batter the door down. No one screamed.

The continuing silence was breaking me out in goose bumps. I didn't even see Bill move. His cool voice came from right beside my ear. 'It is a very young woman. Her hair is dyed white or blond, and it's very short and dark at the roots. She's skinny. She's human. She's scared.'

She wasn't the only one.

I tried like hell to think who my middle-of-the-night caller could be. Suddenly I thought I might know. 'Frannie,' I breathed. 'Quinn's sister. Maybe.'

'Let me in,' a girl's voice said. 'Oh, *please* let me in.'

It was just like a ghost story I'd read once. Every hair on my arms stood up.

'I have to tell you what's happened to Quinn,' Frannie said, and that decided me on the spot.

'Open the door,' I said to Bill in my normal voice. 'We have to let her in.'

'She's human,' Bill said, as if to say, 'How much trouble can she be?' He unlocked the front door.

I won't say Frannie tumbled in, but she sure didn't waste any time getting through the door and slamming it behind her. I hadn't had a good first impression of Frannie, who was long on the aggression and attitude and short on the charm, but I'd come to know her a fraction better as she sat at Quinn's bedside in the hospital after the explosion. She'd had a hard life, and she loved her brother.

'What's happened?' I asked sharply as Frannie stumbled to the nearest chair and sat down.

'You *would* have a vampire here,' she said. 'Can I have a glass of water? Then I'll try to do what Quinn wants.'

I hurried to the kitchen and got her a drink. I turned on the light in the kitchen, but even when I came back to the living room, we kept it dark.

'Where's your car?' Bill asked.

'It broke down about a mile back,' she said. 'But I couldn't wait with it. I called a tow truck and left the keys in the ignition. I hope to God they get it off the road and out of sight.'

'Tell me *right now* what's happening,' I said.

'Short or long version?'

'Short.'

'Some vampires from Vegas are coming to take over Louisiana.'

It was a showstopper.

Chapter 11

Bill's voice was very fierce. 'Where, when, how many?'

'They've taken out some of the sheriffs already,' Frannie said, and I could tell there was just a hint of enjoyment at getting to deliver this momentous news. 'Smaller forces are taking out the weaker ones while a larger force gathers to surround Fangtasia to deal with Eric.'

Bill was on his cell phone before the words had finished leaving Frannie's mouth, and I was left gaping at him. I had come so late to the realization of how weak Louisiana's situation was that it seemed to me for a second that I had brought this about by thinking of it.

'How did this happen?' I asked the girl. 'How did Quinn get involved? How is he? Did he send you here?'

'*Of course* he sent me here,' she said, as if I were the stupidest person she'd ever met. 'He knows you're tied to that vampire Eric, so that makes you part of the target. The Vegas vamps sent someone to have a look at you, even.'

Jonathan.

'I mean, they were evaluating Eric's assets, and you were considered part of that.'

'Why was this Quinn's problem?' I asked, which may not have been the clearest way to put it, but she got my meaning.

'Our mother, our goddamned screwed-up, screw-up *mother*,' Frannie said bitterly. 'You know she got captured and raped by some hunters, right? In Colorado. Like a hundred years ago.' Actually, it had been maybe nineteen years ago, because that was how Frannie had been conceived.

'And Quinn rescued her and killed them all, though he was just a kid, and he went in debt to the local vampires to get them to help him clean up the scene and get his mom away.'

I knew Quinn's mother's sad history. I was nodding frantically by now, because I wanted to get to something I hadn't heard yet.

'Okay, well, my mom was pregnant with me after the rape,' Frannie said, glaring at me defiantly. 'So she had me, but she was never right in the head, and growing up with her was kinda hard, right? Quinn was working off his debt in the pits.' (Think *Gladiator* with wereanimals.) 'She never got right in the head,' Frannie repeated. 'And she's kept getting worse.'

'I get that,' I said, trying to keep my voice level. Bill seemed on the verge of thumping Frannie to speed up her narrative, but I shook my head.

'Okay, so she was in a nice place that Quinn was paying for outside Las Vegas, the only assisted-living center in America where you can send people like my mom.' The Deranged Weretiger Nursing Home? 'But Mom got loose, and she killed some tourist and took her clothes and caught a ride into Vegas and picked up a man. She killed him, too. She robbed him and took his money and gambled until we caught up with her.' Frannie paused and took a deep breath. 'Quinn was still healing from Rhodes, and this about killed him.'

'Oh, no.' But I had a feeling I hadn't heard the bottom line on this incident yet.

'Yeah, what's worse, right? The escape, or the killing?'

Probably the tourists had had an opinion on that.

I vaguely noticed that Amelia had entered the room, and I also realized that she didn't seem startled to see Bill. So she'd been awake when Bill had taken Pam's place. Amelia hadn't met Frannie before, but she didn't interrupt the flow.

'Anyway, there's a huge vampire cartel in Vegas, because the pickings are so rich,' Frannie told us. 'They tracked down Mom before the police could catch her. They cleaned up after her *again*. Turns out that Whispering Palms, the place that lost her, had alerted all the supes in the area to be on the lookout. By the time I got to the casino where they'd grabbed Mom, the vamps were telling Quinn that they'd taken care of everything and now there was more debt for him to work off. He said he was coming off a bad injury and he couldn't go back in the pits. They offered to take me on as a blood donor or a whore for visiting vamps instead, and he just about took out the one who said that.'

Of course. I exchanged a glance with Bill. The offer to 'employ' Frannie had been designed to make anything else look better.

'Then they said they knew of a really weak kingdom that was just about up for grabs, and they meant Louisiana. Quinn told 'em they could get it for free if the King of Nevada would just marry Sophie-Anne, her being in no position to argue. But it turned out the king was right there. He said he detested cripples and no way would he marry a vampire who'd killed her previous husband, no matter how sweet her kingdom was, even with Arkansas thrown in.' Sophie-Anne was the titular head of Arkansas as well as Louisiana since she'd been found innocent of her husband's (the King of Arkansas's) murder in a vampire court. Sophie-Anne hadn't had a chance to consolidate her claim, because of the bombing. But I was sure it was on her to-do list, right after her legs grew back.

Bill flipped his phone open again and began punching in numbers. Whoever he called, he didn't get an answer. His dark eyes were blazing. He was absolutely revved up. He leaned over to pick up a sword he'd left propped against the couch. Yep, he'd come fully armed. I didn't keep items like that in my toolshed.

'They'll want to take us out quietly and quickly so the human news media won't catch on. They'll concoct a story to explain why familiar vampires have been replaced with strange ones,' Bill said. 'You, girl – what part does your brother have to play in this?'

'They made him tell them how many people you-all had and share what else he knew about the situation in Lousiana,' Frannie said. To make matters perfect, she began to cry. 'He didn't want to. He tried to bargain with them, but they had him where they wanted him.' Now Frannie looked about ten years older than she was. 'He tried to call Sookie a million times, but they were watching him, and he was scared he'd be leading them right to her. But they found out anyway. Once he knew what they were going to do, he took a big risk – for both of us – and sent me on ahead. I was glad I'd got a friend to get my car back from you.'

'One of you should have called me, written me, something.' Despite our current crisis, I couldn't stop myself from expressing my bitterness.

'He couldn't let you know how bad it was. He said he knew you'd try to get him out of it somehow, but there was no way out.'

'Well, sure I would have tried to get him out of it,' I said. 'That's what you do when someone's in trouble.'

Bill was silent but I felt his eyes on me. I'd rescued Bill when he'd been in trouble. Sometimes I was sorry I had.

'Your brother, why is he with them now?' Bill asked sharply. 'He's given them information. They are vampires. What do they need with him?'

'They're bringing him with them so he can negotiate with the supe community, specifically the Weres,' Frannie said, sounding suddenly like Miss Corporate Secretary. I felt sort of sorry for Frannie. As the product of a union between a human and a weretiger, she had no special powers to give her an edge or to provide her with a bargaining chip. Her face was streaked with smeared mascara and her nails were chewed down to the quick. She was a mess.

And this was no time to be worried about Frannie, because the vampires of Vegas were taking over the state.

'What had we better do?' I asked. 'Amelia, have you checked the house wards? Do they include our cars?' Amelia nodded briskly. 'Bill, you've called Fangtasia and all the other sheriffs?'

Bill nodded. 'No answer from Cleo. Arla Yvonne answered, and she had already gotten wind of the attack. She said she was going to ground and would try to work her way up to Shreveport. She has six of her nest with her. Since Gervaise met his end, his vampires have been tending the queen, and Booth Crimmons has been their lieutenant. Booth says he was out tonight and his child, Audrey, who was left with the queen and Sigebert, doesn't answer. Even the deputy that Sophie-Anne sent to Little Rock is not responding.'

We were all silent for a moment. The idea that Sophie-Anne might be finally dead was almost unimaginable.

Bill shook himself visibly. 'So,' he continued, 'we might stay here, or we might find another place for you three. When I'm sure you're safe, I have to get to Eric as soon as I can. He'll need every pair of hands tonight if he's to survive.'

Some of the other sheriffs were surely dead. Eric might die tonight. The full realization smacked me in the face with the force of a huge gloved hand. I sucked in a jagged breath and fought to stay on my feet. I just couldn't think about that.

'We'll be fine,' Amelia said stoutly. 'I'm sure you're a great fighter, Bill, but we aren't defenseless.'

With all due respect to Amelia's witchcraft ability, we were so defenseless; at least against vampires.

Bill spun away from us and stared down the hall at the back door. He'd heard something that hadn't reached our human ears. But a second later, I heard a familiar voice.

'Bill, let me in. The sooner, the better!'

'It's Eric,' Bill said with great satisfaction. Moving so fast he was a blur, he went to the rear of the house. Sure enough, Eric was outside, and something in me relaxed. He was alive. I noticed that he was hardly his usual tidy self. His T-shirt was torn, and he was barefoot.

'I was cut off from the club,' he said as he and Bill came up the hall to join us. 'My house was no good, not by myself. I couldn't reach anyone else. I got your message, Bill. So, Sookie, I'm here to ask for your hospitality.'

'Of course,' I said automatically, though I really should have thought about it. 'But maybe we should go to—' I was about to suggest we cut across the graveyard and go to Bill's house, which was larger and would have more facilities for vampires, when trouble erupted from another source. We hadn't been paying any attention to Frannie since she'd finished her story, and the slump she'd experienced once her dramatic news had been delivered had allowed her to think of the potential for disaster we faced.

'I gotta get out of here,' Frannie said. 'Quinn told me to stay here, but you guys are . . .' Her voice was rising and she was on her feet and every muscle in her neck stood out in sharp relief as her head whipped around in her agitation.

'Frannie,' Bill said. He put his white hands on each side of Frannie's face. He looked into the girl's eyes. Frannie fell silent. 'You stay here, you stupid girl, and do what Sookie tells you to do.'

'Okay,' Frannie said in a calm voice.

'Thanks,' I said. Amelia was looking at Bill in a shocked kind of way. I guess she'd never seen a vamp use his whammy before. 'I'm going to get my shotgun,' I said to no one, but before I could move, Eric turned to the closet by the front door. He reached in and extricated the Benelli. He turned to hand it to me with a bemused expression. Our eyes met.

Eric had remembered where I kept the shotgun. He'd learned that when he'd stayed with me while his memory was lost.

When I could look away, I saw Amelia was looking self-consciously thoughtful. Even in my short experience of living with Amelia, I had learned that this was not a look I liked. It meant she was about to make a point, and it was a point I wouldn't care for.

'Are we getting all excited about nothing?' she asked rhetorically. 'Maybe we're panicking for no good reason.'

Bill looked at Amelia as if she'd turned into a baboon. Frannie looked totally unconcerned.

'After all,' Amelia said, wearing a small, superior smile, 'why would anyone come after *us* at all? Or more specifically *you*, Sookie. Because I don't suppose vampires would come after *me*. But that aside, why would they come here? You're not an essential part of the vampire defense system. What would give them a good reason to want to kill or capture you?'

Eric had been making a circuit of the doors and windows. He finished as Amelia was winding up her speech. 'What's happened?' he asked.

I said, 'Amelia is explaining to me why there's no rational reason the vampires would come after me in their attempt to conquer the state.'

'Of course they'll come,' Eric said, barely glancing at Amelia. He examined Frannie for a minute, nodded in approval, and then stood to the side of a living room window to look out. 'Sookie's got a blood tie to me. And now I am here.'

'Yeah,' Amelia said heavily. 'Thanks a lot, Eric, for making a beeline for this house.'

'Amelia. Are you not a witch with much power?'

'Yes, I am,' she said cautiously.

'Isn't your father a wealthy man with a lot of influence in the state? Isn't your mentor a great witch?'

Who had been doing some research on the Internet? Eric and Copley Carmichael had something in common.

'Yeah,' Amelia said. 'Okay, they'd be happy if they could corral us. But still, if Eric hadn't come here, I don't think we'd need to worry about physical injury.'

'You're wondering if we're actually in danger?' I said. 'Vampires, excited, bloodlust?'

'We won't be any use if we're not alive.'

'Accidents happen,' I said, and Bill snorted. I'd never heard him make such an ordinary sound, and I looked at him. Bill was enjoying the prospect of a good fight. His fangs were out. Frannie was staring at him, but her expression didn't change. If there'd been the slightest chance she'd stay calm and cooperative, I might have asked Bill to bring her out of the artificial state. I loved having Frannie still and quiet – but I hated her loss of free will.

'Why did Pam leave?' I asked.

'She can be of more value at Fangtasia. The others have gone to the club, and she can tell me if they are sealed in it or not. It was stupid of me to call them all and tell them to gather; I should have told them to scatter.' From the way he looked now, it wasn't a mistake Eric would ever make again.

Bill stood close to a window, listening to the sounds of the night. He looked at Eric and shook his head. No one there yet.

Eric's phone rang. He listened for a minute, said, 'Good fortune to you,' and hung up.

'Most of the others are in the club,' he told Bill, who nodded.

'Where is Claudine?' Bill asked me.

'I have no idea.' How come Claudine came sometimes when I was in trouble and didn't come at others? Was I just wearing her out? 'But I don't think she'll come, because you guys are here. There's no point in her showing up to defend me if you and Eric can't keep your fangs off of her.'

Bill stiffened. His sharp ears had picked up something. He turned and exchanged a long glance with Eric. 'Not the company I'd have chosen,' Bill said in his cool voice. 'But we'll make a good showing. I do regret the women.' And he looked at me, his deep dark eyes full of some intense emotion. Love? Sorrow? Without a hint or two from his silent brain, I couldn't tell.

'We're not in our graves yet,' Eric said, just as coolly.

Now I too could hear the cars coming down the driveway. Amelia made an involuntary sound of fear, and Frannie's eyes got even wider, though she stayed in her chair as if paralyzed. Eric and Bill sank into themselves.

The cars stopped out front, and there were the sounds of doors opening and shutting, someone walking up to the house.

There was a brisk knock – not on the door, but on one of the porch uprights.

I moved toward it slowly. Bill gripped my arm and stepped in front of me. 'Who is there?' he called, and immediately shifted us three feet away.

He'd expected someone to fire through the door.

That didn't happen.

'It is I, the vampire Victor Madden,' said a cheerful voice.

Okay, unexpected. And especially to Eric, who closed his eyes briefly. Victor Madden's identity and presence had told Eric volumes, and I didn't know what he'd read in those volumes.

'Do you know him?' I whispered to Bill.

Bill said, 'Yes. I've met him.' But he didn't add any details and stood lost in an inner debate. I've never wanted more intensely to know what someone was thinking than I did at that moment. The silence was getting to me.

'Friend or foe?' I called.

Victor laughed. It was a real good laugh – genial, an 'I'm laughing with you, not at you' kind of chortle. 'That's an excellent question,' he said, 'and one only you can answer. Do I have the honor of talking to Sookie Stackhouse, famed telepath?'

'You have the honor of talking to Sookie Stackhouse, barmaid,' I said frostily. And I heard a sort of throaty ruffling noise, a vocalization of an animal. A large animal.

My heart sank into my bare feet.

'The wards will hold,' Amelia was saying to herself in a rapid whisper. 'The wards will hold; the wards will hold.' Bill was gazing at me with his dark eyes, thoughts flickering across his face in rapid succession. Frannie was looking vague and detached, but her eyes were fixed on the door. She'd heard the sound, too.

'Quinn's out there with them,' I whispered to Amelia, since she was the only one in the room who hadn't figured that out.

Amelia said, 'He's on *their* side?'

'They've got his mom,' I reminded her. But I felt sick inside.

'But we've got his sister,' Amelia said.

Eric looked as thoughtful as Bill. In fact, they were looking at each other now, and I could believe they were having a whole dialogue without speaking a word.

All this thoughtfulness wasn't good. It meant they hadn't decided which way they were going to jump.

'May we come in?' asked the charming voice. 'Or may we treat with one of you face-to-face? You seem to have quite a few safeguards on the house.'

Amelia pumped her arm and said, 'Yes!' She grinned at me.

Nothing wrong with a little deserved self-congratulation, though the timing of it might be a bit off. I smiled back at her, though I felt my cheeks would crack.

Eric seemed to gather himself, and after one long last look at each other, he and Bill relaxed. Eric turned to me, kissed me on the lips very lightly, and looked at my face for a long moment. 'He'll spare you,' Eric said, and I understood he wasn't really talking to me but to himself. 'You're too unique to waste.'

And then he opened the door.

Chapter 12

Since the lights were still off in the living room and the security light was on outside, from inside the house we could see pretty well. The vampire standing by himself in the front yard was not particularly tall, but he was a striking man. He was wearing a business suit. His hair was short and curly, and though the light wasn't good for making such a determination, I thought it was black. He stood with an attitude, like a *GQ* model.

Eric was pretty much blocking the doorway, so that was all I could tell. It seemed tacky to go to the window and stare.

'Eric Northman,' said Victor Madden. 'I haven't seen you in a few decades.'

'You've been working hard in the desert,' Eric said neutrally.

'Yes, business has been booming. There are some things I want to discuss with you – rather urgent things, I'm afraid. May I come in?'

'How many are with you?' Eric asked.

'Ten,' I whispered at Eric's back. 'Nine vamps and Quinn.' If a human brain left a buzzing hole in my inner consciousness, a vampire brain left an empty one. All I had to do was count the holes.

'Four companions are with me,' Victor said, sounding absolutely truthful and frank.

'I think you've lost your counting ability,' Eric said. 'I believe there are nine vampires there, and one shifter.'

Victor's silhouette realigned as his hand twitched. 'No use trying to pull the wool over your eyes, old sport.'

'Old sport?' muttered Amelia.

'Let them step out of the woods so I can see,' Eric called.

Amelia and Bill and I abandoned being discreet and went to the windows to watch. One by one, the vampires of Las Vegas came out of the trees. Since they were at the edges of the darkness I couldn't see most of them very well, but I noticed a statuesque woman with lots of brown hair and a man no taller than me who sported a neat beard and an earring.

The last to emerge from the woods was the tiger. I was sure Quinn had shifted into his animal form because he didn't want to look at me face-to-face. I felt horribly sorry for him. I figured that however ripped up inside I was, his insides had to be like hamburger meat.

'I see a few familiar faces,' Eric said. 'Are they all under your charge?'

This had a meaning that I didn't understand.

'Yes,' Victor said very firmly.

This meant something to Eric. He stood back from the doorway, and the the rest of us turned to look at him. 'Sookie,' Eric said, 'it's not for me to invite him in. This is your house.' Eric turned to Amelia. 'Is your ward specific?' he asked. 'Will the ward let in him only?'

'Yes,' she said. I wished she sounded more certain. 'He has to be invited in by someone the ward accepts, like Sookie.'

Bob the cat strolled to the open doorway. He sat in the exact middle of the threshold, his tail wrapped around his paws, and surveyed the newcomer steadily. Victor laughed a little when Bob first appeared, but that died away after a second.

'This is not just a cat,' Victor said.

'No,' I said, loud enough for Victor to hear me. 'Neither is the one out there.' The tiger made a chuffing sound, which I'd read was supposed to be friendly. I guess it was as close as Quinn could come to telling me he was sorry about the whole damn thing. Or maybe not. I came to stand right behind Bob. He raised his head to look at me, and then strolled off with as much indifference as he'd arrived. Cats.

Victor Madden approached the front porch. Evidently the wards would not let him cross the boards, and he waited at the foot of the steps. Amelia flipped on the front porch lights, and Victor blinked in the sudden glare. He was a very attractive man, if not exactly handsome. His eyes were big and brown, and his jaw was decided. He had beautiful teeth displayed in a jaw-cracking smile. He looked at me very carefully.

'Reports of your attractions were not exaggerated,' he said, which took me a minute to decipher. I was too scared to be at my most intelligent. I made out Jonathan the spy among the vampires in the yard.

'Uh-huh,' I said, unimpressed. 'You alone can come in.'

'I'm delighted,' he said, bowing. He took a cautious step up and looked relieved. After that he crossed the porch so smoothly that all of a sudden he was right in front of me, his pocket handkerchief – I swear to God, a snowy white pocket handkerchief – almost touching my white T-shirt. It was all I could do to keep from flinching, but I managed to hold very still. I met his eyes and felt the pressure behind them. He was trying his mind tricks to see what might work on me.

Not much would, in my experience. After I'd let him establish that, I moved back to give him room to enter.

Victor stood quite still just inside the door. He gave everyone in the room a very cautious look, though his smile never faded. When he spotted Bill, the smile actually brightened. 'Ah, Compton,' he said, and though I expected he'd follow up with a more illuminating remark, that didn't happen. He gave Amelia a thorough scrutiny. 'The source of the magic,' he muttered, and inclined his head to her. Frannie got a quicker evaluation. When Victor recognized her, he looked, for one second, severely displeased.

I should have hidden her. I simply hadn't thought about it. Now the Las Vegas group knew that Quinn had sent his sister ahead to warn us. I wondered if we'd survive this.

If we lived until daytime, we three humans could leave in a car, and if the cars were disabled, well, we had cell phones and could call for a pickup. But there was no telling what other day-walking helpers the vampires of Las Vegas had ... besides Quinn. And as far as Eric and Bill being able to fight their way through the line of vampires outside: they could try. I didn't know how far they'd get.

'Please have a seat,' I said, though I sounded about as welcoming as a church lady forced to entertain an atheist. We all moved to the couch and the chairs. We left Frannie where she was. It would be better to maintain every bit of calm we could manage. The tension in the room was almost palpable as it was.

I switched on some lamps and asked the vampires if they would like a drink. They all looked surprised. Only Victor accepted. After a nod from me, Amelia went to the kitchen to heat up some TrueBlood. Eric and Bill were on the couch, Victor had taken the easy chair, and I perched on the edge of the recliner, my hands clenched in my lap. There was a long silence while Victor selected his opening line.

'Your queen is dead, Viking,' he said.

Eric's head jerked. Amelia, entering, stopped in her tracks for a second before carrying the glass of TrueBlood to Victor. He accepted it with a little bow. Amelia stared down at him, and I noticed her hand was hidden in the folds of her robe. Just as I drew in breath to tell her not to be crazy, she moved away from him and came to stand by me.

Eric said, 'I had guessed that was the case. How many of the sheriffs?' I had to hand it to him. You couldn't tell how he felt from his voice.

Victor made a show of consulting his memory. 'Let me see. Oh, yes! All of them.'

I pressed my lips together hard so no sound would escape. Amelia pulled out the straight-backed chair we keep to one side of the hearth. She set it close to me and sank down on it like she was a bag of sand. Now that she was sitting, I could see she had a knife clutched in her hand, the filleting knife from the kitchen. It was real sharp.

'What of their people?' Bill asked. Bill was doing the clean-slate imitation, too.

'There are a few alive. A dark young man named Rasul ... a few servitors of Arla Yvonne. Cleo Babbitt's crew died with her even after an offer of surrender, and Sigebert seems to have perished with Sophie-Anne.'

'Fangtasia?' Eric had saved this for last because he could hardly bear to speak of it. I wanted to go over to him and put my arms around him, but he wouldn't appreciate that at all. It would look weak.

There was a long silence while Victor took a swallow of the True-Blood.

Then he said, 'Eric, your people are all in the club. They have not surrendered. They say they won't until they hear from you. We're ready to burn it down. One of your minions escaped, and she – we think it is a female – is taking out any of my people stupid enough to get separated from the others.'

Yay, *Pam*! I bent my head to hide an involuntary smile. Amelia grinned at me. Even Eric looked pleased, just for a split second. Bill's face didn't alter a bit.

'Why am I alive, of all the sheriffs?' Eric asked – the four-hundred-pound question.

'Because you're the most efficient, the most productive, and the most practical.' Victor had the answer ready at his lips. 'And you have one of the biggest moneymakers living in your area and working for you.' He nodded toward Bill. 'Our king would like to leave you in position, if you will swear loyalty to him.'

'I suppose I know what will happen if I refuse.'

'My people in Shreveport are ready with the torches,' Victor said with his cheerful smile. 'Actually, with more modern devices, but you get the point. And, of course, we can take care of your little group here. You are certainly fond of diversity, Eric. I trail you here thinking to find you with your elite vampires, and we find you in this odd company.'

I didn't even think about bristling. We were an odd company, no doubt about it. I also noticed the rest of us didn't get a vote. This all rested on the question of how proud Eric was.

In the silence, I wondered how long Eric would ponder his decision. If he didn't cave, we'd all die. That would be Victor's way of 'taking care' of us, despite Eric's out-loud thought about me being too valuable to kill. I didn't think Victor gave a fig for my 'value', much less Amelia's. Even if we overwhelmed Victor (and between Bill and Eric that could probably be managed), the rest of the vampires outside had only to set this house on fire as they were threatening to do Fangtasia, and we'd be gone. They might not be able to come in without an invitation, but we certainly had to get out.

My eyes met Amelia's. Her brain was pinging with fear, though she was making a supreme effort to keep her spine stiff. If she called Copley, he would bargain for her life, and he had the wherewithal to bargain effectively. If the Las Vegas crew was hungry enough to invade Louisiana, then they were hungry enough to accept a bribe for the life of the daughter of Copley Carmichael. And surely Frannie would be okay, since her brother was right outside? Surely they would spare Frannie to keep Quinn complaisant? Victor had already pointed out that Bill had skills they needed, because his computer database had proved lucrative. So Eric and I were the most expendable.

I thought about Sam, wished I could call him and talk to him for just a minute. But I wouldn't drag him into this for the world, because that would mean his sure death. I closed my eyes and said good-bye to him.

There was a sound outside the door, and it took me a moment to interpret it as a tiger's noise. Quinn wanted in.

Eric looked at me, and I shook my head. This was bad enough without throwing Quinn into the mix. Amelia whispered, 'Sookie,' and pressed her hand against me. It was the hand with the knife.

'Don't,' I said. 'It won't do any good.' I hoped Victor didn't realize what her intent was.

Eric's eyes were wide and fixed on the future. They blazed blue in the long silence.

Then something unexpected happened. Frannie snapped out of the trance, and she opened her mouth and began to scream. When the first shriek ripped out of her mouth, the door began to thud. In about five seconds Quinn splintered my door by throwing his four hundred and fifty pounds against it. Frannie scrambled to her feet and ran for it, seizing the knob and yanking it open before Victor could grab her, though he missed her by half an inch.

Quinn bounded into the house so quickly he knocked his sister down. He stood over her, roaring at all of us.

To his credit Victor showed no fear. He said, 'Quinn, listen to me.'

After a second, Quinn shut up. It was always hard to say how much humanity was left in the animal form of a shifter. I'd had evidence the Weres understood me perfectly, and I'd communicated with Quinn before when he was a tiger; he'd definitely comprehended. But hearing Frannie scream had uncorked his rage and he didn't seem to know where to aim it. While Victor was paying attention to Quinn, I fished a card out of my pocket.

I hated the thought of using my great-grandfather's Get Out of Jail Free card so soon ('Love ya, Gramps – rescue me!'), and I hated the thought of bringing him without warning into a room full of vampires. But if ever there was a time for fairy intervention, that time would be now, and I might have left it too late. I had my cell phone in my pajama pocket. I pulled it out surreptitiously and flipped it open, wishing I'd put him on speed dial. I looked down, checking the number, and began to press the buttons. Victor was talking to Quinn, trying to persuade him that Frannie was not being hurt.

Did I not do everything right? Did I not wait until I was sure I needed him before I called? Had I not been so clever to have the card on me, to have the phone with me?

Sometimes, when you do everything right, it still turns out all wrong.

Just as the call went through, a quick hand reached around, plucked the phone from my hand, and dashed it against the wall.

'We can't bring him in,' Eric said in my ear, 'or a war will start that will kill all of us.'

I think he meant all of *him*, because I was pretty sure I would be okay if Great-grandpa started a war to keep me that way, but there was no help for it now. I looked at Eric with something very close to hatred.

'There's no one you can call who would help you in this situation,' Victor Madden said complacently. But then he looked a little less pleased with himself, as if he was having second thoughts. 'Unless there is something I don't know about you,' he added.

'There is much you don't know about Sookie,' Bill said. It was the first time he'd spoken since Madden had entered. 'Know this: I will die for her. If you harm her, I'll kill you.' Bill turned his dark eyes on Eric. 'Can you say the same?'

Eric plainly wouldn't, which put him behind in the 'Who Loves Sookie More?' stakes. At the moment, that wasn't so relevant. 'You must also know this,' Eric said to Victor. 'Even more pertinently, if anything happens to her, forces you can't imagine will be set into motion.'

Victor looked deeply thoughtful. 'Of course, that could be an idle threat,' he said. 'But somehow, I believe you are serious. If you're referring to this tiger, though, I don't think he'll kill us all for her, since we have his mother and his sister in our grasp. The tiger already has a lot to answer for, since I see his sister here.'

Amelia had moved over to put her arm around Frannie, both to sooth her and to include herself in the tiger's circle of protection. She looked at me, thinking very clearly, *Should I try some magic? Maybe a stasis spell?*

It was very clever of Amelia to think of communicating this way with me, and I thought about her offer furiously. The stasis spell would hold everything exactly as it was. But I didn't know if her spell could encompass the vampires waiting outside, and I couldn't see the situation would be much improved if she froze only all of us in the room except for herself. Could she be specific about whom the spell affected? I wished that Amelia were telepathic, too, and I'd never wished that on anyone before. As things lay, there was just too much I didn't know. Reluctantly I shook my head.

'This is ridiculous,' Victor said. His impatience was calculated. 'Eric, this is the bottom line and my last offer. Do you accept my king's takeover of Louisiana and Arkansas, or do you want to fight to the death?'

There was another, shorter pause.

'I accept the sovereignty of your king,' Eric said, his voice flat.

'Bill Compton?' Victor asked.

Bill looked at me, his dark eyes dwelling on my face. 'I accept,' he said.

And just like that, Louisiana had a new king, and the old regime was gone.

Chapter 13

I felt the tension whoosh out of me like the air out of a punctured tire.

Eric said, 'Victor, call your people off. I want to hear you tell them.'

Victor, beaming harder than ever, whipped a tiny cell phone from his pocket and called someone named Delilah to give her his orders. Eric used his own cell to phone Fangtasia. Eric told Clancy about the change in leadership.

'Don't forget to tell Pam,' Eric said very clearly, 'lest she kill off a few more of Victor's people.'

There was an awkward pause. Everyone was wondering what came next.

Now that I was pretty sure I was going to live, I hoped Quinn would change back to his human form so I could talk to him. There was a lot to talk about. I wasn't sure I had a right to feel this, but I felt betrayed.

I don't think the world is about me. I could see he'd been forced into this situation.

There was always a lot of forcing around vampires.

As I saw it, this was the second time his mother had set Quinn up, quite inadvertently, to take her fall with the vamps. I got that she wasn't responsible; truly, I did. She'd never wanted to be raped, and she hadn't chosen to become mentally ill. I'd never met the woman and probably never would, but she was surely a loose cannon. Quinn had done what he could. He'd sent his sister ahead to warn us, though I wasn't exactly sure that had ended up helping so very much.

But points for trying.

Now, as I watched the tiger nuzzle Frannie, I knew I'd made mistakes all the way down the line with Quinn. And I felt the anger of betrayal; no matter how I reasoned with myself, the image of seeing my boyfriend on the side of vampires I had to regard as enemies had lit a fire in me. I shook myself, looking around the room.

Amelia had made a dash for the bathroom as soon as she could decently let go of Frannie, who was still crying. I suspected the tension had been too much for my witchy roommate, and sounds from the hall bathroom confirmed that. Eric was still on the phone with Clancy, pretending to be busy while he absorbed the huge change in his circumstances. I couldn't read his mind, but I knew that. He walked down the hall, maybe wanting some privacy to reassess his future.

Victor had gone outside to talk to his cohorts, and I heard one of them say, 'Yeah! *Yes!*' as if his team had scored a winning goal, which I supposed was the case.

As for me, I felt a little weak in the knees, and my thoughts were in such a tumult they could scarcely be called thoughts. Bill's arm went around me, and he lowered me to the chair Eric had vacated. I felt his cool lips brush my cheek. I would have to possess a heart of stone not to be affected by his little speech to Victor – I hadn't forgotten it, no matter how terrifying the night had been – and my heart is not made of stone.

Bill knelt by my feet, his white face turned up to me. 'I hope someday you'll turn to me,' he said. 'I'll never force myself or my company on you.' And he got up and walked outside to meet his new vampire kin.

Okey-dokey.

God bless me; the night wasn't over yet.

I trudged back to my bedroom and pushed the door open, intending to wash my face or brush my teeth or make some stab at smoothing my hair, because I thought it might make me feel a little less trampled.

Eric was sitting on my bed, his face buried in his hands.

He looked up at me as I entered, and he looked shocked. Well, no wonder, what with the very thorough takeover and traumatic changing of the guard.

'Sitting here on your bed, smelling your scent,' he said in a voice so low I had to strain to hear it. 'Sookie . . . I remember everything.'

'Oh, *hell*,' I said, and went in the bathroom and shut the door. I brushed my hair and my teeth and scrubbed my face, but I had to come out. I was being as cowardly as Quinn if I didn't face the vampire.

Eric started talking the minute I emerged. 'I can't believe I—'

'Yeah, yeah, I know, loved a mere human, made all those promises, was as sweet as pie and wanted to stay with me forever,' I muttered. Surely there was a shortcut we could take through this scene.

'I can't believe I felt something so strongly and was so happy for the first time in hundreds of years,' Eric said with some dignity. 'Give me some credit for that, too.'

I rubbed my forehead. It was the middle of the night, I'd thought I was going to die, the man I'd been thinking of as my boyfriend had just turned my whole picture of him upside down. Though now 'his' vamps were on the same side as 'my' vamps, I'd emotionally aligned myself with the vampires of Louisiana, even if some of them had been terrifying in the extreme. Could Victor Madden and his crew be any less scary? I thought not. This very night they'd killed quite a few vamps I'd known and liked.

Coming on top of all these events, I didn't think I could cope with an Eric who'd just had a revelation.

'Can we talk about this some other time, if we have to talk about it?' I asked.

'Yes,' he said after a long pause. 'Yes. This isn't the right moment.'

'I don't know that any time will be right for this conversation.'

'But we're going to have it,' Eric said.

'Eric . . . oh, okay.' I made an 'erase' movement with my hand. 'I'm glad the new regime wants to keep you on.'

'It would hurt you if I died.'

'Yeah, we're blood bound, yadda yadda yadda.'

'Not because of the bond.'

'Okay, you're right. It would hurt me if you died. Also I would have died, too, most likely, so it wouldn't have hurt for long. Now can you please scoot?'

'Oh, yes,' he said with a return of the old Eric flare. 'I'll *scoot* for now, but I'm going to see you later. And rest assured, my lover, we'll come to an understanding. As for the vampires of Las Vegas, they'll be well-suited to running another state that relies heavily on tourism. The King of Nevada is a powerful man, and Victor is not one you can take lightly. Victor is ruthless, but he won't destroy something he may be able to use. He's very good at reining in his temper.'

'So you're not really that unhappy with the takeover?' I couldn't keep the shock out of my voice.

'It's happened,' Eric said. 'There's no goal to be met in being "unhappy" now. I can't bring anyone back to life, and I can't defeat Nevada by myself. I won't ask my people to die in a futile attempt.'

I just couldn't match Eric's pragmatism. I could see his points, and in fact when I'd had some rest, I might agree with him. But not here, not now; he seemed way too cold for me. Of course, he'd had a few hundred years to get that way, and maybe he'd had to go through this process many times.

What a bleak prospect.

Eric paused on his way out the door to bend down to kiss me on the cheek. This was another evening for collecting kisses. 'I'm sorry about the tiger,' he said, and that was the final cap to the night as far as I was concerned. I sat slumped in the little chair in the bedroom corner until I was sure everyone was out of the house. When only one warm brain remained, Amelia's, I peered out of my room to get a visual. Yep, everyone else was gone.

'Amelia?' I called.

'Yeah,' she answered, and I went to find her. She was in the living room, and she was as exhausted as I was.

'Are you going to be able to sleep?' I asked.

'I don't know. I'm going to try.' She shook her head. 'This changes everything.'

'Which this?' Amazingly, she understood me.

'Oh, the vampire takeover. My dad had lots of dealings with the New Orleans vampires. He was going to be working for Sophie-Anne, repairing her headquarters in New Orleans. All her other properties, too. I better call him and tell him. He's going to want to get in there early with the new guy.'

In her own way Amelia was being as practical as Eric. I felt out of tune with the whole world. I couldn't think of anyone I could call who would feel the least bit mournful over the loss of Sophie-Anne, Arla Yvonne, Cleo . . . And the list went on. It made me wonder, for the first time, if vampires might not get inured to loss. Look at all the life that passed them by and then vanished. Generation after generation went to their graves, while still the undead lived on. And on.

Well, this tired human – who would eventually pass on – needed some sleep in the worst possible way. If there was another hostile takeover tonight, it would have to proceed without me. I locked the doors all over again, called up the stairs to Amelia to tell her good night, and crawled back into my bed. I lay awake for at least thirty minutes, because my muscles twitched just when I was about to drift off. I would start up into full wakefulness, thinking someone was coming in the room to warn me about a great disaster.

But finally even the twitching couldn't keep me awake any longer. I fell into a heavy sleep. When I woke, the sun was up and shining in the window, and Quinn was sitting in the chair in the corner where I'd slumped the night before while I was trying to deal with Eric.

This was an unpleasant trend. I didn't want a lot of guys popping in and out of my bedroom. I wanted one who would stay.

'Who let you in?' I asked, propping myself up on one elbow. He looked good for someone who hadn't gotten much sleep. He was a very large man with a very smooth head and huge purple eyes. I had always loved the way he looked.

'Amelia,' he said. 'I know I shouldn't have come in; I should have waited until you were up. You might not want me in the house.'

I went in the bathroom to give myself a minute, another ploy that was getting all too familiar. When I came out, a little neater and more awake than when I'd entered, Quinn had a mug of coffee for me. I took a sip and instantly felt better able to cope with whatever was coming. But not in my bedroom.

'Kitchen,' I said, and we went to the room that had always been the heart of the house. It had been dated when the fire had gotten it. Now I had a brand-new kitchen, but I still missed the old one. The table where my family had eaten for years had been replaced with a modern one, and the new chairs were lots more comfortable than the old ones, but regret still caught at me every now and then when I thought of what had been lost.

I had an ominous feeling that 'regret' was going to be the theme of the day. During my troubled sleep, apparently I'd absorbed a dose of the practicality that had seemed so sad to me the night before. To stave off the conversation we were going to have to have, I stepped to the back door and looked to see that Amelia's car was gone. At least we were alone.

I sat down opposite the man I'd hoped to love.

'Babe, you look like someone just told you I was dead,' Quinn said.

'Might as well have,' I said, because I had to plow into this and look to neither the right nor the left. He flinched.

'Sookie, what could I have done?' he asked. 'What could I have done?' There was an edge of anger in his voice.

'What can I do?' I asked in return, because I had no answer for him.

'I sent Frannie! I tried to warn you!'

'Too little, too late,' I said. I second-guessed myself immediately: Was I being too hard, unfair, ungrateful? 'If you'd called me weeks ago, even once, I might feel different. But I guess you were too busy trying to find your mother.'

'So you're breaking up with me because of my mother,' he said. He sounded bitter and I didn't blame him.

'Yes,' I said after a moment's inner testing of my own resolve. 'I think I am. It's not your mom as much as her whole situation. Your mother will always have to come first as long as she's alive, because she's so damaged. I've got sympathy for that, believe me. And I'm sorry that you and Frannie have a hard row to hoe. I know all about hard rows.'

Quinn was looking down into his coffee mug, his face drawn with anger and weariness. This was probably the worst possible moment to be having this showdown, and yet it had to be done. I hurt too bad to let it last any longer.

'Yet, knowing all this, and knowing I care for you, you don't want to see me anymore,' Quinn said, biting each word out. 'You don't want to try to make it work.'

'I care for you, too, and I had hoped we'd have a lot more,' I said. 'But last night was just too much for me. Remember, I had to find out your past from someone else? I think maybe you didn't tell me about it from the start because you knew it would be an issue. Not your pit fighting – I don't care about that. But your mom and Frannie . . . Well, they're your family. They're . . . dependent. They have to have you. They'll always come first.' I stopped for a moment, biting the inside of my cheek. This was the hardest part. 'I want to be first. I know that's selfish, and maybe unattainable, and maybe shallow. But I just want to come first with someone. If that's wrong of me, so be it. I'll be wrong. But that's the way I feel.'

'Then there's nothing left to talk about,' Quinn said after a moment's thought. He looked at me bleakly. I couldn't disagree. His big hands flat on the table, he pushed to his feet and left.

I felt like a bad person. I felt miserable and bereft. I felt like a selfish bitch.

But I let him walk out the door.

Chapter 14

While I was getting ready for work – yes, even after a night like the one I'd had, I had to go to work – there was a knock at the front door. I'd heard something big coming down the driveway, so I'd tied my shoes hastily.

The FedEx truck was not a frequent visitor at my house, and the thin woman who hopped out was a stranger. I opened the battered front door with some difficulty. It was never going to be the same after Quinn's entrance the night before. I made a mental note to call the Lowe's in Clarice to ask about a replacement. Maybe Jason would help me hang it. The FedEx lady gave a long look at the door's splintered condition when I finally got it open.

'You want to sign for this?' she said as she held out a package, tactfully not commenting.

'Sure.' I accepted the box, a little puzzled. It had come from Fangtasia. Huh. As soon as the truck had wheeled back out to Hummingbird Road, I opened the package. It was a red cell phone. It was programmed to my number. There was a note with it. 'Sorry about the other one, lover,' it read. Signed with a big 'E.' There was a charger included. And a car charger, too. And a notice that my first six months' bill had been paid.

With a kind of bemused feeling, I heard another truck coming. I didn't even bother to move from the front porch. The new arrival was from the Shreveport Home Depot. It was a new front door, very pretty, with a two-man crew to install it. All charges had been taken care of.

I wondered if Eric would clean out my dryer vent.

I got to Merlotte's early so I could have a talk with Sam. But his office door was shut, and I could hear voices inside. Though not unheard of, the closed door was rare. I was instantly concerned and curious. I could read Sam's familiar mental signature, and there was another one that I had encountered before. I heard a scrape of chair legs inside, and I hastily stepped into the storeroom before the door opened.

Tanya Grissom walked by.

I waited for a couple of beats, then decided my business was so urgent I had to risk a conversation with Sam, though he might not be in the mood for it. My boss was still in his creaky wooden rolling chair, his feet propped on the desk. His hair was even more of a mess than usual. He looked like he had a reddish halo. He also looked thoughtful and preoccupied, but when I said I needed to tell him some things, he nodded and asked me to shut the door.

'Do you know what happened last night?' I asked.

'I hear there was a hostile takeover,' Sam said. He tilted back on the springs of his rolling chair, and they squeaked in an irritating way. I was definitely balancing on a thin edge today, so I had to bite my lip to keep from snapping at him.

'Yeah, you might say that.' A hostile takeover was pretty much a perfect way to put it. I told him what had happened at my house.

Sam looked troubled. 'I don't ever interfere in vamp business,' he said. 'The two-natured and vamps don't mix well. I'm really sorry you got pulled into that, Sookie. That asshole Eric.' He looked like there was more he wanted to say, but he pressed his lips together.

'Do you know anything about the King of Nevada?' I asked.

'I know he has a publishing empire,' Sam said promptly. 'And he has at least one casino and some restaurants. He's also the ultimate owner of a management company that handles vampire entertainers. You know, the Elvis Undead Revue with all-vamp Elvis tribute artists, which is pretty funny when you think about it, and some great dance groups.' We both knew that the real Elvis was still around but rarely in any shape to perform. 'If there had to be a takeover of a tourist state, Felipe de Castro is the right vampire for the job. He'll make sure New Orleans gets rebuilt like it ought to be, because he'll want the revenue.'

'Felipe de Castro . . . That sounds exotic,' I said.

'I haven't met him, but I understand he's very, ah, charismatic,' Sam said. 'I wonder if he'll be coming to Louisiana to live or if this Victor Madden will be his agent here. Either way, it won't affect the bar. But there's no doubt it'll affect you, Sookie.' Sam uncrossed his legs and sat up straight in his chair, which shrieked in protest. 'I wish there was some way to get you out of the vampire loop.'

'The night I met Bill, if I'd known what I know now, I wonder if I'd have done anything different,' I said. 'Maybe I would've let the Rattrays have him.' I'd rescued Bill from a sleazy couple who turned out to be not only sleazy, but murderers. They were vampire drainers, people who lured vampires to spots where the vamps could be subdued with silver chains and drained of blood, which sold for big bucks on the black market. Drainers lived hazardous lives. The Rattrays had paid the full price.

'You don't mean that,' Sam said. He rocked in the chair again (*squeak! squeak!*) and rose to his feet. 'You would never do that.'

It felt really pleasant to hear something nice about myself, especially after the morning's conversation with Quinn. I was tempted to talk to Sam about that, too, but he was edging toward the door. Time to go to work, for both of us. I got up, too. We went out and began the usual motions. My mind was hardly on it, though.

To revive my flagging spirits, I tried to think of some bright point in the future, something to look forward to. I couldn't come up with anything. For a long, bleak moment I stood by the bar, my hand on my order pad, trying not to step over the edge into the chasm of depression. Then I slapped myself on the cheek. *Idiot! I have a house, and friends, and a job. I'm luckier than millions of people on the planet. Things will look up.*

For a while, that worked. I smiled at everyone, and if that smile was brittle, by God, it was still a smile.

After an hour or two, Jason came into the bar with his wife, Crystal. Crystal was looking sullen and slightly pregnant, and Jason was looking

. . . Well, he had that hard look about him, the mean look he got sometimes when he'd been disappointed.

'What's up?' I asked.

'Oh, not much,' Jason said expansively. 'You bring us a couple beers?'

'Sure,' I said, thinking he'd never ordered for Crystal before. Crystal was a pretty woman several years younger than Jason. She was a werepanther, but she wasn't a very good one, mostly because of all the inbreeding in the Hotshot community. Crystal had a hard time changing if it wasn't the full moon, and she had miscarried at least twice that I knew of. I pitied her losses, the more so because I knew the panther community considered her weak. Now Crystal was pregnant a third time. That pregnancy had maybe been the only reason Calvin had let her marry Jason, who was bitten, not born. That is, he'd become a panther by being repeatedly bitten – by a jealous male who wanted Crystal for himself. Jason couldn't change into a real panther but into a sort of half-beast, half-man version. He enjoyed it.

I brought them their beers along with two frosted mugs and waited to see if they were going to place a food order. I wondered about Crystal drinking, but decided it wasn't my business.

'I'd like me a cheeseburger with fries,' Jason said. No surprise there.

'What about you, Crystal?' I asked, trying to sound friendly. After all, this was my sister-in-law.

'Oh, *I* don't have enough money to eat,' she said.

I had no idea what to say. I looked at Jason inquiringly, and he gave me a shrug. This shrug said (to his sister), 'I've done something stupid and wrong but I'm not going to back down, because I'm a stubborn shit.'

'Crystal, I'll be glad to stand you lunch,' I said very quietly. 'What would you like?'

She glared at her husband. 'I'd like the same, Sookie.'

I wrote her order down on a separate slip and strode to the hatch to turn them in. I had been ready to get angry, and Jason had lit a match and thrown it on my temper. The whole story was clear in their heads, and as I came to understand what was going on, I was sick of both of them.

Crystal and Jason had settled into Jason's house, but almost every day Crystal rode out to Hotshot, her comfort zone, where she didn't have to pretend anything. She was used to being surrounded by her kin, and she especially missed her sister and her sister's babies. Tanya Grissom was renting a room from Crystal's sister, the room Crystal had lived in until she married Jason. Crystal and Tanya had become instant buddies. Since Tanya's favorite occupation was shopping, Crystal had gone along for the ride several times. In fact, she'd spent all the money Jason had given her for household expenses. She'd done this two paychecks in a row, despite multiple scenes and promises.

Now Jason refused to give her any more money. He was doing all the grocery shopping and picking up any dry cleaning, paying every bill himself. He'd told Crystal if she wanted any money of her own, she had to get a job. The unskilled and pregnant Crystal had not succeeded in finding one, so she didn't have a dime.

Jason was trying to make a point, but by humiliating his wife in public he was making the wrong point entirely. What an idiot my brother could be.

What could I do about this situation? Well . . . nothing. They had to work it out themselves. I was looking at two stunted people who'd never grown up, and I wasn't optimistic about their chances.

With a deep twinge of unease, I remembered their unusual wedding vows; at least, they'd seemed odd to me, though I supposed they were the Hotshot norm. As Jason's closest living relative, I'd had to promise to take the punishment if Jason misbehaved, just as her uncle Calvin had promised the same on Crystal's behalf. I'd been pretty damn rash to make that promise.

When I carried their plates to their table, I saw that the two were in the jaw-clenching, looking-anywhere-but-at-each-other stage of quarreling. I put the plates down carefully, got them a bottle of Heinz ketchup, and skedaddled. I'd interfered enough by buying Crystal lunch.

There was a person involved in this I *could* approach, and I promised myself then and there that I would. All my anger and unhappiness focused on Tanya Grissom. I really wanted to do something awful to that woman. What the hell was she hanging around for, sniffing around Sam? What was her goal in drawing Crystal into this spending spiral? (And I didn't think for a second it was by chance that Tanya's newest big buddy was my sister-in-law.) Was Tanya trying to irritate me to death? It was like having a horsefly buzzing around and lighting occasionally . . . but never quite close enough to swat. While I went about my job on autopilot, I pondered what I could do to get her out of my orbit. For the first time in my life, I wondered if I could forcibly pin another person down to read her mind. It wouldn't be so easy, since Tanya was a wereanimal, but I would find out what was driving her. And I had the conviction that information would save me a lot of heartache . . . a lot.

While I plotted and schemed and fumed, Crystal and Jason silently ate their food, and Jason pointedly paid his own bill, while I took care of Crystal's. They left, and I wondered what their evening would be like. I was glad I wasn't going to be a party to it.

From behind the bar Sam had observed all this, and he asked me in a low voice, 'What's up with those two?'

'They're having the newlywed blues,' I said. 'Severe adjustment problems.'

He looked troubled. 'Don't let them drag you into it,' he said, and then looked like he regretted opening his mouth. 'Sorry, don't mean to give you unwanted advice,' he said.

Something prickled at the corners of my eyes. Sam was giving me advice because he cared about me. In my overwrought state, that was cause for sentimental tears. 'That's okay, boss,' I said, trying to sound perky and carefree. I spun on my heel and went to patrol my tables. Sheriff Bud Dearborn was sitting in my section, which was unusual. Normally he'd pick a seat somewhere else if he knew I was working. Bud had a basket of onion rings in front of him, liberally doused with ketchup, and he was reading a Shreveport paper. The lead story was POLICE SEARCH FOR SIX, and I stopped to ask Bud if I could have his paper when he was through with it.

He looked at me suspiciously. His little eyes in his mashed-in face scanned me as if he suspected he'd find a bloody cleaver hanging from my belt. 'Sure, Sookie,' he said after a long moment. 'You got any of these missing people stowed away at your house?'

I beamed at him, anxiety transforming my smile into the bright grin of someone who wasn't all there mentally. 'No, Bud, I just want to find out what's going on in the world. I'm behind on the news.'

Bud said, 'I'll leave it on the table,' and he began reading again. I think he would have pinned Jimmy Hoffa on me if he could have figured a way to make it stick. Not that he necessarily thought I was a murderer, but he thought I was fishy and maybe involved in things that he didn't want happening in his parish. Bud Dearborn and Alcee Beck had that conviction in common, especially since the death of the man in the library. Luckily for me, the man had turned out to have a record as long as my arm; and not only a record, but one for violent crimes. Though Alcee knew I'd acted in self-defense, he'd never trust me . . . and neither would Bud Dearborn.

When Bud had finished his beer and his onion rings and departed to rain terror on the evildoers of Renard Parish, I took his paper over to the bar and read the story with Sam looking over my shoulder. I had deliberately stayed away from the news after the bloodbath at the empty office park. I'd been sure the Were community couldn't cover up something so big; all they could do was muddy the trail the police would surely be following. That proved to be the case.

After more than twenty-four hours, police remain baffled in their search for six missing Shreveport citizens. Hampering them is their inability to discover anyone who saw any of the missing people after ten o'clock on Wednesday night.

'We can't find anything they had in common,' said Detective Willie Cromwell.

Among the missing is a Shreveport police detective, Cal Myers; Amanda Whatley, owner of a bar in the central Shreveport area; Patrick Furnan, owner of the local Harley-Davidson dealership, and his wife, Libby; Christine Larrabee, widow of John Larrabee, retired school superintendent; and Julio Martinez, an airman from Barksdale Air Force Base. Neighbors of the Furnans say they hadn't seen Libby Furnan for a day prior to Patrick Furnan's disappearance, and Christine Larrabee's cousin says she had not been able to contact Larrabee by phone for three days, so police speculate that the two women may have met with foul play prior to the disappearance of the others.

The disappearance of Detective Cal Myers has the force on edge. His partner, Detective Mike Coughlin, said, 'Myers was one of the newly promoted detectives, and we hadn't had time to get to know each other well. I have no idea what could have happened to him.' Myers, 29, had been with the Shreveport force for seven years. He was not married.

'If they are all dead, you would think at least one body would have turned up by now,' Detective Cromwell said yesterday. 'We have searched all their residences and businesses for clues, and so far we have come up with nothing.'

To add to the mystery, on Monday another Shreveport area resident was murdered. Maria-Star Cooper, photographer's assistant, was slain in her apartment on Highway 3. 'The apartment was like a butcher shop,' said Cooper's landlord, among the first on the scene. No suspects have been reported in the slaying. 'Everyone loved Maria-Star,' said her mother, Anita Cooper. 'She was so talented and pretty.'

Police do not yet know if Cooper's death is related to the disappearances.

In other news, Don Dominica, owner of Don's RV Park, reported the absence of the owners of three RVs parked on his property for a week. 'I'm not sure how many people were in each trailer,' he said. 'They all arrived together and rented the spaces for a month. The name on the rental is Priscilla Hebert. I think at least six people were in each RV. They all seemed pretty normal to me.'

Asked if all their belongings were still in place, Dominica replied, 'I don't know; I haven't been checking. I ain't got time for that. But I haven't seen hide nor hair of them for days.'

Other residents of the RV park had not met the newcomers. 'They kept to themselves,' said a neighbor.

Police Chief Parfit Graham said, 'I'm sure we'll solve these crimes. The right piece of information will surface. In the meantime, if anyone has knowledge of the whereabouts of any of these people, call the Tipster Hotline.'

I considered it. I imagined the phone call. 'All of these people died as a result of the werewolf war,' I would say. 'They were all Weres, and a displaced and hungry pack from south Louisiana decided the dissension in the ranks in Shreveport created an opening for them.'

I didn't think I'd get much of a hearing.

'So they haven't found the site yet,' Sam said very quietly.

'I guess that really was a good place for the meeting.'

'Sooner or later, though . . .'

'Yeah. I wonder what's left?'

'Alcide's crew's had plenty of time now,' Sam said. 'So, not much. They probably burned the bodies somewhere out in the sticks. Or buried them on someone's land.'

I shuddered. Thank God I hadn't had to be part of that; and at least I really *didn't* know where the bodies were buried. After checking my tables and serving some more drinks, I went back to the paper and flipped it open to the obituaries. Reading down the column headed 'State Deaths', I got an awful shock.

SOPHIE-ANNE LECLERQ, prominent businesswoman, residing in Baton Rouge since Katrina, died of Sino-AIDS in her home. Leclerq, a vampire, had extensive holdings in New Orleans and in many places in the state. Sources close to Leclerq say she had lived in Louisiana for a hundred years or more.

I'd never seen an obituary for a vampire. This one was a complete fabrication. Sophie-Anne had not had Sino-AIDS, the only disease that could cross from humans to vampires. Sophie-Anne had probably had an acute attack of Mr Stake. Sino-AIDS was dreaded among vampires, of course, despite the fact that it was hard to communicate. At least it provided a palatable explanation for the human business community as to why Sophie-Anne's holdings were being managed by another vampire, and it was an explanation that no one would question too closely, especially since there was no body to refute the claim. To get it in today's paper, someone must have called it in directly after she'd been killed, perhaps even before she was dead. Ugh. I shivered.

I wondered what had really happened to Sigebert, Sophie-Anne's devoted bodyguard. Victor had implied Sigebert had perished along with the queen, but he hadn't definitely said so. I couldn't believe the bodyguard could still be alive. He would never have let anyone get close enough to kill Sophie-Anne. Sigebert had been at her side for so many years, hundreds upon hundreds, that I didn't think he could have survived her loss.

I left the newspaper open to the obituaries and placed it on Sam's desk, figuring the bar was too busy a place to talk about it even if we had the time. We'd had an influx of customers. I was running my feet off serving them and pocketing some good tips, too. But after the week I'd had, it was not only hard to feel normally happy about the money, it was also impossible to feel normally cheerful about being at work. I just did my best to smile and respond when I was spoken to.

By the time I got off work, I didn't want to talk to anyone about anything.

But of course, I didn't get my druthers.

There were two women waiting in the front yard at my house, and they both radiated anger. One, I already knew: Frannie Quinn. The woman with her had to be Quinn's mother. In the harsh glare of the security light I had a good look at the woman whose life had been such a disaster. I realized no one had ever told me her name. She was still pretty, but in a Goth sort of way that wasn't kind to her age. She was in her forties; her face was gaunt, her eyes shadowed. She had dark hair with more than a touch of gray, and she was very tall and thin. Frannie was wearing a tank top that showed her bra, and tight jeans, and boots. Her mother was wearing pretty much the same outfit but in different colors. I guessed Frannie had charge of dressing her mother.

I parked beside them, because I had no intention of inviting them in. I got out of my car reluctantly.

'You bitch,' Frannie said passionately. Her young face was rigid with anger. 'How could you do that to my brother? He did so much for you!'

That was one way to look at it. 'Frannie,' I said, keeping my voice as calm and level as I could, 'what happens between Quinn and me is really not any of your business.'

The front door opened, and Amelia stepped out on the porch. 'Sookie, you need me?' she asked, and I smelled magic around her.

'I'm coming in, in just a second,' I said clearly, but didn't tell her to go back inside. Mrs Quinn was a pureblood weretiger, and Frannie was half; they were both stronger than me.

Mrs Quinn stepped forward and looked at me quizzically. 'You're the one John loved,' she said. 'You're the one who broke up with him.'

'Yes, ma'am. It just wasn't going to work out.'

'They say I have to go back to that place in the desert,' she said. 'Where they store all the crazy Weres.'

No shit. 'Oh, do they?' I said, to make it clear I had nothing to do with it.

'Yes,' she said, and lapsed into silence, which was kind of a big relief.

Frannie, however, had not done with me. 'I loaned you my car,' she said. 'I came to warn you.'

'And I thank you,' I said. My heart sank. I couldn't think of any magic words to lessen the pain in the air. 'Believe me, I wish things had worked out different.' Lame but true.

'What's wrong with my brother?' Frannie asked. 'He's handsome; he loves you; he's got money. *He's a great guy.* What's wrong with you that you don't want him?'

The bald answer – that I really admired Quinn but didn't want to play second fiddle to his family's needs – was simply unspeakable for two reasons: it was unnecessarily hurtful, and I might be seriously injured as a result. Mrs Quinn might not be compos mentis, but she was listening with growing agitation. If she changed to her tiger form, I had no idea what would happen. She might run off into the woods, or she might attack. All this zoomed through my mind in little pictures. I had to say something.

'Frannie,' I said very slowly and deliberately because I had no idea what I was going to follow that up with. 'There's nothing wrong with your brother at all. I think he's the greatest. But we just have too many strikes against us as a couple. I want him to have the best chance at making a match with some lucky, lucky woman. So I cut him loose. Believe me, I'm hurting, too.' This was mostly true, which helped. But I hoped Amelia had her fingertips primed to deliver some good magic. And I hoped she got the spell right. Just in case, I began shifting away from Frannie and her mother.

Frannie was teetering on the brink of action, and her mother was looking increasingly restless. Amelia had eased forward to the edge of the porch. The smell of magic intensified. For a long moment, the night seemed to catch its breath.

And then Frannie turned away. 'Come on, Mama,' she said, and the two women got into Frannie's car. I took advantage of the moment to run up on the porch. Amelia and I stood shoulder to shoulder wordlessly until Frannie started up the car and drove away.

'Well,' Amelia said. 'So, you broke up with him, I'm gathering.'

'Yeah.' I was exhausted. 'He had too much baggage.' Then I winced. 'Gosh, I never thought I'd catch myself saying that. Especially considering my own.'

'He had his mama.' Amelia was on a perceptive roll that night.

'Yeah, he had his mama. Listen, thanks for coming out of the house and risking a mauling.'

'What are roommates for?' Amelia gave me a light hug and said, 'You look like you need to have a bowl of soup and go to bed.'

'Yeah,' I said. 'That sounds about right.'

Chapter 15

I slept very late the next day. And I slept like a stone. I didn't dream. I didn't toss or turn. I didn't get up to pee. When I woke up, it was close to noon, so it was good I didn't have to be at Merlotte's until evening.

I could hear voices in the living room. This was the downside of having a roommate. There was someone there when you woke up, and sometimes that person had company. However, Amelia was very good about making enough coffee for me when she got up earlier. That prospect got me out of bed.

I had to get dressed since we had company; besides, the other voice sounded masculine. I did a little brisk grooming in the bathroom and threw off my nightgown. I put on a bra and a T-shirt and some khakis. Good enough. I made a beeline for the kitchen and found that Amelia had indeed made a big pot of coffee. And she'd left a mug ready for me. Oh, great. I poured, and popped some sourdough bread in the toaster. The back porch door slammed, and I turned in surprise to see Tyrese Marley enter with an armful of firewood.

'Where do you keep your wood after you bring it in?' he asked.

'I have a rack by the fireplace in the living room.' He'd been splitting the wood Jason had cut and stacked by the toolshed the spring before. 'That's really nice of you,' I said, floundering. 'Um, have you had any coffee, or some toast? Or . . .' I glanced at the clock. 'What about a ham or meatloaf sandwich?'

'Food sounds good,' he said, striding down the hall as though the wood weighed nothing.

So the guest in the living room was Copley Carmichael. Why Amelia's dad was here, I had no clue. I scrambled to assemble a couple of sandwiches, poured some water, and put two kinds of chips by his plate so Marley could pick what he wanted. Then I sat down at the table myself and finally got to drink my coffee and eat my toast. I still had some of my grandmother's plum jam to spread on it, and I tried not to be melancholy every time I used it. No point in letting good jam go to waste. She would have certainly looked at it that way.

Marley returned and sat down opposite me with no sign of discomfort. I relaxed myself.

'I appreciate the work,' I said after he'd had a bite of his food.

'I got nothing else to do while he talks to Amelia,' Marley said. 'Plus, if she's still here all winter, he'll be glad if she can have a fire. Who cut that wood for you and didn't split it?'

'My brother,' I said.

'Humph,' Marley said, and settled into eating.

I finished my toast, poured myself a second mug of coffee, and asked Marley if he needed anything.

'I'm good, thank you,' he said, and opened the bag of barbecue potato chips.

I excused myself to take a shower. It was definitely cooler today, and I got a long-sleeved T-shirt out of a drawer I hadn't opened in months. It was Halloween weather. It was past time to buy a pumpkin and some candy . . . not that I got many trick-or-treaters. For the first time in days, I felt normal: that is to say, comfortably happy with myself and my world. There was a lot to grieve about, and I would, but I wasn't walking around expecting a smack in the face.

Of course, the minute I thought that, I began to brood on bad things. I realized I hadn't heard anything from the Shreveport vampires, and then I wondered why I thought I should or would. This period of adjustment from one regime to another had to be full of tension and negotiation, and it was best to leave them to it. I hadn't heard from the Weres of Shreveport, either. Since the investigation into the disappearance of all those people was still active, that was a good thing.

And since I'd just broken up with my boyfriend, that meant (theoretically) I was footloose and fancy-free. I put on eye makeup as a gesture toward my freedom. And then I added some lipstick. It was hard to feel adventurous, actually. I hadn't wanted to be fancy-free.

As I finished making my bed, Amelia knocked at my door.

'Come on in,' I said, folding my nightgown and putting it in the drawer. 'What's up?'

'Well, my father has a favor to ask you,' she said.

I could feel my face settle into grim lines. Of course, there had to be something Copley wanted if he'd driven up from New Orleans to talk to his daughter. And I could imagine what that request was.

'Go on,' I said, crossing my arms over my chest.

'Oh, Sookie, your body language is already saying no!'

'Ignore my body and speak your piece.'

She heaved a big sigh to indicate how reluctant she was to drag me into her dad's stuff. But I could tell she was tickled pink that he'd asked her to help him. 'Well, since I told him about the Vegas vampire takeover, he wants to reestablish his business link with the vampires. He wants an introduction. He was hoping you could, like, broker that.'

'I don't even know Felipe de Castro.'

'No, but you know that Victor. And he looks like he's got his eyes on his own advancement.'

'You know him as well as I do,' I pointed out.

'Maybe, but what's more important is that he knows who you are, and I'm just the other woman in the room,' Amelia said, and I could see her point – though I hated it. 'I mean, he knows who I am, who my dad is, but he really noticed you.'

'Oh, Amelia,' I moaned, and for just a moment felt like kicking her.

'I know you won't like this, but he said he was ready to pay, like, a finder's fee,' Amelia muttered, looking embarrassed.

I waved my hands in front of me to fan that thought away. I was not going to let my friend's father pay me money to make a phone call or whatever I had to do. At that moment I knew I'd decided I had to do this for Amelia's sake.

We went to the living room to talk face-to-face with Copley.

He greeted me with far more enthusiasm than he'd shown on his previous visit. He fixed his gaze on me, did the whole 'I'm focused on you' thing. I regarded him with a skeptical eye. Since he was no fool, he picked up on that immediately.

'I'm sorry, Miss Stackhouse, for intruding here so soon after my last visit,' he said, laying on the smarm. 'But things in New Orleans are so desperate. We're trying to rebuild to bring the jobs back in. This connection is really important to me, and I employ a lot of people.'

One, I didn't think Copley Carmichael was hurting for business even without the contracts for rebuilding the vampire properties. Two, I didn't for a minute think his sole motivation was the improvement of the damaged city; but after a moment of looking into his head, I was willing to concede that accounted for at least a fraction of his urgency.

Also, Marley had split the wood for the winter and carried a load in. That counted for more with me than any appeal based on emotion.

'I'll call Fangtasia tonight,' I said. 'I'll see what they say. That's the limit of my involvement.'

'Miss Stackhouse, I'm indeed indebted,' he said. 'What can I do for you?'

'Your chauffeur already did it,' I said. 'If he could finish splitting that oak, that would be a great favor.' I'm not a very good wood splitter, and I know because I've tried. Three or four logs done, and I'm wiped out.

'That's what he's been doing?' Copley did a good job of looking astonished. I wasn't sure if it was genuine or not. 'Well, how enterprising of Marley.'

Amelia was smiling and trying not to let her dad notice it. 'Okay, then we're settled,' she said briskly. 'Dad, can I fix you a sandwich or soup? We have some chips or some potato salad.'

'Sounds good,' he said, since he was still trying to be just plain folks.

'Marley and I have already eaten,' I said casually, and added, 'I need to run to town, Amelia. You need anything?'

'I could use some stamps,' she said. 'You going by the post office?'

I shrugged. 'It's on the way. Bye, Mr Carmichael.'

'Call me Cope, please, Sookie.'

I'd just known he was going to say that. Next he was going to try being courtly. Sure enough, he smiled at me with exactly the right blend of admiration and respect.

I got my purse and headed out the back door. Marley was still working on the woodpile in his shirtsleeves. I hoped that had been his very own idea. I hoped he got a raise.

I didn't really have anything to do in town. But I had wanted to dodge any further conversation with Amelia's dad. I stopped by the store and got some more paper towels, bread, and tuna, and I stopped by the Sonic and got an Oreo Blast. Oh, I was a bad girl, no doubt about it. I was sitting in my car working on the Blast when I spied an interesting couple two cars away. They hadn't noticed me, apparently, because Tanya and Arlene were talking steadily. The two were in Tanya's Mustang. Arlene's hair was newly colored, so it was flaming red to the roots, caught up at the back in a banana clip. My former friend was wearing a tiger-print knit top, all I could see of her ensemble. Tanya was wearing a pretty lime green blouse and a dark brown sweater. And she was listening intently.

I tried to believe they were talking about something other than me. I mean, I try not to be too paranoid. But when you see your ex-buddy talking to your known enemy, you have to at least entertain the possibility that the topic of you has come up in an unflattering way.

It wasn't so much that they didn't like me. I've known people all my life who didn't like me. I've known exactly why and how much they didn't like me. That's really unpleasant, as you can well imagine. What bothered me was that I thought Arlene and Tanya were moving into the realm of actually doing something to me.

I wondered what I could find out. If I moved closer, they'd definitely notice me, but I wasn't sure I could 'hear' them from where I was. I bent over like I was fiddling with my CD player, and I focused on them. I tried to mentally skip over or plow through the people in the intervening cars to reach them, which wasn't an easy task.

Finally, the familiar pattern of Arlene helped me to home in. The first impression I got was one of pleasure. Arlene was enjoying herself immensely, since she had the undivided attention of a fairly new audience and she was getting to talk about her new boyfriend's convictions about the need to kill all vampires and maybe people who collaborated with them. Arlene had no hard convictions that she'd formed for herself, but she was great at adopting other people's if they suited her emotionally.

When Tanya had an especially strong surge of exasperation, I zoomed in on her thought pattern. I was in. I remained in my half-concealed position, my hand moving every now and then over the CDs in my little car folder, while I tried to pick out everything I could.

Tanya was still in the pay of the Pelts: Sandra Pelt, specifically. And gradually I came to understand that Tanya had been sent here to do anything she could to make me miserable.

Sandra Pelt was the sister of Debbie Pelt, whom I'd shot to death in my kitchen. (After she'd tried to kill *me*. Several times. Let me point that out.)

Dammit. I was sick to death of the issue of Debbie Pelt. The woman had been a bane to me alive. She had been as malicious and vindictive as her little sister, Sandra. I'd suffered over her death, felt guilty, felt remorseful, felt like I had a huge *C* for 'Cain' on my forehead. Killing a vampire is bad enough, but the corpse goes away and they're sort of . . . erased. Killing another human being changes you forever.

That's how it ought to be.

But it's possible to grow sick of that feeling, tired of that albatross around your emotional neck. And I'd grown both sick and tired of Debbie Pelt. Then her sister and her parents had begun giving me grief, had had me kidnapped. The tables had turned, and I'd held them in my power. In return for me letting them go, they'd agreed to leave me alone. Sandra had promised to stay away until her parents died. I had to wonder if the elder Pelts were still among the living.

I started up my car and began cruising around Bon Temps, waving at familiar faces in almost every vehicle I passed. I had no idea what to do. I stopped at the little town park and got out of my car. I began to stroll, my hands jammed in my pockets. My head was all in a snarl.

I remembered the night I'd confessed to my first lover, Bill, that my great-uncle had molested me when I'd been a child. Bill had taken my story so to heart that he had arranged for a visitor to drop by my great-uncle's house. Lo and behold, my uncle had died from a fall down the stairs. I'd been furious at Bill for taking over my own past. But I couldn't deny that having my great-uncle dead had felt good. That profound relief had made me feel complicit in the assassination.

When I'd been trying to find survivors in the twisted debris of the Pyramid of Gizeh, I'd found someone still living, a vampire who wanted to keep me firmly under his control for the queen's benefit. Andre had been terribly wounded, but he would have lived if an injured Quinn hadn't crawled over and snuffed Andre out. I'd walked away without stopping Quinn or saving Andre, and that had made me several degrees more guilty of Andre's death than of my great-uncle's.

I strode through the empty park, kicking at the stray leaves that came my way. I was struggling with a sick temptation. I had only to say the word to any of many members of the supernatural community, and Tanya would be dead. Or I could set my sights on the source and have Sandra taken out. And again – what a relief her departure from the world would be.

I just couldn't do it.

But I couldn't live with Tanya nipping at my heels, either. She'd done her best to ruin my brother's already shaky relationship with his wife. That was just wrong.

I finally thought of the right person to consult. And she lived with me, so that was convenient.

When I got back to my house, Amelia's dad and his obliging chauffeur had departed. Amelia was in the kitchen, washing dishes.

'Amelia,' I said, and she jumped. 'Sorry,' I apologized. 'I should've walked heavier.'

'I was hoping that my dad and I understood each other a little better,' she confessed. 'But I don't think that's really true. He just needs me to do something for him now and then.'

'Well, at least we got the firewood split.'

She laughed a little and dried off her hands. 'You look like you have something big to say.'

'I want to clear the decks before I tell you this long story. I'm doing your dad a favor, but I'm really doing it for you,' I said. 'I'll call Fangtasia for your father no matter what, because you're my roommate and that'll make you happy. So that's a done deal. Now I'm going to tell you about a terrible thing I did.'

Amelia sat at the table and I sat opposite her, just like Marley and I had done earlier. 'This sounds interesting,' she said. 'I'm ready. Bring it on.'

I told Amelia all about it: Debbie Pelt, Alcide, Sandra Pelt and her parents, their vow that Sandra would never bother me again while they lived. What they had on me and how I felt about it. Tanya Grissom, spy and sneak and saboteur of my brother's marriage.

'Whoa,' she said when I'd finished. She thought for a minute. 'Okay, first off, let's check on Mr and Mrs Pelt.' We used the computer I'd brought back from Hadley's apartment in New Orleans. It took all of five minutes to discover that Gordon and Barbara Pelt had died two weeks before when they'd attempted to make a left turn into a gas station only to be hit broadside by a tractor trailer.

We looked at each other, our noses wrinkled. 'Ewww,' Amelia said. 'Bad way to go.'

'I wonder if she even waited till they were in the ground before she activated the Aggravate Sookie to Death plan,' I said.

'This bitch isn't going to let up. You sure Debbie Pelt was adopted? Because this totally vindictive attitude seems to run in that family.'

'They must have really bonded,' I said. 'In fact, I got the impression that Debbie was more of a sister to Sandra than she was a daughter to her parents.'

Amelia nodded thoughtfully. 'A little pathology going on there,' she said. 'Well, let me think about what I can do. I don't do death magic. And you've said you don't want Tanya and Sandra to die, so I'm taking you at your word.'

'Good,' I said briefly. 'And, uh, I'm willing to pay for this, of course.'

'Poo,' Amelia said. 'You were willing to take me in when I needed to get out of town. You've put up with me all this time.'

'Well, you do pay rent,' I pointed out.

'Yeah, enough to cover my part of the utilities. And you put up with me, and you don't seem to be all up in arms about the Bob situation. So believe me, I'm really glad to do this for you. I've just got to figure out what I'm actually going to do. Do you mind if I consult with Octavia?'

'No, not at all,' I said, trying not to show that I was relieved at the idea of the older witch offering her expertise. 'You got it, right? Got that she was at loose ends? Out of money?'

'Yeah,' Amelia said. 'And I don't know how to give her some without offering offense. This is a good way to do it. I understand that she's stuck in a random corner of the living room in the house of the niece she's staying with. She told me that – more or less – but I don't know what I can do about it.'

'I'll think about it,' I promised. 'If she really, really needs to move out of her niece's, she could stay in my extra bedroom for a little while.' That wasn't an offer that delighted me, but the old witch had seemed pretty miserable. She'd been entertained by going on the little jaunt to poor Maria-Star's apartment, which had been a ghastly sight.

'We'll try to come up with something long-term,' Amelia said. 'I'm going to go give her a call.'

'Okay. Let me know what you-all come up with. I got to get ready for work.'

There weren't too many houses between mine and Merlotte's, but all of them had ghosts hanging from trees, inflated plastic pumpkins in the yard, and a real pumpkin or two sitting on the front porch. The Prescotts had a sheaf of corn, a bale of hay, and some ornamental squash and pumpkins arranged artfully on the front lawn. I made a mental memo to tell Lorinda Prescott how attractive it was when next I saw her at Wal-Mart or the post office.

By the time I got to work, it was dark. I got out my cell phone to call Fangtasia before I went inside.

'Fangtasia, the bar with a bite. Come into Shreveport's premier vampire bar, where the undead do their drinking every single night,' said a recording. 'For bar hours, press one. To schedule a private party, press two. To speak to a live human or a dead vampire, press three. And know this: prank calls are not tolerated. We will find you.'

I was sure the voice was Pam's. She'd sounded remarkably bored. I pressed three.

'Fangtasia, where all your undead dreams come true,' said one of the fangbangers. 'This is Elvira. How may I direct you?'

Elvira, my ass. 'This is Sookie Stackhouse. I need to speak with Eric,' I said.

'Could Clancy help you?' Elvira asked.

'No.'

Elvira seemed stumped.

'The master is very busy,' she said, as if that would be hard for a human like me to understand.

Elvira was definitely a newbie. Or maybe I was getting kind of arrogant. I was irritated with 'Elvira'. 'Listen,' I said, trying to sound pleasant. 'You get Eric on the phone in two minutes or he'll be mighty unhappy with you.'

'*Well*,' Elvira said. 'You don't have to be a bitch about it.'

'Evidently I do.'

'I'm putting you on hold,' Elvira said viciously. I glanced at the employee door of the bar. I needed to hustle.

Click. 'This is Eric,' he said. 'Is this my former lover?'

Okay, even that made things inside me thud and shiver in excitement. 'Yeah, yeah, yeah,' I said, proud of how unshaken I sounded. 'Listen, Eric, for what it's worth, I had a visit today from a New Orleans bigwig named Copley Carmichael. He'd been involved with Sophie-Anne in some business negotiations about rebuilding the headquarters. He wants to establish a relationship with the new regime.' I took a deep breath. 'Are you okay?' I asked, negating in one plaintive question all my cultivated indifference.

'Yes,' he said, his voice intensely personal. 'Yes, I am . . . coping with this. We are very, very lucky we were in a position to . . . We're very lucky.'

I let out my breath very softly so he wouldn't pick up on it. Of course, he would anyway. I can't say I'd been on pins and needles wondering how things were going with the vampires, but I hadn't been resting very easy, either. 'Okay, very good,' I said briskly. 'Now, about Copley. Is there anyone around who'd like to hook up with him about the construction stuff?'

'Is he in the area?'

'I don't know. He was here this morning. I can ask.'

'The vampire I am working with now would probably be the right woman for him to approach. She could meet him at your bar or here at Fangtasia.'

'Okay. I'm sure he'd do either one.'

'Let me know. He needs to call here to set up an appointment. He should ask for Sandy.'

I laughed. 'Sandy, huh?'

'Yes,' he said, sounding grim enough to sober me in a hurry. 'She is not a bit funny, Sookie.'

'Okay, okay, I get it. Let me call his daughter, she'll call him, he'll call Fangtasia, it'll all get set up, and I've done my favor for him.'

'This is Amelia's father?'

'Yes. He's a jerk,' I said. 'But he's her dad, and I guess he knows his building stuff.'

'I lay in front of your fire and talked to you about your life,' he said.

Okay, way out of left field. 'Uh. Yeah. We did that.'

'I remember our shower together.'

'We did that, too.'

'We did so many things.'

'Ah . . . yeah. Okay.'

'In fact, if I didn't have so much to do here in Shreveport, I would be tempted to visit you all by myself to remind you how much you enjoyed those things.'

'If memory serves,' I said sharply, 'you kind of enjoyed them, too.'

'Oh, yes.'

'Eric, I really need to go. I got to get to work.' Or spontaneously combust, whichever came first.

'Good-bye.' He could make even that sound sexy.

'Good-bye.' I didn't.

It took me a second to gather my thoughts back together. I was remembering things I'd tried hard to forget. The days Eric had stayed with me – well, the nights – we'd done a lot of talking and a lot of sexing. And it had been wonderful. The companionship. The sex. The laughing. The sex. The conversations. The . . . well.

Somehow going in to serve beers seemed drab, all of a sudden.

But that was my job, and I owed it to Sam to show up and work. I trudged in, stowed my purse, and nodded to Sam as I tapped Holly on the shoulder to tell her I was here to take over. We switched shifts for the change and convenience but mostly because the night tips were

higher. Holly was glad to see me because she had a date that night
with Hoyt. They were going to a movie and dinner in Shreveport.
She'd gotten a teenager to babysit Cody. She was telling me this as
I was getting it from her contented brain, and I had to work hard
not to get confused. That showed me how rattled I'd been by my
conversation with Eric.

I was really busy for about thirty minutes, making sure everyone
was well-supplied with drinks and food. I caught a moment to call
Amelia soon after that to relay Eric's message, and she told me that
she'd call her dad the minute she hung up. 'Thanks, Sook,' she said.
'Again, you're a great roomie.'

I hoped she'd think of that when she and Octavia were devising a
magical solution to my Tanya problem.

Claudine came into Merlotte's that evening, raising male pulses as
she sauntered to the bar. She was wearing a green silk blouse, black
pants, and black high-heeled boots. That made her at least six foot one,
I estimated. To my amazement, her twin brother, Claude, trailed in
after her. The racing pulses spread to the opposite sex with the speed
of wildfire. Claude, whose hair was as black as Claudine's, though not
as long, was as lovely a hunk as ever posed in a Calvin Klein ad. Claude
was wearing a masculine version of Claudine's outfit, and he'd tied his
hair back with a leather thong. He was also wearing very 'guy' boots.
Since he stripped at a club in Monroe on ladies' night, Claude knew
exactly how to smile at women, though he wasn't interested in them.
I take that back. He was interested in how much money they had in
their purses.

The twins had never come in together; in fact, I didn't recall Claude
setting foot in Merlotte's before. He had his own place to run, his own
fish to fry.

Of course I went over to say hi, and I got a comprehensive hug from
Claudine. To my amazement, Claude followed suit. I figured he was
playing to the audience, which was pretty much the whole bar. Even
Sam was goggling; together, the fairy twins were overwhelming.

We stood at the bar with me sandwiched between them, each with
an arm around me, and I heard brains light up all around the room
with little fantasies, some of which startled even me, and I've seen the

most bizarre things people can imagine. Yep, it's all there for lucky me to see in living color.

'We bring you greetings from our grandfather,' Claude said. His voice was so quiet and liquid that I was sure no one else would be able to hear it. Possibly Sam could, but he was always good for discretion.

'He wonders why you haven't called,' Claudine said, 'especially considering the events of the other night, in Shreveport.'

'Well, that was over with,' I said, surprised. 'Why tell him about something that had already turned out okay? You were there. But I did try to call him the other night.'

'It rang once,' Claudine murmured.

'However, a certain person broke my phone so I couldn't complete the call. He told me it was the wrong thing to do, that it would start a war. I lived through that, too. So that was okay.'

'You need to talk to Niall, tell him the whole story,' Claudine said. She smiled across the room at Catfish Hennessy, who put his beer mug down on the table so hard that it slopped over. 'Now that Niall's made himself known to you, he wants you to confide in him.'

'Why can't he pick up the phone like everyone else in the world?'

'He doesn't spend all his time in this world,' Claude said. 'There are still places for only our kind.'

'Very small places,' Claudine said longingly. 'But very special.'

I was glad to have kin, and I was always glad to see Claudine, who was literally my lifesaver. But the two sibs together were a little overpowering, overwhelming – and when they stood so close with me crowded between them (even Sam was having a visual from that), their sweet smell, the smell that made them so intoxicating to vampires, was drowning my poor nose.

'Look,' Claude said, mildly amused. 'I think we have company.'

Arlene was sidling nearer, looking at Claude as if she'd spied a whole plate of barbecue and onion rings. 'Who's your friend, Sookie?' she asked.

'This is Claude,' I said. 'He's my distant cousin.'

'Well, Claude, nice to meet ya,' Arlene said.

She had some nerve, considering the way she felt about me now and how she'd treated me since she'd started going to the Fellowship of the Sun services.

Claude looked massively uninterested. He nodded.

Arlene had expected more, and after a moment of silence, she pretended to hear someone from one of her tables calling her. 'Gotta go get a pitcher!' she said brightly, and bustled off. I saw her bend over a table, talking very seriously to a couple of guys I didn't know.

'It's always good to see you two, but I *am* at work,' I said. 'So, did you just come to tell me my . . . that Niall wants to know why I called once and hung up?'

'And never called thereafter to explain,' Claudine said. She bent down to kiss my cheek. 'Please call him tonight when you get off work.'

'Okay,' I said. 'I still wish he'd called me himself to ask.' Messengers were all well and good, but the phone was quicker. And I'd like to hear his voice. No matter where my great-grandfather might be, he could wink back into this world to call if he really was that taxed about my safety.

I thought he could, anyway.

Of course, I didn't know what being a fairy prince entailed. Write that down under 'problems I know I'll never face'.

After another round of hugs and kisses, the twins sauntered out of the bar, and many wistful eyes followed them on their progress out the door.

'Hoo, Sookie, you got some hot friends!' Catfish Hennessy called, and there was a general tide of agreement.

'I've seen that guy at a club in Monroe. Doesn't he strip?' said a nurse named Debi Murray who worked at the hospital in nearby Clarice. She was sitting with a couple of other nurses.

'Yeah,' I said. 'He owns the club, too.'

'Looks *and* loot,' said one of the other nurses. Her name was Beverly something. 'I'm taking my daughter next ladies' night. She just broke up with a real loser.'

'Well . . .' I debated explaining that Claude wouldn't be interested in anyone's daughter, then decided that wasn't my responsibility. 'Have a good time,' I said instead.

Since I'd taken time out with my sort-of cousins, I had to hustle to sweeten everyone up. Though they hadn't had my attention during the visit, they had had the entertainment of the twins, so no one was really miffed.

Toward the end of my shift, Copley Carmichael walked in.

He looked funny alone. I assumed Marley was waiting in the car.

In his beautiful suit and with his expensive haircut, he didn't exactly fit in, but I got to give him credit: he acted like he came into places like Merlotte's all the time. I happened to be standing by Sam, who was mixing a bourbon and Coke for one of my tables. I explained to Sam who the stranger was.

I delivered the drink and nodded at an empty table. Mr Carmichael took the hint and settled in.

'Hey! Can I get you a drink, Mr Carmichael?' I said.

'Please get me a single malt scotch,' he said. 'Whatever you've got will be fine. I'm meeting someone here, Sookie, thanks to your phone call. You just tell me the next time you need anything, and I'll do everything in my power to make it happen.'

'Not necessary, Mr Carmichael.'

'Please, call me Cope.'

'Um-hmmm. Okay, let me get your scotch.'

I didn't know a single malt scotch from a hole in the ground, but Sam did, of course, and he gave me a shining clean glass with a very respectable shot of it. I serve liquor, but I seldom drink it. Most folks around here drink the real obvious stuff: beer, bourbon and Coke, gin and tonic, Jack Daniel's.

I set the drink and cocktail napkin on the table in front of Mr Carmichael, and I returned with a little bowl of snack mix.

Then I left him alone, because I had other people to tend to. But I kept track of him. I noticed Sam was keeping a careful eye on Amelia's dad, too. But everyone else was too involved in their own conversations and their own drinking to give much mind to the stranger, one not nearly as interesting as Claude and Claudine.

In a moment when I wasn't looking, a vampire joined Cope. I don't think anyone else knew what she was. She was a real recent vamp, by which I mean she'd died in the past fifty years, and she had prematurely silver hair that was cut in a modest chin-length style. She was small, maybe five foot two, and she was round and firm in all the right places. She was wearing little silver-rimmed glasses that were sheer affectation, because I'd never met a vampire whose eyesight wasn't absolutely perfect and in fact sharper than any human's.

'Can I get you some blood?' I asked.

Her eyes were like lasers. Once she was really giving you her attention, you were sorry.

'You're the woman Sookie,' she said.

I didn't see any need to affirm what she was so sure of. I waited.

'A glass of TrueBlood, please,' she said. 'Quite warm. And I'd like to meet your boss, if you would fetch him.'

Like Sam was a bone. Nonetheless, she was a customer and I was a barmaid. So I heated a TrueBlood for her and told Sam he was wanted.

'I'll be there in a minute,' he said, because he was getting a tray of drinks ready for Arlene.

I nodded and took the blood over to the vampire.

'Thank you,' she said civilly. 'I'm Sandy Sechrest, the new area rep for the King of Louisiana.'

I had no idea where Sandy had grown up, but it had been in the United States and had not been in the south. 'Pleased to meet you,' I said, but not with a whole lot of enthusiasm. Area rep? Wasn't that what sheriffs were, among their other functions? What did that mean for Eric?

At that moment Sam came to the table, and I left because I didn't want to look inquisitive. Besides, I could probably pick it up from his brain later if Sam chose not to tell me what the new vampire wanted. He was good at blocking, but he had to make a special effort to do it.

The three engaged in a conversation for a couple of minutes, then Sam excused himself to get back behind the bar.

I glanced at the vampire and the mogul from time to time in case they needed something more to drink, but neither of them indicated a thirst. They were talking very seriously, and both of them were adept at maintaining a poker face. I didn't care enough to try to latch onto Mr Carmichael's thoughts, and of course Sandy Sechrest was a blank to me.

The rest of the night was the usual stuff. I didn't even notice when the new king's rep and Mr Carmichael left. Then it was time to close everything out and get my tables ready for Terry Bellefleur to come in and clean early in the morning. By the time I really looked around me, everyone was gone but Sam and me.

'Hey, you through?' he said.

'Yeah,' I said after another look around.

'You got a minute?'

I always had a minute for Sam.

Chapter 16

He sat in the chair behind his desk and tilted it back at the usual dangerous angle. I sat in one of the chairs in front of the desk, the one with the most padding in the seat. Most of the lights in the building were out except the one that stayed on over the bar area and the one in Sam's office. The building rang with silence after the cacophony of voices rising over the jukebox and the sounds of cooking, washing, footsteps.

'That Sandy Sechrest,' he said. 'She's got a whole new job.'

'Yeah? What the king's rep supposed to do?'

'Well, as far as I can tell, she'll travel the state pretty much constantly, seeing if the citizens have problems with any vampires, seeing if the sheriffs have everything in order and under control in their own fiefs, and reporting in to the king. She's like an undead troubleshooter.'

'Oh.' I thought that over. I couldn't see that the job would detract from Eric's. If Eric was okay, his crew would be okay. Other than that, I didn't care what the vampires did. 'So, she decided to meet you because . . .?'

'She understood I had associations in the regional supernatural community,' Sam said dryly. 'She wanted me to know she was available to consult in the event 'problems arose'. I have her business card.' He held it up. I don't know if I expected it to drip with blood or what, but it was only a regular business card.

'Okay.' I shrugged.

'What did Claudine and her brother want?' Sam asked.

I was feeling very bad about concealing my new great-grandfather from Sam, but Niall had told me to keep him a secret. 'She hadn't heard from me since the fight in Shreveport,' I said. 'She just wanted to check up, and she got Claude to come with her.'

Sam looked at me a little sharply but he didn't comment. 'Maybe,' he said after a minute, 'this will be a long era of peace. Maybe we can just work in the bar and nothing will happen in the supe community. I'm hoping so, because the time is coming closer and closer when the Weres are going to go public.'

'You think it's soon?' I had no idea how America would react to the news that vampires were not the only things out there in the night. 'You think all the other shifters will announce the same night?'

'We'll have to,' Sam said. 'We're talking on our website about it.'

Sam did have a life that was unknown to me. That sparked a thought. I hesitated, then plowed ahead. There were too many questions in my own life. I wanted to get at least some of them answered.

'How'd you come to settle here?' I asked.

'I'd passed through the area,' he said. 'I was in the army for four years.'

'You were?' I couldn't believe I hadn't known that.

'Yeah,' he said. 'I didn't know what I wanted to do in my life, so I joined when I was eighteen. My mom cried and my dad swore since I'd been accepted to a college, but I'd made up my mind. I was about the stubbornest teenager on the planet.'

'Where'd you grow up?'

At least partly in Wright, Texas,' he said. 'Outside of Fort Worth. Way outside of Fort Worth. It wasn't any bigger than Bon Temps. We moved around all during my childhood, though, because my dad was in the service himself, He got out when I was about fourteen, and my mom's family was in Wright, so that's where we went.'

'Was it hard settling down after moving so much?' I'd never lived anywhere but Bon Temps.

'It was great,' he said. 'I was so ready to stay in one place. I hadn't realized how hard it would be to find my own niche in a group of kids who'd grown up together, but I was able to take care of myself. I played baseball and basketball, so I found my place. Then I joined the army. Go figure.'

I was fascinated. 'Are your mom and dad still in Wright?' I asked. 'It must have been hard for him in the military, with him being a shifter.' Since Sam was a shapeshifter, I knew without him having to tell me that he was the first-born child of pure-blooded shapeshifters.

'Yeah, the full moons were a bitch. There was an herbal drink his Irish grandmother used to make. He learned how to make it himself. It was foul beyond belief, but he drank it on full moons when he had to be on duty and had to be seen all night, and that helped him maintain. . . . But you didn't want to be around him the next day. Dad passed away about six years ago, left me a chunk of money. I'd always liked this area, and this bar was up for sale. It seemed like a good way to invest the money.'

'And your mom?'

'She's still in Wright. She married again about two years after Dad died. He's a good enough guy. He's regular.' Not a shifter or any kind of supernatural. 'So there's a limit to how close I can get to him,' Sam said.

'Your mom's a full-blood. Surely he suspects.'

'He's willfully blind, I think. She has to go out for her evening run, she says, or she's spending the night with her sister in Waco, or she's driving over to visit me, or some other excuse.'

'Must be hard to maintain.'

'I would never try to do that. I almost married a regular girl once, while I was in the service. But I just couldn't marry someone and keep that big a secret. It saves my sanity, having someone to talk to about it, Sookie.' He smiled at me, and I appreciated the trust he was showing. 'If the Weres announce, then we'll all go public. It'll be a great burden off me.'

We both knew there would be new problems to face, but there wasn't any need to talk about future trouble. Trouble always came at its own pace.

'You got any sisters or brothers?' I asked.

'One of each. My sister is married with two kids, and my brother is still single. He's a great guy.' Sam was smiling and his face looked more relaxed than I'd ever seen. 'Craig's getting married in the spring, he says,' Sam went on. 'Maybe you can go to the wedding with me.'

I was so astonished I didn't know what to say, and I was very flattered and pleased. 'That sounds like fun. Tell me when you know the date,' I said. Sam and I had gone out, once, and it had been very pleasant; but it was in the midst of my problems with Bill and the evening had never been repeated.

Sam nodded casually, and the little jolt of tension that had run through me evaporated. After all, this was *Sam*, my boss, and come to think of it, also one of my best friends. He'd clicked into that slot during the past year. I got up. I had my purse, and I pulled on my jacket.

'Did you get an invitation for the Fangtasia Halloween party this year?' he asked.

'No. After the last party they invited me to, they might not want me to come back,' I said. 'Besides, with all the recent losses, I don't know if Eric'll feel like celebrating.'

'You think we ought to have a Halloween party at Merlotte's ?' he asked.

'Maybe not with candy and stuff like that,' I said, thinking hard. 'Maybe a goodie bag for each customer, with dry roasted peanuts? Or a bowl of orange popcorn on each table? And some decorations?'

Sam looked in the direction of the bar as if he could see through the walls. 'That sounds good. Make a thing of it.' Ordinarily we only decorated for Christmas, and that only after Thanksgiving, at Sam's insistence.

I waved good night and left the bar, leaving Sam to check that everything was locked tight.

The night had a cold bite to it. This would be one of the Halloweens that really felt like the Halloweens I'd seen in children's books.

In the center of the parking lot, his face turned up to the sliver of moon, his eyes closed, stood my great-grandfather. His pale hair hung down his back like a thick curtain. His myriad of fine creases were invisible in the moonlight, or else he'd divested himself of them. He was carrying his cane, and once again he was wearing a suit, a black suit. There was a heavy ring on his right hand, the hand gripping the cane.

He was the most beautiful being I'd ever seen.

He didn't look remotely like a human grandfather. Human grand-fathers wore gimme caps from the John Deere place and overalls. They took you fishing. They let you ride on their tractors. They groused at you for being too pampered and then they bought you candy. As for human great-grandfathers, most of us hardly got to know ours.

I became aware of Sam standing by my side.

'Who is that?' he breathed.

'That's my, ah, my great-granddad,' I said. He was right there in front of me. I had to explain.

'Oh,' he said, his voice was full of amazement.

'I just found out,' I said apologetically.

Niall stopped soaking up the moonlight and his eyes opened. 'My great-granddaughter,' he said, as if my presence in the Merlotte's parking lot was a pleasant surprise. 'Who is your friend?'

'Niall, this is Sam Merlotte, who owns this bar,' I said.

Sam extended his hand cautiously, and after a good look at it, Niall touched it with his own. I could feel Sam give a slight jerk, as if my great-grandfather had had a buzzer in his hand.

'Great-granddaughter,' Niall said, 'I hear you were in danger in the fracas between the werewolves.'

'Yes, but Sam was with me, and then Claudine came,' I said, feeling oddly defensive. 'I didn't know there was going to be a fracas, as you put it, when I went. I was trying to be a peacemaker. We were ambushed.'

'Yes, that's what Claudine reported,' he said. 'I understand the bitch is dead?'

By which he meant Priscilla. 'Yes, sir,' I said. 'The bitch is dead.'

'And then you were in danger again one night later?'

I was beginning to feel definitely guilty of something. 'Well, that's not actually my norm,' I said. 'It just happened that the vampires of Louisiana got overrun by the vampires of Nevada.'

Niall seemed only mildly interested. 'But you went as far as dialing the number I left you.'

'Ah, yes, sir, I was pretty scared. But then Eric knocked the phone out of my hand because he thought if you came into the equation, there'd be an out-and-out war. As it turned out, I guess that was for the best, because he surrendered to Victor Madden.' I was still a little angry about it, though, even after Eric's gift of the replacement phone.

'Ahhh.'

I couldn't make head nor tail of that noncommittal sound. This might be the downside of having a great-grandfather on site. I'd been called on the carpet. It was a feeling I hadn't had since I was a young teen and Gran had found out I'd skipped taking out the trash and folding the laundry. I didn't like the feeling now any more than I'd liked it then.

'I love your courage,' Niall said unexpectedly. 'But you are very frail – mortal, breakable, and short-lived. I don't want to lose you just when I finally became able to speak to you.'

'I don't know what to say,' I muttered.

'You don't want me to stop you from doing anything. You won't change. How can I protect you?'

'I don't think you can, not a hundred percent.'

'Then what use am I to you?'

'You don't have to be of use to me,' I said, surprised. He didn't seem to have the emotional set I had. I didn't know how to explain it to him. 'It's enough for me – it's wonderful – just knowing you exist. That you care about me. That I have living family, no matter how distant and different. And you don't think I'm weird or crazy or embarrassing.'

'Embarrassing?' He looked puzzled. 'You're far more interesting than most humans.'

'Thank you for not thinking I'm defective,' I said.

'Other humans think you're *defective*?' Niall sounded genuinely outraged.

'They can't be comfortable sometimes,' Sam said unexpectedly. 'Knowing she can read their minds.'

'But you, shapeshifter?'

'I think she's great,' Sam said. And I could tell he was absolutely sincere.

My back straightened. I felt a flush of pride. In the emotional warmth of the moment, I almost told my great-grandfather about the big problem I'd uncovered today, to prove I could share. But I had a pretty good feeling that his solution to the Sandra Pelt–Tanya Grissom Axis of Evil would be to cause their deaths in a macabre way. My sort-of cousin Claudine might be trying to become an angel, a being I associated with Christianity, but Niall Brigant was definitely from another ethos entirely. I suspected his outlook was, 'I'll take your eye ahead of time, just in case you want mine.' Well, maybe not that preemptive, but close.

'There is nothing I can do for you?' He sounded almost plaintive.

'I'd really like it if you'd just come spend some time with me at the house, when you have some to spare. I'd like to cook you supper. If you want to do that?' It made me feel shy, offering him something I wasn't sure he'd value.

He looked at me with glowing eyes. I could not read his face, and though his body was shaped like a human body, he was not. He was a complete puzzle to me. Maybe he was exasperated or bored or repulsed by my suggestion.

Finally Niall said, 'Yes. I'll do that. I'll tell you ahead of time, of course. In the meantime, if you need anything of me, call the number. Don't let anyone dissuade you if you think I can be of help. I will have words with Eric. He's been useful to me in the past, but he can't second-guess me with you.'

'Has he known I was your kin for very long?' I held my breath, waiting for the answer.

Niall had turned to go. Now he turned back a little, so I saw his face in profile. 'No,' he said. 'I had to know him better, first. I told him only before he brought you to meet me. He wouldn't help me until I told him why I wanted you.'

And then he was gone. It was like he'd walked through a door we couldn't see, and for all I knew, that was exactly what he'd done.

'Okay,' Sam said after a long moment. 'Okay, that was really ... different.'

'Are you all right with all this?' I waved a hand toward the spot where Niall had been standing. Probably. Unless what we'd seen had been some astral projection or something.

'It's not my place to be okay with it. It's your thing,' Sam said.

'I want to love him,' I said. 'He's so beautiful and he seems to care so much, but he's really, really . . .'

'Scary,' Sam finished.

'Yeah.'

'And he approached you through Eric?'

Since apparently my great-grandfather thought it was okay if Sam knew about him, I told Sam about my first meeting with Niall.

'Hmmm. Well, I don't know what to make of that. Vampires and fairies don't interact, because of the vampire tendency to eat fairies.'

'Niall can mask his scent,' I explained proudly.

Sam looked overloaded with information. 'That's another thing I've never heard of I hope Jason doesn't know about this?'

'Oh, God, no.'

'You know he'd be jealous and that would make him mad at you.'

'Since I know Niall and he doesn't?'

'Yep. Envy would just eat Jason up.'

'I know Jason's not the world's most generous person,' I began, to be cut off when Sam snorted. 'Okay,' I said, 'he's selfish. But he's still my brother anyway, and I have to stick by him. But maybe it's better if I never tell him. Still, Niall didn't have any problem showing himself to *you*, after telling me to keep him a secret.'

'I'm guessing he did some checking up,' Sam said mildly. He hugged me, which was a welcome surprise. I felt like I needed a hug after Niall's drop-in. I hugged Sam back. He felt warm, and comforting, and human.

But neither of us was 100 percent human.

In the next instant, I thought, *We are, too.* We had more in common with humans than with the other part of us. We lived like humans; we would die like humans. Since I knew Sam pretty well, I knew he wanted a family and someone to love and a future that contained all the things plain humans want: prosperity, good health, descendants, laughter. Sam didn't want to be a leader of any pack, and I didn't want to be princess of anybody – not that any pureblood fairy would ever think I was anything other than a lowly by-product of their own wonderfulness. That was one of the big differences between Jason and me. Jason would spend his life wishing he was more supernatural than he was; I had spent mine wishing I was less, if my telepathy was indeed supernatural.

Sam kissed me on the cheek, and then after a moment's hesitation, he turned to go into his trailer, walking through the gate in the carefully trimmed hedge and up the steps to the little deck he'd built outside his door. When he'd inserted the key, he turned to smile at me.

'Some night, huh?'

'Yeah,' I said. 'Some night.'

Sam watched while I got in my car, made a pressing gesture to remind me to lock my car doors, waited while I complied, and then went into his trailer. I drove home preoccupied with deep questions and shallow ones, and it was lucky there wasn't any traffic on the road.

Chapter 17

Amelia and Octavia were sitting at the kitchen table the next day when I shambled out. Amelia had used up all the coffee, but at least she'd washed the pot and it took only a few minutes to make myself a much-needed cup. Amelia and her mentor kept a tactful conversation going while I bumbled around getting some cereal, adding some sweetener, pouring milk over it. I hunched over the bowl because I didn't want to dribble milk down my tank top. And by the way, it was getting too cold to wear a tank top around the house. I pulled on a cheap jacket made of sweats material and was able to finish my coffee and cereal in comfort.

'What's up, you two?' I asked, signaling I was ready to interact with the rest of the world.

'Amelia told me about your problem,' Octavia said. 'And about your very kind offer.'

Ah-oh. What offer?

I nodded wisely, as if I had a clue.

'I'll be so glad to be out of my niece's house, you have no idea,' the older woman said earnestly. 'Janesha has three little ones, including one toddler, and a boyfriend that comes and goes. I'm sleeping on the living room couch, and when the kids get up in the morning, they come in and turn on the cartoons. Whether or not I'm up. It's their house, of course, and I've been there for weeks, so they've lost the sense that I'm company.'

I gathered that Octavia was going to be sleeping in the bedroom opposite me or in the extra one upstairs. I was voting for the one upstairs.

'And you know, now that I'm older, I need quicker access to a bathroom.' She looked at me with that humorous deprecation people show when they're admitting to a passage-of-time condition. 'So downstairs would be wonderful, especially since my knees are arthritic. Did I tell you Janesha's apartment is upstairs?'

'No,' I said through numb lips. Geez, this had happened so fast.

'Now, about your problem. I'm not a black witch at all, but you need to get these young women out of your life, both Ms Pelt's agent and Ms Pelt herself.'

I nodded vigorously.

'So,' Amelia said, unable to keep quiet any longer, 'we've come up with a plan.'

'I'm all ears,' I said, and poured myself a second cup of coffee. I needed it.

'The simplest way to get rid of Tanya, of course, is to tell your friend Calvin Norris what she's doing,' Octavia said.

I gaped at her. 'Ah, that seems likely to result in some pretty bad things happening to Tanya,' I said.

'Isn't that what you want?' Octavia looked innocent in a real sly way.

'Well, yeah, but I don't want her to die. I mean, I don't want anything she can't get over to happen to her. I just want her away and not coming back.'

Amelia said, 'Away and not coming back' sounds pretty final to me.'

It sounded that way to me, too. 'I'll rephrase. I want her to be off somewhere living her life but far away from me,' I said. 'Is that clear enough?' I wasn't trying to sound sharp; I just wanted to express myself.

'Yes, young lady, I think we can understand that,' said Octavia with frost in her voice.

'I don't want there to be any misunderstanding here,' I said. 'There's a lot at stake. I think Calvin kind of likes Tanya. On the other hand, I bet he could scare her pretty effectively.'

'Enough to get her to leave forever?'

'You'd have to demonstrate that you were telling the truth,' Amelia said. 'About her sabotaging you.'

'What do you have in mind?' I asked.

'Okay, here's what we think,' Amelia said, and just like that, Phase One was in place. It turned out to be something I could have thought of myself, but the witches' help made the planning run much more smoothly.

I called Calvin at home, and asked him to stop by when he had a minute to spare around lunchtime. He sounded surprised to hear from me, but he agreed to come.

He got a further surprise when he came into the kitchen and found Amelia and Octavia there. Calvin, the leader of the werepanthers who lived in the little community of Hotshot, had met Amelia several times before, but Octavia was new to him. He respected her immediately because he was able to sense her power. That was a big help.

Calvin was probably in his midforties, strong and solid, sure of himself. His hair was graying, but he was straight as an arrow in posture, and he possessed a huge calm that couldn't fail to impress. He'd been interested in me for a while, and I'd only been sorry I couldn't feel the same way. He was a good man.

'What's up, Sookie?' he said after he'd turned down the offer of cookies or tea or Coke.

I took a deep breath. 'I don't like to be a tale-teller, Calvin, but we have a problem,' I said.

'Tanya,' he said immediately.

'Yeah,' I said, not bothering to hide my relief.

'She's a sly one,' he said, and I was sorry to hear an element of admiration in his voice.

'She's a spy,' Amelia said. Amelia could cut right to the chase.

'Who for?' Calvin tilted his head to one side, unsurprised and curious.

I told him an edited version of the story, a story I was extremely sick of repeating. Calvin needed to know that the Pelts had a big beef with me, that Sandra would hound me to my grave, that Tanya had been planted as a gadfly.

Calvin stretched out his legs while he listened, his arms crossed over his chest. He was wearing brand-new jeans and a plaid shirt. He smelled like fresh-cut trees.

'You want to put a spell on her?' he asked Amelia when I'd finished.

'We do,' she said. 'But we need you to get her here.'

'What would the effect be? Would it hurt her?'

'She'd lose interest in doing harm to Sookie and all her family. She wouldn't want to obey Sandra Pelt anymore. It wouldn't hurt her physically at all.'

'Would this change her mentally?'

'No,' Octavia said. 'But it's not as sure a spell as the one that would make her not want to be here anymore. If we cast that one, she'd leave here, and she wouldn't want to come back.'

Calvin mulled this over. 'I kind of like that ole girl,' he said. 'She's a live one. I've been pretty concerned over the trouble she's causing Crystal and Jason, though, and I've been wondering what steps to take about Crystal's crazy spending. I guess this kind of brings the issue front and center.'

'You like her?' I said. I wanted all cards on the table.

'I said that.'

'No, I mean, you *like* her.'

'Well, her and me, we've had some good times now and then.'

'You don't want her to go away,' I said. 'You want to try the other thing.'

'That's about the size of it. You're right: she can't stay and keep on going like she is. She either changes her ways, or she leaves.' He looked unhappy about that. 'You working today, Sookie?'

I looked at the wall calendar. 'No, it's my day off.' I'd have two days in a row off.

'I'll get aholt of her and bring her by tonight. That give you ladies enough time?'

The two witches looked at each other and consulted silently.

'Yes, that will be fine,' Octavia said.

'I'll get her here by seven,' Calvin said.

This was moving with unexpected smoothness.

'Thanks, Calvin,' I said. 'This is really helpful.'

'This'll kill a lot of birds with one stone, if it works,' Calvin said. 'Of

course, if it don't work, you two ladies won't be my favorite people.'
His voice was completely matter-of-fact.

The two witches didn't look happy.

Calvin eyed Bob, who happened to stroll into the room. 'Hello,
brother,' Calvin said to the cat. He gave Amelia a narrowed-eye look.
'Seems to me like your magic don't work all the time.'

Amelia looked guilty and offended simultaneously. 'We'll get this
to work,' she said, tight-lipped. 'You just see.'

'I aim to.'

I spent the rest of the day doing my laundry, redoing my nails,
changing my sheets – all those tasks you save up for your day off.
I went by the library to swap books and absolutely nothing happened.
One of Barbara Beck's part-time assistants was on duty, which was
good. I didn't want to experience the horror of the attack all over
again, as I surely would in every encounter with Barbara for a long
time to come. I noticed the stain was gone from the library floor.

After that, I went to the grocery store. No Weres attacked, no
vampires rose. No one tried to kill me or anyone I knew. No secret
relatives revealed themselves, and not a soul tried to involve me in his
or her problems, marital or otherwise.

I was practically reeking with normality by the time I got home.

Tonight was my cooking night, and I'd decided to fix pork chops.
I have a favorite homemade breading mix that I make in a huge batch,
so I soaked the chops in milk and then dredged them with the mix so
they were ready for the oven. I fixed baked apples stuffed with raisins
and cinnamon and butter and popped them in to bake and I flavored
some canned green beans and some canned corn and put them on low
heat. After a while, I opened the oven to put in the meat. I thought
about making biscuits, but there seemed to be more than enough
calories on board.

While I cooked, the witches were doing stuff in the living room.
They seemed to be having a good old time. I could hear Octavia's
voice, which sounded very much like it was in teaching mode. Every
now and then, Amelia would ask a question.

I did a lot of muttering to myself while I cooked. I hoped this magical
procedure worked, and I was grateful to the witches for being so

willing to help. But I was feeling a little sideswiped on the domestic front. My brief mention to Amelia that Octavia could stay with us for a little while had been a spur of the moment thing. (I could tell I was going to have to be more careful in conversations with my roomie from now on.) Octavia hadn't said she'd be in my house for a weekend, or a month, or any measure of time. That scared me.

I could have cornered Amelia and told her, 'You didn't ask me if Octavia could stay *right now at this moment*, and it's my house,' I supposed. But I *did* have a free room, and Octavia *did* need someplace to stay. It was a little late to discover that I wasn't entirely happy at having a third person in the house – a third person I barely knew.

Maybe I could find a job for Octavia, because regular earnings would allow the older woman her independence and she'd move out of here. I wondered about the state of her house in New Orleans. I assumed it was unlivable. For all the power she had, I guess even Octavia couldn't undo the damage a hurricane had done. After her references to stairs and increased bathroom needs, I'd revised her age upward, but she still didn't seem any older than, say, sixty-three. That was practically a spring chicken, these days.

I called Octavia and Amelia to the table at six o'clock. I had the table set and the iced tea poured, but I let them serve their own plates from the stove. Not elegant, but it did save on dishes.

We didn't talk a lot as we ate. All three of us were thinking about the evening to come. As much as I disliked her, I was a little worried about Tanya.

I felt funny about the idea of altering someone, but the bottom line was, I needed Tanya off my back and out of my life and the lives of those around me. Or I needed her to get a new attitude about what she was doing in Bon Temps. I couldn't see any way around those facts. In line with my new practicality, I'd realized that if I had to choose between continuing my life with Tanya's interference or continuing my life with Tanya altered, there was no contest.

I cleared the plates away. Normally, if one of us cooked, the other did the dishes, but the two women had magical preparations to make. It was just as well; I wanted to keep busy.

We heard the gravel crunching under the wheels of a truck at 7:05.

When we'd asked him to have her here at seven, I hadn't realized he'd bring her as a parcel.

Calvin carried Tanya in over his shoulder. Tanya was compact, but no featherweight. Calvin was definitely working, but his breathing was nice and even and he hadn't broken a sweat. Tanya's hands and ankles were bound, but I noticed he'd wrapped a scarf under the rope so she wouldn't get chafed. And (thank God) she was gagged, but with a jaunty red bandanna. Yes, the head werepanther definitely had a thing for Tanya.

Of course, she was mad as a disturbed rattler, wriggling and twisting and glaring. She tried to kick Calvin, and he slapped her on her butt. 'You stop that now,' he said, but not as if he was particularly upset. 'You've done wrong; you got to take your medicine.'

He'd come in the front door, and now he dumped Tanya on the couch.

The witches had drawn some things in chalk on the floor of the living room, a process that hadn't found much favor with me. Amelia had assured me she could clean it all up, and since she was a champion cleaner, I'd let them proceed.

There were various piles of things (I really didn't want to look too closely) set around in bowls. Octavia lit the material in one bowl and carried it over to Tanya. She wafted the smoke toward Tanya with her hand. I took an extra step back, and Calvin, who was standing behind the couch and holding Tanya by the shoulders, turned his head. Tanya held her breath as long as she could.

After breathing the smoke, she relaxed.

'She needs to be sitting there,' Octavia said, pointing to an area circled by chalky symbols. Calvin plonked Tanya down on a straight-backed chair in the middle. She stayed put, thanks to the mysterious smoke.

Octavia started chanting in a language I didn't understand. Amelia's spells had always been in Latin, or at least a primitive form of it (she'd told me that), but I thought Octavia was more diverse. She was speaking something that sounded entirely different.

I'd been very nervous about this ritual, but it turned out to be pretty boring unless you were one of the participants. I wished I could open the windows to get the smell of the smoke out of the house, and I was glad Amelia had thought to take the batteries out of the smoke detectors. Tanya was clearly feeling something, but I wasn't sure it was the removal of the Pelt effect.

'Tanya Grissom,' Octavia said, 'yank the roots of evil out of your soul and remove yourself from the influence of those who would use you for evil ends.' Octavia made several gestures over Tanya while holding a curious item that looked awfully like a human bone wound around with a vine. I tried not to wonder where she'd gotten the bone.

Tanya squealed beneath her gag, and her back arched alarmingly. Then she relaxed.

Amelia made a gesture, and Calvin bent over to untie the red bandanna that had made Tanya look like a small bandit. He pulled another handkerchief, a clean white one, out of Tanya's mouth. She'd definitely been abducted with affection and consideration.

'I can't believe you're doing this to me!' Tanya shrieked the second her mouth would work. 'I can't believe you kidnapped me like a caveman, you big jerk!' If her hands had been free, Calvin would have taken a pummeling. 'And what the hell is up with this smoke? Sookie, are you trying to burn your house down? Hey, woman, would you get that crap out of my face?' Tanya batted at the vine-wrapped bone with her bound hands.

'I'm Octavia Fant.'

'Well, goody, Octavia Fant. Get me out of these ropes!'

Octavia and Amelia exchanged glances.

Tanya appealed to me. 'Sookie, tell these nuts to let me go! Calvin, I was halfway interested in you before you tied me up and dumped me here! What did you think you were doing?'

'Saving your life,' Calvin said. 'You ain't gonna run now, are you? We got some talking to do.'

'Okay,' Tanya said slowly, as she realized (I could hear her) that something serious was afoot. 'What's all this about?'

'Sandra Pelt,' I said.

'Yeah, I know Sandra. What about her?'

'What's your connection?' Amelia asked.

'What's your interest, Amy?' Tanya countered.

'Amelia,' I corrected, sitting on the big ottoman in front of Tanya. 'And you need to answer this question.'

Tanya gave me a sharp look – she had a repertoire of them – and said, 'I used to have a cousin who was adopted by the Pelts, and Sandra was my cousin's adopted sister.'

'Do you have a close friendship with Sandra?' I said.

'No, not especially. I haven't seen her in a while.'

'You didn't make a bargain with her recently?'

'No, Sandra and I don't see each other too much.'

'What do you think of her?' Octavia asked.

'I think she's a double-barreled bitch. But I sort of admire her,' Tanya said. 'If Sandra wants something, she goes after it.' She shrugged. 'She's kind of extreme for my taste.'

'So if she told you to ruin someone's life, you wouldn't do it?' Octavia was eyeing Tanya intently.

'I got better fish to fry than that,' Tanya said. 'She can go around ruining lives on her own, if she wants to do it so bad.'

'You wouldn't be a part of that?'

'No,' Tanya said. She was sincere, I could tell. In fact, she was beginning to get anxious at our line of questioning. 'Ah, have I done something bad to somebody?'

'I think you got in a little over your head,' Calvin said. 'These nice ladies have intervened. Amelia and Miss Octavia are, ah, wise women. And you know Sookie already.'

'Yeah, I know Sookie.' Tanya gave me a sour look. 'She won't make friends with me no matter what I do.'

Well, yeah, I didn't want you close enough to stab me in the back, I thought, but I didn't say anything.

'Tanya, you've taken my sister-in-law shopping a little too much lately,' I said.

Tanya burst into laughter. 'Too much retail therapy for the pregnant bride?' she said. But then she looked puzzled. 'Yeah, it does seem like we went to the mall in Monroe too many times for my checkbook. Where'd I get the money? I don't even like shopping that much. Why'd I do that?'

'You're not going to do it anymore,' Calvin said.

'You don't tell me what I'm going to do, Calvin Norris!' Tanya shot back. 'I won't go shopping because I don't want to go, not because you tell me not to.'

Calvin looked relieved.

Amelia and Octavia looked relieved.

We all nodded simultaneously. This was Tanya, all right. And she seemed to be minus the destructive guidance of Sandra Pelt. I didn't know if Sandra had whipped up some witchcraft of her own, or if she'd just offered Tanya a lot of money and talked her into thinking Debbie's death was my fault, but the witches appeared to have been successful in excising the tainted Sandra portion of Tanya's character.

I felt oddly deflated at this easy – easy to me, that is – removal of a real thorn in my side. I found myself wishing we could abduct Sandra Pelt and reprogram her, too. I didn't think she'd be as easy to convert. There had been some big pathology going on in the Pelt family.

The witches were happy. Calvin was pleased. I was relieved. Calvin told Tanya he was going to take her back to Hotshot. The somewhat-puzzled Tanya made her departure with a lot more dignity than her entrance. She didn't understand why she'd been in my house and she didn't seem to remember what the witches had done. But she also didn't seem upset about that confusion in her memory.

The best of all possible worlds.

Maybe Jason and Crystal could work things out now that Tanya's pernicious influence was gone. After all, Crystal had really wanted to marry Jason, and she had seemed genuinely pleased that she was pregnant again. Why she was so discontented now . . . I simply didn't get it.

I could add her to the long list of people I didn't understand.

While the witches cleaned up the living room with the windows open – though it was a chilly night, I wanted to get rid of the lingering smell of the herbs – I sprawled on my bed with a book. I found I wasn't focused enough to read. Finally, I decided to go outside, and I threw on a hoody and called to Amelia to let her know. I sat in one of the wooden chairs Amelia and I had bought at Wal-Mart at end-of-summer clearance-sale prices, and I admired the matching table with its umbrella all over again. I reminded myself to take the umbrella down and cover the furniture for the winter. Then I leaned back and let go of my thoughts.

For a while it was nice to simply be outside, smelling the trees and the ground, hearing a whip-poor-will give its enigmatic call from the surrounding woods. The security light made me feel safe, though I knew that was an illusion. If there's light, you can just see what's coming for you a little more clearly.

Bill stepped out of the woods and strolled silently over to the yard set. He sat in one of the other chairs.

We didn't speak for several moments. I didn't feel the surge of anguish I'd felt over the past few months when he was around. He barely disturbed the fall night with his presence, he was so much a part of it.

'Selah has moved to Little Rock,' he said.

'How come?'

'She got a position with a large firm,' he said. 'It was what she told me she wanted. They specialize in vampire properties.'

'She hooked on vamps?'

'I believe so. Not my doing.'

'Weren't you her first?' Maybe I sounded a little bitter. He'd been my first, in every way.

'Don't,' he said, and turned his face toward me. It was radiantly pale. 'No,' he said finally. 'I was not her first. And I always knew it was the vampire in me that attracted her, not the person who was a vampire.'

I understood what he was saying. When I'd learned he'd been ordered to ingratiate himself with me, I'd felt it was the telepath in me that had gotten his attention, not the woman who was the telepath. 'What goes around, comes around,' I said.

'I never cared about her,' he said. 'Or very little.' He shrugged. 'There've been so many like her.'

'I'm not sure how you think this is going to make me feel.'

'I'm only telling you the truth. There has been only one you.' And then he got up and walked back into the woods, human slow, letting me watch him leave.

Apparently Bill was conducting a kind of stealth campaign to win back my regard. I wondered if he dreamed I could love him again. I still felt pain when I thought of the night I'd learned the truth. I figured my regard would be the outer limits of what he could hope to earn. Trust, love? I couldn't see that happening.

I sat outside for a few more minutes, thinking about the evening I'd just had. One enemy agent down. The enemy herself to go. Then I thought of the police search for the missing people, all Weres, in Shreveport. I wondered when they'd give up.

Surely I wouldn't have to deal with Were politics again any time soon; the survivors would be absorbed in setting their house in order.

I hoped Alcide was enjoying being the leader, and I wondered if he'd succeeded in creating yet another little purebred Were the night of the takeover. I wondered who had taken the Furnan children.

As long as I was speculating, I wondered where Felipe de Castro had established his headquarters in Louisiana or if he'd stayed in Vegas. I wondered if anyone had told Bubba that Louisiana was under a new regime, and I wondered if I'd ever see him again. He had one of the most famous faces in the world, but his head had been sadly addled by being brought over at the last possible second by a vampire working in the morgue in Memphis. Bubba had not weathered Katrina well; he'd gotten cut off from the other New Orleans vampires and had had to subsist on rats and small animals (left-behind pet cats, I suspected) until he'd been rescued one night by a search party of Baton Rouge vamps. The last I'd heard, they'd had to send him out of state for rest and recuperation. Maybe he'd wind up in Vegas. He'd always done well in Vegas, when he was alive.

Suddenly, I realized I was stiff with sitting so long, and the night had grown uncomfortably cold. My jacket wasn't doing the job. It was time to go inside and go to bed. The rest of the house was dark, and I figured Octavia and Amelia were exhausted by their witch work.

I heaved myself up from the chair, let the umbrella down, and opened the toolshed door, leaning the umbrella against a bench where the man I'd thought was my grandfather had made repairs. I shut the toolshed door, feeling I was shutting summer inside.

Chapter 18

After a quiet and peaceful Monday off, I went in Tuesday to work the lunch shift. When I'd left home, Amelia had been painting a chest of drawers she'd found at the local junk store. Octavia had been trimming the dead heads off the roses. She'd said they needed pruning back for the winter, and I'd told her to have at it. My grandmother had been the rose person in our household, and she hadn't let me lay a finger on them unless they needed spraying for aphids. That had been one of my jobs.

Jason came into Merlotte's for lunch with a bunch of his coworkers. They put two tables together and formed a cluster of happy men. Cooler weather and no big storms made for happy parish road crews. Jason seemed almost overly animated, his brain a jumble of leaping thoughts. Maybe having the pernicious influence of Tanya erased had already made a difference. But I made a real effort to stay out of his head, because after all, he was my brother.

When I carried a big tray of Cokes and tea over to the table, Jason said, 'Crystal says hey.'

'How's she feeling today?' I asked, to show proper concern, and Jason made a circle of his forefinger and thumb. I served the last mug of tea, careful to put it down evenly so it wouldn't spill, and I asked Dove Beck, a cousin of Alcee's, if he wanted any extra lemon.

'No, thanks,' he said politely. Dove, who'd gotten married the day after graduation, was a whole different kettle of fish from Alcee. At thirty, he was younger, and as far as I could tell – and I could tell pretty far – he didn't have that inner core of anger that the detective did. I'd gone to school with one of Dove's sisters.

'How's Angela?' I asked him, and he smiled.

'She married Maurice Kershaw,' he said. 'They got a little boy, cutest kid in the world. Angela's a new woman – she don't smoke or drink, and she's in church when the doors open.'

'I'm glad to hear that. Tell her I asked,' I said, and began taking orders. I heard Jason telling his buddies about a fence he was going to build, but I didn't have time to pay attention.

Jason lingered after the other men were going out to their vehicles. 'Sook, would you run by and check on Crystal when you get off?'

'Sure, but won't you be leaving work then?'

'I got to go over to Clarice and pick up some chain-link. Crystal wants us to fence in some of the backyard for the baby. So it'll have a safe place to play.'

I was surprised that Crystal was showing that much foresight and maternal instinct. Maybe having the baby would change her. I thought about Angela Kershaw and her little boy.

I didn't want to count up how many girls younger than me had been married for years and had babies – or just had the babies. I told myself envy was a sin, and I worked hard, smiling and nodding to everyone. Luckily, it was a busy day. During the afternoon lull, Sam asked me to help him take inventory in the storeroom while Holly covered the bar and the floor. We only had our two resident alcoholics to serve, so Holly was not going to have to work very hard. Since I was very nervous with Sam's Blackberry, he entered the totals while I counted, and I had to climb up on a stepladder and then back down about fifty times, counting and dusting. We bought our cleaning supplies in bulk. We counted all those, too. Sam was just a counting fool today.

The storeroom doesn't have any windows, so it got pretty warm in there while we were working. I was glad to get out of its stuffy confines when Sam was finally satisfied. I pulled a spiderweb out of his hair as I went by on my way to the bathroom, where I scrubbed my hands and carefully wiped my face, checking my ponytail (as best I could) for any spiderwebs I might have picked up myself.

As I left the bar, I was so looking forward to getting in the shower that I almost turned left to go home. Just in time, I remembered I'd promised to look in on Crystal, so I turned right instead.

Jason lived in my parents' house, and he'd kept it up very nicely. My brother was a house-proud kind of guy. He didn't mind spending his free time on painting, mowing, and basic repairs, a side of him I always found a bit surprising. He'd recently painted the outside a buff color and the trim a glowing white, and the little house looked very spruce. There was a driveway that made a U shape in front. He'd added a branch that led to the porte cochere in back of the house, but I pulled up to the front steps. I stuffed my car keys in my pocket and crossed the porch. I turned the knob because I planned on sticking my head in the door and calling to Crystal, since I was family. The front door was unlocked, as most front doors were during the daytime. The family room was empty.

'Hey, Crystal, it's Sookie!' I called, though I tried to keep my voice subdued so I wouldn't startle her if she were napping.

I heard a muffled sound, a moan. It came from the biggest bedroom, the one my parents had used, which lay across the family room and to my right.

Oh, shit, she's miscarrying again, I thought, and dashed to the closed door. I flung it open so hard it bounced off the wall, but I didn't pay a bit of attention, because bouncing on the bed were Crystal and Dove Beck.

I was so shocked, so angry, and so distraught that as they stopped what they were doing and stared up at me, I said the worst thing I could think of. 'No wonder you lose all your babies.' I spun on my heel and marched out of the house. I was so outraged I couldn't even get in the car. It was really unfortunate that Calvin pulled up behind me and leaped from his truck almost before it stopped.

'My God, what's wrong?' he said. 'Is Crystal okay?'

'Why don't you ask her that?' I said nastily, and climbed into my car only to sit there shaking. Calvin ran into the house as if he had to put out a fire, and I guess that was about the size of it.

'Jason, *dammit*,' I yelled, thumping my fist on my steering wheel. I should have taken the time to listen to Jason's brain. He'd known good and well that since he had business in Clarice, Dove and Crystal would probably take the opportunity to have a tryst. He'd planned on me being dutiful and dropping by. It was just too big a coincidence that Calvin had shown up. He must have also told Calvin to check on Crystal. So there was no deniability, and no chance of hushing this up – not since Calvin and I both knew. I had been right to worry about the terms of the marriage, and now I had something entirely new to worry about.

Plus, I was ashamed. I was ashamed of the behavior of everyone involved. In my code of conduct, which doesn't really make me a very good Christian at all, what single people do in caring relationships is their own business. Even in a more casual relationship – well, if the people respect one another, okay. But a couple who's promised to be faithful, who's pledged that publicly, are governed by a whole different set of rules, in my world.

Not in Crystal's world, or Dove's world, apparently.

Calvin came back down the steps looking years older than he had when he'd bounded up them. He stopped by my car. He wore an expression twin to mine – disillusion, disappointment, disgust. Lots of *dises* there.

'I'll be in touch,' he said. 'We got to have the ceremony now.'

Crystal came out on the porch wrapped in a leopard-print bathrobe, and rather than endure her speaking to me I started the car and left as quickly as I could. I drove home in a daze. When I came in the back door, Amelia was chopping up something on the old cutting board, the one that had survived the fire with only scorch marks. She turned to speak to me and had opened her mouth when she saw my face. I shook my head at her, warning her not to talk, and I went straight into my room.

This would have been a good day for me to be living by myself again.

I sat in my room in the little chair in the corner, the one that had seated so many visitors lately. Bob was curled up in a ball on my bed, a place he was expressly forbidden to sleep. Someone had opened my door during the day. I thought about chewing Amelia out about that, then discarded the idea when I saw a pile of clean and folded underwear lying on top of my dresser.

'Bob,' I said, and the cat unfolded and leaped to his feet in one fluid movement. He stood on my bed, staring at me with wide golden eyes. 'Get the hell out of here,' I said. With immense dignity Bob leaped down from the bed and stalked to the door. I opened it a few inches and he went out, managing to leave the impression that he was doing this of his own free will. I shut the door behind him.

I love cats. I just wanted to be by myself.

The phone rang, and I stood up to answer it.

'Tomorrow night,' Calvin said. 'Wear something comfortable. Seven o'clock.' He sounded sad and tired.

'Okay,' I said, and we both hung up. I sat there a while longer. Whatever this ceremony consisted of, did I have to be a participant? Yeah, I did. Unlike Crystal, I kept my promises. I'd had to stand up for Jason at his wedding, as his closest relative, as a surrogate to take his punishment if he was unfaithful to his new wife. Calvin had stood up for Crystal. And now look what we'd come to.

I didn't know what was going to happen, but I knew it was going to be awful. Though the werepanthers understood the necessity for breeding each available pure male panther to each available pure female panther (the only way to produce purebred baby panthers), they also believed once the breeding had been given a chance, any partnerships formed should be monogamous. If you didn't want to take that vow, you didn't form a partnership or marry. This was the way they ran their community. Crystal would have absorbed these rules from birth, and Jason had learned them from Calvin before the wedding.

Jason didn't call, and I was glad. I wondered what was happening at his house, but only in a dull kind of way. When had Crystal met Dove Beck? Did Dove's wife know about this? I wasn't surprised that Crystal had cheated on Jason, but I was a little astonished at her choice.

I decided that Crystal had wanted to make her betrayal as emphatic as it could possibly be. She was saying, 'I'll have sex with someone else while I'm carrying your child. And he'll be smarter than you, and a different race from you, and he'll even work for you!' Twisting the knife in deeper with every layer. If this was retaliation for the damn cheeseburger, I'd say she'd gotten a steak-size vengeance.

Because I didn't want to seem like I was sulking, I came out for supper, which was lowly and comforting tuna noodle casserole with peas and onions. After stacking the dishes for Octavia to take care of, I retreated back to my room. The two witches were practically tip-toeing up and down the hall because they were so anxious not to disturb me, though of course they were dying to ask me what the problem was.

But they didn't; God bless them. I really couldn't have explained. I was too mortified.

I said about a million prayers before I went to sleep that night, but none of them ended up making me feel any better.

I went to work the next day because I had to. Staying home wouldn't have made me feel any better. I was profoundly glad Jason didn't come into Merlotte's, because I would have thrown a mug at him if he had.

Sam eyed me carefully several times and finally he drew me behind the bar with him. 'Tell me what's happening,' he said.

Tears flooded my eyes, and I was within an ace of making a real scene. I squatted down hastily, as if I'd dropped something on the floor, and I said, 'Sam, please don't ask me. I'm too upset to talk about it.' Suddenly, I realized it would be a big comfort to tell Sam, but I just couldn't, not in the crowded bar.

'Hey, you know I'm here if you need me.' His face was serious. He patted my shoulder.

I was so lucky to have him for a boss.

His gesture reminded me that I had lots of friends who would not dishonor themselves as Crystal had done. Jason had dishonored himself, too, by forcing Calvin and me to witness her cheap betrayal. I had so many friends who would not do such a thing! It was a trick of fate that the one who would was my own brother.

This thought made me feel better and stronger.

I actually had a backbone by the time I got home. No one else was there. I hesitated, wondering whether I could call Tara or beg Sam to take an hour off, or even call Bill to go with me to Hotshot . . . but that was just weakness talking. This was something I had to do by myself. Calvin had warned me to wear something comfortable and not to dress up, and my Merlotte's outfit was certainly both those things. But it seemed wrong to wear my work clothes to an event like this. There might be blood. I didn't know what to anticipate. I pulled on yoga pants and an old gray sweatshirt. I made sure my hair was pulled back. I looked like I was dressed to clean out my closets.

On the drive to Hotshot, I turned up the radio and sang at the top of my lungs to keep myself from thinking. I harmonized with Evanescence and agreed with the Dixie Chicks that I wasn't going to back down . . . a good spine-stiffening song to listen to.

I reached Hotshot well before seven. I'd last been out here at Jason and Crystal's wedding, where I'd danced with Quinn. That visit of Quinn's had been the only time he and I had been intimate. In hindsight, I regretted having taken that step. It had been a mistake. I'd been banking on a future that never came to pass. I'd jumped the gun. I hoped I'd never make that mistake again.

I parked, as I had the night of Jason's wedding, by the side of the road. There weren't nearly as many cars here tonight as there had been then, when many plain human people had been guests. But there were a few extra vehicles. I recognized Jason's truck. The others belonged to the few werepanthers who didn't live in Hotshot.

A little crowd had already assembled in the backyard of Calvin's house. People made way for me until I'd gotten to the center of the gathering and found Crystal, Jason, and Calvin. I saw some familiar faces. A middle-aged panther named Maryelizabeth nodded to me. I saw her daughter nearby. The girl, whose name I couldn't remember, was by no means the only underage observer. I got that creepy feeling that raised the hairs on my arms, the way I did every time I tried to picture everyday life in Hotshot.

Calvin was staring down at his boots, and he didn't look up. Jason didn't meet my eyes, either. Only Crystal was upright and defiant, her dark eyes catching mine, daring me to stare her down. I did dare, and after a moment she dropped her gaze to somewhere in the middle distance.

Maryelizabeth had a tattered old book in her hand, and she opened it to a page she'd marked with a torn piece of newspaper. The community seemed to still and settle. This was the purpose for which they'd assembled.

'We people of the fang and claw are here because one of us broke her vows,' Maryelizabeth read. 'At the marriage of Crystal and Jason, werepanthers of this community, they each promised to remain true to their marriage vows, both in the way of the cat and the way of the human. Crystal's surrogate was her uncle Calvin, and Jason's was his sister, Sookie.'

I was aware of the eyes of all the assembled community moving from Calvin to me. A lot of those eyes were golden yellow. Inbreeding in Hotshot had produced some slightly alarming results.

'Now that Crystal has broken her vows, a fact witnessed by the surrogates, her uncle has offered to take the punishment since Crystal is pregnant.'

This was going to be even nastier than I'd suspected.

'Since Calvin takes Crystal's place, Sookie, do you choose to take Jason's place?'

Oh, *crap*. I looked at Calvin and I knew my whole face was asking him if there was any way out of this. And his whole face told me no. He actually looked sorry for me.

I would never forgive my brother – or Crystal – for this.

'Sookie,' Maryelizabeth prompted.

'What would I have to do?' I said, and if I sounded sullen and grudging and angry, I thought I had a good reason.

Maryelizabeth opened the book again and read the answer. 'We exist by our wits and our claws, and if faith is broken, a claw is broken,' she said.

I stared at her, trying to make sense of that.

'Either you or Jason has to break Calvin's finger,' she said simply. 'In fact, since Crystal broke the faith completely, you have to break two, at least. More would be better. Jason gets to pick, I guess.'

More would be better. Jesus Christ, Shepherd of Judea. I tried to be dispassionate. Who could cause the most damage to my friend Calvin? My brother, no doubt about it. If I was a true friend to Calvin, I would do this. Could I bring myself to? And then it was taken out of my hands.

Jason said, 'I didn't think it would happen this way, Sookie.' He sounded simultaneously angry, confused, and defensive. 'If Calvin stands in for Crystal, I want Sookie to stand in for me,' he told Maryelizabeth. I never thought I could hate my own brother, but at that moment I found out it was possible.

'So be it,' said Maryelizabeth.

I tried to boost myself up mentally. After all, this wasn't maybe quite as bad as I'd anticipated. I'd pictured Calvin being whipped or having to whip Crystal. Or we might have had to do some awful thing involving knives; that would have been way worse.

I tried to believe this might not be so bad right up until the time two of the males carried out a pair of concrete blocks and put them on top of the picnic table.

And then Maryelizabeth produced a brick. She held it out to me.

I began to shake my head involuntarily because I felt a heavy twinge in my stomach. Nausea did flip-flops in my belly. Looking at the common red brick, I began to have an idea what this was going to cost me.

Calvin stepped forward and took my hand. He leaned over to talk very close to my ear. 'Darlin',' he said, 'you have to do this. I accepted this, when I stood up for her when she married. And I knew what she was. And you know Jason. This might easily have been the other way 'round. I might be about to do this to you. And you don't heal as well. This is better. And it has to be. Our people require this.' He straightened and looked me right in the eyes. His own were golden, utterly strange, and quite steady.

I pinched my lips together, and I made myself nod. Calvin gave me a bracing look and took his place by the table. He put his hand on the concrete blocks. With no further ado, Maryelizabeth handed me the brick. The rest of the panthers waited patiently for me to perform the punishment. The vampires would have dressed this all up with a special wardrobe and probably an extraspecial fancy brick from an old temple or something, but not the panthers. It was just a damn brick. I held it with both hands gripping one long side.

After I'd looked at it for a long minute, I said to Jason. 'I don't want to talk to you again. Ever.' I faced Crystal. 'I hope you enjoyed it, bitch,' I said, and I turned as quick as I could and brought the brick down on Calvin's hand.

Chapter 19

Amelia and Octavia hovered around for two days before they decided leaving me alone was the best policy. Reading their anxious thoughts just made me surlier, because I didn't want to accept comfort. I should suffer for what I'd done, and that meant I couldn't accept any easing of my misery. So I gloomed and sulked and brooded and rained my grim mood all over my house.

My brother came into the bar once, and I turned my back on him. Dove Beck didn't choose to drink at Merlotte's, which was a good thing, though he was the least guilty of the bunch as far as I was concerned – though that didn't make him any clean Gene. When Alcee Beck came in, it was clear his brother had confided in him, because Alcee looked even angrier than usual, and he met my eyes every chance he got, just to let me know he was my equal.

Thank God, Calvin didn't show. I couldn't have stood it. I heard enough talk around the bar from his coworkers at Norcross about the accident he'd had while he was working on his truck at home.

Most unexpectedly, on the third night Eric walked into Merlotte's. I took one look at him and suddenly my throat seemed to ease and I felt tears well up in my eyes. But Eric walked through as though he owned the place, and he went into the hall to Sam's office. Moments later Sam stuck his head out and beckoned to me.

After I walked in, I didn't expect Sam to shut the office door.

'What's wrong?' Sam asked me. He'd been trying to find out for days, and I'd been fending off his well-meant queries.

Eric was standing to one side, his arms crossed over his chest. He made a gesture with one hand that said, 'Tell us; we're waiting.' Despite his brusqueness, his presence relaxed the big knot inside me, the one that had kept the words locked in my stomach.

'I broke Calvin Norris's hand into bits,' I said. 'With a brick.'

'Then he was . . . He stood up for your sister-in-law at the wedding,' Sam said, figuring it out quickly. Eric looked blank. The vampires know something about the wereanimals – they have to – but the vamps think they are far superior, so they don't make an effort to learn specifics about the rituals and rhythms of being a were.

'She had to break his hand, which represents his claws in panther form,' Sam explained impatiently. 'She stood up for Jason.' And then Sam and Eric exchanged a look that scared me in its complete agreement. Neither of them liked Jason one little bit.

Sam looked from me to Eric as if he expected Eric to do something to make me feel better. 'I don't belong to him,' I said sharply, since all this was making me feel handled in a major way. 'Did you think Eric coming would make me all happy and carefree?'

'No,' Sam said, sounding a little angry himself. 'But I hoped it would help you talk about whatever was wrong.'

'What's wrong,' I said very quietly. 'Okay, what's wrong is that my brother arranged for Calvin and me to check on Crystal, who's about four months pregnant, and he fixed it so we'd get there at about the same time. And when we checked, we found Crystal in bed with Dove Beck. As Jason knew we would.'

Eric said, 'And for this, you had to break the werepanther's fingers.' He might have been asking if I'd had to wear chicken bones and turn around three times, it was so obvious he was inquiring into the quaint customs of a primitive tribe.

'Yes, Eric, that's what I had to do,' I said grimly. 'I had to break my friend's fingers with a brick in front of a crowd.'

For the first time Eric seemed to realize that he'd taken the wrong approach. Sam was looking at him in total exasperation. 'And I thought you'd be such a big help,' he said.

'I have a few things going in Shreveport,' Eric answered with a shade of defensiveness. 'Including hosting the new king.'

Sam muttered something that sounded suspiciously like, 'Fucking vampires.'

This was totally unfair. I'd expected tons of sympathy when I finally confessed the reason for my bad mood. But now Sam and Eric were so wrapped up in being irritated with each other that neither one of them was giving me a moment's thought. 'Well, thanks, guys,' I said. 'This has been a lot of fun. Eric, big help there – I appreciate the kind words.' And I left in what my grandmother called high dudgeon. I stomped back out into the bar and waited on tables so grimly that some people were scared to call me over to order more drinks.

I decided to clean the surfaces behind the bar, because Sam was still in his office with Eric ... though possibly Eric had left out the back door. I scrubbed and polished and pulled some beers for Holly, and I straightened everything so meticulously that Sam might have a wee problem finding things. Just for a week or two.

Then Sam came out to take his place, looked at the counter in mute displeasure, and jerked his head to indicate I should get the hell out from behind the bar. My bad mood was catching.

You know how it is sometimes, when someone really tries to cheer you up? When you just decide that by golly, nothing in the world is going to make you feel better? Sam had thrown Eric at me like he was throwing a happy pill, yet he was aggravated that I hadn't swallowed it. Instead of being grateful that Sam was fond enough of me to call Eric, I was mad at him for his assumption.

I was in a totally black mood.

Quinn was gone. I'd banished him. Stupid mistake or wise decision? Verdict still out.

Lots of Weres were dead in Shreveport because of Priscilla, and I'd watched some of them die. Believe me, that sticks with you.

More than a few vampires were dead, too, including some I'd known fairly well.

My brother was a devious manipulative bastard.

My great-grandfather wasn't ever going to take me fishing.

Okay, now I was getting silly. Suddenly, I smiled, because I was picturing the prince of the fairies in old denim overalls and a Bon Temps Hawks baseball cap, carrying a can of worms and a couple of fishing poles.

I caught Sam's eye as I cleared a table of plates. I winked at him.

He turned away, shaking his head, but I caught a hint of a smile at the corners of his mouth.

And just like that, my bad mood was officially over. My common sense kicked in. There was no point in lashing myself over the Hotshot incident any longer. I'd had to do what I'd had to do. Calvin understood that better than I did. My brother was an asshole, and Crystal was a whore. These were facts I had to deal with. Granted, they were both unhappy people who were acting out because they were married to the wrong spouse, but they were also both chronologically adults, and I couldn't fix their marriage any more than I'd been able to prevent it.

The Weres had dealt with their own problems in their own way, and I'd done my best to help them. Vampires, ditto . . . sort of.

Okay. Not *all* better, but enough better.

When I got off work, I wasn't completely annoyed to find Eric waiting by my car. He seemed to be enjoying the night, standing all by himself in the cold. I was shivering myself because I hadn't brought a heavy jacket. My Windbreaker wasn't enough.

'It's been nice to be by myself for a while,' Eric said unexpectedly.

'I guess at Fangtasia you're always surrounded,' I said.

'Always surrounded by people wanting things,' he said.

'But you enjoy that, right? Being the big kahuna?'

Eric looked like he was mulling that over. 'Yes, I like that. I like being the boss. I don't like being . . . overseen. Is that a word? I'll be glad when Felipe de Castro and his minion Sandy take their departure. Victor will stay to take over New Orleans.'

Eric was *sharing*. This was almost unprecedented. This was like a normal give-and-take between equals.

'What's the new king like?' Cold as I was, I couldn't resist keeping the conversation going.

'He's handsome, ruthless, and clever,' Eric said.

'Like you.' I could have slapped myself.

Eric nodded after a moment. 'But more so,' Eric said grimly. 'I'll have to keep very alert to stay ahead of him.'

'How gratifying to hear you say so,' said an accented voice.

This was definitely an *Oh, shit!* moment. (An OSM, as I called them to myself.) A gorgeous man stepped out from the trees, and I blinked as I took him in. As Eric bowed, I scanned Felipe de Castro from his gleaming shoes to his bold face. As I bowed, too, belatedly, I realized that Eric hadn't been exaggerating when he said the new king was handsome. Felipe de Castro was a Latin male who threw Jimmy Smits into the shade, and I am a big admirer of Mr Smits. Though perhaps five foot ten or so, Castro carried himself with such importance and straight posture that you couldn't think of him as short – rather, he made other men look too tall. His dark thick hair was clipped close to his head, and he had a mustache and chin strip. He had caramel skin and dark eyes, strong arched eyebrows, a bold nose. The king wore a cape – no kidding, a real full-length black cape. I'll tell you how impressive he was; I didn't even think of *giggling*. Other than the cape, he seemed dressed for a night that might include flamenco dancing, with a white shirt, black vest, and black dress slacks. One of Castro's ears was pierced, and there was a dark stone in it. The overhead security light didn't let me get a better idea of what it might be. Ruby? Emerald?

I'd straightened up and I was staring again. But when I glanced at Eric, I saw he was still bowing. Ah-oh. Well, I wasn't one of his subjects and I wasn't going to do that again. It had gone against my Americanness to do it once.

'Hi, I'm Sookie Stackhouse,' I said, since the silence was getting awkward. I automatically held out my hand, remembered vamps didn't shake, and snatched it back. 'Excuse me,' I said.

The king inclined his head. 'Miss Stackhouse,' he said, his accent strumming my name delightfully. ('Meees Stekhuss.')

'Yes, sir. I'm sorry to meet you and run, but it's really cold out here and I need to get home.' I beamed at him, my lunatic beam I give when I'm really nervous. 'Good-bye, Eric,' I babbled, and stood on tiptoe to kiss him on the cheek. 'Give me a call when you have a minute. Unless you need me to stay, for some crazy reason?'

'No, lover, you need to go home and get into the warmth,' Eric said, clasping both my hands in his. 'I'll call you when my work permits.'

When he let go of me, I did an awkward sort of dip in the king's direction (American! Not used to bowing!) and hopped into my car before either vampire could change his mind about my departure. I felt like a coward – a very relieved coward – as I backed out of my space and drove out of the parking lot. But I was already debating the wisdom of my departure as I turned onto Hummingbird Road.

I was worried about Eric. This was a fairly new phenomenon, one that made me very uneasy, and it had started the night of the coup. Worrying about Eric was like worrying about the well-being of a rock or a tornado. When had I ever had to worry about him before? He was one of the most powerful vampires I'd ever met. But Sophie-Anne had been even more powerful and protected by the huge warrior Sigebert, and look what had happened to her. I felt abruptly, acutely miserable. What was wrong with me?

I had a terrible idea. Maybe I was worried simply because Eric was worried? Miserable because Eric was miserable? Could I receive his emotions this strongly and from this great a distance? Should I turn around and find out what was happening? If the king was being cruel to Eric, I couldn't possibly be of any assistance. I had to pull over to the side of the road. I couldn't drive anymore.

I'd never had a panic attack, but I thought I was having one now. I was paralyzed with indecision; again, not one of my usual characteristics. Struggling with myself, trying to think clearly, I realized I had to turn back whether I wanted to or not. It was an obligation I couldn't ignore, not because I was bonded to Eric, but because I liked him.

I turned the wheel and did a U-turn in the middle of Hummingbird Road. Since I'd seen only two cars since I'd left the bar, the maneuver was no big traffic violation. I drove back a lot faster than I'd left, and when I got to Merlotte's, I found that the customer parking lot was completely empty. I parked in front and pulled my old softball bat out from under the seat. My grandmother had given it to me for my sixteenth birthday. It was a very good bat, though it had seen better days. I crept around the building, taking advantage of the bushes that grew at the foundation for cover. Nandinas. I hate nandinas. They're straggly and ugly and leggy, and I'm allergic to them. Though I was covered with a Windbreaker, pants, and socks, the minute I began threading my way among the plants, my nose began to run.

I peeked around the corner very cautiously.

I was so shocked I couldn't believe what I was seeing.

Sigebert, the queen's bodyguard, had *not* been killed in the coup. No, sirree, he was still among the undead. And he was here in the Merlotte's parking lot, and he was having a lot of fun with the new king, Felipe de Castro, and with Eric, and with Sam, who had been swept up in the net probably by simply leaving his bar to walk to his trailer.

I took a deep breath – a deep but *silent* breath – and made myself analyze what I was seeing. Sigebert was a mountain of a man, and he'd been the queen's muscle for centuries. His brother, Wybert, had died in the queen's service, and I was sure Sigebert had been a target of the Nevada vamps; they'd left their mark on him. Vampires heal fast, but Sigebert had been wounded badly enough that even days after he'd fought, he was still visibly damaged. There was a huge cut across his forehead and a horrible-looking mark just above where I thought his heart would be. His clothes were ripped and stained and filthy. Maybe the Nevada vamps thought he'd disintegrated when in fact he'd managed to get away and hide. *Not important*, I told myself.

The important part was that he'd succeeded in binding both Eric and Felipe de Castro with silver chains. How? *Not important*, I told myself again. Maybe this tendency to mentally wander was coming from Eric, who was looking much more battered than the king. Of course, Sigebert would see Eric as a traitor.

Eric was bleeding from the head and his arm was clearly broken. Castro was bleeding sluggishly from the mouth, so Sigebert had maybe stomped on him. Eric and Castro were both lying on the ground, and in the harsh security light they both looked whiter than snow. Sam had been tied to the bumper of his own truck somehow, and he wasn't damaged at all, at least so far. Thank God.

I tried to figure out how I could conquer Sigebert with my aluminum softball bat, but I didn't come up with any good ideas. If

I rushed him, he'd just laugh. Even as grievously wounded as he was, he was still a vampire and I was no match for him unless I had a great idea. So I watched, and I waited, but in the end I couldn't stand to see him hurting Eric anymore; believe me, when a vampire kicks you, you get plenty hurt. Plus, Sigebert was having a great time with the big knife he had brought.

The biggest weapon at my disposal? Okay, that would be my car. I felt a little pang of regret, because it was the best car I'd ever had, and Tara had sold it to me for a dollar when she'd gotten a newer one. But it was the only thing I could think of that would make a dent in Sigebert.

So back I crept, praying that Sigebert would be so absorbed in his torture that he wouldn't notice the sound of the car door. I laid my head on the steering wheel and thought as hard as I've ever thought. I considered the parking lot and its topography, and I thought about the location of the bound vampires, and I took a deep breath and turned the key. I started around the building, wishing my car could creep through the damn nandina bushes like I had, and I swung wide to allow room to charge, and my lights caught Sigebert, and I hit the accelerator and went straight at him. He tried to get out of the way, but he was none too bright and I'd caught him with his pants down (literally – I really didn't like to think about his next torture plan) and I hit him very hard, and up he bounced, to land on the roof of the car with a huge thud.

I screamed and braked, because this was as far as my plan had gone. He slid down the back of the car, leaving a horrible sheet of dark blood, and disappeared from view. Scared he'd pop up in the rearview mirror, I threw the car into reverse and hit the pedal again. *Bump. Bump.* I yanked the gear stick into park and leaped out, bat in hand, to find Sigebert's legs and most of his torso were wedged under the car. I dashed over to Eric and began fumbling with the silver chain, while he stared at me with his eyes wide. Castro was cursing in Spanish, fluently and fluidly, and Sam was saying, 'Hurry, Sookie, hurry!' which really didn't help my powers of concentration.

I gave up on the damn chains and got the big knife and cut Sam free so he could help. The knife came close enough to his skin to make him yelp a time or two, but I was really doing the best I could, and he didn't bleed. To give him credit, he made it over to Castro in record time and began freeing him while I ran back to Eric, laying the knife on the ground beside us as I worked. Now that I had at least one ally who had the use of his hands and legs, I was able to concentrate, and I got Eric's legs unbound (at least now he could run away – I guess that was my thinking) and then, more slowly, his arms and hands. The silver had been wound around him many times, and Sigebert had made sure it touched Eric's hands. They looked ghastly. Castro had suffered even more from the chains because Sigebert had divested him of his beautiful cape and most of his shirt.

I was unwinding the last strand when Eric shoved me as hard as he could, grabbed the knife, and leaped to his feet so swiftly I saw only a blur. Then he was on Sigebert, who had actually lifted the car to release his own trapped legs. He'd begun dragging himself out from under, and in another minute he would have been ambulatory.

Did I mention it was a big knife? And it must have been sharp, too, because Eric landed by Sigebert, said, 'Go to your maker,' and cut off the warrior vampire's head.

'Oh,' I said shakily, and sat down abruptly on the cold parking lot gravel. 'Oh, wow.' We all remained where we were, panting, for a good five minutes. Then Sam straightened up from the side of Felipe de Castro and offered him a hand. The vampire took it, and when he was upright, he introduced himself to Sam, who automatically introduced himself right back.

'Miss Stackhouse,' the king said, 'I am in your debt.'

Damn straight.

'It's okay,' I said in a voice that wasn't nearly as level as it should be.

'Thank you,' he said. 'If your car is too damaged to repair, I will be very glad to buy you another one.'

'Oh, thanks,' I said with absolute sincerity, as I stood up. 'I'll try to drive it home tonight. I don't know how I can explain the damage. Do you think the body shop would believe I ran over an alligator?' That did happen occasionally. Was it weird that I was worried about the car insurance?

'Dawson would look at it for you,' Sam said. His voice was as odd as mine. He, too, had thought he was going to die. 'I know he's a motorcycle repairman, but I bet he could fix your car. He works on his own all the time.'

'Do what is necessary,' said Castro grandly. 'I will pay. Eric, would you care to explain what just happened?' His voice was considerably more acerbic.

'You should ask your crew to explain,' Eric retorted, with some justification. 'Didn't they tell you Sigebert, the queen's bodyguard, was dead? Yet here he is.'

'An excellent point.' Castro looked down at the crumbling body. 'So that was the legendary Sigebert. He's gone to join his brother, Wybert.' He sounded quite pleased.

I hadn't known the brothers were famous among the vampires, but they'd certainly been unique. Their mountainous physiques, their broken and primitive English, their utter devotion to the woman who'd turned them centuries before – sure, any right-minded vampire would love that story. I sagged where I stood, and Eric, moving faster than I could see, picked me up. It was a very Scarlett and Rhett moment, spoiled only by the fact that there were two other guys there, we were in a humdrum parking lot, and I was unhappy about the damage to my car. Plus not a little shocked.

'How'd he get the jump on three strong guys like you-all?' I asked. I didn't worry about Eric holding me. It made me feel tiny, not a feeling I got to enjoy all that often.

There was a moment of general embarrassment.

'I was standing with my back to the woods,' Castro explained. 'He had the chains arranged for throwing. ... Your word is almost the same. *Lazo.*'

'Lasso,' Sam said.

'Ah, lasso. The first one, he threw around me, and of course, the shock was great. Before Eric could land on him, he had Eric as well. The pain from the silver ... very quickly we were bound. When this one' – he nodded toward Sam – 'came to our aid, Sigebert knocked him unconscious and got rope from the back of Sam's truck and tied him up.'

'We were too involved in our discussion to be wary,' Eric said. He sounded pretty grim, and I didn't blame him. But I decided to keep my mouth shut.

'Ironic, eh, that we needed a human girl to rescue us,' the king said blithely, the very idea that I'd decided not to voice.

'Yes, very amusing,' Eric said in a dreadfully unamused voice. 'Why did you return, Sookie?'

'I felt your, ah, anger at being attacked.' For 'anger' read 'despair'.

The new king looked very interested. 'A blood bond. How interesting.'

'No, not really,' I said. 'Sam, I wonder if you'd mind driving me home. I don't know where you gentlemen left your cars, or if you flew. I *do* wonder how Sigebert knew where to find you.'

Felipe de Castro and Eric shared almost identical expressions of deep thought.

'We'll find out,' Eric said, and set me down. 'And then heads are going to roll.' Eric was good at setting heads to rolling. It was one of his favorite things. I was willing to put my money on Castro sharing that predilection, because the king was looking positively gleeful in anticipation.

Sam fished his keys out of his pocket without a word, and I climbed into the truck with him. We left the two vampires involved in a deep conversation. Sigebert's corpse, still partially under my poor car, was almost gone, leaving a dark greasy residue on the gravel of the parking lot. The good thing about vampires – no corpse disposal.

'I'll call Dawson tonight,' Sam said unexpectedly.

'Oh, Sam, thank you,' I said. 'I'm so glad you were there.'

'It's the parking lot of my *bar*,' he said, and it might have been my own guilty reaction, but I thought I detected some reproach. I suddenly came to the full realization that Sam had walked into a situation in his own backyard, a situation he had no stake or interest in, and that he'd almost died as a result. And why had Eric been in the parking lot back of Merlotte's? To talk to me. And then Felipe de Castro had followed to talk to Eric . . . though I wasn't sure why. But the point was, them being there at all was my fault.

'Oh, Sam,' I said, almost in tears, 'I'm so sorry. I didn't know Eric would wait for me, and I sure didn't know the king would follow him.

I still don't know why he was there. I'm so sorry,' I said again. I would say it a hundred times if it would take that tone out of Sam's voice.

'It's not your fault,' he said. 'I asked Eric to come here in the first place. It's their fault. I don't know how we can pry you loose from them.'

'This was bad, but somehow you're not taking it like I thought you would.'

'I just want to be left in peace,' he said unexpectedly. 'I don't want to get involved in supernatural politics. I don't want to have to take sides in Were shit. I'm not a Were. I'm a shape-shifter, and shifters don't organize. We're too different. I hate vampire politics even more than Were politics.'

'You're mad at me.'

'No!' He seemed to be struggling with what he wanted to say. 'I don't want that for you, either! Weren't you happier before?'

'You mean before I knew any vampires; before I knew about the rest of the world that lies outside the boundaries?'

Sam nodded.

'In some ways. It was nice to have a clear path before me,' I said. 'I do get really sick of the politics and the battles. But my life wasn't any prize, Sam. Every day was a struggle just to act like I was a regular human, like I didn't know all the things I know about other humans. The cheating and infidelity, the little acts of dishonesty, the unkindness. The really severe judgments people pass on each other. Their lack of charity. When you know all that, it's hard to keep going sometimes. Knowing about the supernatural world puts all that in a different perspective. I don't know why. People aren't any better or worse than the supernaturals, but they're not all there is, either.'

'I guess I understand,' Sam said, though he sounded a little doubtful.

'Plus,' I said very quietly, 'it's nice to be valued for the very thing that makes regular people think I'm just a crazy girl.'

'Definitely understand that,' Sam said. 'But there's a price.'

'Oh, no doubt about it.'

'You willing to pay?'

'So far.'

We chugged up my driveway. No lights on. The witchy duo had

gone to bed, or else they were out partying or casting spells.

'In the morning, I'll call Dawson,' Sam said. 'He'll check out your car, make sure you can drive it, or he'll get it towed to his place. Think you can get a ride to work?'

'I'm sure I can,' I said. 'Amelia can bring me in.'

Sam walked me to the back door like he was bringing me home from a date. The porch light was on, which was thoughtful of Amelia. Sam put his arms around me, which was a surprise, and then he just snugged his head in close to mine, and we stood there enjoying each other's warmth for a long moment.

'We survived the Were war,' he said. 'You made it through the vampire coup. Now we lived through the attack of the berserk body-guard. I hope we keep up our record.'

'Now you're scaring me,' I said as I remembered all the other things I'd survived. I should be dead, no doubt about it.

His warm lips brushed my cheek. 'Maybe that's a good thing,' he said, and turned to go back to his truck.

I watched him climb in and reverse, and then I unlocked the back door and went to my room. After all the adrenaline and the fear and the accelerated pace of life (and death) in the parking lot of Merlotte's, my own room seemed very quiet and clean and secure. I'd done my best to kill someone tonight. It was only by chance Sigebert had survived my attempt at vehicular homicide. Twice. I couldn't help but notice that I wasn't feeling remorseful. This was surely a flaw, but at the moment I just didn't care. There were definitely parts of my character I didn't approve of, and maybe from time to time I had moments when I didn't like myself much. But I got through each day as it came to me, and so far I'd survived everything life had thrown at me. I could only hope that the survival was worth the price I'd paid.

Chapter 20

To my relief, I woke up in an empty house. Neither Amelia's nor Octavia's throbbing heads were under my roof. I lay in bed and reveled in the knowledge. Maybe the next time I had a whole day off, I could spend it completely alone. That didn't seem a likely occurrence, but a girl can dream. After I planned my day (call Sam to find out about my car, pay some bills, go to work), I got into the shower and really scrubbed. I used as much hot water as I wanted. I painted my toenails and my fingernails, and I pulled on a pair of sweatpants and a T-shirt and went in to make some coffee. The kitchen was spanking clean; God bless Amelia.

The coffee was great, the toast delicious spread with blueberry jam. Even my taste buds were happy. After I cleaned up from breakfast, I was practically singing with the pleasure of solitude. I went back to my room to make my bed and put on my makeup.

Of course, that was when the knock came at the back door, nearly making me jump out of my skin. I stepped into some shoes and went to answer it.

Tray Dawson was there, and he was smiling. 'Sookie, your car is doing fine,' he said. 'I had to do a little replacing here and there, and it's the first time I ever had to scrape vampire ash off an undercarriage, but you're good to go.'

'Oh, thanks! Can you come in?'

'Just for a minute,' he said. 'You got a Coke in the refrigerator?'

'I sure do.' I brought him a Coke, asked if he wanted some cookies or a peanut butter sandwich to go with it, and when he'd turned that down, I excused myself to finish my makeup. I'd figured Dawson would run me to the car, but he'd driven it over to my place, as it turned out, so I'd need to give him a ride instead.

I had my checkbook out and my pen in hand when I sat at the table opposite the big man and asked him how much I owed him.

'Not a dime,' Dawson said. 'The new guy paid for it.'

'The new king?'

'Yeah, he called me in the middle of the night last night. Told me the story, more or less, and asked me if I could look at the car first thing in the morning. I was awake when he called, so it didn't make me no nevermind. I got over to Merlotte's this morning, told Sam he wasted a phone call since I already knew all about it. I followed him while he drove the car out to my place, and we put it up on the rack and had a good look.'

This was a long speech for Dawson. I put my checkbook back in my purse and listened, silently asking him if he wanted more Coke by pointing at his glass. He shook his head, letting me know he was satisfied. 'We had to tighten up a few things, replace your windshield fluid reservoir. I knew just where another car like yours was at Rusty's Salvage, and it didn't take no time to do the job.'

I could only thank him again. I drove Dawson out to his repair shop. Since the last time I'd driven by, he'd trimmed up the front yard of his home, a modest but tidy frame house that stood next door to the big shop. Dawson had also put all the bits and pieces of motorcycles under cover somewhere, instead of having them strewn around in a handy but unattractive spread. And his pickup was clean.

As Dawson slid out of the car, I said, 'I'm so grateful. I know cars aren't your specialty and I do appreciate your working on mine.' Repairman to the underworld, that was Tray Dawson.

'Well, I did it because I wanted to,' Dawson said, and then he paused. 'But if you could see your way to it, I'd sure like it if you'd put in a word for me with your friend Amelia.'

'I don't have much influence over Amelia,' I said. 'But I'll be glad to tell her what a sterling character you are.'

He smiled very broadly: no suppression there. I didn't think I'd ever seen Dawson crack such a grin. 'She sure looks healthy,' he said, and since I had no idea what Dawson's criteria for admiration were, that was a big clue.

'You call her up, I'll give a reference,' I said.

'It's a deal.'

We parted happy, and he loped across the newly neat yard to his shop. I didn't know if Dawson would be to Amelia's taste or not, but I'd do my best to persuade her to give him a chance.

As I drove home, I listened to the car for any strange noise. It purred away.

Amelia and Octavia came in as I was leaving for work.

'How are you feeling?' Amelia said with a knowing air.

'Fine,' I said automatically. Then I understood she thought I hadn't come home the night before. She thought I'd been having a good time with someone. 'Hey, you remember Tray Dawson, right? You met him at Maria-Star's apartment.'

'Sure.'

'He's going to call you. Be sweet.'

I left her grinning after me as I got into my car.

For once, work was boring and normal. Terry was substituting since Sam hated to work on Sunday afternoons. For a while, he'd even closed for the day. Now we opened late on Sunday and we closed early, so I was ready to start home by seven. No one showed up in the parking lot, and I was able to walk directly to my car without being accosted for a long, weird conversation or being attacked.

The next morning I had errands to run in town. I was short on cash, so I drove to the ATM, waving at Tara Thornton du Rone. Tara smiled and waved back. Marriage was suiting her, and I hoped she and JB were having a happier time of it than my brother and his wife. As I drove away from the bank, to my astonishment I spotted Alcide Herveaux coming out of the offices of Sid Matt Lancaster, an ancient and renowned lawyer. I pulled into Sid Matt's parking lot, and Alcide came over to talk to me.

I should have driven on, hoping he hadn't noticed me.

The conversation was awkward. Alcide had had a lot to deal with, in all fairness. His girlfriend was dead, brutally murdered. Several other members of his pack were also dead. He'd had a huge cover-up to arrange. But he was now the leader of the pack, and he had gotten to celebrate his victory in the traditional way. In hindsight, I suspect he was fairly embarrassed at having sex with a young woman in public, especially so soon after his girlfriend's death. This was quite a bundle of emotions I was reading in his head, and he was flushed when he came to my car window.

'Sookie, I haven't had a chance to thank you for all your help that night. It's lucky for us your boss decided to come with you.'

Yeah, since you wouldn't have saved my life and he did, I'm glad, too. 'No problem, Alcide,' I said, my voice wonderfully even and calm. I was going to have a good day, dammit. 'Have things settled down in Shreveport?'

'The police don't seem to have a clue,' he said, glancing around to make sure no one else was within hearing distance. 'They haven't found the site yet, and there's been a lot of rain. We're hoping sooner rather than later they'll cut back on their investigation.'

'You-all still planning the big announcement?'

'It'll have to be soon. The heads of other packs in the area have been in contact with me. We don't have a meeting of all the leaders like the vampires do, mostly because they have one leader for each state and we have a hell of a lot of packleaders. Looks like we'll all elect a representative from the packleaders, one from each state, and those representatives will go to a national meeting.'

'That sounds like a step in the right direction.'

'Also, we might ask other wereanimals if they want to come in with us. Like, Sam could belong to my pack in an auxiliary way, though he's not a Were. And it would be good if the lone wolves, like Dawson, came to some of the pack parties ... came out howling with us or something.'

'Dawson seems to like his life the way it is,' I said. 'And you'll have to talk to Sam, not me, about whether he wants to associate with you-all formally.'

'Sure. You seem to have a lot of influence with him. Just thought I'd mention it.'

I didn't see it that way. Sam had a lot of influence over me, but whether I had any over him . . . I was dubious. Alcide began making the little shifts in stance that told me as clearly as his brain had that he was about to go his way on whatever business had brought him to Bon Temps.

'Alcide,' I said, seized by an impulse, 'I do have a question.'

He said, 'Sure.'

'Who's taking care of the Furnan children?'

He looked at me, then away. 'Libby's sister. She's got three of her own, but she said she was glad to take them in. There's enough money for their upbringing. When it comes time for them to go to college, we'll see what we can do for the boy.'

'For the boy?'

'He's pack.'

If I'd had a brick in my hand, I wouldn't have minded using it on Alcide. Good God almighty. I took a deep breath. To give him credit, the sex of the child wasn't the issue at all. It was his pure blood.

'There may be enough insurance money for the girl to go, too,' Alcide said, since he was no fool. 'The aunt wasn't too clear about that, but she knows we'll help.'

'And she knows who 'we' is?'

He shook his head. 'We told her it was a secret society, like the Masons, that Furnan belonged to.'

There didn't seem to be anything left to say.

'Good luck,' I said. He'd already had a fair share of that, no matter what you thought about the two dead women that had been his girlfriends. After all, he himself had survived to achieve his father's goal.

'Thank you, and thanks again for your part in that luck. You're still a friend of the pack,' he said very seriously. His beautiful green eyes lingered on my face. 'And you're one of my favorite women in the world,' he added unexpectedly.

'That's a real nice compliment, Alcide,' I said, and drove away. I was glad I'd talked to him. Alcide had grown up a lot in the past few weeks. All in all, he was changing into a man I admired much more than I had the old one.

I'd never forget the blood and the screaming of the horrific night in the abandoned office park in Shreveport, but I began to feel that some good had come out of it.

When I returned home, I found that Octavia and Amelia were in the front yard, raking. This was a delightful discovery. I hated raking worse than anything in the world, but if I didn't go over the yard once or twice during the fall, the pine needle buildup was dreadful.

I had been thanking people all day long. I parked in the back and came out the front.

'Do you bag these up or burn them?' Amelia called.

'Oh, I burn 'em when there's not a burn ban on,' I said. 'It's so nice of you both to think of doing this.' I wasn't aiming to gush – but having your very least favorite chore done for you was really quite a treat.

'I need the exercise,' Octavia said. 'We went to the mall in Monroe yesterday, so I did get some walking in.'

I thought Amelia treated Octavia more like a grandmother than a teacher.

'Did Tray call?' I asked.

'He sure did.' Amelia smiled broadly.

'He thought you were fine-looking.'

Octavia laughed. 'Amelia, you're a femme fatale.'

She looked happy and said, 'I think he's an interesting guy.'

'A bit older than you,' I said, just so she'd know.

Amelia shrugged. 'I don't care. I'm ready to date. I think Pam and I are more buddies than honeys. And since I found that litter of kittens, I'm open for guy business.'

'You really think Bob made a choice? Wouldn't that have been, like, instinct?' I said.

Just then, the cat in question wandered across the yard, curious to see why we were all standing out in the open when there was a perfectly good couch and a few beds in the house.

Octavia gave a gusty sigh. 'Oh, hell,' she muttered. She straightened and held her hands out. '*Potestas mea to in formam veram tuam commutabit natura ips reaffirmet Incantationes praeviae deletae sunt,*' she said.

The cat blinked up at Octavia. Then it made a peculiar noise, a kind of cry I'd never heard come out of a cat's throat before. Suddenly the air around him was thick and dense and cloudy and full of sparks. The cat shrieked again. Amelia was staring at the animal with her mouth wide open. Octavia looked resigned and a little sad.

The cat writhed on the fading grass, and suddenly it had a human leg.

'God almighty!' I said, and clapped a hand over my mouth.

Now it had two legs, two hairy legs, and then it had a penis, and then it began to be a man all over, shrieking all the while. After a horrible two minutes, the witch Bob Jessup lay on the lawn, shaking all over but entirely human again. After another minute, he stopped shrieking and just twitched. Not an improvement, really, but easier on the eardrums.

Then he lunged to his feet, leaped onto Amelia, and made a determined effort to choke her to death.

I grabbed his shoulders to pull him off of her, and Octavia said, 'You don't want me to use magic on you again, right?'

That proved a very effective threat. Bob let go of Amelia and stood panting in the cold air. 'I can't believe you did that to me!' he said. 'I can't believe I spent the last few months as a cat!'

'How do you feel?' I asked. 'Are you weak? Do you need help into the house? Would you like some clothes?'

He looked down at himself vaguely. He hadn't worn clothes in a while, but suddenly he turned red, very nearly all over. 'Yes,' he said stiffly. 'Yes, I would like some clothes.'

'Come with me,' I said. The dusk was coming on as I led Bob into the house. Bob was a smallish guy, and I thought a pair of my sweats might fit him. No, Amelia was a little taller, and a clothes donation from her would be only fair. I spotted the basket full of folded clothes on the stairs where Amelia had left it to carry up the next time she went to her room. Lo and behold, there was an old blue sweatshirt and a pair of black sweat pants. I handed the clothes to Bob wordlessly, and he pulled them on with trembling fingers. I flipped through the stack and found a pair of socks that were plain white. He sat down on the couch to pull them on. That was as far as I could go toward clothing him. His feet were larger than mine or Amelia's, so shoes were out.

Bob wrapped his arms around himself like he feared he was going to disappear. His dark hair was clinging to his skull. He blinked, and I wondered what had happened to his glasses. I hoped Amelia had stored them somewhere.

'Bob, can I get you a drink?' I asked.

'Yes, please,' he said. He seemed to be having a bit of trouble getting his mouth to form the words. His hand moved up to his mouth in a curious gesture, and I realized it was just like my cat Tina's movement when she had raised her paw to lick it before she used it to groom herself. Bob realized what he was doing and lowered his hand abruptly.

I thought about bringing him milk in a bowl but decided that would be insulting. I brought him some iced tea instead. He gulped it but made a face.

'Sorry,' I said. 'I should have asked if you like tea.'

'I do like tea,' he said, and stared at the glass as if he'd just connected tea with the liquid he'd had in his mouth. 'I'm just not used to it anymore.'

Okay, I know this is really awful, but I actually opened my mouth to ask him if he wanted some kibble. Amelia had a bag of 9Lives on the back porch shelf. I bit the inside of my mouth, hard. 'What about a sandwich?' I asked. I had no idea what to talk to Bob about. Mice?

'Sure,' he said. He didn't seem to know what he wanted to do next.

So I made him a peanut butter and jelly, and a ham and pickle on whole wheat with mustard. He ate them both, chewing very slowly and carefully. Then he said, 'Excuse me,' and got up to find the bathroom. He shut the door behind him, and stayed in there for a long time.

Amelia and Octavia had come in by the time Bob emerged.

'I'm so sorry,' Amelia said.

'Me, too,' Octavia said. She looked older and smaller.

'You knew all along how to change him?' I tried to keep my voice level and nonjudgmental. 'Your failed attempt was a fraud?'

Octavia nodded. 'I was scared if you didn't need me, I wouldn't get to visit anymore. I'd have to go stay all day at my niece's. It's so much nicer here. I would have said something soon, because my conscience was bothering me something awful, especially since I'm living here.'

She shook her gray head from side to side. 'I'm a bad woman for letting Bob be a cat for extra days.'

Amelia was shocked. Obviously, her teacher's fall from grace was an amazing development to Amelia, clearly overshadowing her own guilt about what she'd done to Bob in the first place. Amelia was definitely a live-in-the-moment kind of person.

Bob came out of the bathroom. He marched up to us. 'I want to go back to my place in New Orleans,' Bob said. 'Where the hell are we? How did I get here?'

Amelia's face lost all its animation. Octavia looked grim. I quietly left the room. It was going to be very unpleasant, the two women telling Bob about Katrina. I didn't want to be around while he tried to process that terrible news on top of everything else he was trying to handle.

I wondered where Bob had lived, if his house or apartment was still standing, if his possessions were somehow intact. If his family was alive. I heard Octavia's voice rising and falling, and then I heard a terrible silence.

Chapter 21

The next day I took Bob to Wal-Mart to purchase some clothes. Amelia had pressed some money into Bob's hand, and the young man had accepted it because he had no choice. He could hardly wait to get away from Amelia. And I couldn't say as how I blamed him.

As we drove to town, Bob kept blinking around him in a stunned way. When we entered the store, he went to the nearest aisle and rubbed his head against the corner. I smiled brightly at Marcia Albanese, a wealthy older woman who was on the school board. I hadn't seen her since she'd given Halleigh a wedding shower.

'Who's your friend?' Marcia asked. She was both naturally social and curious. She didn't ask about the head rubbing, which endeared her to me forever.

'Marcia, this is Bob Jessup, a visitor from out of town,' I said, and wished I'd prepared a story. Bob nodded at Marcia with wide eyes and held out his hand. At least he didn't poke her with his head and demand to have his ears scratched. Marcia shook hands and told Bob she was pleased to meet him.

'Thanks, nice to meet you, too,' Bob said. Oh, good, he sounded really normal.

'Are you going to be in Bon Temps long, Bob?' Marcia said.

'Oh, God, no,' he said. 'Excuse me, I have to buy some shoes.' And he walked off (very smoothly and sinuously) to the men's shoe aisles.

He was wearing a pair of flip-flops Amelia had donated, bright green ones that weren't quite big enough.

Marcia was clearly taken aback, but I really couldn't think of a good explanation. 'See you later,' I said, and followed in his wake. Bob got some sneakers, some socks, two pairs of pants, two T-shirts, and a jacket, plus some underwear. I asked Bob what he'd like to eat, and he asked me if I could make salmon croquettes.

'I sure can,' I said, relieved he'd asked for something so easy, and got the cans of salmon I'd need. He also wanted chocolate pudding, and that was easy enough, too. He left the other menu selections up to me.

We had an early supper that night before I had to leave for work, and Bob seemed really pleased with the croquettes and the pudding. He looked much better, too, since he'd showered and put on his new clothes. He was even speaking to Amelia. I gathered from their conversation that she'd taken him through the websites about Katrina and its survivors, and he'd been in contact with the Red Cross. The family he'd grown up in, his aunt's, had lived in Bay Saint Louis, in southern Mississippi, and we all knew what had happened there.

'What will you do now?' I asked, since I figured he'd had a while to think about it now.

'I've got to go see,' he said. 'I want to try to find out what happened to my apartment in New Orleans, but my family is more important. And I've got to think of something to tell them, to explain where I've been and why I haven't been in touch.'

We were all silent, because that was a puzzler.

'You could tell 'em you were enchanted by an evil witch,' Amelia said glumly.

Bob snorted. 'They might believe it,' he said. 'They know I'm not a normal person. But I don't think they'd be able to swallow that it lasted so long. Maybe I'll tell them that I lost my memory. Or that I went to Vegas and got married.'

'You contacted them regularly, before Katrina?' I said.

He shrugged. 'Every couple of weeks,' he said. 'I didn't think of us as close. But I would definitely have tried after Katrina. I love them.' He looked away for a minute.

We kicked around ideas for a while, but there really wasn't a credible reason he would have been out of touch for so long. Amelia said she was going to buy Bob a bus ticket to Hattiesburg and he would try to find a ride from there into the most affected area so he could track down his people.

Amelia was clearing her conscience by spending money on Bob. I had no issue with that. She should be doing so; and I hoped Bob would find his folks, or at least discover what had happened to them, where they were living now.

Before I left for work, I stood in the doorway of the kitchen for a minute or two, looking at the three of them. I tried to see in Bob what Amelia had seen, the element that had attracted her so powerfully. Bob was thin and not particularly tall, and his inky hair naturally lay flat to his skull. Amelia had unearthed his glasses, and they were black-rimmed and thick. I'd seen every inch of Bob, and I realized Mother Nature had been generous to him in the man-bits department, but surely that wasn't enough to explain Amelia's ardent sexcapades with this guy.

Then Bob laughed, the first time he'd laughed since he'd become human again, and I got it. Bob had white, even teeth and great lips, and when he smiled, there was a kind of sardonic, intellectual sexiness about him.

Mystery solved.

When I got home, he would be gone, so I said good-bye to Bob, thinking I'd never see him again, unless he decided to return to Bon Temps to get revenge on Amelia.

As I drove into town, I wondered if we could get a real cat. After all, we had the litter box and the cat food. I'd ask Amelia and Octavia in a couple of days. That would surely give them time to stop being so antsy about Bob's cat-dom.

Alcide Herveaux was sitting at the bar talking with Sam when I came into the main room ready for work. Odd, him turning up again. I stopped for a second, and then made my feet move again. I managed a nod, and waved to Holly to tell her I was taking over. She held up a finger, indicating she was taking care of one customer's bill, and then she'd be out of there. I got a hello from one woman and a howdy from another man, and I felt instantly comfortable. This was my place, my home away from home.

Jasper Voss wanted another rum and Coke, Catfish wanted a pitcher of beer for himself and his wife and another couple, and one of our alcoholics, Jane Bodehouse, was ready to eat something. She said she didn't care what it was, so I got her the chicken tender basket. Getting Jane to eat at all was a real problem, and I hoped she'd down at least half of the basket. Jane was sitting at the other end of the bar from Alcide, and Sam jerked his head sideways to indicate I should join them. I turned Jane's order in and then I reluctantly went over to them. I leaned on the end of the bar.

'Sookie,' Alcide said, nodding to me. 'I came to say thank you to Sam.'

'Good,' I said bluntly.

Alcide nodded, not meeting my eyes.

After a moment the new packleader said, 'Now no one will dare to try to encroach. If Priscilla hadn't attacked at the moment she picked, with us all together and aware of the danger we faced as a group, she could have kept us divided and kept picking us off until we'd killed each other.'

'So she went crazy and you got lucky,' I said.

'We came together because of your talent,' Alcide said. 'And you'll always be a friend of the pack. So is Sam. Ask us to do a service for you, any time, any place, and we'll be there.' He nodded to Sam, put some money on the bar, and left.

Sam said, 'Nice to have a favor stashed in the bank, huh?'

I had to smile back. 'Yeah, that's a good feeling.' In fact, I felt full of good cheer all of a sudden. When I looked at the door, I found out why. Eric was coming in, with Pam beside him. They sat at one of my tables, and I went over, consumed with curiosity. Also exasperation. Couldn't they stay away?

They both ordered TrueBlood, and after I served Jane Bodehouse her chicken basket and Sam warmed up the bottles, I was headed back to their table. Their presence wouldn't have rocked any boats if Arlene and her buddies hadn't been in the bar that night.

They were sneering together in an unmistakable way as I put the bottles in front of Eric and Pam, and I had a hard time maintaining my waitress calm as I asked the two if they wanted mugs with that.

'The bottle will be fine,' Eric said. 'I may need it to smash some skulls.'

If I had been feeling Eric's good cheer, Eric was feeling my anxiety.

'No, no, no,' I said almost in a whisper. I knew they could hear me. 'Let's have peace. We've had enough war and killing.'

'Yes,' Pam agreed. 'We can save the killing for later.'

'I'm happy to see both of you, but I'm having a busy evening,' I said. 'Are you-all just out barhopping to get new ideas for Fangtasia, or can I do something for you?'

'We can do something for you,' Pam said. She smiled at the two guys in the Fellowship of the Sun T-shirts, and since she was a wee bit angry, her fangs were showing. I hoped the sight would subdue them, but since they were assholes without a lick of sense, it inflamed their zeal. Pam downed the blood and licked her lips.

'Pam,' I said between my teeth. 'For goodness' sake, stop making it worse.'

Pam gave me a flirty smile, simply so she'd hit all the buttons.

Eric said, 'Pam,' and immediately all the provocation disappeared, though Pam looked a little disappointed. But she sat up straighter, put her hands in her lap, and crossed her legs at the ankle. No one could have looked more innocent or demure.

'Thank you,' Eric said. 'Dear one – that's you, Sookie – you so impressed Felipe de Castro that he has given us permission to offer you our formal protection. This is a decision only made by the king, you understand, and it's a binding contract. You rendered him such service that he felt this was the only way to repay you.'

'So, this is a big deal?'

'Yes, my lover, it is a very big deal. That means when you call us for help, we are obliged to come and risk our lives for yours. This is not a promise vampires make very often, since we grow more and more jealous of our lives the longer we live. You'd think it would be the other way around.'

'Every now and then you'll find someone who wants to meet the sun after a long life,' Pam said, as if she wanted to set the record straight.

'Yes,' Eric said, frowning. 'Every now and then. But he offers you a real honor, Sookie.'

'I'm real obliged to you for bringing the news, Eric, Pam.'

'Of course, I'd hoped your beautiful roommate would come in,' Pam said. She leered at me. So maybe her hanging around Amelia hadn't been entirely Eric's idea.

I laughed out loud. 'Well, she's got a lot to think about tonight,' I said.

I'd been thinking so hard about the vampire protection that I hadn't noticed the approach of the shorter of the FotS adherants. Now he pushed past me in such a way that he rammed my shoulder, deliberately knocking me to the side. I staggered before I managed to regain my balance. Not everyone noticed, but a few of the bar patrons did. Sam had started around the bar and Eric was already on his feet when I turned and brought my tray down on the asshole's head with all the strength I could muster.

He did a little bit of staggering himself.

Those that had noticed the bit of aggravation began applauding. 'Good for you, Sookie,' Catfish called. 'Hey, jerkoff, leave the waitresses alone.'

Arlene was flushed and angry, and she almost exploded then and there. Sam stepped up to her and murmured something in her ear. She flushed even redder and glared at him, but she kept her mouth shut. The taller FotS guy came to his pal's aid and they left the bar. Neither of them spoke (I wasn't sure Shorty *could* speak), but they might as well have had 'You haven't seen the last of us' tattooed on their foreheads.

I could see where the vampires' protection and my friend of the pack status might come in handy.

Eric and Pam finished their drinks and sat long enough to prove they weren't skedaddling because they felt unwelcome and weren't leaving in pursuit of the Fellowship fans. Eric tipped me a twenty and blew me a kiss as he went out the door – so did Pam – earning me an extra-special glare from my former BFF Arlene.

I worked too hard the rest of the night to think about any of the interesting things that had happened that day. After the patrons all left, even Jane Bodehouse (her son came to get her), we put out the Halloween decorations. Sam had gotten a little pumpkin for each table and painted a face on each one. I was filled with admiration, because the faces were really clever, and some of them looked like bar patrons. In fact, one looked a lot like my dear brother.

'I had no idea you could do this,' I said, and he looked pleased.

'It was fun,' he said, and hung a long strand of fall leaves – of course, they were actually made of cloth – around the bar mirror and among some of the bottles. I tacked up a life-size cardboard skeleton with little rivets at the joints so it could be positioned. I arranged this one so it was clearly dancing. We couldn't have any depressing skeletons at the bar. We had to have happy ones.

Even Arlene unbent a little because this was something different and fun to do, though we had to stay a bit later to do it.

I was ready to go home and go to bed when I said good night to Sam and Arlene. Arlene didn't answer, but she didn't throw me the look of disgust she usually awarded me, either.

Naturally, my day wasn't over.

My great-grandfather was sitting on my front porch when I got to the house. It was very strange to see him in the front porch swing, in the odd combination of night and light that the security lamp and the dark hour combined to create. I wished for one moment that I was as beautiful as he was, and then I had to smile at myself.

I parked my car in the front and got out. Tried to walk quietly going up the steps so I wouldn't wake Amelia, whose bedroom overlooked the front. The house was dark, so I was sure they were in bed, unless they'd been delayed at the bus station when they delivered Bob.

'Great-grandfather,' I said. 'I'm glad to see you.'

'You're tired, Sookie.'

'Well, I just got off work.' I wondered if he ever got tired himself. I couldn't imagine a fairy prince splitting wood or trying to find a leak in his water line.

'I wanted to see you,' he said. 'Have you thought of anything I can do for you?' He sounded mighty hopeful.

What a night this was for people giving me positive feedback. Why didn't I have more nights like this?

I thought for a minute. The Weres had made peace, in their own way. Quinn had been found. The vampires had settled into a new regime. The Fellowship fanatics had left the bar with a minimum of trouble. Bob was a man again. I didn't suppose Niall wanted to offer Octavia a room in his own house, wherever that might be. For all I knew, he had a house in a babbling brook or under a live oak somewhere deep in the woods.

'There is something I want,' I said, surprised I hadn't thought of it before.

'What is it?' he asked, sounding quite pleased.

'I want to know the whereabouts of a man named Remy Savoy. He may have left New Orleans during Katrina. He may have a little child with him.' I gave my great-grandfather Savoy's last known address.

Niall looked confident. 'I'll find him for you, Sookie.'

'I'd sure appreciate it.'

'Nothing else? Nothing more?'

'I have to say . . . this sounds mighty ungracious . . . but I can't help but wonder why you seem to want to do something for me so badly.'

'Why would I not? You are my only living kin.'

'But you seem to have been content without me for the first twenty-seven years of my life.'

'My son would not let me come near you.'

'You told me that, but I don't get it. Why? He didn't make an appearance to let me know he cared anything about me. He never showed himself to me, or . . .' Played Scrabble with me, sent me a graduation present, rented a limousine for me to go to the prom, bought me a pretty dress, took me in his arms on the many occasions when I'd cried (growing up isn't easy for a telepath). He hadn't saved me from being molested by my great-uncle, or rescued my parents, one of whom was his son, when they drowned in a flash flood, or stopped a vampire from setting my house on fire while I was sleeping inside. All this guarding and watching my alleged grandfather Fintan had allegedly done had not paid off in any tangible way for me; and if it had paid off intangibly, I didn't know about it.

Would even worse things have happened? Hard to imagine.

I supposed my grandfather could have been fighting off hordes of slavering demons outside my bedroom window every night, but I couldn't feel grateful if I didn't know about it.

Niall looked upset, which was an expression I'd never seen him wear before. 'There are things I can't tell you,' he finally said. 'When I can make myself speak of them, I will.'

'Okay,' I said dryly. 'But this isn't exactly the give-and-take thing I wanted to have with my great-grandfather, I got to say. This is me telling you everything, and you telling me nothing.'

'This may not be what you wanted, but it's what I can give,' Niall said with some stiffness. 'I do love you, and I had hoped that would be what mattered.'

'I'm glad to hear you love me,' I said very slowly, because I didn't want to risk seeing him walk away from Demanding Sookie. 'But acting like it would be even better.'

'I don't act as though I love you?'

'You vanish and reappear when it suits you. All your offers of help aren't help of the practical kind, like the stuff most grandfathers – or great-grandfathers – do. They fix their granddaughter's car with their own hands, or they offer to help with her college tuition, or they mow her lawn so she doesn't have to. Or they take her hunting. You're not going to do that.'

'No,' he said. 'I'm not.' A ghost of a smile crossed his face. 'You wouldn't want to go hunting with me.'

Okay, I wasn't going to think about that too closely. 'So, I don't have any idea of how we're supposed to be together. You're outside my frame of reference.'

'I understand,' he said seriously. 'All the great-grandfathers you know are human, and that I am not. You're not what I expected, either.'

'Yeah, I got that.' Did I even know any other great-grandfathers? Among friends my own age, even grandfathers were not a sure thing, much less great-grandfathers. But the ones I'd met were all 100 percent human. 'I hope I'm not a disappointment,' I said.

'No,' he said slowly. 'A surprise. Not a disappointment. I'm as poor at predicting your actions and reactions as you are at predicting mine.

We'll have to work through this slowly.' I found myself wondering again why he wasn't more interested in Jason, whose name activated an ache deep inside me. Someday soon I was going to have to talk to my brother, but I couldn't face the idea now. I almost asked Niall to check on Jason, but then I changed my mind and kept silent. Niall eyed my face.

'You don't want to tell me something, Sookie. I worry when you do that. But my love is sincere and deep, and I'll find Remy Savoy for you.' He kissed me on the cheek. 'You smell like my kin,' he said approvingly.

And he poofed.

So, another mysterious conversation with my mysterious great-grandfather had been concluded by him on his own terms. Again. I sighed, fished my keys out of my purse, and unlocked the front door. The house was quiet and dark, and I made my way through the living room and into the hall with as little noise as I could make. I turned on my bedside lamp and performed my nightly routine, curtains closed against the morning sun that would try to wake me in a few short hours.

Had I been an ungrateful bitch to my great-grandfather? When I reviewed what I'd said, I wondered if I'd sounded demanding and whiney. In a more optimistic interpretation, I thought I might have sounded like a stand-up woman, the kind people shouldn't mess with, the kind of woman who speaks her mind.

I turned on the heat before I got into bed. Octavia and Amelia hadn't complained, but it had definitely been chilly the past few mornings. The stale smell that always comes when the heat is used the first time filled the air, and I wrinkled my nose as I snuggled under the sheet and the blanket. Then the *whoosh* noise lulled me into sleep.

I'd been hearing voices for some time before I realized they were outside my door. I blinked, saw it was day, and shut my eyes again. Back to sleep. The voices continued, and I could tell they were arguing. I cracked open one eye to peer at the digital clock on the bedside table. It was nine thirty. Gack. Since the voices wouldn't shut up or go away, I reluctantly opened both eyes at one time, absorbed the fact that the day was not bright, and sat up, pushing the covers back. I moved to the window to the left of the bed and looked out. Gray and rainy. As I stood there, drops began to hit the glass; it was going to be that kind of day.

I went to the bathroom and heard the voices outside hush now that I was clearly up and stirring. I threw open the door to find my two housemates standing right outside, which was no big surprise.

'We didn't know if we should wake you,' Octavia said. She looked anxious.

'But I thought we ought to, because a message from a magical source is clearly important,' Amelia said. She appeared to have said it many times in the past few minutes, from the expression on Octavia's face.

'What message?' I asked, deciding to ignore the argument part of this conversation.

'This one,' Octavia said, handing me a large buff envelope. It was made of heavy paper, like a super-fancy wedding invitation. My name was on the outside. No address, just my name. Furthermore, it was sealed with wax. The imprint in the wax was the head of a unicorn.

'Okey-dokey,' I said. This was going to be an unusual letter.

I walked into the kitchen to get a cup of coffee and a knife, in that order, both the witches trailing behind me like a Greek chorus. Having poured the coffee and pulled out a chair to sit at the table, I slid the knife under the seal and detached it gently. I opened the flap and pulled out a card. On the card was a handwritten address: 1245 Bienville, Red Ditch, Louisiana. That was all.

'What does it mean?' Octavia said. She and Amelia were naturally standing right behind me so they could get a good view.

'It's the location of someone I've been searching for,' I said, which was not exactly the truth but close enough.

'Where's Red Ditch?' Octavia said. 'I've never heard of it.' Amelia was already fetching the Louisiana map from the drawer under the telephone. She looked up the town, running her finger down the columns of names.

'It's not too far,' she said. 'See?' She put her finger on a tiny dot about an hour and a half's drive southeast of Bon Temps.

I drank my coffee as fast as I could and scrambled into some jeans. I slapped a little makeup on and brushed my hair and headed out the front door to my car, map in hand.

Octavia and Amelia followed me out, dying to know what I was going to do and what significance the message had for me. But they were just going to have to wonder, at least for right now. I wondered why I was in such a hurry to do this. It wasn't like he was going to vanish, unless Remy Savoy was a fairy, too. I thought that highly unlikely.

I had to be back for the evening shift, but I had plenty of time.

I drove with the radio on, and this morning I was in a country-and-western kind of mood. Travis Tritt and Carrie Underwood accompanied me, and by the time I drove into Red Ditch, I was feeling my roots. There was even less to Red Ditch than there was to Bon Temps, and that's saying something.

I figured it would be easy to find Bienville Street, and I was right. It was the kind of street you can find anywhere in America. The houses were small, neat, boxy, with room for one car in the carport and a small yard. In the case of 1245, the backyard was fenced in and I could see a lively little black dog running around. There wasn't a doghouse, so the pooch was an indoor-outdoor animal. Everything was neat, but not obsessively so. The bushes around the house were trimmed and the yard was raked. I drove by a couple of times, and then I wondered what I was going to do. How would I find out what I wanted to know?

There was a pickup truck parked in the garage, so Savoy was probably at home. I took a deep breath, parked across from the house, and tried to send my extra ability hunting. But in a neighborhood full of the thoughts of the living people in these houses, it was hard. I thought I was getting two brain signatures from the house I was watching, but it was hard to be absolutely sure.

'Fuck it,' I said, and got out of the car. I popped my keys in my jacket pocket and went up the sidewalk to the front door. I knocked.

'Hold on, son,' said a man's voice inside, and I heard a child's voice say, 'Daddy, me! I get it!'

'No, Hunter,' the man said, and the door opened. He was looking at me through a screen door. He unhooked it and pushed it open when he saw I was a woman. 'Hi,' he said. 'Can I help you?'

I looked down at the child who wiggled past him to look up at me. He was maybe four years old. He had dark hair and eyes. He was the spitting image of Hadley. Then I looked at the man again. Something in his face had changed during my protracted silence.

'Who are you?' he said in an entirely different voice.

'I'm Sookie Stackhouse,' I said. I couldn't think of any artful way to do this. 'I'm Hadley's cousin. I just found out where you were.'

'You can't have any claim on him,' said the man, keeping a very tight rein on his voice.

'Of course not,' I said, surprised. 'I just want to meet him. I don't have much family.'

There was another significant pause. He was weighing my words and my demeanor and he was deciding whether to slam the door or let me in.

'Daddy, she's pretty,' said the boy, and that seemed to tip the balance in my favor.

'Come on in,' Hadley's ex-husband said.

I looked around the small living room, which had a couch and a recliner, a television and a bookcase full of DVDs and children's books, and a scattering of toys.

'I worked Saturday, so I have today off,' he said, in case I imagined he was unemployed. 'Oh, I'm Remy Savoy. I guess you knew that.'

I nodded.

'This is Hunter,' he said, and the child got a case of the shys. He hid behind his father's legs and peeked around at me. 'Please sit down,' Remy added.

I shoved a newspaper to one end of the couch and sat, trying not to stare at the man or the child. My cousin Hadley had been very striking, and she'd married a good-looking man. It was hard to peg down what left that impression. His nose was big, his jaw stuck out a little, and his eyes were a little wide-spaced. But the sum of all this was a man most women would look at twice. His hair was that medium shade between blond and brown, and it was thick and layered, the back hanging over his collar. He was wearing a flannel shirt unbuttoned over a white Hanes T-shirt. Jeans. No shoes. A dimple in his chin.

Hunter was wearing corduroy pants and a sweatshirt with a big football on the front. His clothes were brand-new, unlike his dad's.

I'd finished looking at them before Remy'd finished looking at me. He didn't think I had any trace of Hadley in my face. My body was plumper and my coloring was lighter and I wasn't as hard. He thought I looked like I didn't have a lot of money. He thought I was pretty, like his son did. But he didn't trust me.

'How long has it been since you heard from her?' I asked.

'I haven't heard from Hadley since a few months after he was born,' Remy said. He was used to that, but there was sadness in his thoughts, too.

Hunter was sitting on the floor, playing with some trucks. He loaded some Duplos into the back of a dump truck, which backed up to a fire engine very slowly, guided by Hunter's small hands. To the astonishment of the Duplo man sitting in the cab of the fire engines, the dump truck let go of its load all over the fire engine. Hunter got a big kick out of this, and he said, 'Daddy, look!'

'I see it, son.' Remy looked at me intently. 'Why are you here?' he asked, deciding to get right to the point.

'I only found out there might be a baby a couple of weeks ago,' I said. 'Wasn't any point in tracking you down until I heard that.'

'I never met her family,' he said. 'How'd you know she was married? Did she tell you?' Then, reluctantly, he said, 'Is she okay?'

'No,' I said very quietly. I didn't want Hunter to become interested. The boy was loading all the Duplos back into the dump truck. 'She's been dead since before Katrina.'

I could hear the shock detonate like a little bomb in his head. 'She was already a vamp, I heard,' he said uncertainly, his voice wavering. 'That kind of dead?'

'No. I mean really, finally.'

'What happened?'

'She was attacked by another vampire,' I said. 'He was jealous of Hadley's relationship with her, ah, her . . .'

'Girlfriend?' No mistaking the bitterness in her ex-husband's voice and in his head.

'Yeah.'

'That was a shocker,' he said, but in his head all the shock had worn off. There was only a grim resignation, a loss of pride.

'I didn't know about any of this until after she passed.'

'You're her cousin? I remember her telling me she had two. . . . You got a brother, right?'

'Yes,' I said.

'You knew she had been married to me?'

'I found out when I cleaned out her safe-deposit box a few weeks ago. I didn't know there had been a son. I apologize for that.' I wasn't sure why I was apologizing or how I could have known, but I was sorry I hadn't even considered the fact that Hadley and her husband might have had a child. Hadley had been a little older than me, and I guessed Remy was probably thirty or thereabouts.

'You look fine,' he said suddenly, and I flushed, understanding him instantly.

'Hadley told you I had a disability.' I looked away from him, at the boy, who jumped to his feet, announced he had to go to the bathroom, and dashed out of the room. I couldn't help but smile.

'Yeah, she said something. . . . She said you had a hard time of it in school,' he said tactfully. Hadley had told him I was crazy as hell. He was seeing no signs of it, and he wondered why Hadley had thought so. But he glanced in the direction the child had gone, and I knew he was thinking he had to be careful since Hunter was in the house, he had to be alert for any signs of this instability – though Hadley had never specified what form of craziness I had.

'That's true,' I said. 'I had a hard time of it. Hadley wasn't any big help. But her mom, my aunt Linda, was a great woman before the cancer got her. She was real kind to me, always. And we had some good moments now and then.'

'I could say the same. We did have some good moments,' Remy said. His forearms were braced on his knees and his big hands, scarred and battered, hung down. He was a man who knew what hard work was.

There was a sound at the front door and a woman came in without bothering to knock. 'Hey, baby,' she said, smiling at Remy. When she noticed me, her smile faltered and faded away.

'Kristen, this is a relative of my ex-wife's,' Remy said, and there wasn't any haste or apology in his voice.

Kristen had long brown hair and big brown eyes and she was maybe twenty-five. She was wearing khakis and a polo shirt with a logo on the chest, a laughing duck. The legend above the duck read, 'Jerry's Detailing.' 'Nice to meet you,' Kristen said insincerely. 'I'm Kristen Duchesne, Remy's girlfriend.'

'Pleased to meet you,' I said, more honestly. 'Sookie Stackhouse.'

'You didn't offer this woman a drink, Remy! Sookie, can I get you a Coke or a Sprite?'

She knew what was in the refrigerator. I wondered if she lived here. Well, none of my business, as long as she was good to Hadley's son.

'No, thanks,' I said. 'I've got to be going in a minute.' I made a little production out of looking at my watch. 'I got to go to work this evening.'

'Oh, where is that?' Kristen asked. She was a little more relaxed.

'Merlotte's. It's a bar in Bon Temps,' I said. 'About eighty miles from here.'

'Sure, that's where your wife was from,' Kristen said, glancing at Remy.

Remy said, 'Sookie came with some news, I'm afraid.' His hands twisted together, though his voice was steady. 'Hadley is dead.'

Kristen inhaled sharply but she had to keep her comment to herself because Hunter dashed back into the room. 'Daddy, I washed my hands!' he shouted, and his father smiled at him.

'Good for you, son,' he said, and ruffled the boy's dark hair. 'Say hello to Kristen.'

'Hey, Kristen,' Hunter said without much interest.

I stood. I wished I had a business card to leave. This seemed odd and wrong, to just walk out. But Kristen's presence was oddly inhibiting. She picked up Hunter and slung him on her hip. He was quite a load for her, but she made a point of making it look easy and habitual, though it wasn't. But she did like the little boy; I could see it in her head.

'Kristen likes me,' Hunter said, and I looked at him sharply.

'Sure I do,' Kristen said, and laughed.

Remy was looking from Hunter to me with a troubled face, a face that was just beginning to look worried.

I wondered how to explain our relationship to Hunter. I was pretty close to being his aunt, as we reckon things here. Kids don't care about distant cousins.

'Aunt Sookie,' Hunter said, testing the words. 'I got an aunt?'

I took a deep breath. *Yes, you do, Hunter,* I thought.

'I never had one before.'

'You got one now,' I told him, and I looked into Remy's eyes. They were frightened. He hadn't spelled it out to himself yet, but he knew.

There was something I had to say to him, regardless of Kristen's presence. I could feel her confusion and her sense that something was going on without her knowledge. But I didn't have the space on my agenda to worry about Kristen, too. Hunter was the important person.

'You're gonna need me,' I told Remy. 'When he gets a little older, you're gonna need to talk. My number's in the book, and I'm not going anywhere. You understand?'

Kristen said, 'What's going on? Why are we getting so serious?'

'Don't worry, Kris,' Remy said gently. 'Just family stuff.'

Kristen lowered a wriggling Hunter to the floor. 'Uh-huh,' she said, in the tone of someone who knows full well she's having the wool pulled over her eyes.

'Stackhouse,' I reminded Remy. 'Don't put it off till too late, when he's already miserable.'

'I understand,' he said. He looked miserable himself, and I didn't blame him.

'I've got to go,' I said again, to reassure Kristen.

'Aunt Sookie, you going?' Hunter asked. He wasn't quite ready to hug me yet, but he thought about it. He liked me. 'You coming back?'

'Sometime, Hunter,' I said. 'Maybe your dad will bring you to visit me someday.'

I shook Kristen's hand, shook Remy's, which they both thought was odd, and opened the door. As I put one foot on the steps, Hunter said silently, *Bye, Aunt Sookie.*

Bye, Hunter, I said right back.

Dead and Gone

Chapter 1

'Caucasian vampires should never wear white,' the television announcer intoned. 'We've been secretly filming Devon Dawn, who's been a vampire for only a decade, as she gets dressed for a night on the town. Look at that outfit! It's all wrong for her!'

'What was she thinking?' said an acidic female voice. 'Talk about stuck in the nineties! Look at that blouse, if that's what you call it. Her skin just cries out for contrasting color, and what is she putting on? Ivory! It makes her skin look like a Hefty bag.'

I paused in the act of tying my shoe to watch what happened next as the two vampire fashionistas burst in on the hapless victim – oh, excuse me, the lucky vampire – who was about to get an unsolicited makeover. She'd have the additional pleasure of realizing her friends had turned her in to the fashion police.

'I don't think this is going to end well,' Octavia Fant said. Though my housemate Amelia Broadway had sort of slid Octavia into my house – based on a casual invitation I'd issued in a weak moment – the arrangement was working out okay.

'Devon Dawn, here's Bev Leveto from *The Best Dressed Vamp*, and I'm Todd Seabrook. Your friend Tessa called to tell us you needed fashion help! We've been secretly filming you for the past two nights, and – *AAACKK!*' A white hand flashed at Todd's throat, which vanished, leaving a gaping reddish hole. The camera lingered, fascinated, as Todd crumpled to the floor, before it rose to follow the fight between Devon Dawn and Bev.

'Gosh,' said Amelia. 'Looks like Bev's gonna win.'

'Better strategic sense,' I said. 'Did you notice she let Todd go through the door first?'

'I've got her pinned,' Bev said triumphantly on the screen. 'Devon Dawn, while Todd recovers his speech, we're going to go through your closet. A girl who's going to live for eternity can't afford to be tacky. Vampires can't get stuck in their pasts. We've got to be fashion forward!'

Devon Dawn whimpered, 'But I like my clothes! They're part of who I am! You've broken my arm.'

'It'll heal. Listen, you don't want to be known as the little vampire who couldn't, do you? You don't want to have *your* head stuck in the past!'

'Well, I guess not . . .'

'Good! I'll let you up now. And I can tell from the coughing that Todd's feeling better.'

I switched off the television and tied my other shoe, shaking my head at America's new addiction to vampire 'reality' shows. I got my red coat out of the closet. The sight of it reminded me that I myself had some absolutely real problems with a vampire; in the two and a half months since the takeover of the Louisiana vampire kingdom by the vampires of Nevada, Eric Northman had been fully occupied with consolidating his position within the new regime and evaluating what was left of the old.

We were way overdue for a chitchat about Eric's newly recovered memories of our strange and intense time together when he'd temporarily misplaced his memory due to a spell.

'What are you going to do tonight while I'm at work?' I asked Amelia and Octavia, since I didn't need to go another round of imaginary conversations. I pulled on the coat. Northern Louisiana doesn't get the horrific temperatures of the *real* north, but it was in the forties tonight and would be colder when I got off work.

'My niece and her kids are taking me out to dinner,' Octavia said.

Amelia and I gave each other surprised looks while the older woman's head was bent over the blouse she was mending. It was the first time Octavia had seen her niece since she'd moved from the niece's house to mine.

'I think Tray and I are coming to the bar tonight,' Amelia said hastily, to cover the little pause.

'So I'll see you at Merlotte's.' I'd been a barmaid there for years.

Octavia said, 'Oh, I've got the wrong color thread,' and went down the hall to her room.

'I guess you aren't seeing Pam anymore?' I asked Amelia. 'You and Tray are getting to be a regular thing.' I tucked my white T-shirt into my black pants more securely. I glanced in the old mirror over the mantel. My hair was pulled up into its usual ponytail for work. I spotted a stray long blond hair against the red of the coat, and I plucked it off.

'Pam was just a wild hair, and I'm sure she felt the same way about me. I *really* like Tray,' Amelia was saying. 'He doesn't seem to care about Daddy's money, and he's not worried about me being a witch. And he can rock my world in the bedroom. So we're getting along great.' Amelia gave me a cat-eating-the-canary grin. She might look like a well-toned soccer mom – short, gleaming hair, beautiful white smile, clear eyes – but she was very interested in sex and (by my standards) diverse in those interests.

'He's a good guy,' I said. 'Have you seen him as a wolf yet?'

'Nope. But I'm looking forward to it.'

I picked up something from Amelia's transparent head that startled me. 'It's soon? The revelation?'

'Would you *not do* that?' Amelia was normally matter-of-fact about my mind-reading ability, but not today. 'I've got to keep other people's secrets, you know!'

'Sorry,' I said. And I was, but at the same time I was mildly aggrieved. You'd think that I could relax in my own house and loosen the tight wrappings I tried to keep on my ability. After all, I had to struggle every single day at work.

Amelia said instantly, 'I'm sorry, too. Listen, I've got to go get ready. See you later.' She went lightly up the stairs to the second floor, which had been largely unused until she'd come back from New Orleans with me a few months before. She'd missed Katrina, unlike poor Octavia.

'Good-bye, Octavia. Have a good time!' I called, and went out the back door to my car.

As I steered down the long driveway that led through the woods to Hummingbird Road, I wondered about the chances of Amelia and Tray Dawson sticking together. Tray, a werewolf, worked as a motorcycle repairman and as muscle for hire. Amelia was an up-and-coming witch, and her dad was immensely wealthy, even after Katrina. The hurricane had spared most of the materials at his contracting warehouse and provided him with enough work to last for decades.

According to Amelia's brain, tonight was the night – not the night Tray asked Amelia to marry him, but the night Tray came out. Tray's dual nature was a plus to my roommate, who was attracted by the exotic.

I went in the employee entrance and right to Sam's office. 'Hey, boss,' I said when I saw him behind his desk. Sam hated to work on the books, but that was what he was doing. Maybe it was providing a needed distraction. Sam looked worried. His hair was even more tangled than usual, its strawberry waves standing out in a halo around his narrow face.

'Brace yourself. Tonight's the night,' he said.

I was so proud he'd told me, and he'd echoed my own thoughts so closely, I couldn't help but smile. 'I'm ready. I'll be right here.' I dropped my purse in the deep drawer in his desk and went to tie on my apron. I was relieving Holly, but after I'd had a talk with her about the customers at our tables, I said, 'You oughta stick around tonight.'

She looked at me sharply. Holly had recently been letting her hair grow out, so the dyed black ends looked like they'd been dipped in tar. Her natural color, now showing about an inch at the roots, turned out to be a pleasant light brown. She'd colored it for so long that I'd clean forgotten. 'This going to be good enough for me to keep Hoyt waiting?' she asked. 'Him and Cody get along like a house on fire, but I am Cody's mama.' Hoyt, my brother Jason's best buddy, had been co-opted by Holly. Now he was *her* follower.

'You should stay awhile.' I gave her a significant lift of my eyebrows.

Holly said, 'The Weres?' I nodded, and her face brightened with a grin. 'Oh, boy! Arlene's going to have a shit fit.'

Arlene, our coworker and former friend, had become politically sensitized a few months before by one of her string of man friends. Now she was somewhere to the right of Attila the Hun, especially on vampire issues. She'd even joined the Fellowship of the Sun, a church in all but name. She was standing at one of her tables now, having a serious conversation with her man, Whit Spradlin, a FotS official of some sort who had a day job at one of the Shreveport Home Depots. He had a sizeable bald patch and a little paunch, but that didn't make any nevermind to me. His politics did. He had a buddy with him, of course. The FotS people seemed to run in packs – just like another minority group they were about to meet.

My brother, Jason, was at a table, too, with Mel Hart. Mel worked at Bon Temps Auto Parts, and he was about Jason's age, maybe thirty-one. Slim and hard-bodied, Mel had longish light brown hair, a mustache and beard, and a pleasant face. I'd been seeing Jason with Mel a lot lately. Jason had had to fill the gap Hoyt had left, I assumed. Jason wasn't happy without a sidekick. Tonight both men had dates. Mel was divorced, but Jason was still nominally married, so he had no business being out in public with another woman. Not that anyone here would blame him. Jason's wife, Crystal, had been caught cheating with a local guy.

I'd heard Crystal had moved her pregnant self back to the little community of Hotshot to stay with relatives. (She could find a room in any house in Hotshot and be with relatives. It's that kind of place.) Mel Hart had been born in Hotshot, too, but he was the rare member of the tribe who'd chosen to live elsewhere.

To my surprise Bill, my ex-boyfriend, was sitting with another vampire, named Clancy. Clancy wasn't my favorite guy regardless of his nonliving status. They both had bottles of TrueBlood on the table in front of them. I didn't think Clancy had ever dropped in to Merlotte's for a casual drink before, and certainly never with Bill.

'Hey, guys, need a refill?' I asked, smiling for all I was worth. I'm a little nervous around Bill.

'Please,' Bill said politely, and Clancy shoved his empty bottle toward me.

I stepped behind the bar to get two more TrueBloods out of the refrigerator, and I uncapped them and popped them in the microwave. (Fifteen seconds works best.) I shook the bottles gently and put the warm drinks on the tray with some fresh napkins. Bill's cold hand touched mine as I placed his drink in front of him.

He said, 'If you need any help at your place, please call me.'

I knew he meant it kindly, but it sort of emphasized my current manless status. Bill's house was right across the cemetery from mine, and the way he roamed around at night, I figured he was well aware I wasn't entertaining company.

'Thanks, Bill,' I said, making myself smile at him. Clancy just sneered.

Tray and Amelia came in, and after depositing Amelia at a table, Tray went up to the bar, greeting everyone in the place along the way. Sam came out of his office to join the burly man, who was at least five inches taller than my boss and almost twice as big around. They grinned at each other. Bill and Clancy went on alert.

The televisions mounted at intervals around the room cut away from the sports event they'd been showing. A series of beeps alerted the bar patrons to the fact that something was happening on-screen. The bar gradually hushed to a few scattered conversations. 'Special Report' flashed on the screen, superimposed on a newscaster with clipped, gelled hair and a sternly serious face. In solemn tones he said, 'I'm Matthew Harrow. Tonight we bring you a special report. Like newsrooms all across the country, here in Shreveport we have a visitor in the studio.'

The camera moved away to broaden the picture, and a pretty woman came into view. Her face was slightly familiar. She gave the camera a practiced little wave. She was wearing a sort of muumuu, an odd choice for a television appearance.

'This is Patricia Crimmins, who moved to Shreveport a few weeks ago. Patty – may I call you Patty?'

'Actually, it's Patricia,' the brunette said. She was one of the members of the pack that had been absorbed by Alcide's, I remembered. She was pretty as a picture, and the part of her not swathed in the muumuu looked fit and toned. She smiled at Matthew Harrow. 'I'm here tonight as the representative of a people who have lived among you for many years. Since the vampires have been so successful out in the open, we've decided the time's come for us to tell you about ourselves. After all, vampires are dead. They're not even human. But we're regular people just like you-all, with a difference.' Sam turned the volume up. People in the bar began to swivel in their seats to see what was happening.

The newsman's smile had gotten as rigid as a smile could be, and he was visibly nervous. 'How interesting, Patricia! What – what are you?'

'Thanks for asking, Matthew! I'm a werewolf.' Patricia had her hands clasped around her knee. Her legs were crossed. She looked perky enough to sell used cars. Alcide had made a good choice. Plus, if someone killed her right away, well . . . she was the new girl.

By now Merlotte's was silent as the word went from table to table. Bill and Clancy had risen to stand by the bar. I realized now that they were there to keep the peace if they were needed; Sam must have asked them to come in. Tray began unbuttoning his shirt. Sam was wearing a long-sleeved T-shirt, and he pulled it over his head.

'You're saying you turn into a wolf at the full moon?' Matthew Harrow quavered, trying hard to keep his smile level and his face simply interested. He didn't succeed very well.

'And at other times,' Patricia explained. 'During the full moon, most of us *have* to turn, but if we're pure-blooded wereanimals, we can change at other times as well. There are many kinds of wereanimals, but I turn into a wolf. We're the more numerous of all the two-natured. Now I'm going to show you-all what an amazing process this is. Don't be scared. I'll be fine.' She shucked her shoes, but not the muumuu. I suddenly understood she'd worn it so she wouldn't have to undress on camera. Patricia knelt on the floor, smiled at the camera one last time, and began to contort. The air around her shivered with the magic of it, and everyone in Merlotte's went '*Ooooooo*' in unison.

Right after Patricia committed herself to the change on the television screen, Sam and Tray did, too, right then and there. They'd worn underthings they didn't mind ripping to shreds. Everyone in Merlotte's was torn between watching the pretty woman change into a creature with long white teeth, and the spectacle of two people they knew doing the same. There were exclamations all over the bar, most of them not repeatable in polite society. Jason's date, Michele Schubert, actually stood up to get a better view.

I was so proud of Sam. This took a lot of courage, since he had a business that depended to some extent on his likability.

In another minute, it was all over. Sam, a rare pure shapeshifter, turned into his most familiar form, that of a collie. He went to sit in front of me and gave a happy yip. I bent over to pat his head. His tongue lolled out, and he grinned at me. Tray's animal manifestation was much more dramatic. Huge wolves are not often seen in rural northern Louisiana; let's face it, they're scary. People shifted uneasily and might have gotten up to flee from the building if Amelia hadn't squatted by Tray and put her arm around his neck.

'He knows what you're saying,' she told the people at the nearest table encouragingly. Amelia had a great smile, big and genuine. 'Hey, Tray, take them this coaster.' She handed him one of the bar coasters, and Tray Dawson, one of the most implacable fighters both in and out of his wolf form, trotted over to lay the coaster on the lap of the female customer. She blinked, wavered, and finally came down on the side of laughing.

Sam licked my hand.

'Oh, my lord Jesus,' Arlene exclaimed loudly. Whit Spradlin and his buddy were on their feet. But though a few other patrons looked nervous, none of them had such a violent reaction.

Bill and Clancy watched with expressionless faces. They were obviously ready to handle trouble, but all seemed to be going well at the Great Reveal. The vampires' Great Revelation night hadn't gone so smoothly, because it was the first in the series of shocks mainstream society would feel in the years to come. Gradually vampires had come to be a recognized part of America, though their citizenship still had certain limitations.

Sam and Tray wandered among the regulars, allowing themselves to be petted as if they were regular tame animals. While they were doing that, the newscaster on television was visibly trembling as he faced the beautiful white wolf Patricia had become.

'Look, he so scared, he shaking!' D'Eriq, the busboy and kitchen helper, said. He laughed out loud. The drinkers in Merlotte's relaxed enough to feel superior. After all, they'd handled this with aplomb.

Jason's new buddy Mel said, 'Ain't nobody got to be scared of a lady that pretty, even if she does shed some,' and the laughter and relaxation in the bar spread. I was relieved, though I thought it was a little ironic that people might not be so quick to laugh if Jason and Mel had changed; they were werepanthers, though Jason couldn't change completely.

But after the laughter, I felt that everything was going to be all right. Bill and Clancy, after a careful look around, went back to their table.

Whit and Arlene, surrounded by citizens taking a huge chunk of knowledge in their stride, looked stunned. I could hear Arlene being extra confused about how to react. After all, Sam had been our boss for a good many years. Unless she wanted to lose her job, she couldn't cut up. But I could also read her fear and the mounting anger that followed close behind. Whit had one reaction, always, to anything he didn't understand. He hated it, and hate is infectious. He looked at his drinking companion, and they exchanged dark looks.

Thoughts were churning around in Arlene's brain like lottery balls in the popper. It was hard to tell which one would surface first.

'Jesus, strike him dead!' said Arlene, boiling over. The hate ball had landed on top.

A few people said, 'Oh, Arlene!' . . . but they were all listening.

'This goes against God and nature,' Arlene said in a loud, angry voice. Her dyed red hair shook with her vehemence. 'You-all want your kids around this kind of thing?'

'Our kids have always been around this kind of thing,' Holly said equally loudly. 'We just didn't know it. And they ain't come to any harm.' She rose to her feet, too.

'God will *get us* if we don't strike them down,' Arlene said, pointing to Tray dramatically. By now, her face was almost as red as her hair. Whit was looking at her approvingly. 'You don't understand! We're all going to hell if we don't take the world back from them! Look who they got standing there to keep us humans in line!' Her finger swung around to indicate Bill and Clancy, though since they'd resumed their chairs she lost a few points.

I set my tray on the bar and took a step away, my hands clenched in fists. 'We all get along here in Bon Temps,' I said, keeping my voice calm and level. 'You seem to be the only one upset, Arlene.'

She glared around the bar, trying to catch the eyes of various patrons. She knew every one of them. Arlene was genuinely shocked to realize more people weren't sharing her reaction. Sam came to sit in front of her. He looked up at her face with his beautiful doggy eyes.

I took another step closer to Whit, just in case. Whit was deciding what to do, considering jumping Sam. But who would join him in beating up a collie? Even Whit could see the absurdity, and that made him hate Sam all the more.

'How could you?' Arlene screamed at Sam. 'You been lying to me all these years! I thought you were human, not a damn supe!'

'He is human,' I said. 'He's just got another face, is all.'

'And you,' she said, spitting out the words. 'You're the weirdest, the most inhuman, of them all.'

'Hey, now,' Jason said. He leaped to his feet, and after a moment's hesitation, Mel joined him. His date looked alarmed, though Jason's lady friend just smiled. 'You leave my sister alone. She babysat your kids and she cleaned your trailer and she put up with your shit for years. What kind of friend are you?'

Jason didn't look at me. I was frozen in astonishment. This was a very un-Jason gesture. Could he have grown up a little bit?

'The kind that don't want to hang around with unnatural creatures like your sister,' Arlene said. She tore off her apron, said, 'I quit this place!' to the collie, and stomped back to Sam's office to retrieve her purse. Maybe a fourth of the people in the bar looked alarmed and upset. Half of them were fascinated with the drama. That left a quarter on the fence. Sam whined like a sad dog and put his nose between his paws. After that got a big laugh, the discomfort of the moment passed. I watched Whit and his buddy ease out the front door, and I relaxed when they were gone.

Just on the off chance Whit might be fetching a rifle from his truck, I glanced over at Bill, who glided out the door after him. In a moment he was back, nodding at me to indicate the FotS guys had driven away.

Once the back door thunked closed behind Arlene, the rest of the evening went pretty well. Sam and Tray retired to Sam's office to change back and get dressed. Sam returned to his place behind the bar afterward as if nothing had happened, and Tray went to sit at the table with Amelia, who kissed him. For a while, people steered a little clear of them, and there were lots of surreptitious glances; but after an hour, the atmosphere of Merlotte's seemed just about back to normal. I pitched in to serve Arlene's tables, and I made sure to be especially nice to the people still undecided about the night's events.

People seemed to drink heartily that night. Maybe they had misgivings about Sam's other persona, but they didn't have any problem adding to his profits. Bill caught my eye and raised his hand in goodbye. He and Clancy drifted out of the bar.

Jason tried to get my attention once or twice, and his buddy Mel sent big smiles my way. Mel was taller and thinner than my brother, but they both had that bright, eager look of unthinking men who operate on their instincts. In his favor, Mel didn't seem to agree with everything Jason said, not the way Hoyt always had. Mel seemed to be an okay guy, at least from our brief acquaintance; that he was one of the few werepanthers who didn't live in Hotshot was also a fact in his favor, and it may even have been why he and Jason were such big buddies. They were like other werepanthers, but separate, too.

If I ever began speaking to Jason again, I had a question for him. On this major evening for all Weres and shifters, how come he hadn't taken the chance to grab a little of the spotlight for himself? Jason was very full of his altered status as a werepanther. He'd been bitten, not born. That is, he'd contracted the virus (or whatever it was) by being bitten by another werepanther, rather than being born with the ability to change as Mel had been. Jason's changed form was manlike, with hair all over and a pantherish face and claws: really scary, he'd told me. But he wasn't a beautiful animal, and that griped my brother. Mel was a purebred, and he would be gorgeous and frightening when he transformed.

Maybe the werepanthers had been asked to lie low because panthers were simply *too* scary. If something as big and lethal as a panther had appeared in the bar, the reaction of the patrons almost certainly would have been a lot more hysterical. Though wereanimal brains are very difficult to read, I could sense the disappointment the two panthers were sharing. I was sure the decision had been Calvin Norris's, as the panther leader. *Good move, Calvin*, I thought.

After I'd helped close down the bar, I gave Sam a hug when I stopped by his office to pick up my purse. He was looking tired but happy.

'You feeling as good as you look?' I asked.

'Yep. My true nature's out in the open now. It's liberating. My mom swore she was going to tell my stepdad tonight. I'm waiting to hear from her.'

Right on cue, the phone rang. Sam picked it up, still smiling. 'Mom?' he said. Then his face changed as if a hand had wiped off the previous expression. 'Don? What have you done?'

I sank into the chair by the desk and waited. Tray had come to have a last word with Sam, and Amelia was with him. They both stood stiffly in the doorway, anxious to hear what had happened.

'Oh, my God,' Sam said. 'I'll come as soon as I can. I'll get on the road tonight.' He hung up the phone very gently. 'Don shot my mom,' he said. 'When she changed, he shot her.' I'd never seen Sam look so upset.

'Is she dead?' I asked, fearing the answer.

'No,' he said. 'No, but she's in the hospital with a shattered collarbone and a gunshot wound to her upper left shoulder. He almost killed her. If she hadn't jumped . . .'

'I'm so sorry,' Amelia said.

'What can I do to help?' I asked.

'Keep the bar open while I'm gone,' he said, shaking off the shock. 'Call Terry. Terry and Tray can work out a bartending schedule between them. Tray, you know I'll pay you when I get back. Sookie, the waitress schedule is on the wall behind the bar. Find someone to cover Arlene's shifts, please.'

'Sure, Sam,' I said. 'You need any help packing? Can I gas up your truck or something?'

'Nope, I'm good. You've got the key to my trailer, so can you water my plants? I don't think I'll be gone but a couple of days, but you never know.'

'Of course, Sam. Don't worry. Keep us posted.'

We all cleared out so Sam could get over to his trailer to pack. It was in the lot right behind the bar, so at least he could get everything ready in a hurry.

As I drove home, I tried to imagine how Sam's stepdad had come to do such a thing. Had he been so horrified at the discovery of his wife's second life that he'd flipped? Had she changed out of his sight and walked up to him and startled him? I simply couldn't believe you could shoot someone you loved, someone you lived with, just because they had more to them than you'd thought. Maybe Don had seen her second self as a betrayal. Or maybe it was the fact that she'd concealed it. I could kind of understand his reaction, if I looked at it that way.

People all had secrets, and I was in a position to know most of them. Being a telepath is not any fun. You hear the tawdry, the sad, the disgusting, the petty ... the things we all want to keep hidden from our fellow humans, so they'll keep their image of us intact.

The secrets I know least about are my own.

The one I was thinking of tonight was the unusual genetic inheritance my brother and I share, which had come through my father. My father had never known that his mother, Adele, had had a whopper of a secret, one disclosed to me only the past October. My grandmother's two children – my dad and his sister, Linda – were not the products of her long marriage with my grandfather.

Both had been conceived through her liaison with a half fairy, half human named Fintan. According to Fintan's father, Niall, the fairy part of my dad's genetic heritage had been responsible for my mother's infatuation with him, an infatuation that had excluded her children from all but the fringes of her attention and affection. This genetic legacy hadn't seemed to change anything for my dad's sister, Linda; it certainly hadn't helped her dodge the cancer bullet that had ended her life or kept her husband on-site, much less infatuated. However, Linda's grandson Hunter was a telepath like me.

I still struggled with parts of this story. I believed the history Niall had related to be true, but I couldn't understand my grandmother's desire for children being strong enough to lead her to cheat on my grandfather. That simply didn't jibe with her character, and I couldn't understand why I hadn't read it in her brain during all the years that we'd lived together. She must have thought about the circumstances of her children's conceptions from time to time. There was just no way she could've packed those events away for good in some attic of her mind.

But my grandmother had been dead for over a year now, and I'd never be able to ask her about it. Her husband had passed away years before. Niall had told me that my biological grandfather Fintan, too, was dead and gone. It had crossed my mind to go through my grandmother's things in search of some clue to her thinking, to her reaction to this extraordinary passage in her life, and then I would think … *Why bother?*

I had to deal with the consequences here and now.

The trace of fairy blood I carried made me more attractive to supes, at least to some vampires. Not all of them could detect the little trace of fairy in my genes, but they tended to at least be interested in me, though occasionally that had negative results. Or maybe this fairy-blood thing was bull, and vampires were interested in any fairly attractive young woman who would treat them with respect and tolerance.

As to the relationship between the telepathy and the fairy blood, who knew? It wasn't like I had a lot of people to ask or any literature to check, or like I could ask a lab to test for it. Maybe little Hunter and I had both developed the condition through a coincidence – yeah, right. Maybe the trait was genetic but separate from the fairy genes.

Maybe I'd just gotten lucky.

Chapter 2

I went into Merlotte's early in the morning – for me, that means eight thirty – to check the bar situation, and I remained to cover Arlene's shift. I'd have to work a double. Thankfully, the lunch crowd was light. I didn't know if that was a result of Sam's announcement or just the normal course of things. At least I was able to make a few phone calls while Terry Bellefleur (who made ends meet with several part-time jobs) covered the bar. Terry was in a good mood, or what passed for a good mood for him; he was a Vietnam vet who'd had a very bad war. At heart he was a good guy, and we'd always gotten along. He was really fascinated by the Weres' revelation; since the war, Terry had done better with animals than people.

'I bet that's why I've always liked to work for Sam,' Terry said, and I smiled at him.

'I like to work for him, too,' I said.

While Terry kept the beers coming and kept an eye on Jane Bode-house, one of our alcoholics, I started phoning to find a replacement barmaid. Amelia had told me she would help a little but only at night, because she now had a temporary day job covering the maternity leave of a clerk at the insurance agency.

First I phoned Charlsie Tooten. Charlsie, though sympathetic, told me she had the full care of her grandson while her daughter worked, so she was too tired to come in. I called another former Merlotte's employee, but she'd started work at another bar. Holly had said she could double up once but didn't want to do it more than that because of her little boy. Danielle, the other full-time server, had said the same. (In Danielle's case she had twice the excuse because she had two children.)

So, finally, with a huge sigh to let Sam's empty office know how put-upon I was, I called one of my least favorite people – Tanya Grissom, werefox and former saboteur. It took me a while to track her down, but by calling a couple of people out in Hotshot, I was finally able to reach her at Calvin's house. Tanya had been dating him for a while. I liked the man myself, but when I thought of that cluster of little houses at the ancient crossroads, I shuddered.

'Tanya, how you doing? This is Sookie Stackhouse.'

'Really. Hmmm. Hello.'

I didn't blame her for being cautious.

'One of Sam's barmaids quit – you remember Arlene? She freaked about the were thing and walked out. I was wondering if you could take over a couple of her shifts, just for a while.'

'You Sam's partner now?'

She wasn't going to make this easy. 'No, I'm just doing the looking for him. He got called away on a family emergency.'

'I was probably on the bottom of your list.'

My brief silence spoke for itself.

'I figure we can work together,' I said, because I had to say something.

'I got a day job now, but I can help a couple of evenings until you find someone permanent,' Tanya said. It was hard to read anything from her voice.

'Thanks.' That gave me two temporaries, Amelia and Tanya, and I could take any hours they couldn't. This wouldn't be hard on anyone. 'Can you come in tomorrow for the evening shift? If you could be here about five, five thirty, one of us can show you the ropes again, and then you'll be working until the bar closes.'

There was a short silence. 'I'll be there,' Tanya said. 'I got some black pants. You got a T-shirt I can wear?'

'Yep. Medium?'

'That'll do me.'

She hung up.

Well, I could hardly expect to find her happy to hear from me or delighted to oblige since we'd never been fans of each other. In fact, though I didn't believe she remembered, I'd had her bewitched by Amelia and Amelia's mentor, Octavia. I still squirmed when I thought of how I'd altered Tanya's life, but I didn't think I'd had a lot of choices there. Sometimes you just have to regret things and move on.

Sam called while Terry and I were closing the bar. I was so tired. My head was heavy, and my feet were aching.

'How are things going there?' Sam asked. His voice was rough with exhaustion.

'We're coping,' I said, trying to sound perky and carefree. 'How's your mom?'

'She's still alive,' he said. 'She's talking and breathing on her own. The doctor says he thinks she'll recover just fine. My stepfather is under arrest.'

'What a mess,' I said, genuinely distressed on Sam's behalf.

'Mom says she should have told him beforehand,' he told me. 'She was just scared to.'

'Well ... rightly so, huh? As it turns out.'

He snorted. 'She figures if she'd had a long talk with him, then let him see her change after he'd watched the change on TV, he would've been okay.'

I'd been so busy with the bar I hadn't had a chance to absorb the television reports of the reactions around the world to this second Great Revelation. I wondered how it was going in Montana, Indiana, Florida? I wondered if any of the famous actors in Hollywood had admitted to being werewolves. What if Ryan Seacrest was fuzzy every full moon? Or Jennifer Love Hewitt or Russell Crowe? (Which I thought was more than likely.) That would make a huge difference in public acceptance.

'Have you seen your stepfather or talked to him?'

'No, not yet. I can't make myself. My brother went by. He said Don started crying. It was bad.'

'Is your sister there?'

'Well, she's on her way. She had a hard time arranging child care.' He sounded a little hesitant.

'She knew about your mom, right?' I tried to keep the incredulity out of my voice.

'No,' he said. 'Real often, were parents don't tell the kids who aren't affected. My sibs didn't know about me, either, since they didn't know about Mom.'

'I'm sorry,' I said, which stood for a lot of things.

'I wish you were here,' Sam said, taking me by surprise.

'I wish I could be more help,' I said. 'If you can think of anything else I can do, you call me at any hour.'

'You're keeping the business running. That counts for a lot,' he said. 'I better go get some sleep.'

'Okay, Sam. Talk to you tomorrow, okay?'

'Sure,' he said. He sounded so worn-out and sad it was hard not to cry.

I felt relieved that I'd put my personal feelings aside to call Tanya, after that conversation. It had been the right thing to do. Sam's mother being shot for what she was – well, that just put my dislike of Tanya Grissom into perspective.

I fell into bed that night, and I don't think I even twitched after that.

I'd been sure the warm glow generated by Sam's call would carry me through the next day, but the morning started badly.

Sam always ordered the supplies and kept up with the inventory, naturally. Also, naturally, he'd forgotten to remind me that he had some cases of beer coming in. I got a phone call from the truck driver, Duff, and I had to leap out of bed and hurry to Merlotte's. On my way out the door, I glimpsed the blinking light on my answering machine, which I'd been too tired to check the night before. But I didn't have time to worry about missed messages now. I was simply relieved Duff had thought of calling me when he got no answer at Sam's.

I opened the back door of Merlotte's, and Duff wheeled the cases in and put them where they were supposed to go. Somewhat nervously, I signed for Sam. By the time that was done and the truck had pulled out of the parking lot, Sarah Jen, the mail carrier, came by with the bar mail and Sam's personal mail. I accepted both. Sarah Jen had her talking shoes on. She'd heard (already) that Sam's mom was in the hospital, but I didn't feel I had to enlighten her about the circumstances. That was Sam's business. Sarah Jen also wanted to tell me how she wasn't astonished at all that Sam was a wereanimal, because she'd always thought there was something strange about him.

'He's a nice guy,' Sarah Jen admitted. 'I'm not saying he's not. Just . . . something odd there. I wasn't a bit surprised.'

'Really? He's sure said such nice things about you,' I said sweetly, looking down so the line would be a throwaway. I could see the delight flooding Sarah Jen's head as clearly as if she'd drawn me a picture.

'He's always been real polite,' she said, suddenly seeing Sam in the light of a most perceptive man. 'Well, I better be going. I got to finish the route. If you talk to Sam, tell him I'm thinking of his mom.'

After I carried the mail to Sam's desk, Amelia called from the insurance agency to tell me that Octavia had called her to ask if either of us could take her to Wal-Mart. Octavia, who'd lost most of her stuff in Katrina, was stuck out at the house without a car.

'You'll have to take her on your lunch hour,' I said, barely managing not to snap at Amelia. 'I got a full plate today. And here comes more trouble,' I said as a car pulled up beside mine in the employee parking lot. 'Here's Eric's daytime guy, Bobby Burnham.'

'Oh, I meant to tell you. Octavia said Eric tried to call you at home twice. So she finally told Bobby where you were this morning,' Amelia said. 'She figured it might be important. Lucky you. Okay, I'll take care of Octavia. Somehow.'

'Good,' I said, trying not to sound as brusque as I felt. 'Talk to you later.'

Bobby Burnham got out of his Impala and strode up to me. His boss, Eric, was bound to me in a complicated relationship that was based not only on our past history but also on the fact that we'd swapped blood several times.

This hadn't been an informed decision on my part.

Bobby Burnham was an asshole. Maybe Eric had gotten him on sale?

'Miss Stackhouse,' he said, laying the courtliness on thick. 'My master asks that you come to Fangtasia tonight for a sit-down with the new king's lieutenant.'

This was not the summons I'd expected or the kind of conversation I'd foreseen with the vampire sheriff of Area Five. Given the fact that we had some personal issues to discuss, I'd imagined Eric would call me when things had settled down with the new regime, and we'd make some kind of appointment – or date – to talk about the several items on our mutual plate. I wasn't pleased by this impersonal summons by a flunky.

'You ever hear of a phone?' I said.

'He left you messages last night. He told me to talk to you today, without fail. I'm just following orders.'

'Eric told you to spend your time driving over here and asking me to come to his bar tonight.' Even to my own ears, I sounded unbelieving.

'Yes. He said, 'Track her down, deliver the message in person, and be polite.' Here I am. Being polite.'

He was telling me the truth, and it was just killing him. That was almost enough to make me smile. Bobby really didn't like me. The closest I could come to defining why was that Bobby didn't think I was worthy of Eric's notice. He didn't like my less-than-reverent attitude toward Eric, and he couldn't understand why Pam, Eric's right-hand vampire, was fond of me, when she wouldn't give Bobby the time of day.

There was nothing I could do to change this, even if Bobby's dislike had worried me . . . and it didn't. But Eric worried me plenty. I had to talk to him, and I might as well get it over with. It had been late October when I'd last seen him, and it was now mid-January. 'It'll have to be when I get off here. I'm temporarily in charge,' I said, sounding neither pleased nor gracious.

'What time? He wants you there at seven. Victor will be there then.'

Victor Madden was the representative of the new king, Felipe de Castro. It had been a bloody takeover, and Eric was the only sheriff of the old regime still standing. Staying in the good graces of the new regime was important to Eric, obviously. I wasn't yet sure how much of that was my problem. But I was thumbs-up with Felipe de Castro by a happy accident, and I wanted to keep it that way.

'I might be able to get there by seven,' I said after some inner computation. I tried not to think about how much it would please me to lay eyes on Eric. At least ten times in the past few weeks, I'd caught myself before I'd gotten in my car to drive over to see him. But I'd successfully resisted the impulses, because I'd been able to *tell* that he was struggling to maintain his position under the new king. 'I've got to brief the new gal. . . . Yeah, seven is just about doable.'

'He'll be so relieved,' Bobby said, managing to work in a sneer.

Keep it up, asshole, I thought. And possibly the way I was looking at him conveyed that thought, because Bobby said, 'Really, he will be,' in as sincere a tone as he could manage.

'Okay, message delivered,' I said. 'I got to get back to work.'

'Where's your boss?'

'He had a family problem in Texas.'

'Oh, I thought maybe the dogcatcher got him.'

What a howl. 'Good-bye, Bobby,' I said, and turned my back on him to go in the back door.

'Here,' he said, and I turned around, irritated. 'Eric said you would need this.' He handed me a bundle wrapped in black velvet. Vampires couldn't give you anything in a Wal-Mart bag or wrapped in Hallmark paper, oh, no. Black velvet. The bundle was secured with a gold tasseled cord, like you'd use to tie back a curtain.

Just holding it gave me a bad feeling. 'And what would this be?'

'I don't know. I wasn't tasked with opening it.'

I *hate* the word 'tasked', with 'gifted' running close behind. 'What am I supposed to do with this?' I said.

'Eric said, "Tell her to give it to me tonight, in front of Victor."'

Eric did nothing without a reason. 'All right,' I said reluctantly. 'Consider me *messaged*.'

I got through the next shift okay. Everyone was pitching in to help, and that was pleasing. The cook had been working hard all day; this was maybe the fifteenth short-order cook we'd had since I'd begun working at Merlotte's. We'd had every variation on a human being you could imagine: black, white, male, female, old, young, dead (yes, a vampire cook), lycanthropically inclined (a werewolf), and probably one or two I'd completely forgotten. This cook, Antoine Lebrun, was real nice. He'd come to us out of Katrina. He'd outstayed most of the other refugees, who'd moved back to the Gulf Coast or moved on.

Antoine was in his fifties, his curly hair showing a strand or two of gray. He'd worked concessions at the Superdome, he'd told me the day he got hired, and we'd both shuddered. Antoine got along great with D'Eriq, the busboy who doubled as his assistant.

When I went in the kitchen to make sure he had everything he needed, Antoine told me he was really proud to be working for a shapeshifter, and D'Eriq wanted to go over and over his reaction to Sam's and Tray's transformations. After he'd left work, D'Eriq had gotten a phone call from his cousin in Monroe, and now D'Eriq wanted to tell us all about his cousin's wife being a werewolf.

D'Eriq's reaction was what I hoped was typical. Two nights before, many people had discovered that someone they knew personally was a were of some kind. Hopefully, if the were had never shown signs of insanity or violence, these people would be willing to accept that shape-changing was an unthreatening addition to their knowledge of the world. It was even exciting.

I hadn't had time to check reactions around the world, but at least as far as local stuff went, the revelation seemed to be going smoothly. I didn't get the feeling anyone was going to be firebombing Merlotte's because of Sam's dual nature, and I thought Tray's motorcycle repair business was safe.

Tanya was twenty minutes early, which raised her up in my estimation, and I gave her a genuine smile. After we ran over a few of the basics like hours, pay, and Sam's house rules, I said, 'You like being out there in Hotshot?'

'Yeah, I do,' she said, sounding a little surprised. 'The families out in Hotshot, they really get along well. If something goes wrong, they have a meeting and discuss it. Those that don't like the life, they leave, like Mel Hart did.' Almost everyone in Hotshot was either a Hart or a Norris.

'He's really taken up with my brother lately,' I said, because I was a little curious about Jason's new friend.

'Yeah, that's what I hear. Everyone's glad he's found someone to hang with after being on his own so long.'

'Why didn't he fit in out there?' I asked directly.

Tanya said, 'I understand Mel doesn't like to share, like you have to if you live in a little community like that. He's real . . . "What's mine is mine."' She shrugged. 'At least, that's what they say.'

'Jason's like that, too,' I said. I couldn't read Tanya's mind too clearly because of her double nature, but I could read the mood and intent of it, and I understood the other panthers worried about Mel Hart.

They were concerned about Mel making it in the big world of Bon Temps, I guessed. Hotshot was its own little universe.

I was feeling a bit lighter of heart by the time I'd finished briefing Tanya (who had definitely had experience) and hung up my apron. I gathered my purse and Bobby Burnham's bundle, and I hurried out the employee door to drive to Shreveport.

I started to listen to the news as I drove, but I was tired of grim reality. Instead, I listened to a Mariah Carey CD, and I felt the better for it. I can't sing worth a damn, but I love to belt out the lyrics to a song when I'm driving. The tensions of the day began to drain away, replaced by an optimistic mood.

Sam would come back, his mother having recovered, and her husband having made amends and having pledged he'd love her forever. The world would *oooh* and *aaah* about werewolves and other shifters for a while, then all would be normal again.

Isn't it always a bad idea, thinking things like that?

Chapter 3

The closer I got to the vampire bar, the more my pulse picked up; this was the downside to the blood bond I had with Eric Northman. I knew I was going to see him, and I was simply *happy* about it. I should have been worried, I should have been apprehensive about what he wanted, I should have asked a million questions about the velvet-wrapped bundle, but I just drove with a smile on my face.

Though I couldn't help how I felt, I could control my actions. Out of sheer perversity, since no one had told me to come around to the employees' entrance, I entered through the main door. It was a busy night at Fangtasia, and there was a crowd waiting on benches inside the first set of doors. Pam was at the hostess podium. She smiled at me broadly, showing a little fang. (The crowd was delighted.)

I'd known Pam for a while now, and she was as close to a friend as I had among the vampires. Tonight the blond vampire was wearing the obligatory filmy black dress, and she'd camped it up with a long, sheer black veil. Her fingernails were polished scarlet.

'My friend,' Pam said, and came out from behind the podium to hug me. I was surprised but pleased and gladly hugged her back. She'd spritzed on a little perfume to eclipse the faint, rather dry smell of vampire. 'Have you got it?' she whispered in my ear.

'Oh, the bundle? It's in my purse.' I lifted my big brown shoulder bag by its straps.

Pam gave me a look I couldn't interpret through the veil. It appeared to be an expression that compounded exasperation and affection. 'You didn't even look inside?'

'I haven't had time,' I said. It wasn't that I hadn't been curious. I simply hadn't had the leisure to think about it. 'Sam had to leave because his mom got shot by his stepdad, and I've been managing the bar.'

Pam gave me a long look of appraisal. 'Go back to Eric's office and hand him the bundle,' she said. 'Leave it wrapped. No matter who's there. And don't handle it like it was a garden tool he left outside, either.'

I gave her the look right back. 'What am I doing, Pam?' I asked, jumping on the cautious train way too late.

'You're protecting your own skin,' Pam said. 'Never doubt it. Now go.' She gave me a get-along pat on the back and turned to answer a tourist's question about how often vampires needed to get their teeth cleaned.

'Would you like to come very close and look at mine?' Pam asked in a sultry voice, and the woman shrieked with delighted fear. That was why the humans came to vampire bars, and vampire comedy clubs, and vampire dry cleaners, and vampire casinos . . . to flirt with danger.

Every now and then, flirtation became the real thing.

I made my way between the tables and across the dance floor to the rear of the bar. Felicia, the bartender, looked unhappy when she saw me. She found something to do that involved crouching down out of my sight. I had an unfortunate history with the bartenders of Fangtasia.

There were a few vampires seated throughout the bar area, strewn among the gawking tourists, the costumed vampire wannabes, and the humans who had business dealings with the vamps. Over in the little souvenir shop, one of the New Orleans vampire refugees from Katrina was selling a Fangtasia T-shirt to a pair of giggling girls.

Tiny Thalia, paler than bleached cotton and with a profile from an ancient coin, was sitting by herself at a small table. Thalia was actually tracked by fans who had devoted a website to her, though she would not have cared if they'd all burst into flames. A drunken serviceman from Barksdale Air Force Base knelt before her as I watched, and as

Thalia turned her dark eyes on him, his prearranged speech died in his throat. Turning rather pale himself, the strapping young man backed away from the vampire half his size, and though his friends jeered as he returned to his table, I knew he wouldn't approach her again.

After this little slice of bar life, I was glad to knock on Eric's door. I heard his voice inside, telling me to come in. I stepped inside and shut the door behind me. 'Hi, Eric,' I said, and was almost rendered mute by the surge of happiness that swept through me whenever I saw him. His long blond hair was braided tonight, and he was wearing his favorite jeans-and-a-tee combo. The T-shirt tonight was bright green, making him look whiter than ever.

The wave of delight wasn't necessarily related to Eric's gorgeousness or the fact that we'd bumped pelvises, though. The blood bond was responsible. Maybe. I had to fight the feeling. For sure.

Victor Madden, representative of the new king, Felipe de Castro, stood and inclined his curly dark head. Victor, short and compact, was always polite and always well-dressed. This evening he was especially resplendent in an olive suit and brown striped tie. I smiled at him and was just about to tell him I was glad to see him again when I noticed that Eric was eyeing me expectantly. Oh, right.

I shucked off my coat and extracted the velvet bundle from my purse. I dropped the purse and coat in an empty chair, and walked over to Eric's desk with the bundle extended in both hands. This was making as much of the moment as I could, short of getting on my knees and crawling over to him, which I would do when hell froze over.

I laid the bundle in front of him, inclined my own head in what I hoped was a ceremonious manner, and sat down in the other guest chair.

'What has our fair-haired friend brought you, Eric?' Victor asked in the cheerful voice that he affected most of the time. Maybe he was actually that happy, or maybe his mama had taught him (a few centuries ago) that you catch more flies with honey than you do with vinegar.

With a certain sense of theater, Eric untied the golden cord and silently unfolded the velvet. Sparkling like a jewel on the dark material was the ceremonial knife I'd last seen in the city of Rhodes. Eric had used it when he officiated at the marriage of two vampire kings, and he'd used it to nick himself later when he'd taken blood from me and given me blood in return: the final exchange, the one that (from my point of view) had caused all the trouble. Now Eric lifted the shining blade to his lips and kissed it.

After Victor recognized the knife, there was no trace of a smile remaining on his face. He and Eric regarded each other steadily.

'Very interesting,' Victor said finally.

Once again, I had that feeling of drowning when I hadn't even known I was in the pool. I started to speak, but I could feel Eric's will pressing on me, urging me to be silent. In vampire matters, it was smart to take Eric's advice.

'Then I'll take the tiger's request off the table,' Victor said. 'My master was unhappy about the tiger wanting to leave, anyway. And of course, I'll inform my master about your prior claim. We acknowledge your formal attachment to this one.'

From the inclination of Victor's head in my direction, I knew I was 'this one.' And I knew only one male weretiger. 'What are you talking about?' I asked bluntly.

'Quinn requested a private meeting with you,' Victor said. 'But he can't come back to Eric's area without Eric's permission now. It's one of the terms we negotiated when we ... when Eric became our new associate.'

That was a nice way to say, *When we killed all the other vampires in Louisiana except for Eric and his followers. When you saved our king from death.*

I wished I had a moment to think, far away from this room where two vampires were staring at me.

'Does this new rule apply only to Quinn or to all wereanimals who want to come into Louisiana? How could you boss the weres? And when did you put that rule into effect?' I said to Eric, trying to buy some time while I collected myself. I wanted Victor to explain the last part of his little speech, too, that bit about the formal attachment, but I decided to tackle one question at a time.

'Three weeks ago,' Eric said, answering the last question first. His face was calm; his voice was uninflected. 'And the "new rule" applies only to wereanimals who are associated with us in a business way.' Quinn worked for E(E)E, which I suspected was at least partially vampire owned, since Quinn's job was not putting on the weddings and bar mitzvahs the company's human branch dealt with. Quinn's job was staging supernatural events. 'The tiger got his dismissal from you. I heard it from his own lips. Why should he return?' Eric shrugged.

At least he didn't try to sugarcoat it by saying, 'I thought he might bother you' or 'I did it for your own good.' No matter how bonded we were – and I was actually struggling against the temptation to smile at him – I felt the hair on the back of my neck rising at Eric managing my life like this.

'Now that you and Eric are openly pledged,' Victor said in a silky voice, 'you certainly won't want to see Quinn, and I'll tell him so.'

'We're *what?*' I glared at Eric, who was looking at me with an expression I can only describe as bland.

'The knife,' Victor said, sounding even happier. 'That's its significance. It's a ritual knife handed down over the centuries and used in important ceremonies and sacrifices. It's not the only one of its kind, of course, but it's rare. Now it's only used in marriage rituals. I'm not sure how Eric came to have possession of it, but its presentation from you to Eric, and his acceptance, can only mean that you and Eric are pledged to each other.'

'Let's all step back and take a deep breath,' I said, though I was the only person in the room who was breathing. I held up my hand as though they'd been advancing on me and my 'halt' gesture would stop them. 'Eric?' I tried to pack everything into my voice, but one word can't carry that much baggage.

'This is for your protection, dear heart,' he said. He was trying to be serene so that some of that serenity would run through our bond and drown my agitation.

But a few gallons of serenity wouldn't calm me down. 'This is so high-handed,' I said in a choked voice. 'This is sheer gall. How could you do this without talking to me about it? How could you think I would let you commit me to something without talking about it first? We haven't even seen each other in months.'

'I've been a little busy here. I'd hoped your sense of self- preservation would kick in,' Eric said, which was honest, if not tactful. 'Can you doubt that I want what's best for you?'

'I don't doubt that you want what *you think* is best for me,' I said. 'And I don't doubt that that marches right along with what you think is good for *you*.'

Victor laughed. 'She knows you well, Eric,' he said, and we both glared at him. 'Ooops,' he said, and pretended to zip his mouth shut.

'Eric, I'm going home. We'll talk about this soon, but I don't know when. I'm running the bar while Sam's gone. There's trouble in his family.'

'But Clancy said the announcement went well in Bon Temps.'

'Yes, it did, but at Sam's own family home in Texas, it didn't go so well.'

Eric looked disgusted. 'I did my best to help. I sent at least one of my people around to every public venue. I went to watch Alcide himself shift at the Shamrock Casino.'

'That went okay?' I asked, temporarily sidetracked.

'Yes, only a few drunkards acted up. They were quelled quite easily. One woman even offered herself to Alcide in his wolf form.'

'Ewww,' I said, and got up, grabbing my purse. He'd distracted me long enough.

Eric rose and vaulted over the desk in a movement that was as startling as it was impressive. Suddenly he was right in front of me, and his arms went around me, and he held me to him. It took every-thing I had to keep my back stiff, to keep from relaxing against him. It's hard to explain how the bond made me feel. No matter how furious I got with Eric, I was happier when I was with him. It wasn't that I yearned for him uncontrollably when we were separated; it was just that I was aware of him. All the time. I wondered if it was the same for him.

'Tomorrow night?' he said, releasing me.

'If I can get away. We have a lot to talk about.' I gave Victor a stiff nod, and I left. I glanced back once to see the knife shining against the black velvet as it lay on Eric's desk.

I knew how Eric had gotten the knife. He'd simply kept it rather than returning it to Quinn, who'd been in charge of the wedding ritual between two vampires, a ceremony I'd witnessed in Rhodes. Eric, who was some kind of mail-order priest, had officiated at the service, and afterward, he'd evidently kept the knife just on the chance it would come in handy. How he'd retrieved it from the wreck of the hotel, I didn't know. Maybe he'd gone back during the night, after the daytime explosion. Maybe he'd sent Pam. But he'd gotten it, and now he'd used it to pledge me to him.

And thanks to my own dazed affection . . . or warmth . . . or infatuation . . . for the Viking vampire, I had done exactly what he'd asked without consulting my common sense.

I didn't know who I was angrier with – myself, or Eric.

Chapter 4

I spent a restless night. I would think of Eric and feel the warm rush of joy, and then think of Eric and want to punch him in the face. I thought of Bill, the first man I'd ever dated more than once, the first man I'd ever gone to bed with; when I remembered his cool voice and body, his contained calm, and contrasted it with Eric, I couldn't believe I had fallen for two such different males, especially when my all-too-brief episode with Quinn was factored in. Quinn had been warm-blooded in every respect, and impulsive, and kind to me, and yet so scarred by his past, he hadn't shared it with me – which, in my view, had led to our relationship being ruined. I'd dated Alcide Herveaux, pack leader, too, but it had never gone further.

Sookie Stackhouse's All-Male Revue.

Don't you just hate nights like that, when you think over every mistake you've made, every hurt you've received, every bit of meanness you've dealt out? There's no profit in it, no point to it, and you need sleep. But that night, men were on my mind, and not in a happy way.

When I'd exhausted the topic of my problems with the male sex, I launched into worrying about the responsibility of the bar. I finally got three hours' sleep after I made myself admit that there was no way I could run Sam's business into the ground in a few days.

Sam called the next morning while I was still at home to tell me his mother was better and was definitely going to recover. His brother and sister were now dealing with the family revelations in a much calmer way. Don, of course, was still in jail.

'If she keeps improving, I may be able to start back in a couple of days,' he said. 'Or even sooner. Of course, the doctors keep telling us they can't believe how fast she's healing.' He sighed. 'At least we don't have to conceal that now.'

'How's your mom handling the emotional part?' I asked.

'She's quit insisting they should release him. And since she had a frank talk with the three of us, she's admitting she and Don might have to get a divorce,' he said. 'She's not happy about the idea, but I don't know if you can completely reconcile with someone who's shot you.'

Though I'd answered the phone by my bed and was still comfortably prone, I found it impossible to go back to sleep after we'd hung up. I'd hated to hear the pain in Sam's voice. Sam had enough to fret about without troubling him with my problems, so I hadn't even seriously considered bringing up the knife incident, though I would have been relieved to share my worries with Sam.

I was up and dressed by eight o'clock, early for me. Though I was moving and thinking, I felt as rumpled and wrinkled as my bedsheets. I wished someone could yank me smooth and orderly, the way I yanked the sheets. Amelia was home (I checked to see if her car was parked out back when I made the coffee) and I'd glimpsed Octavia shuffling into the hall bathroom, so it was shaping up to be a typical morning, as mornings went nowadays at my house.

The pattern was broken by a knocking at the front door. Usually I'm warned by the crunching of the gravel driveway, but in my heavier-than-usual morning fog, I'd missed it.

I looked through the peephole to see a man and a woman, both dressed in proper business suits. They didn't look like Jehovah's Witnesses or home invaders. I reached out to them mentally and found no hostility or anger, only curiosity.

I opened the door. I smiled brilliantly. 'Can I help you?' I said. The cold air gusted around my bare feet.

The woman, who was probably in her early forties, smiled back. Her brown hair had a little gray in it and was cut in a simple chin-length style. She'd parted it very precisely. Her pantsuit was charcoal with a black sweater underneath, and her shoes were black. She carried a black bag, which wasn't exactly like a purse, more like a laptop case.

She held out her hand to shake, and when I touched her, I knew more. It was hard to keep the shock off my face. 'I'm from the New Orleans office of the FBI,' she said, which is a bombshell of an opener for your average conversation. 'I'm Agent Sara Weiss. This is Special Agent Tom Lattesta from our Rhodes office.'

'You're here about . . .?' I kept my face pleasantly blank.

'May we come in? Tom's come all the way from Rhodes to talk to you, and we're letting all your warm air out.'

'Sure,' I said, though I was far from sure. I was trying hard to get a fix on their intent, but it wasn't easy. I could only tell they weren't there to arrest me or anything drastic like that.

'Is this a convenient time?' Agent Weiss asked. She implied she'd be delighted to come back later, though I knew that wasn't true.

'This is as good as any,' I said. My grandmother would have given me a sharp look for my ungraciousness, but then, Gran had never been questioned by the FBI. This was not exactly a social call. 'I do have to leave for work pretty soon,' I added to give myself an escape hatch.

'That's bad news, about your boss's mother,' Lattesta said. 'Did the big announcement go well at your bar?' From his accent, I could tell he'd been born north of the Mason-Dixon Line, and from his knowledge of Sam's whereabouts and identity, he'd done his homework, down to investigating the place I worked.

The sick feeling that had started up in my stomach intensified. I had a moment of wanting Eric there so badly it made me a little dizzy, and then I looked out the window at the sunshine and felt only anger at my own longing. *This is what you get,* I told myself.

'Having werewolves around makes the world more interesting, doesn't it?' I said. The smile popped onto my face, the smile that said I was really strained. 'I'll take your coats. Please, have a seat.' I indicated the couch, and they settled on it. 'Can I get you some coffee or some iced tea?' I said, thanking Gran's training for keeping the words flowing.

'Oh,' Weiss said. 'Some iced tea would be wonderful. I know it's cold outside, but I drink it year-round. I'm a southern woman born and bred.'

And laying it on a little too thick, in my opinion. I didn't think Weiss would become my best friend, and I didn't plan to swap any recipes. 'You?' I looked at Lattesta.

'Sure, great,' he said.

'Sweet or unsweet?' Lattesta thought it would be fun to have the famous southern sweet tea, and Weiss accepted sweet as a matter of bonding. 'Let me tell my roommates we have company,' I said, and I called up the stairs, 'Amelia! The FBI is here!'

'I'll be down in a minute,' she called back, not sounding surprised at all. I knew she'd been standing at the top of the stairs listening to every word.

And here came Octavia in her favorite green pants and striped long-sleeved shirt, looking as dignified and sweet as an elderly white-haired black woman can look. Ruby Dee has nothing on Octavia.

'Hello,' she said, beaming. Though she looked like everyone's favorite granny, Octavia was a powerful witch who could cast spells with almost surgical precision. She'd had a lifetime of practice in concealing her ability. 'Sookie didn't tell us she was expecting company, or we would have cleaned up the house.' Octavia beamed some more. She swept a hand to indicate the spotless living room. It would never be featured in *Southern Living*, but it was clean, by golly.

'Looks great to me,' Weiss said respectfully. 'I wish my house looked this neat.' She was telling the truth. Weiss had two teenagers and a husband and three dogs. I felt a lot of sympathy – and maybe some envy – for Agent Weiss.

'Sookie, I'll bring tea for your guests while you talk,' Octavia said in her sweetest voice. 'You just sit down and visit a spell.' The agents were settled on the couch and looking around the shabby living room with interest when she returned with napkins and two glasses of sweet tea, ice rattling in a pleasant way. I rose from the chair opposite the couch to put napkins in front of them, and Octavia placed the glasses on the napkins. Lattesta took a large swallow. The corner of Octavia's mouth twitched just a little when he made a startled face and then did his best to amend his expression to pleased surprise.

'What did you-all want to ask me?' Time to get down to brass tacks. I smiled at them brightly, my hands folded in my lap, my feet parallel, and my knees clamped together.

Lattesta had brought in a briefcase, and now he put it on the coffee table and opened it. He extracted a picture and handed it to me. It had been taken in the middle of the afternoon in the city of Rhodes a few months before. The picture was clear enough, though the air around the people in it was blighted with the clouds of dust that had billowed up from the collapsed Pyramid of Gizeh.

I kept my eyes on the picture, I kept my face smiling, but I couldn't stop my heart from sinking into my feet.

In the picture, Barry the Bellboy and I were standing together in the rubble of the Pyramid, the vampire hotel that a splinter Fellowship group had blown up the previous October. I was somewhat more recognizable than my companion, because Barry was standing in profile. I was facing the camera, unaware of it, my eyes on Barry's face. We were both covered in dirt and blood, ash and dust.

'That's you, Miss Stackhouse,' Lattesta said.

'Yes, it is.' Pointless to deny the woman in the picture was me, but I sure would have loved to have done so. Looking at the picture made me feel sick because it forced me to remember that day all too clearly.

'So you were staying at the Pyramid at the time of the explosion?'

'Yes, I was.'

'You were there in the employ of Sophie-Anne Leclerq, a vampire businesswoman. The so-called Queen of Louisiana.'

I started to tell him there had been no 'so-called' about it, but discretion blocked those words. 'I flew up there with her,' I said instead.

'And Sophie-Anne Leclerq sustained severe injuries in the blast?'

'I understand she did.'

'You didn't see her after the explosion?'

'No.'

'Who is this man standing with you in the picture?'

Lattesta hadn't identified Barry. I had to keep my shoulders stiff so they wouldn't sag with relief. I shrugged. 'He came up to me after the blast,' I said. 'We were in better shape than most, so we helped search for survivors.' Truth, but not the whole truth. I'd known Barry for months before I'd encountered him at the convention at the Pyramid. He'd been there in the service of the King of Texas. I wondered how much about the vamp hierarchy the FBI actually knew.

'How did the two of you search for survivors?' Lattesta asked.

That was a very tricky question. At that time, Barry was the only other telepath I'd ever met. We'd experimented by holding hands to increase our 'wattage', and we'd looked for brain signatures in the piles of debris. I took a deep breath. 'I'm good at finding things,' I said. 'It seemed important to help. So many people hurt so bad.'

'The fire chief on-site said you seemed to have some psychic ability,' Lattesta said. Weiss looked down at her tea glass to hide her expression.

'I'm not a psychic,' I said truthfully, and Weiss immediately felt disappointed. She felt she could be in the presence of a poseur or a nut job, but she had hoped I'd admit I was the real thing.

'Chief Trochek said you told them where to find survivors. He said you actually steered the rescue crews to the living.'

Amelia came down the stairs then, looking very respectable in a bright red sweater and designer jeans. I met her eyes, hoping she'd see I was silently asking for help. I hadn't been able to turn my back on a situation where I could actually save lives. When I'd realized I could find people – that teaming up with Barry would result in saving lives – I couldn't turn away from the task, though I was scared of being exposed to the world as a freak.

It's hard to explain what I see. I guess it's like looking through infrared goggles or something. I see the heat of the brain; I can count the living people in a building, if I have time. Vampire brains leave a hole, a negative spot; I can usually count those, too. Plain old dead people don't register with me at all. That day when Barry and I had held hands, the joining had magnified our abilities. We could find the living, and we could hear the last thoughts of the dying. I wouldn't wish that on anyone. And I didn't want to experience it again, ever.

'We just had good luck,' I said. That wouldn't convince a toad to hop.

Amelia came forward with her hand extended. 'I'm Amelia Broadway,' she said, as if she expected them to know who she was.

They did.

'You're Copley's daughter, right?' Weiss asked. 'I met him a couple of weeks ago in connection with a community program.'

'He's so involved in the city,' Amelia said with a dazzling smile. 'He's got his fingers in a dozen pies, I guess. Dad's real fond of the Sook, here.' Not so subtle, but hopefully effective. *Leave my roommate alone. My father's powerful.*

Weiss nodded pleasantly. 'How'd you end up here in Bon Temps, Ms Broadway?' she asked. 'It must seem real quiet here, after New Orleans.' *What's a rich bitch like you doing in this backwater? By the way, your dad's not around to run interference for you.*

'My house got damaged during Katrina,' Amelia said. She left it at that. She didn't tell them that she'd been in Bon Temps already when Katrina happened.

'And you, Ms Fant?' Lattesta asked. 'Were you an evacuee also?' He'd by no means abandoned the subject of my ability, but he was willing to go along with the social flow.

'Yes,' Octavia said. 'I was living with my niece under cramped circumstances, and Sookie very kindly offered me her spare bedroom.'

'How'd you know each other?' Weiss asked, as if she was expecting to hear a delightful story.

'Through Amelia,' I said, smiling just as happily back at her.

'And you and Amelia met—?'

'In New Orleans,' Amelia said, firmly cutting off that line of questioning.

'Did you want some more iced tea?' Octavia asked Lattesta.

'No, thank you,' he said, almost shuddering. It had been Octavia's turn to make the tea, and she did have a heavy hand with the sugar. 'Ms Stackhouse, you don't have any idea how to contact this young man?' He indicated the picture.

I shrugged. 'We both helped to look for bodies,' I said. 'It was a terrible day. I don't remember what name he gave.'

'That seems strange,' Lattesta said, and I thought, *Oh, shit.* 'Since someone answering your description and a young man answering his description checked into a motel some distance from the explosion that night and shared a room.'

'Well, you don't have to know someone's name to spend the night with them,' Amelia said reasonably.

I shrugged and tried to look embarrassed, which wasn't too hard. I'd rather they think me sexually easy than decide I was worthy of more attention. 'We'd shared a horrible, stressful event. Afterward, we felt really close. That's the way we reacted.' Actually, Barry had collapsed in sleep almost instantly, and I had followed soon afterward. Hanky-panky had been the furthest thing from our minds.

The two agents stared at me doubtfully. Weiss was thinking I was lying for sure, and Lattesta suspected it. He thought I knew Barry very well.

The phone rang, and Amelia hurried to the kitchen to answer it. She came back looking green.

'Sookie, that was Antoine on his cell phone. They need you at the bar,' she said. And then she turned to the FBI agents. 'Probably you should go with her.'

'Why?' Weiss asked. 'What's up?' She was already on her feet. Lattesta was stuffing the picture back into his briefcase.

'A body,' Amelia said. 'A woman's been crucified behind the bar.'

Chapter 5

The agents followed me to Merlotte's. There were five or six cars parked across the spot where the front parking lot ended and the back parking began, effectively blocking access to the back. But I leaped out of my car and picked a path between them, and the FBI agents were right on my heels.

I had hardly been able to believe it, but it was true. There was a traditional cross erected in the employee parking lot, back by the trees where the gravel gave way to dirt. A body was nailed to it. My eyes scanned it, took in the distorted body, the streaks of dried blood, came back up to the face.

'Oh, no,' I said, and my knees folded.

Antoine, the cook, and D'Eriq, the busboy, were suddenly on either side of me, pulling me up. D'Eriq's face was tearstained, and Antoine looked grim, but the cook had his head together. He'd been in Iraq and in New Orleans during Katrina. He'd seen things that were worse.

'I'm sorry, Sookie,' he said.

Andy Bellefleur was there, and Sheriff Dearborn. They walked over to me, looking bigger and bulkier in their waterproof quilted coats. Their faces were hard with suppressed shock.

'Sorry about your sister-in-law,' Bud Dearborn said, but I could barely pay attention to the words.

'She was pregnant,' I said. 'She was pregnant.' That was all I could think about. I wasn't amazed that someone would want to kill Crystal, but I was really horrified about the baby.

I took a deep breath and managed to look again. Crystal's bloody hands were panther paws. The lower part of her legs had changed, too. The effect was even more shocking and grotesque than the crucifixion of a regular human woman and, if possible, more pitiful.

Thoughts raced through my head with no logical sequence. I thought of who needed to know that Crystal had died. Calvin, not only head of her clan but also her uncle. Crystal's husband, my brother. Why was Crystal left here, of all places? Who could have done this?

'Have you called Jason yet?' I said through numb lips. I tried to blame that on the cold, but I knew it was shock. 'He would be at work this time of day.'

Bud Dearborn said, 'We called him.'

'Please don't make him look at her,' I said. There was a bloody mess trailing down the wood of the cross to the ground at its base. I gagged, got myself under control.

'I understand she cheated on him, and that their breakup was pretty public.' Bud was trying to be dispassionate, but the effort was costing him. Rage was in the back of his eyes.

'You can ask Dove Beck about that,' I said, instantly on the defensive. Alcee Beck was a detective for the Bon Temps police department, and the man Crystal had chosen to cheat with was Alcee's cousin Dove. 'Yeah, Crystal and Jason had separated. But he would never do anything to his baby.' I knew Jason would not have done such a horrific thing to Crystal no matter what the provocation, but I didn't expect anyone else to believe me.

Lattesta walked over to us, Agent Weiss following close behind. She looked a little white around the mouth, but her voice was steady. 'From the condition of the body, I believe this woman was a . . . werepanther.' She said the word as if it was hard to get it through her lips.

I nodded. 'Yes, ma'am, she was.' I was still fighting to gain control of my stomach.

'Then this could be a hate crime,' Lattesta said. His face was locked down tight, and his thoughts were orderly. He was composing a mental list of phone calls he should make, and he was trying to figure out if there was any way he could take charge of the case. If the murder had been a hate crime, he had a good shot at being in on the investigation.

'And who might you be?' Bud Dearborn asked. He had his hands on his belt, and he was looking at Weiss and Lattesta as if they were pre-need burial plot salesmen.

While the law enforcement types were all introducing themselves and saying profound things about the crime scene, Antoine said, 'I'm sorry, Sookie. We had to call 'em. But we called your house right after.'

'Of course you had to call them,' I said. 'I just wish Sam was here.' Oh, gosh. I pulled my cell phone out of my pocket and pressed his speed-dial number.

'Sam,' I said when he picked up. 'Can you talk?'

'Yes,' he said, sounding apprehensive. He could already tell some-thing was wrong.

'Where are you?'

'I'm in my car.'

'I have bad news.'

'What's happened? Did the bar burn down?'

'No, but Crystal's been murdered in the parking lot. Out back by your trailer.'

'Oh, shit. Where's Jason?'

'He's on his way here, near as I can find out.'

'I'm sorry, Sookie.' He sounded exhausted. 'This is going to be bad.'

'The FBI is here. They're thinking it might be a hate crime.' I skipped the explanation of why they'd happened to be in Bon Temps.

'Well, a lot of people didn't like Crystal,' Sam said cautiously, sur-prise in his voice.

'She was crucified.'

'Dammit to *hell*.' A long pause. 'Sook, if my mom is still stable and nothing's happening legally with my stepfather, I'll start back later today or early tomorrow.'

'Good.' I couldn't begin to pack enough relief into that one word. And it was no use pretending I had everything under control.

'I'm sorry, *cher*,' he said again. 'Sorry you're having to handle it, sorry Jason will be suspected, sorry about the whole thing. Sorry for Crystal, too.'

'I'll be glad to see you,' I said, and my voice was shaky with incipient tears.

'I'll be there.' And he hung up.

Lattesta said, 'Ms Stackhouse, are these men other bar employees?'

I introduced Antoine and D'Eriq to Lattesta. Antoine's expression didn't change, but D'Eriq was completely impressed that he'd met an FBI agent.

'Both of you knew this Crystal Norris, right?' Lattesta said mildly.

Antoine said, 'Just by sight. She come in the bar some.'

D'Eriq nodded.

'Crystal Norris Stackhouse,' I said. 'She's my sister-in-law. The sheriff's called my brother. But you need to call her uncle, Calvin Norris. He works at Norcross.'

'He her nearest living relative? Besides the husband?'

'She's got a sister. But Calvin's the leader of—' I stopped, not sure if Calvin had endorsed the Great Reveal. 'He raised her,' I said. Close enough.

Lattesta and Weiss huddled with Bud Dearborn. They were deep in conversation, probably about Calvin and the tiny community out at the bleak crossroads. Hotshot was a group of small houses containing lots of secrets. Crystal had wanted to escape from Hotshot, but she also felt most secure there.

My eyes returned to the tortured figure on the cross. Crystal was dressed, but her clothes had ripped when her arms and legs had changed to panther limbs, and there was blood everywhere. Her hands and feet, impaled with nails, were crusted with it. Ropes did the work of holding her to the crossbar, kept the flesh from ripping free of the nails.

I'd seen a lot of awful things, but this was maybe the most pathetic. 'Poor Crystal,' I said, and found tears were rolling down my cheeks.

'You didn't like her,' Andy Bellefleur said. I wondered how long he'd been out here, looking at the ruin of what had once been a living, breathing, healthy woman. Andy's cheeks were patched with stubble, and his nose was red. Andy had a cold. He sneezed and excused himself to use a handkerchief.

D'Eriq and Antoine were talking to Alcee Beck. Alcee was the other Bon Temps police detective, and that didn't make the investigation look too promising. He wouldn't be too regretful about Crystal's death.

Andy faced me again after he'd stuffed his handkerchief in his pocket. I looked at his weary, broad face. I knew he'd do his best to find out who'd done this. I trusted Andy. Square-built Andy, some years my senior, had never been a smiley kind of guy. He was serious and suspicious. I didn't know if he'd chosen his occupation because it suited him, or if his character had altered in response to his occupation.

'I hear she and Jason had split,' he said.

'Yes. She cheated on him.' This was common knowledge. I wasn't going to pretend otherwise.

'Pregnant and all, like she was?' Andy shook his head.

'Yeah.' I spread my hands. *That was the way she was.*

'That's sick,' Andy said.

'Yeah, it is. Cheating with your husband's baby in your stomach between you . . . that's just specially icky.' It was a thought I'd had but never voiced.

'So, who was the other man?' Andy asked casually. 'Or men?'

'You're the only guy in Bon Temps who doesn't know she was screwing Dove Beck,' I said.

This time it registered. Andy glanced over at Alcee Beck and back to me. 'I know now,' he said. 'Who hated her that much, Sookie?'

'If you're thinking Jason, you can just think again. He would never do that to his baby.'

'If she was so free with herself, maybe it wasn't his baby,' Andy said. 'Maybe he found that out.'

'It was his,' I said with a firmness I wasn't sure I felt. 'But even if it wasn't, if some blood test says it wasn't, he wouldn't kill anybody's baby. Anyway, they weren't living together. She'd moved back in with her sister. Why would he even go to the trouble?'

'Why were the FBI at your house?'

Okay, so this questioning thing was going to go one way. 'Some questions about the explosion in Rhodes,' I said. 'I found out about Crystal while they were there. They came along out of professional curiosity, I guess. Lattesta, the guy, thinks this might be a hate crime.'

'That's an interesting idea,' he said. 'This is undoubtedly a hate crime, but whether or not it's the kind of thing they should investigate, I don't know yet.' He strode off to talk to Weiss. Lattesta was looking up at the body, shaking his head, as if he was noting a level of awfulness he'd thought couldn't be reached.

I didn't know what to do with myself. I was in charge of the bar, and the crime scene was on bar property, so I was determined to stay.

Alcee Beck called, 'All people on the scene who are not police officers, leave the area! All police officers who are nonessential to the crime scene, step into the front parking lot!' His gaze fell on me, and he jabbed a finger toward the front. So I went back to lean against my car. Though it was cold enough, it was lucky for all of us that the day was bright and the wind wasn't blowing. I pulled my coat collar up around my ears and reached into the car to get my black gloves. I tugged them on and waited.

Time passed. I watched various police officers come and go. When Holly showed up for her shift, I explained what had happened and sent her home, telling her I'd call when I'd gotten permission to reopen. I couldn't think of any other course of action. Antoine and D'Eriq had left long ago, after I'd entered their cell numbers on my phone.

Jason's truck screeched to a halt beside my car, and he leaped out to stand in front of me. We hadn't spoken in weeks, but this was no time to talk about our differences. 'Is it true?' my brother asked.

'I'm sorry. It's true.'

'The baby, too?'

'Yeah.'

'Alcee come out to the job site,' he said numbly. 'He come asking how long it had been since I'd seen her. I haven't talked to her in four or five weeks, except to send her some money for the doctor visits and her vitamins. I saw her once at Dairy Queen.'

'Who was she with?'

'Her sister.' He took a long, shuddering breath. 'You think . . . was it bad?'

No point beating around the bush. 'Yes,' I said.

'Then I'm sorry she had to go that way,' he said. He wasn't used to expressing complex emotions, and it sat awkwardly on him, this combination of grief and regret and loss. He looked five years older. 'I was so hurt by her and mad at her, but I wouldn't want her to suffer and be afraid. God knows we probably wouldn't have been good as parents, but we didn't get a chance to try.'

I agreed with every part of what he'd said.

'Did you have company last night?' I said finally.

'Yeah, I took Michele Schubert home from the Bayou,' he said. The Bayou was a bar in Clarice, only a few miles away.

'She stay all night?'

'I made her scrambled eggs this morning.'

'Good.' For once my brother's promiscuity paid off – Michele was a single divorcée without children and forthright to boot. If anyone would be willing to tell the police exactly where she'd been and what she'd done, Michele was the woman. I said as much.

'The police have already talked to her,' Jason told me.

'That was fast.'

'Bud was in the Bayou last night.'

So the sheriff would have seen Jason leave and would have noted whom he'd left with. Bud hadn't kept the job of sheriff this long without being shrewd. 'Well, that's good,' I said, and couldn't think of anything else to say.

'You think maybe she was killed because she was a panther?' Jason asked hesitantly.

'Maybe. She was partially changed when she was killed.'

'Poor Crystal,' he said. 'She would have hated anyone to see her like that.' And to my amazement, tears ran down his face.

I didn't have the slightest idea how to react. All I could do was fetch a Kleenex from the box in my car and shove it in his hand. I hadn't seen Jason cry in years. Had he even cried when Gran had died? Maybe he really had loved Crystal. Maybe it hadn't been solely wounded pride that had caused him to set up her exposure as an adulteress. He'd fixed it so both her uncle Calvin and I would catch her in the act. I'd been so disgusted and furious with being forced to be a witness – and with the consequences – that I'd avoided Jason for weeks. Crystal's death had shunted aside that anger, at least for the moment.

'She's beyond that now,' I said.

Calvin's battered truck pulled up on the other side of my car. Quicker than my eye could track, he stood in front of me, while Tanya Grissom scrambled out the other side. A stranger looked out of Calvin's eyes. Normally a peculiar yellowish color, those eyes were now almost golden, and the irises were so large that there was almost no visible white. His pupils had elongated. He was not even wearing a light jacket. It made me cold to look at him in more ways than one.

I held up my hands. 'I'm so sorry, Calvin,' I said. 'You need to know Jason did *not* do this.' I looked up, not too far, to meet his eerie eyes. Calvin was a little grayer now than he'd been when I'd first met him several years ago, and a little stockier. He still looked solid and dependable and tough.

'I need to smell her,' he said, ignoring my words. 'They have to let me back there to smell her. I'll know.'

'Come on then; we'll go tell them that,' I said, because not only was that a good idea, but also I wanted to keep him away from Jason. At least Jason was smart enough to stay on the far side of my car. I took Calvin's arm and we began to walk around the building, only to be stopped by the crime scene tape.

Bud Dearborn moved over to the other side of the tape when he saw us. 'Calvin, I know you're rattled, and I'm real sorry about your niece,' he began, and with a flash of claw Calvin ripped down the tape and began walking over to the cross.

Before he'd gotten three steps, the two FBI agents moved to intercept him. Suddenly they were on the ground. There was a lot of shouting and tumult, and then Calvin was being held back by Bud, Andy, and Alcee, with Lattesta and Weiss trying to assist from their undignified positions.

'Calvin,' Bud Dearborn wheezed. Bud was not a young man, and it was clear that holding Calvin back was taking every bit of strength he possessed. 'You gotta stay away, Calvin. Any evidence we collect is gonna be tainted if you don't stay away from the body.' I was astonished at Bud's restraint. I would have expected him to crack Calvin in the head with his baton or a flashlight. Instead, he seemed as sympathetic as a strained and taxed man could be. For the first time, I understood that I wasn't the only one who'd known about the secret of the Hotshot community. Bud's wrinkled hand patted Calvin's arm in a gesture of consolation. Bud took care to avoid touching Calvin's claws. Special Agent Lattesta noticed them, and he drew in a harsh breath, making an incoherent warning noise.

'Bud,' Calvin said, and his voice came out in a growl, 'if you can't let me over there now, I have to smell her when they take her down. I'm trying to catch the scent of the ones who did this.'

'I'll see if you can do that,' Bud said steadily. 'For right now, buddy, we got to get you out of here because they gotta pick up all this evidence around here, evidence that'll stand up in court. You got to stay away from her. Okay?'

Bud had never cared for me, nor I for him, but at that moment I sure thought well of him.

After a long moment, Calvin nodded. Some of the tension went out of his shoulders. Everyone who was holding on to him eased up on their grip.

Bud said, 'You stay out front; we'll call you. You got my word.'

'All right,' Calvin said. The law enforcement crowd let go. Calvin let me put my arm around him. Together, we turned to make for the front parking lot. Tanya was waiting for him, tension in every line of her body. She'd had the same expectations I'd had: that Calvin was going to get a good beating.

'Jason didn't do this,' I said again.

'I don't care about your brother,' he said, turning those strange eyes on me. 'He doesn't matter to me. I don't think he killed her.'

It was clear that he thought my anxiety about Jason was blocking my concern about the real problem, the death of his niece. It was clear he didn't appreciate that. I had to respect his feelings, so I shut my mouth.

Tanya took his hands, claws and all. 'Will they let you go over her?' she asked. Her eyes never left Calvin's face. I might as well not have been there.

'When they take the body down,' he said.

It would be so great if Calvin could identify the culprit. Thank God the werecreatures had come out. But ... that might have been why Crystal had been killed.

'You think you'll be able to get a scent?' Tanya said. Her voice was quiet, intent. She was more serious than I'd ever seen her in our spotty acquaintance. She put her arms around Calvin, and though he was not a tall man, she only reached his upper sternum. She looked up at him.

'I'll get a score of scents after all these folks have touched her. I can only try to match them all. I wish I'd been here first.' He held Tanya as if he needed to lean on someone.

Jason was standing a yard away, waiting for Calvin to notice him. His back was stiff, his face frozen. There was an awful moment of silence when Calvin looked over Tanya's shoulder and noted Jason's presence.

I don't know how Tanya reacted, but every muscle in my body twanged from the tension. Slowly Calvin held out a hand to Jason. Though it was a human hand again, it was obviously battered. The skin was freshly scarred and one of the fingers was slightly bent.

I had done that. I'd stood up for Jason at his wedding, and Calvin had stood up for Crystal. After Jason had made us witness Crystal's infidelity, we'd had to stand in for them when the penalty had been pronounced: the maiming of a hand or paw. I'd had to bring a brick down on my friend's hand. I hadn't felt the same about Jason since then.

Jason bent and licked the back of the hand, emphasizing how subservient he was. He did it awkwardly, because he was still new to the ritual. I held my breath. Jason's eyes were rolled up to keep Calvin's face in sight. When Calvin nodded, we all relaxed. Calvin accepted Jason's obeisance.

'You'll be in at the kill,' Calvin said, as if Jason had asked him something.

'Thanks,' Jason said, and then backed away. He stopped when he'd gone a couple of feet. 'I want to bury her,' he said.

'We'll all bury her,' Calvin said. 'When they let us have her back.' There was not a particle of concession in his voice.

Jason hesitated a moment and then nodded.

Calvin and Tanya got back in Calvin's truck. They settled in. Clearly they planned to wait there until the body was brought down from the cross. Jason said, 'I'm going home. I can't stay here.' He seemed almost dazed.

'Okay,' I said.

'Are you . . . do you plan on staying here?'

'Yes, I'm in charge of the bar while Sam is gone.'

'That's a lot of trust he has in you,' Jason said.

I nodded. I should feel honored. I did feel honored.

'Is it true his stepdad shot his mom? That's what I heard at the Bayou last night.'

'Yes,' I said. 'He didn't know that Sam's mom was, you know, a shapeshifter.'

Jason shook his head. 'This coming-out thing,' he said. 'I don't know that's it been such a good idea after all. Sam's mom got shot. Crystal is dead. Someone who knew what she was put her up there, Sookie. Maybe they'll come after me next. Or Calvin. Or Tray Dawson. Or Alcide. Maybe they'll try to kill us all.'

I started to say that couldn't happen, that the people I knew wouldn't turn on their friends and neighbors because of an accident of birth. But in the end, I didn't say that, because I wondered if it was the truth.

'Maybe they will,' I said, feeling an icy tingle run down my back. I took a deep breath. 'But since they didn't go after the vampires – for the most part – I'm thinking they'll be able to accept weres of all sorts. At least, I hope so.'

Mel, wearing the slacks and sports shirt he wore daily at the auto parts place, got out of his car and walked over. I noticed that he was carefully not looking at Calvin, though Jason was still standing right beside the panther's pickup. 'It's true, then,' Mel said.

Jason said, 'She's dead, Mel.'

Mel patted Jason's shoulder in the awkward way men have when they have to comfort other men. 'Come on, Jason. You don't need to be around here. Let's go to your house. We'll have a drink, buddy.'

Jason nodded, looking dazed. 'Okay, let's go.' After Jason left for home with Mel following right behind, I climbed back in my own vehicle and fished the newspapers for the past few days from the backseat. I often picked them up from the driveway when I came out to go to work, tossed them in the back, and tried to read at least the front page within a reasonable length of time. What with Sam leaving and my business with the bar, I hadn't caught a glimpse of the news since the weres went public.

I arranged the papers in order and began to read.

The public reaction had ranged from the panicked to the calm. Many people claimed they'd had a suspicion that the world contained more than humans and vampires. The vampires themselves were 100 percent behind their furry brethren, at least in public. In my experience, the two major supernatural groups had had a very bumpy relationship. The shifters and Weres mocked the vampires, and the vampires jeered right back. But it looked like the supernaturals had agreed to present a united front, at least for a while.

The reactions of governments varied wildly. I think the U.S. policy had been formed by werewolves in place within the system, because it was overwhelmingly favorable. There was a huge tendency to accept the weres as if they were completely human, to keep their rights as Americans exactly on a par with their previous status when no one knew they were two-natured. The vampires couldn't be too pleased about that, because they hadn't yet obtained full rights and privileges under the law. Legal marriage and inheritance of property were still forbidden in a few states, and vampires were barred from owning certain businesses. The human casino lobby had been successful in banning the vamps from direct ownership of gambling establishments, which I still couldn't understand, and though vampires could be police officers and firefighters, vampire doctors were not accepted in any field that included treating patients with open wounds. Vampires weren't allowed in competition sports, either. That I could understand; they were too strong. But there were already lots of athletes whose ancestry included full- and part-weres, because sports were a natural bent for them. The military ranks, too, were filled with men and women whose grandparents had bayed under the full moon. There were even some full-blooded Weres in the armed services, though it was a very tricky occupation for people who had to find somewhere private to be three nights a month.

The sports pages were full of pictures of some part- and whole-weres who'd become famous. A running back for the New England Patriots, a fielder for the Cardinals, a marathon runner ... they'd all confessed to being wereanimals of one kind or another. An Olympic champion swimmer had just discovered that his dad was a wereseal, and the number-one ranked women's tennis player in Britain had gone on record as saying that her mother was a wereleopard. The sports world hadn't been in such a tumult since the last drug scandal. Did these athletes' heritage give them an unfair advantage over other players? Should their trophies be taken away from them? Should their records be allowed to stand? Another day, I might enjoy debating this with someone, but right now I just didn't care.

I began to see an overall picture. The outing of the two-natured was a much different revelation than the vampires' announcement. The vampires had been completely off the human grid, except in legend and lore. They'd lived apart. Since they could subsist on the Japanese synthetic blood, they had presented themselves as absolutely non-threatening. But wereanimals had been living among us all the time, integrated into our society yet maintaining their secret lives and alli-ances. Sometimes even their children (those who weren't firstborn and therefore not weres) didn't know what their parents were, especially if they were not wolves.

'I feel betrayed,' one woman was quoted as saying. 'My granddad turns into a lynx every month. He runs around and kills things. My beautician, I've been going to her for fifteen years, and she's a coyote. I didn't know! I feel I've been deceived in an ugly way.'

Some people thought it was fascinating. 'Our principal is a were-wolf,' said a kid in Springfield, Missouri. 'How cool is that?'

The very fact of the existence of wereanimals frightened some people. 'I'm scared I'll shoot my neighbor by accident if I see him trotting down the road,' said a farmer in Kansas. 'What if he gets after my chickens?'

Various churches were thrashing out their policy on weres. 'We don't know what to think,' a Vatican official confessed. 'They're alive, they're among us, they must have souls. Even some priests are were-animals.' The fundamentalists were equally stymied. 'We were worried about Adam and Steve,' a Baptist minister said. 'Should we have been more worried about Rover and Fluffy?'

While my head had been in the sand, all hell had broken loose.

Suddenly it was easier to see how my werepanther sister-in-law had ended up on a cross at a bar owned by a shifter.

Chapter 6

The moment the nails came out of her hands and feet, Crystal's body reverted to looking completely human. I watched from behind the crime scene tape. This process drew the horrified attention of everyone on the site. Even Alcee Beck flinched back. I'd been waiting for hours by then; I'd read all the newspapers twice, found a paperback in the glove compartment and gotten about a third of the way through it, and had a limp conversation with Tanya about Sam's mother. After we'd rehashed that news, she mostly talked about Calvin. I gathered that she had moved in with him. She'd gotten a part-time job at Norcross in the main office, doing something clerical. She loved the regular hours. 'And I don't have to stand up all day,' she said.

'Sounds good,' I said politely, though I'd hate that kind of job. Working with the same people every day? I'd get to know them all too well. I wouldn't be able to stay out of their thoughts, and I'd reach the point of wanting to get away from them because I knew too much about them. At the bar, there were always different people coming in to keep me distracted.

'How'd the Great Reveal go for you?' I asked.

'I told 'em at Norcross the next day,' she said. 'When they found out I was a werefox, they thought that was funny.' She looked disgusted. 'Why do the big animals get all the press? Calvin got huge respect out in the plant from his crew. I get jokes about bushy tails.'

'Not fair,' I agreed, trying not to smile.

'Calvin is completely wiped out about Crystal,' Tanya said abruptly. 'She was his favorite niece. He felt awful bad for her when it turned out she was such a poor shifter. And about the babies.' Crystal, the product of a lot of inbreeding, had taken forever to change into her panther form and had had a hard time reversing the process when she wanted to become a human again. She'd miscarried several times, too. The only reason she'd been allowed to marry Jason was that it had become obvious she would probably never carry a pureblood baby to term.

'Could be this baby was lost before the murder, or she aborted during the murder,' I said. 'Maybe the – whoever did this – didn't know.'

'She was showing, but not a whole lot,' Tanya said, nodding. 'She was real picky about her food, 'cause she was determined to keep her figure.' She shook her head, her face bitter. 'But really, Sookie, does it really make any difference if the killer knew or not? The end is the same. The baby is dead, and so is Crystal, and she died afraid and alone.'

Tanya was absolutely right.

'Do you think Calvin can track whoever did this from the smell?' I asked.

Tanya looked uneasy. 'There were lots of scents,' she said. 'I don't know how he can tell which one's *the* scent. And look, they're all touching her. Some of 'em are wearing rubber gloves, but those have an odor, you know. See, there's Mitch Norris helping take her down, and he's one of us. So how will Calvin know?'

'Besides, it might be one of them,' I said, nodding toward the group gathered around the dead woman. Tanya looked at me sharply.

'You mean law enforcement might be in on it?' she said. 'Do you know something?'

'No,' I said, sorry I'd opened my big mouth. 'It's just ... we don't know anything for sure. I guess I was thinking about Dove Beck.'

'He's the one she was in bed with that day?'

I nodded. 'That big guy, there – the black guy in the suit? That's his cousin Alcee.'

'Think he might have had something to do with it?'

'Not really,' I said. 'I was just . . . speculating.'

'I'll bet Calvin's thought of that, too,' she said. 'Calvin's very sharp.'

I nodded. There was nothing flashy about Calvin, and he hadn't managed to go to college (I hadn't either), but there was nothing wrong with his brain.

Bud beckoned to Calvin then, and he got out of his truck and went over to the body, which had been laid on a gurney spread with an open body bag. Calvin approached the body carefully, his hands behind his back so he wouldn't touch Crystal.

We all watched, some with loathing and distaste, some with indifference or interest, until he'd finished.

He straightened, turned, and walked back in the direction of his truck. Tanya got out of my car to meet him. She put her arms around him and looked up at him. He shook his head. I'd lowered my window so I could hear. 'I couldn't make out much on the rest of her,' he said. 'Too many other smells. She just smelled like a dead panther.'

'Let's go home, Calvin,' Tanya said.

'Okay.' They each raised a hand to me to let me know they were leaving, and then I was by myself in the front parking lot, still waiting. Bud asked me to open the employee entrance to the bar. I handed him the keys. He returned after a few minutes to tell me that the door had been securely locked and that there was no sign anyone had been inside the bar since it had closed. He handed the keys to me.

'So we can open up?' I asked. A few police vehicles had left, the body was gone, and it seemed to me that the whole process was winding down. I was willing to wait there if I could get into the building soon.

But after Bud told me it might be two or three more hours, I decided I'd go home. I'd spoken to every employee I could reach, and any customers could clearly see from the tape put across the parking lot that the bar was closed. I was wasting my time. My FBI agents, who'd spent hours with their cell phones clamped to their ears, seemed now to be more concerned about this crime than about me, which was great. Maybe they'd forget all about me.

Since no one seemed to be watching me or to care what I was doing, I started my car up and left. I didn't have the heart to run any errands. I went straight back to the house.

Amelia had long ago left for work at the insurance agency, but Octavia was home. She had set up the ironing board in her room. She was pressing the hem on a pair of pants she'd just shortened, and she had a pile of her blouses ready to iron. I guess there wasn't any magic spell to get the wrinkles out. I offered to drive her into town, but she said her trip with Amelia the day before had taken care of all her needs. She invited me to sit on the wooden chair by the bed while she worked. 'Ironing goes faster when you have someone to talk to,' she said, and she sounded so lonely I felt guilty.

I told her about the morning I'd had, about the circumstances of Crystal's death. Octavia had seen some bad stuff in her time, so she didn't freak out. She made the appropriate answers and expressed the shock almost anyone would feel, but she hadn't really known Crystal. I could tell there was something on her mind.

Octavia put down the iron and moved to face me directly. 'Sookie,' she said, 'I need to get a job. I know I'm a burden to you and Amelia. I used to borrow my niece's car during the day when she was working the night shift, but since I've moved out here, I've been having to ask you-all for rides. I know that gets old. I cleaned my niece's house and cooked and helped to watch the kids to pay her for my room and board, but you and Amelia are such cleaners that my two cents wouldn't really be a help.'

'I'm glad to have you, Octavia,' I said, not entirely truthfully. 'You've helped me in a lot of ways. Remember that you got Tanya off my back? And now she seems to be in love with Calvin. So she won't be pestering me anymore. I know you'd feel better if you could get a job, and maybe something will come up. In the meantime, you're fine here. We'll think of something.'

'I called my brother in New Orleans,' she said to my astonishment. I hadn't even known she had a living brother. 'He says the insurance company has decided to give me a payment. It's not much, considering I lost almost everything, but it'll be enough to buy a good secondhand car. There won't be anything there for me to go back to, though. I'm not going to rebuild, and there aren't too many places I could afford on my own.'

'I'm sorry,' I said. 'I wish there was something I could do about it, Octavia. Make things better for you.'

'You've already made things better for me,' she said. 'I'm grateful.'

'Oh, please,' I said miserably. 'Don't. Thank Amelia.'

All I know how to do is magic,' Octavia said. 'I was so glad to help you out with Tanya. Does she seem to remember?'

'No,' I said. 'I don't think she remembers anything about Calvin bringing her over here, or the spell casting. I'll never be her favorite person, but at least she's not trying to make my life miserable anymore.'

Tanya had been sent to sabotage me by a woman named Sandra Pelt, who bore me a grudge. Since Calvin had clearly taken a shine to Tanya, Amelia and Octavia had worked a little magic on her to cut her free from Sandra's influence. Tanya still seemed abrasive, but that was just her nature, I figured.

'Do you think we should do a reconstruction to find out who Crystal's killer was?' Octavia offered.

I thought it over. I tried to imagine staging an ectoplasmic reconstruction in the parking lot of Merlotte's. We'd have to find at least one more witch, I thought, because that was a large area, and I wasn't sure Octavia and Amelia could handle it by themselves. They'd probably think they could, though.

'I'm afraid we'd be seen,' I said finally. 'And that would be bad for you and Amelia. Besides, we don't know where the actual death took place. And you have to have that, right? The death site?'

Octavia said, 'Yes. If she didn't die there in the parking lot, it wouldn't do a bit of good.' She sounded a bit relieved.

'I guess we won't know until the autopsy if she died there or before they put up the cross.' I didn't think I could stand to witness another ectoplasmic reconstruction, anyway. I'd seen two. Watching the dead – in a watery but recognizable form – reenact the last minutes of their lives was an indescribably eerie and depressing experience.

Octavia went back to her ironing, and I wandered into the kitchen and heated up some soup. I had to eat something, and opening a can was about as much effort as I could expend.

The dragging hours were absolutely negative. I didn't hear from Sam. I didn't hear from the police about opening Merlotte's. The FBI agents didn't return to ask me more questions. Finally I decided to drive to Shreveport. Amelia had returned from work, and she and Octavia were cooking supper together when I left the house. It was a homey scene; I was simply too restless to join in.

For the second time in as many days, I found myself on the way to Fangtasia. I didn't let myself think. I listened to a black gospel station all the way over, and the preaching helped me feel better about the awful events of the day.

By the time I arrived, it was full night, though it was too early for the bar to be crowded. Eric was sitting at one of the tables in the main room, his back to me. He was drinking some TrueBlood and talking to Clancy, who ranked under Pam, I thought. Clancy was facing me, and he sneered when he saw me walking toward the table. Clancy was no Sookie Stackhouse fan. Since he was a vampire, I couldn't discover why, but I thought he simply didn't like me.

Eric turned to see me approaching, and his eyebrows rose. He said something to Clancy, who got up and stalked back to the office. Eric waited for me to sit down at his table. 'Hello, Sookie,' he said. 'Are you here to tell me how angry you are at me about our pledging? Or are you ready to have that long talk we must have sooner or later?'

'No,' I said. We sat for a while in silence. I felt exhausted but oddly peaceful. I should be giving Eric hell about his highhanded handling of Quinn's request and the knife presentation. I should be asking him all kinds of questions . . . but I couldn't summon up the necessary fire.

I just wanted to sit beside him.

There was music playing; someone had turned on the all-vampire radio station, KDED. The Animals were singing 'The Night'. After he finished his drink and there was only a red residue staining the sides of the bottle, Eric lay his cold white hand on top of mine. 'What happened today?' he asked, his voice calm.

I began to tell him, starting with the FBI visit. He didn't interrupt to exclaim or to ask questions. Even when I ended my tale with the removal of Crystal's body, he didn't speak for a while. 'Even for you, that's a busy day, Sookie,' he said finally. 'As for Crystal, I don't think I ever met her, but she sounds worthless.'

Eric never waffled around to be polite. Though I actually enjoyed that, I was also glad it wasn't a widely held trait. 'I don't know that anyone is worthless,' I said. 'Though I have to admit, if I had to pick one person to get in a lifeboat with me, she wouldn't have made even my long list.'

Eric's mouth quirked up in a smile.

'But,' I added, 'she was pregnant, that's the thing, and the baby was my brother's.'

'Pregnant women were worth twice as much if they were killed in my time,' Eric said.

He'd never volunteered much information about his life before he'd been turned. 'What do you mean, worth?' I asked.

'In war, or with foreigners, we could kill whom we pleased,' he said. 'But in disputes between our own people, we had to pay silver when we killed one of our own.' He looked like he was dredging up the memory with an effort. 'If the person killed was a woman with child, the price was double.'

'How old were you when you got married? Did you have children?' I knew Eric had been married, but I didn't know anything else about his life.

'I was counted a man at twelve,' he said. 'I married at sixteen. My wife's name was Aude. Aude had . . . we had . . . six children.'

I held my breath. I could tell he was looking down the immense swell of time that had passed between his present – a bar in Shreveport, Louisiana – and his past – a woman dead for a thousand years.

'Did they live?' I asked very quietly.

'Three lived,' he said, and he smiled. 'Two boys and a girl. Two died at birth. And with the sixth child, Aude died, too.'

'Of what?'

He shrugged. 'She and the baby caught a fever. I suppose it was from some sort of an infection. Then, if people got sick, they mostly died. Aude and the baby perished within hours of each other. I buried them in a beautiful tomb,' he said proudly. 'My wife had her best broach on her dress, and I laid the baby on her breast.'

He had never sounded less like a modern man. 'How old were you?'

He considered. 'I was in my early twenties,' he said. 'Perhaps twenty-three. Aude was older. She had been my elder brother's wife, and when he was killed in battle, it fell to me to marry her so our families would still be bonded. But I'd always liked her, and she was willing. She wasn't a silly girl; she'd lost two babies of my brother's, and she was glad to have more that lived.'

'What happened to your children?'

'When I became a vampire?'

I nodded. 'They can't have been very old.'

'No, they were small. It happened not long after Aude's death,' he said. 'I missed her, you see, and I needed someone to raise the children. No such thing as a househusband then.' He laughed. 'I had to go raiding. I had to be sure the slaves were doing what they ought in the fields. So I needed another wife. One night I went to visit the family of a young woman I hoped would marry me. She lived a mile or two away. I had some worldly goods, and my father was a chief, and I was thought a handsome man and was a noted fighter, so I was a good prospect. Her brothers and her father were glad to greet me, and she seemed ... agreeable. I was trying to get to know her a bit. It was a good evening. I had high hopes. But I had a lot to drink there, and on my way home that night ...' Eric paused, and I saw his chest move. In remembering his last moments as a human, he had actually taken a deep breath. 'It was the full moon. I saw a man lying hurt by the side of the road. Ordinarily I would have looked around to find those who had attacked him, but I was drunk. I went over to help him; you can probably guess what happened after that.'

'He wasn't really hurt.'

'No. But I was, soon after. He was very hungry. His name was Appius Livius Ocella.' Eric actually smiled, though without much humor. 'He taught me many things, and the first was not to call him Appius. He said I didn't know him well enough.'

'The second thing?'

'How to get to know him.'

'Oh.' I figured I understood what that meant.

Eric shrugged. 'It was not so bad . . . once we left the area I knew. In time, I stopped pining after my children and my home. I had never been away from my people. My father and mother were still alive. I knew my brothers and my sisters would make sure the children were brought up to be as they ought, and I had left enough to keep them from being a burden. I worried, of course, but there was no helping it. I had to stay away. In those days, in small villages, any stranger was instantly noticed, and if I ventured anywhere close to where I'd lived, I'd be recognized and hunted. They would know what I was, or at least know I was . . . wrong.'

'Where did you and Appius go?'

'We went to the biggest cities we could find, which were few enough then. We traveled all the time, parallel to the roads so we could prey on travelers.'

I shuddered. It was painful to imagine Eric, so flamboyant and quick-witted, skulking through the woods in search of easy blood. It was awful to think of the unfortunates he'd ambushed.

'There were not so many people,' he said. 'Villagers would miss their neighbors immediately. We had to keep moving. Young vampires are so hungry; at first, I killed even when I didn't mean to.'

I took a deep breath. This was what vampires did; when they were young, they killed. There had been no substitute for fresh blood then. It was kill, or die. 'Was he good to you? Appius Livius Ocella?' How much worse could you have it than to be the constant companion of the man who had murdered you?

'He taught me all he knew. He had been in the legions, and he was a fighter, as I was, so we had that in common. He liked men, of course, and that took some getting used to. I had never done that. But when you're a new vampire, anything sexual seems exciting, so even that I enjoyed . . . eventually.'

'You had to comply,' I said.

'Oh, he was much stronger . . . though I was a bigger man than him – taller, longer arms. He had been vampire for so many centuries, he'd lost count. And of course, he was my sire. I had to obey.' Eric shrugged.

'Is that a mystical thing or a made-up rule?' I asked, curiosity finally getting the better of me.

'It's both,' Eric said. 'It's a compulsion. It's impossible to resist, even when you want to ... even when you're desperate to get away.' His white face was closed and brooding.

I couldn't imagine Eric doing something he didn't want to do, being in a subservient position. Of course, he had a boss now; he wasn't autonomous. But he didn't have to bow and scrape, and he made most of his own decisions.

'I can't imagine it,' I said.

'I wouldn't want you to.' His mouth pulled down at one corner, a wry expression. Just when I began to ponder the irony of that, since he'd perhaps married me vampire-style without asking me, Eric changed the subject, slamming shut the door on his past. 'The world has changed a great deal since I was human. The past hundred years have been especially exciting. And now the Weres are out, and all the other two-natured. Who knows? Maybe the witches or the fae will step forward next.' He smiled at me, though it was a little stiff.

His idea gave me a happy fantasy of seeing my great- grandfather Niall every day. I'd only learned of his existence a few months before, and we hadn't spent much time together, but learning I had a living ancestor had been very important to me. I had so few blood kin. 'That would be wonderful,' I said wistfully.

'My lover, it will never happen,' Eric said. 'The creatures that make up the fae are the most secret of all the supernatural beings. There are not many remaining in this country. In fact, there are not so many remaining in the world. The number of their females, and the fertility of those females, is dropping every year. Your great-grandfather is one of the few survivors with royal blood. He would never condescend to treat with humans.'

'He talks to me,' I said, because I wasn't sure what 'treat' meant.

'You share his blood.' Eric waved his free hand. 'If you didn't, you would never have seen him.'

Well, no, Niall wasn't going to stop in at Merlotte's for a brew and a chicken basket and shake hands all around. I looked at Eric unhappily. 'I wish he'd help Jason out,' I said, 'and I never thought I'd say that.

Niall doesn't seem to like Jason at all, but Jason's going to be in a lot of trouble about Crystal's death.'

'Sookie, if you're asking for my thoughts, I have no idea why Crystal was killed.' And he really didn't care much. At least with Eric, you could tell where you stood.

In the background the KDED DJ said, 'Next, Thom Yorke's "And It Rained All Night".' While Eric and I had been having our one-on-one, the bar sounds had seemed muted, faraway. Now they came back with a rush.

'The police and the werepanthers, they'll track whoever did it,' he said. 'I'm more concerned about these FBI agents. What is their goal? Do they want to take you away? Can they do that in this country?'

'They wanted to identify Barry. Then they wanted to find out what Barry and I could do, and how we could do it. Maybe they were supposed to ask if we'd work for them, and Crystal's death interrupted our conversation before they could say anything.'

'And you don't want to work for them.' Eric's bright blue eyes were intent on my face. 'You don't want to leave.'

I pulled my hand out from under his. I watched my hands clasp each other, twist. 'I don't want people to die because I wouldn't help them,' I said. I felt my eyes brim with tears. 'But I'm selfish enough that I don't want to go wherever they send me, trying to find dying people. I couldn't stand the wear and tear of seeing disaster every day. I don't want to leave home. I've been trying to imagine what it would be like, what they might have me do. And it scares me to death.'

'You want to own your own life,' Eric said.

'As much as anyone can.'

'Just when I think you're very simple, you say something complex,' Eric said.

'Are you complaining?' I tried to smile, failed.

'No.'

A heavy girl with a big jaw came up and thrust an autograph book in front of Eric. 'Could you please sign this?' she said. Eric gave her a blinding smile and scribbled on the blank page. 'Thank you,' she said breathlessly, and went back to her table. Her friends, all women just old enough to be in the bar, were exclaiming at her courage, and she leaned forward, telling them all about her encounter with the vampire. As she finished, one of the human waitresses drifted up to their table and took another order for drinks. The staff here was well-trained.

'What was she thinking?' Eric asked me.

'Oh, she was very nervous and she thought you were lovely, but . . .' I struggled to put it into words. 'Not handsome in a way that was very real to her, because she would never think she would actually get to have you. She's very . . . she doesn't think much of herself.'

I had one of those flashes of fantasy. *Eric would walk over to her, bow to her, give her a reverent kiss on the cheek, ignore her prettier friends. This gesture would make every man in the bar wonder what the vampire saw in her that they couldn't see. Suddenly the plain girl would be overwhelmed with attention from the men who'd witnessed the interchange. Her friends would give her respect because Eric had. Her life would change.*

But none of that happened, of course. Eric forgot about the girl as soon as I'd finished speaking. I didn't think it would work out like my fantasy, even if he did approach her. I felt a flash of disappointment that fairy tales didn't come true. I wondered if my fairy great-grand-father had ever heard one of what we thought of as a fairy tale. Did fairy parents tell fairy children human tales? I was willing to bet they didn't.

I felt a moment of disconnect, as if I were standing back from my own life and viewing it from afar. The vampires owed me money and favors for my services to them. The Weres had declared me a friend of the pack for my help during the just-completed war. I was pledged to Eric, which seemed to mean I was engaged or even married. My brother was a werepanther. My great-grandfather was a fairy. It took me a moment to pull myself back into my own skin. My life was too weird. I had that out-of-control feeling again, as if I were spinning too fast to stop.

'Don't talk to the FBI people alone,' Eric was saying. 'Call me if it's at night. Call Bobby Burnham if they come in the day.'

'But he hates me!' I said, dragged back into reality and thus not too cautious. 'Why would I call him?'

'What?'

'Bobby hates me,' I said. 'He'd love it if the feds carted me off to some underground bunker in Nevada for the rest of my life.'

Eric's face looked frozen. 'He said this?'

'He didn't have to. I can tell when someone thinks I'm slime.'

'I'll have a talk with Bobby.'

'Eric, it's not against the law for someone to dislike me,' I said, remembering how dangerous it could be to complain to a vampire.

He laughed. 'Maybe I'll make it against the law,' he said teasingly, his accent more apparent than usual. 'If you can't reach Bobby – and I am absolutely sure he will help you – you should call Mr Cataliades, though he's down in New Orleans.'

'He's doing well?' I hadn't seen or heard from the half-demon lawyer since the collapse of the vampire hotel in Rhodes.

Eric nodded. 'Never better. He is now representing Felipe de Castro's interests in Louisiana. He would help if you asked him. He's quite fond of you.'

I stored that piece of information away to ponder. 'Did his niece survive?' I asked. 'Diantha?'

'Yes,' Eric said. 'She was buried for twelve hours, and the rescuers knew she was there. But there were beams wedged over the place where she was trapped, and it took time to remove them. They finally dug her out.'

I was glad to hear Diantha was alive. 'And the lawyer, Johan Glassport?' I asked. 'He had a few bruises, Mr Cataliades said.'

'He recovered fully. He collected his fee and then he vanished into the depths of Mexico.'

'Mexico's gain is Mexico's loss,' I said. I shrugged. 'I guess it takes a lawyer to get your money when the hirer is dead. I never got mine. Maybe Sophie-Anne thought Glassport did more for her, or he had the wits to ask even though she'd lost her legs.'

'I didn't know you weren't paid.' Eric looked displeased all over again. 'I'll talk to Victor. If Glassport collected for his services to Sophie, you certainly should. Sophie left a large estate, and no children. Victor's king owes you a debt. He'll listen.'

'That would be great,' I said. I may have sounded a little too relieved.

Eric eyed me sharply. 'You know,' he said, 'if you need money, you have only to ask. I will not have you going without anything you need, and I know you enough to be sure you wouldn't ask for money for something frivolous.'

He almost didn't sound like that was such an admirable attribute. 'I appreciate the thought,' I said, and I could hear my voice get all stiff. 'I just want what's due me.'

There was a long silence between us, though the bar was at its usual noise level around Eric's table.

'Tell me the truth,' Eric said. 'Is it possible you came here simply to spend time with me? You haven't yet told me how angry you are with me that I tricked you over the knife. Apparently you're not going to, at least not tonight. I haven't yet discussed with you all my memories of the time we spent together when you were hiding me at your house. Do you know why I ended up so close to your home, running down that road in the freezing cold?'

His question was so unexpected that I was struck silent. I wasn't sure I wanted to know the answer. But finally I said, 'No, I don't.'

'The curse contained within the witch, the curse that activated when Clancy killed her . . . it was that I would be close to my heart's desire without ever realizing it. A terrible curse and one that Hallow must have constructed with great subtlety. We found it dog-eared in her spell book.'

There was nothing for me to say. I'd think about that, though.

It was the first time I'd come to Fangtasia simply to talk, without having been called there for some vampire reason. Blood bond or something much more natural? 'I think . . . I just wanted some company,' I said. 'No soul-shaking revelations.'

He smiled. 'This is good.'

I didn't know if it was or not.

'You know we're not really married, right?' I said. I had to say something, as much as I wanted to forget the whole thing had ever happened. 'I know vamps and humans can get married now, but that wasn't a ceremony I recognize, nor does the State of Louisiana.'

'I know that if I hadn't done it, you'd be sitting in a little room in Nevada right now, listening to Felipe de Castro while he does business with humans.'

I hate it when my suspicions are correct. 'But I saved him,' I said, trying not to whine. 'I saved his life, and he promised I had his friend-ship. Which means his protection, I thought.'

'He wants to protect you right by his side now that he knows what you can do. He wants the leverage having you would give him over me.'

'Some gratitude. I should have let Sigebert kill him.' I closed my eyes. 'Dammit, I just can't come out ahead.'

'He can't have you now,' Eric said. 'We are wed.'

'But, Eric . . .' I thought of so many objections to this arrangement I couldn't even begin to voice them. I had promised myself I wouldn't start arguing about this tonight, but the issue was like the eight-hundred-pound gorilla. It simply couldn't be ignored. 'What if I meet someone else? What if you . . . Hey, what are the ground rules of being officially married? Just tell me.'

'You're too upset and tired tonight for a rational conversation,' Eric said.

He shook his hair back over his shoulders, and a woman at the next table said, '*Ooooooooooh.*'

'Understand that he can't touch you now, that no one can unless they petition me first. This is under penalty of final death. And this is where my ruthlessness will be of service to both of us.'

I took a deep breath. 'Okay. You're right. But this isn't the end of the subject. I want to know everything about our new situation, and I want to know I can get out of this if I can't stand it.'

His eyes looked as blue as a clear autumn sky, and as guileless. 'You will know everything when you want to know,' he said.

'Hey, does the new king know about my great-grandfather?'

Eric's face settled into lines of stone. 'I can't predict Felipe's reaction if he finds out, my lover. Bill and I are the only ones who have that knowledge now. It has to stay that way.'

He reached over to take my hand again. I could feel each muscle, each bone, through the cool flesh. It was like holding hands with a statue, a very beautiful statue. Again, I felt oddly peaceful for a few minutes.

'I have to go, Eric,' I said, sorry but not sorry to be leaving. He leaned over to me and kissed me lightly on the lips. When I pushed back my chair, he rose to walk me to the door. I felt the wannabes hammer me with looks of envy all the way out of Fangtasia. Pam was at her station, and she looked at us with a chilly smile.

Lest we part on too lovey-dovey a note, I said, 'Eric, when I'm back to being myself, I'm going to nail your ass for putting me in this position of being pledged to you.'

'Darling, you can nail my ass anytime,' he said charmingly, and turned to go back to his table.

Pam rolled her eyes. 'You two,' she said.

'Hey, this isn't any of *my* doing,' I said, which wasn't entirely true. But it was a good exit line, and I took advantage of it to leave the bar.

Chapter 7

The next morning, Andy Bellefleur called to give me the green light to reopen.

By the time the crime scene tape was down, Sam had returned to Bon Temps. I was so glad to see my boss that my eyes got weepy. Managing Merlotte's was a lot harder than I'd ever realized. There were decisions to make every day and a huge crowd of people who needed to be kept happy: the customers, the workers, the distributors, the deliverymen. Sam's tax guy had called with questions I couldn't answer. The utility bill was due in three days, and I didn't have check-writing privileges. There was a lot of money that needed to be deposited into the bank. It was almost payroll time.

Though I felt like blurting out all these problems the minute Sam walked in the back door of the bar, I drew in a calming breath and asked about his mother.

After giving me a half hug, Sam had thrown himself into his creaking chair behind his desk. He swiveled to face me directly. He propped his feet up on the edge of the desk with an air of relief. 'She's talking, walking, and mending,' he said. 'For the first time, we don't have to make up a story to cover how fast she can heal. We took her home this morning, and she's already trying to do stuff around the house. My brother and sister are asking her a million questions now that they've gotten used to the idea. They even seem kind of envious I'm the one who inherited the trait.'

I was tempted to ask about his stepfather's legal situation, but Sam seemed awful anxious to get back into his normal routine. I waited a moment to see if he would bring it up. He didn't. Instead, he asked about the utility bill, and with a sigh of relief I was able to refer him to the list of things that needed his attention. I'd left it on his desk in my neatest handwriting.

First on the list was the fact that I'd hired Tanya and Amelia to come in some evenings to make up for Arlene's defection.

Sam looked sad. 'Arlene's worked for me since I bought the bar,' he said. 'It's going to be strange, her not being here. She's been a pain in the butt in the past few months, but I figured she'd swing around to being her old self sooner or later. You think she'll reconsider?'

'Maybe, now that you're back,' I said, though I had severe doubts. 'But she's gotten to be so intolerant. I don't think she can work for a shifter. I'm sorry, Sam.'

He shook his head. His dark mood was no big surprise, considering his mom's situation and the not-completely-ecstatic reaction of the American populace to the weird side of the world.

It amazed me that, once upon a time, I hadn't known, either. I hadn't realized some of the people I knew were werewolves because I didn't comprehend there was such a thing. You can misinterpret every mental cue you get if you don't understand where it's coming from. I'd always wondered why some people were so hard to read, why their brains gave me a different image from others. It simply hadn't occurred to me it was because those brains belonged to people who literally turned into animals.

'You think business'll slack off because I'm a shapeshifter or because of the murder?' Sam asked. Then he shook himself and said, 'Sorry, Sook. I wasn't thinking about Crystal being your in-law.'

'I wasn't ever nuts about her, as you well know,' I said, as matter-of-factly as I could. 'But I think it's awful what was done to her, no matter what she was like.'

Sam nodded. I'd never seen his face so gloomy and serious. Sam was a creature of sunshine.

'Oh,' I said, getting up to leave, and then I stopped, shifting from foot to foot. I took a deep breath. 'By the way, Eric and I are married now.' If I'd hoped I'd get to make my exit on a light note, my judgment was way, way off. Sam leaped to his feet and grabbed me by the shoulders.

'What have you done?' he asked. He was deadly serious.

'I haven't done anything,' I said, startled by his vehemence. 'It was Eric's doing.' I told Sam about the knife.

'Didn't you realize there was some significance to the knife?'

'I didn't know it was a knife,' I said, beginning to feel pretty pissed but still maintaining my reasonable voice. 'Bobby didn't tell me. I guess he didn't know himself, so I couldn't very well pick it up from his brain.'

'Where was your sense? Sookie, that was an *idiotic* thing to do.'

This was not exactly the reaction I had anticipated from a man I'd been worried about, a man on whose behalf I'd been working my butt off for days. I gathered my hurt and pride around me like a jacket. 'Then let me just take my *idiotic* self home, so you won't have to put up with my idiocy any longer,' I said, my voice even enough to support a level. 'I guess I'll go home now that you're back and I don't have to be here *every single minute of my day* to make sure things are running okay.'

'I'm sorry,' he said, but it was too late. I was on my high horse, and I was riding it out of Merlotte's.

I was out the back door before our heaviest drinker could have counted to five, and then I was in my car and on the way home. I was mad, and I was sad, and I suspected that Sam was right. That's when you get the angriest, isn't it? When you know you've done something stupid? Eric's explanation hadn't exactly erased my concerns.

I was scheduled to work that evening, so I had until then to get my act together. There was no question of my not showing up. Whether or not Sam and I were on the outs, I had to work.

I wasn't ready to be at home, where I'd have to think about my own confused feelings.

Instead of going home, I turned and went to Tara's Togs. I hadn't seen a lot of my friend Tara since she'd eloped with JB du Rone. But my inner compass was pointing in her direction. To my relief, Tara was in the store alone. McKenna, her 'helper', was not a full-time employee. Tara came out of the back when the bell on the door rang. She looked a little surprised to see me at first, but then she smiled. Our friendship has had its ups and downs, but it looked like we were okay now. Great.

'What's up?' Tara asked. She looked attractive and snuggly in a teal sweater. Tara is taller than I am, and real pretty, and a real good businesswoman.

'I've done a stupid thing, and I don't know how I feel about it,' I said.

'Tell me,' she commanded, and we went to sit at the table where the wedding catalogs were kept. She shoved the box of Kleenex over to me. Tara knows when I'm going to cry.

So I told her the long story, beginning with the incident in Rhodes where I'd exchanged blood with Eric for what turned out to be one too many times. I told her about the weird bond we had as a result.

'Let me get this straight,' she said. 'He offered to take your blood so an even worse vamp wouldn't bite you?'

I nodded, dabbing at my eyes.

'Wow, such self-sacrifice.' Tara had had some bad experiences with vampires. I wasn't surprised at her sarcastic summation.

'Believe me, Eric doing it was by far the lesser of two evils,' I assured her.

Suddenly, I realized *I'd be free now if Andre had taken my blood that night*. Andre had died at the bombing site. I considered that for a second and moved on. That hadn't happened and I wasn't free, but the chains I wore now were a lot prettier.

'So how are you feeling about Eric?' Tara asked.

'I don't know,' I said. 'There are things I almost love about him, and things about him that scare the hell out of me. And I really ... you know ... *want* him. But he pulls tricks for what *he* says is my own good. I believe he cares about me. But he cares about himself mostly.' I took a deep breath. 'I'm sorry, I'm babbling.'

'This is why I married JB,' she said. 'So I wouldn't have to worry about shit like this.' She nodded, confirming her own good decision.

'Well, you've taken him, so I can't do that,' I said. I tried to smile. Marriage to someone as simple as JB sounded really relaxing. But was marriage supposed to be like settling back in a La-Z-Boy? *At least spending time with Eric is never boring*, I thought. Sweet as he was, JB had a finite capacity for entertaining conversation.

Plus, Tara was always going to have to be in charge. Tara was no fool, and she'd never be blinded by love. Other things, maybe, but not love. I knew Tara clearly understood the rules of her marriage to JB, and she didn't seem to mind. For her, being the navigator/captain was a comforting and empowering role. I definitely liked to be in charge of my own life – I didn't want anyone owning me – but my concept of marriage was more in the nature of a democratic partnership.

'So, let me summarize,' Tara said in a good imitation of one of our high school teachers. 'You and Eric have done the nasty in the past.'

I nodded. Boy howdy, had we.

'Now the whole vampire organization owes you for some service you performed. I don't want to know what it was, and I don't want to know why you did it.'

I nodded again.

'Also, Eric more or less owns a piece of you because of this blood-bond thing. Which he didn't necessarily plan out in advance, to give him credit.'

'Yep.'

'And now he's maneuvered you into the position of being his fiancée? His wife? But you didn't know what you were doing.'

'Right.'

'And Sam called you idiotic because you obeyed Eric.'

I shrugged. 'Yeah, he did.'

Tara had to help a customer then, but only for a couple of minutes. (Riki Cunningham wanted to pay on a prom dress she'd put on layaway for her daughter.) When Tara resumed her seat, she was ready to give me feedback. 'Sookie, at least Eric does care about you some, and he's never hurt you. You could've been smarter. I don't know if you weren't because of this bond thing you have with him or because you're so gone on him that you don't ask enough questions. Only you can figure that out. But it could be worse. No humans need to know about this knife thing. And Eric can't be around during the day, so you'll have Eric-free time to think. Also, he's got his own business to run, so he's not going to be following you around. And the new vampire execs have to leave you alone because they want to keep Eric happy. Not so bad, right?' She smiled at me, and after a second, I smiled back.

I began to perk up. 'Thanks, Tara,' I said. 'You think Sam will stop being mad?'

'I wouldn't exactly expect him to apologize for saying you acted like an idiot,' Tara warned me. 'A, it's true, and B, he's a man. He's got that chromosome. But you two have always gotten along great, and he owes you for you taking care of the bar. So he'll come around.'

I pitched my used Kleenex into the little trash can by the table. I smiled, though it probably wasn't my best effort.

'Meanwhile,' Tara said, 'I have some news for you, too.' She took a deep breath.

'What is it?' I asked, delighted that we were back on best-friend footing.

'I'm going to have a baby,' Tara said, and her face froze in a grimace.

Ah-oh. *Dangerous* footing. 'You don't look super-happy,' I said, cautiously.

'I hadn't planned on having children at all,' she said. 'Which was okay with JB.'

'So . . .?'

'Well, even multiple birth control methods don't always work,' Tara said, looking down at her hands, which were folded on top of a bridal magazine. 'And I just can't have it taken care of. It's ours. So.'

'Might . . . might you come around to being glad about this?'

She tried to smile. 'JB is really happy. It's hard for him to keep it a secret. But I wanted to wait for the first three months to pass. You're the first one I've told.'

'I swear,' I said, reaching over to pat her shoulder, 'you'll be a good mother.'

'You really think so?' She looked, and felt, terrified. Tara's folks had been the kind of parents who occasionally get shot-gunned by their offspring. Tara's abhorrence of violence had prevented her from taking that path, but I don't think anyone would have been surprised if the older Thorntons had vanished one night. A few people would have applauded.

'Yeah, I really think so.' I meant it. I could *hear*, directly from her head, Tara's determination to wipe out everything her own mother had done to her by being the best mother she could be to her own child. In Tara's case, that meant she would be sober, gentle-handed, clean of speech, and full of praise.

'I'll show up at every classroom open house and teacher conference,' she said, now in a voice that was almost frightening in its intensity. 'I'll bake brownies. My child will have new clothes. Her shoes will fit. She'll get her shots, and she'll get her braces. We'll start a college fund next week. I'll tell her I love her every damn day.'

If that wasn't a great plan for being a good mother, I couldn't imagine what a better one could be.

We hugged each other when I got up to leave. *This is the way it's supposed to be*, I thought.

I went home, ate a belated lunch, and changed into my work clothes.

When the phone rang, I hoped it was Sam calling to smooth things over, but the voice on the other end was an older man's and unfamiliar.

'Hello? Is Octavia Fant there, please?'

'No, sir, she's out. May I take a message?'

'If you would.'

'Sure.' I'd answered the phone in the kitchen, so there was a pad and pencil handy.

'Please tell her Louis Chambers called. Here's my number.' He gave it to me slowly and carefully, and I repeated it to make sure I'd put it down correctly. 'Ask her to call me, please. I'll be glad to take a collect call.'

'I'll make sure she gets your message.'

'Thank you.'

Hmmm. I couldn't read thoughts over the phone, which normally I considered a great relief. But I would have enjoyed learning a little more about Mr Chambers.

When Amelia came home a little after five, Octavia was in the car. I gathered Octavia had been walking around downtown Bon Temps filling out job applications, while Amelia had put in an afternoon at the insurance agency. It was Amelia's evening to cook, and though I had to leave for Merlotte's in a few minutes, I enjoyed watching her leap into action, creating spaghetti sauce. I handed Octavia her message while Amelia was chopping onions and a bell pepper.

Octavia made a choked sound and grew so still that Amelia stopped chopping and joined me in waiting for the older woman to look up from the piece of paper and give us a little backstory. That didn't happen.

After a moment, I realized Octavia was crying, and I hurried to my bedroom and got a tissue. I tried to slip it to Octavia tactfully, like I hadn't noticed anything amiss but just happened to have an extra Kleenex in my hand.

Amelia carefully looked down at the cutting board and resumed chopping while I glanced at the clock and began fishing around in my purse for my car keys, taking lots of unnecessary time to do it.

'Did he sound well?' Octavia asked, her voice choked.

'Yes,' I said. There was only so much I could get from a voice on the other end of a phone line. 'He sounded anxious to talk to you.'

'Oh, I have to call him back,' she said, and her voice was wild.

'Sure,' I said. 'Just punch in the number. Don't worry about calling collect or anything; the phone bill'll tell us how much it was.' I glanced over at Amelia, cocking an eyebrow. She shook her head. She didn't know what the hell was going on, either.

Octavia placed the call with shaking fingers. She pressed the phone to her ear after the first ring. I could tell when Louis Chambers answered. Her eyes shut tight, and her hand clenched the phone so hard the muscles stood out.

'Oh, Louis,' she said, her voice full of raw relief and amazement. 'Oh, thank God. Are you all right?'

Amelia and I shuffled out of the kitchen at that point. Amelia walked to my car with me. 'You ever heard of this Louis guy?' I asked.

'She never talked about her private life when she was working with me. But other witches told me Octavia had a steady boyfriend. She hasn't mentioned him since she's been here. It looks like she hasn't heard from him since Katrina.'

'She might not have thought he survived,' I said, and we widened our eyes at each other.

'That's big stuff,' Amelia said. 'Well. We may be losing Octavia.' She tried to stifle her relief, but of course, I could read it. As fond as Amelia was of her magical mentor, I'd realized that for Amelia, living with Octavia was like living with one of your junior high teachers.

'I got to go,' I said. 'Keep me posted. Text me if there's any big news.' Texting was one of my new Amelia-taught skills.

Despite the chilly air, Amelia sat on one of the lawn chairs that we'd recently hauled out of the storage shed to encourage ourselves to anticipate spring. 'The minute I know something,' she agreed. 'I'll wait here a few minutes, then go check on her.'

I got in my car and hoped the heater would warm up soon. In the gathering dusk, I drove to Merlotte's. I saw a coyote on the way. Usually they were too clever to be seen, but this one was trotting along the side of the road as if he had an appointment in town. Maybe it was really a coyote, or maybe it was a person in another form. When I considered the possums and coons and the occasional armadillo I saw squashed by the road every morning, I wondered how many werecreatures had gotten killed in their animal forms in such careless ways. Maybe some of the bodies the police labeled murder victims were actually people killed by accident in their alternate form. I remembered all animal traces had vanished from Crystal's body when she'd been taken down from the cross, after the nails had been removed. I was willing to bet those nails had been silver. There was so much I didn't know.

When I came in Merlotte's back door, full of plans to reconcile with Sam, I found my boss having an argument with Bobby Burnham. It was almost dark now, and Bobby should be off the clock. Instead, he was standing in the hall outside of Sam's office. He was red in the face and fit to be tied.

'What's up?' I said. 'Bobby, did you need to talk to me?'

'Yeah. This guy wouldn't tell me when you were going to get here,' Bobby said.

'This guy is my boss, and he isn't obliged to tell you anything,' I said. 'Here I am. What do you need to say to me?'

'Eric sent you this card, and he ordered me to tell you I'm at your disposal whenever you need me. I'm supposed to wash your car if you want me to.' Bobby's face went even redder as he said this.

If Eric had thought Bobby would be made humble and compliant after a public humiliation, he was nuts. Now Bobby would hate me for a hundred years, if he lived that long. I took the card Bobby handed me and said, 'Thanks, Bobby. Go back to Shreveport.'

Before the last syllable left my mouth, Bobby was out the back door. I examined the plain white envelope and then stuck it in my purse. I looked up to meet Sam's eyes.

'Like you needed another enemy,' he said, and stomped into his office.

Like I needed another friend acting like an asshole, I thought. So much for us having a good laugh over our disagreement. I followed Sam in to drop my purse in the drawer he kept empty for the barmaids. We didn't say a word to each other. I went to the storeroom to get an apron. Antoine was changing his stained apron for a clean one.

'D'Eriq bumped into me with a jar full of jalapeños, and the juice slopped out,' he said. 'I can't stand the smell of 'em.'

'Whoo,' I said, catching a whiff. 'I don't blame you.'

'Sam's mama doing okay?'

'Yeah, she's out of the hospital,' I said.

'Good news.'

As I tied the strings around my waist, I thought Antoine was about to say something else, but if he was, he changed his mind. He crossed the hall to knock on the kitchen door, and D'Eriq opened it from the inside and let him in. People had wandered into the kitchen by mistake too often, and the door was kept locked all the time. There was another door from the kitchen that led directly out back, and the Dumpster was right outside.

I walked past Sam's office without looking in. He didn't want to talk to me; okay, I wouldn't talk to him. I realized I was being childish.

The FBI agents were still in Bon Temps, which shouldn't have surprised me. Tonight, they came into the bar. Weiss and Lattesta were sitting opposite another in a booth, a pitcher of beer and a basket of French-fried pickles between them, and they were talking intently. And at a table close to them, looking regal and beautiful and remote, was my great-grandfather Niall Brigant.

This day was going to win a prize for most peculiar. I blew out a puff of air and went to wait on my great-grandfather first. He stood as

I approached. His pale straight hair was tied back at the nape of his neck. He was wearing a black suit and a white shirt, as he always did. Tonight, instead of the solid black tie he usually wore, he had on a tie I'd given him for Christmas. It was red, gold, and black striped, and he looked spectacular. Everything about him gleamed and shone. The shirt wasn't simply white – it was snowy and starched; and his coat wasn't just black – it was spotlessly inky. His shoes showed not a speck of dust, and the myriad of fine, fine wrinkles in his handsome face only set off its perfection and his brilliant green eyes. His age enhanced rather than diminished his looks. It almost hurt to look at him. Niall put his arms around me and kissed my cheek.

'Blood of my blood,' he said, and I smiled into his chest. He was so dramatic. And he had such a hard time looking human. I'd had one glimpse of him in his true form, and it had been nearly blinding. Since no one else in the bar was gasping at the sight of him, I knew they weren't seeing him the same way I did.

'Niall,' I said. 'I'm so happy to see you.' I always felt pleased and flattered when he visited. Being Niall's great-granddaughter was like being kin to a rock star; he lived a life I couldn't imagine, went places I would never go, and had power I couldn't fathom. But every now and then he spent time with me, and that time was always like Christmas.

He said very quietly, 'These people opposite me, they do nothing but talk of you.'

'Do you know what the FBI is?' Niall's fund of knowledge was incredible, since he was so old he'd stopped counting at a thousand and sometimes missed accurate dates by more than a century, but I didn't know how specific his information about the modern day might be.

'Yes,' he said. 'FBI. A government agency that collects data about law breakers and terrorists inside the United States.'

I nodded.

'But you're such a good person. You're not a killer or terrorist,' Niall said, though he didn't sound as if he believed my innocence would protect me.

'Thank you,' I said. 'But I don't think they want to arrest me. I suspect they want to find out how I get results with my little mental condition, and if they decide I'm not nuts, they probably want me to work for them. That's why they came to Bon Temps . . . but they got sidetracked.' And that brought me to the painful subject. 'Do you know what happened to Crystal?'

But some other customers called me then, and it was a while before I got back to Niall, who was waiting patiently. He somehow made the scarred chair look like a throne. He picked the conversation up right where we'd left off.

'Yes, I know what happened to her.' His face didn't seem to change, but I felt the chill rolling off of him. If I'd had anything to do with Crystal's death, I would have felt very afraid.

'How come you care?' I asked. He'd never paid any attention to Jason; in fact, Niall seemed to dislike my brother.

Niall said, 'I'm always interested in finding out why someone connected to me has died.' Niall had sounded totally impersonal when he spoke of Crystal's death, but if he was interested, maybe he would help. You'd think he'd want to clear Jason, since Jason was his great-grandson just as surely as I was his great-granddaughter, but Niall had never shown any sign of wanting to meet Jason, much less get to know him.

Antoine rang the bell in the kitchen to tell me one of my orders was up, and I scurried off to serve Sid Matt Lancaster and Bud Dearborn their cheesy chili bacon fries. The recently widowed Sid Matt was so old I guess he figured his arteries couldn't harden much more than they already had, and Bud had never been one for health food.

When I could return to Niall, I said, 'Do you have any idea who did it? The werepanthers are searching, too.' I put down an extra napkin on the table in front of him so I'd look busy.

Niall didn't disdain the panthers. In fact, though fairies seemed to consider themselves apart and superior to all other species of supernaturals, Niall (at least) had respect for all shapechangers, unlike the vampires, who regarded them as second-rate citizens. 'I'll look a little. I've been preoccupied, and that is why I haven't visited. There is trouble.' I saw that Niall's expression was even more serious than usual.

Oh, shit. More trouble.

'But you need not concern yourself,' he added regally. 'I will take care of it.'

Did I mention Niall is a little proud? But I couldn't help but feel concerned. In a minute I'd have to go get someone else another drink, and I wanted to be sure I understood him. Niall didn't come around often, and when he did, he seldom dallied. I might not get another chance to talk to him. 'What's up, Niall?' I asked directly.

'I want you to take special care of yourself. If you see any fairies other than myself or Claude and Claudine, call me at once.'

'Why would I worry about other fairies?' The other shoe dropped. 'Why would other fairies want to hurt me?'

'Because you are my great-granddaughter.' He stood, and I knew I'd get no more explanation than that.

Niall hugged me again, kissed me again (fairies are very touchy-feely), and left the bar, his cane in his hand. I'd never seen him use it as an aid to walking, but he always had it with him. As I stared after him, I wondered if it had a knife concealed inside. Or maybe it might be an extra-long magic wand. Or both. I wished he could've stuck around for a while, or at least issued a more specific danger bulletin.

'Ms Stackhouse,' said a polite male voice, 'could you bring us another pitcher of beer and another basket of pickles?'

I turned to Special Agent Lattesta. 'Sure, be glad to,' I said, smiling automatically.

'That was a very handsome man,' Sara Weiss said. Sara was feeling the effects of the two glasses of beer she'd already had. 'He sure looked different. Is he from Europe?'

'He does look foreign,' I agreed, and took the empty pitcher and fetched them a full one, smiling all the while. Then Catfish, my brother's boss, knocked over a rum and Coke with his elbow, and I had to call D'Eriq to come with a washcloth for the table and a mop for the floor.

After that, two idiots who'd been in my high school class got into a fight about whose hunting dog was better. Sam had to break that up. They were actually quicker to come to their senses now that they knew what Sam was, which was an unexpected bonus.

A lot of the discussion in the bar that evening dealt with Crystal's death, naturally. The fact that she'd been a werepanther had seeped into the town's consciousness. About half of the bar patrons believed she'd been killed by someone who hated the newly revealed underworld. The other half wasn't so sure that she'd been killed because she was a werepanther. That half thought her promiscuity was enough motivation. Most of them assumed Jason was guilty. Some of them felt sympathy for him. Some of them had known Crystal or her reputation, and they felt Jason's actions were justifiable. Almost all of these people thought of Crystal only in terms of Jason's guilt or innocence. I found it real sad that most people would only remember her for the manner of her death.

I should go see Jason or call him, but I couldn't find it in my heart. Jason's actions over the past few months had killed something in me. Though Jason was my brother, and I loved him, and he was showing signs of finally growing up, I no longer felt that I had to support him through all the trials his life had brought him. That made me a bad Christian, I realized. Though I knew I wasn't a deep theological thinker, I sometimes wondered if crisis moments in my life hadn't come down to two choices: be a bad Christian or die.

I'd chosen life every time.

Was I looking at this right? Was there another point of view that would enlighten me? I couldn't think of anyone to ask. I tried to imagine the Methodist minister's face if I asked him, 'Would it be better to stab someone to keep yourself safe, or let them go on and kill you? Would it be better to break a vow I made in front of God, or refuse to break my friend's hand to bits?' These were choices I had faced. Maybe I owed God a big debt. Or maybe I was protecting myself like he wanted me to. I just didn't know, and I couldn't think deep enough to figure out the Ultimate Right Answer.

Would the people I was serving laugh, if they knew what I was thinking? Would my anxiety over the state of my soul amuse them? Lots of them would probably tell me that all situations are covered in the Bible, and that if I read the Book more, I'd find my answers there.

That hadn't worked for me so far, but I wasn't giving up. I abandoned my circular thoughts and listened in on the people around me to give my brain a rest.

Sara Weiss thought that I seemed like a simple young woman, and she decided I was incredibly lucky to have been given a gift, as she considered it. She believed everything Lattesta had told her about what had happened at the Pyramid, because underneath her practical approach to life there was a streak of mysticism. Lattesta, too, thought it was almost possible I was psychic; he'd listened to accounts of the Rhodes first responders with great interest, and now that he'd met me, he'd come to think they were speaking the truth. He wanted to know what I could do for my country and his career. He wondered if he'd get a promotion if he could get me to trust him enough to be my handler throughout my time of helping the FBI. If he could acquire my male accomplice, as well, his upward trajectory would be assured. He would be stationed at FBI headquarters in Washington. He would be launched up the ladder.

I considered asking Amelia to lay a spell on the FBI agents, but that seemed like cheating somehow. They weren't supes. They were just doing what they'd been told to do. They didn't bear me any ill will; in fact, Lattesta believed he was doing me a favor, because he could get me out of this parish backwater and into the national limelight, or at least high in the esteem of the FBI.

As if that mattered to me.

As I went about my duties, smiling and exchanging chitchat with the regular customers, I tried to imagine leaving Bon Temps with Lattesta. They'd devise some test to measure my accuracy. They'd finally believe I wasn't psychic but telepathic. When they found out what the limits of my talent were, they'd take me places where awful things had happened so I could find survivors. They'd put me in rooms with the intelligence agents of other countries or with Americans they suspected of awful things. I'd have to tell the FBI whether or not those people were guilty of whatever crime the FBI imagined they might have committed. I'd have to be close to mass murderers, maybe. I imagined what I might see in the mind of such a person, and I felt sick.

But wouldn't the knowledge I gained be a great help to the living? Maybe I'd learn about plots far enough in advance to prevent deaths.

I shook my head. My mind was wandering too far afield. All that *might* happen. A serial killer *might* be thinking of where his victims were buried just at the moment I was listening to his thoughts. But in my extensive experience, people seldom thought, 'Yes, I buried that body at 1218 Clover Drive under the rosebush,' or, 'That money I stole sure is safe in my bank account numbered 12345 in the Switzerland National Bank.' Much less, 'I'm plotting to blow up the XYZ building on May 4, and my six confederates are . . .'

Yes, there would be some good I could do. But whatever I could achieve would never reach the expectations of the government. And I'd never be free again. I didn't think they'd hold me in a cell or anything – I'm not that paranoid. But I didn't think I'd ever get to live my own life as I wanted.

So once again, I decided that maybe I was being a bad Christian, or at least a bad American. But I knew that unless I was forced to do so, I wasn't going to leave Bon Temps with Agent Weiss or Special Agent Lattesta. Being married to a vampire was way better.

Chapter 8

I was mad at almost everybody when I drove home that night. Every now and then, I had spells like that; maybe everyone does. It's hormonal or cyclical in some other way. Or maybe it's just the chance alignment of the stars.

I was angry with Jason because I'd been angry with him for months. I was angry with Sam in a kind of hurt way. I was pissed at the FBI agents because they were here to put pressure on me – though in truth they hadn't done that yet. I was outraged at Eric's stunt with the knife and his high-handed banishment of Quinn, though I had to admit Eric had spoken the truth when he said I'd given Quinn the heave-ho first. That didn't mean I never wanted to see him again. (Or did it?) It *sure* didn't mean that Eric could dictate to me who I saw and who I didn't.

And maybe I was angry with myself, because when I'd had the chance to confront Eric about all kinds of stuff, I'd gone all goopy and listened to his reminiscences. Like the flashbacks on *Lost*, Eric's Viking memories had broken into the flow of the current story.

To make me even angrier, there was a car I didn't recognize parked at the front door, where only visitors parked. I went to the back door and up the porch steps, frowning and feeling totally contrary. I didn't want company. All I wanted to do was put on my pajamas, wash my face, and get into bed with a book.

Octavia was sitting at the kitchen table with a man I'd never met. He was one of the blackest men I'd ever seen, and his face was tattooed with circles around the eyes. Despite his fearsome decorations, he looked calm and agreeable. He rose to his feet when I came in.

'Sookie,' Octavia said in a trembling voice, 'this is my friend Louis.'

'Nice to meet you,' I said, and extended my hand for him to shake. He gave mine a carefully gentle grip, and I sat down so he would. Then I noticed the suitcases sitting in the hall. 'Octavia?' I said, pointing at them.

'Well, Sookie, even us old ladies have some romance in our lives,' Octavia said, smiling. 'Louis and I were close friends before Katrina. He lived about ten minutes' drive away from me in New Orleans. After it happened, I looked for him. I gave up, finally.'

'I spent a lot of time trying to find Octavia,' Louis said, his eyes on her face. 'I finally tracked down her niece two days ago, and her niece had the phone number here. I couldn't believe I'd finally found her.'

'Did your house survive the . . .?' Incident, catastrophe, disaster, apocalypse; pick your word, they all would serve.

'Yes, praise the gods, it did. And I have electricity. There's a lot to do, but I have light and heat. I can cook again. My refrigerator's humming and my street's almost clean. I put my own roof back on. Now Octavia can come home with me to a place fit for her.'

'Sookie,' she said very gently, 'you've been so kind, letting me stay with you. But I want to be with Louis, and I need to be back in New Orleans. There'll be something I can do to help rebuild the city. It's home to me.'

Octavia obviously felt she was delivering a heavy blow. I tried to look chagrined. 'You have to do what's best for you, Octavia. I've loved having you in my house.' I was so grateful Octavia wasn't telepathic. 'Is Amelia here?'

'Yes, she's upstairs getting something for me. Bless her heart, she got me a good-bye present somehow.'

'Awww,' I said, trying not to overdo it. I got a sharp look from Louis, but Octavia beamed at me. I'd never seen Octavia beam before, and I liked the look on her.

'I'm just glad I was able to be a help to you,' she said, nodding wisely.

It was a little trouble to maintain my slightly-sad-but-brave smile, but I managed. Thank goodness Amelia clattered down the stairs at that moment with a wrapped package in her hands, a thin, flimsy red scarf tied around it and secured with a big bow. Without looking at me, Amelia said, 'Here's a little something from Sookie and me. I hope you enjoy it.'

'Oh, you're so sweet. I'm sorry I ever doubted your skill, Amelia. You're one heck of a witch.'

'Octavia, it means so much to me to hear you say that!' Amelia was genuinely touched and tearful.

Thank goodness Louis and Octavia got up then. Though I liked and respected the older witch, she had provided a series of speed bumps in the smooth running of the household Amelia and I had formed.

I actually found myself breathing a profound sigh of relief when the front door shut on her and her partner. We'd all said good-bye to one another over and over, and Octavia had thanked both of us for various things repeatedly, and she'd also found ways to remind us of all sorts of mysterious things she'd done for us that we were having a hard time recalling.

'Heavens be praised,' said Amelia, collapsing on the stairs. Amelia was not a religious woman, or at least she wasn't a conventional Christian religious woman, so this was a quite a demonstration from her.

I sat on the edge of the couch. 'I hope they're very happy,' I said.

'You don't think we should have checked up on him somehow?'

'A witch as strong as Octavia can't take care of herself?'

'Good point. But did you see those tattoos?'

'They were something, weren't they? I guess he's some kind of sorcerer.'

Amelia nodded. 'Yeah, I'm sure he practices some form of African magic,' she said. 'I don't think we need to worry about the high crime rate in New Orleans affecting Octavia and Louis. I don't think anyone's going to be mugging them.'

'What was the present we gave her?'

'I called my dad, and he faxed me a gift certificate to his home supplies store.'

'Hey, good idea. What do I owe you?'

'Not a dime. He insisted it be on him.'

At least this happy incident took the edge off my generalized anger. I felt more companionable with Amelia, too, now that I no longer harbored a vague resentment for her bringing Octavia into my house. We sat in the kitchen and chatted for about an hour before I turned in, though I was too exhausted to try to explain the saga of what had been happening lately. We went to bed better friends than we'd been in weeks.

As I was getting ready for bed, I was thinking about our practical gift to Octavia, and that reminded me of the card Bobby Burnham had handed me. I got it out of my purse and slit the envelope with my nail file. I pulled out the card inside. Enclosed in it was a picture I'd never seen, clearly taken during Eric's photo shoot for the calendar you could buy in the gift shop at Fangtasia. In the calendar shot, Eric (Mr January) stood by a huge bed made up all in white. The background was gray, with glittering snowflakes hanging down all around. Eric had one foot on the floor, the other knee bent and resting on the bed. He was holding a white fur robe in a strategic position. In the picture Eric had given me today, he was in somewhat the same pose, but he was holding a hand out to the camera as if he was inviting the viewer to come join him on the bed. And the white fur wasn't covering quite everything. 'I wait for the night you join me,' he'd written on the otherwise blank card in his crabbed handwriting.

Faintly cheesy? Yes. Gulp inducing? Oh, you betcha. I could practically feel my blood heat up. I was sorry I'd opened it right before I climbed in the bed. It definitely took me a long time to drift off to sleep.

It felt funny not to hear Octavia buzzing around the house when I woke up the next morning. She'd vanished from my life as quickly as she'd entered it. I hoped that in some of their time together, Octavia and Amelia had discussed Amelia's status with what remained of her New Orleans coven. It was hard to believe Amelia could turn a young man into a cat (during the course of some very adventurous sex), I thought, as I watched my roommate hurry out the back door to get to the insurance office. Amelia, dressed in navy pants and a tan and navy sweater, looked like she was ready to sell Girl Scout cookies.

When the door slammed behind her, I drew a long breath. I was alone in the house for the first morning in ages.

The solitude didn't last long. I was drinking a second cup of coffee and eating a toasted biscuit when Andy Bellefleur and Special Agent Lattesta came to the front door. I hastily pulled on some jeans and a T-shirt to answer the door.

'Andy, Special Agent Lattesta,' I said. 'Come on in.' I led the way back to the kitchen. I wasn't going to let them keep me away from my coffeepot. 'Do you want a cup?' I asked them, but they both shook their heads.

'Sookie,' Andy said, his face serious, 'we're here about Crystal.'

'Sure.' I bit off some biscuit, chewed, and swallowed. I wondered if Lattesta was on a diet or something. He followed my every move. I dipped into his brain. He wasn't happy that I wasn't wearing a bra, because my boobs distracted him. He was thinking I was a bit too curvy for his taste. He was thinking he'd better not think about me that way anymore. He was missing his wife. 'I figured that would take priority over the other thing,' I said, forcing my attention back to Andy.

I couldn't tell how much Andy knew – how much Lattesta had shared – about what had happened in Rhodes, but Andy nodded. 'We think,' he said, after glancing from me to Lattesta, 'that Crystal died three nights ago, sometime between one a.m. and three or four a.m.'

'Sure,' I said again.

'You knew that?' Lattesta went practically on point, like a bird dog.

'It stands to reason. There's always someone around the bar until one or two, and then normally Terry comes in to clean the floors sometime between six and eight a.m. Terry wasn't coming so early that day because he'd been tending bar and needed to sleep late, but most people wouldn't think of that, right?'

'Right,' Andy said after an appreciable pause.

'So,' I said, my point made, and poured myself some more coffee.

'How well do you know Tray Dawson?' Andy asked.

That was a loaded question. The accurate answer was, 'Not as well as you think.' I'd once been caught in an alley with Tray Dawson and he'd been naked, but it wasn't what people thought. (I'd been aware they'd thought quite a bit.) 'He's been dating Amelia,' I said, which was pretty safe to say. 'She's my roommate,' I reminded Lattesta, who was looking a little blank. 'You met her two days ago. She's at work right now. And of course, Tray's a werewolf.'

Lattesta blinked. It would take a while for him to get used to people saying that with straight faces. Andy's own expression didn't change.

'Right,' Andy said. 'Was Amelia out with Tray the night Crystal died?'

'I don't remember. Ask her.'

'We will. Has Tray ever said anything to you about your sister-in-law?'

'I don't recall anything. Of course, they knew each other, at least a little bit, since they were both wereanimals.'

'How long have you known about ... werewolves? And the other wereanimals?' Andy asked, as though he just couldn't help himself.

'Oh, for a while,' I said. 'Sam first, and then others.'

'And you didn't tell anyone?' Andy asked incredulously.

'Of course not,' I said. 'People think I'm weird enough as it is. Besides, it wasn't my secret to tell.' It was my turn to give him a look. 'Andy, you knew, too.' After that night in the alley when we'd been attacked by a were-hater, Andy had at least heard Tray in his animal form and then seen him as a naked human. Any basic connect-the-dots would draw a picture of a werewolf.

Andy looked down at the notepad he'd taken out of his pocket. He didn't write anything down. He took a deep breath. 'So that time I saw Tray in the alley, he had just changed back? I'm kind of glad. I never figured you for the kind of woman who'd have sex in public places with someone she scarcely knew.' (That surprised me; I'd always thought Andy believed just about anything bad about me.) 'What about that bloodhound that was with you?'

'That was Sam,' I said, rising to rinse out my coffee cup.

'But at the bar he changed into a collie.'

'Collies are cute,' I said. 'He figured more people would relate. It's his usual form.'

Lattesta's eyes were bugging out. He was one tightly wound guy. 'Let's get back on topic,' he said.

'Your brother's alibi seems to be true,' Andy said. 'We've talked to Jason two or three times, and we've talked to Michele twice, and she's adamant that she was with him the whole time. She told us everything that happened that night in detail.' Andy half smiled. 'Too much detail.'

That was Michele. She was forthright and downright. Her mom was the same way. I'd gone to vacation Bible school one summer when Mrs Schubert was teaching my age group. 'Tell the truth and shame the devil,' she'd advised us. Michele had taken that adage to heart, though maybe not in the way her mother had intended it.

'I'm glad you believe her,' I said.

'We also talked to Calvin.' Andy leaned on his elbows. 'He gave us the background on Dove and Crystal. According to him, Jason knew all about their affair.'

'He did.' I shut my mouth tight. I wasn't going to talk about that incident if I could help it.

'And we talked to Dove.'

'Of course.'

'Dove Beck,' Lattesta said, reading from his own notes. 'He's twenty-six, married, two kids.'

Since I knew all that, I had nothing to say.

'His cousin Alcee insisted on being there when we talked to him,' Lattesta said. 'Dove says he was home all that night, and his wife corroborates that.'

'I don't think Dove did it,' I said, and they both looked surprised.

'But you gave us the lead that she and Dove had had an affair,' Andy said.

I flushed with mortification. 'I'm sorry I did. I hated it when everyone looked at Jason like they were sure he'd done it, when I knew he hadn't. I don't think Dove murdered Crystal. I don't think he cared enough about her to do that to her.'

'But maybe she ruined his marriage.'

'Still, he wouldn't do that. Dove would be mad at himself, not at her. And she was pregnant. Dove wouldn't kill a pregnant woman.'

'How can you be so sure?'

Because I can read his mind and see his innocence, I thought. But the vampires and Weres had come out, not me. I was hardly a supernatural creature. I was just a variation on human. 'I don't think that's in Dove,' I said. 'I don't see it.'

'And we're supposed to accept that as proof?' Lattesta said.

'I don't care what you do with it,' I said, stopping short of offering a suggestion as to exactly what he might try. 'You asked me; I answered you.'

'So you do think this was a hate crime?'

It was my turn to look down at the table. I didn't have a notepad to scribble on, but I wanted to consider what I was about to say. 'Yes,' I told them finally. 'I think it was a hate crime. But I don't know if it was personal hate, because Crystal was a slut . . . or racial hate, because she was a werepanther.' I shrugged. 'If I hear anything, I'll tell you. I want this solved.'

'Hear anything? In the bar?' Lattesta's expression was avid. Finally, a human man saw me as intensely valuable. Just my luck he was happily married and thought I was a freak.

'Yes,' I said. 'I might hear something in the bar.'

They left after that, and I was glad to see them go. It was my day off. I felt I should do something special today to celebrate, since I was coming off such a difficult time, but I couldn't think of anything to do. I looked at the Weather Channel and saw the high for today was supposed to be in the sixties. I decided winter was officially over, even though it was still January. It would get cold again, but I was going to enjoy the day.

I got my old chaise longue out of the storage shed and set it up in the backyard. I slicked my hair up in a ponytail and doubled it over so it wouldn't hang down. I put on my smallest bikini, which was bright orange and turquoise. I covered myself in tanning lotion. I took a radio and the book I was reading and a towel, and went out to the yard. Yep, it was cool. Yep, I got goose bumps when a breeze came up. But this was always a happy day on my calendar, the first day I got to sunbathe. I was going to enjoy it. I needed it.

Every year I thought of all the reasons I shouldn't lie out in the sun. Every year I added up my virtues: I didn't drink, I didn't smoke, and I very seldom had sex, though I was willing to change that. But I loved my sun, and it was bright in the sky today. Sooner or later I'd pay for it, but it remained my weakness. I wondered if maybe my fairy blood would give me a pass on the possibility of skin cancer. Nope: my aunt Linda had died of cancer, and she'd had more fairy blood than I had. Well . . . dammit.

I lay on my back, my eyes closed, dark glasses keeping the glare to a minimum. I sighed blissfully, ignoring the fact that I was a little on the cold side. I carefully didn't think about many things: Crystal, mysterious ill-wishing fairies, the FBI. After fifteen minutes, I switched to my stomach, listening to the country-and-western station from Shreveport, singing along from time to time since no one was around to hear me. I have an awful voice.

'Whatchadoing?' asked a voice right by my ear.

I'd never levitated before, but I think I did then, rising about six inches off the low folding chaise. I squawked, too.

'Jesus Christ, Shepherd of Judea,' I wheezed when I finally realized that the voice belonged to Diantha, part-demon niece of the half-demon lawyer Mr Cataliades. 'Diantha, you scared me so bad I almost jumped out of my skin.'

Diantha was laughing silently, her lean, flat body bobbing up and down. She was sitting cross-legged on the ground, and she was wearing red Lycra running shorts and a black-and-green patterned T-shirt. Red Converses with yellow socks completed her ensemble. She had a new scar, a long red puckered one that ran down her left calf.

'Explosion,' she said when she saw I was looking at it. Diantha had changed her hair color, too; it was a gleaming platinum. But the scar was bad enough to recapture my attention.

'You okay?' I asked. It was easy to adopt a terse style when you were talking to Diantha, whose conversation was like reading a telegram.

'Better,' she said, looking down at the scar herself. Then her strange green eyes met mine. 'My uncle sent me.' This was the prelude to the message she had come to deliver, I understood, because she said it so slowly and distinctly.

'What does your uncle want to tell me?' I was still on my stomach, propped on my elbows. My breathing was back to normal.

'He says the fairies are moving around in this world. He says to be

careful. He says they'll take you if they can, and they'll hurt you.'
Diantha blinked at me.

'Why?' I asked, all my pleasure in the sun evaporating as if it had never been. I felt cold. I cast a nervous glance around the yard.

'Your great-grandfather has many enemies,' Diantha said slowly and carefully.

'Diantha, do you know why he has so many enemies?' That was a question I couldn't ask my great-grandfather himself, or at least I hadn't worked up the courage to do so.

Diantha looked at me quizzically. 'They're on one side; he's on the other,' she said as if I were slow. 'Theygotyergrandfather.'

'They . . . these other fairies killed my grandfather Fintan?'

She nodded vigorously. 'Hedidn'ttellya,' she said.

'Niall? He just said his son had died.'

Diantha broke into a hoot of shrill laughter. 'Youcouldsaythat,' she said, and doubled over, still laughing. 'Choppedintapieces!' She slapped me on the arm in her excess of amusement. I winced.

'Sorry,' she said. 'Sorrysorrysorry.'

'Okay,' I said. 'Just give me a minute.' I rubbed the arm vigorously to restore the feeling. How did you protect yourself if marauding fairies were after you?

'Who exactly am I supposed to be scared of?' I asked.

'Breandan,' she said. 'Itmeanssomething; Iforgot.'

'Oh. What does 'Niall' mean?' Easily sidetracked, that was me.

'Cloud,' Diantha said. 'All Niall's people got sky names.'

'Okay. So Breandan is after me. Who is he?'

Diantha blinked. This was a very long conversation for her. 'Your great-grandfather's enemy,' she explained carefully, as if I were very dense. 'The only other fairy prince.'

'Why did Mr Cataliades send you?'

'Didyerbest,' she said in one breath. Her unblinking bright eyes latched onto mine, and she nodded and very gently patted my hand.

I *had* done my best to get everyone out of the Pyramid alive. But it hadn't worked. It was kind of gratifying to know that the lawyer appreciated my efforts. I'd spent a week being angry at myself because I hadn't uncovered the whole bombing plot more quickly. If I'd paid more attention, hadn't let myself get so distracted by the other stuff going on around me . . .

'Also, yercheck'llcome.'

'Oh, good!' I could feel myself brighten, despite the worry caused by the rest of Diantha's message. 'Did you bring a letter for me, or anything like that?' I asked, hoping for a little more enlightenment.

Diantha shook her head, and the gelled spikes of her bright platinum hair trembled all over her head, making her look like an agitated porcupine. 'Uncle has to stay neutral,' she said clearly. 'Nopaper-nophonecallsnoemails. That's why he sent me.'

Cataliades had really stuck his neck out for me. No, he'd stuck *Diantha's* neck out. 'What if they capture you, Diantha?' I said.

She shrugged a bony shoulder. 'Godownfightin',' she said. Her face grew sad. Though I can't read demon minds in the same way I can read human ones, any fool could tell Diantha was thinking about her sister, Gladiola, who had died from the sweep of a vampire's sword. But after a second, Diantha looked simply lethal. 'Burn'em,' Diantha said. I sat up and raised my eyebrows to show I didn't understand.

Diantha turned her hand up and looked at the palm. A tiny flicker of flame hovered right above it.

'I didn't know you could do that,' I said. I was not a little impressed. I reminded myself to always stay on Diantha's good side.

'Little,' she said, shrugging. I deduced from that that Diantha could make only a small flame, not a large one. Gladiola must have been taken completely by surprise by the vampire who'd killed her, because vampires were flammable, much more so than humans.

'Do fairies burn like vamps?'

She shook her head. 'Buteverything'llburn,' she said, her voice certain and serious. 'Sooner, later.'

I suppressed a shiver. 'Do you want a drink or something to eat?' I asked.

'Naw.' She got up from the ground, dusted off her brilliant outfit. 'Igottago.' She patted me on the head and turned, and then she was gone, running faster than any deer.

I lay back down on the chaise to think about all this. Now Niall had warned me, Mr Cataliades had warned me, and I felt well and truly scared.

But the warnings, though timely, didn't give me any practical information about how to guard against this threat. It might materialize at any time or in any place, as far as I could tell. I could assume the enemy fairies wouldn't storm Merlotte's and haul me out of there, since the fae were so secretive; but other than that, I didn't have a clue about what form the attack would take or how to defend myself. Would locked doors keep fairies out? Did they have to be granted entry, like vampires? No, I couldn't recall having to tell Niall he could come in, and he'd been to the house.

I knew fairies weren't limited to the night, as the vamps were. I knew they were very strong, as strong as vampires. I knew the fae who were actual fairies (as opposed to the fae who were brownies or goblins or elves) were beautiful and ruthless; that even vampires respected the ferocity of the fairies. The oldest fairies didn't always live in this world, as Claudine and Claude did; there was somewhere else they could go, a shrinking and secret world they found vastly preferable to this one: a world without iron. If they could limit their exposure to iron, fairies lived so long that they couldn't keep track of the years. Niall, for example, tossed around hundreds of years in his conversational chronology in a very inconsistent way. He might describe some event as being five hundred years ago, when another event that predated it was earmarked two hundred years ago. He simply couldn't keep track of the passage of time, maybe partly because he didn't spend most of that time in our world.

I wracked my brain for any other information. I did know one other thing, and I couldn't believe I'd forgotten it even momentarily. If iron is bad for fairies, lemon juice is even worse. Claude and Claudine's sister had been murdered with lemon juice.

Now that I thought of them, I thought it might be helpful for me to talk to Claude and Claudine. Not only were they my cousins, but Claudine was my fairy godmother, and she was supposed to help me. She'd be at work at the department store where she handled complaints and wrapped packages and took layaway payments. Claude would be at the male strip club he now owned and managed. He'd be easier to reach. I went inside to look up the number. Claude actually answered the phone himself.

'Yes,' he said, managing to convey indifference, contempt, and boredom in the one word.

'Hi, sweetie!' I said brightly. 'I need to talk to you face-to- face. Can I run over there, or are you busy?'

'No, don't come here!' Claude sounded almost alarmed at the idea. 'I'll meet you at the mall.'

The twins lived in Monroe, which boasted a nice mall.

'Okay,' I said. 'Where and when?'

There was a moment of silence. 'Claudine can get off late for lunch. We'll meet you in an hour and a half in the food court, around Chick-fil-A.'

'See you there,' I said, and Claude hung up. Mr Charm. I hustled into my favorite jeans and a green and white T-shirt. I brushed my hair vigorously. It had gotten so long I found it a lot of trouble to deal with, but I couldn't bring myself to cut it.

Since I'd exchanged blood with Eric several times, not only had I not caught so much as a cold, but I didn't even have split ends. Plus, my hair was shinier and actually looked thicker.

I wasn't surprised that people bought vampire blood on the black market. It did surprise me that people were foolish enough to trust the sellers when they said that the red stuff was actually genuine vampire blood. Often the vials contained TrueBlood, or pig's blood, or even the Drainer's own blood. If the purchaser did get genuine vampire blood, it was aged and might easily drive the consumer mad. I would never have gone to a Drainer to buy vampire blood. But now that I'd had it several times (and very fresh), I didn't even need to use makeup base. My skin was flawless. Thanks, Eric!

I don't know why I bothered with being proud of myself, because no one was going to look at me twice when I was with Claude. He's close to six feet tall, with rippling black hair and brown eyes, the physique of a stripper (six-pack abs and all), and the jaw and cheekbones of a Renaissance statue. Unfortunately, he has the personality of a statue, too.

Today Claude was wearing khakis and a tight tank top under an open green silk shirt. He was playing with a pair of dark glasses. Though Claude's facial expressions when he wasn't 'on' ranged from blank to sullen, today he actually seemed nervous. He scanned the food court area as if he suspected that someone had followed me, and he didn't relax when I dropped into a chair at his table. He had a Chick-fil-A cup in front of him, but he hadn't gotten anything to eat, so I didn't, either.

'Cousin,' he said, 'are you well?' He didn't even try to sound sincere, but at least he said the right words. Claude had gotten marginally more polite when I'd discovered my great-grandfather was his grand-father, but he'd never forget I was (mostly) human. Claude had as much contempt for humans as most fairies did, but he was definitely fond of bedding humans – as long as they had beard stubble.

'Yes, thank you, Claude. It's been a while.'

'Since we met? Yes.' And that was just fine with him. 'How can I help you? Oh, here comes Claudine.' He looked relieved.

Claudine was wearing a brown suit with big gold buttons and a brown, cream, and tan striped blouse. She dressed very conservatively for work, and though the outfit was becoming, something about the cut made her look somewhat less slim, I noticed. She was Claude's twin; there had been another sister, their triplet Claudette, but Clau-dette had been murdered. I guess if there are two remaining out of three, you call the living two 'twins'? Claudine was as tall as Claude, and as she bent to kiss him on the cheek, their hair (exactly the same shade) mingled in a cascade of dark ripples. She kissed me, too. I wondered if all the fae are as into physical contact as the fairies are. My cousin had a trayful of food: French fries, chicken nuggets, some kind of dessert, a big sugary drink.

'What kind of trouble is Niall in?' I asked, going directly to the point. 'What kind of enemies does he have? Are they all actual fairies? Or are they some other kind of fae?'

There was a moment of silence while Claudine and Claude noted my brisk mood. They weren't at all surprised at my questions, which I thought was significant.

'Our enemies are fairies,' Claudine said. 'The other fae don't mix in our politics, as a rule, though we're all variations on the same theme –

like pygmies, Caucasians, and Asians are variations on human beings.' She looked sad. 'All of us are less than we used to be.' She tore open a ketchup package and squirted it all over her fries. She stuck three fries in her mouth at one time. Wow, hungry.

'It would take hours to explain our whole lineage,' Claude said, but he wasn't dismissing me. He was simply stating a fact. 'We come from the line of fairies that claims kinship to the sky. Our grandfather, your great-grandfather, is one of the few surviving members of our royal family.'

'He's a prince,' I said, because that was one of the few facts I knew. *Prince Charming Prince Valiant. Prince of the City.* The title carried a lot of weight.

'Yes. There is another prince, Breandan.' Claude pronounced it 'Bren-DAWN.' Diantha had mentioned Breandan. 'He is the son of Niall's older brother, Rogan. Rogan claimed kinship to the sea, and from there his influence spread to all bodies of water. Rogan recently has gone to the Summerlands.'

'Dead,' Claudine translated before she took a bite of her chicken.

Claude shrugged. 'Yes, Rogan's dead. He was the only one who could rein in Breandan. And you should know, Breandan's the one who—' But Claude stopped in midsentence, because his sister had her hand clamped down on his arm. A woman who was feeding a little boy French fries looked over at us curiously, her attention attracted by Claudine's sudden gesture. Claudine gave Claude a look that could blister paint. He nodded, removed his arm from her grip, and began to speak again. 'Breandan disagrees very strongly with Niall about policy. He . . .'

The twins looked at each other. Finally Claudine nodded.

'Breandan believes all the humans with fairy blood should be eradicated. He believes every time one of us mates with a human, we lose some of our magic.'

I cleared my throat, trying to get rid of the lump of fear that had risen to block it. 'So Breandan's an enemy. Any more royalty on Niall's side?' I asked in a choked voice.

'A less-than-prince. His title doesn't translate,' Claude said. 'Our father, Dillon son of Niall, and his first wife, Branna. Our mother is

Binne. If Niall goes to the Summerlands, Dillon will replace him as prince. But of course he must wait.'

The names were unfamiliar. The first one sounded almost like Dylan, the second sounded like BEE-nah. 'Spell those, please,' I said, and Claudine said, 'B-I-N-N-E. D-I-L-L-O-N. Niall didn't live happily with Branna, and it took him a long time to love our father, Dillon. Niall preferred his half-human sons.' She smiled at me to reassure me that humans were okay with her, I guess.

Niall had told me once I was his only living relative. But that wasn't true. Niall was definitely swayed by emotion, not facts. I needed to remember that. Claude and Claudine didn't seem to blame Niall's partiality on me, to my huge relief.

'So who's on Breandan's side?' I asked.

'Dermot,' said Claudine. She looked at me expectantly.

I knew that name. I struggled to remember where I'd heard it.

'He's my grandfather Fintan's brother,' I said slowly. 'Niall's other son by Einin. But he's half human.' Einin had been a human woman seduced by Niall centuries ago. (She'd thought he was an angel, which gives you some idea how good fairies can look when they don't need to look human.) My half-human great-uncle was trying to kill his dad?

'Did Niall tell you that Fintan and Dermot were twins?' Claude asked.

'No,' I said, astonished.

'Dermot was the younger by a few minutes. The twins were not identical, you understand,' he said. He was enjoying my ignorance. 'They were ...' He paused, looked baffled. 'I don't know the right term,' he said.

'Fraternal. Okay, interesting, but so?'

'Actually,' Claudine said, looking down intently at her chicken, 'your brother, Jason, is the spitting image of Dermot.'

'Are you suggesting that ... What are you suggesting?' I was ready to be indignant, once I knew why.

'We're only telling you that this is why Niall has been naturally inclined to favor you over your brother,' Claude said. 'Niall loved Fintan, but Dermot defied Niall at every turn. He openly rebelled against our grandfather and pledged his loyalty to Breandan, though

Breandan despises him. In addition to Dermot's resemblance to Jason, which is only a quirk of genes, Dermot is an asshole like Jason. You can see why Niall doesn't claim kinship with your brother.'

I felt a moment's pity for Jason until my common sense woke me up. 'So Niall has enemies besides Breandan and Dermot?'

'They have their own followers and associates, including a few assassins.'

'But your dad and your mom are on Niall's side?'

'Yes. Others are, too, of course. All of us sky people.'

'So I have to watch out for any approaching fairies, and they might attack me at any time because I'm Niall's blood.'

'Yes. The fae world is too dangerous. Especially now. That's one reason we live in the human world.' Claude glanced at Claudine, who was wolfing chicken nuggets like she'd been starving.

Claudine swallowed, patted her mouth with the paper napkin, and said, 'Here's the most important point.' She popped in another nugget and glanced at Claude, signaling him to take over.

'If you see someone who looks like your brother, but isn't ...' Claude said.

Claudine swallowed. 'Run like hell,' she advised.

Chapter 9

I drove home more confused than ever. Though I loved my great-grandfather as much as I could on our short acquaintance . . . and I was absolutely ready to love him even more, and I was willing to back him up to the limit because we were kin . . . I still didn't know how to fight this war, or how to dodge it, either. Fairies did not want to be known to the human world, and they never would. They weren't like the wereanimals or the vampires, who wanted to share in the planet with us. There was much less reason for the fairies to keep in line with human policies and rules. They could do anything they wished and vanish back into their secret place.

For about the millionth time, I wished I had a normal great-grandfather instead of this improbable, glorious, and inconvenient fairy prince version.

Then I was ashamed of myself. I should be happy for what I'd been given. I hoped God hadn't noticed my lapse of appreciation.

I'd already had a busy day, and it was only two o'clock. This wasn't shaping up to be my normal day off. Usually I did laundry, cleaned house, went to the store, read, paid bills. . . . But today was so pretty I wanted to stay outside. I wanted to work on something that would allow me to think at the same time. There sure was plenty to mull over.

I looked at the flower beds around the house and decided to weed. This was my least-favorite chore, maybe because it was the one I'd often been assigned as a child. Gran had believed we should be brought up to work. It was in her honor that I tried to keep the flower beds looking nice, and now I sighed and made up my mind to get the job done. I'd start with the bed by the driveway, on the south side of the house.

I went over to our metal toolshed, the latest in a series of toolsheds that had served the Stackhouse family over the generations we'd lived on this spot. I opened the door with the familiar mingled feelings of pleasure and horror, because someday I was going to have to put in some serious work cleaning out the interior. I still had my grandmother's old trowel; there was no telling who'd used it before her. It was ancient but so well taken care of that it was better than any modern substitute. I stepped into the shadowy shed and found my gardening gloves and the trowel.

I knew from watching *Antiques Roadshow* that there were people who collected old farm implements. This toolshed would be an Aladdin's cave to such a collector. My family didn't believe in letting things go if they still worked. Though chock-full, the shed was orderly, because that had been my grandfather's way. When we'd come to live with him and Gran, he'd drawn an outline for every commonly used tool. That was where he'd wanted that tool to be replaced every time it was used, and that was where it was still kept now. I could reach unerringly for the trowel, which was maybe the oldest tool in the shed. It was heavy, sharper, and narrower than its modern counterparts, but its shape was familiar to my hand.

If it had been really, truly spring, I'd have changed back into my bikini to combine business with pleasure. But though the sun was still shining, I wasn't in a carefree mood any longer. I pulled my gardening gloves on, because I didn't want to ruin my fingernails. Some of these weeds seemed to fight back. One grew on a thick, fleshy stalk, and it had sharp points on its leaves. If you let it grow long enough, it blossomed. It was really ugly and prickly, and it had to be removed by its roots. There were quite a few of them springing up among the emerging cannas.

Gran would have had a fit.

I crouched and set to work. With my right hand, I sank the trowel in the soft dirt of the flower bed, loosening the roots of the nasty weed, and pulled it up with my left hand. I shook the stalk to get the dirt off the roots and then tossed it aside. Before I'd started I'd put a radio out on the back porch. In no time at all, I was singing along with LeAnn Rimes. I began to feel less troubled. In a few minutes, I had a respectable pile of uprooted weeds and a glow of virtue.

If he hadn't spoken, it would have ended differently. But since he was full of himself, he had to open his mouth. His pride saved my life.

Also, he picked some unwise words. Saying, 'I'll enjoy killing you for my lord,' is just not the way to make my acquaintance.

I have good reflexes, and I erupted from my squatting position with the trowel in my hand and I drove it upward into his stomach. It slid right in, as if it were designed to be a fairy-killing weapon.

And that was exactly what it turned out to be, because the trowel was iron and he was a fairy.

I leaped back and dropped into a half crouch, still gripping the bloody trowel, and waited to see what he'd do. He was looking down at the blood seeping through his fingers with an expression of absolute amazement, as if he couldn't believe I'd ruined his ensemble. Then he looked at me, his eyes pale blue and huge, and there was a big question on his face, as if he were asking me if I'd really done that to him, if it wasn't some kind of mistake.

I began backing up to the porch steps, never taking my eyes from him, but he wasn't a threat any longer. As I reached behind me to open the screen door, my would-be murderer crumpled to the ground, still looking surprised.

I retreated into the house and locked the door. Then I walked on trembling legs over to the window above the kitchen sink and peered out, leaning as far over the sink as I could. From this angle I could see only a bit of the crumpled body. 'Okay,' I said out loud. '*Okay.*' He was dead, looked like. It had been so *quick.*

I started to pick up the wall phone, noticed how my hands were shaking, and spotted my cell phone on the counter where I'd been charging it. Since this was a crisis that definitely called for the head honcho, I speed-dialed my great-grandfather's big, secret emergency number. I thought the situation qualified A male voice, not Niall's, answered. 'Yes?' the voice said with a cautious tone.

'Ah, is Niall there?'

'I can reach him. Can I help you?'

Steady, I told myself. *Steady.* 'Would you please tell him I've killed a fairy and he's laid out in my yard and I don't know what to do with the body?'

There was a moment of silence.

'Yes, I'll tell him that.'

'Pretty soon, you think? Because I'm alone and I'm kind of freaked out.'

'Yes. Quite soon.'

'And someone will come?' Geez Louise, I sounded whiny. I made my spine stiffen. 'I mean, I can load him in my car trunk, I guess, or I could call the sheriff.' I wanted to impress this unknown with the fact that I wasn't completely needy and helpless. 'But there's the whole thing with you guys being secret, and he didn't seem to have a weapon, and obviously I can't prove this guy said he'd enjoy killing me.'

'You . . . have killed a fairy.'

'I *said* that. Way back.' Mr Slow-on-the-Uptake. I peered out the window again. 'Yeah, he's still not moving. Dead and gone.'

This time the silence lasted so long that I thought I must have blanked out and missed something. I said, 'I'm sorry?'

'Are you really? We'll be there very soon.' And he hung up.

I couldn't not look, and I couldn't bear to look. I'd seen the dead before, both human and nonhuman. And since the night I'd met Bill Compton in Merlotte's, I'd seen more than my share of bodies. Not that that was Bill's fault, of course.

I had goose pimples all over.

In about five minutes, Niall and another fairy walked out of the woods. There must be some kind of portal out there. Maybe Scotty had beamed them up. Or down. And maybe I wasn't thinking too clearly.

The two fairies stopped when they saw the body and then exchanged a few words. They seemed astonished. But they weren't scared, and they weren't acting like they expected the guy to get up and fight, so

I crept across the back porch and out the screen door.

They knew I was there, but they continued their eyeballing of the body.

My great-grandfather raised his arm and I crept under it. He held me to him, and I glanced up to see that he was smiling.

Okay, *that* was unexpected.

'You're a credit to our family. You've killed my enemy,' he said. 'I was so right about humans.' He looked proud as punch.

'This is a good thing?'

The other fairy laughed and looked at me for the first time. He had hair the color of butterscotch, and his eyes matched his hair, which to me was so weird that it was really off-putting – though like all the fairies I'd met, he was gorgeous. I had to suppress a sigh. Between the vampires and the fairies, I was doomed to be a plain Jane.

'I'm Dillon,' he said.

'Oh, Claudine's dad. Nice to meet you. I guess your name means something, too?' I said.

'Lightning,' he said, and gave me a particularly winsome smile.

'Who is this?' I said, jerking my head at the body.

'He was Murry,' Niall said. 'He was a close friend of my nephew Breandan.'

Murry looked very young; to the human eye, he'd been perhaps eighteen. 'He said he was looking forward to killing me,' I told them.

'But instead, you killed him. How did you do it?' Dillon asked, as if he was asking how I rolled out a flaky piecrust.

'With my grandmother's trowel,' I said. 'Actually, it's been in my family for a long time. Not like we make a fetish of gardening tools or anything; it just works and it's there and there's no need to buy another one.' Babbling.

They both looked at me. I couldn't tell if they thought I was nuts or what.

'Could you show us this gardening tool?' Niall said.

'Sure. Do you-all want some tea or something? I think we've got some Pepsi and some lemonade.' No, no, not lemonade! They'd die! 'Sorry, cancel the lemonade. Tea?'

'No,' said Niall quite gently. 'I think not now.'

I'd dropped the bloody trowel in among the cannas. When I picked it up and approached them, Dillon flinched. 'Iron!' he said.

'You don't have the gloves on,' Niall said to his son chidingly, and took the trowel from me. His hands were covered with the clear flexible coating developed in fairy-owned chemical factories. Coated with this substance, fairies were able to go out in the human world with some degree of assurance that they wouldn't get poisoned in the process.

Dillon looked chastened. 'No, sorry, Father.'

Niall shook his head as if he were disappointed in Dillon, but his attention was really on the trowel. He might have been prepared to handle something poisonous to him, but I noticed he still handled it very carefully.

'It went into him really easily,' I said, and had to repress a sudden wave of nausea. 'I don't know why. It's sharp, but it's not that sharp.'

'Iron can part our flesh like a hot knife in butter,' Niall said.

'Ugh.' Well, at least I knew I hadn't suddenly gotten superstrong.

'He surprised you?' Dillon asked. Though he didn't have the fine, fine wrinkles that made my great-grandfather even more beautiful, Dillon looked only a little younger than Niall, which made their relationship all the more disorienting. But when I looked down at the corpse once more, I was completely back in the present.

'He sure did surprise me. I was just working away weeding the flower bed, and the next thing you know, he was standing right there telling me how much he was looking forward to killing me. I'd never done a thing to him. And he scared me, so I kind of came up in a rush with the trowel, and I got him in the stomach.' Again, I wrestled with my own stomach's tendency to heave.

'Did he speak any more?' My great-grandfather was trying to ask me casually, but he seemed pretty interested in my answer.

'No, sir,' I said. 'He kind of looked surprised, and then he . . . he died.' I walked over to the steps and sat down rather suddenly and heavily.

'It's not exactly like I feel guilty,' I said in a rush of words. 'It's just that he was trying to kill me and he was happy about it and I never did a thing to him. I didn't know anything about him, and now he's dead.'

Dillon knelt in front of me. He looked into my face. He didn't exactly look kind, but he looked less detached. 'He was your enemy, and now he is dead,' he said. 'This is cause for rejoicing.'

'Not exactly,' I said. I didn't know how to explain.

'You're a *Christian*,' he said, as if he'd discovered I was a herm-aphrodite or a fruitarian.

'I'm a real bad one,' I said hurriedly. His lips compressed, and I could see he was trying hard not to laugh. I'd never felt less like mirth, with the man I'd killed lying a few feet away. I wondered how many years Murry had walked this earth, and now he was crumpled in a lifeless heap, his blood staining my gravel. Wait a minute! He wasn't anymore. He was turning to . . . dust. It wasn't anything like the gradual flaking away of a vampire; it was more like someone was erasing Murry.

'Are you cold?' Niall asked. He didn't seem to think the dis-appearance of bits of the body was anything unusual.

'No, sir. I'm just all upset. I mean, I was sunbathing and then I went to see Claude and Claudine, and now here I am.' I couldn't take my eyes off the body's incremental disappearance.

'You've been lying in the sun and gardening. We like the sun and sky,' he said, as if that was proof positive I had a special relationship with the fairy branch of my family. He smiled at me. He was so beautiful. I felt like an adolescent when I was around him, an ado-lescent with acne and baby fat. Now I felt like a *murderous* adolescent.

'Are you going to gather up his . . . ashes?' I asked. I rose, trying to look brisk and purposeful. Action would make me feel less miserable.

Two pairs of alien eyes stared at me blankly.

'Why?' Dillon asked.

'To bury them.'

They looked horrified.

'No, not in the *ground*,' Niall said, trying to sound less revolted than he was. 'That isn't our way.'

'Then what are you going to do with them?' There was quite a heap of glittering powder on my driveway and in my flower bed, and there was still his torso remaining. 'I don't mean to be pushy, but Amelia might come home anytime. I don't get a lot of other visitors, but there's the odd UPS delivery person and the meter reader.'

Dillon looked at my great-grandfather as if I'd suddenly begun speaking Japanese. Niall said, 'Sookie shares her house with another woman, and this woman may return at any moment.'

'Is anyone else going to come after me?' I asked, diverted from my question.

'Possibly,' Niall said. 'Fintan did a better job of protecting you than I am doing, Sookie. He even protected you from me, and I only want to love you. But he wouldn't tell me where you were.' Niall looked sad, and harried, and tired for the first time since I'd met him. 'I've tried to keep you out of it. I imagined I only wanted to meet you before they succeeded in killing me, and I arranged it through the vampire to make my movements less noticeable, but in arranging that meeting I've drawn you into danger. You can trust my son Dillon.' He put his hand on the younger fairy's shoulder. 'If he brings you a message, it's really from me.' Dillon smiled charmingly, displaying supernaturally white and sharp teeth. Okay, he was scary, even if he was Claude and Claudine's dad.

'I'll talk to you soon,' Niall said, bending over to give me a kiss. The fine, gleaming pale hair fell against my cheek. He smelled so good; fairies do. 'I'm sorry, Sookie,' he said. 'I thought I could force them all to accept ... Well, I couldn't.' His green eyes glowed with intensity and regret. 'Do you have – yes, a garden hose! We could gather up most of the dust, but I think it more practical if you simply ... distribute it.'

He put his arms around me and hugged me, and Dillon gave me a mocking salute. The two took a few steps to the trees, and then they simply vanished into the undergrowth as deer do when you encounter them in the woods.

So that was that. I was left in my sunny yard, all by myself, with a sizeable pile of glittering powdery dust in a body-shaped heap on the gravel.

I added to my mental list of the odd things I'd done that day. I'd entertained the police, sunbathed, visited at a mall with some fairies, weeded, and killed someone. Now it was powdered corpse removal time. And the day wasn't over yet.

I turned on the faucet, unwound the hose enough so the flow would reach the right area, and compressed the spray head to aim the water at the fairy dust.

I had a weird, out-of-body feeling. 'You'd think I'd be getting used to it,' I said out loud, startling myself even more. I didn't want to add up the people I'd killed, though technically most of them weren't people. Before the past two years (maybe even less if I counted down the months), I'd never laid a finger on another person in anger, aside from hitting Jason in the stomach with my plastic baseball bat when he tore my Barbie's hair out.

I pulled myself up sharply. The deed was done now. No going back.

I released the spray head and turned the hose off at the faucet.

In the fading sunlight, it was a little hard to tell, but I thought I'd dispersed the dust pretty thoroughly.

'But not from my memory,' I said seriously. Then I had to laugh, and it sounded a little crazy. I was standing out in my backyard hosing down fairy blood and making melodramatic statements all to myself. Next I'd be doing the *Hamlet* soliloquy that I'd had to memorize in high school.

This afternoon had brought me down hard, to a real bad place.

I bit down on my bottom lip. Now that I was definitely over the intoxication of having a living relative, I had to face the fact that Niall's behavior was charming (mostly) but unpredictable. By his own admission, he'd inadvertently put me at great risk. Maybe I should have wondered before this what my grandfather Fintan had been like. Niall had told me he'd watched over me without ever making himself known, an image that seemed creepy but touching. Niall was creepy and touching, too. Great-uncle Dillon just seemed creepy.

The temperature was dropping with the creeping darkness, and I was shivering by the time I went in the house. The hose might freeze tonight, but I couldn't bring myself to care. There were clothes in the dryer, and I had to eat since I'd missed eating lunch at the mall. It was getting closer to suppertime. I had to concentrate on small things.

Amelia phoned while I was folding the laundry. She told me she was about to leave work and was going to meet Tray for dinner and a movie. She asked me if I wanted to come along, but I said I was busy.

Amelia and Tray didn't need a third wheel, and I didn't need to feel like one.

It would have been nice to have some company. But what would I have done for social chitchat? *Wow, that trowel slid into his stomach like it was Jell-O.*

I shuddered and tried to think of what to do next. An uncritical companion, that was who I needed. I missed the cat we'd called Bob (though he hadn't been born a cat and wasn't one now). Maybe I could get another cat a real one. It wasn't the first time I'd considered going to the animal shelter. I'd better wait until this fairy crisis was over before I did that. There wasn't any point in picking out a pet if I was liable to be abducted or killed at any moment, right? Wouldn't be fair to the animal. I caught myself *giggling*, and I knew that couldn't be good.

Time to stop brooding; time to get something done. First, I'd clean off the trowel and put it away. I carried it to the kitchen sink, and I scrubbed it and rinsed it. The dull iron seemed to have a new gloss on it, like a bush that had gotten watered after a drought. I held it to the light and stared at the old tool. I shook myself.

Okay, that had really been an unpleasant simile. I banished the idea and scrubbed. When I thought the trowel looked spotless, I washed it and dried it all over again. Then I walked quickly out the back door and through the dark to hang the damn thing back in the toolshed on its designated hook.

I wondered if I might not get a cheap new trowel at Wal-Mart after all. I wasn't sure I could use the iron one the next time I wanted to move some jonquil bulbs. It would feel like using a gun to pry out nails. I hesitated, the trowel poised to hang from its designated hook. Then I made up my mind and carried it back to the house. I paused on the back steps, admiring the last streak of light for a few moments until my stomach growled.

What a long day it had been. I was ready to settle in front of the television with a plate of something bad for me, watching some show that wouldn't improve my mind at all.

I heard the crunching of a car coming up the driveway as I was opening the screen door. I waited outside to see who my caller might be. Whoever it was, they knew me a little, because the car proceeded around to the back.

In a day full of shocks, here was another: my caller was Quinn, who was not supposed to stick his big toe into Area Five. He was driving a Ford Taurus, a rental car.

'Oh, *great*,' I said. I'd wanted company earlier, but not this company. As much as I'd liked and admired Quinn, this conversation promised to be just as upsetting as the day had been.

He got out of his car and strode over to me, his walk graceful, as always. Quinn is a very large shaved-bald man with pansy purple eyes. He is one of the few remaining weretigers in the world and probably the only male weretiger on the North American continent. We'd broken up the last time I'd seen him. I wasn't proud of how I'd told him or why I'd done it, but I thought I'd been pretty clear about us not being a couple.

Yet here he was, and his big warm hands were resting on my shoulders. Any pleasure I might have felt at seeing him again was drowned by the wave of anxiety that swept over me. I felt trouble in the air.

'You shouldn't be here,' I said. 'Eric turned down your request; he told me so.'

'Did he ask you first? Did you know I wanted to see you?' The darkness was now intense enough to trigger the outside security light. Quinn's face had harsh lines in the yellow glare. His gaze locked with mine.

'No, but that's not the point,' I said. I felt rage on the wind. It wasn't my rage.

'I think it is.'

It was sunset. There simply wasn't time to get into an extended argument. 'Didn't we say it all last time?' I didn't want to go through another scene, no matter how fond I was of this man.

'You said what you thought was all, babe. I disagree.'

Oh, great. Just what I needed! But since I really do know that not everything is about me, I counted to ten and said, 'I know I didn't give you any slack when I told you we shouldn't see each other anymore, Quinn, but I did mean what I said. What's changed in your personal situation? Is your mom able to take care of herself now? Or has Frannie grown up enough to be able to manage your mom if she escapes?' Quinn's mom had been through an awful time, and she'd come out of it more or less nuts. Actually, more. His sister, Frannie, was still a teenager.

He bowed his head for a moment, as if he were gathering himself. Then he looked directly into my eyes again. 'Why are you harder on me than on anyone else?' he asked.

'I am not,' I said instantly. But then I thought, *Am I?*

'Have you asked Eric to give up Fangtasia? Have you asked Bill to give up his computer enterprise? Have you asked Sam to turn his back on his family?'

'What . . .?' I began, trying to work out the connection.

'You're asking me to give up other people I love – my mother and my sister – if I want to have you,' he said.

'I'm not asking you to do *anything*,' I said, feeling the tension inside me ratchet up to an almost intolerable level. 'I told you that I wanted to be first with the guy in my life. And I figured – I still figure – that your family has got to come first with you because your mom and your sister are not exactly stand-on-their-own-two-feet kind of women. I haven't asked Eric to give up Fangtasia! Why would I do that? And where does Sam come into it?' I couldn't even think of a reason to mention Bill. I was so over him.

'Bill loves his status in the human and vampire worlds, and Eric loves his little piece of Louisiana more than he'll ever love you,' Quinn said, and he sounded almost sorry for me. That was ridiculous.

'Where did all the hating come from?' I asked, holding my hands spread in front of me. 'I didn't quit dating you because of any feelings I had for someone else. I quit dating you because I thought your plate was full already.'

'He's trying to wall you off from everyone else who cares for you,' Quinn said, focusing on me with unnerving intensity. 'And look at all the dependents *he* has.'

'You're talking about Eric?' All Eric's 'dependents' were vampires who could damn well take care of themselves.

'He'll *never* dump his little area for you. He'd never let his little pack of sworn vamps serve someone else. He'll never—'

I couldn't stand this anymore. I gave a scream of sheer frustration. I actually stomped my foot like a three-year-old. 'I haven't asked him to!' I yelled. 'What are you talking about? Did you show up to tell me no else will ever love me? What's wrong with you?'

'Yes, Quinn,' said a familiar, cold voice. 'What's wrong with you?'

I swear I jumped at least six inches. I'd let my quarrel with Quinn absorb my attention, and I hadn't felt Bill's arrival.

'You're frightening Sookie,' Bill said from a yard behind me, and my spine shivered at the menace in his voice. 'That won't happen, tiger.'

Quinn snarled. His teeth began growing longer, sharper, before my eyes. Bill stood at my side in the next second. His eyes were glowing an eerie silvery brown.

Not only was I afraid they'd kill each other, I realized that I was really tired of people popping on and off of my property like it was a train station on the supernatural railroad.

Quinn's hands became clawed. A growl rumbled deep in his chest.

'No!' I said, willing them to listen to me. This was the day from hell.

'You're not even on the list, vampire,' Quinn said, and his voice wasn't really his any longer. 'You're the past.'

'I will make you a rug on my floor,' Bill said, and his voice was colder and smoother than ever, like ice on glass.

The two idiots launched themselves at each other.

I started to jump in to stop them, but the functioning part of my brain told me that would be suicidal. I thought, *My grass is going to get sprinkled by a little more blood this evening*. What I should have been thinking was, *I need to get the hell out of the way*. In fact, I should have run inside and locked the door and left them to it.

But that was hindsight. Actually, what I did was stand there for a moment, hands fluttering uselessly, trying to figure out how to separate them ... and then the two grappling figures lurched and staggered. Quinn threw Bill away from him with all his strength. Bill cannoned into me with such force that I actually went up in the air an inch or two – and then, very decisively, down I came.

Chapter 10

Cold water trickled over my face and neck. I spluttered and choked as some trickled into my mouth.

'Too much?' asked a hard voice, and I pried open my eyes to see Eric. We were in my room, and only the bathroom light was on.

'Enough,' I said. The mattress shifted as Eric got up to carry the washrag into my bathroom. In a second he was back with a hand towel, dabbing at my face and neck. My pillow was damp, but I decided not to worry about it. The house was cooling off now that the sun was gone, and I was lying there in my underwear. 'Cold,' I said. 'Where are my clothes?'

'Stained,' Eric said. There was a blanket at the end of the bed, and he pulled it up over me. He turned his back to me for a moment, and I heard his shoes hit the floor. Then he got under the blanket with me and propped himself up on an elbow. He was looking down at me. His back was to the light coming from the bathroom, so I couldn't discern his expression. 'Do you love him?' he said.

'Are they alive?' No point in deciding if I loved Quinn or not if he was dead, right? Or maybe Eric meant Bill. I couldn't decide. I realized I felt a little odd.

'Quinn drove away with a few broken ribs and a broken jaw,' Eric told me, his voice quite neutral. 'Bill will heal tonight, if he hasn't already.'

I considered that. 'I guess you had something to do with Bill being here?'

'I knew when Quinn disobeyed our ruling. He was sighted within half an hour of crossing into my area. And Bill was the closest vampire to send to your house. His task was to make sure you weren't being harassed while I made my way here. He took his role a little too seriously. I'm sorry you were hurt,' Eric said, his voice stiff. He wasn't used to making apologies, and I smiled in the darkness. It was almost impossible for me to feel anxious, I noticed in a distant kind of way. And yet surely I ought to be upset and angry?

'So they stopped fighting when I hit the ground, I hope.'

'Yes, the collision ended the . . . scuffle.'

'And Quinn left on his own?' I ran my tongue around my mouth, which tasted funny: kind of sharp and metallic.

'Yes, he did. I told him I would take care of you. He knew he'd crossed too many lines by coming to see you, since I'd told him not to enter my area. Bill was less accepting, but I made him return to his house.'

Typical sheriff behavior. 'Did you give me some of your blood?' I asked.

Eric nodded quite casually. 'You had been knocked unconscious,' he said. 'And I know that is serious. I wanted you to feel well. It was my fault.'

I sighed. 'Mr High-handed,' I muttered.

'Explain. I don't know this term.'

'It means someone who thinks he knows what's best for everyone. He makes decisions for them without asking them.' Maybe I had put a personal spin on the term, but so what?

'Then I am high-handed,' Eric said with no shame whatsoever. 'I'm also very . . .' He dipped his head and kissed me slowly, leisurely.

'Horny,' I said.

'Exactly,' he said, and kissed me again. 'I've worked with my new masters. I've shored up my authority. I can have my own life now. It's time I claimed what is mine.'

I'd told myself I'd make up my own mind, no matter how Eric and I were tied by our blood exchanges. After all, I still had free will.

But whether or not the inclination had been planted by Eric's blood donation, I found that my body was strongly in favor of returning the kiss and of trailing the palm of my hand down Eric's broad back. Through the fabric of his shirt, I could feel the muscles and tendons and the bones of his spine as they moved. My hands seemed to remember the map of Eric's topography even as my lips remembered the way he kissed. We went on this way very slowly for a few minutes as he reacquainted himself with me.

'Do you really remember?' I asked him. 'Do you really remember staying with me before? Do you remember what it felt like?'

'Oh, yes,' he said, 'I remember.' He had my bra unhooked before I'd even realized his hand was back there. 'How could I forget these?' he said, his hair falling around his face as his mouth fastened on my breast. I felt the tiny sting of his fangs and the sharp pleasure of his mouth. I touched the fly of his jeans, brushed my hand against the bulge inside, and suddenly the moment for being tentative was over.

His jeans were off, and his shirt, too, and my panties vanished. His long cool body pressed full-length against my warm one. He kissed me over and over in a kind of frenzy. He made a hungry noise, and I echoed it. His fingers probed me, fluttering against the hard nub in a way that made me squirm.

'Eric,' I said, trying to position myself underneath him. 'Now.'

He said, 'Oh, yes.' He slid inside as if he'd never been gone, as if we'd made love every night for the past year. 'This is best,' he whispered, and his voice had that accent I caught occasionally, that hint of a time and place that were so far distant I could not imagine them. 'This is *best*,' he said again. 'This is *right*.' He pulled out a little, and I made a choked noise.

'Not hurting?' he asked.

'Not hardly,' I said.

'I am too big for some.'

'Bring it on,' I said.

He shoved forward.

'Omigod,' I said through clenched teeth. My fingers were digging hard into the muscles of his arms. 'Yes, again!' He was as deep inside me as he could get without an operation, and he glowed above me, his white skin shining in the darkness of the room. He said something in a language I didn't recognize; after a long moment, he repeated it. And then he began to move quicker and quicker until I thought I would be pounded into pieces, but I kept up. I kept up, until I saw his fangs glisten as he bent over me. When he bit my shoulder, I left my body for a minute. I'd never felt anything so good. I didn't have enough breath to scream or even speak. My arms were around Eric's back, and I felt him shudder all over as he had his own good minute.

I was so shaken I couldn't have talked if my life had depended on it. We lay in silence, exhausted. I didn't mind his weight on me. I felt safe.

He licked the bite mark in a lazy way, and I smiled into the darkness. I stroked his back as if I were soothing an animal. I felt better than I'd felt in months. It had been a while since I'd had sex, and this was like . . . *gourmet* sex. Even now I felt little jolts of pleasure ripple out from the epicenter of the orgasm.

'Will this change the blood bond?' I asked. I was careful not to sound like I was accusing him of something. But of course, I was.

'Felipe wanted you. The stronger our bond, the less chance there is he can maneuver you away.'

I flinched. 'I can't do that.'

'You won't need to,' Eric said, his voice flowing over me like a feather quilt. 'We are pledged with the knife. We are bonded. He can't take you from me.'

I could only be grateful I didn't have to go to Las Vegas. I didn't want to leave home. I couldn't imagine how it would feel to be surrounded by so much greed; well, yes, I could. It would be awful. Eric's big, cool hand cupped my breast, and he stroked with his long thumb.

'Bite me,' Eric said, and he meant it literally.

'Why? You said you already gave me some.'

'Because it makes me feel good,' he said, and moved on top of me again. 'Just . . . for that.'

'You can't be . . .' But he *was* ready again.

'Would you like to be on top?' Eric asked.

'We could do that for a while,' I said, trying not to sound too femme fatale. In fact, it was hard not to growl. Before I could even gather myself, we'd reversed positions. His eyes were intent on mine. His hands went up to my breasts, caressing and pinching gently, and his mouth followed after his hands.

I was afraid I was losing control of my leg muscles, I was so relaxed. I moved slowly, not very regularly. I felt the tension gradually beginning to build again. I began to focus, to move steadily.

'Slow,' he said, and I reduced the pace. His hands found my hips and began to direct me.

'Oh,' I said, as a sharper pleasure began to seep through me. He'd found my pleasure center with his thumb. I began to speed things up, and if he tried to slow me after that, I ignored it. I rose and fell faster and faster, and then I took his wrist, and I bit with all my strength, sucked on the wound. He yelled, an incoherent sound of release and relief. That was enough to finish me, and I collapsed on top of him. I licked his wrist lazily, though I didn't have the coagulant in my saliva that he possessed.

'Perfect,' he said. 'Perfect.'

I started to tell him he couldn't possibly mean that, as many women as he'd had over the centuries, but I figured, *Why spoil the moment? Let it be.* In a rare moment of wisdom, I listened to my own advice.

'Can I tell you what happened today?' I asked after we'd drowsed for a few minutes.

'Of course, my lover.' His eyes were half open. He was lying on his back beside me, and the room smelled of sex and vampire. 'I'm all ears – for the moment, at least.' He laughed.

This was the real treat, or at least one of the real treats – having someone with whom to share the day's events. Eric was a good listener, at least in his postcoital relaxed state. I told him about Andy and Lattesta's visit, about Diantha's appearance while I was sunbathing.

'I thought I tasted the sun on your skin,' he said, stroking my side. 'Go on.'

So off I babbled like a brook in the spring, telling him about my rendezvous with Claude and Claudine and all they'd told me about Breandan and Dermot.

Eric was more alert when I was talking about the fairies. 'I smelled fairies around the house,' he said. 'But in my overwhelming anger at seeing your tiger-striped suitor, I put the thought aside. Who came here?'

'Well, this bad fairy named Murry, but don't worry, I killed him,' I said. If I'd ever doubted I had Eric's full attention, I didn't doubt it any longer.

'How did you do that, my lover?' he asked very gently.

I explained, and by the time I got to the part where my great-grandfather and Dillon showed up, Eric sat up, the blanket falling away. He was completely serious and alert.

'The body is gone?' he asked for the third time, and I said, 'Yes, Eric, it is.'

'It might be a good idea for you to stay in Shreveport,' Eric said. 'You could even stay in my house.'

That was a first. I'd never been invited to Eric's house before. I had no idea where it was. I was astonished and sort of touched.

'I really appreciate that,' I said, 'but it would be awful hard for me to commute from Shreveport back here to work.'

'You would be much safer if you left your job until this problem with the fairies is resolved.' Eric cocked his head while he looked at me, his face quite expressionless.

'No, thanks,' I said. 'Nice of you to offer. But it would be really inconvenient for you, I bet, and I know it would be for me.'

'Pam is the only other person I've invited to my home.'

I said brightly, 'Only blondes permitted, huh?'

'I honor you with the invitation.' Still not a clue on his face. If I hadn't been so used to reading peoples' minds, maybe I could have interpreted his body language better. I was too accustomed to knowing what people *really* meant, no matter what words they spoke.

'Eric, I'm clueless,' I said. 'Cards on the table, okay? I can tell you're waiting for me to give you a certain reaction, but I have no idea what it is.'

He looked baffled; that's what he looked.

'What are you after?' he asked me, shaking his head. The beautiful golden hair tumbled around his face in tangles. He was a total mess since we'd made love. He looked better than ever. Grossly unfair.

'What am I after?' He lay back down, and I turned on my side to face him. 'I don't think I'm after anything,' I said carefully. 'I was after an orgasm, and I got plenty of those.' I smiled at him, hoping that was the right answer.

'You don't want to quit your job?'

'Why would I quit my job? How would I live?' I asked blankly. Then, finally, I got it. 'Did you think that since we made whoopee and you said I was yours, I'd want to quit work and keep house for you? Eat candy all day, let you eat me all night?'

Yep, that was it. His face confirmed it. I didn't know how to feel. Hurt? Angry? No, I'd had enough of all that today. I couldn't pump another strong emotion to the surface if I had all night. 'Eric, I like to work,' I said mildly. 'I need to get out of the house every day and mingle with people. If I stay away, it's like a deafening clamor when I get back. It's much better for me to deal with people, to stay used to keeping all those voices in the background.' I wasn't explaining very well. 'Plus, I like being at the bar. I like seeing everyone I work with. I guess giving people alcohol isn't exactly noble or a public service; maybe the opposite. But I'm good at what I do, and it suits me. Are you saying . . . What are you saying?'

Eric looked uncertain, an expression that sat oddly on his normally self-assured face. 'This is what other women have wanted from me,' he said. 'I was trying to offer it before you asked for it.'

'I'm not anyone else,' I said. It was hard to shrug in my position on the bed, but I tried.

'You're mine,' he said. Then he noticed my frown and amended his words hastily. 'You're only my lover. Not Quinn's, not Sam's, not Bill's.' There was a long pause. 'Aren't you?' he said.

A relationship discussion initiated by the guy. This was different, if I went by the stories I'd heard from the other barmaids.

'I don't know if the – comfort – I feel with you is the blood exchange or a feeling I would've had naturally,' I said, picking each word carefully. 'I don't think I would have been so ready to have sex with you tonight if we didn't have a blood bond, because today has been one hell of a day. I can't say, 'Oh, Eric, I love you, carry me away,' because I don't know what's real and what's not. Until I'm sure, I have no intention of changing my life drastically.'

Eric's brows began to draw together, a sure sign of displeasure.

'Am I happy when I'm with you?' I put my hand against his cheek. 'Yes, I am. Do I think making love with you is the greatest thing ever? Yes, I do. Do I want to do it again? You bet, though not right now since I'm sleepy. But soon. And often. Am I having sex with anyone else? No. And I won't, unless I decide the bond is all we have.'

He looked as if he were thinking of several different responses. Finally he said, 'Do you regret Quinn?'

'Yes,' I said, because I had to be honest. 'Because we had the beginning of something good going, and I may have made a huge mistake sending him away. But I've never been seriously involved with two men at the same time, and I'm not starting now. Right now, that man is you.'

'You love me,' he said, and he nodded.

'I appreciate you,' I said cautiously. 'I have big lust for you. I enjoy your company.'

'There's a difference,' Eric said.

'Yes, there is. But you don't see me bugging you to spell out how you feel about me, right? Because I'm pretty damn sure I wouldn't like the answer. So maybe you better rein it in a little yourself.'

'You don't want to know how I feel about you?' Eric looked incredulous. 'I can't believe you're a human woman. Women *always* want to know how you feel about them.'

'And I'll bet they're sorry when you tell them, huh?'

He lifted one eyebrow. 'If I tell them the truth.'

'That's supposed to put me in a confiding mood?'

'I always tell you the truth,' he said. And there wasn't a trace of that smile left on his face. 'I may not tell you everything I know, but what I tell you . . . it's true.'

'Why?'

'The blood exchange has worked both ways,' he said. 'I've had the blood of many women. I've had almost utter control over them. But they never drank mine. It's been decades, maybe centuries since I gave any woman my blood. Maybe not since I turned Pam.'

'Is this the general policy among vampires you know?' I wasn't quite sure how to ask what I wanted to know.

He hesitated, nodded. 'For the most part. There are some vampires who like to take total control over a human . . . make that human their Renfield.' He used the term with distaste.

'That's from *Dracula*, right?'

'Yes, Dracula's human servant. A degraded creature . . . Why someone of Dracula's eminence would want so debased a man as that . . .' Eric shook his head disgustedly. 'But it does happen. The best of us look askance at a vampire who makes servant after servant. The human is lost when the vampire assumes too much control. When the human goes completely under, he isn't worth turning. He isn't worth anything at all. Sooner or later, he has to be killed.'

'Killed! Why?'

'If the vampire who's assumed so much control abandons the Renfield, or if the vampire himself is killed . . . the Renfield's life is not worth living after that.'

'They have to be put down,' I said. Like a dog with rabies.

'Yes.' Eric looked away.

'But that's not going to happen to me. And you won't ever turn me.' I was absolutely serious.

'No. I won't ever force you into subservience. And I will never turn you, since you don't want it.'

'Even if I'm going to die, don't turn me. I would hate that more than anything.'

'I agree to that. No matter how much I may want to keep you.'

Right after we'd met, Bill had not changed me when I had been close to death. I'd never realized he might have been tempted to do so. He'd saved my human life instead. I put that away to consider later. Tacky to think about one man when you're in bed with another.

'You saved me from being bonded to Andre,' I said. 'But it cost me.'

'If he'd lived, it would have cost me, too. No matter how mild his reaction, Andre would have paid me back for my intervention.'

'He seemed so calm about it that night,' I said. Eric had persuaded Andre to let him be his proxy. I'd been very grateful at the time, since Andre gave me the creeps and he didn't give a damn about me, either. I remembered my talk with Tara. *If I'd let Andre share blood that night,*

I'd be free now, since he's dead. I still couldn't decide how I felt about that – probably three different ways.

Tonight was turning out to be a huge one for realizations. They could just stop coming any old time now.

'Andre never forgot a challenge to his will,' Eric said. 'Do you know how he died, Sookie?'

Ah-oh.

'He got stuck in the chest with a big splinter of wood,' I said, swallowing a little. Like Eric, I didn't always tell the whole truth. The splinter hadn't gotten in Andre's chest by accident. Quinn had done that.

Eric looked at me for what seemed like a very long time. He could feel my anxiety, of course. I waited to see if he'd push the issue. 'I don't miss Andre,' he said finally. 'I regret Sophie-Anne, though. She was brave.'

'I agree,' I said, relieved. 'By the way, how are you getting along with your new bosses?'

'So far, so good. They're very forward-thinking. I like that.'

Since the end of October, Eric had had to learn the structure of a new and larger organization, the characters of the vampires who made it work, and how to liaise with the new sheriffs. Even for him, that was a big bite to chew.

'I bet the vamps you had with you before that night are extra glad they pledged loyalty to you, since they survived when so many of the other vamps in Louisiana died that night.'

Eric smiled broadly. It would have been really scary if I hadn't seen the fang display before. 'Yes,' he said with a whole bunch of satisfaction. 'They owe me their lives, and they know it.'

He slid his arms around me and held me against his cool body. I was content and sated, and my fingers trailed through the happy trail of golden hair that led downward. I thought of the provocative picture of Eric as Mr January in the 'Vampires of Louisiana' calendar. I liked the one he'd given me even more. I wondered if I could get a poster-sized blowup.

He laughed when I asked him. 'We should think of producing another calendar,' he said. 'It was a real earner for us. If I can have a picture of you in the same pose, I'll give you a poster of me.'

I thought about it for twenty seconds. 'I don't think I could do a nude picture,' I said with some regret. 'They always seem to show up to bite you in the ass.'

Eric laughed again, low and husky. 'You talk a lot about that,' he said. 'Shall I bite you in the ass?' This led to a lot of other things, wonderful and playful things. After those things had come to a happy completion, Eric glanced at the clock beside my bed.

'I have to go,' he whispered.

'I know,' I said. My eyes were heavy with sleep.

He began to dress for his return to Shreveport, and I pulled down the covers and snuggled into the bed properly. It was hard to keep my eyes open, though watching him move around my bedroom was a sweet sight.

He bent to kiss me, and I put my arms around his neck. For a second, I knew he was thinking of crawling back in the bed with me; I hoped it was his body language and his murmur of pleasure that cued me to his thoughts. Every now and then, I got a flash from a vampire mind, and it scared me to death. I didn't think I'd last long if vampires realized I could read their minds, no matter how seldom that occurred.

'I want you again,' he said, sounding a little surprised. 'But I have to go.'

'I'll see you soon, I guess?' I was awake enough to feel uncertain.

'Yes,' he said. His eyes were bright and his skin glowed. The mark on his wrist was gone. I touched where it had been. He leaned over to kiss the place on my neck where he'd bitten me, and I shivered all over. 'Soon.'

Then he was gone, and I heard the back door close quietly behind him. With the last bit of energy in my muscles, I rose and passed through the kitchen in the dark to shoot the dead bolt. I saw Amelia's car parked by mine; at some point, she'd returned home.

I went to the sink to get a drink of water. I knew the dark kitchen like the back of my hand, so I didn't need a light. I drank and realized how thirsty I was. As I turned to go back to bed, I saw something move at the edge of the woods. I froze, my heart pounding in a very unpleasant way.

Bill stepped out of the trees. I knew it was him, though I couldn't see his face clearly. He stood looking up, and I knew he must have watched Eric take flight. Bill had recovered from the fight with Quinn, then.

I expected to be angry that Bill was watching me, but the anger never rose. No matter what had happened between us, I could not rid myself of the feeling that Bill had not simply been spying on me – he had been watching over me.

Also – more practically – there was nothing to be done about it. I could hardly throw open the door and apologize for having male company. At this moment, I wasn't the least bit sorry I'd gone to bed with Eric. In fact, I felt as sated as if I'd had the Thanksgiving feast of sex. Eric didn't look anything like a turkey – but after I had a happy mental image of him lying on my kitchen table with some sweet potatoes and marshmallows, I was able to think only of my bed. I slid under the covers with a smile on my face, and almost as soon as my head hit the pillow, I was asleep.

Chapter 11

I should have known my brother would come to see me. I should only have felt surprised that he hadn't appeared earlier. When I got up the next day at noon, feeling as relaxed as a cat in a pool of sunshine, Jason was in the backyard on the chaise I'd used the day before. I thought it was smart of him not to come inside, considering we were at odds with each other.

Today wasn't going to be nearly as warm as the day before. It was cold and raw. Jason was bundled in a heavy camo jacket and a knit cap. He was staring up into the cloudless sky.

I remembered the twins' warning, and I looked at him carefully; but no, it was Jason. The feel of his mind was familiar, but maybe a fairy could impersonate even that. I listened in for a second. No, this was definitely my brother.

It was strange to see him sitting idle and even stranger to see him alone. Jason was always talking, drinking, flirting with women, working at his job, or working on his house; and if he wasn't with a woman, he nearly always had a male shadow – Hoyt (until he'd been preempted by Holly) or Mel. Contemplation and solitude were not states I associated with my brother. Watching him stare at the sky as I sipped my mug of coffee, I thought, *Jason's a widower now.*

That was a strange new identity for Jason, a heavy one he might not be able to manage. He'd cared for Crystal more than she'd cared for him. That had been a new experience for Jason, too. Crystal – pretty, stupid, and faithless – had been his female counterpart. Maybe her infidelity had been an attempt to reassert her independence, to struggle against the pregnancy that had tied her more securely to Jason. Maybe she'd just been a bad woman. I'd never understood her, and now I never would.

I knew I'd have to go talk to my brother. Though I'd told Jason to stay away from me, he wasn't listening. When had he ever? Maybe he'd taken the temporary truce caused by Crystal's death as a sign of a new state of things.

I sighed and went out the back door. Since I'd slept so late, I'd showered before I'd even made my coffee. I grabbed my old quilted pink jacket off the rack by the back door and pulled it over my jeans and sweater.

I put a mug of coffee on the ground by Jason, and I sat on the upright folding chair close to him. He didn't turn his head, though he knew I was there. His eyes were hidden behind dark glasses.

'You forgiven me?' he asked after he'd taken a gulp of coffee. His voice sounded hoarse and thick. I thought he'd been crying.

'I expect that sooner or later I might,' I said. 'But I'll never feel the same about you again.'

'God, you've gotten hard. You're all the family I've got left.' The dark glasses turned to face me. *You have to forgive me, because you're all I have who can forgive.*

I looked at him, feeling a little exasperated, a little sad. If I was getting harder, it was in response to the world around me. 'If you need me so much, I guess you should have thought twice before you set me up like that.' I rubbed my face with my free hand. He had some family he didn't know about, and I wasn't going to tell him. He would only try to use Niall, too.

'When will they release Crystal's body?' I asked.

'Maybe in a week,' he said. 'Then we can have the funeral. Will you come?'

'Yes. Where will it be?'

'There's a chapel out close to Hotshot,' he said. 'It doesn't look like much.'

'The Tabernacle Holiness Church?' It was a peeling, white ramshackle building way out in the country.

He nodded. 'Calvin said they do the burials for Hotshot from there. One of the guys in Hotshot is the pastor for it.'

'Which one?'

'Marvin Norris.'

Marvin was Calvin's uncle, though he was four years younger.

'I think I remember seeing a cemetery out back of the church.'

'Yeah. The community digs the hole, one of them puts together the coffin, and one of them does the service. It's real homey and personal.'

'You've been to a funeral there before?'

'Yeah, in October. One of the babies died.'

There hadn't been an infant death listed in the Bon Temps paper in months. I had to wonder if the baby had been born in a hospital or in one of the houses in Hotshot; if any trace of its existence had ever been recorded.

'Jason, have the police been by any more?'

'Over and over. But I didn't do it, and nothing they say or ask can make that change. Plus, the alibi.'

I couldn't argue that.

'How are you fixed as far as work goes?' I wondered if they would fire Jason. It wasn't the first time he'd been in trouble. And though Jason was never guilty of the worst crimes attributed to him, sooner or later his reputation as being a generally okay guy would simply crumple for good.

'Catfish said to take time off until the funeral. They're going to send a wreath to the funeral home when we get her body back.'

'What about Hoyt?'

'He hasn't been around,' Jason said, sounding puzzled and hurt.

Holly, his fiancée, wouldn't want him hanging around with Jason. I could understand that.

'Mel?' I asked.

'Yeah,' Jason said, brightening. 'Mel comes by. We worked on his truck yesterday, and this weekend we're going to paint my kitchen.' Jason smiled at me, but it faded fast. 'I like Mel,' he said, 'but I miss Hoyt.'

That was one of the most honest things I'd ever heard Jason say.

'Haven't you heard anything about this, Sookie?' Jason asked me. 'You know – the way you *hear* things? If you could steer the police in the right direction, they could find out who killed my wife and my baby, and I could get my life back.'

I didn't think Jason was ever going to get his old life back. I was sure he wouldn't understand, even if I spelled it out. But then I saw what was in his head in a moment of true clarity. Though Jason couldn't verbalize these ideas, he *did* understand, and he was pretending, pretending hard, that everything would be the same ... if only he could get out from under the weight of Crystal's death.

'Or if you tell us,' he said, 'we'll take care of it, Calvin and me.'

'I'll do my best,' I said. What else could I say? I climbed out of Jason's head and swore to myself I wouldn't get inside again.

After a long silence, he got up. Maybe he'd been waiting to see if I'd offer to make lunch for him. 'I guess I'll go back home, then,' he said.

'Good-bye.'

I heard his truck start up a moment later. I went back in, hanging the jacket back where I'd gotten it.

Amelia had left me a note stuck to the milk carton in the refrigerator. 'Hey, roomie!' it said by way of opening. 'Sounded like you had company last night. Did I smell a vampire? Heard someone shut the back door about three thirty. Listen, be sure and check the answering machine. You got messages.'

Which Amelia had already listened to, because the light wasn't blinking anymore. I pressed the Play button.

'Sookie, this is Arlene. I'm sorry about everything. I wish you'd come by to talk. Give me a call.'

I stared at the machine, not sure how I felt about this message. It had been a few days, and Arlene had had time to reconsider stomping out of the bar. Could she possibly mean she wanted to recant her Fellowship beliefs?

There was another message, this one from Sam. 'Sookie, can you come in to work a little early today or give me a call? I need to talk to you.'

I glanced at the clock. It was just one p.m., and I wasn't due at work until five. I called the bar. Sam picked up.

'Hey, it's Sookie,' I said. 'What's up? I just got your message.'

'Arlene wants to come back to work,' he said. 'I don't know what to tell her. You got an opinion?'

'She left a message on my answering machine. She wants to talk to me,' I said. 'I don't know what to think. She's always on some new thing, isn't she? Do you think she could have dropped the Fellowship?'

'If Whit dropped her,' he said, and I laughed.

I wasn't so sure I wanted to rebuild our friendship, and the longer I thought about it, the more doubtful I became. Arlene had said some hurtful and awful things to me. If she'd meant them, why would she want to mend fences with a terrible person like me? And if she hadn't meant them, why on earth had they passed her lips? But I felt a twinge when I thought of her children, Coby and Lisa. I'd kept them so many evenings, and I'd been so fond of them. I hadn't seen them in weeks. I found I wasn't too upset about the passing of my relationship with their mother – Arlene had been killing that friendship for some time now. But the kids, I did miss them. I said as much to Sam.

'You're too good, *cher*,' he said. 'I don't think I want her back here.' He'd made up his mind. 'I hope she can find another job, and I'll give her a reference for the sake of those kids. But she was causing trouble before this last blowup, and there's no point putting all of us through the wringer.'

After I'd hung up, I realized that Sam's decision had influenced me in favor of seeing my ex-friend. Since Arlene and I weren't going to get the opportunity to gradually make peace at the bar, I'd try to at least fix things so we could nod at each other if we passed in Wal-Mart.

She picked up on the first ring. 'Arlene, it's Sookie,' I said.

'Hey, hon, I'm glad you called back,' she said. There was a moment of silence.

'I thought I'd come over to see you, just for a minute,' I said awkwardly. 'I'd like to see the kids and talk to you. If that's okay.'

'Sure, come over. Give me a few minutes, so I can pick up the mess.'

'You don't need to do that for me.' I'd cleaned Arlene's trailer many a time in return for some favor she'd done me or because I didn't have anything else to do while she was out and I was there to babysit.

'I don't want to slide back into my old ways,' she said cheerfully, sounding so affectionate that my heart lifted . . . for just a second.

But I didn't wait a few minutes.

I left immediately.

I couldn't explain to myself why I wasn't doing what she'd asked me to do. Maybe I'd caught something in Arlene's voice, even over the phone. Maybe I was recalling all the times Arlene had let me down, all the occasions she'd made me feel bad.

I don't think I'd let myself dwell on these incidents before, because they revealed such a colossal pitifulness on my part. I'd needed a friend so badly I'd clung to the meager scraps from Arlene's table, though she'd taken advantage of me time after time. When her dating wind had blown the other way, she hadn't thought twice about discarding me to win favor with her current flame.

In fact, the more I thought, the more I was inclined to turn around and head back to my house. But didn't I owe Coby and Lisa one more try to mend my relationship with their mom? I remembered all the board games we'd played, all the times I'd put them to bed and spent the night in the trailer because Arlene had called to ask if she could spend the night away.

What the hell was I doing? Why was I trusting Arlene *now*?

I wasn't, not completely. That's why I was going to scope out the situation.

Arlene didn't live in a trailer park but on an acre of land a little west of town that her dad had given her before he passed away. Only a quarter acre had been cleared, just enough for the trailer and a small yard. There was an old swing set in the back that one of Arlene's former admirers had assembled for the kids, and there were two bikes pushed up against the back of the trailer.

I was looking at the trailer from the rear because I'd pulled off the road into the overgrown yard of a little house that had stood next door until its bad wiring had caused a fire a couple of months before. Since then, the frame house had stood half-charred and forlorn, and the former renters had found somewhere else to live. I was able to pull behind the house, because the cold weather had kept the weeds from taking over.

I picked a path through the fringe of high weeds and trees that separated this house from Arlene's. Working through the thickest growth, I made my way to a vantage point where I could see part of the parking area in front of the trailer and all of the backyard. Only Arlene's car was visible from the road, since it had been left in the front yard.

From my vantage point, I could see that behind the trailer was parked a black Ford Ranger pickup, maybe ten years old, and a red Buick Skylark of approximately the same vintage. The pickup was loaded down with pieces of wood, one long enough to protrude beyond the truck bed. They measured about four by four, I estimated.

As I watched, a woman I vaguely recognized came out of the back of the trailer onto the little deck. Her name was Helen Ellis, and she'd worked at Merlotte's about four years before. Though Helen was competent and so pretty she'd drawn the men in like flies, Sam had had to fire her for repeated lateness. Helen had been volcanically upset. Lisa and Coby followed Helen onto the deck. Arlene was framed in the doorway. She was wearing a leopard print top over brown stretch pants.

The kids looked so much older than the last time I'd seen them! They looked reluctant and a little unhappy, especially Coby. Helen smiled at them encouragingly and turned back to Arlene to say, 'Just let me know when it's over!' There was a pause while Helen seemed to struggle with how to phrase something she didn't want the kids to understand. 'She's only getting what she deserves.' I could see Helen only in profile, but her cheerful smile made my stomach heave. I swallowed hard.

'Okay, Helen. I'll call you when you can bring 'em back,' Arlene said. There was a man standing behind her. He was too far back in the interior for me to identify with certainty, but I thought he was the man I'd hit on the head with a tray a couple of months back, the man who'd been so ugly to Pam and Amelia. He was one of Arlene's new buddies.

Helen and the kids drove off in the Skylark.

Arlene had closed the back door against the chill of the day. I shut my eyes and located her inside the trailer. I found there were two men in there with her. What were they thinking about? I was a little far, but I stretched out with my extra sense.

They were thinking about doing awful things to me.

I crouched under a bare mimosa, feeling as bleak and miserable as I've ever felt. Granted, I'd known for some time that Arlene wasn't truly a good person or even a faithful person. Granted, I'd heard her rant and rave about the eradication of the supernaturals of the world. Granted, I'd come to realize that she'd slipped into regarding me as one of them. But I'd never let myself believe that whatever affection she'd ever felt for me had slipped away entirely, transmuted by the Fellowship's policy of hate.

I pulled my cell phone out of my pocket. I called Andy Bellefleur.

'Bellefleur,' he said briskly.

We were hardly buddies, but I sure was glad to hear his voice.

'Andy, it's Sookie,' I said, taking care to keep my voice quiet. 'Listen, there are two guys in Arlene's trailer with her, and there're some long pieces of wood in the back of their pickup. They don't realize I know they're in the trailer with Arlene. They're planning on doing the same thing to me that was done to Crystal.'

'You got anything I could take to court?' he asked cautiously. Andy had always been a closet believer in my telepathy, though that didn't mean he was necessarily a fan of mine.

'No,' I said, 'they're waiting for me to show up.' I crept closer, hoping like hell they weren't looking out the back windows. There was a box of extra-long nails in the pickup bed, too. I had to close my eyes for second as the horror crawled all over me.

'I've got Weiss and Lattesta with me,' Andy said. 'Would you be willing to go in if we were there to back you up?'

'Sure,' I said, feeling anything but. I simply knew I was going to have to do this. It could be the end of any lingering suspicion of Jason. It could mean recompense or at least retribution for the death of Crystal and the baby. It could put at least a few of the Fellowship fanatics behind bars and maybe serve as a good lesson to the rest. 'Where are you?' I asked, shaking with fear.

'We were already in the car to go to the motel. We can be there in seven minutes,' Andy said.

'I parked behind the Freer house,' I said. 'I gotta go. Someone's coming out the back of the trailer.'

Whit Spradlin and his buddy, whose name I couldn't recall, came down the steps and unloaded the wood beams from the pickup. The pieces were already formed into the correct lengths. Whit turned to the trailer and called something, and Arlene opened the door and came down the back steps, her purse over one shoulder. She walked toward the cab of the pickup.

Dammit, she was going to get in and drive away, leaving her car parked in front as though she were there! Any lingering tenderness I'd harbored in my heart burned away at that moment. I looked at my watch. Maybe three more minutes until Andy arrived.

She kissed Whit and waved at the other man, and they went into the trailer to hide so I wouldn't see them. According to their plan, I'd come to the front, knock on the door, and one of them would fling it open and drag me in.

Game over.

Arlene opened the truck door, the keys in her hand.

She had to stay. She was the weak link. I knew this in every way I could know it – intellectually, emotionally, and with my other sense.

This was going to be awful. I braced myself.

'Hi, Arlene,' I said, stepping out of my cover.

She shrieked and jumped. 'Jesus Christ, Sookie, what are you doing in my backyard?' She made an elaborate fuss of collecting herself. Her head was a snarled tangle of anger and fear and guilt. And regret. There was some, I swear.

'I've been waiting to see you,' I said. I had no idea what to do now, but I'd slowed her down a little. I might have to physically tackle her. The men inside hadn't noticed my abrupt appearance, but that wouldn't last long unless I got extremely lucky. And I hadn't had a run of luck, much less extreme luck, lately.

Arlene was standing still, keys in hand. It was easy to get inside her head and rummage around, reading the awful story in there.

'What you doing, getting ready to go, Arlene?' I asked, keeping my voice very quiet. 'You're supposed to be inside, waiting for me to get here.'

She saw everything, and her eyes closed. Guilty, guilty, guilty. She had tried to construct a bubble to keep the men's intent hidden from herself, to keep it from touching her heart. That hadn't worked – but it hadn't stopped her treachery today, either. Arlene stood exposed to herself.

I said, 'You got in too deep.' My own voice sounded detached and level. 'No one will understand that or forgive it.' Her eyes went wide with the knowledge that what I was saying was true.

But I was in for my own kind of shock. I knew, suddenly and surely, that she had not killed Crystal and neither had these men; they'd planned to crucify me in emulation of Crystal's death because it seemed like such a great idea, such an open statement of their opinion of the shapeshifters' announcement. I'd been selected as the sacrificial lamb, despite the fact that they knew for sure I wasn't a shapeshifter; in fact, they thought I wouldn't put up as much of a fight since I was only a shapeshifter sympathizer, not one of the two-natured. I wouldn't be as strong, in their opinion. I found this incredible.

'You're a poor excuse for a woman,' I said to Arlene. I couldn't seem to stop, and I couldn't seem to sound anything but matter-of-fact. 'You've never told the truth to yourself in your whole life, have you? You still see yourself as a pretty, young thing of twenty-five, and you still think some man will come along and recognize that in you. Someone will take care of you, let you quit working, send your kids to private schools where they'll never have to talk to anyone different from them. That's not gonna happen, Arlene. This is your life.' And I swept an open hand at the trailer in its weedy yard, the old truck. It was the meanest thing I'd ever said, and every word of it was true.

And she screamed. She couldn't seem to stop screaming. I looked into her eyes. She kept trying to look away, but she couldn't seem to do that. 'You witch!' she sobbed. 'You're a witch. There are such things, and you're one of 'em!'

If she'd been right, I could have prevented what happened next.

At that moment, Andy pulled into the Freer yard, just as I had. For all he knew, there was still time to creep up on the trailer. I heard his car more or less at my back. My whole attention was concentrated on Arlene and the rear door of the trailer. Weiss, Lattesta, and Andy came up behind me just as Whit and his friend burst from the back door of the trailer, rifles in hands.

Arlene and I were standing between two armed camps. I felt the sun on my arms. I felt a cold breeze pick up my hair and toss a lock playfully across my face. Over Arlene's shoulder, I saw the face of Whit's friend, and I finally remembered his name was Donny Boling. He'd had a recent haircut. I could tell from the white half inch at the base of his neck. He was wearing an Orville's Stump Grinding T-shirt. His eyes were a muddy brown. He was aiming at Agent Weiss.

'She has children,' I called. 'Don't do it!'

His eyes widened with fright.

Donny swung the rifle toward me. He thought, *Shoot HER.*

I flung myself to the ground as the rifle went off.

'Lay down your arms!' Lattesta screamed. 'FBI!'

But they didn't. I don't think his words even registered.

So Lattesta fired. But you couldn't say he hadn't warned them.

Chapter 12

In the moments following Special Agent Lattesta's demand that the two men lay down their arms, bullets flew through the air like pine pollen in the spring.

Though I was in an exposed position, none of them hit me, which I found absolutely amazing.

Arlene, who didn't dive as fast as I did, got a crease across her shoulder. Agent Weiss took the bullet – the same one that creased Arlene – in the upper right side of her chest. Andy shot Whit Spradlin. Special Agent Lattesta missed Donny Boling with his first shot, got him with his second. It took weeks to establish the sequence, but that's what happened.

And then the firing was over. Lattesta was calling 911 while I was still prone on the ground, counting my fingers and toes to make sure I was intact. Andy was equally quick calling the sheriff's department to report that shots had been fired and an officer and civilians were down.

Arlene was screaming over her little wound like she'd been gut shot.

Agent Weiss was lying in the weeds bleeding, her eyes wide with fear, her mouth clamped shut. The bullet had gone in under her raised arm. She was thinking of her children and her husband and of dying out here in the sticks, leaving them behind. Lattesta pulled off her vest and put pressure on her wound, and Andy ran over to secure the two shooters.

I slowly pushed up to a sitting position. There was no way I could stand. I sat there in the pine needles and dirt and looked at Donny Boling, who was dead. There was not the faintest trace of activity in his brain. Whit was still alive though not in good shape. After Andy gave Arlene a cursory examination and told her to shut up, she quit shrieking and settled down to cry.

I have had lots of things to blame myself about in the course of my life. I added this whole incident to the list as I watched the blood seeping into the dirt around Donny's left side. No one would have gotten shot if I'd just climbed back in my car and driven away. But no, I had to try to catch Crystal's killers. And I knew now – too late – that these idiots weren't even the culprits. I told myself that Andy had asked me to help, that Jason needed me to help . . . but right now, I couldn't foresee feeling okay about this for a long time.

For a brief moment I considered lying back down and wishing myself dead.

'Are you okay?' Andy called after he'd cuffed Whit and checked on Donny.

'Yeah,' I said. 'Andy, I'm sorry.' But he'd run into the front yard to wave down the ambulance. Suddenly there were a lot more people around.

'Are you all right?' asked a woman wearing an EMT uniform. Her sleeves were folded up neatly to show muscles I didn't know women could develop. You could see each one rippling under her mocha skin. 'You look kind of out of it.'

'I'm not used to seeing people get shot,' I said. Which was mostly true.

'I think you better come sit on this chair over here,' she said, and pointed to a folding yard chair that had seen better days. 'After I tend to the ones that are bleeding, I'll check you out.'

'Audrey!' called her partner, a man with a belly like a bay window. 'I need another pair of hands here.' Audrey hustled over to help, and another team of EMTs came running around the trailer. I had nearly the same dialogue with them.

Agent Weiss left for the hospital first, and I gathered that the plan was to stabilize her at the hospital in Clarice and then airlift her to

Shreveport. Whit was loaded into the second ambulance. A third arrived for Arlene. The dead guy waited for the coroner to appear.

I waited for whatever would happen next.

Lattesta stood staring blankly into the pines. His hands were blood-stained from pressing on Weiss's wound. As I watched, he shook himself. The purpose flooded back into his face, and his thoughts began flowing once again. He and Andy began to consult.

By now the yard was teeming with law enforcement people, all of whom seemed to be very pumped. Officer-involved shootings are not that ordinary in Bon Temps or in Renard Parish. When the FBI is represented at the scene, the excitement and tension were practically quadrupled.

Several more people asked me if I was all right, but no one seemed to be anxious to tell me what to do or to suggest I remove myself, so I sat in the rickety chair with my hands in my lap. I watched all the activity, and I tried to keep my mind blank. That wasn't possible.

I was worried about Agent Weiss, and I was still feeling the ebbing power of the huge wave of guilt that had washed over me. I should have been upset that the Fellowship guy was dead, I suppose. But I wasn't.

After a while, it occurred to me that I was also going to be late for work if this elaborate process didn't get a move on. I knew that was a trivial consideration, when I was staring at the blood that had soaked into the ground, but I also knew it wouldn't be trivial to my boss.

I called Sam. I don't remember what I said, but I remember I had to talk him out of coming to get me. I told Sam there were plenty of people on-site and most of them were armed. After that, I had nothing to do but stare off into the woods. They were a tangle of fallen branches, leaves, and various shades of brown, broken up by little pines of various heights that had volunteered. The bright day made the patterns of shadow and shade fascinating.

As I looked into the depths of the woods, I became aware that something was looking back. Yards back within the tree line, a man was standing; no, not a man – a fairy. I can't read fairies at all clearly; they're not as blank as vampires, but they're the closest I've found.

It was easy to read the hostility in his stance, though. This fairy was not on my great-grandfather's side. This fairy would have been glad to see me lying on the ground bleeding. I sat up straighter, abruptly aware I had no idea whether all the police officers in the world could keep me safe from a fairy. My heart thudded once again with alarm, responding to the adrenaline in a sort of tired way. I wanted to tell someone that I was in danger, but I knew that if I pointed the fairy out to any one of the people present, not only would he fade back into the woods, but I might be endangering the human. I'd done enough of that this day.

As I half rose from the lawn chair with no very good plan in mind, the fairy turned his back on me and vanished.

Can't I have a moment's peace? At this thought, I had to bend over and cover my face with my hands because I was laughing, and it wasn't good laughter. Andy came over and squatted in front of me, tried to look into my face. 'Sookie,' he said, and for once his voice was gentle. 'Hey, girl, get it together. You got to come talk to Sheriff Dearborn.'

Not only did I talk to Bud Dearborn, I also had to talk to lots of other people. Later, I couldn't remember any of the conversations I had. I told the truth to whoever asked me questions.

I didn't mention seeing the fairy in the woods simply because no one asked me, 'Did you see anyone else here this afternoon?' When I had a second of not feeling stunned and miserable, I wondered why he'd shown himself, why he'd come. Was he tracking me somehow? Was there some kind of supernatural bug planted on me?

'Sookie,' Bud Dearborn said. I blinked.

'Yessir?' I stood up, and my muscles were trembling.

'You can go now, and we'll talk to you again later,' he said.

'Thanks,' I told him, hardly aware of what I was saying. I climbed into my car, feeling absolutely numb. I told myself to drive home and put on my waitress outfit and get to work. Hustling drinks would be better than sitting at home recycling the events of the day, if I could manage to stand up that long.

Amelia was at work, so I had the house to myself as I pulled on my working pants and my long-sleeved Merlotte's T-shirt. I felt cold to the bone and wished for the first time that Sam had thought about stocking a Merlotte's sweatshirt. My reflection in the bathroom mirror was awful: I was white as a vampire, I had big circles under my eyes, and I guessed I looked exactly like someone who'd seen a lot of people bleeding that day.

The evening felt cold and still as I walked out to my car. Night would fall soon. Since Eric and I had bonded, I'd found myself thinking of him every day as the sky grew dark. Now that we'd slept together, my thoughts had turned into cravings. I tried to stuff him in the back of my mind on the drive to the bar, but he persisted in popping to the fore.

Maybe because the day had been such a nightmare, I discovered I would give my entire savings account to see Eric *right now*. I trudged toward the employee door, gripping the trowel stuffed in my shoulder bag. I thought I was ready for an attack, but I was so preoccupied I didn't send out my extra sense to detect another presence, and I didn't see Antoine in the shadow of the Dumpster until he stepped out to greet me. He was smoking a cigarette.

'Geez Louise, Antoine, you scared me to death.'

'Sorry, Sookie. You planning on doing some planting?' He eyed the trowel I'd whipped out of my bag. 'We ain't too busy this evening. I took me a minute to have a smoke.'

'Everybody calm tonight?' I stuffed the trowel down into my purse without trying to explain. Maybe he would chalk it up to my general strangeness.

'Yeah, no one preaching to us; no one getting killed.' He smiled. 'D'Eriq's full of talk about some guy showing up earlier that D'Eriq thought was a fairy. D'Eriq's on the simple side, but he can see stuff no one else can. But – fairies?'

'Not fairy like gay, but fairy like Tinker Bell?' I'd thought I didn't have enough remaining energy to be alarmed. I'd thought wrong. I glanced around the parking lot with considerable alarm.

'Sookie? It's true?' Antoine was staring at me.

I shrugged weakly. Busted.

'Shit,' Antoine said. 'Well, shit. This ain't the same world I was born into, is it?'

'No, Antoine. It isn't. If D'Eriq says anything else, please tell me. It's important.' Could have been my great-grandfather watching over me, or his son Dillon. Or it could have been Mr Hostile who'd been lurking in the woods. What had set the fae world off? For years, I'd never seen one. Now you couldn't throw a trowel without hitting a fairy.

Antoine eyed me doubtfully. 'Sure, Sookie. You in any trouble I should know about?'

Hip-deep in alligators. 'No, no. I'm just trying to avoid a problem,' I said, because I didn't want Antoine to worry and I especially didn't want him to share that worry with Sam. Sam was sure to be worried enough.

Of course, Sam had heard several versions of the events at Arlene's trailer, and I had to give him a quick summary as I got ready to work. He was deeply upset about the intentions of Donny and Whit, and when I told him Donny was dead, he said, 'Whit should have got killed, too.'

I wasn't sure I was hearing him right. But when I looked into Sam's face, I could see he was really angry, really vengeful. 'Sam, I think enough people have died,' I said. 'I haven't exactly forgiven them, and maybe that's not even something I can do, but I don't think they were the ones who killed Crystal.'

Sam turned away with a snort and put a bottle of rum away with such force that I thought it might shatter.

Despite a measure of alarm, as it turned out I treasured that evening . . . because nothing happened.

No one suddenly announced that he was a gargoyle and wanted a place at the American table.

No one stomped out in a hissy. No one tried to kill me or warn me or lie to me; no one paid me any special attention at all. I was back to being part of the ambience at Merlotte's, a situation that used to make me bored. I remembered the evenings before I'd met Bill Compton, when I'd known there were vampires but hadn't actually met one or seen one in the flesh. I remembered how I'd longed to meet an actual vampire. I'd believed their press, which alleged that they were victims of a virus that left them allergic to various things (sunlight, garlic, food) and only able to survive by ingesting blood.

That part, at least, had been quite true.

As I worked, I thought about the fairies. They were different from the vampires and the Weres. Fairies could escape and go to their very own world, however that happened. It was a world I had no desire to visit or see. Fairies had never been human. At least vampires might remember what being human was like, and Weres were human most of the time, even if they had a different culture; being a Were was like having dual citizenship, I figured. This was an important difference between the fairies and other supernaturals, and it made the fairies more frightening. As the evening wore on and I plodded from table to table, making an effort to get the orders right and to serve with a smile, I had times of wondering whether it would have been better if I'd never met my great-grandfather at all. There was a lot of attraction in that idea.

I served Jane Bodehouse her fourth drink and signaled to Sam that we needed to cut her off. Jane would drink whether we served her or not. Her decision to quit drinking hadn't lasted a week, but I'd never imagined it would. She'd made such resolutions before, with the same result.

At least if Jane drank here, we would make sure she got home okay. *I killed a man yesterday.* Maybe her son would come get her; he was a nice guy who never took a sip with alcohol in it. *I saw a man get shot dead today.* I had to stand still for a minute because the room seemed to be a little lopsided.

After a second or two, I felt steadier. I wondered if I could make it through the evening. By dint of putting one foot in front of the other and blocking out the bad stuff (from past experience I was an expert at that), I made it through. I even remembered to ask Sam how his mother was doing.

'She's getting better,' he said, closing out the cash register. 'My stepdad's filed for divorce, too. He says she doesn't deserve any alimony because she didn't disclose her true nature when they got married.'

Though I'd always be on Sam's side, whatever it was, I had to admit (strictly to myself) that I could see his stepdad's point.

'I'm sorry,' I said inadequately. 'I know this is a tough time for your mom, for your whole family.'

'My brother's fiancée isn't too happy about it, either,' Sam said.

'Oh, no, Sam. She's freaked out by the fact that your mom—?'

'Yeah, and of course she knows about me now, too. My brother and sister are getting used to it. So they're okay – but Deidra doesn't feel that way. And I don't think her parents do, either.'

I patted Sam's shoulder because I didn't know what to say. He gave me a little smile and then a hug. He said, 'You've been a rock, Sookie,' and then he stiffened. Sam's nostrils flared. 'You smell like – there's a trace of vampire,' he said, and all the warmth had gone out of his voice. He released me and looked at me hard.

I'd really scrubbed myself and I'd used all my usual skin products afterward, but Sam's fine nose had picked up that trace of scent Eric had left behind.

'Well,' I said, and then stopped dead. I tried to organize what I wanted to say, but the past forty hours had been so tiring. 'Yes,' I said, 'Eric was over last night.' I left it at that. My heart sank. I'd thought of trying to explain to Sam about my great-grandfather and the trouble we were in, but Sam had enough troubles of his own. Plus, the whole staff was feeling pretty miserable about Arlene and her arrest.

There was too much happening.

I had another moment of sickening dizziness, but it passed quickly, as it had before. Sam didn't even notice. He was lost in gloomy reflection, at least as far as I could read his twisty shapeshifter mind.

'Walk me to my car,' I said impulsively. I needed to get home and get some sleep, and I had no idea if Eric would show up tonight or not. I didn't want anyone else to pop up and surprise me, as Murry had done. I didn't want anyone trying to lure me to my doom or shooting guns in my vicinity. No more betrayal by people I cared for, either.

I had a long list of requirements, and I knew that wasn't a good thing.

As I pulled my purse out of the drawer in Sam's office and called good night to Antoine, who was still cleaning in the kitchen, I realized that the height of my ambition was to get home and go to bed without talking to anyone else, and to sleep undisturbed all night.

I wondered if that was possible.

Sam didn't say anything else about Eric, and he seemed to attribute my asking him to escort me as an attack of nerves after the incident at the trailer. I could have stood just inside the bar door and looked out with my other sense, but it was best to be double careful; my telepathy and Sam's nose made a good combination. He was eager to check the parking lot. In fact, he sounded almost disappointed when he announced there was nothing out there but us.

As I drove away, in my rearview mirror I saw Sam leaning on the hood of his truck, which was parked in front of his trailer. He had his hands in his pockets, and he was glaring at the gravel on the ground as if he hated the sight of it. Just as I pulled around the corner of the bar, Sam patted the truck's hood in an absentminded way and walked back into the bar, his shoulders bowed.

Chapter 13

'Amelia, what works against fairies?' I asked. I'd gotten a full night's sleep, and I was feeling much better in consequence. Amelia's boss was out of town, so she had the afternoon off.

'You mean something that'll act as a fairy repellent?' she asked.

'Yeah, or cause fairy death even,' I said. 'That's preferable to me getting killed. I need to defend myself.'

'I don't know too much about fairies, since they're so rare and secretive,' she said. 'I wasn't sure they still existed until I heard about your great-grandfather. You need something like Mace for fairies, huh?'

I had a sudden idea. 'I've already got some, Amelia,' I said, feeling happier than I had in days. I looked in the racks on the door of the refrigerator. Sure enough, there was a bottle of ReaLemon. 'Now all I got to do is buy a water pistol at Wal- Mart,' I said. 'It's not summer, but surely they've got some over in the toy department.'

'That works?'

'Yeah, a little-known supernatural fact. Just contact with it is fatal. I understand if it's ingested, the result's even quicker. If you could squirt it in a fairy's open mouth, that would be one dead fairy.'

'Sounds like you're in big trouble, Sookie.' Amelia had been reading, but now she laid her book on the table.

'Yeah, I am.'

'You want to talk about it?'

'It's complicated. Hard to explain.'

'I understand the definition of "complicated".'

'Sorry. Well, it might not be safe for you to learn the ins and outs of it. Can you help? Will your wards work against fairies?'

'I'll check my sources,' Amelia said in that wise way she had when she didn't have a clue. 'I'll call Octavia if I have to.'

'I'd appreciate it. And if you need some kind of spell-casting ingredients, money is no object.' I'd gotten a check in the mail that very morning from Sophie-Anne's estate. Mr Cataliades had come through with the money she'd owed me. I was going to run it to the bank this afternoon, since the drive-through would be open.

Amelia took a deep breath, stalled. I waited. Since she's an exceptionally clear broadcaster, I knew what she wanted to talk about, but to keep our relationship on an even keel, I simply held out until she spoke out loud.

'I heard from Tray, who's got a couple friends on the police force – though not many – that Whit and Arlene are denying up and down that they killed Crystal. They . . . Arlene says they planned on making you an example of what happens to people who hang around with the supernatural; that it was Crystal's death that gave them the idea.'

My good mood evaporated. I felt a profound depression settle on my shoulders. Hearing this spoken out loud made it seem even more horrible. I could think of no comment to offer. 'What does Tray hear about what might happen to them?' I said finally.

'Depends on whose bullet hit Agent Weiss. If it was Donny's – well, he's dead. Whit can say he was being shot at, so he shot back. He can say he didn't know anything about a plan to harm you. He was visiting his girlfriend and happened to have some pieces of wood in the back of his pickup.'

'What about Helen Ellis?'

'She told Andy Bellefleur she just came to the trailer to pick up the kids because they'd done really well on their report cards, and she'd promised to take them to the Sonic for an ice cream treat. Any more than that, she doesn't know diddlysquat.' Amelia's face expressed extreme skepticism.

'So Arlene is the only one talking.' I dried the baking sheet. I'd made biscuits that morning. Baking therapy, cheap and satisfying.

'Yeah, and she may recant any minute. She was real shaken up when she talked, but she'll wise up. Maybe too late. At least we can hope so.'

I'd been right; Arlene *was* the weakest link. 'She gotten a lawyer?'

'Yeah. She couldn't afford Sid Matt Lancaster, so she hired Melba Jennings.'

'Good move,' I said thoughtfully. Melba Jennings was only a couple of years older than me. She was the only African-American woman in Bon Temps who'd been to law school. She had a hard-as-nails facade and was confrontational in the extreme. Other lawyers had been known to take incredible detours to dodge Melba if they saw her coming. 'Makes her look less of a bigot.'

'I don't think it's going to fool anyone, but Melba's like a pit bull.' Melba had been in Amelia's insurance agency on behalf of a couple of clients. 'I better go make my bed,' Amelia said, standing and stretching. 'Hey, Tray and I are going to the movies in Clarice tonight. Want to come?'

'You've really been trying to include me on your dates. You're not getting bored with Tray already, I hope?'

'Not a bit,' Amelia said, sounding faintly surprised. 'In fact, I think he's great. Tray's buddy Drake has been pestering him, though. Drake's seen you in the bar, and he wants to get to know you.'

'He a Were?'

'Just a guy. Thinks you're pretty.'

'I don't do regular guys,' I said, smiling. 'It just doesn't work out very well.' It 'worked out' disastrously, as a matter of fact. Imagine knowing what your date thinks of you every single minute.

Plus, there was the issue of Eric and our undefined but intimate relationship.

'Keep the possibility on the back burner. He's really cute, and by cute, I mean hotter than a steam iron.'

After Amelia had tromped up the stairs, I poured myself a glass of tea. I tried to read, but I found I couldn't concentrate on the book. Finally, I slid my paper bookmark in and stared into space, thinking about a lot of things.

I wondered where Arlene's children were now. With Arlene's old aunt, who lived over in Clarice? Or still with Helen Ellis? Did Helen like Arlene enough to keep Coby and Lisa?

I couldn't rid myself of a nagging feeling of responsibility for the kids' sad situation, but it was going to have to be one of those things I simply suffered. The person really responsible was Arlene. There was nothing I could do for them.

As if thinking of children had triggered a nerve in the universe, the phone rang. I got up and went to the wall-mounted unit in the kitchen. 'Hello,' I said without enthusiasm.

'Ms Stackhouse? Sookie?'

'Yes, this is she,' I said properly.

'This is Remy Savoy.'

My dead cousin Hadley's ex, father of her child. 'I'm glad you called. How's Hunter?' Hunter was a 'gifted' child, God bless him. He'd been 'gifted' the same way I had been.

'He's fine. Uh, about that thing.'

'Sure.' We were going to talk telepathy.

'He's going to need some guidance soon. He'll be starting kinder-garten. They're going to notice. I mean, it'll take a while, but sooner or later . . .'

'Yeah, they'll notice all right.' I opened my mouth to suggest that Remy bring Hunter over on my next day off or that I could drive to Red Ditch. But then I remembered that I was the target of a group of homicidal fairies. Not a good time for a young 'un to come visiting, and who's to say they couldn't follow me to Remy's little house? So far none of them knew about Hunter. I hadn't even told my great-grandfather about Hunter's special talent. If Niall himself didn't know, maybe none of the hostiles had uncovered the in-formation.

On the whole, better to take no risks.

'I really want to meet with him and get to know him. I promise I'll help him as much as I can,' I said. 'Right now, it just isn't possible. But since we have a little time to spare before kindergarten . . . maybe in a month or so?'

'Oh,' Remy said in a nonplussed way. 'I was hoping to bring him over on my day off.'

'I have a little situation here that I have to resolve.' If I was alive after it was resolved . . . but I wasn't going to imagine that. I tried to think of a palatable excuse, and of course, I did have one. 'My sister-in-law just died,' I told Remy. 'Can I call you when I'm not so busy with the details of . . .' I couldn't think of a way to wrap up that sentence. 'I promise it'll be soon. If you don't have a day off, maybe Kristen could bring him?' Kristen was Remy's girlfriend.

'Well, that's part of the problem,' Remy said, and he sounded tired but also a little amused. 'Hunter told Kristen that he knew she didn't really like him, and that she should stop thinking about his daddy without any clothes on.'

I drew a deep breath, tried not to laugh, didn't manage it. 'I *am* sorry,' I said. 'How did Kristen handle that?'

'She started crying. Then she told me she loved me but my kid was a freak, and she left.'

'Worst possible scenario,' I said. 'Ah . . . do you think she'll tell other people?'

'Don't see why she wouldn't.'

This sounded depressingly familiar: shades of my painful childhood. 'Remy, I'm sorry,' I said. Remy had seemed like a nice guy on our brief acquaintance, and I had been able to see he was devoted to his son. 'If it makes you feel any better, I survived that somehow.'

'But did your parents?' There was a trace of a smile in his voice, to his credit.

'No,' I said. 'However, it didn't have anything to do with me. They got caught by a flash flood when they were driving home one night. It was pouring rain, visibility was terrible, the water was black like the road, and they just drove down onto the bridge and got swept away.' Something buzzed in my brain, some kind of signal that this thought was significant.

'I'm sorry, I was just joking,' Remy was saying in a shocked voice.

'No, no problem. Just one of those things,' I said, the way you do when you don't want the other person to fuss about your feelings.

We left it that I would call him when I had 'some free time'. (That actually meant 'when no one's trying to kill me,' but I didn't explain that to Remy.) I hung up and sat on the stool by the kitchen counter.

I was thinking about my parents' deaths for the first time in a while. I had some sad memories, but that was the saddest of all. Jason had been ten, and I had been seven, so my recollection wasn't precise, but we'd talked about it over the years, of course, and my grandmother had recounted the story many times, especially as she grew older. It never varied. The torrential rain, the road leading down into the little hollow where the creek ran, the black water . . . and they'd been swept away into the dark. The truck had been found the next day; their bodies, a day or two after that.

I got dressed for work automatically. I slicked my hair up in an extra-tight ponytail, making sure any stray hairs were gelled into place. As I was tying my shoes, Amelia dashed downstairs to tell me that she'd checked her witch reference books.

'The best way to kill fairies is with iron.' Her face was lit with triumph. I hated to rain on her parade. Lemons were even better, but it was kind of hard to slip a fairy a lemon without the fairy realizing it.

'I knew that,' I said, trying not to sound depressed. 'I mean, I appreciate the effort, but I need to be able to knock them out.' So I could run away. I didn't know if I could stand to have to hose down the driveway again.

Of course, killing the enemy beat the alternative: letting them catch me and do what they wished with me.

Amelia was ready for her date with Tray. She was wearing high heels with her designer jeans, an unusual look for Amelia.

'What's with the heels?' I asked, and Amelia grinned, displaying her excellent white teeth.

'Tray likes 'em,' she said. 'With the jeans on *or* off. You should see the lingerie I'm wearing!'

'I'll pass,' I said.

'If you want to meet us after you get off work, I'm betting Drake will be there. He's seriously interested in getting to know you. And he's cute, though his looks may not exactly appeal to you.'

'Why? What's this Drake look like?' I asked, mildly curious.

'That's the freaky part. He looks a lot like your brother.' Amelia looked at me doubtfully. 'That might weird you out, huh?'

I felt all the blood drain out of my face. I'd gotten to my feet to leave, but I sat down abruptly.

'Sookie? What's the matter? Sookie?' Amelia was hovering around me anxiously.

'Amelia,' I croaked, 'you got to avoid this guy. I mean it. You and Tray get away from him. And for God's sake, don't answer any questions about me!'

I could see from the guilt on her face she had already answered quite a few. Though she was a clever witch, Amelia couldn't always tell when people weren't really *people*. Evidently, neither could Tray – though the sweet smell of even a half fairy should have alerted a Were. Maybe Dermot had the same scent-masking ability that his father, my great-grandfather, did.

'Who is he?' Amelia asked. She was scared, which was good.

'He's . . .' I tried to formulate the best explanation. 'He wants to kill me.'

'Does this have something to do with Crystal's death?'

'I don't think so,' I said. I tried to give the possibility some rational consideration, found my brain simply couldn't deal with the idea.

'I don't get it,' Amelia said. 'We have months – well, weeks – of nothing but plain old life, and then, all of a sudden, here we are!' She threw up her hands.

'You can move back to New Orleans if you want to,' I said, my voice faltering. Of course, Amelia knew she could leave anytime she wanted, but I wanted to make it clear I wasn't sucking her into my problems unless she chose to be sucked. So to speak.

'No,' she said firmly. 'I like it here, and my house in New Orleans isn't ready, anyway.'

She kept saying that. Not that I wanted her to leave, but I couldn't see what the delay was. After all, her dad was a builder.

'You don't miss New Orleans?'

'Of course I do,' Amelia said. 'But I like it here, and I like my little suite upstairs, and I like Tray, and I like my little jobs that keep me going. And I also like – a *hell* of a lot – being out of my dad's line of sight.' She patted me on the shoulder. 'You go off to work and don't worry. If I haven't thought of anything by morning, I'll call Octavia.

Now that I know the deal about this Drake, I'll stonewall him. And Tray will, too. No one can stonewall like Tray.'

'He's very dangerous, Amelia,' I said. I couldn't impress that on my roommate emphatically enough.

'Yeah, yeah, I get that,' she said. 'But you know, I'm not any little honey myself, and Dawson can fight with the best of 'em.'

We gave each other a hug, and I allowed myself to immerse in Amelia's mind. It was warm, busy, curious, and . . . forward-looking. No brooding on the past for Amelia Broadway. She gave me a pat on the back to signal she was letting go, and we stepped back from each other.

I ran by the bank, then I stopped at Wal-Mart. After a bit of searching, I found one little rack of water guns. I got a two-pack of the clear plastic version, one blue and one yellow. When I thought of the ferocity and strength of the fairy race, and the fact that it took all I had to open the damn blister pack and extricate the water pistols, my chosen method of defense seemed ludicrous. I'd be armed with a plastic water pistol and a trowel.

I tried to clear my mind of all the worries that were plaguing me. There was so much to think about. . . . Actually, there was so much to fear. It might be time to take a leaf from Amelia's book and look forward. What did I need to do *tonight*? Which one of my ongoing worries could I actually do something to solve? I could listen in the bar tonight for clues about Crystal's death, as Jason had asked me to do. (I would have done it anyway, but it seemed even more important to track down her killers now that danger seemed to be piling up from all directions.) I could arm myself against fairy attack. I could be alert for any more Fellowship gangs. And I could try to arrange some more defense.

After all, I was supposed to be under the protection of the Shreveport Were pack because I'd helped them out. I was also under the protection of the new vampire regime because I'd saved their leader's ass. Felipe de Castro would have been a pile of ash if not for me; for that matter, so would Eric. Wasn't this the best time in the world to call in those markers?

I got out of my car behind Merlotte's. I looked up at the sky, but it was cloudy. I thought it was only a week after the new moon. And it was definitely full dark. I pulled my cell phone out of my purse. I'd discovered Eric's cell number scrawled on the back of one of his business cards, tucked halfway under my bedside phone. He answered on the second ring.

'Yes,' he said, and I was able to tell by that one word that he was with others.

A little shiver went down my spine at the sound of his voice.

'Eric,' I said, and then wished I'd spent a little time framing my request. 'The king said he owed me,' I continued, realizing this was a little bald and bold. 'I'm in real danger. I wonder what he could do about that.'

'The threat involving your older kin?' Yes, he was definitely with other people.

'Yes. The, ah, enemy has been trying to get Amelia and Tray to introduce him to me. He doesn't seem to realize I would recognize him, or maybe he's very good at pretending. He's supposed to be on the anti-human side, but he's half human. I don't understand his behavior.'

'I see,' Eric said after an appreciable pause. 'So protection is necessary.'

'Yes.'

'And you ask this as . . .?'

If he'd been with his own underlings, he'd have told them to leave so he could talk to me frankly. Since he hadn't done that, he was probably with one of the Nevada vamps: Sandy Sechrest, Victor Madden, or Felipe de Castro himself, though that was unlikely. Castro's far more lucrative business ventures in Nevada required his presence most of the time. I finally realized Eric was trying to find out if I was asking as his bed buddy and 'wife,' or as someone he owed big-time.

'I ask this as someone who saved Felipe de Castro's life,' I said.

'I'll present this petition to Victor, since he's here at the bar,' Eric said smoothly. 'I'll get back to you this night.'

'Great.' Mindful of vamps' extreme hearing, I added, 'I appreciate that, Eric,' as if we were friendly acquaintances.

Mentally dodging the question of what we actually were to each other, I tucked away the cell phone and went into work, hustling because I was a couple of minutes late. Now that I'd talked to Eric, I felt much more optimistic about my chances of survival.

Chapter 14

I kept my mental ears open that night, so it was a hard evening for me. After years of practice and some help from Bill, I'd learned to block out most of the thoughts of the humans around me. But tonight was just like the bad old days, when I'd smiled all the time to cover the confusion in my head caused by the constant bombardment of mental mutterings.

When I walked past the table where Bud Dearborn and his ancient crony Sid Matt Lancaster were having chicken baskets and beers, I heard, *Crystal's no great loss, but no one gets crucified in Renard Parish. . . . We gotta solve that case*, and *Got me some genuine werewolves for clients. I wish Elva Deane had lived to see this; she woulda loved it.* But mostly Sid Matt was thinking about his hemorrhoids and his spreading cancer.

Oh, gosh, I hadn't known. My next pass by his table, I patted the venerable lawyer on the shoulder. 'Let me know if you need anything,' I said, and met his turtlelike stare with a blank face. He could take it any way he chose, as long as he knew I was willing to help.

When you throw out your net that wide, you come up with a lot of trash. I found out over the course of the evening that Tanya thought she might be settling down permanently with Calvin, that Jane Bodehouse thought she had chlamydia and wondered who was responsible, and that Kevin and Kenya, police officers who always requested the same shift, were actually living together now. Since Kenya was black and Kevin couldn't be whiter, this was causing Kevin's folks some problems, but he was standing firm. Kenya's brother wasn't too happy about her living situation, either, but he wasn't going to beat up Kevin or anything like that. I gave them a big smile when I brought them bourbon and Cokes, and they smiled back. It was so rare to see Kenya crack a grin that I almost laughed. She looked about five years younger when she smiled.

Andy Bellefleur came in with his new wife, Halleigh. I liked Halleigh, and we hugged each other. Halleigh was thinking she might be pregnant, and it would be mighty early in the marriage for them to start a family, but Andy was quite a bit older than her. This maybe-pregnancy hadn't been planned, so she was pretty worried about how Andy would take the news. Since I was laying myself out there tonight, I tried something new. I sent my extra sense down into Halleigh's belly. If she really was pregnant, it was too soon for the little brain to be registering.

Andy was thinking Halleigh had been quiet the past couple of days, and he was worried something was wrong with her. He was also worried about the investigation of Crystal's death, and when he felt Bud Dearborn's eyes on him, he wished he'd picked any other place in Bon Temps for his evening out. The gunfight at Arlene's trailer was haunting his dreams.

Other people in the bar were thinking about typical stuff.

What are the all-time most popular thoughts? Well, they're really, really boring.

Most people think about their money problems, what they need from the store, what housework they have to do, how their jobs are going. They worry about their kids . . . a lot. They brood over issues with their bosses and their spouses and their coworkers and other members of their churches.

On the whole, 95 percent of what I hear is nothing anybody'd want to write down in her diary.

Every now and then the guys (less often, the women) think about sex with someone they see in the bar – but honestly, that's so common I can brush it aside, unless they're thinking about me. That's pretty disgusting. The sex ideas multiply with the drinks consumed; no surprise there.

The people thinking about Crystal and her death were the law enforcement people charged with finding out who'd killed her. If one of the culprits was in the bar, he was simply not thinking about what he'd done. And there had to be more than a single person involved. Setting up a cross was not something a man on his own could handle; at least not without a *lot* of preparation and some elaborate arrangement of pulleys. You'd have to be some kind of supernatural to pull it off by yourself.

This was Andy Bellefleur's train of thought while he waited for his crispy chicken salad.

I had to agree with him. I'd bet Calvin had already considered that scenario. Calvin had sniffed the body, and he hadn't said he'd smelled another wereanimal of any kind. But then I recalled that one of the two men who'd been wheeling the body out had been a supe.

As far as learning anything new, I was drawing a blank until Mel came in. Mel, who lived in one of Sam's rental duplexes, looked like a reject from the cast of *Robin Hood, the Musical* tonight. His longish light brown hair, neat mustache and beard, and tight pants gave him a theatrical air.

Mel surprised me by giving me a half hug before he sat down, as if I were a good buddy of his.

If this behavior was because he and my brother were both panthers . . . but that still didn't make a lot of sense. None of the other werepanthers got cozy with me because of Jason – far from it. The Hotshot community had been a lot warmer toward me when Calvin Norris had been thinking of asking me to be his mate. Did Mel have a secret yearning to go out with me? That would be . . . unpleasant and unwelcome.

I took a little trip into Mel's head, where I saw no lusty thoughts about me. If he'd been attracted, he'd have been thinking them, since I was right in front of him. Mel *was* thinking about the things Catfish Hennessy, Jason's boss, had been saying about Jason in Bon Temps Auto Parts that day. Catfish's tolerance balloon had burst, and he'd told Mel he was thinking about firing Jason.

Mel was plenty worried about my brother, bless his heart. I'd wondered my whole life how someone as selfish as my brother could attract such faithful friends. My great-grandfather had told me that people with a trace of fairy blood were more attractive to other humans, so maybe that explained it.

I went behind the bar to pour some more tea for Jane Bodehouse, who was trying to be sober today because she was trying to compile a list of the guys who might have given her chlamydia. A bar is a bad place to start a sobriety program – but Jane had hardly any chance of succeeding, anyway. I put a slice of lemon in the tea and carried it to Jane, watched her hands shake as she picked up the glass and drank from it.

'You want something to eat?' I asked, keeping my voice low and quiet. Just because I'd never seen a drunk reform in a bar, that didn't mean it couldn't happen.

Jane shook her head silently. Her dyed brown hair was already escaping the clip that held it back, and her heavy black sweater was covered with bits of this and that. Her makeup had been applied with a shaky hand. I could see the lipstick caked in the creases in her lips. Most of the area alcoholics might stop in Merlotte's every now and then, but they based themselves at the Bayou. Jane was our only 'resident' alkie since old Willie Chenier had died. When Jane was in the bar, she always sat on the same stool. Hoyt had made a label for it when he'd had too much to drink one night, but Sam had made him take it off.

I looked in Jane's head for an awful minute or two, and I watched the slow shifting of thoughts behind her eyes, noticed the broken veins in her cheeks. The thought of becoming like Jane was enough to scare almost anyone sober.

I turned away to find Mel standing beside me. He was on his way to the men's room, because that's what was in his head when I looked.

'You know what they do in Hotshot with people like that?' he asked quietly, nodding his head toward Jane as if she couldn't see or hear him. (Actually, I thought he was right about that. Jane was turned so inward that she didn't seem to be acknowledging the world much today.)

'No,' I said, startled.

'They let them die,' he said. 'They don't offer them food or water or shelter, if the person can't seek it for himself or herself.'

I'm sure my horror showed on my face.

'It's kindest in the end,' he said. He drew a deep, shuddering breath. 'Hotshot has its ways of getting rid of the weak.'

He went on his way, his back stiff.

I patted Jane on the shoulder, but I'm afraid I wasn't really thinking about her. I was wondering what Mel had done to deserve his exile to a duplex in Bon Temps. If it had been me, I would have been happy to be rid of the multiple ties of kinship and the microscopic hierarchy of the little cluster of houses huddled around the old crossroads, but I could tell that wasn't the way Mel felt about it.

Mel's ex-wife had a margarita in Merlotte's from time to time. I thought I might do a little research on my brother's new buddy the next time Ginjer dropped by.

Sam asked me a couple of times if I was okay, and I was surprised by the strength of my desire to talk to him about everything that had happened lately. I was astonished to realize how often I confided in Sam, how much he knew about my secret life. But I knew that Sam had enough on his plate right now. He was on the phone with his sister and his brother several times during the evening, which was really unusual for him. He looked harassed and worried, and it would be selfish to add to that load of worry.

The cell phone in my apron pocket vibrated a couple of times, and when I had a free moment, I ducked into the ladies' room and checked my text messages. One from Eric. 'Protection coming,' it said. That was good. There was another message, and this one was from Alcide Herveaux, the Shreveport pack leader. 'Tray called. Trouble Ur way?' it read. 'We owe U.'

My chances of survival had risen considerably, and I felt much more cheerful as I finished out my shift.

It was good to have stockpiled favors with both vampires and werewolves. Maybe all the shit I'd gone through last fall would prove to have been worth it after all.

All in all, though, I had to say my project for the evening had been a washout. Sure, after asking Sam for permission, I'd filled both the plastic water guns with juice from the lemons in the refrigerator (intended for iced tea). I thought maybe real lemons would somehow be more potent than the bottled lemon juice at home. So I felt a little safer, but the sum total of my knowledge about the death of Crystal had not increased by one fact. Either the murderers hadn't come in the bar, weren't fretting over the evil thing they'd done, or weren't thinking about it at the moment I was looking inside their heads. Or, I thought, *all of the above.*

Chapter 15

I had vampire protection, of a sort, waiting for me after work. Bubba was standing by my car when I left Merlotte's. He grinned when he saw me, and I was glad to give him a hug. Most people wouldn't have been pleased to see a mentally defective vampire with a penchant for cat blood, but I'd become fond of Bubba.

'When did you get back in town?' I asked. Bubba had gotten caught in New Orleans during Katrina, and he'd required a long recovery. The vampires were willing to accommodate him, because he had been one of the most famous people in the world until he'd been brought over in a morgue in Memphis.

''Bout a week ago. Good to see you, Miss Sookie.' Bubba's fangs slid out to show me how glad. Just as quickly, they snicked back into concealment. Bubba still had talent. 'I've been traveling. I've been staying with friends. But I was in Fangtasia tonight visiting Mr Eric, and he asked if I'd like the job of keeping watch over you. I told him, 'Miss Sookie and me, we're real good friends, and that would suit me just fine.' Have you gotten another cat?'

'No, Bubba, I haven't.' Thank God.

'Well, I got me some blood in a cooler in the back of my car.' He nodded toward a huge old white Cadillac that had been restored with time and trouble and lots of cash.

'Oh, the car's beautiful,' I said. I almost added, 'Did you own it while you were alive?' But Bubba didn't like references to his former state of existence; they made him upset and confused. (If you put it very carefully, from time to time he'd sing for you. I'd heard him do 'Blue Christmas.' Unforgettable.)

'Russell give that to me,' he said.

'Oh, Russell Edgington? The King of Mississippi?'

'Yeah, wasn't that nice? He said since he was king of my home state, he felt like giving me something special.'

'How's he doing?' Russell and his new husband, Bart, had both survived the Rhodes hotel bombing.

'He's feeling real good now. He and Mr Bart are both healed up.'

'I'm so glad to hear it. So, are you supposed to follow me home?'

'Yes'm, that's the plan. If you'll leave your back door unlocked, close to morning I'll get into that hidey-hole in your guest bedroom; that's what Mr Eric said.'

Then it was doubly good that Octavia had moved out. I didn't know how she would have reacted if I'd told her that the Man from Memphis needed to sleep in her closet all day long.

When I got home, Bubba pulled in right behind me in his amazing car. I saw that Dawson's truck was there, too. I wasn't surprised. Dawson worked as a bodyguard from time to time, and he was in the area. Since Alcide had decided he wanted to help, Tray Dawson was an obvious choice, regardless of his relationship with Amelia.

Tray himself was sitting at my kitchen table when Bubba and I came in. For the first time since I'd known him, the big man looked seriously startled. But he was smart enough not to blurt anything out.

'Tray, this is my friend Bubba,' I said. 'Where's Amelia?'

'She's upstairs. I got some business to talk with you.'

'I figured. Bubba's here for the same reason. Bubba, this is Tray Dawson.'

'Hey, Tray!' Bubba shook hands, laughing because he'd made a rhyme. He hadn't translated real well. The spark of life had been so faint by the time a morgue attendant of the fanged persuasion had gotten hold of him, and the drugs in his system so pervasive, that Bubba had been lucky to survive the bringing over as well as he had, which wasn't too well.

'Hey,' Tray said cautiously. 'How are you doing . . . Bubba?'

I was relieved Tray'd picked up on the name.

'I'm real good, thank you. Got me some blood in the cooler out there, and Miss Sookie keeps some TrueBlood in the refrigerator, or at least she used to.'

'Yes, I have some,' I said. 'You want to sit down, Bubba?'

'No, ma'am. I think I'll just grab me a bottle and settle down out in the woods. Bill still live across the cemetery?'

'Yes, he does.'

'Always good to have friends close.'

I wasn't sure I could call Bill my friend; our history was too complicated for that. But I was absolutely sure that he'd help me if I was in danger. 'Yes,' I said, 'that's always good.'

Bubba rummaged around in the refrigerator and came out with a couple of bottles. He raised them to me and Tray, and took his leave smiling.

'Good God Almighty,' Tray said. 'That who I think it is?'

I nodded and took a seat opposite him.

'Explains all the sightings,' he said. 'Well, listen, you got him out there and me in here. That okay with you?'

'Yes. I guess you've talked to Alcide?'

'Yeah. I'm not trying to get in your business, but it would have been better to hear all this from you directly. Especially since you talked to Amelia about this guy Drake, and Amelia's all upset because apparently she's been blabbing to the enemy. If we'd known about your troubles, she would have kept her mouth shut. I would have killed him when he first introduced himself. Saved all of us a lot of trouble. You think about that?'

Bluntness was the way to go with Tray. 'I think you are kind of getting in my business, Tray. When you're here as my friend and Amelia's boyfriend, I tell you what I think I can without endangering you or Amelia. It never occurred to me that Niall's enemies would think of getting information through my roommate. And it was news to me that you couldn't tell a fairy from a human.' Tray winced. 'You may not want to be responsible for guarding me, with the personal complication of having your girlfriend under the same roof as the woman you're supposed to protect. Is this too big a conflict of interest for you?'

Tray regarded me steadily. 'No, I want the job,' he said, and even though he was a Were, I could tell that his real goal was keeping Amelia safe. Since she lived with me, he could kill two birds with one stone by getting paid for protecting me. 'For one thing, I owe that Drake payback. I never knew he was a fairy, and I don't know how he managed that. I got a good nose.'

Tray's pride had been bruised. I could understand that. 'Drake's dad can mask his smell, even from vampires. Maybe Drake can, too. Also, he's not completely fae. He's half-human, and his real name is Dermot.'

Tray absorbed this, nodded. I could tell he felt a little better. I was trying to figure out if I did.

I had misgivings about the arrangement. I thought of calling Alcide and explaining why Tray might be a less than perfect bodyguard, but I decided against it. Tray Dawson was a great fighter and would do his best for me . . . up to the point where he had to make a choice between Amelia and me.

'So?' he said, and I realized I'd been quiet for too long.

'The vampire can take the nights and you can take the days,' I said. 'I should be okay while I'm at the bar.' I pushed back my chair and left the kitchen without saying anything else. I had to admit that instead of feeling relieved, I was even more worried. I'd thought I'd been so clever asking for an extra layer of protection; instead, now I was going to worry about the safety of the men providing that layer.

I got ready for bed slowly, finally admitting to myself that I was hoping Eric would put in an appearance. I'd love to have his brand of relaxation therapy to help me sleep. I expected to lie awake anticipating the next attack. As it turned out, I was so tired from the night before that I drifted off to sleep very quickly.

Instead of my usual boring dreams (customers calling me constantly while I hurried to catch up, mold growing in my bathroom), that night I dreamed of Eric. In my dream, he was human and we walked together under the sun. Oddly enough, he sold real estate.

When I looked at the clock the next morning, it was very early, at least for me: not quite eight o'clock. I woke up with a feeling of alarm. I wondered if I'd had another dream, one I didn't remember.

I wondered if my telepathic sense had caught something even while I slept, something wrong, something askew.

I took a moment to scan my own house, not my favorite way to start the day. Amelia was gone, but Tray was here and in trouble.

I put on a bathrobe and slippers and stepped out into the hall. The moment I opened my door, I could hear him being sick in the hall bathroom.

There are some moments that should be completely private, and the moments when you're throwing up are at the top of that list. But werewolves are normally completely healthy, and this was the guy who'd been sent to guard me, and he was obviously (excuse me) sick as a dog.

I waited until a lull in the sound. I called, 'Tray, is there anything I can do for you?'

'I've been poisoned,' he said, choking and gagging.

'Should I call the doctor? A human one? Or Dr Ludwig?'

'No.' That sounded definite enough. 'I'm trying to get rid of it,' he gasped, after another bout of retching. 'But it's too late.'

'You know who gave it to you?'

'Yeah. That new girlfriend . . .' He faded out for a few seconds. 'Out in the woods. Vampire Bill's new fuck.'

I had an instinctive reaction. 'He wasn't with her, right?' I called.

'No, she—' More awful noises. 'She came from the direction of his house, said she was his . . .'

I knew, without a doubt, that Bill didn't have a new girlfriend. Though it embarrassed me to admit it to myself, I was so sure because I knew he wanted me back. I knew he wouldn't jeopardize that by taking someone else to his bed or by permitting such a woman to roam in the woods where I might encounter her.

'What was she?' I said, resting my forehead against the cool wood of the door. I was getting tired of yelling.

'She was some fangbanger.' I felt Tray's brain shift around through the fog of sickness. 'At least, she felt like a human.'

'The same way Dermot felt human. And you drank something she handed you.' It was kind of mean of me to sound incredulous, but honestly!

'I couldn't help it,' he said very slowly. 'I was so thirsty. I had to drink it.'

He'd been under some kind of compulsion spell. 'And what was it? The stuff you drank?'

'It tasted like wine.' He groaned. 'Goddammit, it must have been vampire blood! I can taste it in my mouth now!'

Vampire blood was still the hot drug on the underground marketplace, and human reactions to it varied so widely that drinking the blood was very much like playing Russian roulette, in more ways than one. Vampires hated the Drainers who collected the blood because the Drainers often left the vampire exposed to the day. So vampires also loathed the users of the blood, since they created the market. Some users became addicted to the ecstatic sensation that the blood could offer, and those users sometimes tried to take the blood right from the source in a kind of suicide attack. But every now and then, the user went berserk and killed other humans. Either way, it was all bad press for the vamps who were trying to mainstream.

'Why would you do that?' I asked, unable to keep the anger out of my voice.

'I couldn't help it,' he said, and the bathroom door finally opened. I took a couple of steps back. Tray looked bad and smelled worse. He was wearing pajama pants and nothing else, and a vast expanse of chest hair was right at my eye level. It was covered in goose pimples.

'How come?'

'I couldn't . . . not drink it.' He shook his head. 'And then I came back here and got in bed with Amelia, and I tossed and turned all night. I was up when the K— when Bubba came in and went to bed in your closet. He said something about a woman talking to him, but I was feeling really bad by then, and I don't remember what he said. Did Bill send her over here? Does he hate you that bad?'

I looked up then and met his eyes. 'Bill Compton loves me,' I said. 'He would never hurt me.'

'Even now that you're screwing the big blond?'

Amelia couldn't keep her mouth shut.

'Even now that I'm screwing the big blond,' I said.

'You can't read vampire minds, Amelia says.'

'No, I can't. But some things you just know.'

'Right.' Though Tray didn't have enough energy to look skeptical, he gave it a good shot. 'I have to go to bed, Sookie. I can't take care of you today.'

I could see that. 'Why don't you go back to your own house and try to get some rest in your own bed?' I said. 'I'm going to work today, and I'll be around someone.'

'No, you gotta be covered.'

'I'll call my brother,' I said, surprising even myself. 'He's not going to work now, and he's a panther. He should be able to watch my back.'

'Okay.' It was a measure of Tray's wretchedness that he didn't argue, though he wasn't a Jason fan by any means. 'Amelia knows I'm not feeling good. If you talk to her before I do, tell her I'll call her tonight.'

The werewolf staggered out to his truck. I hoped he was good to drive home, and I called after him to make sure, but he just waved a hand at me and drove down the driveway.

Feeling oddly numb, I watched him go. I'd done the prudent thing for once; I'd called in my markers and gotten protection. And it hadn't done me a bit of good. Someone who couldn't attack me in my home – because of Amelia's good magic, I had to assume – had arranged to attack me in other ways. Murry had turned up outside, and now some fairy had met up with Tray in the woods, compelling him to drink vampire blood. It might have sent him mad; he might have killed all of us. I guess, for the fairies, it was a win-win situation. Though he hadn't gone crazy and killed me or Amelia, he'd gotten so sick that he was effectively out of the bodyguard business for a while.

I walked down the hall to go into my room and pull on some clothes. Today was going to be a hard day, and I always felt better when I was dressed while handling a crisis. Something about putting on my underwear makes me feel more capable.

I got my second shock of the day when I was about to turn into my room. There was a movement in the living room. I stopped dead and took a huge, ragged breath. My great-grandfather was sitting on the couch, but it took me an awful moment to recognize Niall. He got up, regarding me with some astonishment while I stood gasping, my hand over my heart.

'You look rough today,' he said.

'Yeah, well, not expecting visitors,' I said breathlessly. He wasn't looking so great himself, which was a first. His clothes were stained and torn, and unless I was much mistaken, he was sweating. My fairy prince great-grandfather was actually less than gorgeous for the very first time.

I moved into the living room and looked at him more closely. Though it was early, I had my second stab of anxiety for the day. 'What's up?' I asked. 'You look like you've been fighting.'

He hesitated for a long moment, as if he was trying to pick among several items of news. 'Breandan has retaliated for the death of Murry,' Niall said.

'What has he done?' I scrubbed my dry hands across my face.

'He caught Enda last night, and now she is dead,' he said. I could tell from his voice that her death had not been a quick one. 'You didn't meet her; she was very shy of humans.' He pushed back a long strand of his pale hair so blond it looked white.

'Breanden killed a fairy woman? There aren't that many fairy women, right? So doing that . . . isn't that extra awful?'

'It was intended to be,' Niall said. His voice was bleak.

For the first time, I noticed that my great-grandfather's slacks were soaked with blood around the knees, which was probably why he hadn't come closer to hug me.

'You need to get out of those clothes,' I said. 'Please, Niall, go climb in the shower, and I'll put your stuff in the washing machine.'

'I have to go,' he said, and I could tell my words hadn't registered. 'I came here to warn you in person, so you would take the situation very seriously. Powerful magic surrounds this house. I could appear here only because I'd been in here before. Is it true that the vampires and the Weres are looking out for you? You have extra protection; I can feel it.'

'I have a bodyguard night and day,' I lied, because he didn't need to be worrying about me. He was hip-deep in alligators himself. 'And you know that Amelia is a strong witch. Don't worry about me.'

He stared at me, but I didn't think he was seeing me at all. 'I have to go,' he said abruptly. 'I wanted to be sure of your well-being.'

'Okay . . . thanks a lot.' I was trying to think of an improvement on this limp response when Niall poofed right out of my living room.

I'd told Tray I was going to call Jason. I wasn't sure how sincere I'd been about that, but now I knew I had to. The way I saw it, Alcide's favor to me had expired; he'd asked Tray to help, and now Tray was out of commission in the course of duty. I sure wasn't going to request that Alcide himself come guard me, and I wasn't close to any of his pack members. I took a deep breath and called my brother.

'Jason,' I said when he answered the phone.

'Sis. What's up?' He sounded oddly jazzed, as if he'd just experienced something exciting.

'Tray had to leave, and I think I need some protection today,' I said. There was a long silence. He didn't rush into questioning me, which was strange. 'I was hoping you could go around with me? What I plan on doing today,' I began, and then tried to figure out what that was. It was hard to have a good crisis when real life kept asking to be lived. 'Well, I need to go to the library. I need to pick up a pair of pants at the dry cleaners.' I hadn't checked the label before that particular purchase. 'I have to work the day shift at Merlotte's. I guess that's it.'

'Okay,' Jason said. 'Though those errands don't sound exactly urgent.' There was a long pause. Suddenly he said, 'Are you okay?'

'Yeah,' I said cautiously. 'Should I not be?'

'The weirdest thing happened this morning. Mel slept at my place last night, since he was the worse for wear after he met me at the Bayou. So early this morning, there was a knock at the door. I answered it, and this guy was there, and he was, I don't know, nuts or something. The strangest part was, this guy looked a lot like me.'

'Oh, no.' I sat on the stool abruptly.

'He wasn't right, sis,' Jason said. 'I don't know what was wrong with him, but he wasn't right. He just started talking when Mel answered the door, like we knew who he was. He was saying crazy stuff. Mel tried to get between him and me, and he threw Mel clear across the room and called him a killer. Mel might've broken his neck if he hadn't landed on the couch.'

'Mel's okay, then.'

'Yeah, he's okay. Pretty mad, but you know . . .'

'Sure.' Mel's feelings were not the most important issue here. 'So what did he do next?'

'He said some shit about now that he was face-to-face with me he could see why my great-grandfather didn't want me around, and crossbreeds should all die, but I was clearly blood of his blood, and he'd decided I should know what's going on around me. He said I was ignorant. I didn't understand a lot of it, and I still don't get what he was. He wasn't a vamp, and I know he wasn't a shifter of any kind or I'd've smelled him.'

'You're okay – that's the big thing, right?' Had I been wrong all along about keeping Jason out of the fairy loop?

'Yeah,' he said, his voice abruptly going all cautious and wary. 'You're not going to tell me what this is all about, are you?'

'Come over here, and we'll talk about it. Please, please, don't open the door unless you know who's there. This guy is bad, Jason, and he's not picky about who he hurts. I think you and Mel were real lucky.'

'You got someone there with you?'

'Not since Tray left.'

'I'm your brother. I'll come over if you need me,' Jason said with unexpected dignity.

'I really appreciate that,' I said.

I got two for the price of one. Mel came with Jason. This was awkward, because I had some family stuff to tell Jason, and I couldn't with Mel around. With unexpected tact, Mel told Jason that he had to run home and get an ice pack for his shoulder, which was badly bruised. While Mel was gone, I sat Jason down on the other side of the kitchen table, and I said, 'I got some things to tell you.'

'About Crystal?'

'No, I haven't heard anything about that yet. This is about us. This is about Gran. You're going to have a hard time believing this.' I'd given him fair warning. I remembered how upset I'd been when my great-grandfather had told me about how my half-fairy grandfather, Fintan, had met my grandmother, and how she'd ended up having two children with him, our dad and our aunt Linda.

Now Fintan was dead – murdered – and our grandmother was dead, and our father and his sister were dead. But we were living, and just a small part fairy, and that made us a target for our great-grandfather's enemies.

'And one of those enemies,' I said after I'd told him our family history, 'is our half-human great-uncle, Fintan's brother, Dermot. He told Tray and Amelia that his name was Drake, I guess because it sounded more modern. Dermot looks like you, and he's the one who showed up at your house. I don't know what his deal is. He joined up with Breandan, Niall's big enemy, even though he's half-human himself and, therefore, exactly what Breandan hates. So when you said he was crazy, I guess there's your explanation. He seems to want to connect with you, but he hates you, too.'

Jason sat staring at me. His face was completely vacant. His thoughts had gotten caught in a traffic jam. Finally he said, 'You tell me he was trying to get Tray and Amelia to introduce you? And neither of them knew what he was?'

I nodded. There was some more silence.

'So why did he want to meet you? Did he want to kill you? Why'd he need to meet you first?'

Good question. 'I don't know,' I said. 'Maybe he just wanted to see what I was like. Maybe he doesn't know what he really wants.' I couldn't figure this out, and I wondered if Niall would come back to explain it to me. Probably not. He had a war on his hands, even if it was a war being fought mostly away from human view. 'I don't get it,' I said out loud. 'Murry came right here to attack me, and he was all fairy. Why is Dermot, who's on the same side, being all . . . indirect?'

'Murry?' Jason asked, and I closed my eyes. Shit.

'He was a fairy,' I said. 'He tried to kill me. He's not a problem now.'

Jason gave me an approving nod. 'You go, Sookie,' he said. 'Okay, let me see if I'm getting this straight. My great-grandfather didn't want to meet me because I look a lot like Dermot, who's my . . . great-uncle, right?'

'Right.'

'But Dermot apparently likes me a little better, because he actually came to my house and tried to talk to me.'

Trust Jason to interpret the situation in those terms. 'Right,' I said.

Jason hopped to his feet and took a turn around the kitchen. 'This is all the vampires' fault,' he said. He glared at me.

'Why do you think so?' This was unexpected.

'If they hadn't come out, none of this would be happening. Look at what's happened since they went on TV. Look at how the world has changed. Now *we're* out. Next, the fucking fairies. And the fae are bad news, Sookie; Calvin warned me about 'em. You think they're all pretty and sweetness and light, but they're not. He's told me stories about them that would make your hair curl. Calvin's dad knew a fairy or two. From what he's said, it would be a good thing if they died out.'

I couldn't decide if I was surprised or angry. 'Why are you being so mean, Jason? I don't need you arguing with me or saying bad things about Niall. You don't know him. You don't . . . Hey, you're part fairy, remember!' I had an awful feeling that some of what he'd said was absolutely true, but it sure wasn't the time to have this discussion.

Jason looked grim, every plane of his face tense. 'I'm not claiming kin to any fairy,' he said. 'He don't want me; I don't want him. And if I see that crazy half-and-half again, I'll kill the son of a bitch.'

I don't know what I would have said, but at that moment Mel came in without knocking, and we both turned to look at him.

'I'm sorry!' he said, obviously flustered and disturbed by Jason's anger. He seemed, for a second, to think Jason had been talking about him. When neither of us gave him a guilty reaction, he relaxed. 'Excuse me, Sookie. I forgot my manners.' He was carrying an ice bag in his hand, and he was moving a little slowly and painfully.

'I'm sorry you got hurt by Jason's surprise visitor,' I said. You're always supposed to put your company at ease. I hadn't put a whole lot of thought into Mel, but right at that second I realized I would have been happier if Jason's former BFF, Hoyt, had been here instead of the werepanther. It wasn't that I disliked Mel, I thought. It was just that I didn't know him very well, and I didn't feel an automatic trust in him the way you feel about people from time to time. Mel was different. Even for a werepanther, he was hard to read, but that didn't mean he was impossible.

After offering Mel something to drink, which was only polite, I asked Jason if he was going to stay the day, run around on my errands with me. I had serious doubts he would say yes. Jason was feeling rejected (by a fairy great-grandfather he'd never met and didn't want to acknowledge), and that was a state of affairs Jason didn't handle well.

'I'll go around with you,' he said, unsmiling and stiff. 'First, let me run over to the house and check out my rifle. I'll need it, and it hasn't been sighted in a coon's age. Mel? You coming with me?' Jason simply wanted to be out of my presence to calm down. I could read it as easily as if he'd written it on the grocery list pad by the telephone.

Mel rose to go with Jason.

'Mel, what did you make of Jason's visitor this morning?' I asked.

'Aside from the fact that he could throw me across the room and looked enough like Jason to make me turn to make sure your brother was coming out of his bedroom? Not much,' Mel said. Mel had managed to dress in his usual khakis and polo shirt, but the blue bruises on his arms kind of ruined his neat appearance. He shrugged on a jacket with great care.

'See you in a while, Sookie. Come around to get me,' Jason said. Of course, he'd want to ride in my car and burn up my gas, since we were running my errands. 'In the meantime, you got my cell number.'

'Sure. I'll see you in an hour or so.'

Since being alone hadn't been a normal state of affairs for me lately, I would have actually enjoyed the feeling of having the house to myself if I hadn't been worried that a supernatural killer was after me.

Nothing happened. I ate a bowl of cereal. Finally, I decided to risk taking a shower despite my *Psycho* memories. I made sure all the outside doors were locked, and I locked the bathroom door, too. I took the quickest shower on record.

Nobody had tried to kill me yet. I dried off, put on some makeup, and dressed for work.

When it was time to go, I stood on the back porch and eyeballed the distance between the steps and my car door, over and over. I figured I'd have to take ten steps. I unlocked the car with the keypad. I took a few deep breaths and unlocked the screen door. I pushed it open and fairly leaped off the porch, bypassing the steps entirely. In an undignified scramble, I yanked open the car door, slid inside, and slammed and locked the door. I looked around me.

Nothing moved.

I laughed a little breathlessly. Silly me!

Being so tense was making all the scary movies I'd ever seen pop into my head. I was thinking of *Jurassic Park* and dinosaurs – maybe my thought link was that fairies were the dinosaurs of the supernatural world – and I half expected a piece of goat to fall on my windshield.

That didn't happen, either. Okay . . .

I inserted the key and turned it, and the motor turned over. I didn't blow up. There was no Tyrannosaurus in my rearview mirror.

So far, so good. I felt better once I'd begun going slowly down the driveway through the woods, but I was sure keeping my eyes busy. I felt a compulsion to get in touch with someone, to let someone know where I was and what I was doing.

I whipped my cell phone out of my purse and called Amelia. When she answered, I said, 'I'm driving over to Jason's. Since Tray is so sick, Jason's going around with me today. Listen, you know Tray was spelled by a fairy into drinking rotten vampire blood?'

'I'm at work here,' Amelia said, caution in her voice. 'Yes, he called ten minutes ago, but he had to go throw up. Poor Tray. At least the house was okay.'

Amelia's point was that her wards had held. Well, she had a right to be proud of that.

'You're great,' I said.

'Thanks. Listen, I'm really worried about Tray. I tried calling him back after a few minutes, but he didn't answer. I hope he's just sleeping it off, but I'm going over there after I leave work. Why don't you meet me there? We can figure out what to do about getting you some more security.'

'Okay,' I said. 'I'll come over right after I get off work, probably around five.' Phone in my hand, I jumped out and grabbed the mail from my mailbox, which sat up on Hummingbird Road. Then I got back in my car quick as I could.

That had been stupid. I could have gone without checking the mail for one day. Habits are very hard to break, even when they're unimportant habits. 'I really am lucky you live with me, Amelia,' I said.

That might have been spreading it on a little thick, but it was the absolute truth.

But Amelia had gone off on another mental path. 'You're speaking to Jason again? You told him? About *things?*'

'Yeah, I had to. Great-grandfather can't have everything his own way. Stuff has happened.'

'It always does, around you,' Amelia said. She didn't sound angry, and she wasn't condemning me.

'Not always,' I said after a sharp moment of doubt. *In fact*, I thought, as I turned left at the end of Hummingbird Road to go to my brother's, *that point Jason made about everything changing when the vamps came out ... that just might have been something I really agree with.*

Prosaically, I realized my car was almost out of gas. I had to pull into Grabbit Quik. While I was pumping the liquid gold into my car, I fell back to puzzling over what Jason had told me. What would be urgent enough to bring a reclusive and human-hating half fairy to Jason's door? Why would he tell Jason ...? I shouldn't be thinking about this.

This was stupid, and I should be watching out for myself instead of trying to solve Jason's problems.

But after a few more seconds of turning the conversation over in my head, I began to have a sneaking suspicion that I understood it a little better.

I called Calvin. At first he didn't get what I was saying, but then he agreed to meet me at Jason's house.

I caught a glimpse of Jason in the backyard when I pulled into the circular driveway of the neat, small house my dad had built when he and my mother were first married. It was out in the country, out farther west than Arlene's trailer, and though it was visible from the road, it had a pond and several acres lying behind it. My dad had loved to hunt and fish, and my brother did, too. Jason had recently put in a makeshift range, and I could hear the rifle.

I decided to come through the house, and I took care to yell when I was at the back door.

'Hey!' Jason called back. He had a 30–30 in his hands. It had been our father's. Mel was standing behind him, holding a box of ammo. 'We decided we better get in some practice.'

'Good idea. I wanted to be sure you didn't think I was your crazy caller, come back to yell some more.'

Jason laughed. 'I still don't understand what good Dermot thought he'd do, coming up to the front door like that.'

'I think I do,' I said.

Jason held out his hand without looking, and Mel gave him some bullets. Jason opened the rifle and began loading. I looked over at the sawhorse he'd set up, noted all the empty milk jugs lying on the ground. He'd filled them with water so they'd sit steady, and thanks to the bullet holes, the water was flowing out onto the ground.

'Good shooting,' I said. I took a deep breath. 'Hey, Mel, you want to tell me about Hotshot funerals? I haven't ever been to one, and Crystal's will take place as soon as the body comes back, I reckon.'

Mel looked a little surprised. 'You know I haven't lived out there for years,' he protested. 'It's just not for me.' Except for the fading bruises, he didn't look like he'd been thrown across the room by anyone, much less a crazed half fairy.

'I wonder why that guy threw you around instead of Jason,' I said, and felt Mel's thoughts ripple with fear. 'Are you hurt?'

He moved his right shoulder a little. 'I thought I'd broken something. But I guess it's just going to be sore. I wonder what he was. Not one of us.'

He hadn't answered my question, I noticed.

Jason looked proud that he hadn't blabbed.

'He's not entirely human,' I said.

Mel looked relieved. 'Well, that's good to know,' he said. 'My pride was pretty much shot to hell when he threw me around. I mean, I'm a full-blood panther, and it was like I was kindling or something.'

Jason laughed. 'I thought he'd come on in and kill me then, thought I was a goner. But once Mel was down, this guy just started talking to me. Mel was playing possum, and here's this fella looks a lot like me, telling me what a favor he's done me . . .'

'It was weird,' Mel agreed, but he looked uncomfortable. 'You know I'd've been on my feet if he'd started punching on you, but he really rang my bell, and I figured I might as well stay down once it looked like he wasn't going to go after you.'

'Mel, I hope you're really okay.' I made my voice concerned, and I moved a little closer. 'Let me have a look at that shoulder.' I extended my hand, and Jason's eyebrows knit together.

'Why do you need to . . .?' An awful suspicion was creeping over his face. Without another word, he stepped behind his friend and held him firm, his hands gripping Mel on either side right below Mel's shoulders. Mel winced with pain, but he didn't say anything, not a word; he didn't even pretend to be indignant or surprised, and that was almost enough.

I put a hand on either side of Mel's face, and I closed my eyes, and I looked in his head. And this time Mel was thinking about Crystal, not Jason.

'He did it,' I said. I opened my eyes and looked at my brother's face across Mel's shoulder. I nodded.

Jason screamed, and it wasn't a human sound. Mel's face seemed to melt, as if all the muscles and bones had shifted. He hardly looked human at all.

'Let me look at you,' Mel pleaded.

Jason looked confused, since Mel *was* looking at me; he couldn't look anywhere else, the way Jason was holding him. Mel wasn't struggling, but I could see every muscle under his skin standing out, and I didn't think he'd be passive forever. I bent down and picked up the rifle, glad Jason had reloaded it.

'He wants to look at you, not me,' I told my brother.

'Goddammit,' Jason said. His breathing was heavy and ragged as if he'd been running, and his eyes were wide. 'You have to tell me *why*.'

I stepped back and raised the rifle. At this distance, even I couldn't miss. 'Turn him around, since he wants to talk to you face-to-face.'

They were in profile to me when Jason spun Mel around. Jason's grip refastened on the werepanther, but now Jason's face was a foot from Mel's.

Calvin walked around the house. Crystal's sister, Dawn, was with him. There was also a boy of about fifteen trailing along. I remembered meeting the boy at the wedding. He was Jacky, Crystal's oldest first cousin. Adolescents practically reek of emotion and confusion, and Jacky was no exception. He was struggling to conceal the fact that he was both nervous and excited. Maintaining a cool demeanor was just killing him.

The three newcomers took in the scene. Calvin shook his head, his face solemn. 'This is a bad day,' he said quietly, and Mel jerked at the sound of his leader's voice.

Some of the tension leaked out of Jason when he saw the other werepanthers.

'Sookie says he did it,' he said to Calvin.

'That's good enough for me,' Calvin said. 'But, Mel – you should tell us yourself, brother.'

'I'm not your brother,' Mel said bitterly. 'I haven't lived with you for years.'

'That was your own choice,' Calvin said. He walked around so he could see Mel's face, and the other two followed him. Jacky was snarling; any pretense at being cool had vanished. The animal was showing through.

'There isn't anyone else in Hotshot like me. I would have been alone.'

Jason looked blank. 'There are lots of guys in Hotshot like you,' he said.

'No, Jason,' I said. 'Mel's gay.'

'We're not okay with that?' my brother asked Calvin. Jason hadn't yet gotten the party line on a few issues, apparently.

'We're okay with people doing what they want to do in bed after they've done their duty to the clan,' Calvin said. 'Purebred males have to father a young 'un, no matter what.'

'I couldn't do it,' Mel said. 'I just plain couldn't do it.'

'But you were married once,' I said, and wished I hadn't spoken. This was a matter for the clan now. I hadn't called Bud Dearborn; I'd called Calvin. My word was good enough for Calvin, not for court.

'Our marriage didn't work in that department,' Mel said. His voice sounded almost normal. 'Which was okay with her. She had her own fish to fry. We never had . . . conventional sex.'

If I found this distressing, I could only imagine how hard it had been for Mel. But when I remembered what Crystal had looked like up on that cross, all my sympathy drained away in a hurry.

'Why did you do that to Crystal?' I asked. I could tell from the rage building in the brains around me that the time for talking was almost over.

Mel looked beyond me, past my brother, away from his leader, his victim's sister and cousin. He seemed to be focused on the winter-bare limbs of the trees around the still, brown pond. 'I love Jason,' he said. 'I love him. And she abused him and his child. Then she taunted me. She came here that day. . . . I'd stopped off to get Jason to help me build some shelves at the shop, but he wasn't here. She drove up while I was out in the yard writing Jason a note. She began to say . . . she said awful things. Then she told me I had to have sex with her, that if I did, she'd tell them at Hotshot and I'd be able to go back to live there, and Jason could come live with me. She said, 'His baby's inside me; doesn't that get you all hot?' And it got worse and worse. The bed of the truck was down because the wood I'd bought was sticking out, and she kind of backed up to it and lay down, and I could see her. It was . . . she was . . . she kept telling me what a pussy I was and that Jason would never care about me . . . and I slapped her as hard as I could.'

Dawn Norris turned to one side as though she was going to throw up. But she pressed her lips together in a hard line and straightened up. Jacky wasn't that tough.

'She wasn't dead, though.' My brother forced the words between his clenched teeth. 'She bled all down the cross. She lost the baby after she'd been hung up.'

'I'm sorry about that,' Mel said. His gaze returned from the pond and the trees and focused on my brother. 'I thought the blow had killed her – I really did. I would never have left her to go in the house if I'd thought she was still alive. I would never have let someone else get her. What I did was bad enough, because I intended for her to die. But I didn't crucify her. Please believe me. No matter what you think of me for hurting her, I would never have done that. I thought if I took her somewhere else, no one would think you did it. I knew you were going out that night, and I figured if I put her somewhere else, you'd have an alibi. I figured you'd end up spending the night with Michele.'

Mel smiled at Jason, and it was such a tender look that my heart ached. 'So I left her in the back of the truck, and I came in the house to have a drink. And when I came back out, she was gone. I couldn't believe it. I thought she'd gotten up and walked away. But there wasn't any blood, and the wood was gone, too.'

'Why Merlotte's?' Calvin said, and his voice came out like a growl.

'I don't know, Calvin,' Mel said. His face was almost sublime with his relief from the load of his guilt, with the release of confessing his crime and his love for my brother. 'Calvin, I know I'm about to die, and I swear to you that I have no idea what happened to Crystal after I went into the house. I did not do that horrible thing to her.'

'I don't know what to make of that,' Calvin said. 'But we have your confession, and we'll have to proceed.'

'I accept that,' Mel said. 'Jason, I love you.'

Dawn turned her head just a fraction so her eyes could meet mine. 'You better go,' she said. 'We got things to do.'

I walked off with the rifle, and I didn't turn to look even when the other panthers began to tear Mel apart. I could hear it, though.

He didn't scream after a second.

I left Jason's rifle on his back porch, and I drove to work. Somehow having a bodyguard didn't seem important anymore.

Chapter 16

As I served beers and daiquiris and vodka collinses to the people stopping by on their way home from work, I stood back and eyed myself in amazement. I'd worked for hours, serving and smiling and hustling, and I'd never broken down at all. Sure, I'd had to ask four people to repeat their orders. And I'd walked past Sam twice, and he'd said something to me to which I hadn't responded – I knew this because he'd stopped me to tell me so. But I'd gotten the right plates and drinks to the right tables, and my tips were running about average, which meant I'd been agreeable and hadn't forgotten anything crucial.

You're doing so good, I told myself. *I'm so proud of you. You just have to get through this. You can go home in fifteen minutes.*

I wondered how many women had given themselves the same lecture: the girl who'd held her head up at a dance where her date was paying attention to another classmate; the woman who'd been passed by for promotion at her job; the woman who had listened to a dire diagnosis and yet kept her face together. I knew men must have days like this, too.

Well, maybe not too many people had days *exactly* like this.

Naturally, I'd been turning over in my head Mel's strange insistence that he was not responsible for Crystal's crucifixion, during which she'd actually died. His thoughts had had the ring of truth. And really, there was no reason why he would've balked at confessing everything when he'd already confessed so much, found peace doing so. Why would someone steal the half-dead Crystal and the wood, and do a deed so disgusting? It would've had to have been someone who'd hated Crystal an awful lot, or maybe someone who had hated Mel or Jason. It was an inhuman act, yet I found myself believing in Mel's dying assertion that he had not done it.

I was so glad to leave work that I began driving home on automatic pilot. When I'd gotten almost to the turnoff into my driveway, I remembered that I'd told Amelia hours before that I'd meet her at Tray's house.

I'd completely forgotten.

I could forgive myself, considering the day I'd had – if Amelia was okay. But when I remembered Tray's mean state and his ingestion of vampire blood, I felt a jolt of panic.

I looked at my watch and saw I was more than forty-five minutes late. Turning around in the next driveway, I drove back to town like a bat out of hell. I was trying to pretend to myself I wasn't scared. I wasn't doing a very good job.

There weren't any cars in front of the small house. Its windows were dark. I could see the bumper of Tray's truck peering out from the carport behind the house.

I drove right by and turned around on a county road about half a mile farther out. Confused and worried, I returned to park outside Tray's. His house and the adjacent workshop were outside the Bon Temps city limits but not isolated. Tray had maybe a half-acre lot; his little home and the large metal building housing his repair business were right next to a similar setup owned by Brock and Chessie Johnson, who had an upholstery shop. Obviously, Brock and Chessie had retreated to their house for the night. The living room lights were on; as I watched, Chessie pulled the curtains shut, which most people out here didn't bother to do.

The night was dark and quiet; the Johnsons' dog was barking, but that was the only sound. It was too cold for the chorus of bugs that often made the night come alive.

I thought of several scenarios that could explain the dead look of the house.

One. The vampire blood still had hold over Tray, and he'd killed Amelia. Right now, he was in his house, in the dark, thinking of ways to kill himself. Or maybe he was waiting for me to come, so he could kill me, too.

Two. Tray had recovered from his ingestion of vamp blood, and when Amelia had appeared on his doorstep, they'd decided to treat their free afternoon as a honeymoon. They wouldn't be at all happy if I interrupted them.

Three. Amelia had come by, found no one at home, and was now back at the house cooking supper for herself and me, because she expected me to drive up at any moment. At least that explanation accounted for the absence of Amelia's car.

I tried to think of an even better series of events, but I couldn't. I pulled out my cell phone and tried my home number. I heard my own voice on the answering machine. Next, I tried Amelia's cell. It went to voice mail after three rings. I was running out of happy options. Figuring that a phone call would be less intrusive than a knock at the door, I tried Tray's number next. I could hear the faint ring of the phone inside . . . but no one answered it.

I called Bill. I didn't think about it for more than a second. I just did it.

'Bill Compton,' said the familiar cool voice.

'Bill,' I said, and then couldn't finish.

'Where are you?'

'I'm sitting in my car outside of Tray Dawson's house.'

'The Were who owns the motorcycle repair shop.'

'Right.'

'I'm coming.'

He was there in less than ten minutes. His car pulled up behind mine. I was pulled over on the shoulder, because I hadn't wanted to drive up onto the gravel in front of the house.

'I'm weak,' I said, when he got in beside me. 'I shouldn't have called you. But I swear to God, I didn't know what else to do.'

'You didn't call Eric.' It was a simple observation.

'Take too long,' I said. I told him what I'd done. 'I can't believe I forgot Amelia,' I said, stricken by my self-centeredness.

'I think forgetting one thing after such a day is actually permissible, Sookie,' Bill said.

'No, it isn't,' I said. 'It's just that . . . I can't go in there and find them dead. I just can't do it. My courage has just collapsed.'

He leaned over and kissed me on the cheek. 'What's one more dead person to me?' he said. And then he was out of the car and moving silently in the faint light peeking around the curtains of the house next door. He got to the front door, listened intently. He didn't hear anything, I knew, because he opened the door and stepped inside.

Just as he vanished, my cell phone rang. I jumped so hard I almost hit my head on the roof. I dropped the phone and had to grope for it.

'Hello?' I said, full of fear.

'Hey, did you call? I was in the shower,' Amelia said, and I collapsed over the steering wheel, thinking, *Thank you God thank you God thank you thank you.*

'You okay?' Amelia asked.

'Yes,' I said. 'I'm okay. Where is Tray? Is he there with you?'

'Nope. I went to his house, but he wasn't there. I waited a while for you, but you didn't show, so I figured he'd gone to the doctor, and I decided you must have been held up at work or something. I went back to the insurance agency, and I just got home about thirty minutes ago. What's up?'

'I'll be there soon,' I said. 'Lock the doors and don't let anyone in.'

'Doors are locked; no one's knocking,' she said.

'Don't let me in,' I said, 'unless I give you the password.'

'Sure, Sookie,' she said, and I could tell she thought I'd gone over the edge. 'What's the password?'

'Fairypants,' I said, and how I came up with that I have no idea. It simply seemed super unlikely that anyone else in the world would say it.

'I got it,' Amelia said. 'Fairypants.'

Bill was back at the car. 'I've got to go,' I said, and hung up. When he opened the door, the dome light showed his face. It looked grim.

'He's not there,' he said immediately. 'But there's been a fight.'

'Blood?'

'Yes.'

'Lots?'

'He could still be alive. From the way it smelled, I don't think it was all his.'

My shoulders slumped. 'I don't know what to do,' I confessed, and it felt almost good to say it out loud. 'I don't know where to go to find him or how to help him. He's supposed to be working as my bodyguard. But he went out in the woods last night and met up with a woman who said she was your new girlfriend. She gave him a drink. It was bad vampire blood, and it made him sick as the flu.' I looked over at Bill. 'Maybe she got it from Bubba. I haven't seen him to ask. I'm kind of worried about him.' I knew Bill could see me far more clearly than I could see him. I spread my hands in query. Did he know this woman?

Bill looked at me. His mouth curved up in a rather bitter little smile. 'I'm not dating anyone,' he said.

I decided to completely ignore the emotional slant. I didn't have the time or the energy tonight. I'd been right when I'd discounted the mysterious woman's identity. 'So this was someone who could pretend to be a fangbanger, someone convincing enough to overcome Tray's good sense, someone who could put him under a spell so he'd drink the blood.'

'Bubba doesn't have much good sense at all,' Bill said. 'Even though some fairy magic doesn't work on vampires, I don't think he'd be hard to bespell.'

'Have you seen him tonight?'

'He came over to my place to put drinks in his cooler, but he seemed weak and disoriented. After he drank a couple of bottles of TrueBlood, he seemed to be better. The last I saw of him, he was walking across the cemetery toward your house.'

'I guess we better go there next.'

'I'll follow you.' Bill went to his own car, and we set off to drive the short distance to my place. But Bill caught the light at the intersection of the highway and Hummingbird Road, and I was ahead of him by quite a few seconds. I pulled up in back of the house, which was well-lit. Amelia had never worried about an electric bill in her life; it just made me want to cry sometimes when I followed her around turning off switch after switch.

I got out of the car and hurried for the back steps, all ready to say, 'Fairypants!' when Amelia came to the door. Bill would be there in less than a minute, and we could make a plan on how to find Tray. When Bill got there, he'd check on Bubba; I couldn't go out in the woods. I was proud of myself for not rushing into the trees to find the vampire.

I had so much to think about that I didn't think about the most obvious danger.

There's no excuse for my lack of attention to detail.

A woman by herself always has to be alert, and a woman who's had the experiences I've had has extra cause for alarm when blips are on her radar. The security light was still on at the house and and the backyard looked normal, it was true. I had even glimpsed Amelia in the kitchen through a window. I hurried to the back steps, my purse slung over my shoulder, my trowel and water guns inside it, my keys in my hand.

But anything can be hiding in the shadows, and it takes only a moment's inattention for a trap to spring.

I heard a few words in a language I didn't recognize, but for a second I thought, *He's mumbling*, and I couldn't imagine what a man behind me would be mumbling, and I was about to put my foot on the first step to the back porch.

And then I didn't know a thing.

Chapter 17

I thought I was in a cave. It felt like a cave: cool, damp. And the sound was funny.

My thoughts were anything but speedy. However, the sense of wrongness rose to the top of my consciousness with a kind of dismaying certainty. I was not where I was supposed to be, and I shouldn't be wherever I was. At the moment, these seemed like two separate and distinct thoughts.

Someone had bopped me on the head.

I thought about that. My head didn't feel sore, exactly: it felt thick, as if I had a bad cold and had taken a serious decongestant on top of that. So, I concluded (with all the speed of a turtle), I had been knocked out magically rather than physically. The result was about the same. I felt like hell, and I was scared to open my eyes. At the same time, I very much wanted to know who was in this space with me. I braced myself and made my eyelids open. I caught a glimpse of a lovely and indifferent face, and then my eyelids clamped shut again. They seemed to be operating on their own timetable.

'She's joining us,' said someone.

'Good; we can have some fun,' said another voice.

That didn't sound promising at all. I didn't think the fun was going to be anything I could enjoy, too.

I figured I could get rescued anytime now, and that would be just fine.

But the cavalry didn't ride in. I sighed and forced my eyes open again. This time the lids stayed apart, and by the light of a torch – a real, honest-to-God flaming wood torch – I examined my captors. One was a male fairy. He was as lovely as Claudine's brother Claude and just about as charming – which is to say, not at all. He had black hair, like Claude's, and handsome features and a buff body, like Claude's. But his face couldn't even simulate interest in me. Claude was at least able to fake it when circumstances required that.

I looked at Kidnapper Number Two. She hardly seemed more promising. She was a fairy, too, and therefore lovely, but she didn't appear to be any more lighthearted or fun-loving than her companion. Plus, she was wearing a body stocking, or something very like one, and she looked good in it, which in and of itself was enough to make me hate her.

'We have the right woman,' Two said. 'The vampire-loving whore. I think the one with short hair was a bit more attractive.'

'As if any human can truly be lovely,' said One.

It wasn't enough to be kidnapped; I had to be insulted, too. Though their words were the last thing in the world I needed to be worrying about, a little spark of anger lit in my chest. *Just keep that up, asshole,* I thought. *You just wait till my great-grandfather gets ahold of you.*

I hoped they hadn't hurt Amelia or Bubba.

I hoped Bill was all right.

I hoped he'd called Eric and my great-grandfather.

That was a lot of hoping. As long as I was in the wishful-thinking zone, I wished that Eric was tuned in to my very great distress and my very real fear. Could he track me by my emotions? That would be wonderful, because I was certainly full of them. This was the worst fix I'd ever been in. Years ago, when Bill and I had exchanged blood, he'd told me he'd be able to find me. I hoped he'd been telling the truth, and I hoped that ability hadn't faded with time. I was willing to be saved by just about anybody. Soon.

Kidnapper One slid his hands under my armpits and yanked me to a sitting position. For the first time, I realized my hands were numb. I looked down to see they were tied with a strip of leather. Now I was propped up against a wall, and I could see I was not actually in a cave.

We were in an abandoned house. There was a hole in the roof, and I could see stars through it. The smell of mildew was strong, almost choking, and under it trailed the scents of rotting wood and wallpaper. There was nothing in the room but my purse, which had been tossed into a corner, and an old framed photograph, which hung crookedly on the wall behind the two fairies. The picture had been taken outside, probably in the nineteen twenties or thirties, and it was of a black family dressed up for their picture-taking adventure. They looked like a farming family. At least I was still in my own world, I figured, though probably not for long.

While I could, I smiled at Thing One and Thing Two. 'My great-grandfather is going to kill you,' I said. I even managed to sound pretty happy about that. 'You just wait.'

One laughed, tossing his black hair behind him in a malemodelly gesture. 'He'll never find us. He'll yield and step down rather than see you killed in a slow and painful way. He *loooooves* humans.'

Two said, 'He should have gone to the Summerland long ago. Consorting with humans will kill us off even faster than we are dying already. Breandan will seal us off. We'll be safe. Niall is out of date.'

Like he'd expired on the shelves or something.

'Tell me you have a boss,' I said. 'Tell me you're not the brains of the operation.' I was sort of aware that I was seriously addled, probably as a result of the spell that had knocked me out, but knowing I wasn't myself didn't seem to stop me talking, which was a pity.

'We owe allegiance to Breandan,' One said proudly, as if that would make everything clear to me.

Instead of connecting their words with my great-grandfather's arch-enemy, I pictured the Brandon I'd gone to high school with, who'd been a running back on the football team. He'd gone to Louisiana Tech and then into the air force. 'He got out of the service?' I said.

They stared at me with a total lack of comprehension. I couldn't really fault them for that. 'Service of whom?' asked Two.

I was still blaming her for saying I was a skank, and I decided I wasn't speaking to her. 'So, what's the program?' I asked One.

'We wait to hear from Niall, who will respond to Breandan's

demands,' he said. 'Breandan will seal us all in Faery, and we will never have to deal with your like again.'

At the moment, that seemed like an excellent plan, and I was temporarily on Breandan's side.

'So Niall doesn't want that to happen?' I said, trying to keep my voice steady.

'No, he wants to visit the likes of you. While Fintan hid the knowledge of you and your brother, Niall behaved himself, but when we removed Fintan—'

'Bit by bit!' said Two, and laughed.

'He was able to find enough information to track you down. And so did we. We found your brother's house one day, and there was a gift outside in a truck. We decided to have some fun with it. We followed your scent to where you work, and we left your brother's wife and the abomination outside for all to see. Now we're going to have some fun with you. Breandan has said we can do with you what we will, short of death.'

Maybe my slow wits were speeding up a little. I understood that they were enforcers for my great-grandfather's enemy, and that they had killed my grandfather Fintan and crucified poor Crystal.

'I wouldn't, if I were you,' I said, quite desperately. 'Hurt me, that is. Because after all, what if this Breandan doesn't get what he wants? What if Niall wins?'

'In the first place, that's not likely,' Thing Two said. She smiled. 'We plan to win, and we plan to have a *lot* of fun. Especially if Niall wants to see you; surely he'll demand proof you're alive before he surrenders. We have to leave you breathing . . . but the more terrible your plight, the faster the war will be over.' She had a mouthful of the longest, sharpest teeth I'd ever seen. Some of them were capped with gleaming silver points. It was a ghastly touch.

At the sight of those teeth, those awful shining teeth, I threw off the remnants of the magic they'd laid on me, which was a great pity.

I was completely and utterly lucid for the next hour, which was the longest of my life.

I found it bewildering – and utterly shocking – that I could feel such pain and not die of it.

I would have been glad to die.

I know a lot about humans, since I see into their minds every day, but I didn't know a lot about fairy culture. I had to believe Thing One and Thing Two were in a league of their own. I couldn't imagine that my great-grandfather would have laughed when I began to bleed. And I had to hope that he wouldn't enjoy cutting a human with a knife, either, as One and Two did.

I'd read books where a person being tortured went 'somewhere else' during the ordeal. I did my best to find somewhere else to go mentally, but I remained right there in the room. I focused on the strong faces of the farming family in the photograph, and I wished it wasn't so dusty so I could see them clearly. I wished the picture was straight. I just knew that good family would have been horrifed at what they were witnessing now.

At moments when the fairy duo wasn't hurting me, it was very hard to believe I was awake and that this was really happening. I kept hoping I was suffering through a particularly horrible dream, and I would wake from it . . . sooner, rather than later. I'd known from a very early age that there was cruelty in the world – believe me, I'd learned that – but I was still shocked that the Things were *enjoying themselves*. I had no personhood to them – no identity. They were completely indifferent to the plans I'd had for my life, the pleasures I'd hoped to enjoy. I might have been a stray puppy or a frog they'd caught by the creek.

I myself would have thought doing these things to a puppy or a frog was horrible.

'Isn't this the daughter of the ones we killed?' One asked Two while I was screaming.

'Yes. They tried to drive through water during a flood,' Two said in a tone of happy reminiscence. 'Water! When the man had sky blood! They thought the iron can would protect them.'

'The water spirits were glad to pull them under,' One said.

My parents hadn't died in an accident. They'd been murdered. Even through my pain, I registered that, though at the moment it was beyond me to form a feeling about the knowledge.

I tried to talk to Eric in my head in the hope he could find me through our bond. I thought of the only other adult telepath I knew,

Barry, and I sent him messages – though I knew damn good and well that we were too far away from each other to transmit our thoughts. To my everlasting shame, toward the end of that hour I even considered trying to contact my little cousin Hunter. I knew, though, that not only was Hunter too young to understand, but also . . . I really couldn't do that to a child.

I gave up hope, and I waited for death.

While they were having sex, I thought of Sam and how happy it would make me if I could see him now. I wanted to say the name of someone who loved me, but my throat was too hoarse from screaming.

I thought about vengeance. I wanted One and Two to die with a craving that burned through my gut. I hoped someone, any one of my supe friends – Claude and Claudine, Niall, Alcide, Bill, Quinn, Tray, Pam, Eric, Calvin, Jason – would tear these two limb from limb. Perhaps the other fairies could take the same length of time with them that they were taking with me.

One and Two had said that Breandan wanted them to spare me, but it didn't take a telepath to realize they weren't going to be capable of holding off. They were going to get carried away with their fun, as they had with Fintan and Crystal, and there would be no repairing me.

I became sure I was going to die.

I began to hallucinate. I thought I saw Bill, which made no sense at all. He was in my backyard probably, wondering where I was. He was back in the world that *made sense*. But I could swear I saw him creeping up behind the creatures, who were enjoying working with a pair of razor blades. He had his finger over his mouth as if he were telling me to keep silent. Since he wasn't there, and my throat was too raw to speak anyway (I couldn't even produce a decent scream anymore), that was easy. There was a black shadow following him, a shadow topped with a pale flame.

Two jabbed me with a sharp knife she'd just pulled from her boot, a knife that shone like her teeth. They both leaned close to me to drink in my reaction. I could only make a raspy noise. My face was crusted with tears and blood.

'Little froggy croaking,' One said.

'Listen to her. Croak, froggy. Croak for us.'

I opened my eyes and looked into hers, meeting them squarely for the first time in many long minutes. I swallowed and summoned up all my remaining strength.

'You're going to die,' I said with absolute certainty. But I'd said it before, and they didn't pay any more attention now than they had the first time.

I made my lips move up in a smile.

The male had just enough time to look startled before something gleaming flashed between his head and his shoulders. Then, to my intense pleasure, he was in two pieces and I was covered in a wash of fresh red blood. It ran over me, drenching the blood already dried on my skin. But my eyes were clear, so I could see a white hand gripped Two's neck, lifting her, spinning her around, and her shock was intensely gratifying as teeth almost as sharp as her own ripped into her long neck.

Chapter 18

I wasn't in a hospital.

But I was in a bed, not my own. And I was a little cleaner than I had been, and bandaged, and in a lot of pain; in fact, a dreadful amount of pain. The part where I was cleaner and bandaged – oh, a wholly desirable state. The other part, the pain – well, that was expected, understandable, and finite. At least no one was trying to hurt me any worse than I'd already been hurt. So I decided I was excellent.

I had a few holes in my memory. I couldn't remember what had happened between being in the decrepit shack and being here; I could recall flashes of action, the sound of voices, but I had no coherent narrative to connect them. I remembered One's head becoming detached, and I knew someone had bitten Two. I hoped she was as dead as One. But I wasn't sure. Had I really seen Bill? What about the shadow behind him?

I heard a *click, click, click.* I turned my head very slightly. Claudine, my fairy godmother, was sitting by the bed, knitting.

The sight of Claudine knitting was just as surrealistic as the sight of Bill appearing in the cave. I decided to go back to sleep – a cowardly retreat, but I thought I was entitled.

'She's going to be all right,' Dr Ludwig said. Her head came up past the side of my bed, which told me for sure that I wasn't in a modern hospital bed.

Dr Ludwig takes care of the cases who can't go to the regular human hospital because the staff would flee screaming at the sight of them or the lab wouldn't be able to analyze their blood. I could see Dr Ludwig's coarse brown hair as she walked around the bed to the door. Dr Ludwig had a deep voice. I suspected she was a hobbit – not really, but she sure did look like one. Though she wore shoes, right? I spent some moments trying to remember if I'd ever caught a glimpse of Dr Ludwig's feet.

'Sookie,' she said, her eyes appearing at my elbow. 'Is the medicine working?'

I didn't know if this was a second visit of hers, or if I'd blanked out for a few moments. 'I'm not hurting as much,' I said, and my voice was very rough and whispery. 'I'm starting to feel a little numb. That's just . . . excellent.'

She nodded. 'Yes,' she said. 'Considering you're human, you're very lucky.'

Funny. I felt better than when I'd been in the shack, but I couldn't say I felt lucky. I tried to scrape together some appreciation of my good fortune. There wasn't any there to gather up. I was all out. My emotions were as crippled as my body.

'No,' I said. I tried to shake my head, but even the painkillers couldn't disguise the fact that my neck was too sore to twist. They'd choked me repeatedly.

'You're not dead,' Dr Ludwig pointed out.

But I'd come pretty damn close; I'd sort of stepped over the line. There'd been an optimum rescue time. If I'd been liberated before that time, I would have laughed all the way to the secret supernatural clinic, or wherever I was. But I'd looked at death too closely – close enough to see all the pores in Death's face – and I'd suffered too much. I wouldn't bounce back this time.

My emotional and physical state had been sliced and gouged and pinched and bitten to a rough, raw surface. I didn't know if I could spackle myself back into my pre-kidnap smoothness. I said this, in much simpler words, to Dr Ludwig.

'They're dead, if that helps,' she said.

Yes indeedy, that helped quite a bit. I'd been hoping I hadn't imagined that part; I'd been a little afraid their deaths had been a delightful fantasy.

'Your great-grandfather beheaded Lochlan,' she said. So he'd been One. 'And the vampire Bill Compton tore the throat out of Lochlan's sister, Neave.' She'd been Two.

'Where's Niall now?' I said.

'Waging war,' she said grimly. 'There's no more negotiation, no more jockeying for advantage. There's only killing now.'

'Bill?'

'He was badly hurt,' the little doctor said. 'She got him with her blade before she bled to death. And she bit him back. There was silver in her knife and silver caps on her teeth. It's in his system.'

'He'll get better,' I said.

She shrugged.

I thought my heart was going to plunge down out of my chest, through the bed. I could not look this misery in the face.

I struggled to think of something besides Bill. 'And Tray? He's here?'

She regarded me silently for a moment. 'Yes,' she said finally.

'I need to see him. And Bill.'

'No. You can't move. Bill's in his daytime sleep for now. Eric is coming tonight, actually in a couple of hours, and he'll bring at least one other vampire with him. That'll help. The Were is too badly wounded for you to disturb.'

I didn't absorb that. My mind was racing ahead. It was a mighty slow race, but I was thinking a little more clearly. 'Has someone told Sam, do you know?' How long had I been out? How much work had I missed?

Dr Ludwig shrugged. 'I don't know. I imagine so. He seems to hear everything.'

'Good.' I tried to shift positions, gasped. 'I'm going to have to get up to use the bathroom,' I warned her.

'Claudine,' Dr Ludwig said, and my cousin put away her knitting and rose from the rocking chair. For the first time, I registered that my beautiful fairy godmother looked like someone had tried to push her through a wood chipper. Her arms were bare and covered with scratches, scrapes, and cuts. Her face was a mess. She smiled at me, but it was painful.

When she lifted me in her arms, I could feel her effort. Normally Claudine could heft a large calf without any trouble if she chose to.

'I'm sorry,' I said. 'I can walk. I'm sure.'

'Don't think of it,' Claudine said. 'See, we're already there.'

When our mission was accomplished, she scooped me up and took me back to bed.

'What happened to you?' I asked her. Dr Ludwig had departed without another word.

'I got ambushed,' she said in her sweet voice. 'Some stupid brownies and one fairy. Lee, his name was.'

'I guess they were allied with this Breandan?'

She nodded, fished out her bundle of knitting. The item she was working on appeared to be a tiny sweater. I wondered if it was for an elf. 'They were,' she said. 'They are bits of bone and flesh now.' She sounded quite pleased.

Claudine would never become an angel at this rate. I wasn't quite sure how the progression worked, but reducing other beings to their component parts was probably not the route of choice. 'Good,' I said. The more of Breandan's followers who met their match, the better. 'Have you seen Bill?'

'No,' Claudine said, clearly not interested.

'Where is Claude?' I asked. 'Is he safe?'

'He's with Grandfather,' she said, and for the first time, she looked worried. 'They're trying to find Breandan. Grandfather figures that if he takes out the source, Breandan's followers will have no choice but to stop the war and pledge an oath to him.'

'Oh,' I said. 'And you didn't go, because . . .?'

'I'm guarding you,' she said simply. 'And lest you think I chose the path of least danger, I'm sure Breandan is trying to find this place. He must be very angry. He's had to enter the human world, which he hates so much, now that his pet killers are dead. He loved Neave and Lochlan. They were with him for centuries, and both his lovers.'

'Yuck,' I said from the heart, or maybe from the pit of my stomach.

'Oh, *yuck*.' I couldn't even think about what kind of 'love' they would make. What I'd seen hadn't looked like love. 'And I would never accuse you of taking the path of least danger,' I said after I'd gotten over being nauseated. 'This whole world is dangerous.' Claudine gave me a sharp look. 'What kind of name is Breandan?' I asked after a moment of watching her knitting needles flash with great speed and panache. I wasn't sure how the fuzzy green sweater would turn out, but the effect was good.

'Irish,' she said. 'All the oldest ones in this part of the world are Irish. Claude and I used to have Irish names. It seemed stupid to me. Why shouldn't we please ourselves? No one can spell those names or pronounce them correctly. My former name sounds like a cat coughing up a fur ball.'

We sat in silence for a few minutes.

'Who's the little sweater for? Are you going to have a bundle of joy?' I asked in my wheezy, whispery new voice. I was trying to sound teasing, but instead, I just sounded creepy.

'Yes,' she said, raising her head to look at me. Her eyes were glowing. 'I'm going to have a baby. A pure fairy child.'

I was startled, but I tried to cover that with the biggest smile I could paste on my face. 'Oh. That's great!' I said. I wondered if it would be tacky to inquire as to the identity of the father. Probably.

'Yes,' she said seriously. 'It's wonderful. We're not really a very fertile race, and the huge amount of iron in the world has reduced our birthrate. Our numbers decline every century. I am very lucky. It's one of the reasons I never take humans to bed, though from time to time I would love to; they are so delicious, some of them. But I'd hate to waste a fertile cycle on a human.'

I'd always assumed it was her desired ascension to angel status that had kept Claudine from bedding any of her numerous admirers. 'So, the dad's a fairy,' I said, kind of pussyfooting around the topic of the paternal identity. 'Did you date for a while?'

Claudine laughed. 'I knew it was my fertile time. I knew he was a fertile male; we were not too closely related. We found each other desirable.'

'Will he help you raise the baby?'

'Oh, yes, he'll be there to guard her during her early years.'

'Can I meet him?' I asked. I was really delighted at Claudine's happiness, in an oddly remote way.

'Of course – if we win this war and passage between the worlds is still possible. He stays mostly in Faery,' Claudine said. 'He is not much for human companionship.' She said this in much the same way she would say he was allergic to cats. 'If Breandan has his way, Faery will be sealed off, and all we have built in this world will be gone. The wonderful things that humans have invented that we can use, the money we made to fund those inventions . . . that'll all be gone. It's so intoxicating being with humans. They give off so much energy, so much delicious emotion. They're simply . . . fun.'

This new topic was a fine distraction, but my throat hurt, and when I couldn't respond, Claudine lost interest in talking. Though she returned to her knitting, I was alarmed to notice that after a few minutes she became increasingly tense and alert. I heard noises in the hall, as if people were moving around the building in a hurry. Claudine got up and went over to the room's narrow door to look out. After the third time she did this, she shut the door and she locked it. I asked her what she was expecting.

'Trouble,' she said. 'And Eric.'

One and the same, I thought. 'Are there other patients here? Is this, like, a hospital?'

'Yes,' she said. 'But Ludwig and her aide are evacuating the patients who can walk.'

I'd assumed I'd had as much fear as I could handle, but my exhausted emotions began to revive as I absorbed some of her tension.

About thirty minutes later, she raised her head and I could tell she was listening. 'Eric is coming,' she said. 'I'll have to leave you with him. I can't cover my scent like Grandfather can.' She rose and unlocked the door. She swung it open.

Eric came in very quietly; one moment I was looking at the door, and the next minute, he filled it. Claudine gathered up her paraphernalia and left the room, keeping as far from Eric as the room permitted. His nostrils flared at the delicious scent of fairy. Then she was gone, and Eric was by the bed, looking down at me. I didn't feel happy or content, so I knew that even the bond was exhausted, at least temporarily. My face hurt so much when I changed expressions that I knew it was covered with bruises and cuts. The vision in my left eye was awfully blurry. I didn't need a mirror to tell me how terrible I looked. At the moment, I simply couldn't care.

Eric tried hard to keep the rage from his face, but it didn't work.

'Fucking *fairies*,' he said, and his lip curled in a snarl.

I couldn't remember hearing Eric curse before.

'Dead now,' I whispered, trying to keep my words to a minimum.

'Yes. A fast death was too good for them.'

I nodded (as much as I could) in wholehearted agreement. In fact, it would almost be worth bringing them back to life just to kill them again more slowly.

'I'm going to look at your wounds,' Eric said. He didn't want to startle me.

'Okay,' I whispered, but I knew the sight would be pretty gross. What I'd seen when I pulled up my gown in the bathroom had looked so awful I hadn't had any desire to examine myself further.

With a clinical neatness, Eric folded down the sheets and the blanket. I was wearing a classic hospital gown – you'd think a hospital for supes would come up with something more exotic – and of course, it was scooted up above my knees. There were bite marks all over my legs – deep bite marks. Some of the flesh was missing. Looking at my legs made me think of Shark Week on the Discovery Channel.

Ludwig had bandaged the worst ones, and I was sure there were stitches under the white gauze. Eric stood absolutely still for a long moment. 'Pull up the gown,' he said, but when he realized that my hands and arms were too weak to cooperate, he did it.

They'd enjoyed the soft spots the most, so this was really unpleasant, actually disgusting. I couldn't look after one quick glance. I kept my eyes shut, like a child who's wandered into a horror film. No wonder the pain was so bad. I would never be the same person again, physically or mentally.

After a long time, Eric covered me and said, 'I'll be back in a minute,' and I heard him leave the room. He was back quickly with a couple of bottles of TrueBlood. He put them on the floor by the bed.

'Move over,' he said, and I glanced up at him, confused. 'Move over,' he said again with impatience. Then he realized I couldn't, and he put an arm behind my back and another under my knees and shifted me easily to the other side of the bed. Fortunately, it was much larger than a real hospital bed, and I didn't have to turn on my side to make room for him.

Eric said, 'I'm going to feed you.'

'What?'

'I'm going to give you blood. You'll take weeks to heal otherwise. We don't have that kind of time.'

He sounded so briskly matter-of-fact that I felt my shoulders finally relax. I hadn't realized how tightly wound I'd been. Eric bit into his wrist and put it in front of my mouth. 'Here,' he said, as if there was no question I'd take it.

He slid his free arm under my neck to raise my head. This was not going to be fun or erotic, like a nip during sex. And for a moment I wondered at my own unquestioning acquiescence. But he'd said we didn't have time. On one level I knew what that meant, but on another I was too weak to do more than consider the time factor as a fleeting and nearly irrelevant fact.

I opened my mouth and swallowed. I was in so much pain and I was so appalled by the damage done to my body that I didn't think more than once about the wisdom of what I was doing. I knew how quick the effects of ingesting vampire blood would be. His wrist healed once, and he reopened it.

'Are you sure you should do this?' I asked as he bit himself for the second time. My throat rippled with pain, and I regretted trying a whole sentence.

'Yes,' he said. 'I know how much is too much. And I fed well before I came here. You need to be able to move.' He was behaving in such a practical way that I began to feel a little better. I couldn't have stood pity.

'Move?' The idea filled me with anxiety.

'Yes. At any moment, Breandan's followers may – will – find this place. They'll be tracking you by scent now. You smell of the fairies who hurt you, and they know now Niall loves you enough to kill his own kind for you. Hunting you down would make them very, very happy.'

At the thought of any more trouble, I stopped drinking and began crying. Eric's hand stroked my face gently, but he said, 'Stop that now. You must be strong. I'm very proud of you, you hear me?'

'Why?' I put my mouth on his wrist and drank again.

'You are still together; you are still a person. Lochlan and Neave have left vampires and fairies in rags – literally, rags . . . but you survived and your personality and soul are intact.'

'I got rescued.' I took a deep breath and bent back to his wrist.

'You would have survived much more.' Eric leaned over to get the bottle of TrueBlood, and he drank it down quickly.

'I wouldn't have wanted to.' I took another deep breath, aware that my throat was aching still but not as sharply. 'I hardly wanted to live after . . .'

He kissed my forehead. 'But you did live. And they died. And you are mine, and you will be mine. They will not get you.'

'You really think they're coming?'

'Yes. Breandan's remaining forces will find this place sooner or later, if not Breandan himself. He has nothing to lose, and his pride to retain. I'm afraid they'll find us shortly. Ludwig has removed almost all the other patients.' He turned a little, as if he were listening. 'Yes, most of them are gone.'

'Who else is here?'

'Bill is in the next room. He's been getting blood from Clancy.'

'Were you not going to give him any?'

'If you were irreparable . . . no, I would have let him rot.'

'Why?' I asked. 'He actually came to rescue me. Why get mad at him? Where were you?' Rage bubbled up my throat.

Eric flinched almost a half inch, a big reaction from a vampire his age. He looked away. I could not believe I was saying these things.

'It's not like you were obliged to come find me,' I said, 'but I hoped the whole time – I hoped you would come, I prayed you would come, I thought over and over you might hear me. . . .'

'You're killing me,' he said. 'You're killing me.' He shuddered beside me, as if he could scarcely endure my words. 'I'll explain,' he said in a muted voice. 'I will. You will understand. But now, we don't have enough time. Are you healing yet?'

I thought about it. I didn't feel as miserable as I had before the blood. The holes in my flesh were itching almost intolerably, which meant they were healing. 'I'm beginning to feel like I'll be better sometime,' I said carefully. 'Oh, is Tray Dawson still here?'

He looked at me with a very serious expression. 'Yes; he can't be moved.'

'Why not? Why didn't Dr Ludwig take him?'

'He would not survive being moved.'

'No,' I said, shocked even after all that I'd been through.

'Bill told me about the vampire blood he ingested. They hoped he'd go crazy enough to hurt you, but his leaving you alone was good enough. Lochlan and Neave were delayed; a pair of Niall's warriors found them, attacked them, and they had to fight. Afterward, they decided to stake out your house. They wanted to be sure Dawson wouldn't come to help you. Bill called me to tell me that you and he went to Dawson's house. By that time, they already had Dawson. They had fun with him before they had . . . before they caught you.'

'Dawson's that hurt? I thought the effects of the bad vamp blood would wear off by now.' I couldn't imagine the big man, the toughest Were I knew, being defeated.

'The vampire blood they used was just a vehicle for the poison. They'd never tried it on a Were, I suppose, because it took a long time to act. And then they practiced their arts on him. Can you rise?'

I tried to gather my muscles to make the effort. 'Maybe not yet.'

'I'll carry you.'

'Where?'

'Bill wants to talk to you. You have to be brave.'

'My purse,' I said. 'I need something from it.'

Wordlessly Eric put the soft cloth purse, now spoiled and stained, on the bed beside me. With great concentration, I was able to open it and slide my hand inside. Eric raised his eyebrows when he saw what I'd pulled out of the purse, but he heard something outside that made him looked alarmed. Eric was up and sliding his arms under me, and then he straightened as easily as if I'd been a plate of spaghetti. At the door he paused, and I managed to turn the knob for him. He used his foot to push it open, and out we went into the corridor. I was able to see that we were in an old building, some kind of small business that had been converted to its present purpose. There were doors up and down the hall, and there was a glass-enclosed control room of some kind about midway down. Through the glass on its opposite side, I could see a gloomy warehouse. There were a few lights on in it, just enough to disclose that it was empty except for some discards, like dilapidated shelving and machine parts.

We turned right to enter the room at the end of the hall. Again, I performed the honors with the knob, and this time it wasn't quite as agonizing to grip the knob and turn it.

There were two beds inside this room.

Bill was in the right-hand bed, and Clancy was sitting in a plastic chair pulled up right against the side. He was feeding Bill the same way Eric had fed me. Bill's skin was gray. His cheeks had caved in. He looked like death.

Tray Dawson was in the next bed. If Bill looked like he was dying, Tray looked like he was already dead. His face was bruised blue. One of his ears had been bitten off. His eyes were swollen shut. There was crusted blood everywhere. And this was just what I could see of his face. His arms were lying on top of the sheet, and they were both splinted.

Eric laid me down beside Bill. Bill's eyes opened, and at least they were the same: dark brown, fathomless. He stopped drinking from Clancy, but he didn't move or look better.

'The silver is in his system,' Clancy said quietly. 'Its poison has traveled to every part of his body. He'll need more and more blood to drive it out.'

I wanted to say, 'Will he get better?' But I couldn't, not with Bill lying there. Clancy rose from beside the bed, and he and Eric began having a whispered conversation – a very unpleasant one, if Eric's expression was any indication.

Bill said, 'How are you, Sookie? Will you heal?' His voice faltered.

'Exactly what I want to ask you,' I said. Neither of us had the strength or energy to hedge our conversation.

'You will live,' he said, satisfied. 'I can smell that Eric has given you blood. You would have healed anyway, but that will help the scarring. I'm sorry I didn't get there faster.'

'You saved my life.'

'I saw them take you,' he said.

'What?'

'I saw them take you.'

'You . . .' I wanted to say, 'You didn't stop them?' But that seemed too horrendously cruel.

'I knew I couldn't defeat the two of them together,' he said simply. 'If I'd tried to take them on and they'd killed me, you would have been as good as dead. I know very little about fairies, but even I had heard of Neave and her brother.' These few sentences seemed to exhaust Bill. He tried to turn his head on the pillow so he could look directly into my face, but he managed to turn only an inch. His dark hair looked lank and lusterless, and his skin no longer had the shine that had seemed so beautiful to me when I'd seen it the first time.

'So you called Niall?' I asked.

'Yes,' he said, his lips barely moving. 'Or at least, I called Eric, told him what I'd seen, told him to call Niall.'

'Where was the old house?' I asked.

'North of here, in Arkansas,' he said. 'It took a while to track you. If they'd gotten in a car . . . but they moved through the fae world, and with my sense of smell and Niall's knowledge of fae magic, we were able to find you. Finally. At least your life was saved. I think it was too late for the Were.'

I hadn't known Tray was in the shack. Not that the knowledge would have made any difference, but maybe I would have felt a little less lonely.

Of course, that was probably why the two fairies hadn't let me see him. I was willing to bet there wasn't much about the psychology of torture that Neave and Lochlan hadn't known.

'Are you sure he's . . .'

'Sweetheart, look at him.'

'I haven't passed yet,' Tray mumbled.

I tried to get up, to go over to him. That was still a little out of my reach, but I turned on my side to face him. The beds were so close together that I could hear him easily. I think he could sort of see where I was.

'Tray,' I said, 'I'm so sorry.'

He shook his head wordlessly. 'My fault. I should have known . . . the woman in the woods . . . wasn't right.'

'You did your best. If you had resisted her, you would have been killed.'

'Dying now,' he said. He made himself try to open his eyes. He almost managed to look right at me. 'My own damn fault,' he said.

I couldn't stop crying. He seemed to fall unconscious. I slowly rolled over to face Bill. His color was a little better.

'I would not, for anything, have had them hurt you,' he said. 'Her dagger was silver, and she had silver caps on her teeth. . . . I managed to rip her throat out, but she didn't die fast enough. . . . She fought to the end.'

'Clancy's given you blood,' I said. 'You'll get better.'

'Maybe,' he said, and his voice was as cool and calm as it had always been. 'I'm feeling some strength now. It will get me through the fight. That will be time enough.'

I was shocked almost beyond speech. Vampires died only from staking, decapitation, or from a rare severe case of SinoAIDS. Silver poisoning?

'Bill,' I said urgently, thinking of so many things I wanted to say to him. He'd closed his eyes, but now he opened them to look at me.

'They're coming,' Eric said, and all those words died in my throat.

'Breandan's people?' I said.

'Yes,' Clancy said briefly. 'They've found your scent.' He was scornful even now, as if I'd been weak in leaving a scent to track.

Eric drew a long, long knife from a sheath on his thigh. 'Iron,' he said, smiling.

And Bill smiled, too, and it wasn't a pleasant smile. 'Kill as many as you can,' he said in a stronger voice. 'Clancy, help me up.'

'No,' I said.

'Sweetheart,' Bill said, very formally, 'I have always loved you, and I will be proud to die in your service. When I'm gone, say a prayer for me in a real church.'

Clancy bent to help Bill out of the bed, giving me a very unfriendly look while he did so. Bill swayed on his feet. He was as weak as a human. He threw off the hospital gown to stand there clad only in drawstring pajama pants.

I didn't want to die in a hospital gown, either.

'Eric, have you a knife to spare for me?' Bill asked, and without turning from the door, Eric passed Bill a shorter version of his own knife, which was halfway to being a sword, according to me. Clancy was also armed.

No one said a word about trying to shift Tray. When I glanced over at him, I thought he might have already died.

Eric's cell phone rang, which made me jump a couple of inches. He answered it with a curt, 'Yes?' He listened and then clicked it shut. I almost laughed, the idea of the supes communicating by cell phones seemed so funny. But when I looked at Bill, gray in the face, leaning against the wall, I didn't think anything in the world would ever be funny again.

'Niall and his fae are on the way,' Eric told us, his voice as calm and steady as if he were reading us a story about the stock market. 'Breandan's blocked all the other portals to the fae land. There is only one opening now. Whether they'll come in time, I don't know.'

'If I live through this,' Clancy said, 'I'll ask you to release me from my vow, Eric, and I'll seek another master. I find the idea of dying in the defense of a human woman to be disgusting, no matter what her connection to you is.'

'If you die,' Eric said, 'you'll die because I, your sheriff, ordered you into battle. The reason is not pertinent.'

Clancy nodded. 'Yes, my lord.'

'But I will release you, if you should live.'

'Thank you, Eric.'

Geez Louise. I hoped they were happy now they'd gotten that settled.

Bill was swaying on his feet, but neither Eric nor Clancy regarded him with anything but approval. I couldn't hear what they were hearing, but the tension in the room mounted almost unbearably as our enemies came closer.

As I watched Bill, waiting with apparent calm for death to come to him, I had a flash of him as I'd known him: the first vampire I'd ever met, the first man I'd ever gone to bed with, the first suitor I'd ever loved. Everything that followed had tainted those memories, but for one moment I saw him clearly, and I loved him again.

Then the door splintered, and I saw the gleam of an ax blade, and I heard high-pitched shouts of encouragement from the other fairies to the ax wielder.

I resolved to get up myself, because I'd rather perish on my feet than in a bed. I had at least that much courage left in me. Maybe, since I'd had Eric's blood, I was feeling the heat of his battle rage. Nothing got Eric going like the prospect of a good fight. I struggled to my feet. I found I could walk, at least a little bit. There were some wooden crutches leaning against the wall. I couldn't remember ever seeing wooden crutches, but none of the equipment at this hospital was standard human-hospital issue.

I took a crutch by the bottom, hefted it a little to see if I could swing it. The answer was 'Probably not.' There was a good chance I'd fall over when I did, but active was better than passive. In the meantime, I had the weapons in my hand that I'd retrieved from my purse, and at least the crutch would hold me up.

All this happened quicker than I can tell you about it. Then the door was splintering, and the fairies were yanking hanging bits of wood away. Finally the gap was large enough to admit one, a tall, thin male with gossamer hair, his green eyes glowing with the joy of the fight. He struck at Eric with a sword, and Eric parried and managed to slash his opponent's abdomen. The fairy shrieked and doubled over, and Clancy's blow caught him on the back of the neck and severed his head.

I pressed my back against the wall and tucked the crutch under one arm. I gripped my weapons, one in each hand. Bill and I were side by side, and then he slowly and deliberately stepped in front of me. Bill threw his knife at the next fairy through the door, and the point went right into the fairy's throat. Bill reached back and took my grandmother's trowel.

The door was almost demolished by now, and the assaulting fairies seemed to move back. Another male stepped in through the splinters and over the body of the first fae, and I knew this must be Breandan. His reddish hair was pulled back in a braid and his sword slung a spray of blood from its blade as he raised it to swing at Eric.

Eric was the taller, but Breandan had a longer sword. Breandan was already wounded, for his shirt was drenched with blood on one side. I saw something bright, a knitting needle, protruding from Breandan's shoulder, and I was sure the blood on his sword was Claudine's. A rage went through me, and that held me up when I would have collapsed.

Breandan leaped sideways, despite Eric's attempts to keep him engaged, and a very tall female warrior jumped into the spot Breandan had occupied and swung a mace – a mace, for God's sake – at Eric. Eric ducked, and the mace continued its path and hit Clancy in the side of the head. Instantly his red hair was even redder, and he went down like a bag of sand. Breandan leaped over Clancy to face Bill, his sword slicing off Clancy's head as he cleared the body. Breandan's grin grew brighter. 'You're the one,' he said. 'The one who killed Neave.'

'I took out her throat,' Bill said, and his voice seemed as strong as it ever had been. But he swayed on his feet.

'I see she's killed you, too,' Breandan said, and smiled, his guard relaxing slightly. 'I'll only be the one to make you realize it.'

Behind him, forgotten on the corner bed, Tray Dawson made a superhuman effort and gripped the fairy's shirt. With a negligent gesture, Breandan twisted slightly and brought the gleaming sword down on the defenseless Were, and when he pulled the sword back, it was freshly coated with red. But in the moment it took Breandan to do this, Bill thrust my trowel under Breandan's raised arm. When Breandan turned back, his expression was startled. He looked down at the hilt as if he couldn't imagine how it came to be sticking out of his side, and then blood ran from the corner of his mouth.

Bill began to fall.

Everything stood still for a moment, but only in my mind. The space in front of me was clear, and the woman abandoned her fight with Eric and leaped on top of the body of her prince. She screamed, long and loud, and since Bill was falling she aimed the thrust of her sword at me.

I squirted her with the lemon juice in my water pistol.

She screamed again, but this time in pain. The juice had fallen on her in a spray, across her chest and upper arms, and where the lemon had touched her smoke began to rise from her skin. A drop had hit her eyelid, I realized, because she used her free hand to rub at the burning eye. And while she did that, Eric swung his long knife and severed her arm, and then he stabbed her.

Then Niall filled the doorway of the room, and my eyes hurt to see him. He wasn't wearing the black suit he wore when he met me in the human world but a sort of long tunic and loose pants tucked into boots. Everything about him was white, and he shone . . . except where he was splashed with blood.

Then there was a long silence. There was no one left to kill.

I slid to the floor, my legs as weak as Jell-O. I found myself slumped against the wall by Bill. I couldn't tell if he was alive or dead. I was too shocked to weep and too horrified to scream. Some of my cuts had reopened, and the scent of the blood and the reek of fairy lured Eric, pumped full of the excitement of battle. Before Niall could reach me, Eric was on his knees beside me, licking the blood from a slice on my cheek. I didn't mind; he'd given me his. He was recycling.

'Off her, vampire,' said my great-grandfather in a very soft voice.

Eric raised his head, his eyes shut with pleasure, and shuddered all over. But then he collapsed beside me. He stared at Clancy's body. All the exultation drained from his face and a red tear made its way down his cheek.

'Is Bill alive?' I asked.

'I don't know,' he said. He looked down at his arm. He'd been wounded, too: a bad slash on his left forearm. I hadn't even seen it happen. Through the torn sleeve, I watched the cut begin to heal.

My great-grandfather squatted in front of me.

'Niall,' I said, my lips and mouth working with great effort. 'Niall, I didn't think you would come in time.'

Truthfully, I was so stunned I hardly knew what I was saying or even which crisis I was referring to. For the first time, keeping on living seemed so difficult I wasn't sure it was worth the trouble.

My great-grandfather took me in his arms. 'You are safe now,' he said. 'I am the only living prince. No one can take that away from me. Almost all of my enemies are dead.'

'Look around,' I said, though I lay my head on his shoulder. 'Niall, look at all that's been taken.' Tray Dawson's blood trickled slowly down the soaked sheet to patter on the floor. Bill was crumpled against my right thigh. As my great-grandfather held me close and stroked my hair, I looked past his arm at Bill. He'd lived for so many years, survived by hook or by crook. He'd been ready to die for me. There is no female – human, fairy, vamp, Were – who wouldn't be affected by that. I thought of the nights we'd spent together, the times we'd talked lying together in bed – and I cried, though I felt almost too tired to produce tears.

My great-grandfather sat back on his heels and looked at me. 'You need to go home,' he said.

'Claudine?'

'She's in the Summerland.'

I couldn't stand any more bad news.

'Fairy, I leave cleaning this place to you,' Eric said. 'Your great-granddaughter is my woman, mine and mine alone. I'll take her to her home.'

Niall glared at Eric. 'Not all the bodies are fae,' Niall said with a pointed glance at Clancy. 'And what must we do with that one?' He jerked his head toward Tray.

'*That one* needs to go back into his house,' I said. 'He has to be given a proper burial. He can't just vanish.' I had no idea what Tray would have wanted, but I couldn't let the fairies shovel his body into a pit somewhere. He deserved far better than that. And there was Amelia to tell. Oh, God. I tried to pull my legs up preparatory to standing, but my stitches yanked and pain shot through me. '*Ahh,*' I said, and clenched my teeth.

I stared down at the floor while I got my breath back. And while I was staring, one of Bill's fingers twitched.

'He's alive, Eric,' I said, and though it hurt like the dickens, I could smile about that. 'Bill's alive.'

'That's good,' Eric said, though he sounded too calm. He flipped open his cell phone and speed-dialed someone. 'Pam,' he said. 'Pam, Sookie lives. Yes, and Bill, too. Not Clancy. Bring the van.'

Though I lost a little time somewhere in there, eventually Pam arrived with a huge van. It had a mattress in the back, and Bill and I were loaded in by Pam and Maxwell Lee, a black businessman who just happened to be a vampire. At least, that was the impression Maxwell always gave. Even on this night of violence and conflict, Maxwell looked neat and unruffled. Though he was taller than Pam, they got us into the back with gentleness and grace, and I appreciated it very much. Pam even forewent making any jokes, which was a welcome change.

As we drove back to Bon Temps, I could hear the vampires talking quietly about the end of the fairy war.

'It will be too bad if they leave this world,' Pam said. 'I love them so much. They're so hard to catch.'

Maxwell Lee said, 'I never had a fairy.'

'Yum,' Pam said, and it was the most eloquent 'yum' I've ever heard.

'Be quiet,' Eric said, and they both shut up.

Bill's fingers found mine, gripped them.

'Clancy lives on in Bill,' Eric told the other two.

They received this news in a silence that seemed respectful to me.

'As you live on in Sookie,' Pam said very quietly.

My great-grandfather came to see me two days later. After she let him in, Amelia went upstairs to cry some more. She knew the truth, of course, though the rest of our community was shocked that someone had broken into Tray's house and tortured him. Popular opinion said that his assailants must have believed Tray was a drug dealer, though there was absolutely no drug paraphernalia found in an intensive search of his house and shop. Tray's ex-wife and his son were making the funeral arrangements, and Tray would be buried at Immaculate Conception Catholic Church. I was going to try to go to support Amelia. I had another day to get better, but today I was content to lie on my bed, dressed in a nightgown. Eric couldn't give me any more blood to complete my healing. For one thing, in the past few days he'd already given me blood twice, to say nothing of the nips we'd exchanged during lovemaking, and he said we were dangerously close to some undefined limit. For another thing, Eric needed all his blood to heal himself, and he took some of Pam's, too. So I itched and healed, and saw that the vampire blood had filled in the bitten-out flesh of my legs.

That made my explanation of my injuries (a car accident; I'd been hit by a stranger who'd driven away) just feasible if not too many people examined the wounds. Of course, Sam had known right away that wasn't the truth. I had ended up telling him what had happened the first time he came to see me. The patrons of Merlotte's were very sympathetic, he reported when he came the second time. He had brought me daisies and a chicken basket from Dairy Queen. When he'd thought I wasn't watching, Sam had looked at me with grim eyes.

After Niall pulled a chair close to the bed, he took my hand. Maybe the events of the past few days had made the fine wrinkles in his skin a fraction deeper. Maybe he looked a little sad. But my royal great-grandfather was still beautiful, still regal, still strange, and now that I knew what his race could do . . . he looked frightening.

'Did you know Lochlan and Neave killed my parents?' I asked.

Niall nodded after a perceptible pause. 'I suspected,' he said. 'When you told me your parents had drowned, I had to consider it possible. They all had an affinity to water, Breandan's people.'

'I'm glad they're dead,' I said.

'Yes, I am, too,' he said simply. 'And most of Breandan's followers are dead, as well. I spared two females, since we need them so much, and though one of them was the mother of Breandan's child, I let her live.'

He seemed to want my praise for that. 'What about the child?' I asked.

Niall shook his head, and the sheet of pale hair moved with the gesture.

He loved me, but he was from a world even more savage than mine.

As if he had heard my thoughts, Niall said, 'I'm going to finish blocking the passage to our land.'

'But that's what the war was over,' I said, bewildered. 'That was what Breandan wanted.'

'I have come to think that he was right, though for the wrong reason. It isn't the fae who need to be protected from the human world. It's the humans who need to be protected from us.'

'What will that mean? What are the consequences?'

'Those of us who've been living among the humans will have to choose.'

'Like Claude.'

'Yes. He'll have to cut his ties with our secret land, if he wants to live out here.'

'And the rest? The ones who live there already?'

'We won't be coming out anymore.' His face was luminous with grief.

'I won't get to see you?'

'No, dear heart. It's better not.'

I tried to summon up a protest, to tell him that it was *not* better, it was awful, since I had so few relatives, that I would not talk to him again. But I just couldn't make the words come out of my mouth. 'What about Dermot?' I said instead.

'We can't find him,' Niall said. 'If he's dead, he went to ash somewhere we haven't discovered. If he's here, he's being very clever and very quiet. We'll keep trying until the door closes.'

I hoped devoutly that Dermot was on the fairy side of that door.

At that moment, Jason came in.

My great-grandfather – *our* great-grandfather – leaped to his feet. But after a moment, he relaxed. 'You must be Jason,' he said.

My brother stared at him blankly. Jason had not been himself since the death of Mel. The same edition of our local paper that had carried the story about the awful discovery of the body of Tray Dawson had carried another story about the disappearance of Mel Hart. There was wide conjecture that maybe the two events were connected somehow.

I didn't know how the werepanthers had covered up the scene in back of Jason's house, and I didn't want to know. I didn't know where

Mel's body was, either. Maybe it had been eaten. Maybe it was at the bottom of Jason's pond. Maybe it lay in the woods somewhere.

The last was what I suspected. Jason and Calvin had told the police that Mel had said he was going hunting by himself, and Mel's truck was found parked at a hunting preserve where he had a share. There were some bloodstains discovered in the back of the truck that made police suspect Mel might know something about Crystal Stackhouse's awful death, and now Andy Bellefleur had been heard to say he wouldn't be surprised if old Mel hadn't killed himself out in the woods.

'Yeah, I'm Jason,' my brother said heavily. 'You must be . . . my great-grandfather?'

Niall inclined his head. 'I am. I've come to bid your sister good-bye.'

'But not me, huh? I'm not good enough.'

'You are too much like Dermot.'

'Well, crap.' Jason threw himself down on the foot of the bed. 'Dermot didn't seem too bad to me, *Great-grandfather*. Least, he came to warn me about Mel, let me know that Mel had killed my wife.'

'Yes,' Niall said remotely. 'Dermot may have been partial to you because of the resemblance. I suppose you know that he helped to kill your parents?'

We both stared at Niall.

'Yes, the water fae who followed Breandan had pulled the truck into the stream, as I hear it, but only Dermot was able to touch the door and pull your parents out. Then the water nymphs held them underwater.'

I shuddered.

'Ask me, I'm glad you're saying good-bye,' Jason said. 'I'm glad you're leaving. I hope you never come back, not a one of you.'

Pain flitted over Niall's face. 'I can't dispute your feeling,' he said. 'I only wanted to know my great-granddaughter. But I've brought Sookie nothing but grief.'

I opened my mouth to protest, and then I realized he was telling the truth. Just not all the truth.

'You brought me the reassurance that I had family who loved me,' I said, and Jason made a choking sound. 'You sent Claudine to save my life, and she did, more than once. I'll miss you, Niall.'

'The vampire is not a bad man, and he loves you,' Niall said. He rose. 'Good-bye.' He bent and kissed my cheek. There was power in his touch, and I suddenly felt better. Before Jason could gather himself to object, Niall kissed his forehead, and Jason's tense muscles relaxed.

Then my great-grandfather was gone before I could ask him which vampire he meant.

Acknowledgments – All Together Dead

There are a few people I've thanked before and need to thank again: Robin Burcell, former cop and present writer, and FBI Agent George Fong, who were great about answering my questions about security and bomb disposal. I appreciate the input of Sam Saucedo, the former newscaster and now writer, who explained a few things about border politics to me. I also need to thank S. J. Rozan, who was happy to answer my questions about architecture, though the vampire part was a distinct shock. I may have misused the information given me, but it was in a good cause. As always, I owe a great debt to my friend Toni L. P. Kelner, who read my first draft without laughing in my face. And my new continuity person, Debi Murray, gets a tip of the hat; from now on if I make mistakes, I have someone to blame. I owe a lot to the many wonderful readers who visit my website (www.charlaineharris.com) and leave messages of encouragement and interest. Beverly Batillo, my fan club president, has given me a boost many a time when I was down in the dumps.

Acknowledgements – From Dead to Worse

A tip of the hat to Anastasia Luettecke, who was a perfectionist in supplying me with Octavia's Latin. And thanks to Mury Sellars for being the go-between. As always, I owe a great debt of thanks to Toni L. P. Kelner and Dana Cameron for their valuable comments and the gift of their time. My one and only minion, Debi Murray, assisted me with her encyclopedic knowledge of the Sookie universe. The group of enthusiastic readers known as Charlaine's Charlatans gave me moral (and morale) support; and I hope this book will serve as their reward.

Acknowledgments – Dead and Gone

There are lots of people who've helped me along the way, and that help has put me where I am today. I want to give thanks to just a few. The current moderators of my website (Katie, Michele, MariCarmen, Victoria, and Kerri) make my life so much easier, and the moderators emeriti (Beverly and Debi) deserve a tip of the hat, too. The readers who visit www.charlaineharris.com to offer their comments, theories, and pats on the back are always a source of encouragement.

Backed by a cast of thousands – okay, four – Toni Kelner and Dana Cameron are a constant source of support, encouragement, commiseration, and enthusiasm. I wouldn't know what to do without them.

*Hungry for more Sookie? Turn the page for the
first chapter of* Dead in the Family,
the next book in the Sookie Stackhouse series.

Available now from Gollancz.

MARCH
The First Week

'I feel bad that I'm leaving you like this,' Amelia said. Her eyes were puffy and red. They'd been that way, off and on, ever since Tray Dawson's funeral.

'You have to do what you have to do,' I said, giving her a very bright smile. I could read the guilt and shame and ever-present grief roiling around Amelia's mind in a ball of darkness. 'I'm lots better,' I reassured her. I could hear myself babbling cheerfully along, but I couldn't seem to stop. 'I'm walking okay, and the holes are all filled in. See how much better?' I pulled down my jeans waistband to show her a spot that had been bitten out. The teeth marks were hardly perceptible, though the skin wasn't quite smooth and was visibly paler than the surrounding flesh. If I hadn't had a huge dose of vampire blood, the scar would've looked like a shark had bitten me.

Amelia glanced down and hastily away, as if she couldn't bear to see the evidence of the attack. 'It's just that Octavia keeps e-mailing me and telling me I need to come home and accept my judgment from the witches' council, or what's left of it,' she said in a rush. 'And I need to check all the repairs to my house. And since there are a few tourists again, and people returning and rebuilding, the magic store's reopened. I can work there part-time. Plus, as much as I love you and I love living here, since Tray died . . .'

'Believe me, I understand.' We'd gone over this a few times.

'It's not that I blame you,' Amelia said, trying to catch my eyes.

She really didn't blame me. Since I could read her mind, I knew she was telling me the truth.

Even *I* didn't totally blame myself, somewhat to my surprise.

It was true that Tray Dawson, Amelia's lover and a Were, had been killed while he'd been acting as my bodyguard. It was true that I'd requested a bodyguard from the Were pack nearest me because they owed me a favor and my life needed guarding. However, I'd been present at the death of Tray Dawson at the hands of a sword-wielding fairy, and I knew who was responsible.

So I didn't feel guilty, exactly. But I felt heartsick about losing Tray, on top of all the other horrors. My cousin Claudine, a full-blooded fairy, had also died in the Fae War, and since she'd been my real, true fairy godmother, I missed her in a lot of ways. And she'd been pregnant.

I had a lot of pain and regret of all kinds, physical and mental. While Amelia carried an armful of clothes downstairs, I stood in her bedroom, gathering myself. Then I braced my shoulders and lifted a box of bathroom odds and ends. I descended the stairs carefully and slowly, and I made my way out to her car. She turned from depositing the clothes across the boxes already stowed in her trunk. 'You shouldn't be doing that!' she said, all anxious concern. 'You're not healed yet.'

'I'm fine.'

'Not hardly. You always jump when someone comes into the room and surprises you, and I can tell your wrists hurt,' she said. She grabbed the box and slid it into the backseat. 'You still favor that left leg, and you still ache when it rains. Despite all that vamp blood.'

'The jumpiness'll get better. As time passes, it won't be so fresh and at the front of my mind,' I told Amelia. (If telepathy had taught me anything, it was that people could bury the most serious and painful of memories, if you gave them enough time and distraction.) 'The blood is not just any vampire's. It's Eric's blood. It's strong stuff. And my wrists are a lot better.' I didn't mention that the nerves were jumping around in them like hot snakes just at this moment, a result of their having been tied together tightly for several hours. Dr Ludwig, physician to the supernatural, had told me the nerves – and the wrists – would be back to normal, eventually.

'Yeah, speaking of the blood ...' Amelia took a deep breath and steeled herself to say something she knew I wouldn't like. Since I heard it before she actually voiced it, I was able to brace myself. 'Had you thought about ... Sookie, you didn't ask me, but I think you better not have any more of Eric's blood. I mean, I know he's your man, but you got to think about the consequences. Sometimes people get flipped by accident. It's not like it's a math equation.'

Though I appreciated Amelia's concern, she'd trespassed into private territory. 'We don't swap,' I said. *Much.* 'He just has a sip from me at, you know ... the happy moment.' These days Eric was having a lot more happy moments than I was, sadly. I kept hoping the bedroom magic would return; if any male could perform sexual healing, that male would be Eric.

Amelia smiled, which was what I'd been aiming for. 'At least ... She turned away without finishing the sentence, but she was thinking, *At least you feel like having sex.*

I didn't so much feel like having sex as I felt like I ought to keep trying to enjoy it, but I definitely didn't want to discuss that. My ability to cast aside control, which is the key to good sex, had been pinched out of existence during the torture. I'd been absolutely helpless. I could only hope that I'd recover in that area, too. I knew Eric could feel my lack of completion. He'd asked me several times if I was sure I wanted to engage in sex. Nearly every time, I said yes, operating on the bicycle theory. Yes, I'd fallen off. But I was always willing to try to ride it again.

'So, how's the relationship doing?' she said. 'Aside from the whoopee.' Every last thing was in Amelia's car. She was stalling, dreading the moment when she actually got into her car and drove away.

It was only pride that was keeping me from bawling all over her.

'I think we're getting along pretty well,' I said with a great effort at sounding cheerful. 'I'm still not sure what I feel as opposed to what the bond is making me feel.' It was kind of nice to be able to talk about my supernatural connection to Eric, as well as my regular old man-woman attraction. Even before my injuries during the Fae War, Eric and I had established what the vampires called a blood bond, since we'd exchanged blood several times. I could sense Eric's general location and his mood, and he could feel the same things about me. He was always faintly present in the back of my mind – sort of like turning on a fan or an air filter to provide a little buzz of noise that would help you get to sleep. (It was good for me that Eric slept all day, because I could be by myself at least part of the time. Maybe he felt the same way after I went to bed at night?) It wasn't like I heard voices in my head or anything – at least no more than usual. But if I felt happy, I had to check to make sure it was me and not Eric who felt happy. Likewise for anger; Eric was big on anger, controlled and carefully banked anger, especially lately. Maybe he was getting that from me. I was pretty full of anger myself these days.

I'd forgotten all about Amelia. I'd stepped right into my own trough of depression.

She snapped me out of it. 'That's just a big fat excuse,' she said tartly. 'Come on, Sookie. You love him, or you don't. Don't keep putting off thinking about it by blaming everything on your bond. Wah, wah, wah. If you hate the bond so much, why haven't you explored how you can get free of it?' She took in the expression on my face, and the irritation faded out of her own. 'Do you want me to ask Octavia?' she asked in a milder voice. 'If anyone would know, she would.'

'Yes, I'd like to find out,' I said, after a moment. I took a deep breath. 'You're right, I guess. I've been so depressed I've put off making any decisions, or acting on the ones I've already made. Eric's one of a kind. But I find him . . . a little overwhelming.' He was a strong personality, and he was used to being the big fish in the pond. He also knew he had infinite time ahead of him.

I did not.

He hadn't brought that up yet, but sooner or later, he would.

'Overwhelming or not, I love him,' I continued. I'd never said it out loud. 'And I guess that's the bottom line.'

'I guess it is.' Amelia tried to smile at me, but it was a woeful attempt. 'Listen, you keep that up, the self-knowledge thing.' She stood for a moment, her expression frozen into the half smile. 'Well, Sook, I better get on the road. My dad's expecting me. He'll be all up in my business the minute I get back to New Orleans.'

Amelia's dad was rich, powerful, and had no belief in Amelia's power at all. He was very wrong not to respect her witchcraft. Amelia had been born with the potential for the power in her, as every true witch is. Once Amelia had some more training and discipline, she was going to be really scary – scary on purpose, rather than because of the drastic nature of her mistakes. I hoped her mentor, Octavia, had a program in place to develop and train Amelia's talent.

After I waved Amelia down the driveway, the broad smile dropped from my face. I sat on the porch steps and cried. It didn't take much for me to be in tears these days, and my friend's departure was just the trigger now. There was so much to weep about.

My sister-in-law, Crystal, had been murdered. My brother's friend Mel had been executed. Tray and Claudine and Clancy the vampire had been killed in the line of duty. Since both Crystal and Claudine had been pregnant, that added two more deaths to the list.

Probably that should have made me long for peace above all else. But instead of turning into the Bon Temps Gandhi, in my heart I held the knowledge that there were plenty of people I wanted dead. I wasn't directly responsible for most of the deaths that were scattered in my wake, but I was haunted by the feeling that none of them would have happened if it weren't for me. In my darkest moments – and this was one of them – I wondered if my life was worth the price that had been paid for it.